EAGLE AND EMU

Manfred Jurgensen is Head of the Department of German at the University of Queensland. In 1991 Professor Jurgensen was awarded a Doctorate of Letters (DLitt) by the University of Queensland "in recognition of his great international distinction as a literary scholar". He has published extensively on German literature. His scholarly works include studies on Goethe, Grass, Frisch, Bachmann and Bernhard. His best-known critical publications are *The Fictional I (Das fiktionale Ich)* and *Narrative Forms of the Fictional I (Erzählformen des fiktionalen Ich)*. Jurgensen is the editor of two series of international book anthologies, *Queensland Studies in German* and *German-Australian Studies*. He is the founding editor of the multicultural literary journal *Outrider*, a bilingual novelist, poet and critic and a specialist in intercultural aesthetics. Professor Jurgensen holds a Personal Chair and is a Fellow of the Alexander von Humboldt Foundation.

EAGLE AND EMU

GERMAN-AUSTRALIAN WRITING
1930-1990

Manfred Jurgensen

University of Queensland Press

First published 1992 by University of Queensland Press
Box 42, St Lucia, Queensland 4067 Australia

© Manfred Jurgensen 1992

This book is copyright. Apart from any fair dealing
for the purposes of private study, research, criticism
or review, as permitted under the Copyright Act, no
part may be reproduced by any process without written
permission. Enquiries should be made to the publisher.

The typeset text for this book was supplied by the author in
   camera-ready form
Printed in Australia by The Book Printer, Melbourne

Distributed in the USA and Canada by
International Specialized Book Services, Inc.,
5602 N.E. Hassalo Street, Portland, Oregon 97213-3640

Cataloguing in Publication Data
National Library of Australia

Jurgensen, Manfred, 1940-
   Eagle and emu: German-Australian writing 1930-1990.

   Bibliography.
   Includes index.

   1. German literature — 20th century — History and criticism.
   2. Australia in literature. 3. Public opinion — Germany. 4.
   Australia — Foreign public opinion, German. I. Title.

830.91

ISBN 0 7022 2357 3

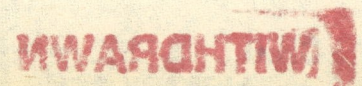

In memoriam

Richard H. Samuel

"Ein ehemaliges Vaterland gibt es nicht."

Thomas Mann (1941)

"...the country which receives culture from abroad, without having anything to give in return, and the country which aims to impose its culture on another, without accepting anything in return, will both suffer from this lack of reciprocity."

T. S. Eliot (1948)

"...es gibt doch auch für dieses Land ein Außen, in dem gedacht, gefühlt, gedichtet wird..."

Paul Hatvani (1973)

Contents

Illustrations ix
Acknowledgments x

Introduction 1

1 THE THIRTIES
  Away From Europe: Adventure, Discovery and
  Germans in Australia 11

2 THE FORTIES
  Blood and Culture: The Old Language in Search
  of the New Land 111

3 THE FIFTIES
  The New Challenge: Boys' Own Geography
  and Domestic Reconstruction 132

4 THE SIXTIES
  Migrants, Adventure and Social Conscience:
  German Workmanship 150

5 THE SEVENTIES
  Look Back in Wonder: Visitors from Another
  Republic of Letters 193

6 THE EIGHTIES
  Tourist Guides and Television Images:
  Full Circle 229

7 INTERNATIONAL SOCIALISM AND MIGRATION:
  The GDR Connection 1956-1987 269

8 JOINING THE "MAINSTREAM":
　　　　　First-Generation Australian Writers 1967-1989 301
Conclusion 393

Notes 397
Bibliography 408
Index 419

Illustrations

Letter of *Schweizerische Schillerstiftung* to Esther Landolt, 1939
Letter of Esther Landolt to *Schweizerische Schillerstiftung*, 1939
Werner Fels, Sydney, 1938
Walter Kaufmann, Berlin, 1985
Joachim Specht, Dessau, 1988
Margaret Diesendorf, Sydney, 1986
Rudi Krausmann, Sydney, 1989

Acknowledgments

I wish to express my gratitude to the University of Queensland for a Special Project Grant and the Australian Research Grant Scheme for its support of this first history of German-Australian literature from the 1930s to the present day. I am grateful for the professional research assistance provided by Marga Lange (Sydney) and Roslyn Orr (Canberra). My colleague Malcolm McInnes was invaluable as critical reader of the manuscript. Further thanks are due to Dr Andreas Bode of the International Youth Library, Schloß Blutenburg (Munich); to members of the Mitchell Library Sydney; to Marguerite S. Jurgensen (Basel); to the Deutsche Literaturarchiv Marbach and to the many contemporary authors in Germany and in Australia who so generously gave their time for interviews and provided vital material. Professor Elizabeth Perkins (James Cook University, Townsville) and Marga Lange contributed independently to this work. Special thanks are due to these co-authors who handled a difficult task with energy and skill. Finally, it is my pleasure to acknowledge the professionalism and commitment of Alec Waskiw from the University of Queensland's Prentice Computer Centre.

Introduction

There is no *a priori* recognised body of bicultural literature. Thus the term "German-Australian Writing" relates not to a history of literature in the accepted sense but to a sociohistorical analysis of German-Australian interculturalism. Nor does this study have much in common with the academic discipline of comparative literature. Rather, it aims to trace German perceptions of Australia, as reflected in travelogues, narrative fiction and poetry. Inherent in these literary invocations is the cultural self-concept of what it means "to be German". Perceptions and projections of the Fifth Continent may vary from decade to decade, but Australia remains the central, all-embracing point of reference. This perspective serves both sociopolitical escapism and cultural self-reflection. It is its continuity of theme which has prompted the construct of a "German-Australian literature". No author knowingly contributed to it as a *corpus sui generis*. All references to "literature" are therefore to be understood in the most liberal sense. Without such frame (or scaffolding) many of these authors would be condemned to literary oblivion at odds with the historical impact of much of their writing. With the emergence of German migrant writers (from the fifties to the eighties) this rescue from antiquarianism assumes greater significance. For with these German-Australian authors the nature of bi- or intercultural literature takes on very specific dimensions. In the context of a multicultural Australian literature German-born writers (i.e. of German language origin) transform the qualitative function of their native culture. A German literary sensibility begins to assert itself in a body of literature no longer determined by one exclusive "national" culture. Seventy writers in sixty years: the existence of a German-Australian "literature" cannot be called into doubt. Nor can it be questioned that such a body of writing reflects the changing nature of political, commercial and cultural relations between the German-speaking countries and Australia. Indeed, if such writing can be classified and discussed under one heading, it would have to be called a literature of bicultural relations. For all the divergence of individual works and the general preoccupations of historical periods, the one overriding concern prevails: German responses to Australia and, to a lesser extent, Australian responses to Germany. The specific area and character of these reactions vary considerably, ranging from travelogue impressions to experiences of German migrants, centred on socio-literary key concepts such as "adventure", "the exotic", "colonialism" or "bi-culturalism". Each decade since the thirties articulates its own preoccupations, both stylistically and thematically.

Although there has been some German-Australian writing prior to the 1930s — discussed over four pages in Augustin Lodewyckx's authoritative study *Die Deutschen in Australien* (Stuttgart 1932) — its quantity and quality does not warrant renewed attention.[1] It seemed appropriate to begin the present survey with a period which saw not only the rise of German fascism (and its implied aspirations for world conquest) but also a strong aftermath of German colonialism, both responses to Germany's defeat in the First World War. The sheer quantity of German literary works about Australia during this time — by far the most strongly represented decade — indicates the intense nature of German-Australian relations in that crucial period. Australia became increasingly a point of reference in German cultural self-assessment and a code for "adventurous" escapism. From the beginning, Australia features as "the other", the far-away place in which opposites are realised, a distant continent of challenge, land of freedom imagined and feared, the subject of German longing and territorial ambition, both the radically foreign and the familiar dream of escape. It also represents the German desire to "overcome history", to live ahistorically, metaphysically; Australia is perceived as the "geschichtslose, unbekannte Kontinent".[2] Living in Australia thus holds the promise of a new beginning.[3]

This history records different ways by which German culture tried to "claim", to grasp and to evaluate Australia. It is in the nature of a literature of relations that it is always a form of self-reflection. Perhaps the works of German-language authors writing about Australia over the past sixty years provide more reliable information on their native country's sociopolitical and cultural developments than on the country of their literary presentation. One of the key aspects to emerge from this analysis of German-Australian literature is the paradox of exploration as a form of escape. It has been a characteristic feature of German culture generally, reflected in the escape from social challenges into philosophy and art. German literature's "flight from reality"

(Wirklichkeitsflucht) has been demonstrated (by Hans Mayer[4] and, from an Anglo-German perspective, by Michael Hamburger[5]) as its ambiguous nature. Australia assumes a recognisable function in such context: it becomes part of a fictionally codified target of German "longing" *(Sehnsucht),* part of a world to be conquered as a means of escape. With emigration this German dichotomy gains sociopolitical reality. For the persecuted, the refugee or the migrant for economic gain the need to leave a native country is imperative. Fleeing from an unsettling home leads to discoveries of a newly adopted life.

Yet it constitutes one of the anomalies of German-Australian writing that it addresses itself very rarely to the realisation of a key aspect of German culture: the escape into a new knowledge, experienced in the act of migration. It may well be that such cultural uprooting is not considered sufficiently philosophic and hence not worthy of literary reflection. German migration to Australia is frequently discussed as part of a travelogue's report on the make-up of this country's European population or account of German settlements in South Australia or Queensland. But few German migrant authors have written about the most important event of their lives. A migrant's consciousness is of course involved in any literary work of cultural transformation. Bilingualism is a further expression of German migrant culture.

There are basically four groups of writers who feature in this survey of German-Australian literature. The majority are short-term visitors to this country who report on their experiences, often fictionalising them into tales of exotic adventure. It is fair to say that most of this kind of writing lacks the imaginative and creative qualities of literary art. They have little in common with a handful of major German writers who accepted invitations to come to this country in recognition of their status, lecturing and reading from their works. Their subsequent literary response to Australia is characterised by an artistic transformation of first impressions, the ability to turn their experience into a poetic composition. Australia in their writing becomes the image of a deeper, more embracing discovery. The third group of authors consists of German language migrants who live in Australia and publish in both English and German. They see themselves as Australian writers of German cultural background and feature prominently in what has come to be known as "multicultural" literature in Australia. The final group is made up of German-language writers who migrated to Australia, lived in the country for a number of years and then returned to

Germany. East German authors are most strongly represented in this category; many of them also write in German as well as in English.

This study's title *Eagle and Emu* is an attempt to allude to the changes and difficulties in intercultural writing. Only a few established German authors manage to express their vision of Australia "in full flight". Most German writers in Australia have lost their wings, migrants and visitors alike, although such loss does not exclusively refer to literary quality. Many works discussed are a mixture of German cultural origin and Australian influences. In extreme cases the cultural loss extends to severe problems in the use of the German language. Occasionally, there are similar difficulties in visiting German authors' handling of Australian English. Complete linguistic and imaginative integration is rare; alienation remains at the very heart of German-Australian writing. In one sense, it could be argued that this is the history of a crippled literature, consisting of "exotic" pieces by reputable German writers, more or less inapt travelogues and narrative sketches by minor authors, similarly awkward and naive writings by migrant chroniclers and attempts of a bilingual, bicultural German-Australian literary imagination to create its own art.

There is no denying the divergence of quality, aim and kind. On the other hand, like migration itself, this very volatility may yet lead to a new and transformed quality of writing in which many of the earlier German contributions serve as literary undergrowth. If the study of German-Australian literature is to be more than an interest in esoteric antiquarianism, it must be undertaken with an eye to its cultural transformation into Australian writing. The aim of this survey is not a documentation of minor works for their own sake; rather it is to trace the historical developments of German-Australian literary relations in order to highlight the quantitative and qualitative transformation into a new, self-conscious, Australian writing of bicultural origin.

The academic tools, the terminological and conceptual resources for the study of such literary developments are limited. If German-Australian writing is at least in part a crippled literature, it is also a literature in the making. Like the cultures of many other "ethnic" minorities in this country, the German contribution to Australian literature is a process of intercultural mediation and transformation which has reached a critical stage. Either German writing about Australia continues to be a subject-related, minor (in quality and output) part of German literature, and German migrant authors writing in Australia remain exiled in the confines of a culturally alienated ghetto. Or both streams contribute, albeit by dissociation (i.e. by detachment of themes, perspective and cultural values), to a symbiotic German-Australian writing which sees itself as part of a "mainstream" multicultural literature of this migrant country.[6] If the latter applies, there is a purpose and direction in the critical differentiation between the three kinds of writing. If not, the history of German-Australian literature will be little more than a chronology of oddities and minor talents.

It is significant, however, that each decade since the thirties includes at least one major literary figure, often writers whose main work forms a recognised part of German literature. As the history of German-Australian writing progresses, more reputable authors emerge who choose Australia as a prominent, if not the main, theme of their œuvre, while major German writers continue to be attracted to the subject (Lenz, Bienek, Artmann, Bichsel). The eighties saw extensive screenings of Australian films on German-language television, which in turn led to the production of a number of German television films in Australia. The impact of Australia in the electronic media had its literary consequence.

It is no coincidence that West Germany's leading TV talk-show host and film actor (Joachim Fuchsberger) decides to live in Sydney and joins the German-Austrian actress Luise Ullrich in writing about their personal view of Australia. Other writers during this period repeatedly refer to film and television images of this country, comparing their experience with the media's projections. It is, of course, not a uniquely German-Australian phenomenon: Australia conquered the media landscape of both Europe and the United States during that time. One of the specific effects of that influence on German-Australian writing is the visualisation of images; cinematography and photography combine to present mythological landscapes of an "archaic continent".[7]

In contrast, the seventies were characterised by literary images and verbal symbolism created by some of the most outstanding representatives of contemporary German literature. In many ways, it proved the most "literary" period of the past sixty years. Australia became the target of literary wit and imaginative characterisation. Life was blown into clichés, distorted perspectives of Eurocentric cultural arrogance were readjusted, and Australia was turned into a theme of literary art. The image was poetic composition, not the mindless repetition of predefined clichés.

The sixties and fifties do not compare well with the literary standards of the following decade. They do not boast recognised writers of major talent, but address themselves to a number of social issues, among them the welfare of Aborigines. In this era, more than before or since, German authors plead for racial tolerance and an Australian society of multicultural coexistence. Where migration to this country is discussed, it is seen as a path to a new social and cultural consciousness. The sixties in particular produce works of fiction and social reportage which assert a vision of Australia inseparably linked to Aboriginal culture. It is more than speculation that such enlightened racial views are the result of Nazi Germany's barbaric racism: Germans feel the continued need to dissociate themselves from the "culture" of their immediate past. In the economic boom of the sixties during which German exports begin to "conquer the world" a new confidence arises which allows a critical assessment of the Third Reich's more sinister aspirations for world dominance. The sociocultural background of most German-Australian publications of the fifties is Germany's economic and moral reconstruction. The pioneering spirit of migrants and settlers in Australia is celebrated as a model for young Germans. There is a clear analogy drawn between the adventurous challenges of life in Australia and the opportunity to participate in the creation of what came to be known as the German "economic miracle". Commercial success is equated with moral integrity; it provides the alibi for a new beginning.

Not surprisingly, the forties present a curious mixture of blood and soil mythology, a glorification of nature's inherent creativity and variations of ahistorical adventures. Towards the end of the decade there are first calls for a socially tolerant migrant society. Style and literary form tend to be traditional, reinforcing the aim of cultural continuity. German-Australian writing during this period is a denazified propagation of allegedly timeless values, which includes the literary and philosophical virtues of classical antiquity.

The most appropriate way to characterise the thirties is to classify German-Australian works of fiction as a continuation of earlier colonial literature. Migration to this country is integrated into a pattern of German global colonisation. German migrants are perceived as part of the German people still, temporarily resident in foreign countries which themselves may, sooner or later, fall under German influence. The term *Deutschtum* assumes cultural, racial and political superiority which motivates a literature of propaganda serving an ideological vision to

"Germanize" the world. Emigration is therefore inseparably linked to power-political expansionism. All non-German cultures are more or less "exotic"; the settlement and cultural conversion of such foreign countries the "adventure" of German heroes, extolled in colonial and fascist literature. If in philosophical terms the world is not "home", this metaphysical alienation could be reduced to some extent by making the world "German". Most of this nationalistic writing lacks intellectual substance as well as imaginative quality. It shares the underlying assumptions of Nazi Germany's *Weltanschauung*. Nor can it be said that all German-Australian settlers dissociate themselves from such a view. There is evidence of strong endorsement of Nazi ideology and Hitler worship in German-language publications of various clubs and associations.[8] Among such a flood of fascist and racist literature the visit to Australia by Egon Erwin Kisch and the subsequent publication of his *Landung in Australien* mark an all-too-rare resistance against fascist cultural politics. His social reportage demonstrates a new and extremely effective way of exposing political and ideological collusion. Kisch's *Landfall in Australia* deserves to be read more widely, both for its ability to capture the spirit of Australian society during the thirties and for its exposure of Australian-German collaboration at the highest government level.

Most writers address themselves to Australia on an occasional basis, prompted by visits or migration. However, a number of authors became writers in direct consequence of their residence in this country. Their response to Australia is a continuing process, extending over several decades. They are of special interest in this study, as it was the experience of migration which in some way prompted them to write and hence may be called, with greater justification than other German-Australian authors, "migrant writers". As Australia continues to be a country of active migration, there is no conflict between the designation of an "Australian" and a "migrant" writer. Anglo-Australian literature has not always acknowledged this obvious fact leading back to its own origins of migration.[9]

Although not the only GDR writers to have published on Australia, Walter Kaufmann and Joachim Specht represent a continuing German socialist perspective on this country. Both emigrated to Australia (Kaufmann in 1942, Specht in 1952), both returned to (East) Germany (Kaufmann in 1956, Specht in 1955). Their work experience in Australia not only informs their writing about this land, it also leads them to an ideological endorsement of international socialism.

Returning "home" to a German communist state holds special philosophical meaning to these authors. The majority of their work published in the GDR retains the Australian connection, thematically as well as sociopolitically. Living conditions in Australia as well as this country's defence alliance with the United States remain dominant subjects of narrative analyses. Kaufmann's identification with Australia seems greater; he not only holds an Australian passport, but also writes most of his prose in English, frequently translating his own works into German. But both writers display an obvious affection for Australia, balanced by strong social criticism, especially in the area of Aboriginal rights, trade unions, militarism and migration. In the context of international socialism "migration" assumes a somewhat different significance: a global solidarity of the working class accepts the migrant worker in any country as part of the one consciousness, the one "world" of comrades. Australia thus becomes the setting of a paradigmatic social and ideological conflict. It is a feature of German-Australian literature that it has produced a virtually uninterrupted flow of socialist writings about Australia since the publication of Kisch's celebrated *Landfall*.

Another group of writers is made up of adoptive Australians born in Austria, West or East Germany and Switzerland who write almost exclusively in English, their second tongue. Most of them are also active as translators and general mediators between German and Australian culture. There is no doubt that they see themselves as Australian writers belonging to an Australian literature. Together, they have published a formidable body of works, in virtually all literary genres. They are rightly listed in the *Oxford Companion to Australian Literature*[10] and remain anxious to dissociate themselves from a concept of ghetto or "ethnic" writing. It is significant that all of them are active in the literary life of the nation, editing or co-editing journals (such as *Aspect, Outrider, Poetry Australia* and *etymspheres*[11]), reading and lecturing. If the various streams of German-Australian writing come together to form part of a multicultural Australian literature, it is in the representatives of this group.

German-Australian literature thus covers a wide range of writing, thematically as well as qualitatively. Its cultural ideology and social politics vary as dramatically as its aesthetics and imaginative vision. Because of the heavy emphasis on "adventure" much of German-Australian writing can be classified as juvenile fiction. If many of these narratives are included in the present survey, it is because they reflect the changing ideological concepts of *Abenteuer*. A literature addressing itself to new beginnings has a natural affinity for the young. Australia is perceived as an old country but a young nation. It thus reflects certain aspects of Germany's own cultural and political history. The mostly simple and naive tone characteristic of much German writing about Australia is well-suited for the style of juvenile adventure novels. To ignore German *Jugendliteratur* about this country is to exclude a fundamental aspect of German-Australian writing.[12] Even well-established authors adopt the position of childlike innocents when confronted with radically different experiences during their stay in Australia. Certainly the visitors' gesture of learning and willingness to explore new territory lends much of their literary responses a frequently stylised and self-conscious quality of juvenile study.

This overview of German-Australian literature does not include the works of second-generation German Australians such as Eric Otto Schlunke (1906–1960), an "unjustly neglected writer", as Geoffrey Dutton rightly claims.[13] Schlunke's narrative, "Henrys Gefangener" appeared in German translation in Frank Auerbach's anthology of Australian short stories *Eine Frau im Busch und andere australische Erzählungen* (1970).[14] Nor does this history consider academic publications by German-Australians (except in the broadest sense), including scholarly works on German literature and contributions to German-Australian literary or general cultural relations. The history of Australian *Germanistik* still waits to be written. At least some of its outstanding representatives deserve to be named in this context: Augustin Lodewyckx, Richard Samuel, Anthony Stephens, Gero von Wilpert, Gerhard Schulz and Leslie Bodi — the latter two responsible for major contributions to the study of German-Australian literature and culture. (In 1987 the University of Queensland's German Department established a Research Unit of German-Australian Relations.) Despite extensive national and international research no claim is made that this survey deals with all authors who have contributed to the development of German-Australian writing. In particular, it has excluded occasional poetry in Australia's German-language press and devotional verse published in mainly Lutheran outlets. While it lists, and makes reference to, academic studies relative to German-Australian literature, no critical appraisal of secondary literature has been attempted.

The aim, then, is to offer an analysis of representative texts which belong to a body of writing about Australia — by German visitors and migrants whose responses reflect certain aspects of German-Australian cultural relations during this century. The scope of the survey could have been extended considerably, had German influences on Australian literature been taken into account.[15] It is a field of research already well covered by various individual and general studies. Similarly, no German translations and other mediations of Australian literature have been considered. (It should be noted that an association of German Australianists has been formed in 1987 and a series of book publications, *Deutsch-Australische Studien,* was founded in 1990.[16]) The temptation to discuss Hans Magnus Enzensberger's translation of John Tranter's poetry (*Der falsche Atlas*) had to be resisted.[17] With few exceptions, the literature of translation remained outside the range of the present study. The purpose of this history is a first stock-taking of the primary material, its sociocultural classification and an examination of its literary character. One basic assumption in the presentation of such writing has been the need to include works of little artistic merit alongside those by reputable authors. The intercultural dimensions of German-Australian writing cannot be analysed in the manner of traditional disciplines (including the study of comparative literature) if they are to be understood as vital ingredients of a branch of symbiotic Australian literature in the making. Left in isolation, the majority of these works will remain little more than antiquarian curiosities, footnotes or appendices of a German-language literary culture or a minor thread in an Australian literature of migration and cultural assimilation. Gathered in what might be termed a coalition of minor forces, including individual or isolated works by major writers otherwise considered obscure or of limited interest and value, they contribute to a German-culture section of Australian literature. There is overwhelming evidence that such tributaries continue to provide, in affirmation and in conflict, a confluence of recognisably German-inspired writing as part of "mainstream" Australian literature.

Chapter One

Away From Europe: Adventure, Discovery and Germans in Australia

> "War es nicht ein stolzer Gedanke, auf diesem fremden, fernen Boden ein neues Geschlecht deutscher Menschen zu begründen?"
>
> O.E.H. Becker, *Das australische Abenteuer*

THE THIRTIES

In the politically volatile years of the thirties German writing about Australia consisted mainly of travelogues turned into popular fiction. The authors were overwhelmingly short-term visitors to this country. A great deal of their fictionalising continued the tradition of adventure novels, written, more specifically, as exotic narratives of *Kolonialliteratur*. Germany's aspirations as a world power perceived migrants in Australia (and elsewhere) as *Auslandsdeutsche*, Germans in exile, still part of the German people (*Volksgemeinschaft*) separated from their tribal home (*Stammesheimat*). The relatively close proximity of former German colonies in the Pacific reinforced the implication that Australia, too, could become the (eventual) target of German expansionism. The *Deutschtumspolitik* of Germany, especially during the "Third Reich", has been documented and leaves no doubt about the cultural and political intentions of the home country.[1] Colonial adventure stories from South-West Africa, Togo, Cameroon or East Africa followed the same general pattern of themes, plot, characterisation and political imperialism. (Bismarck began to develop Germany's colonial expansion in 1884–85. Under Kaiser Wilhelm II the Germans acquired further overseas bases in "Ciautschou" (1898) and the South Sea islands of the Carolines, the Marianas and the Palaus

(1899). European imperialism and colonialism were characterised as a struggle for a "place in the sun".[2]) It is in this context that most of the German narratives about Australia in the thirties have to be read. The adventure of discoveries served a transparent political purpose.

Australia is described in this prose as wild and untouched, as a land largely unknown. Some authors, like *Joseph M. Velter* (1931), lament the loss of German colonies, such as South-West Africa, and perceive Australia as a colonial alternative. They see themselves as *Abenteuerdichter*, writers of adventure stories, whose sense of adventure is derived from the experience of war. Their political stance is conservative, reactionary, in strong opposition to democratic forces. As such, they reject the political and cultural developments of the Weimar Republic (1919–1933). Among their social values camaraderie rates highly, the shared experience of soldiers. In Australia, these soldiers may become battlers, pioneers in a struggle to tame the land. But here, too, comradeship of Germans remains paramount. German migrants are described as colonisers (*Kolonisator*[3]), determined to regain lost colonies. Much of this writing may be seen as a continuation of colonial literature with strong and explicit political aims. Needless to say, these fictional travelogues were written for domestic, i.e. German, consumption. They propagate supposedly German qualities, such as industriousness, reliability and orderliness. Not surprisingly, there are frequent appeals to a "responsible *Auslandsdeutschtum*" (those of German stock living abroad). Migrants who have become settlers are still considered to be part of the German people. Germans in Australia remain integrated into German politics. Thus, any manifestation of socialism in Australia is branded as un-German and undesirable. Among the many distortions and misunderstandings of Australian society the equation of the concepts of mateship and German *Kameradschaft* features prominently. The overall attitude of these writers is anti-democratic and anti-socialist.

There is a strong sense in all of this writing that history can be overcome by "adventure". Emigration is seen as something "in the blood" of all Germans — yet as part of a longing which, it is claimed, must remain inexpressible, enigmatic and ultimately without direction. Such Romantic *Sehnsucht* may indeed be interpreted as a form of *Weltflucht*[4], an escape from the here and now. Australia is especially appropriate for such explorative travel or emigration: it is an "unknown" (*unbekannte*[5]) continent. Significantly, part of this adventure is the knowledge and guarantee of an ancestral estate, an heirloom, "back home". The entailed estate plays an important symbolic part in many of the narrative works written during this period. Emigration, adventure, discovery and travel are all related to a home which is never questioned. If *Auswandererlust* is described as being in the blood of Germans (presumably as an extension of *Wanderlust*), so is the *Abenteuerlust* — love of adventure. "The blood hungers for adventure", one novelist writes[6], applying a pre-fascist mythology of blood and soil. Appropriately for such a concept of blood adventure, the *Abenteuer* in Australia may consist of being reunited with one's family, in particular with one's father (as in fatherland).

Part of such blood ideology is, inevitably, it would seem, a racism expressing itself violently, if inconsistently, in many of the prose works of the thirties. There is evidence of anti-semitism and of racist attitudes towards Aborigines, both expressed in the crudest and most extreme form. Even anti-Italian sentiments find their way into a novel about Germans in Australia[7]. In other works, however, Aborigines are seen in a more positive light: as part of German adventure, they rescue the superior colonist; following the pattern of *Robinson Crusoe*, there can be a useful relationship with a Man Friday, even if it does not qualify for *Kameradschaft*. Generally, the description of Aborigines is negative and condescending. They do not understand the value of work. They are referred to as "Niggers"[8], nomads who live on the lowest level of culture, savages who suffer superstitious fears[9]. The occasional contrast of idealised portrayals of Aborigines owes much to the writings of Karl May (1842–1912), the German *Abenteuerschriftsteller* whose many novels about the American West centred around the figure of Winnetou, a Red Indian and archetype of the noble savage. There are similar conflicts between, on the one hand, the historical reasons for emigration (including references to the 1848 migrants from Germany), and, on the other hand, the yearning for a no-man's-land (*Niemandsland*). The longing (*Sehnsucht*) is directed at oblivion — a central feature of much of German culture. A native history of Australia is never considered; the country's record begins with the penal colonies of the British Empire. Adventure is the only history worthy to be told.

Germans living in Australia are shown to be homesick, longing to return to the fatherland. Their highest treasure is work, yet it is the commitment to work which makes Germans unpopular in the strange, bizarre country. Few writers of the period do not refer to the treatment of Germans in Australia during the First World War. Internment, censorship and persecution of German migrants are denounced with considerable passion. There is joy in being able to report that the German language may be used again. German centres are described with affection and pride, mainly as outposts of German civilisation, much less as part of an emerging Australian nation. Significantly, one author speaks of German "Kraftzentren"[10]. The main refuge of German culture is seen to be the Lutheran Church, which in turn is interpreted as part of German soil. Many writers refer to Ludwig Leichhardt's expeditions in Australia — without interpreting his discoveries as part of Australian history and culture. Rather, Leichhardt is being celebrated as a German heroic epic (*deutsches Heldenepos*)[11]. There is an heroic dimension in German emigration as well. Together with other European migrants, they are seen as an outpost of the white race. Even writers of travelogues and of narrative fiction see themselves in the footsteps of explorers such as Leichhardt. It is all part of a semi-spiritual quest of cultivating the barren land with German work and vision. Even writing about Australia is a kind of literary conquest and discovery.

Almost all of these books are aimed at the popular reading market, many specifically at young readers. Their tone is generally didactic, mixed with a generous dosage of "boys' own" adventure. Most of the novels' subtitles refer explicitly to *Abenteuer*, *Fahrten* or *Erlebnisse*, adventurous journeys and exotic adversities. Some are published in series which characterise the nature and aim of these narrative works: "Länder, Abenteuer, Helden — Eine Jugendschriftenreihe"[12], "Vieras Spannende Wild-Süd-Jugendbücher"[13], "Bunte Jugendbücher"[14], "Sammlung Aus weiter Welt"[15] or "Neueste Hefte der Deutschen Jugendbücherei"[16]. They are, in the main, cheaply mass-produced, in the form of paper-covered booklets, occasionally retaining the appearance of a periodical. To illustrate the range and thematic preoccupations of such series, in particular the colonial interconnections of "German adventures", a representative list of titles may be revealing: *Die Fahrt nach der Goldküste, Sandfeldschrecken. Ein südafrikanisches Erlebnis, Jacks Abenteuer. Erlebnisse eines Deutschen in Südafrika, Schwere Tage in Südwest, Tigerjagd auf Java. Erlebnisse deutscher Kolonisten, Deutsches Pflanzerleben in der Südsee, Mafell. Abenteuer in der Südsee, Bruder Leichtfuß in Australien, Grünhorn in Australien. Auswanderer-Erlebnisse*[17]. Other narrative works appear in more expensive hardback editions, but their style and didactic aim hardly differ from the cheaper journalistic versions. The colonial adventure serves to reinforce a sense of national and racial identity; the German adventurers (re)discover their native roots. There is explicit reference to a "longing for one's own race"[18]: the lure of the exotic leads back to a reaffirmed home, the foreign world creates or reinforces the concept of a national home. Longing leads to a revitalised sense of belonging. Adventure means to leave home, face the unfamiliar and return home with an affirmation of the familiar. Australia, as part of a strange world, is always looked at from the native culture's, i.e. German, perspective. No attempt is made to adapt to the strange, to let the foreign become familiar, to assimilate it into a home culture experience. On the contrary: these narratives all emphasise, and find their very *raison d'être* in, the otherness, the difference and the potential threats of other places, other people, other cultures. In the final analysis they are a literature which could be likened to a colonial curiosity shop. Its adventurous fiction of the exotic serves to reassure the reader of the safety of his home, he remains an armchair traveller who is informed again and again that the world can merely confirm the superiority of the German nation and its people. The political didacticism of such adventure travelogues needs no labouring: they strongly reinforce cultural conservatism. Colonial imperialism, in literature too, serves the domestic market and internal politics.

While there is considerable variance in the level of literary style, the writing of German-Australian travelogue fiction in the thirties may be summed up by the term "aesthetics of otherness" (*Ästhetik der Fremdartigkeit*). All authors concentrate on the unusual; their descriptions aim for startling effects — not produced by the imaginative quality of the text, but by the strange and surprising nature of a foreign country. There is a strong underlying tone of humour in some of the narrative accounts, more often than not the travel writer is amused by what he sees. Antipodean inversions are a constant source of comedy. The foreign qualities of a land are related back to the familiar knowledge of home: learning and adjusting can be a mixture of good-natured humour and self-righteous arrogance.

Australia is generally seen as a land preserved for whites. Many books pose as ethnological reports, claiming to pass on factual information about the fifth continent. The same semi-documentary style is retained when Australia is described as the outpost of the white race or when it is argued that whites can populate the tropics. There is a characteristic overlapping of travelogue geography and political ideology, including racism and colonial imperialism. All texts can and must be related back to the historical developments in Germany and

Australia. Thus, some writers not only express anti-semitic and anti-communist sentiments, but go so far as to recommend Adolf Hitler as a model leader for Australia. The majority of narrative works of this period are written by nationalists, right-wing conservatives, military reactionaries and fascists. Their readers were potential Hitler youths and young Germans destined to fight a world war. The cultural ideology of most texts is transparently obvious, the writing of many prose narratives depressingly poor in imaginative quality, rich in political slogans and repetitive clichés. They need to be recorded in the history of German-Australian literature not for their literary excellence, but for their crude expression of the spirit of the age (*Zeitgeist*).

There is, among all the nationalist prose, a remarkable minority voice of the socialist Left: the classic reportage by Egon Erwin Kisch, *Landung in Australien*, first published in 1937 in Amsterdam, then, in various editions, from 1948 to 1962 in Berlin (GDR), and in 1975, for the first time in the Federal Republic of Germany, in Darmstadt/Neuwied. The special style of Kisch's reportage has by now received its belated recognition. It is the new and unique quality of a reporting style which is both factual and personal. Kisch's reports are biased, in some ways they could even be termed political pamphlets. But the power of observation and intelligence of his prose achieves its own status of objectivity. Whereas the right-wing travelogues relate to a concept of the exotic epitomising the strange and unusual — a notion of the frequently unverifiable — Kisch claims that nothing is more exotic than our environment: "nichts ist exotischer als unsere Umwelt"[19]. Australia thus becomes an extended part of a social and political environment, to be observed with the same precision and ideological commitment as places and events in Europe. Upon his return from Australia, Kisch addresses the Writers Congress For The Defence of Culture in June 1935; the title of his talk is "Reportage as a Form of Art and Ideological Struggle" ("Reportage als Kunstform und Kampfform"). Autobiographical experience is presented as socially representative, paradigmatic in its political significance. Kisch's social reportage of his experiences in Australia gives a well-informed account of this country's exotic everyday political reality. Unlike his conservative *Deutschtum* colleagues, he writes about contemporary Australia from the point of view of a global anti-fascist. His subject is Australian society and its relationship with the rest of the world. Of special interest are the bilateral relations between Nazi-Germany and Australia.

Walter Stölting

Australien. Das Land von morgen

Walter Stölting's introduction to Australia appeared in 1930. It offers a general survey of Australian life in the earlier part of the century. Stölting rejects the attempt to write a travelogue. He explains that the actual travelling time was of far less significance than his research.

Stölting's account of Australia concentrates on a number of recurring features: the railway system, the road structure, the Australian home, the contrast between city and country, irrigation. The book is indeed much more than impressionistic description; the author is well informed and anxious to make Australia, not himself, the "hero" of his narrative. It is significant that he begins with an observation about the special light, the "starkes Licht"(9), prevailing on the continent. Stölting instantly grasps the non-European features of Australia's landscape. His descriptions fluctuate between factual explanations and enraptured anthropomorphising. The author concentrates on unique Australian features in natural and in social life. His discussion of Australia's low rainfalls thus leads directly to an account of everyday life and features of housing, architecture and local customs. Stölting's book is an entertaining mixture of anthropology, sociology and imaginative adaptation of geographical data.

The author rightly reminds his readers that he is writing about a European Australia. England is still the motherland, a source of economic investment and military protection against expansionist Japan. Interestingly, Stölting believes England had learnt from the loss of her American colonies and therefore made every effort to remain on friendly terms with Australia. The book offers a precise description of the six states of the Commonwealth of Australia, including the political structure of federal and state governments. A brief historical survey of penal settlement gives a general background to information about contemporary social and political conditions. Stölting's history of migration to Australia is sketchy, but factually reliable. It concentrates on its economic impact.

Significantly, Stölting declares an affinity of Australians with the (classical) Greeks: it is an analogy which helps explain his own classicist poetry written in this country. His idealism amounts to a vision of cultural regeneration and a "new race". It is hardly surprising, therefore, that Stölting devotes an entire chapter to what he calls "the new man". He has no doubt that "a new race" ("eine neue Rasse") is growing in Australia. This "neue Menschenrasse"(82) will not follow the example of the North-American; its racial ingredients are English, Welsh, Scottish and Irish, with contributions from Germany, Scandinavia and "perhaps" ("vielleicht auch") Italy. In Stölting's view, this will make "the Australian race" purer ("viel reiner und eigener",Ibid.) than Americans. Interestingly, the author praises the equality of man and woman in an Australian marriage, indeed, generally the Australian male's attitude to women and warns against applying European concepts of parental (or other) love to Australians. Again and again, Stölting compares the emerging Australian "race" with the Greeks of classical antiquity. He sees Australians involved in non-European pleasures ("Vergnügen",101), such as exercising a trade for a hobby. The face of the Australian of the future will be similar to the "Gesicht...der wirklichkeitsnahen klassischen Vergangenheit".(102) It will be free of want, but, unlike ancient Greece, also free of the luxuries gained by exploitation, as slavery is unknown in Australia. His vision of this new man will be realised, he believes, in the fourth or fifth generation of native white Australians.

Stölting stresses that Germans have been a vital part of the history of white settlement from the very beginning. The reports of the German botanists and naturalists R. and G. Forster formed part of Cook's official submission to the British Government and thus were largely responsible for the decision to colonise the land. Stölting reminds his readers that Captain Phillip's father was a German from Frankfurt am Main. He quotes a newspaper article from Adelaide describing the reception of early German settlers in South Australia. They were perceived as a "Volk von Bauern"(195), hard-working, frugal, disciplined, polite and proud. Stölting tells the story of the well-known German geologist Menge who, in 1836 (the year of laying of the foundation stone of Adelaide), together with a number of German miners, vine-growers and farmers, went to South Australia, preparing the ground for the first major transport of German migrants two years later. He also informs his readers of another small group of German vine-growers who arrived in 1837 and settled in New South Wales, "Winzer aus Hattenheim im Rheingau, die sich in Neu-Süd-Wales niederließen".(196) Stölting concentrates on the well-documented history of German migration to South Australia, its historical background of religious persecution in Silesia and, later (after 1848), post-revolutionary conflicts, and quotes the long list of German townships and settlements: "Langmeil, Lobetal, Blumberg,

Friedensberg, Bethanien, Schönberg, Neukirch, Rheintal" etc.(197) Tanunda, although Aboriginal in name, and Hahndorf, named after the Danish captain Hahn who transported 200 Germans in 1838 to Adelaide, receive special mention. Stölting explains that after 1848 highly-educated Germans followed, under the leadership of Dr Richard Schomburgk and Dr Mücke. He records and analyses the different waves of German migration to all Australian colonies or states.

After listing impressive achievements by German settlers Stölting turns to the rise of anti-Germanism at the beginning of the century. It is here that the term *Deutschtum* reveals its ambiguity. (It must be borne in mind, of course, that Stölting's account precedes the policy of *Deutschtum* in Australia by the Nazis.) Anti-German sentiments were incited by the "Entente Cordiale" and increased armament of Germany, the author explains. He refers to New South Wales' Premier, Sir Henry Parkes, whose aim it became to keep Australia free of Germans and the Irish. Stölting accuses Australians of deceptive war propaganda, of lies and distortions in the treatment of Germans. He describes the virtual destruction of German-Australian culture, the closing of newspapers, the renaming of German townships (there were 48 in South Australia alone), the closing of German schools and German clubs. There can be little doubt that in many cases the persecution of German migrants in this country was extreme and unjustified. More often than not, it was the result of zealous naivety, rather than vicious hatred or informed judgement. Stölting's defence of *Deutschtum*, in Australia and elsewhere, would have read very differently a few years later.

Stölting's introduction to Australia proves well-informed, engagingly written and idealistically argumentative. Behind a wealth of documentary and statistical information the reader detects glimpses of the author's vision. It is a "Vision Splendid", a utopian rebirth of Greek culture in the Antipodes. However, this very ideal is itself an extension of the dream of German Classicism, of the "classically" educated German *Bildungsbürgertum* (middle class), an "imported" cultural conception. Stölting's creative writing shows the tragic incongruity of such vision. In the context of a German-Australian literature, Stölting's vision came to be replaced by the ideology of blood and soil, the Nazi "philosophy" of fatherland and race.

Peter Mattheus

Minnewitt und Knisterbusch

This book of juvenile fiction is one of many illustrating the similarity between *Jugendliteratur* and narratives about Australia written for adult readers. The "ingredients" of plot and characterisation remain largely the same, as does the very motivation for writing the work. The language may vary slightly (though not as much as one would expect), but what is being said is virtually indistinguishable. The common theme is "das sonderbare Land Australien", or, as the book's subtitle puts it more precisely, "Lustige und abenteuerliche Erlebnisse in dem 'sonderbaren Land Australien'". Mattheus' novel consists of what might be termed a narrative stock-taking of the Australian landscape and of the Australian way of life. Its humour is derived from the exotic and incongruous, the foreign and antipodean; the adventure is modelled on American westerns and Colonial exploration.

Peter Mattheus offers an extreme example of attempts to "translate" Australian colloquialisms by employing German everyday talk, more specifically the racy jargon of young people. Their inappropriateness highlights a genuine problem: the challenge of transcultural language in German-Australian fiction. Most authors follow the option chosen by Mattheus, to draw no distinction between the speech of Australians and Germans in Australia, apart from occasional terms or phrases of Australian English. It leads to inherent difficulties. A foreign character is linguistically, stylistically and culturally drawn in a manner which falsifies or takes away his alien status and identity. Once integrated into another language (German), his distinctive otherness has to be recomposed — in terms of that language's native culture. Few, if any, German-Australian writers have succeeded in this art of cultural mediation. It calls for an imaginative strength which proved beyond them. (Several writers use extensive bilingual dialogues in the hope of bypassing this difficulty.)

Such problems contribute to the lack of authenticity in so many narrative works about Australia: it all "sounds" and "reads" wrong, even where a wealth of factual information is presented. These books are, of course, for domestic consumption, determined to reinforce native values and perceptions. *Minnewitt und Knisterbusch* is representative because it is a German book with German characters (even where they pretend to be Australian) and a German interpretation of the "sonderbare Land Australien". It shares with novels of adult fiction the one-dimensional quality of character and plot. Most figures are no more than vessels to be filled with information regarding national customs or carriers and providers of that information. The description of the Australian countryside ("Steppe" and "Buschwald", 31) consists of enumerations of un-European features, relating the exotic back to the familiar by comparing it to a German zoo.

Only once does the novel depart from the predictable listing of "exotic" Australiana. Approaching the outskirts of Adelaide, young Michel registers the curiously characteristic juxtaposition of old and new, rich and poor, beautiful and ugly. Unlike his descriptions of bush and country, the author seems close to a kind of social realism all too rare in German-Australian writing when he draws the streets and houses of the city. Such recognisably accurate observation could have led to a more substantial dealing with Australia, even in young adult fiction. Yet, the promise of social analysis and realistic reporting remains unfulfilled.

COLIN ROSS

Der unvollendete Kontinent

Of Ross' three publications dealing, directly or indirectly, with Australia, this is by far the most influential and authoritative. *Der unvollendete Kontinent* appeared 1930 in the prestigious Brockhaus Verlag Leipzig. Its title concept soon became a generally accepted slogan. Ross applies the idea of an "incomplete continent" — geographically a tautologous or at best a dubious description — not only to the country, but also to its people: Australians are paradigmatically "incomplete" in their development.

The country creates a population in its own image. Ross remains tantalisingly vague about which inhabitants of Australia he is referring to. Is it the total, black and white, population, the indigenous people, or only the white colonists and immigrants? Migration brought about such rapid growth, Colin Ross argues, that Australia "jumped" various stages of progress and quickly became an "overcomplete" ("übervollendete") development. It is this paradox which fascinates him and motivates his book.

Australia thus is a model case study for him, both as geographer and social historian. Ross believes that geography is *the* science of the twentieth century, a precondition for politics and economics on an international scale. Interestingly, he envisages and propagates a United Europe, based on a willingness and ability to think world-wide: "wenn es den europäischen Nationen eine Selbstverständlichkeit geworden ist, über Europa hinaus zu denken."(3) His book about Australia is part of that vision, in that sense also a political statement.

Like most authors of the thirties (and before), Ross sees Australia as a country of the Nordic white race, comparing it with living conditions in California and South Africa. He is surprised to discover "keine kulturlosen Wilden" (251), and he admires "die religiösen und kosmischen Ideen" in the "Weltbild des australischen Eingeborenen".(252) Yet his language and general preoccupation with race show him to be firmly entrenched in German nationalistic racist ideology. He continues to speak of the "reinblütig weiße Mann"(32) and is surprised to find that he carries out work in the tropics that is normally done by "Mischlinge oder Farbige" (Ibid.).

As a German writer, he is especially interested in South Australia, its history and settlement by Germans. He calls the state's foundation a "literary" event: "...es (gab) eine Literarische Gesellschaft für Südaustralien, ehe auch nur der erste Siedler seinen Fuß auf südaustralischen Boden gesetzt hatte."(38) Adelaide thus becomes the city of education, the "Stadt für Erziehung".(39)

Ross addresses himself to German-Australian relations by conceding that anti-German feelings were understandable in the light of the many casualties Australia suffered during the First World War. He differentiates between "Deutschaustralier" and other "Auslandsdeutsche" by arguing that the former continue to cling fiercely to religious doctrine and have remained cultural rebels. A special definition of "German" is applicable to them. It is not "Deutschtum in politischem Sinn". Colin Ross offers a precise cultural interpretation: "Das 'Deutsche' ist für sie das Herz, ist ein Reich, das nicht von dieser Welt ist. Deutsch bedeutet für die südaustralischen Deutschen Religion, Seele, Gott."(56) It is this spiritual otherworldliness which Australians failed to understand when they began to persecute German migrants for their alleged sympathies with the national aspirations of the country of their ancestors. Ross has no doubt that these German-Australians would have never been politically active on behalf of a Germany their forebears left behind. But he also predicts (accurately) that this kind of German piety will not survive.

Like other German writers, Ross lists various aspects and features of the Australian landscape. But what makes Colin Ross' book remarkable is that it goes beyond the usual inventory of Australian characteristics and terminology. The author offers a well-informed discussion of Australian urbanization, with its social and cultural consequences. His observations on Australia's desperate search for its own history and national identity are as relevant today as they were in 1930. Ross interprets Australia's involvement in the First World War as a passionate desire to become part of history. Yet he suggests that Australia's uniqueness and potential greatness are to be found in the very lack of (white man's) history. He advises against a borrowing of European history and finds Australia's cultural void the real challenge, a hope not only for Australians, but for the world at large.

There is no doubt that Colin Ross is sympathetic to Australia as a whole. He sees ideals of European social democracy realised and finds this country far more truly democratic than the United States. Whatever is going to happen to the "australische Zukunftsstaat"(163), the author is convinced that it is a place where social relations may be studied for the benefit of Germany and the whole of Europe. Ross' Australia assumes model character; he never looks at it in isolation, for or by itself. There is a lot to be learnt from what he believes to be a social experiment on a grand scale.

In that context he praises Australia's egalitarianism and the high living standard. But he criticises the mediocrity which he thinks is the inevitable consequence of such social equality. Colin Ross cannot be accused of the crude kind of outbursts against socialism which characterise so much of German-Australian popular fiction of the twenties and the thirties, yet he too is clearly concerned about the socialist challenge. Australia, he argues, is the land of mass mediocrity and as such the ideal of the socialist state of the future(166).

Colin Ross may hold racist views and share other values with an emerging German nationalism, but he is neither a colonialist nor a fascist. His book on Australia is a part geographical, part anthropological travelogue which relates problems and features of a foreign country to his own by way of comparison and contrast. The meaningful perspective is not to look at Australia from a European point of view, he argues, but to look (back) at Europe from the antipodean vantage point of Australia. Ross' claim that only then may Europeans read social changes in the future is as extravagant as his belief that Australia offers a reflection of the history of European civilisation. He does not doubt that "the incomplete continent" can be held up as a "prophetic mirror" to future developments in Germany and elsewhere.

The assessment of Australia as "das größte kulturelle Experiment der Menschheit"(228) is made with incongruous conviction, for Ross calls it at the same time a premature and unjustified interference with the natural order of things. He criticises in particular various natural and cultural importations from Europe. But the real problem, as he sees it, lies in the lack of determination to populate the continent. He thinks Australia was discovered 150 years too early. The reader senses the allusion to "Lebensraum", a concept held not only by Nazis. There is a strong implication in everything Ross writes that the Australian continent could be used to feed "60 Millionen"(230). He despairs over the reluctance of Australians to open up their land. His attitude to Australia, though essentially positive, is coloured by the model character he chooses to extend to it. His reservations almost always refer to a transference of Australian conditions to a Germany or a Europe of the future. His own discussion of Australia's economy proves well-informed and knowledgeable, especially in his references to agriculture.

Ross calls the White Australia policy a "national dogma"(263), comparable to the Monroe Doctrine in the USA or the "gloire" of France. At the time of the writing of his book this was undeniably true. Ross highlights the shortcomings of such a policy, both economically and militarily. He has no doubt that "Nordaustralien liegt jedem Einfall gegenüber offen und schutzlos da... (es ist) überhaupt nicht zu verteidigen"(272). The argument that the North of the continent cannot be defended is still with us; it is clear that Colin Ross shares the Australian fear of a "yellow peril". There is considerable confusion in his argument for a White Australia to be defended against non-white Asian expansionism: it is never quite clear whether he is arguing for the emancipation of the "Aryan" Aborigines or for massive white European migration or for both. Yet, it would be unfair to link Colin Ross with the racism of Nazi ideology. Indeed, he attacks Australia's own racist creed, a dogma shared by all political parties: "...die 'nordische Mythe' ist hier ja geistiges Dogma und politisches Credo, und zwar für alle Parteien."(276) He closes his critical analysis of "the incomplete continent" with a qualified endorsement of Australia's "Freisein vom Produktionswahn, dem Rausch der großen Zahl"(277–278). The refusal to produce for the sake of production and to chase questionable records of "progress" distinguishes Australia from the United States — for Ross, a commendable distinction. At the same time he correctly predicts Australia's Depression and believes that within fifty years it will have to choose between an "olive" and a "yellow" peril: "ich glaube, daß es keine andere Chance hat als zu wählen zwischen der 'olivfarbenen' und der 'gelben' Gefahr"(278).

Das Buch der fernen Welt

One year after the publication of *Der unvollendete Kontinent* Colin Ross wrote the introduction to a book of photographs of Asia, Africa, Australia and America, *Das Buch der fernen Welt*. It is a remarkable essay, with a few comments particularly relevant to Australia. Ross addresses himself to the effect that modern standardisation has had on the perception of beauty, especially the beauty of nature as experienced by the traveller. Already, he suggests, there are "Anglo-Saxon travellers" who can only respond to the beauty of countries if it is predefined and "normed" by travelogues, films or tourist brochures. He arrives at an indirect description of beauty which is of vital concern to the art of travel literature and reflects back upon his own "Reisebuch" *Der unvollendete Kontinent* (as well as his other travelogues): it is the degree of strangeness — "der Grad ihrer Fremdartigkeit" — which determines our judgement of natural beauty ("Naturschönheit"). Citing the example of Europeans' ecstatic response to palm trees, Ross declares: "Gerade die Fremdartigkeit ist es, die in hohem Grade unser Schönheitsurteil bestimmt".(vi)[20] He perceives the unfamiliar as a decisive part of the European bourgeois concept of beauty. He further believes in a "law of rhythm" which operates under maximum conditions where different vegetations come together. He calls it "die Kontrastwirkung, die so wichtig für die Beurteilung der Schönheit der Welt ist".(vii) What Colin Ross offers is an aesthetic model of travelling and narrative geography.

"Wenn von der Schönheit der Welt die Rede ist", Ross maintains, "muß auch von Australien ein Wort gesagt werden".(xi) He uses his concepts of contrast, rhythm and the unfamiliar to plead for a particular brand of Australian beauty. They are applied to the interior and the coastline of the continent, but also, quite specifically, to the harbour of Sydney which he compares with the harbours of Rio de Janeiro and Hongkong. Australia as an incomplete divine creation remains Ross' cultural and aesthetic vision of the continent. He continues to be fascinated and excited by the *strange beauty* of the place.

Haha Whenua — das Land, das ich gesucht

This travelogue, published in 1933, deals with the author's experiences in the South Sea, including New Zealand and Papua New Guinea. The only section dealing with Australia is Part Three, "In den Korallengärten des Großen Barriereriffs"(96–120). It gives Ross the opportunity to write about Captain Cook's journey through the same waters, especially about the damages to the "Endeavour" caused by the reef and its repairs carried out at what is now known as Cooktown. Ross' narrative invokes a central theme of German-European longing: the tropical island of dreams, the exotic, idyllic getaway. Chapter Fifteen is actually called "Die Insel meiner Träume". It is the island of a collective dream, not the escapist longing of an individual; an archetypal manifestation of the European imagination. To this day such islands feature prominently in German popular culture[21].

Ross knows how to appeal to, and keep alive, national myths and collective dreams. The Barrier Reef seems a curiously appropriate backdrop for such travelogues of identity and belief. Colin Ross ends his Australian section of *Haha Whenua* with a philosophical reflection on the illusion of the world. He is praising a country which, despite the perceptive realism of his descriptions, ultimately does not exist.

JOSEPH M. VELTER

Australien kreuz und quer

Velter's novel is described as "ein packendes Abenteuerbuch"[22] combining factual information with imaginative fiction. The narrative carries the subtitle "Fahrten durch Busch und Wüste". It is in fact an autobiographical travelogue, written in the tradition of German adventure novels.

Two young Germans seek "adventure" in books written about far-away countries. Australia is presented to them as "ein phantastisch fremder, wilder und unberührter Kontinent".(Ibid.) They immediately decide: "das war endlich unser gesuchtes, gelobtes Land!"(Ibid.) It is an unknown land which attracts them. "Adventure" means to them to explore the unknown, to gain knowledge through travel and personal experience. In that specific sense Australia becomes their place of longing, located in a "Welt der Abenteuer".(Ibid.) In addition, they are guided by a desire to return to nature, to escape a corrupt civilisation. Their trip to Australia is also a flight from what they call "decadent mankind" ("entarteten Menschen",12); they express their feelings of frustration in the outcry "Fort in die Wildnis zur ehrlichen Mutter Erde...".(Ibid.)

There is a great measure of romantic idealisation in the image of Australia which the novel both exposes and reinforces. Its style expresses a cultural conflict which the author emphasises at the end of his book. Commenting on his own alienation in Australia, he concludes: "Wir sehen ja nicht nur die Welt, sondern uns selbst in ihr."(160) The "adventures" he narrates are in fact experiences of cultural alienation; their ultimate aim is to reaffirm the young reader's concept of home.

Velter's portrayal of Aborigines is strongly influenced by his need to introduce a primitive and dangerous counter-culture threatening the safety and self-concept of the white "adventurers". Australia is a country in which there are still "savages" ("noch Wilde gab", 33). Velter thus follows the pattern of German adventure stories. But he adds a further dimension. His young heroes aim to follow in the footsteps of Australia's explorers: they plan to cross the continent from south to north, from Adelaide to Palmerston-Port Darwin.(96) Not surprisingly, Chapter Five contains explicit references to Leichhardt, confirming the intentional analogy.

Unfortunately, Velter confuses Leichhardt's final expedition with his first journey from the Darling Downs to Port Essington. In a grotesque vision he speculates that Leichhardt may have died by drowning in a lagoon.(Ibid.) As so often, facts are subjected to the needs of narrative adventure. This makes Velter's book a curious mixture of information and misinformation. Its general tendency is to see nature as a hostile force, especially where it takes the form of non-European wilderness. The "adventure" consists of destroying it.

Australien kreuz und quer introduces a variety of Australianisms, mainly from the bush. As the title promises, the book offers a cross-section of Australiana, almost always to stress the exotic nature of the land and its people. The overall impression is that it is a strange country in which Germans have difficulty feeling at home. There is little joy in its discovery. Velter laments the absence of a written history and sees an urgent need to "humanize" the land. Australia remains a foreign place. The author offers a general "atmospheric" introduction to the continent, stylising it to a European "adventure".

Velter predicts the extinction of the Aborigines ("das aussterbende Volk der Schwarzen", 106) and treasures the "adventure" of meeting "real savages". The reader never feels that the author has any affinity with Australia. It is one of many settings for his adventurous narratives. A list of his other works indicates the preoccupation with the exotic: *Das blaue Phantom, Elfenbein vom Aldan, Die Otterinsel, Silber am Sandawaku, Die Totenschwemme* and *Überfall auf die Goldwasserfarm*[23]. The place itself is the "adventure". It is an inherent logic that Velter's concept of "adventure" does not allow for familiarity. As a result, Australia is not allowed to lose its strangeness, and the narrator makes no attempt to delve below the surface of its foreign appearance.

Die Farm der guten Hoffnung

This Velter novel first appeared in 1935 and forms part of the German-Australian "colonial" adventure tradition. The very title invokes the colonial aspirations of Germany in Southern Africa, mixed with the adventurous challenge of sailing round Cape Hope. It is in fact a book about Germans in Australia who see themselves as either hunters or explorers. Their background is a paradigmatic disillusionment with post-war German politics. Velter's protagonist laments the loss of the German colony in South-West Africa and links this disappointment with his decision to come to Australia instead. The extension of German colonial life to Australia has rarely been stated so unequivocally. The search for "Raum" was to become a major part of Hitler's expansionist policy of "Volk ohne Raum".

The image of Australia presented in this novel follows the pattern set by earlier travelogues. It is again the total "otherness", the strange, exotic quality of the land which Velter stresses. Australia seems not to be part of the rest of the world. The landscape is seen as belonging to another planet. Australia thus is a country which cannot be grasped ("Unfaßliches Land!",17), in which German adventurers, hunters and settlers have to learn to rethink ("umlernen", 18): everything is different. Living in this country is a challenge, a re-education. The Aborigines are part of the Australian "otherness" Germans try to come to terms with. It is the horror of a defeated white man's civilisation which haunts the German settler. The Australian bush is only described as a threat to the Europeans.

One major effect of such exposure to the Australian "otherness" is the disorientation or loss of identity of Velter's protagonists. Individual lives are revealed as insignificant, yet incomprehensible. Life in Australia discloses a cruel and senseless fate. The Australian landscape is seen as the correlative of a cruel fate. In addition, it externalises the European's desperate state of mind. It is an agent of "fate", actively shaping or destroying individual lives. Like a ghost town, the German settlers are in danger of being reclaimed by the country they tried to "civilise".

Die Farm der guten Hoffnung is the story of settlement involving a defeat of the native land. Germany is left behind. When the clearing and cultivating is completed the European settlers are infatuated with a sense of victory over the hostile country. Settling is experienced as a conquest. Jochen Flindt, addressing his men, speaks of their achievement in military terms. Their work was their battle; it leads to a camaraderie essential to the German literary concept of adventure. Part of its tradition is the threat of betrayal: a comrade in arms is lured into desertion. Velter allocates that task to a woman who is defeated by the land.

Woman personifies a destructive power negating the triumph of settlement, her very being is unsettled, volatile, intimidatory. She has no place anywhere — rather she is identified with an unsettling sensuality, a tropical cycle of wilful regeneration and destruction — the very force the farmers have to defeat and hope to replace with an order of European civilisation. The camaraderie of the men will not be triumphant unless this soulless woman is destroyed. Velter uses set "forces" in his adventure novels; they are not motivated or analysed in any detail, it is more important to record the heroes' reaction to their challenge. Little attempt is made to try to discover the true nature of those who have a different attitude to the land. Adventurers are meant to fight the "unknown" and the "unknowable".

Velter succeeds in conveying the contradictory nature of Europeans living in the Australian bush. There is a hint of recognition of an emerging Australian settler's and bushman's character. It is never presented as a comprehensive vision, never articulated in detail. The author allows only a frustrating glimpse of a white Australian identity.

Contemporary reviews praised Joseph M. Velter as "the great German narrative poet of adventure" (Jakob Kneip)[24]. They emphasised "die Abenteuerlust der Phantasie", adventures of the imagination, claiming that Velter had given "dem deutschen Abenteuerroman der

Gegenwart eine gültige Kunstform..., die ihm größeren literarischen Wert und längeren Bestand sichert"[25]. It is clear from his novels' reception that their literary pretensions were respected. Velter is seen as "ein Dichter, der zu einem Barden der Natur, der Jahreszeiten, der Jagdgefühle, des fremden Klimas wird". He is appreciated as author "des guten Abenteuerromanes"[26]. He earns special praise for having elevated "die Stoffgattung der Abenteuergeschichte" to the level of "gepflegte Unterhaltungsliteratur" and for lending the genre "einen neuen...Wortgehalt", a new quality of literary imagination[27]. Others simply endorse him as a writer of "kraftvolle Abenteuerbücher"[28]. However one interprets these enthusiastic responses, it is clear that Velter was seen as the archetypal narrator of adventure stories, the most convincing exponent of a genre of fiction which enjoyed great prominence in Germany, especially during the thirties.

Jürgen in Australien. Eine Jungengeschichte

In the same year as *Die Farm der guten Hoffnung* – 1935 – Velter published a narrative addressed especially to young German boys, *Jürgen in Australien*. It is a story of friendship and "boys' own adventure" remarkably free from the contemporary extremes of German nationalism or fascism. The settlement of Germans in Australia is treated as something only slightly unusual; migration itself is accepted as a fact of life. The German migrants are shown as well integrated first-generation Australians.

There are no conflicts, no cultural tensions, despite the reaffirmation that Australia is completely different from Germany. The difference is experienced as a pleasant learning process. Some of the narrator's terminology may be suspect — he continues to speak of "Cowboys"(44) in Australia — nonetheless the book offers a reasonable introduction to life in the Australian country. Velter makes use of all the well-known clichés of travelogues and adventure stories.

Velter's book is an authentic reflection of first-generation settlers meeting German visitors. The "mistakes" are, sociologically speaking, documentary; the author's narrative style, is, whether consciously or not, an expression of tolerance and openness refreshing in a work written and published in the mid-thirties. *Jürgen in Australien* is a reaffirmation of the family, its loyalty, its values and its home — wherever it might be.

Willi Vahldiek

Um Gold

Um Gold appeared in July 1931 as Volume 92 of the Ensslin & Laiblins series "Aus weiter Welt". Vahldiek was 52 years old at the time. He introduces himself to his readers by writing about his early Karl May phantasies, his induction into the army at the age of nineteen and his participation in the war in China in 1900. "Mein Reisetrieb führte mich 1902 nach Australien", he reports, adding that in 1904 he moved on to the "deutschen Sonnenland Südwestafrika". Like all of his fellow-writers in this series, Vahldiek retains more than a nostalgic attachment to the former German colonies. Indeed, he describes himself as a "Colonial writer". He concludes his biographical sketch with the comment: "Ich liebe die weite Welt, besonders aber unsere früheren Kolonien. Und wer von den altern Überseern täte das nicht"(2).

The context in which the story *Um Gold* is told thus needs no further explanation. Three Germans and an Austrian meet in Darwin in 1928; together, they venture into the interior, only to be welcomed by another German on his lonely farm. It seems that Germans made up a large part of the population. The farmer's name is Bradhering, a North German, who found refuge in Australia at the outbreak of the First World War. He assures his vivitors that he is happy in the Australian bush. Then he tells them about a young white man he thinks he has seen living with Aborigines. Mindful of his task as commissioned author, Vahldiek lets his character explain: "...daraus könnt ihr ersehen, daß es hier doch etwas gibt, das zu Abenteuern führen kann"(7). Although the four visitors are really sailors waiting for a boat to take them out of Darwin, they decide to travel into Arnhemland, following the tracks of the white man among a tribe of savages ("Wilden", Ibid.). "Hein Trinau aus Hamburg", "Fritz Müller aus Berlin", "Georg Wenzel aus Danzig" and "Xaver Zentgraf aus Wien"(5) cannot resist the temptation to experience a real adventure — "ein seltenes Abenteuer zu bestehen".(8) Needless to say, Bradhering, the Outback farmer from Schleswig-Holstein, joins them. "Es hat noch keiner vermocht", he tells his new friends, "das, was uns im Busch festhält, treffend zu erklären."(9) Even the German sailors begin to feel "die Seele des Landes".(10) They link up with a mysterious "alte Buschläufer" named John, whose real name is Johann Rabe who started out as a gold-miner in Western Australia.(11) He believes he is responsible for the death of another German gold-digger named Fritz Becker whose money and gold he stole and whose three-year-old son Klaus he deserted in the North Australian bush. The first stage of John's unmasking occurs when he suddenly speaks German.

Such operatic revelations occur in the context of exotic flora and fauna. While a monstrous crime has to be atoned for, nature haunts criminal and innocent alike. The native population, of which the lost son Klaus now is a part, appears as a life "totally different", "totally foreign". It is above all the "otherness" which makes Australia and its indigenous people an attractive subject for exotic adventure tales. Racism is an obvious ingredient of such narrative fiction. The Aborigines are described as ugly, inferior beings. When the young German is discovered, it is his racial superiority which is stressed.

The Germans rescue their fellow countryman, suffering many deprivations on their return to civilisation. *Um Gold* centres around "miracles" in nature and in man. No punishment is needed for intended murder. Vahldiek gives the topos of "lost in the bush" his own special twist. German sailors on leave in the Australian bush are heroes and saviours in the name of race.

As is to be expected in popular writing of this kind, style and language do not stand up to closer scrutiny. The author employs an unfortunate mixture of racy colloquialism and pseudo-poetic sentimentality, attempting to convey the impression of casual, natural, "inspired" speech. Vahldiek's formal education was limited, but he knows his readers' expectations and aims to use what might be termed an anecdotal language. He tells a yarn of no literary pretension, in the hope of entertaining a large, unsophisticated readership anxious to hear strange tales of exotic places and adventurous happenings. Australian adventure stories form part of a wider range of "colonial", antipodean or "overseas" ("Übersee") narratives, keeping the dream of German colonies and territories alive whilst reminding their readers of the natural superiority of the Germanic or Nordic race.

Johann Carl Martin

Himmelsstürmer, Grünhorn in Australien

Like Willi Vahldiek, J.C. Martin is a regular contributor to the popular series "Aus weiter Welt". His two publications *Himmelsstürmer* (1930) and *Grünhorn in Australien* (1931) follow the familiar pattern of personal adventure stories in far-away places. By the time *Himmelsstürmer* appeared, Martin was 67 years old; he had first come to Australia at the age of 25. He returned to Australia in the early years of the new century, visiting Tasmania and other parts of the continent, without a prolonged stay. His *Himmelsstürmer* bears the subtitle "Selbsterlebte Abenteuer in Australien", and in fact appears to be a fictionalised version of his experiences as a young migrant. Australia teaches him the value of work. As with most narratives of exotic adventures, the reader's longing for a distant world is reassured by confirmations of home truths. German virtues have to be practised all over the globe. *Himmelsstürmer* is written in the first person singular, in line with the description of its subtitle. It records various work experiences in Australia. Australia is described as an extension of Germany, albeit in a strange environment.

After the tiring work of the day, the authorial narrator finds time to read Australian literature and discovers that his hosts and employers know little of their own national writing. The report throws interesting light on early German-Australian literary relations at popular level. The farmer Werner is described as a first-generation Australian of German extraction; his father is one of the many Silesian peasants who emigrated in the wake of the 1848 Revolution. The reader is told that he found gold at Ballarat and bought himself land from the proceeds.

Martin presents the obligatory list of Australian native animals, not without some incongruous mistakes. Like many other migrants, he describes the "Heimweh nach dem Vaterland" on the occasion of the first "Weihnachtsfest in Australien".(15) Interestingly, he meets an Anglo-Australian farmer who has travelled widely and instils in him a renewed longing to see the world:

> Seine Reiseerinnerungen und Raritäten aus Afrika, Ägypten und Ceylon, die teils die Wände schmückten, teils eine Ecke seines Studierzimmers ausfüllten, durfte ich eingehend besichtigen, und oft drängte sich mir der Wunsch auf: Wenn ich doch auch einmal die weite Welt bereisen und derartige Sammlungen anlegen könnte!(17)

J.C. Martin did just that: he not only published in the series "Aus weiter Welt", he travelled the world and started a conchological collection documenting his journeys. His passage epitomises the *raison d'être* of the Ensslin & Laiblins booklets, as the author articulates and enacts the longings of his readers.

There is some historical interest in Martin's description of Melbourne in the late nineteenth century ("Melbourne zählte damals rund 250,000 Einwohner", 18), especially in his attendance of the World Exhibition at Carlton.(17–19) It includes an account of investment speculations, "ein dankbares Feld für Jobber (Makler, Börsenspieler").(19) A visit of a "Weinstube" in "Collinsstreet"(20) adds authenticity to "the local touch". Martin concludes his report with his brief return to Australia some twenty years later, this time as "scientific collector".

A renewed meeting takes place between him and the man whose worldly collection he is trying to emulate. The author's "Australia Revisited" merely confirms the lessons learnt when he first visited the continent. There is no need for him to return, he has learnt all there is to learn from an Australia consisting of honest work and fierce determination. In future, he will collect samples of the world elsewhere.

Grünhorn in Australien is another version of J.C.Martin's "Auswanderer-Erlebnisse", overlapping with his preceding *Himmelsstürmer*. In its opening paragraph he makes the much repeated claim that Germans are "born" with a longing to emigrate, a trivialisation of what, more often than not, was the dramatic consequence of extreme situations of need. It is a sentimental generalisation in support of the reader's armchair longing for escape, as well as the justification of Martin's own "unstillbare Drang nach fernen Ländern". Indeed, the further away the country of migration, the more attractive it appears. No reasons are given why a young man of twenty-five should wish to escape his native country. Social or political considerations do not play an important part in adventure series such as Ensslin & Laidlin's "Aus weiter Welt". The "longing" of its protagonists is "existential", it has no particular causes. Martin, like his many fellow commissioned authors, suggests it is above all a disposition of temperament, akin to the well-known German "Wanderlust". Australia becomes the code of "otherness", of being "far away", of a different life on the other side of the world. Martin alludes to its exotic appeal when he calls it "das Leben im Lande der Kakadus und Farnbäume".(4)

Yet, for all its romantic stereotyped falsification and coding, *Grünhorn in Australien* does offer an eye-witness account of the actual procedures of migration from Germany to Australia in 1888. Martin writes about his travelling on the "Heim für Auswanderer" in Bremen(5) and gives an indication of the financial investment of a migrant, the length of the train journey to Bremen and the conditions on migrant trains and boats. Not until Joachim Specht's *Peterborough Story* does a narrative work of German-Australian literature offer such detailed account of life on a migrant ship. Written in autobiographical style, from the perspective of a twenty-five-year-old, the language's simplicity and naivety do not seem out of character. Martin relates the usual problems of a migrant's first few days in Australia. Despite his knowledge of English, he must admit: "Den australischen 'Slang' verstand ich nur schwer, andererseits wurde auch ich nicht immer verstanden".(17) But Melbourne offers much to comfort the young Germans. They witness the completion of the Exhibition Building in Carlton and enjoy the relaxation of the Botanical Gardens designed by the German Baron von Müller. The struggle for a living is described in realistic terms. Martin recalls how they manage to find a modest cottage on the outskirts of the city. And he reports the difficulty of being a German migrant in Melbourne looking for work. This is the usual response he gets from prospective employers: "...wir stellen ungern Deutsche ein, weil wir schlechte Erfahrungen mit ihnen gemacht haben. Sie laufen nach ein paar Jahren weg und gründen in unseren eigenen Artikeln ein Geschäft".(19) Ironically, it is the Germans' commercial enterprise which is held against them.

If Martin's *Grünhorn in Australien* has any qualities, it is not in the realm of literature but as a document of social history. Despite some misinformation (including occasional misspellings, such as "Freemantle"(14) and comical mistranslations, such as "Muttonhead", "Schafskopf",25), the narrative is a fairly authentic account of the difficulties of finding work in the cities during the 1880s and 1890s in Australia. A century before Brisbane's World Expo unemployed workers are looking for part-time work at the World Expo in Melbourne. The author and his friends are unsuccessful. Incongruously, a German opera singer shows them the way. It is difficult not to see the comedy of such a conclusion to *Grünhorn in Australien*. If it needs a migrant opera singer to discover work in this country — presumably not in one's original profession — Australia's social history may be in need of such unlikely testimony as J.C. Martin's autobiographical fiction.

Hans-Joachim Mühlen-Schulte

Drei Millionärsanwärter starten in Australien

This is a typical example of young adult fiction centering on Australia as a "land of limitless opportunities", a place of adventurous challenge. Like America, Australia is referred to as "Drüben"(9), a "beyond" where heaven or paradise exists in the form of rich uncles, a spectacular career or limitless freedom. It would be fair to interpret the German concept of "Drüben" as a kind of secular, social and political redemption. If today's political metaphysics still looks to America for "salvation", it is steeped in the tradition of German migration. Australia holds a less prominent place in the same projection of leaving frustrations and native limitations behind. Mühlen-Schulte's 1932 narrative for German adolescents follows this pattern very closely. The rich uncle found gold in Australia. The history of German-Australian writing demonstrates the similarity between juvenile and adult literature: they share the same assumptions and follow the same model. Lack of opportunity back home and limitless opportunity in the New Country are the formula of hope for all migration and form the basis of narrative fiction dealing with this subject. Its inherent naivety makes for disarming and amusing descriptions; in writings for adults it often leads to a perpetuation of painful misconceptions or to a trivialised narrative style. It could be said that a great many works of German-Australian fiction retain an infantile quality, both in their perception and in their expression of a predefined vision.

Drei Millionärsanwärter carries such naive expectations in its title and playfully exposes the myth. Addressed to young readers, the novel offers a range of exaggerated and unbelievable experiences under the usual heading of "adventures". As the moral of the book is stated explicitly at its end, the didactic purpose of its unlikely tales cannot be doubted. All adventures in Australia lead to the Protestant work ethic. The transparency of incredible events, even for young readers, makes the didactic exercise enjoyable. Many of the laughable absurdities of "adult" fiction are exposed, yet the great Australian dream is not altogether demythologised. Stubborn perseverance in work, not coincidental luck, can create a fortune. Like all adventure novels, Mühlen-Schulte's book is written for domestic consumption. Despite occasional homage to German nationalism the book is refreshingly free from jingoistic tirades so common in German-Australian writing during the thirties.

All the usual ingredients of an Australian adventure are to be found in this novel: the "Waldbrand" (bushfire), the young kangaroo, the dramatic change of weather, the drought ("die große Dürre"), plagues (rats, rabbits), the poisonous snakes and spiders and wealthy squatters. Yet all this is set against the background of German adventure stories for the young (Karl May etc.). Such adaptations illustrate the extent to which the Australian scene is interchangeable with the American. It helps explain why Aborigines are mostly seen as the equivalent of American Red Indians. The author needlessly reminds his readers: "Hanne hatte seine Indianerbücher aufmerksam gelesen".(76) So have a lot of writers of German-Australian literature. Australia thus is a testing ground for "manhood", an exotic place of challenge. "Adventure" means specifically to conquer any lack of determination in a young person and to learn to accept responsibility. It is a pedagogic concept used as a genre of didactic fiction for the young.

The mysterious magic emanating from the place is the *Abenteuerroman's* correlative of the adolescent's urge to find and to define himself. There is an eros of self-discovery inherent in such "adventure". Australia is a "sign", the manifestation of this aim to search for oneself. Any other far-away country could fulfil the same function. "Aber Australien ist ja...genau wie Amerika", says the author.(87) Any attempt to draw his attention to the vast differences between the two countries would be missing the point; it is not the place that matters. Although the setting is Australia, the lesson to be learnt could have been projected into any setting.

The presentation of Australia as a pedagogic province is a central feature of German-Australian "adventure" fiction. The special character of Mühlen-Schulte's novel for young readers is that its protagonists remain in Australia. Reunification of the family may be another cliché of German adventurers in Australia, but in this case the three adults joining the boys from Germany are apprentices in the craft of moral self-fulfilment. They, too, want to enter "paradise", the heavenly continent of golden labour. Life in Australia is a confirmation of German values; as such, it promises blissful self-affirmation.

Augustin Lodewyckx

Die Deutschen in Australien

The author, of Belgian extraction, was Associate Professor of Germanic Languages at the University of Melbourne from 1922 to 1946. His *Die Deutschen in Australien* is the most authoritative publication on its subject to date. It first appeared in 1932 as part of a series of cultural histories in the "Schriften des Deutschen Ausland-Instituts Stuttgart" (Volume 32). Although in need of updating, this history of Germans in Australia remains a reliable compilation. No single comparable book has been written since.[28] Lodewyckx's work consists of thirteen chapters dealing with a wide range of German contributions to Australian society and culture. Almost one-third is devoted to church and mission activities. In his Introduction the author rightly argues "daß gerade die wichtigste Gruppe der Deutschaustralier sich im Kirchlichen ausgelebt hat".(5) Lodewyckx offers a general historical survey of German participation in the discovery (or discoveries) of Australia and other parts of the Pacific region, linking it with a precise summary of Australia's history. This is followed by a detailed account of German immigration and settlement in all Australian states over a period of 150 years.

Lodewyckx stresses the achievements of Germans in the area of economics, art and science. His chapter "Die Deutschen in der australischen Wirtschaft" illustrates the extent of German contributions to agriculture, wine-growing, mining and trade in Australia. Chapters on German schools in Australia and on science and art demonstrate a similar commitment in those fields. In the final three chapters Lodewyckx deals with German-Australian relations. "In diesen Abschnitten habe ich", he comments, "wie in den vorigen, die Tatsachen ihre eigene Sprache reden lassen. Ein Urteil über die Geschehnisse überlasse ich meistens dem Leser selbst."(Ibid.) The author does indeed show impartiality in an area of notorious conflicts of ideological and cultural bias.

The German contribution to literature, the emergence of a "deutschaustralische Literatur", is discussed in Chapter Eight: "Die deutsche Sprache in Australien, Literatur, Presse".(170–182) Lodewyckx foreshadows the result of his analysis as early as in the Introduction where he states: "In der Dichtkunst, wir müssen es gestehen, ist die Ernte eine nicht sehr reiche".(5) A similar judgement opens the section on "Deutschaustralische Literatur"(178): "Von einer deutsch-australischen Literatur kann nur in sehr beschränktem Maße die Rede sein." This may explain why the author does not attempt a definition of the concept. He does not, for example, clarify whether works written in English may also fall under the heading of German-Australian literature. (The title of his chapter would seem to indicate that he is only interested in "the German language in literature". Yet his brief listings include a passing reference to authors of German extraction in an "Australian literature written in English": "Auch in der australischen Literatur englischer Sprache haben ein paar Männer deutscher Abstammung einen guten Namen erworben." He goes on to list the Jewish writers Nathan F. Spielvogel and I.A. Rosenblum as well as Leon Gellert. By such criterion contemporary writers like David Martin would certainly belong to a "deutschaustralische Literatur". What is remarkable in the light of a concept of multicultural literature in Australia is Lodewyckx's unquestioning distinction of an "Australian literature in English", assuming a broader range of Australian literature, written in community languages.) At the close of his discussion, Lodewyckx does acknowledge the ambiguity of the term "deutschaustralische Literatur":

> Was wir daher unter dem etwas anspruchsvollen Titel "Deutschaustralische Literatur" zusammenfassen, sind lauter Werke von in Deutschland oder in der Schweiz geborenen Verfassern, die sich entweder dauernd oder vorübergehend in Australien niederließen.(182)

It is a terminological uncertainty which has remained. Lodewyckx's claim that little of literary consequence was written by German settlers is justified for the period covered by his history. Ironically, in the late thirties (August von der Flatt) and forties that was about to change, albeit on a moderate scale. With that, the concept of a German-Australian literature gained a new dimension of legitimacy. What is missing in Lodewyckx's discussion is a contextualising of the European German-Australian literature, relating the few authors to German literary, social and ideological backgrounds. He does not describe the writings of C.F. Behrens, the Forsters, Chamisso, Gerstäcker and Theodor Müller as part of a German tradition of travelogues, nor does he emphasise the fundamental interrelationship between travel literature, narratives (or journals) of exploration and adventure fiction — arguably *the* prominent feature of German-Australian writing. It is curious that Lodewyckx should devote a quarter of the space reserved to German-Australian literature to excerpts from Stefan von Kotze's *Australische Skizzen*, lines he believes offer "in poetic sublimation" a description of the gold-rush ("in welchen von Kotze dichterisch verklärt die unwiderstehliche Macht schildert, die den Goldsucher in die Wildnis treibt", 180). The quotations display no exceptional literary quality.

Lodewyckx's study *Die Deutschen in Australien* includes an excellent survey of the German press in Australia. As the examples of Hermann Püttmann and L.L. Politzer illustrate, literary and journalistic activities often complemented each other. Lodewyckx's own work is characterised by a style he himself calls "schlicht und einfach"(5), a happy mixture of academic precision and general readability. His text is notably free of scholarly jargon and ideological prejudice. There is clear evidence that the book was a labour of love; its subject is obviously close to the author's heart. *Die Deutschen in Australien* is crowded with facts and documentation, yet it retains the quality of an historical narrative. Augustin Lodewyckx lacks the vision of a Manning Clark or Geoffrey Blainey, but he is equally reliable in his careful presentation of facts and in the gatherings of evidence. He does speak of the "Deutschtum in Australien"(235) or the "deutschaustralische Volkstum"(6), but these ideologically loaded terms do not lead him to a position of aggressive nationalism. He does not doubt that "die Deutschen und ihre Kultur...in der Zukunft noch eine sehr bedeutende Rolle...in Australien (spielen werden)".(245) If there is a slight irritation, it is Lodewyckx's appeal to young German-Australians to grow into "würdige Führer ihres Volkes".(Ibid.) It raises the basic question whether "second generation" Australians of German background should wish to aspire to such leadership. Whose "Volk" *is* theirs, worthy of their representation? And is it realistic or wise to expect Australian-born "Germans" to speak for a Germany they may have inherited under politically and ideologically volatile circumstances? Amazingly, Lodewyckx does not address himself to the subject of integration. His title seems to imply that "Germans in Australia" remain German forever, irrespective of the circumstances. The history of German assimilation in this country tells a different story. The author writes about a German culture in Diaspora, without acknowledging in his survey of clubs and cultural organisations that the image of Germany cultivated is retrospective. It is in the nature of national groups in migrant countries to be conservative. Their aim is to preserve the memory of what was left behind. Lodewyckx would have done well to retain some critical detachment in his description of German nationalism in Australia.

Kurt Faber

Im australischen Busch, Als Landstreicher durch Australien

These seemingly different publications are actually edited versions of the same book, consisting of two separate short stories. The first edition appeared in 1933 as Volume 391 of the "Deutsche Jugendbücherei", the other shortly afterwards in the Ensslin & Laiblins series "Bunte Bücher" (Heft 230). Both are in fact excerpts from Kurt Faber's full-length book publication *Tausend und ein Abenteuer*, published by Rainer Wunderlich Verlag in Tübingen, which reached its fourth edition in 1932. Kurt Faber had died in the winter of 1929–30 in Canada. *Tausend und ein Abenteuer* is described by the publisher as the last work edited by the author, the author himself as "ein Vorkämpfer wahren Deutschtums".(33) Curiously, *Als Landstreicher durch Australien* bears a different title inside, i.e. *Unter Landstreichern und Schafscherern. Erlebnisse eines Deutschen in Australien*. Perhaps just as curiously, it is edited by the "Lehrervereinigung für Kunstpflege in Berlin". *Im australischen Busch* and *Als Landstreicher durch Australien* both consist of the two stories "Paradies der Landstreicher" and "Romantik der Wolle". It seems that after the death of the author the publishers "utilised" excerpts from his last book in various popular series and did not hesitate to abbreviate, rewrite or edit the text whenever necessary.

Not that the literary quality of Faber's narratives could be said to have suffered from these various adaptations. The level of his writing can only be called modest or uncomplicated. Like so many other *Deutschtum* authors in foreign countries, Kurt Faber's attraction to a mass readership lay in his life, in the "heroic travels", adventures and explorations which he recorded in his travelogues. He specialises in translation of foreign terms. (Much of German-Australian literature is based on such mediation of the "exotic".) His descriptions of Australia are, on the whole, informative and reliable, if occasionally exaggerated or stylised for effect. The geography of a foreign, far-away country is of special interest to his imaginary world travellers. He compares the Australian countryside with other parts of the word. This kind of travelogue adventure thrives on comparisons between countries; the readers themselves have accumulated a knowledge anxious to be tested.

Kurt Faber provides plenty of factual information about the antipodean continent, dressed in anecdotal narratives of personal experience. They are designed to persuade his readers that Australia is indeed a "paradise for vagabonds". He romanticises the swagman culture to a mixture of socialist egalitarianism and criminal underworld. This is the real subject of his first story: Australia as a home for "Landstreicher". He concludes his narrative with a vision of "die große Freimaurerei des wandernden Volkes", praising the life-style of the many vagabonds he met all over the world: "so wie ich es überall gefunden habe auf dieser Erde: die schlimmsten Teufel und die reinsten Engel und Himmel und Hölle noch immer auf der Landstraße".(15) Australia is merely one variation of this all-embracing, universal life on the road.

For all its atmospheric invocation, the author somehow fails to capture the authentic spirit of an Australian setting. Perhaps he has simply done too much travelling. Some of his scenes seem interchangeable or variations of a more general representation. Kurt Faber remains an outsider whose preconceived ideas prevent him from greater empathy with foreign landscapes and their inhabitants. It is fair to say that the author's sensibility is at odds with the local temperament. All the more surprising therefore, when Faber occasionally employs the Australian idiom in translation: "...'s ist ein Monat von Sonntagen, seit wir uns nicht mehr gesehen."(18) It is doubtful whether his German readers appreciate what narrative style is being employed.

More than in the preceding tale, "Romantik der Wolle" reveals the writer's uneasiness with his subject. He is more explicit about his fear of what he believes is a criminal characteristic in Australia's city population. Almost all Australians, he argues, have a natural disposition to cheat or to exploit their fellow men. Faber's contempt for the Australian country town is based on generalised observation and loses further credibility when he mocks the faded beauty of country women by quoting from Goethe's *Faust*:

> Man weiß, das Volk taugt aus dem Grunde nichts,
> geschnürten Leibs, geschminkten Angesichts,
> man weiß, man sieht's, man kann es greifen,
> und dennoch tanzt man, wie sie pfeifen.

The incongruity of such quotation speaks for itself. The champion of vagabonds and swagmen has great difficulty coming to terms with the ordinary humanity of simple country folk. (Significantly, the *Faust* quotation is left out in *Als Landstreicher durch Australien*. The editors of the later publication may have sensed the credibility problem of their author.)

Faber is more sympathetic to the early pioneers of Australian farming. He spends much time explaining the duties of a "Boundaryrider (Grenzreiter)" and the "Stationshände" and reinvokes life on a "homestead".(20) Yet when it comes to describing the life of ordinary Australian workers the author's attitude is somewhat ambivalent. He believes Australians generally are more independent-minded than their American cousins. He acknowledges that in no country of the world wages are as high as in Australia, but argues that this is achieved at the expense of vast unemployment, especially in the cities. The author is particularly unhappy about unionism in the country.

One of Faber's most interesting reports concerns a "black birder (schwarzen Vogelfänger)" who used to lure kanakas from the South Sea islands to the sugar plantations in Queensland. After initial denials the slave catcher identifies himself to the narrator as a German who "mit List und lockenden Versprechungen, oft auch mit roher Gewalt die Kanaken in ihren Inselparadiesen aufgriff und gegen gutes Kopfgeld nach den Zuckerrohrplantagen in Queensland verfrachtete."(23) It is an aspect of German migrant activity about which little is known to this day.

Such bursts of disturbing realism are quickly interrupted by a return to Europeanised distortions of sheep-farming and other activities on the land. "So ist das Schäferleben in diesem modernen Arkadien", writes Faber. "Eine beschauliche Verbannung in behaglicher Verzweiflung zwischen Herde und Hütte."(25) It is indicative of the uneven style of the narrative, fluctuating between pseudo-literary and pedestrian. Faber retells some bush yarns, even quotes the occasional bush ballad ("In des Gummibaumes Schatten,/des Gummibaumes Schatten,/ist des Herdenmannes Grab!"[29]), and generally tries hard to convey aspects of what has been called Australiana. If he fails, it may well be because he finds it difficult to identify with those very people his literary *persona* derives from. Kurt Faber is not a vagabond, even less a swaggie, but a German middle-class traveller posing as narrative adventurer. His Australia is an ultimately unattractive, strange and primitive place which he has visited on behalf of his cult readers, not a country of comfortable travel or great excitement á la Karl May or James Fenimore Cooper.

Hans Bertram

Flug in die Hölle

Bertram's "Atlantis Expedition" is one of the best documented "adventures" by Germans on Australian soil. This "Bericht" ("report") appeared in 1933 in Berlin. As recently as 1986 a filmed version of the German flyers' experiences was shown on Australian television[29]. Hans Bertram speaks of "unser großes Australienerlebnis"(152) when describing the dramatic events of his and his co-pilot's flight from Kupang/Timor to Northern Australia in 1932. His report sees itself as a kind of factual "Robinsonade". Throughout the narrative Bertram is defensive about his writing ability — "ein Dichter müßte man sein"(3), he says at the very beginning. At least part of his difficulty lies in the contrast between a cold, sunless Berlin in which the narrative account is written and the beauty of the South Sea islands:

> Diese Zeilen schreibe ich in Berlin, eingeengt von einem kalten, sonnenlosen Himmel, von erdrückenden Steinhaufen moderner Baukunst. Wie soll man da von der Südsee erzählen können, von diesen Trauminseln, den Farbensymphonien von Wasser, Strand, Palmenwald und Himmel? (Ibid.)

It is the familiar image of the antipodean paradise. Bertram, the non-professional writer, pleads with his readers to invoke their dreams.

"Unreal" and "supernatural" are key terms in his description, stressing the fearful unfamiliarity of the terrain in which he and his co-pilot Klausmann have to survive. The constant addresses to the reader convey more than the usual attempt to establish rapport, there is an urgency to communicate an experience beyond the level of exotic adventure. The author speaks of their "Leidenszeit" ("passion") and at the end of this report hopes to have "borne witness" ("Zeugnis zu geben",152) to something greater than chance survival. The strong sense of a religious "miracle" is borne out by the book's final words: "Gott lebt! — Hans!"(Ibid.) It is a test of faith as much as the story of wrecked ambition.

Flug in die Hölle must indeed be read as a kind of thanksgiving. Part of this gratitude has religious dimensions. Bertram keeps referring to the "Wunder der 53 Tage" ("miracle of the 53 days",134). Earlier, he writes: "Die Kraft holten wir uns im Gebet und im Glauben an die Mutter".(122) Against such background, he interprets their survival in the wilderness in explicitly Christian terms. Hans Bertram's

Robinsonade turns more and more into a religious narrative of didactic intent. "These notes", he determines, "shall be a Song of Praise for our God who sent out white and black messengers to save us!"(134) The book's title assumes theological dimensions.

Australia is experienced in such terms. "Kann es denn ein derartiges Land auf der Welt geben?" asks Bertram, a land which is dead, "vollkommen ausgestorben".(113) He notes that the Kimberleys are as large as his native Germany.(114) But that is about all the factual or geographical information he is able to pass on. Australia is basically a spiritual landscape for Bertram. Even the *topos* of a bushfire is transformed into spiritual dimension.

Against such extraordinary vision the historical and natural Australia fades into insignificance; it is merely the backdrop of a miracle of survival. The landscape of "hell" is essentially metaphysical and to that extent interchangeable. For all the goodwill and gratitude Bertram expresses towards the Aborigines, it is as messengers of salvation that they feature and matter in his story. From "Ekel" and "Abscheu"(94) his feelings for black Australians change to intense admiration — as a result of the Germans' salvation. They are now "diese prachtvollen Gestalten".(137) Although he promises to "have a closer look at them"(Ibid.), it is clear that such approach will not lead to an anthropological description. Bertram does not really see the Aborigine, any more than he sees the Australian landscape. The author constructs a "noble savage" to glorify his own salvation. Only when Bertram actually describes a meal he and his friend share with the Aborigines does the reader sense an element of realism.(143–145) As part of his idealised version of an Australian "heaven" and "hell" Hans Bertram is savagely critical of European civilisation. We ("wir Menschen der Zivilisation",Ibid.) have lost Christian charity or love for one's fellow-man and have to re-learn it from the "wild natives" of Australia. Instead of the original "Ekel" he felt for the Aborigine, he now feels "Ekel" for the civilisation he so desperately longed for in the North Australian wilderness — mainly because of attempts to sensationalise his experience. *Flug in die Hölle* is an eye-witness report of a "saved soul" where believing is seeing. Back in Berlin, Bertram reinforces German concepts of the exotic by transforming the antipodean adventure into spiritual testimony. Our "Robinsondasein"(89) is reduced to lost souls waiting to be found.

C.M.H. Clark relates Hans Bertram's volatile mixture of will and faith to an ultimate subservience to German fascism. It is true that in his *Flug in die Hölle* (published as *Flight Into Hell* in 1985) he states: "Und die Wahrheit ist, — ich rufe sie laut in alle Welt –: Du Mensch brauchst im Leben zwei Dinge: du brauchst einen Willen und einen Glauben!"(107) That interdependence of will and faith characterises his own book and his own *Weltanschauung*: he believes what he wants to believe, his *Flug in die Hölle* is a kind of *Triumph des Willens*. Bertram's subsequent "faith" in Hitler revealed the peculiarly aesthetised idealism he shared with Leni Riefenstahl, especially in black natives and tribal culture, and the nationalistic dimensions of his "salvation". Clark's *History of Australia* (Volume VI) offers a more sober and sombre account of Bertram's and Klausmann's fateful flight:

> They were on a flight from Germany to the Far East to stake a claim for German aviation in the forthcoming competition for control of passenger and freight air traffic between Europe and the East...Bertram never forgot his debt to (the) nomads of the deserts of Australia. Yet soon after his return to Germany early in 1933 he fell under the spell of Adolf Hitler, the apologist for the Germans as a 'master race'. He believed in this man. He believed that only those with an iron will and an unbreakable faith could survive.(426)[30]

The "faith" and "charity" of Hans Bertram need no further elaboration. The "spiritual epiphany" revealed itself as a glorification of fascist "will to power".

KARL EY

Kolonisten in Ketten

This book appeared in 1935, published by the Dünen Verlag Bremen. It propagates a "wertvolle und zeitgemäße Beitrag zur Kolonialfrage und zu den Aufgaben eines seiner Verantwortung bewußten Auslandsdeutschtums". The dream of Germany's resurgence as a colonial power still persists, and Germans living abroad are seen as natural allies in such aspiration. A glorification of combat and "manhood" form further part in the nationalist and imperialist concept of "Abenteuer" during the thirties. The publisher's blurb declares: "Der Krieg konnte ihnen wohl Freiheit und Besitz rauben, niemals aber den Glauben an ihre Heimat, an Deutschland".(203) Adventures are undertaken for the glory of the "fatherland"; living in "colonies" (or potential colonies) is seen as an extension of a German home. Migrants and settlers are expected to retain strong links with their native country, to interpret their position as outposts of a German empire. German plans for world domination were never well hidden.

Kolonisten in Ketten carries the subtitle "Der Roman eines Erdteils", and its author does present history in the form of a novel. Karl Ey motivates his narrative composition by constructing a story within a story ("Rahmenerzählung"). A brief "Einleitung" (1–8) and "Schluß"(199–202) form the "pretext" for the historical novel. An old Australian aboard an ocean-liner is asked by a young American woman to tell her the history of his country, as they are entering Sydney Harbour. Like other novels of the thirties, *Kolonisten in Ketten* emphasises the racial "purity" of Australia's population — albeit by distortion and misinformation. The historical narrative begins in November 1786. In a curious mixture of fictional narrative and historical documentation the author describes the background to Australia's initial colonisation. He quotes James Cook's diary and reports on Prime Minister Pitt's appointment of Captain Arthur Phillip to lead the expedition. This leads to a sudden authorial intrusion, a kind of nationalistic narrative comment:

> Unter all den Männern, die an der Besiedlung einer neuen Welt teilhaben sollen, unter all den Menschen in blitzenden Uniformen und bunter Sträflingstracht ist zweifellos Kapitän Phillip die aufrechteste und sympathischste Erscheinung, eine Tatsache, die uns nicht unangenehm berührt, denn in den Adern des Kapitäns rollt deutsches Blut.(32)

The reader is taken on board the deportation fleet leaving Portsmouth on 13 May 1787. The novel's aim is to create the impression of an eye-witness account. Extracts from Captain Phillip's diary are integrated into the narrative. Ey presents reliable statistics on the loadings of HMS "Sirius", HMS "Supply" and the other three ships sailing to Botany Bay ("Borrowdale", "Fishburne" and "Golden Grove"). The author succeeds in conveying the enormity of the challenge. From the beginning, he draws "Pioniere in roten Militärröcken" and "Pioniere in Ketten".(40) When a planned mutiny is discovered, Phillip's action is described as "typically German":

> Gouverneur Phillip begnügt sich aber nicht mit der Bestrafung der Meuterer. Mit echt deutscher Gründlichkeit untersucht er die Zustände auf den Gefangenenschiffen und ist entsetzt.(42)

"Kolonisten in Ketten...".(49) The phrase is often used as an expression or sign of irony, contrast or moral indignation. The "Gouverneur" continues to be shown as a man of German temperament. After the raising of the flag on 26 January 1788, Phillip spends the night taking stock of his manpower, assets, food and money. The narrator describes the governor's inventory thus: "Mit der Gewissenhaftigkeit eines deutschen Beamten gibt sich der Herr eines neuen Erdteils...nicht nur mit der Eintragung der Sträflinge in die erste 'Bürgerrolle' Australiens zufrieden...".(55)

Like so many German writers about Australia, Ey refers to the folly of the importation of five rabbits. Breaking out of the strictly sequential historical narrative, it is the present which gives many of Ey's historical accounts their special relevance. He writes about the first land decree printed on the Australian continent, reproduces the document in full and traces the biography of Tom Barry, the convict printer responsible for its production. The novel describes Tom Barry's career as Australia's first newspaper publisher who founded *The Sydney Bulletin* and in characteristic updating comments:

> Einer der größten Zeitungsverleger Australiens heißt heute Thomas W. Barry. Man konnte kürzlich lesen, daß er mit seiner Motorjacht zum Besuch des amerikanischen Zeitungskönigs Hearst in Los Angeles eingetroffen sei.(78)

Fact and fiction intermingle in the old Australian's report to the young American woman.

The novel's narrator reminds his readers that Phillip was responsible for the first reliable reports about the Aborigines. Wherever possible, Phillip is allowed to speak himself, usually by quoting his diaries. Ey uses somewhat heavy-handed introductions to such excerpts, for example: "Hören wir, was Kapitän Phillip selbst darüber in seinen Erinnerungen sagt:".(96) Phillip's interest in Aborigines is explained in some detail, including the story of "Koalbays" and "Bänaläng"(sic).(101–102) Refreshingly, Karl Ey refers to the Aborigines as "die Australier".(102)

Kolonisten in Ketten includes a fictional plot centred around the convicts Jenny Day and Montgomery Clark. It is a transparent construction allowing the narrator to be identified at the end of the book.(202) Ey did not believe his readers would remain interested in a country's history without a human interest story holding it together. Unfortunately, Jenny and "Monty" cannot match the far more exciting plot of building a nation. The author writes about the fate of many "Emanzipisten"(108), the liberated convicts in the colony. Inevitably, he cannot resist the temptation to write about "Bushrangers"(109) as well. He accurately reports the criminal activities of some military officers.

Occasionally, Ey's novel sets out to interpret social history. It is in this area that some of the book's most interesting passages occur. Thus the author relates the fate of "eine ganze Theatergesellschaft" which was deported from Dublin "weil sie in einem Stück patriotische irische Propaganda betrieben haben sollte".(117) And he records the arrival of "die ersten Privatpersonen in Australien"(Ibid.) as well as the forming of "die Vigilanten von Neusüdwales"(127), a vigilante group against crime in the colony. In these episodes the author succeeds in creating the impression of authenticity, both in characterisation and in social history. The narrator continues to quote from contemporary sources. However, the extracts are such that it is not always possible to distinguish between quotation as fictional form and authentic documentation. The transparency of the narrative structure calls for more than the usual suspension of disbelief. The astonishing thing is that Karl Ey does succeed in creating the illusion of authentic social history, at least in parts. One such event is the report on Sydney's first theatre: "Das erste Theater in Sydney wird errichtet!"(135) Another is the discovery of fertile land beyond the mountains and the subsequent extension of Sydney beyond Parramatta.

Not always does the "human interest" story interrelate as successfully with the country's history. Remarkably for the time in which this novel was written, Ey's portrayal of Aborigines remains sympathetic throughout. The author makes no attempt to hide the confiscation of land by the white settlers. The title of his novel thus steadily gains in irony. Jenny's and "Monty's" freedom and wealth are correlated to the Aborigines' suppression and poverty. Ey does not go beyond stating this contrast. The reader is left to wonder whether the irony in the novel's description of Aborigines working for white "emancipist" settlers is intentional.

The novel's final chapter deals, among other things, with the Rum Rebellion. Ey again employs authentic as well as fictional quotations from contemporary sources to describe the living conditions in and around Sydney. The restoration of law and order in Sydney under Governor Macquarie takes up much space, as does Macquarie's refusal to accept women convicts. Queen Victoria's decision to allow "unbescholtene Jungfrauen"(174) to emigrate to Australia is described in a curious mixture of the usual quotations from public pronouncements (including newspapers) and a reluctant mind-reading of a profoundly, if somewhat comically, royalist narrator.

In the context of real or fictional documentation as literary style for an historical novel the authorial comments, reflections or other intrusions almost read like alienation effects. Is Ey's narrator serious when he "interprets" the voluntary migration of young British "virgins" as a moral surplus with its own impact on the male convict population? "Daß dieser Gedanke nicht falsch war", he reflects, "ist vielleicht durch den aufrechten, kernigen, ehrlichen Charakter bewiesen, der den heutigen Australier auszeichnet."(178) As so often in this book, it is not altogether clear whether something is meant seriously or not. Like America, Australia is seen as a strange place, full of contradictions and possibilities. Striking it rich in a far-away country of migration has always been a popular myth, not only in Germany. There is a lot of mythology in Karl Ey's *Kolonisten in Ketten*, such as the fate of the barber MacThomas who became "der reichste Mann eines Kontinents".(191) His "story" is reported in the *Sydney Bulletin* (1885) and retold by the narrator Montgomery Clark.

The novel thus culminates in an affirmation of wealth and good fortune to be gained in Australia. In the Conclusion ("Schluß") the skyline of Sydney inspires a discussion of the distribution of wealth, comparing the Australian situation with that of the United States. The old Australian, Montgomery Clark, asks the young American lady: "Hat man in den USA nicht von Anbeginn der geschäftlichen Spekulation zu großen Spielraum gegeben?" Clark, who has inherited the name of his father and grandfather, claims that Sydney was built with far less financial speculation: "der Australier schätzt die Arbeit mehr als den leichten Gewinn", he informs the US lady — and the amazed reader. Australia's wealth is built on "die fleißigen Hände aus England, Irland und Deutschland".(200) *Kolonisten in Ketten* thus almost ends a migrants' brochure, propagating an Anglo-German work ethic and promising just rewards. Like all of this novel's claims, it is an interpretation of fact and fiction, a mixture of reliable information and fanciful speculation. Perhaps there is no reason to expect anything different from a work of popular literature — or, indeed, from any attempt to "actualise" history. Whatever the literary qualities of this narrative vision — and they are clearly limited — *Kolonisten in Ketten* remains noteworthy for its relative resistance to Nazi or even excessively nationalistic sentiments. Karl Ey has written a refreshingly "liberal" book about Australia at a time when that in itself was no mean achievement.

Kurt Heyd

Christophs Abenteuer in Australien

The author calls his narrative "eine Erzählung aus der Goldgräberzeit". In his short "Vorrede" Heyd claims that the adventures told in his book were in fact his grandfather's. He first heard them during the long winters of the war years when the boy was told one or two stories a day. "...sie waren so fremdartig und so reich an Abenteuern," Heyd remembers, "daß sie nicht ausgelöscht werden konnten."(5) *Christophs Abenteuer in Australien* are therefore re-told mainly for young readers and continues the German interpretation of Australian history as "strange" ("fremdartig") and "adventurous". The book was released in Berlin in the summer of 1935.

It is a pleasant enough novel about young Christoph who in July 1854 follows his parents who have migrated to Australia. No specific reasons are given why the family has to leave Germany. The reader may assume that it took place in the aftermath of 1848. Although his teacher informs him that Australia is a penal colony of ill repute, Christoph confidently announces: "Ich fahre jetzt auch nach Australien; ich will dort Goldgräber oder Forschungsreisender werden."(8) In his naive expectations he does reflect a widespread assumption among German readers about the most likely themes of narrative fiction dealing with Australia. Heyd stresses the social equality in the gold fields, a classless society in which even a young boy may find his place. In the "Goldminen...gab es keinen Unterschied zwischen alt und jung, zwischen Grafen und Bauern, Adligen und Handwerkern..."(28). Perhaps that is why the narrator immediately refers to "die neue Heimat"(30) when, after exactly one hundred days, the migrant ship reaches Port Phillip Bay.

Kurt Heyd's account of Melbourne around the middle of the nineteenth century does not lack authenticity. He describes the "Hafenviertel St. Kilda"(32) with great enthusiasm, but his protagonist is taken aback by the sight of the rest of the city: "Das war ja nur ein riesengroßes Dorf aus Holzbaracken und halbfertigen Steinhäusern," Christoph exclaims.(34) The author invokes a half-completed town under the spell of the gold-rush, a place where bourgeois morality, law and order have largely broken down. Much of Heyd's fictional adventure has a solid historical basis.

With the inevitable move to the bush young Christoph learns the special language of Australians. The author does not extend this perspective beyond Australia's flora and fauna. Although the narrative does stress the characteristic egalitarianism among gold-diggers, no attempt is made to offer a sociological interpretation of "mateship" as a form of political inversion. The bushranger theme is treated as a variation of the *topos* of mistaken identity. The novel carries it to the extreme of including the boy's own father in the search and confusion.

As with most German novels about Germans in Australia, the plot centres on "ethnic" settings. Christoph has no difficulty finding "ein großes, von Deutschen bevorzugtes Hotel" in Sydney (113) or "Deutsche, die in die Minen wollten"(115). Part of the theme of Germans in Australia is invariably a description of a "deutsche Weihnachtsfeier"(116), a Christmas celebration reminding the migrants what they have left behind. It is a time of longing and reflection. But Heyd rightly stresses the "multicultural" component of life in the diggings. It is seen as the potential genesis of a truly democratic, non-racist society. Against such credible social realism there are "adventurous" passages of pure phantasy demanding more than the usual share of willing suspension of disbelief. The unlikely story ends in a German folksong celebrating the joys of travelling the world.

Kurt Heyd's book is a tantalising mixture of historical narrative and escapist phantasy. Its cheerful tone throughout tempers any didactic ambition. The novel is free from racist or fascist elements, in itself a refreshing sign of moral and political independence in German youth literature of 1935. For all its superficialities and exaggerations, the author does succeed in offering a narrative introduction to Australia a hundred years ago which retains some authenticity. It takes its place in the context of young adult fiction not for its literary qualities, but for its glimpses of historical and social impacts which have shaped the future Australian nation.

A.E. JOHANN

Känguruhs, Kopra und Korallen

This author, whose real name is Alfred Wollschläger, has a penchant for title alliterations; in addition to the Australian travelogue released in Berlin in 1936, Johann published the following three titles with Ullstein, Berlin: *Kulis, Kapitäne und Kopfjäger* (1936), *Präsident, Prärien und Pelztiere* (1937) and *Generäle, Geishas und Gedichte*

(1938). Interestingly, these books are not listed among his 38 novels, stories and travelogues, as they appear in *Kürschners Deutscher Literatur-Kalender*[31]. If Wollschläger's narrative report of Australia is anything to go by, the author's self-censorship appears to be a case of "de-Nazification". The work is unashamedly fascist and racist. This is what he has to say in his chapter "Wo in Australien der deutsche Wein wächst":

> Im australischen Deutschtum wie überall auf der ganzen Welt hat die Wiedergeburt Deutschlands die schon in Vergessenheit sinkende alte Heimat wieder neu zu Ehren gebracht. Selten habe ich so begierigen Zuhörern über die Wege und Ziele des neuen Deutschland berichten können wie hier in den Hügeln Südaustraliens...Diese Menschen,...die längst dem Paß nach Australier sind, haben im Herzen die alte Heimat nicht verloren, wenn es auch — wie überall — nicht an Verrätern und Renegaten mangelt.(69–70)

Such profoundly disturbing statements are not isolated. They lend weight to the much maligned Australian government's fear and precaution regarding German migrants. (It makes Australia's collusion with the Nazi government in the case of Egon Erwin Kisch all the more deplorable.) Lutheran pastors are called "Frontkämpfer".(82) Johann tells the story of Pastor Rösenmann who in the First World War has to bury Australian soldiers of German extraction. The Lutheran man of God finds it impossible to reconcile such conflict: "Sie waren doch alle rein deutsch? Revoltierte ihr Blut nicht, wenn sie auf Deutsche schossen?"(75) Blood and race are of central importance to this author whose Australian travelogue often degenerates into pure Nazi propaganda. It is an apologia of racist *Deutschtum* rarely displayed in such explicit terms.

Johann's attitude to Aborigines is predictable: he calls them "diese häßliche, plattnasige, wulstlippige Rasse" and declares they belong "zu den unentwickelsten Menschenarten, die es überhaupt auf der Erde gibt".(15) He not only holds them in contempt, he confidently predicts their extinction: "Ihre Tage sind gezählt".(Ibid.) The visitor to Australia never misses a chance to mock and to insult the native population of the host country. In Darwin he meets a "Steinzeitmensch im Tropenhelm, ...der gerade wieder einmal dabei (war), als arbeitsloser Wilder seine Ferien zu genießen".(14) It would be simple to ignore such "reporting" as beneath contempt, if this author did not express an attitude which has helped shape the image of Australia and the Aborigines to this day. Johann shares with almost all writers of the thirties (and some of later periods) the obsession that this fertile and rich land must not be lost to the white man ("dem weißen Mann nicht verlorengehen soll",17). Like many Australians then (and since), he fears that the country may fall into the hands of a mixed race, the Chinese or the Japanese ("Sonst wird das Land früher oder später den Mischlingen, den Chinesen, den Japanern zufallen...",18). It is against such ideological and political background that *Känguruhs, Kopra und Korallen* offers the author's travelling impressions.

Wollschläger-Johann remembers Ludwig Leichhardt by drawing attention to the fact that he is travelling the same path, albeit in greater comfort and less danger. The important point is that it was a German who explored the North of Australia: "Ein Deutscher also war es, der dies Nordaustralien als erster aufhellte."(111) Leichhardt continues to serve as model explorer even for Johann's travelogue. He refers to Leichhardt's fate as "das Heldenepos eines deutschen Forschers"(112), an heroic epic, a classical tragedy.(Ibid.) The subject of his admiration has turned into literature.

Generally, the book adheres to a perspective of German cultural superiority, with Australia an antipodean oddity of at least some entertainment value. Johann's focus on German concerns leads him to discuss the Flying Doctor Service only with reference to the "deutsche Flieger Bertram".(149) Again and again, he reminds his readers that longing for far-away foreign places is an intrinsic part of the German soul: "Deutschen...scheint die unbezwingliche Fernsucht am drängendsten eingeboren zu sein"(153), another feature of racial superiority. Germans need to conquer the world.

Among such heavy reflection on born leadership and the burden of conquest a chapter entitled "Die Mädchen in Queensland und sonst in Australien"(sic!) may have been planned as light, or even comical, relief. Whatever the author's intentions, the message reads loud and clear: Queensland's women are proud to belong to a nordic white race which can survive in the tropics. They are living proof "daß...die hellhäutige Rasse selbst die glühenden Tropen sich auch ohne farbige Diener zur Wohnstatt von Eltern, Kindern und Kinderskindern machen kann, wenn sie es nun einmal so beschlossen hat".(165) Queensland is described as a "weißes Tropenland" in which healthy Germans have settled: "im Süden Queenslands hat ein starkes, gesundes Deutschtum Wurzel geschlagen".(Ibid.) Not surprisingly, therefore, many Queensland women turn out to be "gute Kameraden" in the "tropisch schönen und gefährlichen Queensland".(166) The dangers of

Queensland are not elaborated upon. The Nazi traveller praises the racial beauty of German Queensland women. The extravagant compliment must be read in the context of his earlier pronouncements that the Australian native population consists of "abschreckend häßliche Menschen".(106) There is little in this book which does not relate back to fascist ideology and racism.

A.E. Johann uses stories of individuals or families to illustrate general life-styles or social patterns. He thereby invokes the impression of a reportage, creating the illusion of authenticity. Like a reporter, he employs "human interest" features to attract or to regain the reader's attention. *Känguruhs, Kopra und Korallen* appears to integrate into its narrative a documentation of Australia's social life. But these "illustrations" are as arbitrary and constructed as the book's title. There is little information about contemporary Australian society which is reliable; it is the unusual, the far-fetched and the exotic which interest the author. Both from a literary and from a socio-historical point of view, Johann-Wollschläger's narrative on Australia is worthless. It merely demonstrates some of the excesses of Nazi "literature" on a continent where *Deutschtum* struggled to assert itself in a challenge of racial and cultural superiority.

WOLFGANG MARKEN

Das große Australiengeheimnis

The author of this extraordinarily confused and confusing novel, published in 1936, falls into the category of what is usually termed "popular writing". (Unlike French and English literature, German writing has been unable to reconcile highbrow and lowbrow fiction in a good quality popular narrative.) Wolfgang Marken turned out "novels" made to order at enormous speed. Just prior to his *Das große Australiengeheimnis* he published *Kompagnie Olympia,* in time for the Olympic Games in Berlin, *Kämpfer im Meere, Das Kreuz in Franken* and *Der dicke Müller siedelt.* Not surprisingly in the context of German fascism, Marken wrote mainly about people toiling the earth or preparing for war. *Kompagnie Olympia* bears the revealing subtitle "Ein deutscher Schicksalsroman". *Schicksal* (fate) served as code for the need to do battle in most Nazi publications. This novel deals with "die deutsche Jugend, die im Dienste für Volk und Vaterland in der

Wehrmacht ihre Pflicht erfüllt".

Das große Australiengeheimnis is not quite as explicit. Read in terms of political history, it is an interesting document illustrating the Nazi's desperate attempts to present the British as elective allies and racial cousins. There is a "natural" North-South axis in the novel's characterisation: the Nordic figures prove morally and racially superior in every situation.

The great Australian secret referred to in the novel's title is the existence of a subterranean river-system reaching from the Great Sandy Desert to Lake Macdonald, discovered, or rediscovered, by a second generation Nordic expert of the divining-rod. The novel further invents a German-Baltic explorer who spent his life studying the Great Sandy Desert. Strangely, he uses a Maori as his guide through North-Western Australia. As a vital concession to the novel's concept of "adventure", the subterranean waters lead to massive deposits of gold. The search for this wealth assumes political dimensions: not only Germans, Swedes and English aristocrats are anxious to claim it ("for the good of mankind"), there is also a certain Dr. Ussu and his daughter Malo who direct their submarine to the underground wealth of Australia in the name of Japanese world dominance. Any attempts, however, to pursue such aim by way of personal relationships with Northern Europeans are doomed to failure. Colonisation, commercial exploitation for nationalist political aims, remains a central theme of German-Australian literature during the thirties.

A significant sub-plot of *Das große Australiengeheimnis* is an alleged conspiracy on behalf of an emerging India against the British crown. In what amounts to a mixture of Restoration Drama and Comedy of Manners, Marken's novel abounds with characters of false identity and operatic situations of confusion. On one level, however, *Das große Australiengeheimnis* is a "family novel", a book about family values and German decency. A young woman is left in no doubt about her place in the moral scheme of things. She is urged to start building her "temple of love" and motherliness in which the man may regain his strength to do battle. "Kampf" seems inevitable. A strong and racially pure family structure and colonial properties are seen as vital ingredients in the preparation for this struggle.

The "great Australian secret" is called "Goldenhall". Marken creates a new antipodean *Valhalla*, the mythical secret of a continent ("das große Geheimnis dieses Erdteils",177) consisting of a "cathedral of gold" underneath its largest desert. Australia hides the wealth with which Germany and Japan could finance their aspirations for world dominance. It is an adventurous vision directed at more than the young. Marken reflects the aspirations of many German "Kolonisten" in Australia and elsewhere when one of his characters declares: "Alle sollen zurück in die Heimat. Und keiner ist mehr arm."(185) The novel uses traditional devices of adventure stories to propagate ideological beliefs in the superiority of Nordic people. The British, the Scandinavians and the Germans are seen as racial brothers who have a natural right to share the wealth of the world — because they will distribute it morally, responsibly, wisely. The enemy is seen as a half-caste, or, in terms of the adventure novel, as a pirate. Crimes against "life" and "racial purity" played a particularly gruesome part in Nazi "justice".

Although Wolfgang Marken's novel does not address itself to life in Australia (most of its plot takes place around Indonesia), it does express a symptomatic concept of the country. Marken exploits the mystique still associated with the continent. It is above all the empty space which holds attraction to the author and reader in fascist Germany. In the name of German-British friendship *Das große Australiengeheimnis* designs its adventurous plot and characterisation along the lines of a family reunion. When that is achieved the novel's protagonist reaffirms "das, was mir am teuersten war, meine Heimat, mein Vaterland".(283) In the context of the work it hardly matters whether that "Vaterland" is England, Germany or Scandinavia. What is important is that the hero can prove his dedication to the "fatherland". In an interesting phrase he speaks of having "fled" home ("Ich floh heim!",287), a revealing concept applied to many other Germans who, after years in Australia or other "colonies", returned home to a fascist regime.

Das große Australiengeheimnis is a stylistically and imaginatively impoverished novel. Its discussion can be justified only in the context of a social history of German-Australian literary relations. Wolfgang Marken's work is that of a *Vielschreiber*, an ideological and narrative opportunist. That Australia should have been conceived of, albeit in a novel of this kind, as a treasure-trove for Nordic racist visions of world dominance does indeed seem worthy of being recorded.

Egon Erwin Kisch

Landung in Australien

Of all the German authors writing about Australia in the thirties, only Egon Erwin Kisch (1885–1948) succeeds in portraying the sociopolitical reality of the country he visits. His *Landung in Australien* (1937) is a demonstration of the quality and dimension of the reportage, a literary art form struggling for emancipation from the limits of routine journalism. Aesthetically, as well as socio-historically, Kisch's "Weg zu den Antipoden" (the first of thirteen reports about his stay in Australia) must be considered one of the most outstanding examples of this genre. In the autumn of 1934 Kisch is appointed European delegate to an anti-war congress in Melbourne. His special task is to report on the struggle of the resistance against the Nazis. Hitler's diplomats in Australia attempt to prevent Kisch's landing in Australia. In Melbourne he, quite literally, jumps ship; in his attempt to force a landing he breaks his leg. The question whether Kisch may set foot on Australian soil grows into a major conflict of domestic and international politics. His report describes sources of ideological conflicts, relying on irony and wit as means of exposure. Kisch stayed in Australia from 6 November 1934 to 11 March 1935, from his arrival in Fremantle to his departure in Sydney.

Understandably, the desperate (if pathetic) attempts of the Australian authorities to prevent Kisch's landing form the larger part of his reportage. Kisch opens his account ("Weg zu den Antipoden", also referred to as "Sprung zu den Antipoden")[32] with a description of the historical background of his trip to Australia, the hounding of Czech citizens in Europe as a result of the assassination of Alexander II of Serbia. For a short while the reader may be forgiven for thinking that the book deals with the escape of the assassin. However, the narrator soon introduces his protagonist, albeit in a provocatively general, representative identity, as "the man" or "our man". Playfully, even flirtatiously, Kisch reveals: "Uns: das sind wir, die wir dieses Buch schreiben, der Mann ist dieses Buches Held...er steht uns nahe,...wir solidarisieren, ja, wir identifizieren uns geradezu mit ihm."(8) Specificity and generality coincide, Kisch relates his reporting to a role-playing identity. Autobiography is turned into semi-detached narration. Author, narrator and protagonist overlap, without ever fully coinciding, thus opening up effective possibilities of social humour. The reader, too, is drawn into the narrative: he is either addressed with an intimate, identifying *du*, or as a separate role identity of the report (cf. "ebensowenig dem Leser etwas verraten wie dem Mann...", 9). It is clear from the beginning that when Kisch speaks of the "bevorstehende Abenteuer"(8), he relates to a very different concept of adventure from that propagated by the *Deutschtum* authors of the thirties. His adventure refers to the risks and tensions of participating in world-wide social developments, more specifically to his own role as socialist at a time of international conflict culminating in the Second World War.

Egon Erwin Kisch's reason for travelling to Australia is thus vastly different from that of the other German authors of travelogues during this decade. Kisch hopes for exchange of social and political information; as antifascist he plans to report to Australians about the atrocities of Hitler's Germany. The tone of his narrative is therefore geared to authentic communication; verifiable, documentary and argumentative in character. *Landung in Australien* contains traditional devices of narrative fiction, such as dialogue and characterisation; but it also provides precise reproductions of documents, such as passports, legal papers or newspaper reports. Part of this aim for authenticity is the translation of any term or phrase the author or narrator consider significant. Generally, the context of Kisch's reportage is a world of news, a time of historically important events. The background of his own report is drawn by statements such as: "Die Radio-News melden...".(16) The narrator acts as one carrier and witness of news among many. Nor is literature left outside the realm of factual events and authentic experience. Kisch plays with literary quotations, "updating" them in a form of alienation. The constellation of the Southern Cross, for example, he introduces via a quotation from Dante's *Purgatorio*.(17) Most important of all, Kisch allows his narrator to make his own problems — for example, his difficulties with the Australian language (19) — an integral part of the experience he is trying to report. At no stage does Kisch surrender his European perspective of Australia. Even on his journey to the Antipodes he reinvokes the history lessons of his school years, without however failing to give them a new twist. (About Vasco da Gama he writes that because he was welcomed in Calicut, he later returned to subjugate his hosts.[20])

On his arrival in Perth Kisch is not allowed to leave the ship. He tells reporters that he has not come to agitate against Germany but against the Nazis.(27) His contact with Australians is limited to customs officials, police, and journalists. An Australian reporter tells him "daß das Hitlerregime dem Charaker der Deutschen entspricht".(Ibid.) Kisch's protagonist *unser Mann* strongly objects to this Australian image of Germans. The narrator at this stage reproduces several newspaper reports, both in Australia and in Germany, about his arrival in Fremantle. Kisch's style is witty, elegant and sarcastic. In clever montage of part authentic, part fictional documentation he plays with the manipulation of the fascist and the non-fascist press.

> Auf dem Wedding und in Neukölln, am Potsdamer Platz und vor der Gedächtniskirche rufen die Zeitungsjungen aus: "...wird nich nach Australjen jelassen! Der rasende Reporta entrüstet! Nachtausjabe!" Wir (die Beobachter) trennen unseren Astralleib von dem australischen und kaufen einem Zeitungshändler, der eben das Wort "entrüstet" dramatisch in die Berliner Luft schmettert, ein Blatt ab...(29)

The extravagance of Kisch's narrative style conveys an authentic simultaneity, the travelling of news and the coinciding of different interpretations of the same event. Returning to Australia, the report now expresses German-European satisfaction over the world's belated recognition of the true character of German emigrants ("den wahren Charakter der Emigranten aus Deutschland zu begreifen beginnt...",Ibid.). The narrator manipulates the news as it manipulates his protagonist. As always with Kisch, stylistic devices serve the art of exposure.

Part of his reporting consists of observations, reflections or commentaries on events and their political background. Kisch rightly points out that Australia has suffered as a result of the First World War, both in human life and economically. He follows his reminder with the comment: "Und da errichtet man ein Kriegerdenkmal, den Shrine von Melbourne, der an Aufwand alles Dagewesene übertrifft".(31) He reports the protest of Australian writers and intellectuals against the refusal to let Kisch land in their country, only to remark: "Kühl und höhnisch läßt Mister Menzies, Generalstaatsanwalt und Minister, diesen Sturm zu seinen Füßen branden."(32) To be sure, there is stylisation, fictionalisation in such responses, there are rhetorical and political gestures of opposition or defiance. Kisch succeeds in lending them, too, the quality of authentic reporting. He accepts the politics of role manipulation. As he is described "ein ausländischer Agent, der Australien aufwiegeln will"(36), Kisch's narrator projects his own roles in the unfolding of a sociopolitical drama.

Reading Kisch's *Landung in Australien* draws a very different image of Germans in Australia from the one presented in the *Abenteuerbücher* written by conservative travellers. Instead of the nationalistic and sentimental idealisation of German settlements in South Australia, places where local German-language presses advocated a Hitlerian concept of leadership for Australia[33], Kisch reports in a matter-of-fact tone. There is, he claims, a great thirst of knowledge about the political events in Germany. "Davon weiß man wenig in Australien."(Ibid.) It seems that Kisch's plan to enlighten Australians of all backgrounds about the nature of German fascism was welcomed by at least some migrants from the "home country". Other German emissaries, such as Count Luckner, found a rather more enthusiastic hearing from the migrant community.[34] As one would expect, there were differing responses to German fascism among German migrants in Australia, reflecting perhaps not merely the general reaction, in the early stage, to the rise of Hitlerism in Germany itself, but also the curious contradiction of migration itself: progressively multinational and conservatively nationalistic. Kisch leaves no doubt about the constant interference of German Nazis in Australia during his four-month-stay in the country. ("Das Verbot erfolgte auf Wunsch der deutschen Nationalsozialisten in Australien...",49.) It is quite clear from his account that the Australian Government acted in collusion with the Nazi Government in Germany. Interestingly, one attempt to denigrate Kisch's status and credibility was to question the quality of his writing. The Minister for Customs doubted Kisch's success as a writer: "Jedenfalls steht fest, daß keines seiner Bücher jemals in die englische Sprache übersetzt wurde."(47)

Confrontation is a stylistic as well as an ideological device for Kisch. He often juxtaposes opposing views or differing reports. A quotation is followed by an "anti-quotation". The result is that untruths expose themselves. Kisch uses this technique most effectively when he quotes the Berlin Nazi paper *Angriff*, only to counter-quote from an Australian daily.(50) His introduction to these excerpts is characteristically ironical, playfully self-deprecatory:

> Man wird verstehen, daß wir nicht selbst sagen, was sich ereignet hat, sondern es weniger Beteiligten, unberufen Berufeneren zu sagen überlassen.(Ibid.)

Referring to the Australian newspaper, he offers the professional comment of a journalist: "Wer dem Tatort näher ist, kommt dem

Tatbestand näher."(Ibid.) It is an article of faith which lies at the heart of his reportage. Kisch narrates by quoting himself, his narrator comes close to the place of action and quotes a social report to authenticate the evidence *(Tatbestand)*. So-called facts are understandable, and hence reportable, only as social dynamics; they are a "state of affairs", voices Kisch is trying to capture in dialectic conflict and authenticity.

Part of Kisch's polemics or *Parteilichkeit* (Lukács) is expressed in fictionalised documentation which adds considerably to his political characterisation of friend and enemy. After previous quotations and other forms of documentary authenticity, he can quote his own projections without losing his overall credibility. Kisch has already established his trustworthiness and his reader is prepared to follow him in statements such as this:

> Nun hat er seinen Fuß auf Australien gesetzt und ihn dabei gebrochen. Mister Menzies kann lachen. Und auch der Nazidiplomat, der durch seine Intervention das Landungsverbot veranlaßt hat, und die Gestapo in Berlin lachen sich ins blutige Fäustchen.(52)

There is nothing untrue about his projection, even if it cannot be verified in the usual manner. The reporter is interpreting contemporary history, based on a collection of authenticated personal experience. Kisch writes a chapter of Australian history; his *Landung in Australien* narrates a representative personal history. The interpretation of events is part of that history, assuming the same historical status as so-called facts. Like all authors, Kisch lures his readers into collusion. He confides in them. His humour almost always serves the function of drawing the reader into a position of intimacy and trust. Consider the following passage:

> Gut gebrüllt, Löwe, raunt er sich ins Ohr, wir aber haben es doch gehört, und mißbilligen dieses Eigenlob, obwohl wir mildernde Umstände nicht versagen.(73)

The reader is made a witness of the narrator's temperament, his mind and his emotions. It is on the basis of such knowledge that the relationship between author and reader is one of trust. When a newspaper is quoted, it is interrupted by the narrative voice, thus integrating the author's own thoughts and feelings into the report. This logic even applies where a sarcastic aside is added to the text, such as: "fix gearbeitet, deutsches Konsulat!"(83). It forms part of the narrative report. If it reveals bias, it is part of Kisch's reportage of opinions. *Landung in Australien* is a collection of views, described and contextualised by a social historian, written at a time of worldwide political crisis.

The role of literature in Kisch's concept of ideological conflict is obvious: it helps shape and disseminate opinions, values and critical awareness. Kisch mocks the bourgeois hierarchy of literary value which puts reporting the truth at the bottom and *Dichtung* (poetical works/fiction) at the very top.[35] He recruits literature into the struggle for a socialist humanism. Throughout his Australia reportage Kisch makes constant reference to writers, their works and their actions. When Poet Laureate John Masefield attends a meeting of the Fellowship of Australian Writers, Kisch regrets the English poet's abandoning of his early revolutionary work. He is embarrassed by Masefield's lack of social concern.(89–91) By contrast, he quotes from a handwritten collection of Hölderlin's poetry, given to him by a female comrade in Melbourne.(53) His montage of quotations demonstrates the relevance and sociopolitical dimensions of imaginatively precise writing. Kisch does not differentiate between so-called high and low literature, nor does he approach literary work with the kind of awe characteristic of the German bourgeois middle class. He takes it more seriously than that: to him it is of the same urgency as the latest news, it *is* news, and as such worthy to be reported. Kisch acknowledges (in an amused way) his friendship with Lion Feuchtwanger (38), appreciates the irony of being told that he is not a major writer (46–47) and mocks the conventions of literary scholarship ("Autorisierte Übersetzung von uns",61). One possible defence against the absurdity of the Australian language test for the "migrant" Kisch is "Engels' Meisterreportage" ("Lage der arbeitenden Klasse in England") (96) — a literary document, a social report. It is with further irony and amusement, rather than triumph, that Kisch's narrator can report the sudden availability of two of his books in Sydney — in English translation.(101) He is equally amused when P.R. Stephenson[36](sic!) introduces him at a writer's meeting, in the presence of Katharine Susannah Prichard, with a somewhat outdated biographical extract from a Czech encyclopaedia. (He would have been somewhat less amused, had he known about "Inky" Stephensen's notorious anti-communism and anti-semitism.) Needless to say, Kisch established contact with many Australian writers during his short stay[37]. His final day he spends in the company of Katharine Susannah Prichard, whom he visits at her home in the Darling Ranges. Yet, significantly, the reportage "Weg zu den Antipoden" ends with the Red-Front battle hymn confronting the

Nazi Horst-Wessel-Song. It is not the aesthetic values of any kind of writing that interest Kisch, but its commitment to ideological visions. When signing his autograph, Kisch adds the words "ein Springer" to his name, to indicate that in Australia he is less known as a writer than as an acrobat. A less playful negation of literary ambition is his signing of a copy of Hitler's *Mein Kampf*, stating it is the first time in his life that he has put his name on such nonsense ("auf solch stupides Zeug").(91) Writers, too, have to be reported on, and Kisch consistently does not exclude himself from this task.

Landung in Australien faithfully reports the part played by the Australian press, in particular the *Sydney Morning Herald* and the *Bulletin*, in Kisch's political struggle in this country. It exposes the latter's anti-semitism, and quotes the former's public admission of dishonest journalism.(106–118)

Kisch gives further account of his travels in Australia, including his visit to Queensland's area of German settlements. In three paragraphs he sketches the cultural conflicts of generations of migrants. He draws a brief but precise historical survey of gradual assimilation. Kisch is sensitive to the tragedy of third generation Australians of German background retaining a loving interest and longing for the "Land von Großmütterchens Märchen", only to be told by him that this fairy-tale has turned into a nightmare. He was on a mission of conflict: Australia did not know about Nazi Germany, in many cases it did not want to know. Kisch's meeting with German migrants was going to be especially difficult. Their loyalty towards the home culture was severely tested by the political realities of contemporary Germany. Perhaps Kisch's style of reportage may be summed up by one of his own sentences towards the end of his "Weg zu den Antipoden": "Es ist so, aber es kann nicht so sein."(124) His reporting remains factual and historical, but with a direction and a purpose to help bring about change.

It is Australian society and its contemporary politics Kisch is interested in. Many of his remarks read prophetic, some have kept their validity to this day. He demonstrates a genuine concern for the political liberation of Aborigines(123–125). The Australian Labor Party Kisch accuses of not being a socialist workers party, he repeatedly likens its history to that of liberal parties in Europe. In a memorable, witty phrase he speaks of the party's fear of radical politics: "Vorsicht ist die Mutter der Labor Party...".(127) "Weg zu den Antipoden" is the longest and the weightiest of Kisch's reports from Australia. It must be ranked among the world's most outstanding social reportages. It is knowledgeable, empathetic, observant, precise, analytical, witty and engaging. In the context of a German-Australian literature, Kisch's *Landung in Australien* establishes a genre or tradition of left-wing social narratives (Walter Kaufmann, Joachim Specht).

The remaining sketches or reports address themselves to specific aspects of Australian life and history. "An Botany Bay sitzend" is a brilliant reflection on the nature of Australia's colonisation. His thoughts include Australia's fear of an invasion by an unknown or unnamed force, its deception and exploitation at Gallipoli (pointing out that Russian documents concerning the claim of the peninsula were never published in Australia) and the two national "battles" of Glenrowan and the Eureka Stockade. Kisch concludes his Botany Bay reflections with the claim that Australians are not really interested in their country, even though they find their home worthy of love and comfortable ("liebenswert und angenehm"). He states that most Australians do not know their own continent, that more have visited Europe than other parts of Australia. The Australian Kisch encountered retains the shortsightedness and attitude of the first white landing at Botany Bay who did not move further to discover the true beauty of the land. "An Botany Bay sitzend" thus acquires its special double meaning.

Kisch's following essay "Die Ahnen" continues to delve into Australia's past, — the short-lived history of white Australia. As always, he is prompted by a concrete occasion, this time the national celebrations of 26 January, to reflect upon the past and the present of social history. Kisch decides to ask Australians in the street what they know about their national day. In what reads like a demonstration of multicultural Australia long before the concept was developed, he quotes the answers of a Mister Barches, formerly of Tel-Aviv, and a Mister Pletwichka, a migrant from Czechoslovakia, none of whom can explain the reason for the special day. It is a kind of national embarrassment or shame which, Kisch argues, leads Australians to be evasive about the date when the First Fleet landed at Botany Bay. Kisch even suggests that the term "First Fleet" is a euphemism to hide the convict past. He imagines the conditions on board the first convict ships and reports them in the form of an imaginative documentary. His historical fiction is well-informed and includes statistical information.(153) He describes his projected authenticity in contrast to a festive regatta on Sydney Harbour celebrating Australia Day. The yachts of the rich and idle are confronted by the memories of sailing ships carrying convict ancestors. Kisch's reconstructed authenticity concludes with the explicit acknowledgement of its hypothetical nature: "So mag es am 26 Januar 1788 ausgesehen haben."(155)

Unlike Australian writers of the same period, Kisch is strongly aware of the coincidental nature of British colonisation, and unlike them, he feels no urge to hide the fact that a very large portion of the Australian population was never Anglo-Saxon or Anglo-Celtic (in itself, of course, a rather dubious term). Of the epitome of Australian manhood, the "Diggers", he says that the majority were the offspring not of the first wave of settlers, but of the gold-diggers of the fifties. If he thereby demythologises Australia's ancestors, he concludes his reflections on an affirmative note: these forefathers, Kisch maintains, have produced worthy descendants.

The treatise on Aborigines, "Schwarz-Australien", follows naturally as a vital part of Australia's past. Kisch writes about the original Australians in the fictional form of a talk to a young boy, a reader of Karl May's adventure stories about cowboys and Indians. The boy's eager anticipation to learn about Australia's wild natives ("Wilde") is disappointed because Kisch is determined to report "wie es wirklich war und wie es wirklich ist", — a formula equally applicable to all his narrative accounts of Australia.(159) Characteristically, he advises his fictional young friend to read historical documents rather than self-indulgent adventure stories. Kisch's exposure has the quality of black humour about it. His deconstructed version of historical events is incongruously, offensively direct, revealing the true motives behind rhetoric and mythology. It is an art of reporting the essential, reducing appearance to being. Kisch not merely reports the genocide of Aborigines, he also interprets the reasons behind such action. To him, it is the unsuitability of the Aboriginal population to be used as work slaves which brought about their destruction. He exposes the socioeconomic considerations which led to the Aborigines being decimated. Kisch quotes Engels ("Der Ursprung der Familie") when discussing tribal relations and Georg Forster in his account of the "Frazer Massaker".(162–163) He succeeds in conveying the horror and distrust Aborigines must fear in their dealings with white Australians, using both Australian and German sources. His "Schwarz-Australien" is another example of cultural mediation.

With great empathy Kisch explains that imprisonment of Aborigines amounts to a death sentence, a fact disregarded by the white Australian authorities to this day. (Walter Kaufmann's *Tod in Fremantle* deals, not coincidentally, with alleged suicides of Aboriginal prisoners. In this, as in so many other narrative themes, he is following a direction first indicated by Egon Erwin Kisch.) It is difficult not to read Kisch's account of the situation as a document of continued relevance, indeed, of ever-increasing urgency.

"Sträflinge außer Dienst" continues Kisch's narrative enquiry into the past. His immediate inspiration is a visit to the island of Pinchgut, "die kriminal-historische Insel".(172) Kisch traces Australia's convict past back to the present day, Pinchgut is today's Fort Denison — "und hat Form und Inhalt verändert".(174) Australia as a whole has changed in a similar manner. Thus the island's history becomes a representative example of the history of the continent since white settlement. Kisch rightly stresses the violence which lies at the basis of Australian civilisation. And he again relates Australia's past to contemporary politics. Whilst deploring the excesses of sadistic violence in the 18th and 19th century, he points out that they have been surpassed by the terror of Nazi Germany.

History remains contemporary, a living point of reference and means of orientation. Kisch's sarcastic description of the exploitation of workers in terms of a grammar of ownership is another striking example of updating or keeping alive historical events by exposing their sociopolitical background. He alludes to a language of slave-keepers where brutality is merely a means of "progress". His reporting combines historical description with socioeconomical interpretation; Kisch's ideological commitment quotes history as verifiable evidence. Readers should bear in mind that this text was written against the background of fascist racism turning large sections of European society into convicts. To Kisch, this essay must have seemed of antipodean topicality in more ways than one.

Not surprisingly, Kisch is very interested in the history of Australia's trade union movement, in fact, he calls Australia the "Kontinent der Gewerkschaften". His well-informed narrative survey covers 100 years, i.e. from 1835 to 1935, retracing the events, characters and places of the growth of the union. Kisch sees evidence of the workers' power in the very early determination to eliminate competition between convict labour and the work of free men. It further demonstrates, according to Kisch, the fact that the interests of the working class are identical to those of mankind in general.(185) The *Gewerkschafts*-essay consists of 18 sections, each covering one year or a specific period in the history of Australia's trade unions, listing the achievements, the problems and the specific contribution to the movement. The exploitation of English farm labourers, Kisch reminds his readers, was reported back to England and their treatment in Australia is in fact described at the end of the first volume of Marx's *Kapital*. He naturally integrates Australia's labour and trade union movement into the international class struggle.

Kisch comments on the excessive multiplication of unions in Australia after the strikes of the nineties and the failure, in 1918, to form "One Big Union". His most scathing attack is reserved for a German economist who published the study *Die Wirtschaftskrise in Australien*. Dr. Hans Schmidt's exploitation of the workers in the name of "Produktivität des Landes" is likened to E.G. Wakefield's suppression of labour in the interest of "Nationalreichtum". As always with Kisch, Australian social conditions are related to the situation in Germany. His narrative history of trade unions in Australia ends with a curious analogy; the movement is likened to a kangaroo. It carries in its pouch a new breed, a higher form of Australian worker — Marxists in the making. The didactic intent is directed as much at German as at Australian workers. Australia's social history serves as illustration of world-wide developments.

As part of his attempt to characterise the nature of Australian society and what might be termed the Australian national temperament, Kisch devotes one essay to horse racing. In "Von Pferderennen und Rennpferden" (another characteristic play with words) he captures an authentic part of Australian culture. As usual, he traces the history of the most important races, in particular the Melbourne Cup. The origins are, of course, proletarian: boundary riders were the first jockeys. A vital connection is established when he learns that Australia's leading bushrangers stole racehorses. Racing is thus part of Australia's national mythology, an expression of reckless courage and love of freedom. Kisch reveals the sociopolitical dimensions of a people's passion. His reportage proves at the same time amusing and critically alert, both entertaining and ideologically didactic.

"Kohle unter dem Meer" is a narrative, at times almost anecdotal, report of Australia's coalfields and the turbulent history of the mining industry. Kisch visits Wonthaggi, Birchgrove (Sydney), Newcastle and Dudley, combining impressionistic descriptions of life in a coal town with political and economic reflections. His political criticism emerges from the very act of reporting; he has no need for explicit moralising.

Kisch's essays are filled with factual information, not always political in nature. The autobiographical, "experiential" dimension of Kisch's reporting is ever present; here it reaches its highlight in his visit of an underwater mine in Dudley. Kisch, still suffering a broken leg, is carried down the shaft by miners — another oddity, "newsworthy", an "exotic" extravagance. The title "Kohle unter dem Meer" denotes the authenticity of a personal adventure.

Addressing himself to the "Fremdling" (stranger), Kisch's narrative "Merkwürdiges über Haifische sowie anderes, zum Teil vorsintflutliches Getier" aims for the unusual, gruesome and adventurous. Making extensive (and very effective) use of irony, Kisch's narrative voice impersonates an absurdly incongruous or contradictory Australian attitude: whilst there are numerous reports of shark attacks and expensive plans for shark-netting popular beaches, the visitor is told that there are no sharks to worry about. The reporter Kisch quotes the macabre story of the thirteen-year-old shark victim Elsie Morrin. The girl who lost both her arms haunts the author of this story. He links it to another bizarre event, the "Shark Murder Case", as it came to be known in Sydney. Kisch likens his account of it to a Schillerian ballad, facetiously suggesting the title "(der) Fisch des Polykrates".(232)

Like so many other German writers dealing with Australia, Kisch feels that the very unusual nature of this country's flora and fauna calls for a somewhat distorted kind of description. In an attempt to humanise his subject, he tends to use an anecdotal style — like all good feature writers. However, he does not turn these animals into tourist attractions, nor does he fall back on the cliché descriptions of other popular writers. He applies the same kind of unconventional, slightly "off-beat", wit and humour to comment on their character. Who else but Kisch would compare a platypus with Napoleon!

The title of Kisch's next essay sets its tone: the biblical "Anbetung des Heiligen Lammes" projects a mock-heroic and mock-religious interpretation of the very worldly history of sheep farming in Australia. The purpose of Kisch's pseudo-religious language is to expose, by way of incongruous juxtaposition, the truth of secular brutality that shaped the progress of wool in this country. Captain John Macarthur is described as "der wucherischste, geldgierigste and skrupelloseste" of English thieves, yet his arrival in Australia is dressed in biblical rhetoric. Macarthur is stylised into the Apostle of Lamb Breeding ("der Apostel der Lämmerzucht") and Thomas Sutcliffe, the pioneer of the wool trade, to the Apostle of Wool Trade ("der Apostel des Wollhandels", 244). Capitalist suppressors and exploiters have been honoured, Kisch implies, like religious heroes, with their own monuments erected at Sydney's Macquarie Place. Kisch applies Marxist criteria, both to economics and to "religion". He offers an historical survey of the wool industry in Australia (including an account of the shearer's strike in the nineties), and presents detailed statistical information about import and export. Kisch predicts the ever-increasing economic might of Japan (250) and Australia's dependence on its far-eastern neighbour. He also foresees the rise of synthetic fibre and marvels at the dogmatic faith of conservatives in the Temple of Doom. The report on the Australian Lamb ends with open mockery, equating the Bible with bad economic management. An outdated belief is stated, then exposed, finally played out against itself. Kisch's quotations, even where they are stylistically manipulated, are carriers of judgement.

"Wir fahren zum Ölschiefer", one of Kisch's lesser reportages, offers another account of an industry in crisis. The production of shale oil at Newnes closed down in 1922 and has not been reopened since. Kisch travels to the town to witness the social life of a deserted working community. There is grim humour in his description and it is on the level of casual pertness that Kisch's report ignites and operates. The logic and wit of his style carries the "moral" of his prose, its sociopolitical commitment and a role collusion with the reader. It is clear that Kisch's report sees the closing down of a national industry as part of a global bankruptcy of capitalism.

His "Illustrationen zu einem Lenin-Zitat" further demonstrates Kisch's interpretation of, and interest in, Australia as an example of certain bourgeois-capitalist developments, moving towards an inevitable crisis. Kisch begins by quoting Lenin's amazement at Australia in 1913 where workers control the Upper House and are in control of the Lower House, without threatening the capitalist system in any shape or form.(262) Kisch agrees with Lenin's assertion that the Australian Labor Party is liberal-bourgeois, rather than socialist. It represents, in its purest form, he argues, non-socialist unions. Lenin sees no revolutionary potential in such labour forces. Kisch puts Lenin's claims to the test by surveying the history of the Australian Labor Party. He sees that it embraced conflicting ideas from its very inception.(265) His analysis of labour leaders makes it clear that most of them were liberals. Kisch takes a closer look at the inner structure and ideology of the Labor Party. He is critical of Labor's Caucus system, arguing that it replaces a non-existent party program and a non-existent social theory.(267) He is further critically mindful of Labor's racist workers and migration policy, both designed (by the trade unions) to retain a British Australia.(270) Kisch argues that it was this refusal to allow an intake of non-British migrant workers which was responsible for a widespread lack of industrialisation and the failure to populate the tropical and subtropical North.(Ibid.)

Kisch notes the emergence of the Australian Communist Party in the thirties, but acknowledges the difficulties of its struggle and the limitations of its influence. Australia can hardly be described as a worker's paradise ("Arbeitsparadies",275). Parts of Sydney seem more impoverished than Whitechapel when Marx was in London. "Illustrationen zu einem Lenin-Zitat" is another narrative sketch successfully combining historical survey and ideological agitation. Not the least impressive feature of Kisch's report is the wealth and reliability of his facts, including new or little-known information — the hallmark of a good social historian.

Kisch's final text in the collection *Landung in Australien* shows once again how "tuned-in" he is to the Australian national psyche (as it projects itself). "Die Gefahren der Bodyline" is an affectionate account of the infamous cricket test series between Australia and England in 1932–1933. Kisch proves well-informed, even in the sport of cricket. But he does not really write about the game and its rules; he is much more interested in the social rules surrounding it. The "game" continues, the class struggle takes place in a context of agreed positions. Kisch's wily comment at the end of his report: "Vorläufig hat die Sache mit der Bodyline die Landkarte der Welt nicht verändert"(287) should be recognised for what it is — the witty double-talk of a social realist, a precise observer and a committed fighter.

Egon Erwin Kisch's contribution to the history of German-Australian literature is considerable. Like no other writer of his time he looks at Australian society, offering precise and well-informed observation. Indeed, it may be said that Kisch is responsible for a second discovery of Australia[38]. His reportages combine epic narrative with social documentation. Kisch elevates the journalistic feature to the level of art. His careful compositions are the expression of a disciplined and a profoundly political imagination. Like all good reporters, Kisch has an instinct for what is new and what is important. He writes about the junctures of ideological conflict, the places of political tension, the genesis of social drama. It is as social historian that Kisch addresses himself to Australia. In "Weg zu den Antipoden" the reporter himself becomes news, the writer his own protagonist. Kisch's creation of a narrative *persona* is an ironic self-fictionalisation allowing playfully critical reflections on the perceiver and the perceived. By extension, many of his descriptions assume the nature of documentary fiction. The author's political commitment is a bias carried by his dialectic style; the final impression is one of authenticity. The stylistic role-playing of the political writer is an effective device reflecting the general drama of social conflict in which both author and reader have their parts.

Kisch came to Australia for a specific purpose, as delegate of the Paris Committee Against War and Fascism: he intended to inform the Melbourne Anti-War Congress of conditions in Nazi Germany and to report on his own experiences as a prisoner of the fascist regime. While informing Australians about Hitler's Germany, *Landung in Australien* became a major literary report informing Germans of the social and political situation in Australia. His work constitutes one of the few serious attempts of German writers to analyse Australian society. Kisch's method, his style and composition, have remained exemplary. To date, only Walter Kaufmann and Joachim Specht have attempted to follow his form of sociopolitical narrative. (Kaufmann's concept of "faction" clearly owes a great deal to Kisch's reporting.) If Australia has largely remained a little-known, exotic continent for German readers, it is because too few writers were prepared to abandon the tourist's vision and take a closer look at the real country, its social conditions and its political culture.

HEINZ GECK

Umweg über Australien

Geck joins the long list of German authors specialising in exotic adventure stories. Among his other publications are the "Abenteuer-Roman" of India, *Sturm über dem Khaiberpass*, and the "Abenteuerliche Roman aus der Südsee", *Der Grüne Stein*. *Umweg über Australien* also bears the subtitle "Ein abenteuerlicher Roman", illustrating its didactic concept of "adventure" in exemplary fashion: Australia is merely a "detour" ("Umweg") in the rediscovery of the real, German home.

Two reasons come together for the hero, Peter Dobeneck, to flee his "fatherland". Ironically, his own father had turned to reading too many adventure novels after his mother's death, resulting in neglect and bad management of the family farm. Geck reveals the *raison d'être* of his own genre when he describes it as a form of "Weltflucht", a kind of *ersatz* world travel and substitute for personal experience. One reason, then, why Peter Dobeneck finds himself at the age of twenty-eight "without any hope" is

> weil Vater die Zügel schleifen ließ nach Mutters Tod und lieber mit einem Schmöker über die sieben Meere abenteuerte, als den Pflugsterz in die Hand nahm...(10).

In terms of Nazi ideology that constitutes "desertion of the soil", something the son will, sooner or later, have to rectify. The other reason for Peter Dobeneck's flight from Germany is an Australian woman, June Haslitt. "...ich war ihr verfallen vom ersten Augenblick an," he confesses.(25) There is irony in that seduction as well. Like other writers of the Nazi period, Geck subscribes to the blood and soil philosophy of the "master race". There is constant reference to blood throughout the novel. Peter Dobeneck, narrating his own story, first speaks of his "Blut hungrig auf Abenteuer".(11) As a young man he is haunted by "das plötzlich wache Blut".(12–13) Meeting June Haslitt he feels "das Klopfen ihres Blutes" as well as the "Singen des eigenen Blutes".(26) Later, he discovers the disturbing fact that June's grandmother "hatte Maoriblut".(33) When in Australia, the hero finds that "schießen...lag mir im Blut".(120) It seems, then, that "blood" may both lead a young man astray and remind him of his innate qualities. In much the same way, he may spend his time on an Australian soil largely owned by Jewish interests ("heute gehört die ganze Station, ich selber eingeschlossen, dem Herrn Nathan Myers in Melbourne",124), only to return to his own "Erbhof" ("entailed estate") in Germany, his "eigene Scholle".(240) It is thus "blood" and "soil" which make the novel's protagonist take "detours" to his true destiny. Although it is asserted that "Fernweh", the longing for travel and far-away places, is another natural ingredient of German blood, almost all novels of German-Australian adventures cite the lost war as the real reason for having left the country, either as migrant or as travelling "adventurer". Geck, too, interprets the Weimar Republic as chaotic and in its democratic structure as "un-German". The motivation for "detouring" the world is therefore clearly political. A trip to Australia is a strong protest against the political developments in the fatherland. Readers of

Geck's novel know quite well how to deconstruct the myth of the great Australian adventure. The author's contemporaries recognised the tragedy of such a dramatic move. Australia, whatever else it may have been, was primarily the place farthest away from Germany and thus a code for extreme detachment from domestic politics. *Umweg über Australien* is the narrative record of a homecoming. The novel ends with an harmonious vision of *Blut und Boden* ideology. The "adventure" therefore serves a very concrete purpose.

The narrator's image of Australia is somewhat hazy. It is precisely the unknown qualities of the continent which attract him; it is a negative fascination linked to his concept of adventure. There can be no clear and positive vision, as it is really an escape from the familiar. By 1937 Colin Ross' slogan of the "unvollendete Kontinent" had received widespread acceptance. Geck freely quotes it to suggest the incompleteness of his protagonist's development for as long as he remains in Australia. Australia and Germany are presented in terms of positive and negative correlatives. There is a strong suggestion that the Australian Aborigines correspond, as a national problem, to the German Jews. Given Geck's enthusiastic endorsement of Nazi ideology of blood and soil, it is hardly surprising that he shares its racism as well. Aborigines are almost always called "Nigger"(69) or "Buschnigger"(71), their appearance is "von erstaunlicher Häßlichkeit".(125) There are no women in the world, the author informs his readers, who are as horrifyingly ugly as "the racially unimproved" female Aborigine.(136) Male Aborigines trying to defend their land are described as "ölbemalte schwarze Satane".(186) Surprisingly or carelessly, Geck on one occasion refers to them as "Australier".(188) Yet even after such unwitting acknowledgement of the primary inhabitants of the continent they remain "verdammte Nigger".(190)

Australia, then, is a "mistake"; the novel's hero is misled by a woman, "June...ein gefährliches Spielzeug", racially impure.(33) *Umweg über Australien* is thus also an affirmation of German love and of a racially pure, Aryan marriage. The "adventure" with a part-Maori woman is an Australian "detour", a correlative "mistake". In accordance with its etymology, it is an adventure which leads to an arrival — or a return to the roots of one's being. All the exotic ingredients of Peter Dobeneck's adventures enforce a negative polarity pointing home.

The literary weakness of the novel lies in its lack of authenticity.

Set pieces of terminological explanations cannot bring to life what are in effect cardboard characters and cliché situations. The protagonist's search for an allegedly dead man to collect an insurance policy links up with the stock plot of getting lost in the bush (despite the intriguing warning: "Sieh zu, daß du nicht gebuscht wirst...",128). Credibility is stretched by a number of extreme "coincidences". The author has taken his own statement "In diesem Land war alles möglich"(137) too literally. Geck's narrative suffers most when it tries to describe the behaviour of Aborigines. It is then that his reading knowledge of natives "all over the world" becomes all too apparent. As he confuses white Australians with Canadians ("Mounties",82), so he makes Aborigines behave like Red Indians. Geck tries to motivate the derivative nature of his adventure tale by stringing together a collection of anecdotal stories passed on by various fictional characters. Although he claims to be writing his own story, the narrative protagonist relies heavily on hearsay information, reducing many of his figures to mere mouth-pieces and himself to an unimaginative gatherer of second-hand knowledge.

Heinz Geck's "abenteuerlich Roman" *Umweg über Australien* uses a narrative detour to propagate Nazi blood and soil ideology. The attempt to dress up second-hand information as authentic personal experience of paradigmatic importance fails because of a general lack of imaginative strength. Style and language are uninspired, despite the dominance of the ideological message. The novel's didacticism remains heavy-handed. The book is one more unnecessary, unpleasant and unimaginative adventure travelogue written during the "Third Reich". As an illustration of Nazi Germany's image of Australia, it deserves to be remembered.

Alfred Herzog

Mädels, Ochsen und Halunken

Published in 1937 by the Traditions-Verlag Berlin, this novel is symptomatic for the kind of writing produced during the rule of fascism. It bears the (almost obligatory) subtitle "Australisches Abenteuer", but the "adventures" of Alfred Herzog are little more than Nazi-German propaganda. The book is explicitly fascist, anti-semitic, anti-trade union and racist. As such, it demonstrates an extreme aspect of German-Australian literature in paradigmatic fashion and deserves closer analysis.

Its protagonist is a thirty-seven-year-old "Auslandsdeutscher", Robert Ried, who in 1932 finds that his native Germany is governed by the Social Democrats. His return home is a great disappointment. Robert's father lost his colonial property in 1915; since then his son barely survived "in der Südsee". No specific place is referred to, the novel simply uses the term "drüben". Germans are persecuted because they are better, more reliable workers. Herzog sees his "Auslandsdeutsche" as "Kolonisatoren"; working for someone else, especially for the native population which owns the land, is out of the question: "das kann der deutsche Kolonisator nicht vertragen".(12) Migration automatically means colonisation. Work is seen as a means of conquest. A labour movement in Germany attempting to establish a fair distribution of wealth is ideologically abhorrent to such colonial mentality. Much of Herzog's novel is devoted to denigrating the socialists, in Germany and elsewhere. Although he says he has never been to Australia, Robert claims: "Ein australischer Sozialdemokrat geht heute schnurstracks zur Polizei und zeigt dich an, weil du als eingewanderter Deutscher eine Arbeit angenommen hast. Wo bleibt da die internationale Verbrüderung?"(13) As a German colonist in the South Sea he witnessed "wie bei Kriegsausbruch die Deutschen mißhandelt wurden, wie man brutal und gemein deutsche Frauen und Kinder abtransportierte, um sie ins Zuchthaus nach Neuseeland zu bringen".(Ibid.) Much of Herzog's book is made up of agitation. It serves as motivation for a military revenge. Robert Ried, too, finds (temporary) refuge in the German navy; confronted with a democratic government in his "fatherland", he is horrified and demands that only those who participated in the "Great War" be appointed to positions of power, the "Ehrenstellen des Staatsbetriebes".(14)

Herzog's hero suffers the social, moral and political dislocation of a soldier after a lost war. He longs for a continuation of his military life and hopes to bring this about by calling for a military government. Robert Ried's friendship with the docker Karl Leeken represents the totalitarian concept of the common interests and the essential oneness of a people, — what National Socialists called "Volksgemeinschaft". It was a conception embracing the entirety of a race, expressed in the term "the nation as a whole". The docker Leeken is seen as the victim of incompetent democratic governments: he is an unemployed worker who turns to communism. Ried, the repatriated German abroad, is doubly homeless: he is an unemployed ex-soldier whose politics are the far Right. Together they embody the central ideology of Nazism. Alfred Herzog throws light on the by no means insignificant role played in the emergence of fascist Germany by colonists, migrants or settlers abroad returning home. Nor is the dream of colonialism surrendered; it grows harmoniously into the greater vision of world dominance. German *Kulturpolitik* in Australia was made to serve the aims of Nazi expansionism. Robert's "Draußen" is "das Ausland, in dem deutsche Staatsangehörige wohnten"(51), whose real home is Germany.

Australia is something of a litmus test measuring the ideological commitment of Germans at home and abroad. For Robert Ried, Germans living in the antipodes are suffering from racial deprivation. The German colonist in New Zealand or Tahiti has lost his identity twice: "Er sehnt sich nach den Menschen seiner Rasse"(90) and he is the victim of German-language journalism writing about "versumpfte Kolonialwirtschaft"(91). Robert carries the burden of Germany's honour: "Deutschlands Ehre und Ansehen ist geschändet worden," he laments.(Ibid.) He takes a boat to Sydney and is farewelled with the heartfelt advice "Bleiben Sie ein guter Deutscher, Kamerad!"(99)

Not surprisingly, Australia is presented as a land of socialists and trade unionists. Herzog severely criticises "those responsible" for Australia's inability to look into the future. Australia is not, he argues, the "land of tomorrow". Robert Ried's problems will continue; Australia does not seem very different from Germany. The author attacks the myth of an Australian "Arbeiterparadies". Strikes rate highly among his many objections to workers protecting themselves. In an amazing turnabout from the novel's own racism, Herzog claims that the Australian unions have done nothing for the coloureds and blacks. His tone is triumphantly mocking and scathingly aggressive. In a similar application of different criteria, he describes Italian, Rumanian, Russian, French and English migrants as "inferior" members of their national cultures: "Sie alle gehörten sicher nicht zu den Auserwählten ihrer Nationen."(132) It appears only Germans living in Australia belong to that category. Herzog disapproves of the strong influence of "the church" in Australia.

The author's language is that of Nazism. Its tone is sloppy, vulgar and arrogant. Unwittingly, Herzog's style documents paradigmatic features of fascist "values". Australia is seen as an extension of British interests, and Germans are not welcome as settlers — unless they invest their capital.(152) The author's "Kameraden" in Australia despair over the loss of respect for their native country. They call for a will so strong "daß sich das Ausland wieder dazu bequemt, in uns ein starkes Volk zu sehen".(154) In despair they fear the equation of German migrants with coloureds and blacks. They think they know the image of Germany Australian children are taught at school and appeal for a "starkes Volk" to counter such distortion and humiliation. A "rejuvenation" of Germans will have to take the path of asserting their racial "superiority". At times, the narrative text reads like a speech by Goebbels.(162) It acknowledges the aim of ideological change and is an explicit preparation for war.

Mädels, Ochsen und Halunken is not so much a novel about German fascism in Australia as about the genesis of fascism in the context of colonialisation and migration. Anti-semitism evolves as an important ingredient to counterbalance the feeling of national inferiority, as does racism in general.(174,191,202,205,etc.) The novel's (and its author's) own philosophy of German-Australian relations during the rise of fascism is expressed in the following sentence: "Ich glaube, daß...Deutsche auch in Australien Deutschland dienen können, damit die Lügen vernichtet werden, die man über uns ausstreut."(Ibid.) The presence of Germans in Australia is to serve Germany, more specifically to destroy the "lies" and misinformation spread about the German nation and its people. Herzog's propaganda novel makes sure that it is a discredited character who attempts to resist fascism in Germany. It is the "honest", likeable Thomas who defends Nazism in Australia. The novel culminates in moral appeals to "ein anständiger Deutscher"(234), without ever allowing for a meaningful definition of the emotive term or succeeding in correlating it to democratic political values. Herzog champions the *Deutschtum* ideology among German migrants and settlers in Australia. "Die Mehrzahl der Germans stehen für ihr Deutschtum ein," says Thomas.(Ibid.)

In the final passages of the novel the author equates "den Kampf im Leben" with the concept of "ehrliche Arbeit", — a central idea in all *Deutschtum* literature, as well as a basic equation in Nazi ideology. Bearing in mind the subtitle of the novel, it is perhaps surprising the "Abenteurer" are now defined as "Halunken"(237), unable to participate in honest combat and labour. Herzog ends his narrative with a description of the German settlers' response:

(es) leuchteten die Augen, und sie erzählten von Treue und Liebe zur Heimat, die weit über den Wassern liegt, die man niemals vergessen kann, wenn man ein rechter German ist.(238)

It underlines the emotionalism of its appeal. The novel demonstrates, albeit by default, the extent of political, moral and cultural confusion which characterised the situation of German migrants in Australia during the period of German fascism. Unwittingly, Alfred Herzog's piece of muddled propaganda bears witness to the volatile issue of nationalism in exile. Both German and Australian sociopolitical life are invoked only by way of clichés, generalisations and prejudices. As seems inevitable with propagandistic novels of the past, there is much involuntary humour. Yet it is in the end the fear and disgust, articulated in a language of rhetoric and hate, which leave the most lasting impression. Herzog's style is slanderous and barbaric, the novel a prolonged tour-de-force of hatred and of impoverished imagination. As a piece of Nazi sentimentality and fascist nationalism it remains a profoundly disturbing document.

August Von Der Flatt (J.F.W. Schulz)

Jugenderinnerungen und Allgemeine Beobachtungen

Johann Friedrich W. Schulz published three titles under the pseudonym of August von der Flatt at the Auricht's Printing Office in Tanunda. They are all written in a pidgin German, made up of his inherited Silesian dialect and Germanised Australianisms, and appeared in 1937 and 1938. The first is called *Jugenderinnerungen und Allgemeine Beobachtungen*. At the age of fifty the author recalls his childhood and youth in South Australia. He remembers the German school he attended at Robertstown and his friendship with an Australian boy who visits "de englische Schule".(3) Schulz invokes the spirit of German settlements in the earlier part of this century. As his adopted name implies, he identifies himself with the area, the plane or flatness of the region of German settlement. His *nom de plume* purports to be a personification of the area, a role *persona* embodying the spirit of the community. Part of "August von der Flatt's" temperament is his pronounced anti-intellectual attitude. School, to him, is a waste of time. One can only wonder to what extent such sentiments reflect the general feeling of the German-Australian social unity in South Australia at that time. There is a marked element of fundamentalist religious "logic" in this author's deliberations. World trade in commodities is criticised for interfering with God's divine plan.(5) In a characteristically simplistic manner August von der Flatt asks why people still die of starvation while trade agreements are in force. He has similar complaints about German and French wines pricing each other out of the market. Schulz creates a popular ethnic figure dispensing no-nonsense judgements and opinions, the kind of thought typical of regional rural settlers. The "earthy" language is an integral part of this posture. August von der Flatt's reflections of the common man are motivated by his work: "Wenn mon 'n ganzen Tag hinter 'n Flug oder hinter de Aegen harloft, do hutt mon Zeit ieber alles, woaste in de Zeitungen schtieht, nachzudenken," he explains, and proudly adds: "denn de Zeitungen kriegn ber hier uff de Flatt ooch, ooch welche von Deutschland und Amerika".(6) Much of his thinking is the result of such monotonous work and a prolonged reaction to the reading of newspapers.

Schulz is, of course, an Australian-born ethnic German who writes for a culturally cohesive group of German-Australians. His thoughts on the world and on Australia are, as it were, for local consumption. Although August von der Flatt's popular literature is hardly more than a gossipy conversation at the local or the barber's, it is an authentic record of more than personal feelings. It may be assumed that he expresses ideas supported by most, if not all, in his community.

He continues with a critique of all Australian states. Queensland's decision to use white labourers in the cane fields has led to sugar price increases, with the absurd result, he claims, "Dass ber fer insern eegnen Zucker nu mehr bezoahln missen als andere Länder". In despair he exclaims: "Is doas anne Wirtschoft!"(7) The reader senses the amused and angry approval of his mates. New South Wales, he argues, has many corrupt officials, and in a touch of grotesque irony he suggests to deport them all to Africa, "mit a Lendentuch um Leib und anne Haue in der Hand, un nu — feiht for juhrself".(Ibid.) Phonetic transcriptions such as in the final phrase are a feature of von der Flatt's language. He has no hesitation in using the word "Texpeher" ("taxpayer"), for example. In his "Germanized" English vocabulary he retains the German gender. Reading his texts thus often leads to intriguing or comical encounters, sometimes in support of, occasionally in contrast to, what is being said. Perhaps predictably, he criticises New South Wales and Victoria for their frequent strikes. As the record of German trade unionism shows, to strike is an essentially "un-German" protest; it is in conflict with the high cultural value attached to work, especially in Protestantism. In too many "Fektris" workers "schtreikn".(8) The entire economy of the land is an "Eirisch Schtuh" ("Irish Stew").(10) August von der Flatt also has a solution to the rabbit plague: he plans to start a "Karnickel Farm" and if he does not get a fair price for his breed he intends to release the animals in Parliament. Western Australia's plans to secede from the Commonwealth do not surprise von der Flatt, any more than the political problems in Tasmania.

This criticism of all Australian states and of the Australian economy in generally leads to the recommendation to take Hitler as model saviour. As he stated earlier, he does get German newspapers in the Barossa Valley and "knows what he is talking about". August von der Flatt believes that Hitler's anti-democratic, anti-semitic, anti-free press and anti-communist stand is exactly what Australia needs to resolve her present difficulties. The author Johann Friedrich Wilhelm Schulz expresses Nazi sympathies in conjunction with a reaffirmed loyalty to Australia. The support for Hitler by a representative "literary" figure of the South Australian ethnic German community must be taken as a strong indication of the extent of fascist sympathies among these people. It is thus a passage of historic importance and deserves to be quoted in full.

> Und wie sull de Korre nu wieder aus 'n Dreck raus? Well, do scheint blussig een Weg zu sein, und doas is dar, dann dar Hitler in Deutschland genumm hutt. Dar hutt sich rechts und links ins Parlament reingehaun, bis a Reichskanzler wurde. Do hutt a zunächst de Juden on de Loden gekriegt. A hutt gezeigt, doss mon dar verlognen Presse doch 's Maul schtuppen konn...Und de Kommunisten und Uffwiegler missen aus 'n Lande raus, doss 's mon su rocht. Von schmutzige Bilder und schlechte Bicher wird a Feuer gemacht, doss eem doas Herz dabei woarm wird. Kirchen und kristliche Schuln warden versurgt und de gottlusen Schuln warden zugemacht.
>
> Wenn ich monchesmoal in de Zeitungen lasen tu (nich etwo in inse englische verlogene Zeitungen, denn die hoabn de Juden ooch in de Hände), wenn ich in de deutschen Zeitungen lasen tu, oder in Briefe, die de von Deutschland kumm, und sah wies jitzt do zugieht, do möcht ich mer an 'n Malli Knippel in de Hand nahm und in inse verführten Unempleud reinschpringn und rechts und links zuhaun.(Ibid.)

The "advice" is so explicit and extreme that it can only be considered frightening. All popular humour has suddenly disappeared. The recurring counsel is "reinhaun" or "zuhaun", to smash up and to beat up. The violence extends to the burning of books and the destruction of "degenerate" art, to the censorship of the press and the punishment of the unemployed. Von der Flatt's "popular wisdom" is so horrendous that readers may need to remind themselves of its sources. German newspapers under Nazi control and letters from German relatives who were themselves subjected to fascist suppression appear to have been the basis for this extraordinary outburst. The author never experienced the terror he is advocating. Nonetheless, it is a profoundly disturbing document of Australian-born ethnic German Nazi support during the late thirties in this country. The remarkable naivety of advocating an Australian Hitler to turn the continent into "a richtiges Paradies"(Ibid.) seems to have been shared by more than a minority of German settlers. Perhaps it is an unwitting admission of guilt when von der Flatt ends his political comments with the remark that there is not much call for intellectual prowess in the Barossa Valley, "do freu ich mer, doss ich hier uff dar Flatt bin, wu ber blussig su klug sein, wie's nötig is".(12) For all the previous reflections on world politics, the statement expresses a characteristic self-satisfied sense of withdrawal from the broader problems of life. The Lutheran spirit of Protestantism has formulated its rebellious gesture, only to return to a moral inwardness. The German community of fundamentalist Christians will not, in the end, be affected by anything happening in the world.

The first section of the booklet ends with a somewhat less sinister complaint about Australia's "Tekseschen" ("taxation"). Some of the author's popular humour reappears, including the ability to laugh at himself. Yet the fervent belief in one's own righteousness creates a special kind of Diaspora. It is a tone which characterises the thought and language of von der Flatt's Barossa Valley German community, even where its expressions are light-hearted and humorous.

The second part of this publication consists of letters sent by August von der Flatt to his "Noachbar", "Fritz Wurscht"(11), or "Fritz vom Schkrupp".(16) Schulz's epistolary style proves no different from his earlier narration: it is essentially social small talk, gossip and political pub talk. He predicts the end of Australia as a result of forthcoming elections: if Labor wins, no one will work any more; if the Liberals win, there will be a drought. Such is von der Flatt's humour. By inventing a politics of natural seasons he poses as the champion of his people. The city people lack real understanding of the man on the land ("von der Flatt"). He also attacks his own young people for dressing up and for not keeping their "beautiful German names": "Inse scheene deutsche Näme sein hin."(Ibid.) August von der Flatt is appointed by a local meeting to travel to the city "and create order" ("und Urdnung schoffn"). His comment on city life is as profound as are his other observations on Australian social scenes: "Ber koam ooch glücklich in de Schtoadt on. Mei Wort, lofen do Menschen rim, immer hin und har."(21) It may be assumed that Schulz knew the work of "Steele Rudd" (1868–1935), the pen-name of Arthur Hoey Davis, author of the humorous characters Dad and Dave. Rudd founded and edited *Steele Rudd's Magazine* (1904–1930) and is best known for his short stories in *On Our Selection* (first published in *The Bulletin* in 1899). Schulz's "August von der Flatt" is clearly modelled on the life of the "cocky" farmer invented by "Steele Rudd". There is the same naivety, the same wit, the same "local colour". It is remarkable that the German migrant community should follow so closely the rural model of Australian popular literature.

While in "Adlied" ("Adelaide"), August von der Flatt wants to attend church. He is disturbed to realise that he has left his "great Breslau hymn-book" at home, "...'s fehlt mer ooch mei grusses Breslauer Gesangbuch unterm Orm".(23) Asking his way to a church, he speaks German and is surprised to find that the first person can show him the way in his language. There is a moment of dogmatic theological conflict when he is asked "Welche?" ("which Lutheran church?"). "Ich soag: De lutherische. A froagt: Welche? Do hoast wull a Knix, denk ich, weils doch blussig eene lutherische Kirche gibt...".(Ibid.) He ends up attending a Methodist service. Later he comes across "de Salweschen Armi" ("the Salvation Army"), but does not respond to their form of worship. A few days later, he visits South Australia's State Parliament, where he is allowed to sit "in de Schtrenschers Gallerie" ("strangers' gallery").(24) His description of parliamentary proceedings makes for amusing comparison with his own later *Anne Gemeende-Versammlung uff der Flatt*.(1938) He intervenes in a discussion about starvation of workers, reverting to his Hitlerian impulse to smash things up ("doss ich...dreinschloagn tu"), until "Mister Schpieker" calls him to "Seilens!"(25) Democracy and social tolerance are not August von der Flatt's strong points.

While in Adelaide ("wu keen Mensch woas von ins uff der Flatt wissen will"), he discovers a German section in the local paper ("fer de Kriegsleute uffs deutsche Kriegsschiff, de 'Köln'"). The crew of the German battleship visits Tanunda a few days later and this causes the author to describe a German cultural reunion with overtly political overtones. He comments particularly on those German settlers who under Australian pressure had given up speaking their language and now find that they can speak it once again. To Schulz, this is a case of German "law and order", a return to respect shown for German language and culture. The highlight of August von der Flatt's narrative epistle is his invitation to board the German battleship. It ends with a dream-vision of peculiar anti-French sentiments: an English and a German battleship fire on a French boat from cannons loaded with Bavarian beer...On that note of German *Kulturpolitik* the narrative concludes. The thirty-five-page publication contains a number of Tanunda-German advertisements which are in themselves of great interest, not only for the social historian.

Meine irschte Reese noach Bethesda und meine zweete noach Hermannsburg

Meine irschte Reese noach Bethesda und meine zweete noach Hermannsburg, like its predecessor published in Tanunda, follows the narrative form of a diary-type letter to "Fritz vom Schkrupp". It is a kind of travelogue, written in a casual, colloquial and intimate style. August von der Flatt uses plenty of "fill-words", such as "Ennihau" ("anyhow") or "Enuff sed!" ("enough said!"), to convey the tone of friendly conversation. The journey itself is described in rather pedestrian terms, leading the reader to wonder perhaps why the report was undertaken. It is only when the group arrives at the former Bethesda ("das ehemoalige Bethesda",7) that his interest may be aroused. The abandoned mission station, long reclaimed by nature, prompts an emotional response in the travellers. Most houses are covered in sand. "Du konnst im Sand uff de Decke lohfen."(Ibid.) The author includes his own photos to illustrate the extent of nature's takeover. Schulz quotes some reactions among the German-Australians who have worked there as missionaries and teachers. "Hie hoab ich gewohnt — do Schule gehalten, do schtund de Kirche".(8) Yet no deeper reflection of their loss is expressed.

Instead, von der Flatt realises the inhuman treatment of the Aborigines by the Australian government. His response is characteristically confused. What appears to be support for the indigenous population is in reality an objection to their natural food and way of life.

The section "Noach Hermannsburg" opens with the quotation of the proverb "...'s keen Rest fer de Wicked" ("there's no rest for the wicked"). Such transcriptions make up much of the oddities and interest of a text which over lengthy passages has little else to offer. The following is a brief range of phonetic adaptations: "schtarting Hendel" ("starting handle"), "Tuhl Bäg" ("tool bag"), "Nau trei her" ("now try her") (16), "Schwäg" ("swag"), "Metress, Blenkits" ("mattress, blankets"), "o Keh" ("okay"), "Exhohst" ("exhaust") (17), "Intehk" ("intake"), "Netting Fenz" ("netting fence"), "de Wehtress" ("waitress"), "schtreht out" ("straight out"), "Eil giw her e go" ("I'll give her a go") (18). Readers of (High) German and English are required to be versatile in their adjustments. There are plenty of practical matters von der Flatt discusses; in fact, his descriptions are largely a kind of stock-taking of tools, machines and objects. The most appropriate analysis of the text would indeed be an inventory of corresponding terms. There are a few humorous sketches about sleeping in the open and riding camels. Despite an exhaustive listing of all his activities, von der Flatt's journey to Hermannsburg simply lacks interest. Occasionally he touches on a potentially controversial subject, such as provocation of Aborigines in Alice Springs by the whites, but the author immediately changes the subject again. It is clearly a publication addressing itself to a very restricted readership. What deserves to be noted is the German Lutheran appeal at the end of the letter: the natives' welfare is a categorical imperative in a commitment to the white man's burden.

Anne Gemeende-Versammlung uff der Flatt

Finally, there is a brief comedy featuring August von der Flatt, Fritz vom Schkrupp, der Vorsitzende (chairman) and die Versammlung (assembly), called *Anne Gemeende-Versammlung uff der Flatt*. It is a light-hearted play combining documentation with self-irony. The script reads like a short drama. But the text is also a valuable document of social history. The meeting begins and ends with a song, presumably a Lutheran hymn. Immediately after the opening a language conflict arises: August von der Flatt objects to English being used during their discussion. As in his earlier publication, he criticises the young for not honouring the tongue of their parents. He fears: "inse schiene deutsche Schproache is hin."(1) (It is, of course, highly contentious whether his own dialect could be equated with the "schiene deutsche Schproache".

It is not clear whether Schulz is aware of the irony of the claim.) Another member of the congregation displays the conflict of bilingualism in his response: "Ich verstehe auch deutsch, but if I want to speak I can express myself better in English."(Ibid.) What follows is a comedy of confusion concerning August von der Flatt's parrot who was taught to speak English. It is easier, he claims, to teach a cockatoo English, an argument which convinces the assembly to remain bilingual during its deliberations. August von der Flatt appears as a contradictory but good-natured member of an ethnic community whose humour is an expression of cultural dislocation. Schulz's *persona* is a stylised self-projection of a German Australian in fear of losing his identity. In the mini-society of a township congregation this social role-playing becomes the dramatic expression of cultural assertion in Diaspora.

Heinrich Hauser

Last Port of Call

This 1938 seafaring novel of 301 pages devotes approximately ten per cent to the arrival of the ship *Notre Dame* in Australia, more precisely, its deliberate wrecking on the Australian coast "in thick, stormy weather, some miles north of Cape Catastrophe".(300) Hauser's narrative centres around the figures of Captain Andersson and the sailor Jorg Borcke whose eighty-nine days aboard the vessel have forged a special bond between them. They share the secret determination not to allow the ship to be sold for scrap. Jorg repeats the captain's pronouncement: "we are sailing into eternity".(286) For this Scandinavian crew Australia assumes the meaning of an end to freedom, a place where life itself — a European life — must cease. But this death is a suicide, a ritualistic defiance. The captain is unwilling to start a new life, to take over a new vessel. In symbolism reminiscent of Joseph Conrad the novel's adventure captures a cultural and a spiritual journey of negation. "They had died a great, a magnificent death," the narrator records.(299) Yet while the captain dies, Jorg Borcke reaches land. The noise he hears beyond the dunes is the pounding motor of a car — modern technology, rejected by Captain Andersson, catches up with him. The wrecked *Notre Dame* makes way for machines and engineering progress at sea, while Jorg is carried to safety by transport's rapid advance. In a conflict of generations a mechanical future destroys Andersson and rescues Borcke. Australia is presented as the testing ground for this trial of strength. It is the "last port of call" for "the masts, the yards, the topmasts, the sails, the rigging".(282) The century "marches in engine time".(Ibid.)

It is in the light of such conflict that Australia assumes its special significance. It is a continent where "science had arrived just in time to see the last men of the Stone Age on our globe".(274) The destination of the journey thus reflects the challenge of civilisation faced by the crew of the *Notre Dame*. There is brutal irony in the description of the Aborigines who "have gone over at a bound into the Iron Age" and "are dying of it as of a plague".(Ibid.) The land which rescues Jorg remains a place of hostile tension. The narrator describes it in overwhelmingly negative terms: "it was as if one had been hurled out of the ether with an enormous impact upon a strange planet".(300) Progress causing the death of a culture unites the lives of sailors and Aborigines: both have to adapt to new conditions, to a new life-style. Hauser's *Last Port of Call* attempts to draw this analogy with subtle force, yet does so by quoting Jorg Borcke's sketchy unsympathetic reading knowledge of Australia's native population, flora and fauna.

> He read about Australia. What a strange contradictory country! (Its animals) caused a shudder, a breath from that subterranean of primitive ages from which even man had once ascended.(270)

There are indeed "subterranean", "primitive" forces operating in the minds of the European sailors on their final voyage to "eternity". The contradiction between progress and decay forms a vital part of the novel's theme. Again, Australia is presented as reflecting such variance.

> And Australian water! It was the most contradictory water in the world...There was no depending on this water.(271)

The Aborigines are described by their "primitive characteristics"(Ibid.), with "revoltingly ugly, completely distorted" faces.(Ibid.) The narrator records that they "were probably the oldest type among the surviving men of the earth".(Ibid.) The irony is that they never actually appear in the novel, except as quotation from Jorg's reading. They not only remain literature, the validity of which has been written about them (by unnamed authors) is highly questionable. The men are likened to "old prophets, religious fanatics, hermits of the desert"(272) — and as such bear a resemblance to the crew of the *Notre Dame*. Jorg's and Barossa's support of the suicidal captain may be compared to the description of Aboriginal behaviour: "They held tight to the dying man, trying literally to keep him alive".(Ibid.) Hauser correlates the people of the desert with a European seafaring tribe. They share a spirituality related to their respective environment. The mythology of the sea is analogous to the Australian wilderness: "The desert was peopled by an ancestor cult which went back to the very beginnings of the race."(Ibid.) Captain Andersson practises and inspires a similar ancestral devotion on the *Notre Dame*, aptly named as allusion to a spiritual vessel. Referring to the ship's emergency pumps, the narrator reminds his readers "with what disdain" Jorg Borcke "had looked at these clumsy, primitive machines...antiquated as they were...".(282) The inference is unmistakable. Sailing will no longer follow the ancient rites, it will not survive modern technology, any more than the Aborigines will adjust to the white man's life and values. The *Notre Dame* sails into the end of sailing, the Australian shore. Progress progresses into the death of a "primitive" people and their culture. It is from this perspective that the coastline of South Australia is characterised as "unfriendly and inhospitable".(278) The arrival in Australia will be the final showdown for the captain and his crew, by extension, for European civilisation on this continent.

Hauser has written a *Landung in Australien* very different from Kisch's: instead of the sociopolitical, his novel concentrates on the cultural-mythological. Once again, Australia has been interpreted as a realm of myth, a spiritual projection, a manifestation of ancient conflicts. The significance of the symbol is stressed when the captain declares: "It's not very different here from at home."(287) The "last port of call" is drawn into a native European imagination and acquires its recognisable meaning. "It was easy to understand," the narrator remarks earlier, "that coasts are nothing but dangers to a ship like *Notre Dame*".(278) Approaching the "shore", the European becomes "primitive man" once more. Suddenly, there is "the old Jorg", tradition and progress, culture and civilisation, "eternity" and the future. When the vessel is finally wrecked, it is described as "a great piece of seamanship".(300) "The last Viking was dead. Dead was the *Notre Dame*, which no power on earth could free from this coast. They had died a great, a magnificent death."(299) Landing in Australia here means a suicidal farewell to a culture of the past, the ritualistic killing of the old and the bitter acceptance of the new. Unlike the captain, Jorg is prepared to undergo this violent transformation. To him, Australia is both the ancient land and the country of the future; it is a continent on which the conflict of cultures rages. His ultimate acceptance of this dynamic of human progress expresses itself in the ecstatic, spiritual joy over his salvation. Hauser's *Last Port of Call* ends with a symbolic narrative gesture characteristic of its style throughout: "Jorg fell forward, got his mouth full of sand, and tasted in ecstasy the flavour of the earth".(301) He "falls" into a future which he will share with "the earth". Hauser's hero identifies himself with the spiritual and social dimensions of Australia, the land of challenging "salvation".

HERMANN KEMPCKE

Ludwig Leichhardt: 125. Geburtstag — 90 Jahre verschollen

Kempcke's essay on Ludwig Leichhardt appeared in 1938.[39] It commemorates the achievements of the German explorer in Australia and presents a well-researched history of his life prior to his departure in 1841 for Sydney. Kempcke writes with obvious love and pride of the man who grew up in his part of the Mark Brandenburg. His study includes illustrations from the Museum of Local History at Beeskow where Hermann Kempcke worked for many years. He refers to Leichhardt as "unser Landmann".(48) The text, described as "Ein Erinnerungsblatt an den Australienforscher Ludwig Leichhardt und seine Familie", is a memorial address and homage, a poetic tribute and a scientific report. It is this peculiar mixture which makes Kempcke's commemoration interesting.

The author opens with a lyrical outburst, lamenting and celebrating the tragic nature of human life. The silence of the Australian desert is likened to the forgetfulness of ordinary Germans. While Leichhardt's reputation is secured and honoured by scientists, the general populace knows nothing about his timeless achievements. Ludwig Leichhardt is seen as the archetypal hero whose bold exploits are soon forgotten. Despite such hero worship, the author does not succumb to nationalistic glorification, — a remarkable feat, considering the time and place of publication. Kempcke's genealogical investigation provides reliable data about Ludwig Leichhardt's grandfather and father and traces the family's move to the shire of Beeskow-Storkow in 1803. The father's (Christian Leichhardt's) life-long interest in literature and general ambition to educate himself — he was a peat-cutter — is stressed, as is his mother's (Charlotte Sophie Strählow's) love of fables, fairy-tales and sagas. Her influence on the young Ludwig prompts Kempcke to another paradigmatic observation: "Und auch hier zeigt sich wieder, wie so oft bei großen Männern, der geistige Zusammenhang einer bedeutenden Mutter mit dem Sohn."(50) His is an obituary celebrating the didacticism of the exemplary.

The author traces Ludwig Leichhardt's activities at primary school, emphasising that each child was allocated a piece of land on which it had to grow various plants and collect insects, flowers, butterflies and herbs. Ludwig Leichhardt's collections thus began at a very early stage; the home was crowded with the boy's herbariums and entomological boxes. Kempcke throws light on Leichhardt's years at grammar school, during which he both failed to move up, as a result of his sickly constitution, and later graduated as best student. Two passions of the young Leichhardt stand out: the call of the open air and debating. Kempcke convincingly explains how Leichhardt, under the influence of fellow-student William Nicholson, changes his university studies from philology to science and medicine, while rejecting his father's advice to devote himself to theology. In a letter, quoted in the essay, he informs his brother-in-law Barth that his studies are to lead him to something greater than a doctorate, a first allusion to his concrete plans of travelling as a natural scientist and explorer (8 July, 1834). Herman Kempcke believes that the urge to travel was shared by most members of the Leichhardt family. Ludwig Leichhardt's contact with Count Pückler and his friends, mostly writers of travelogues, further influenced his decision to leave university. (Curiously, Kempcke does not provide any information when and how Leichhardt achieved his doctorate; by the time he joins his friend William in London, the author simply refers to his hero as "Dr. Ludwig Leichhardt".) Understandably, the obituary does not attempt to throw light on the ambivalent nature of the friendship between Leichhardt and Nicholson. William is simply honoured as sponsor of Leichhardt's journey to Australia.

When sketching his activities in Europe, Kempcke endorses Leichhardt's own sense of a mission, his "Sendung für dieses Erdenleben".(52) After the failures of his other ventures, the author argues, Leichhardt must have felt that "to lift the mysterious veil" ("den geheimnisvollen Schleier", Ibid.) of Australia's flora and fauna was his true "Mission".(Ibid.) Kempcke places heavy emphasis on Leichhardt's religious faith, his patriotism, his modesty and his moral commitment. He values Leichhardt's letters very highly, both as a source for further research and as documents "of the nobility of his spirit" ("hohen Adel seiner Gesinnung", Ibid.). Kempcke reminds his readers of the total lack of social contacts which complicated Leichhardt's ambitions in Australia. He rightly calls his hero "a poor emigrant" ("armen Auswanderer",53) who knows nothing about the land and its people. "Die Natur des Landes kannte er gar nicht, die Menschen waren ihm fremd."(Ibid.) Such handicaps strengthen the author's conviction that Leichhardt was indeed a man with a mission.(Ibid.) He explicitly endorses Leichhardt's own motto, taken from Goethe's *Iphigenie auf Tauris* (1787): "Die Götter brauchen manchen guten Mann zu ihrem Dienst auf dieser weiten Erde."(Ibid.) Kempcke's homage combines factual historical information with a mild form of mythologising. Leichhardt's expedition to Port Essington is not discussed in any detail; the author is more interested in the celebration of his hero after the event. He shows a keen awareness of the commercial significance of the journey.(54) Addressing himself to Leichhardt's own commitment to Australia, he calls him an archetypal German ("ein kerndeutscher Mann", Ibid.) who has discovered an elective home ("seine neue Wahlheimat", Ibid.) he will not leave. Although he plans to visit his native Germany again after his second expedition, he has no intention of settling there. The "poor migrant" has become an Australian in mind and spirit. Leichhardt's failed second "Forschungsreise"(Ibid.) still inspires Kempcke to hope and a vision of greatness. The disappearance of the "kühne wagemutige Deutsche"(Ibid.), the courageously daring German, is not fully accepted. Why should it not be possible, the author asks, to discover the "secrets of the desert" with the aid of modern technology. He has not given up hope that Leichhardt and his lost party may be found. It is the hope of resurrection of the myth, the faith of legends. Kempcke acknowledges the generous assistance to Leichhardt's mother by the Australian government and criticises the lack of support and recognition in the explorer's native Prussia. In Australia, the author informs his readers, suburbs, streets, districts, parks and mountains are named in honour of the famous German-Australian. Science has immortalised him by applying his name to a coral, an Australian cypress and a kangaroo. In his elective country a statue of the explorer celebrates his achievements, whereas in Prussia only Georg Fränz's biographical sketch of 1915, a simple plaque outside the school of Falkenberg (1923) and a Leichhardt Room in the local museum of Beeskow bear witness to the "treue märkische Heimatsohn".(55) Kempcke's commemorative article culminates in an appeal to honour a great German in Australia, to recognise and to remember a forgotten hero.

125 Geburtstag — 90 Jahre verschollen is an informative, passionate contribution to German-Australian literature. In its mixture of scholarly and popular mythological style it seems an appropriate expression of the fate and fame of Ludwig Leichhardt. It deserves to be considered in the continuing discussion of this explorer's contribution to Australia. E. M. Webster's authoritative biography *Whirlwinds in the plain. Ludwig Leichhardt. Friends foes & history* does not, for instance, refer to Hermann Kempcke. It is as complementary perception of a native Australian vision that his contribution remains of real value. The Prussian version of a cultural hero does not sit uncomfortably with the literary, historical and mythological projections of Ludwig Leichhardt in Australia.

Heinrich Hauser

Australien. Der menschenscheue Kontinent

In many ways this is one of the most authoritative travelogues in the history of German-Australian literature. It presents a wealth of useful, first-hand, factual information, and it does so in a style which is a happy mixture of personal experience and a collection of data, anecdotal reflection and objective knowledge. Hauser's 1939 Australia book is eminently readable. It covers most aspects of life in this country, its brief history, flora and fauna, as well as the temperament, values and distinctive nature of its people. It is no coincidence that the author's description of Australia ends with a chapter on "der australische Mensch".(252) Hauser spent in all about a year in Australia, first during the summer of 1922–23, then again during the same period in 1936–37. Whilst one year may not be a sufficient period of time to write about a country authoritatively, Hauser's two visits were a decade and a half apart, allowing for reassessment, recognition of change and an appreciation of development and growth.

Heinrich Hauser's introduction bears the programmatic title "'Volk ohne Raum' — 'Raum ohne Volk'".(7) The variation and juxtaposition of Hitler's slogan propagating German conquest and annexation lead to an antipodean inversion summarising the author's social, political and cultural interpretation of Australia. The "otherness" is seen to be the opposite; Australia is "'anders', ...sehr anders"(8), so different that it may reflect on the German dilemma. "Wir sind 'Volk ohne Raum' —

und drüben ist 'Raum ohne Volk'", Hauser formulates.(9) It is important, therefore, to recognise the ideological implications of his introduction to a continent about which very little is known in Germany. The author's decision to write this book can only be understood in these terms. German Australians should have been leading the way in forging special German-Australian relations, especially after the declaration of the Third Reich. As so many other German authors, Hauser never questions the ultimate loyalty of German migrants to their native country, whatever their reasons for leaving it. They are to be used as "mediators", as "ambassadors" of a "new" Germany. In such context the reassurance that Australia "has nothing to fear from Germany" remains less than comforting. The nature of German-Australian relations is revealed in Hauser's repeated discussion of race, anti-semitism and blood and soil ideology. Australia's fear of the Japanese and Chinese and her increasing detachment from Great Britain are manipulated into friendly relations or ideological analogies with Nazi Germany. In Australia's policy to preserve a white population Hauser recognises "wiederum eine erstaunliche Verwandtschaft mit den Ideen des neuen Deutschlands".(218) He explicitly states that only Germans can fully appreciate the ideals of a white Australia policy. Racism and colonialism come together in his vision of a great South Land reserved for whites only.(220) German-Australian relations here mean collusion in the ideology of racial colonialism.

In a highly revealing description of Australia's immigration law Hauser exposes its racist policy. As the case of Kisch demonstrates, this policy was not only applied to racially undesirable migrants. In Hauser's own interpretation this is "German" statecraft, part of an ideological affinity between Germany and Australia. Both peoples share the belief "daß Völker verschiedener Moralauffassung (sic!) sich nicht miteinander vertragen".(218) As part of such German-Australian relations, the author is anxious to dispel the anti-German image formed as a result of the First World War. He appeals to Australians to recognise the different type of German migrant who has come more recently to settle in their land. It is a sophisticated Northern European settler of racially pure origin sharing their ideological vision of a white Australia. "Deutsche, die etwa heute nach Australien einwandern," he continues, "sind nicht mehr dieselben anspruchslosen Bauern, die nichts als eine religiöse Freistatt suchten wie die vor hundert Jahren."(222) In 1939 Germans in Australia want more than religious freedom; they seek active participation in the shaping of their new country's future, and wish to do so in the context of friendly German-Australian relations. Hauser warns that the decision to strip Germany of her colonies will, of necessity, be "avenged".(216) German-Australian relations must be understood in this context. If Australia cannot be turned into a German colony, a shared racial ideology is the next best thing: racism constitutes its own brand of colonialism. Hauser speaks of "viel Raum in der Welt" which is kept "in verbrecherischer Weise verschlossen und...künstlich leer".(214–215) It is a criminal conspiracy, he argues, to keep underpopulated parts of the world beyond the reach of European colonialists. The three major conspirators, according to Hauser (and, indeed, official Nazi policy), are "England, Frankreich und Amerika".(215)

It is clear from such deliberations that Heinrich Hauser's Australian travelogue is much more than a tourist's record. His aim is to foster Australian-German relations in the interests of a fascist Germany of neocolonial, expansionist aspirations. His definition of "the Australian" is entirely in terms of German racial mediation and transformation:

> Sein Gesamtbild erinnert an das jener Germanen, die ins Südland wanderten, dessen Wärme ihre nordische Härte löste.(259)

German-Australian friendship is expressed in terms of a shared racial superiority. It is hardly surprising that the author refers to the Aborigines as "die schon reichlich entarteten Eingeborenen"(112); he is in the habit of employing Nazi terminology even where he is anxious to express sympathy. Hauser's general description of Australia's native population reads like that of other German writers of Nazi sympathies (Geck et al.): "Das Profil ist oft geradezu semitisch...".(114)[40]

He laments that a man whose great-grandfather was an Aboriginal should find the urge to return to his native tribe, thus becoming "ein der weißen Rasse völlig verlorener Mann".(120) Hauser emphasises why he writes about the case: Germans are more preoccupied with racial questions than other peoples. ("Für uns Deutsche, die wir uns mehr als andere Völker mit Rassenfragen beschäftigen, ist der...Fall interessant.",119) There can be no doubt about Hauser's Nazi racism and its application in his narrative description of German-Australian relations.

Like Colin Ross, Hauser stresses that German settlers in Australia were primarily concerned with spiritual matters. Indeed, their German ethnicity expressed itself almost entirely in their religion. This meant that on the one hand it was impossible to erase it, on the other hand Hauser regrets that Germans never had the kind of political influence their numbers would have justified. He is anxious to replace religious loyalty with a more worldly cause; otherwise, he fears, Germans in Australia are in danger of disappearing.

It is symptomatic that in his interpretation of Australian history Hauser traces a development which he describes as "Vom 'Konzentrationslager' zum Staatenbund".(174) The penal colony is called a concentration camp; again, Nazi terminology is superimposed on the presentation of a foreign culture. Hauser's discussion of the rise of Australian nationalism between 1856 and 1900 culminates in the disturbing conclusion:

> Soviel steht fest: Australien, dessen öffentliche Meinung unser neues Deutschland aus Mangel an Aufklärung völlig abzulehnen scheint, — dies Australien ist viel "nationalsozialistischer", als es selber glaubt.(189)

In the light of the Australian government's contacts with the Nazi government in Berlin at the time of this book's publication and, indeed, throughout the thirties, such a statement is profoundly unsettling. Hauser sees Australian society as essentially egalitarian; workers subscribe to a kind of undogmatic socialism while aiming to advance to the ranks of small-time capitalists. The Australian workers' union has never joined the "Internationale", the trade union movement has never fought for socialisation of enterprises — it was committed to a nationalisation of industries instead. Hauser comments: "Wir sehen auch hier wieder eine überraschende Verwandtschaft mit den Ideen des Dritten Reiches."(208) He praises Australia for recognising the folly of a racial melting pot as practised by the United States. Multiracism and multiculturalism are derided as "Jewish ideas".(209)

It is surprising that *Australien. Der menschenscheue Kontinent* still manages to offer more than Nazi propaganda and attempts to manipulate German-Australian relations in the interest of German fascist aspirations. Yet it does express such a bias in the context of a wealth of authoritative, well-written observations and reliable information about Australia. It is a thorough study and a stimulating survey, shining with intelligence, bursting with vigour. Without its fascist bias, Hauser's book could serve as a model of good travel writing. Its style is not without elegance and wit, the author's anecdotal narration capturing the spirit of the place and its people. His description of the Australian landscape is enthusiastic, almost passionate — a reflection of his first impressions when he was nineteen years of age. Throughout, Hauser relates his findings back to Germany, expressing similarities, contrasts, analogies.

He draws valid and useful comparisons between German and Australian agriculture, stressing the industrial nature of Australian farming. Hauser favours the term "Roman" (novel) whenever he realises the need to offer an historical perspective on a central aspect of Australian life. (It is, of course, a German colloquialism much in vogue at that time.) "Roman" always refers to a colourful history and in Hauser's usage becomes synonymous with "exotic". It is hardly surprising, then, that so much in Australia, including the decision to immigrate, is associated with this author's concept of "Roman". In one chapter Hauser shows that Australians, too, can be affected by "Romane": he tells the story of a young man who as a result of having read the novels of Walter Scott felt the urge to travel to England. "Vor einem Jahr war er von zu Hause fortgelaufen, weil die Romane Walter Scotts eine unstillbare Sehnsucht nach dem alten Land in ihm erweckt hatten."(235) Hauser's own travelogue assumes the character of such a novel.

His book contains all the usual Australianisms in need of explanation. But it describes, interprets and assesses them better than most other travelogues. Hauser is simply better informed in most cases. He not only records that the first ploughing in Australia took place in 1795, he also writes about McKay's invention of the combined harvester in 1884 and offers a detailed history of exports of Australian produce. He gives a good briefing on the term "sundowner"(54) and informs his readers that Australians consume three times more tea per head than the English or the Chinese. To illustrate various points, he translates passages from Australian bush ballads and other literary works. Australian art, he argues, is at its best wherever it remains free from European influences.(61) Hauser's book has an excellent chapter on "Forscher und Pioniere"(63) and on the different stages of the discovery of Australia. (It seems amazing that he consistently misspells Leichhardt as "Leichardt", 64ff.) Given his habitual analogies of the unusual, exotic or epic and the "novel", it is not surprising that he should devote an entire chapter to the family saga of the Duracks. When writing about early contacts between Europeans and Aborigines the author stresses the cultural clash by relating it to episodes in James Fenimore Cooper's novels and other narrative works dealing with the American West.(110)

Hauser draws a brief, but empathetic picture of all of Australia's larger cities, comparing them, wherever possible, with German state capitals or well-known larger towns. "Freemantle (sic!) und Perth stehen in ähnlichem Verhältnis zueinander wie etwa Warnemünde und Rostock."(155) Curiously, he argues that Australian cities have no slums. ("Elendsviertel und Mietskasernen gibt es in Australien so gut wie überhaupt nicht."156) He likens Perth to Hamburg: "Auf flachen Landzungen, die sich weit in die Seen erstrecken und an den Hügelhängen dehnt sich das größere Perth dem Alster-Viertel Hamburgs nicht ganz unähnlich."(157) Melbourne is described as Australia's London.(159) Perhaps the most wilful comparison is reserved for the nation's capital: "Tatsächlich ist Canberra ein Staat im Staat, etwa wie der Kirchenstaat in Italien."(171) The ACT as Australia's Vatican?

A central argument of the book maintains that it is the vastness of the land which has shaped an Australian "race". One aspect of this influence is the anti-authoritarian, anti-bureaucratic temperament of the Australian. Hauser thereby explains the conflicts between squatters and the government.(184) He relates this anti-authoritarianism to the failure of European lecturers in Australia:

> Der Australier glaubt nicht an Autorität; er besitzt ein natürliches Mißtrauen gegen jedermann, der sich autoritär gebärdet — daher der Mißerfolg fast aller europäischer Kapazitäten, die sich auf Vortragsreisen nach Australien begeben.(259)

This is an interesting, if controversial, comment on the difficulty of cultural mediation. Hauser does not merely refer to a different attitude, he believes in the existence, or emergence, "einer australischen Rasse"(254) and proceeds to characterise its physical features.

An undeniable achievement of Hauser's *Australien. Der menschenscheue Kontinent* is his earnest attempt to convey to his readers an appreciation of an Australian culture. He claims that "von einer rein australischen Kunst kann noch kaum die Rede sein"(236), yet writes knowledgeably of the *Bulletin* school, discusses Aeneas Gunn's *We of the Never-Never* ("zweifellos einer der besten Romane über das Leben im australischen Busch",241), acknowledges the existence of a "selbständige australische Kunstkritik"(Ibid.) and refers to "eine impressionistische Malerschule...in Melbourne.(Ibid.) Whatever its shortcomings, Hauser's survey of an emerging Australian culture of art and science deserves recognition. He rightly complains of the incongruous classicist writing up to the eighties and remarks on the

"European eyes" of early Australian painters. In his report on Australian universities he notes that "pure science and humanism" have little place; his comments have lost none of their validity to this day:

> (Die Universitäten) vermitteln Zweckwissen, Machtwissen, nicht das, was wir "reine" Wissenschaft nennen würden. Die Ideen des Humanismus haben in Australien wenig Kraft; neue Lehrstühle werden nicht für Sanskrit, klassische Geschichte oder Griechisch geschaffen, wohl aber für Landwirtschaft, Biologie, Zoologie, Japanisch und Chinesisch.(238–239)

Heinrich Hauser is, on the whole, a well-informed, reliable reporter, albeit of an ideological persuasion which has soured German-Australian relations for many decades during this century.

ALEXANDER TROLL (ED.)

Australien. In Busch und Sand

Although L.L. Politzer lists Alexander Troll's collection *Australien. In Busch und Sand* as having been published in 1939, it did in fact appear in 1928 (August Scherl Verlag Berlin). The book is featured as part of a series entitled "Der Weltwanderer. Dichtung und Erlebnis", which consists of a sequence of individual volumes devoted to particular continents, countries, cities or places. Much of German-Australian literature is written in the tradition of world travelogues, a genre aiming to combine imaginative literature with biographical experience. Unfortunately, too many works fall below the level of artistically creative writing, relying instead on the authenticity of personal observation. However, even this claim of eye-witness reporting proves to be without substance on more than one occasion. Troll's selection of short texts about aspects of Australian life presents a number of recurring themes, motives and *topoi*, as treated by eight different authors, themselves representative of the kind of writing, and the nationality of writers, dealing with Australia and its people. One is American, two are white Australians, one is the collective voice of Aboriginal mythology, four are Germans, two of whom are academics and two professional narrators.

Mark Twain's brief account of an arrival in Sydney ("Ankunft in Sydney") deals with the most common opening of travelogues about Australia. His short narrative endorses and anticipates countless similar fictional and factual arrivals in German-Australian prose.

It is followed by an extract from Albert Daibler's *Geschichten aus Australien* (Teubner Verlag Leipzig), three chapters republished under the title "Zweiunddreißig Jahre unter Menschenfressern im australischen Busch". It retells the story of William Buckley, the English convict at Port Phillip Bay who escaped into the Australian bush and spent thirty-two years among Aborigines. In his summary of "The Life and Adventures of William Buckley" by the Tasmanian John Morgan (first published in Hobart in 1852) Daibler takes up the theme of an exotic and dangerous Australia. His convicts enter "den geheimnisvollen Boden des fast noch unbekannten australischen Kontinents".(13) Cannibalism and the Australian bush fit into the German concept of "adventure" in distant places. Daibler combines the didacticism of historical information with the aim of exciting and entertaining — a pattern followed by most German-Australian writers. It is a mixture of popular literature attractive to both young and old readers, making the distinction between children's, young adult's and general fiction difficult. Daibler further uses the opportunity to introduce to his readers a wide range of Australian plants and animals and generally describe the natural landscape of the continent. In theme, style and narrative design his "Geschichten aus Australien" are truly representative.

Alfred Kötz's account of "Dr. Ludwig Leichhardts erste Reise durch Nordaustralien" is an excerpt from his work of narrative fiction entitled *Mimboka, eine Erzählung aus dem Leben der Austral-Neger* (published by the C. Heinrich Verlag in Dresden) and follows the same lines as Daibler's text. It, too, is a "Nacherzählung", representing in popular form the events recorded in Leichhardt's *Journal of an Overland Expedition*. Kötz stresses the fact that the explorer was a German; his story appeals to his readers' national pride. Such literary nationalism remains a vital part in the history of German-Australian writing. Whereas Daibler looks at Aborigines as part of Australian "nature", Kötz fictionalises their role in Leichhardt's explorations by applying Aboriginal mythology to his characterisation and plot. His narrative is essentially historical fiction.

The three stories by Friedrich Gerstäcker (1816–1872) are all taken from his best-known work dealing with Australia, *Im Busch*. Gerstäcker was one of Germany's leading authors of adventure novels in the nineteenth century, whose *Reisen um die Welt*, a fictionalised travelogue in six volumes, first appeared in 1847/48. The extracts in Troll's anthology all deal with the gold rush in New South Wales, another recurring theme in German-Australian literature. Gerstäcker's narrative employs and explains Australian terms such as "Bushranger"(52) or "Dray"(54), occasionally translating or mixing English and German names, as in "Gumbaum oder Wattelbusch".(67) Remarkably, the author refers to life in the gold-fields as "eine Art von Kommunismus"(57), and generally displays a keen eye for social behaviour. He, too, mixes fact with fiction, giving clear preference to a good story. His writing does convey the impression of historical authenticity, even where the accuracy cannot be substantiated.

Stefan von Kotze's (1869–1909) "Eine Känguruhjagd" is taken from his *Australische Skizzen* (1903), capturing an aspect of life in the Australian country. The descriptions are well-informed, humorous and mildly didactic. They include references to historical events, such as the building of the overland telegraph, and provide information about contemporary society. Von Kotze's humour is not without venom, as this account of an uprising in a North Queensland cane farm illustrates:

> Aber die anwesenden Weißen sprangen auf ihre Pferde, lösten den Bügelriemen aus und veranstalteten eine Kavallerieattacke auf die schäumenden Wilden mit glänzendem Ergebnis. Selbst ein Negerschädel widersteht einem solchen Hieb nicht. Das Bügeleisen ist auch in den schwächsten Händen eine gefährliche Waffe — selbst bei unseren Frauen.(85)

Unfortunately, there is a lot of this type of "wit" in German-Australian writing.

The last three contributions to Alexander Troll's collection *Australien. In Busch und Sand* are by Australians. "Dürre" is credited to one Davell O'Reilly; it may be safely assumed that the reference is to Dowell O'Reilly (1865–1923), the friend of Henry Lawson and father of Eleanor Dark, the novelist. His story, and the following, "Des Überländers Weib" by Henry Lawson, are taken from Stefan von Kotze's anthology *Aus einer neuen Literatur. Australische Erzählungen und Plaudereien* (Dom-Verlag, Berlin). There are occasional inaccuracies in the translation or retelling of the original (cf. "in der Reverina", 92), but the overall quality and tone of the Australian narrative style are preserved. Literary translations play an important part in German-Australian writing. Troll's anthology ends with a "Volksmärchen der Australneger". Some of the intercultural problems are shown by the translation of Aboriginal myths and legends as "Volksmärchen". But there can be no doubting the genuine desire to communicate to German readers the tribal imagination of Aborigines.

Similar attempts are frequently made in the history of German-Australian literature.

It is the collective impact of Troll's selection which gives this publication its special character. The editor succeeds in presenting central themes of German-Australian writing. The inclusion of an American travelogue and three Australian texts in translation authenticates the anthology's aim to collect representative responses to the land and its people. It thus serves as an influential introduction to both readers and writers. The popularity of the book further indicates the continued interest in Australian "adventures" and in travel descriptions of the land "down under". Although not an author of original writing, Alexander Troll thus deserves to be included in a survey of the development of German-Australian literary relations. His *Australien. In Busch und Sand* is a collection of themes and motives, of content and style, which remain a vital part in literary interpretations of Australia by German writers.

Berend Von Tiefenhausen

Deutsche in Australien

Published 1939 in the series *Deutsche in Übersee* (edited by E. Barth von Wehrenalp), the work's stock-taking of Germans in this country has unmistakable overtones of expansionist aspirations on the part of Nazi Germany. It is proudly announced at the beginning of the book that "Es war ein Deutscher, der das australische Land für die britische Krone in Besitz nahm."(5) This exaggerated claim is characteristic of its tone and philosophy throughout. Berend von Tiefenhausen speaks exclusively of "Deutschtum", with an implied pretension to a "Reich" extending to German migration all over the world. Indeed, he presents a map of Australia listing "Deutschtumsgebiete" in Victoria, New South Wales, Queensland, South Australia and Western Australia.(4) If these German-Australians could not be returned "home" ("heim ins Reich"), they were called upon to represent German culture and Nazi ideology in their part of the world — a world which would, sooner or later, be "Germanized" ("am deutschen Wesen soll die Welt genesen").

It is in that vein that the author opens his chapter "Der Weltkrieg bricht aus" with the reproach: "Die schwerste Prüfung für das Deutschtum in Australien brachte der Weltkrieg. Nicht nur die

Reichsdeutschen, sondern auch naturalisierte Staatsbürger wurden verfolgt."(22) Whilst there can be no denying the cruelty and folly of Australian officialdom in interning and persecuting naturalised German-Australians, the term "Prüfung" reveals ambitions of a conquering German presence in this country. Not surprisingly von Tiefenhausen repeatedly refers to the nationalist German author A.E. Johann in his attempt to arouse outrage and patriotic fervour in his readers.(Ibid., 26) He laments that German-Australians were "forced" to go to war against the country of their forefathers. The author further "exposes" the deaths of many Germans and "German-Austrians" ("Deutschösterreicher", Ibid.) in Australian internment camps, "ein ebenso erschütterndes Wahrzeichen der Geschichte des Auslandsdeutschtums".(Ibid.) The lesson is to remain loyal to the fatherland and to beware of the intentions of the host country.

There is a constant appeal to a continuing responsibility of German settlers in Australia for the well-being of their native land or country of cultural origin. No attempt is made to respect German-Australians' loyalty to their new country. "Deutschtum" is used as a means of cultural politics, designed to instil a sense of pride in those who in the past have felt the need to leave the fatherland. *Deutsche in Australien* is anxious to remind German-Australians of German superiority in virtually all areas, especially in manufacturing. Despite tariff protection and anti-German sentiments Australia was forced to import German goods after the First World War.(26) With the seizure of power by the Nazis von Tiefenhausen welcomes the "clearer guidelines" of Germany's foreign policy.(27) He also informs his readers of the kind of political representation Nazi-Germany enjoyed in Australia during the thirties. Some aspects of such diplomatic representation and other matters of Nazi-Germany's cultural politics in Australia have since been researched and published (John Moses, 1988).[41] Von Tiefenhausen correctly stresses the role played by Lutheran churches in keeping alive the traditions of German culture ("daß das Volkstumsbewußtsein bei den Australiendeutschen lebendig blieb", 29). More precisely, it is the concept of one people spread all over the world which they sponsored. "Volkstum" and "Deutschtum" are synonymous; national characteristics assume racial, philosophical and spiritual dimensions. A world lost and (re)gained is the basically metaphysical concept of the "Third Reich". How Germans saw their own emigrants in the world is a clear reflection of Nazi ideology and mythology. *Deutsche in Australien* is part of that record.

O.E.H. BECKER

Das australische Abenteuer

This work was first published in the year 1939. Like Esther Landolt's novels set in Australia it was written and read during the period of German fascism. The Nazi movement encouraged traditional concepts of adventure, heroism and excitement. Part of the attraction of the Hitler youth movement lay in this commitment to "masculine", "Germanic" activities. It is easy to see, then, that a narrative bearing the title *Das australische Abenteuer* must have held very real appeal to a German reading public exposed to almost total cultural control by the Nazis. As with Landolt, this does not, of course, mean that Becker's work is in itself fascist; it is rather a significant aspect of the book's genre, theme and general preoccupation. Like so many German books about Australia, it is written in the tradition of the *Abenteuerroman*. In this case, the novel's title carries a double meaning: it is not only the narrative account of its protagonist's adventure(s) in Australia but also a reference to the "adventure" of the new country itself. Becker gave his novel the subtitle "Ein Roman vom Leben, vom Gold und von der Geschichte des fünften Kontinents", a descriptive summary of the book's aims. The author keeps this promise: *Das australische Abenteuer* is as didactic as it is "adventurous". The early history of Australia becomes an integral part of the novel's narrative. Its readers are reliably informed of important events, dates and outstanding figures of Australian colonial history. Personal experience remains inextricably linked with a developing nation's history; the book propagates the adventure of discovering an individual and a collective identity.

What must immediately be said is that Becker's concept of Australia and Australian-ness differs significantly from the way Anglo-Saxon settlers saw themselves. Not surprisingly, he introduces a large number of German migrants, especially in his descriptions of Adelaide and South Australia. The reader gains the impression of an early Australia which was, in today's terminology, a multicultural society. It may be assumed that the narration relates back to the middle of the 19th century. (Its protagonist remarks at the beginning of the novel that Sydney is 70 years old.)

The book's main character is the Prussian adventurer Friedrich von Pannwitz who as second son receives his parents' permission to travel the world, provided he not only enjoys himself but also studies the countries and continents he visits.(41) Sydney's cosmopolitan wealth impresses the German visitor who has taken a boat from San Francisco to Botany Bay. The first Australian Pannwitz meets is the son of one of the original convicts who came to this country on the First Fleet in 1788. The narrator informs his readers that, like so many victims of deportation, John Hunter was punished unjustly. Yet after his release he became a rich man devoting his life to the wool trade and other import-export business. He retired in Manly where he and his wife lived next to George Howe, a fellow sufferer and founder of the first Australian newspaper, the *Sydney Herald*. This historical information is presented by the author, not by one of his fictional characters. From the beginning, his novel is anxious to tell the history of Australia; the book is a programmatic mixture of fiction and documentation. (It is interesting to note, by the way, that John Hunter's grandson is not in Sydney at the time of Pannwitz's visit; he has been sent to London by his father Henry Hunter to receive an education ["nach London zur Erziehung geschickt", 9]. Thus began a social and cultural ritual which was largely responsible for the continued Anglo-Saxon domination of Australian education and institutions.)

From this casual introduction to an historical/fictional character, other "stories" follow. One of Henry Hunter's friends is William Ruse, the grandson of James Ruse, the first released convict who was allowed to settle in Australia. Pannwitz has already read about James Ruse in a book on the colony's early settlement he studied in San Francisco.(11) James Ruse, too, is described as a victim of an unjust system of deportation and the author does not miss the opportunity to let Hunter comment on New South Wales' contemporary attempts to put an end to the practice.(12) Ruse's grandson William offers Pannwitz stories about the colonial past. The ensuing exchange between Mrs. Hunter and Ruse is symptomatic of the narrative logic of Becker's novel. She remarks that these stories are in reality the story and history of his grandfather. William Ruse's reply is categorical and to the point: "It is," he explains, "the unfolding history of New South Wales, Mr. von Pannwitz!"(13) The novel's narrative authenticity is derived from this interaction of personal and social history. When Ruse begins with his narration he reminds his listeners "Ich bin also streng historisch!"(Ibid.) O.E.H. Becker applies the same logic of narrative poetics to the novel as a whole; the author is a collector and occasional witness of history in the making. Even episodes which may well be no more than gossip or rumour assume historical significance where they characterise the spirit of the age. Ultimately, Becker's novel adheres to the Aristotelian belief that fiction is a most reliable expression of history. Throughout *Das australische Abenteuer* numerous "stories" are told by various characters, almost in the manner of *Rahmenerzählungen*. Occasionally the dialogue serves as no more than a pretext to introduce yet another anecdote or tale of recent events. It is fair to say that as a result the dialogue is stilted and increasingly artificial.

Becker puts the need to introduce characters with stories to tell to good use. It allows him, for example, to describe landscapes and dwellings and to pass on information about them. Thus the reader is informed that at one time Parramatta had more inhabitants than Sydney and that its original name was "Rosehill".(17) When Pannwitz is invited to meet Johannes Scheffer who runs a cattle station around Dubboo (sic!) he is told a great deal about the countryside, the life of a squatter and the dangers of being attacked by bushrangers.(21) As he crosses the Blue Mountains in a coach the narrator relates the history of their conquest by Wentworth, Lawson and Blaxland. The plains of Bathurst thus assume their specific meaning to Pannwitz: he appreciates the discovery of fertile land and the determination of squatters like the German Scheffer. The meeting with this settler leads to a first confrontation. Pannwitz witnesses a family which has succeeded in retaining its German identity, yet become truly Australian. He is told that Johannes Scheffer's father was the first German to arrive in Australia, after having been sold to fight for the British in the North American War. His personal "adventure" is described as another instance of social, indeed world, history. On the one hand Pannwitz discovers "Hier war Deutschland wirklich nicht vergessen!"(32), on the other hand he is made aware of the Australian character of this family. When he falls in love with Eleanor Scheffer he is faced with a situation familiar to many migrants since. At the close of the novel's first chapter Pannwitz's response to Australia is summed up in the exclamation "Merkwürdiges Land, merkwürdige Verhältnisse!"(22) At the beginning of the fourth chapter he experiences the first stage of a very real conflict of loyalty. He loves "die freie Lebensweise"(61) he encounters in Australia. More importantly, he feels that he cannot ask Eleanor to spend her married life with him in Germany. Significantly, the narrator speaks of "seine Liebe zu der Australierin".(62)

> Oder sollte er etwa im Lande bleiben? Noch schauderte er, wenn er daran dachte und diese so ganz andere Welt mit der gehegten, von jahrtausendealter Kultur gewandelten und verschönten Landschaft

Deutschlands verglich. Dort lagen seine Wurzeln, dorthin zog ihn alles zurück.(61–62)

The conflict is not merely socio-cultural; it is suffered as an intensely personal crisis. Suddenly the term *Abenteuer* assumes a negative meaning: "Er war ein Abenteurer und nichts sonst. War es nicht besser, aufzubrechen, zu fliehen vor sich selbst...?"(62) The choice between two cultures focuses as an issue of personal identity, or, more precisely, as the possibility of free self-determination. A cultural identity is not merely forced upon the individual; he can choose a bi- or transcultural self-concept. Pannwitz can enter the "adventure" of an Australian/German marriage. The Scheffers have adopted a perspective which implies the acceptance of home and identity as a dynamic relationship. Instead of a static definition inherited at birth the family derives an understanding of its place by differentiation, endorsing aspects of various cultures while developing its own characteristic lifestyle. The Scheffers do not live a ghetto culture; their station is no Diaspora. The visitor informs Eleanor that his home in Silesia was near the countryside invoked in the writings of Joseph von Eichendorff. He then puts a question which alludes to another form of "multiculturalism", a question, however, which (perhaps significantly) remains unanswered: "ich weiß nicht, ob jemals seine Erzählungen und Gedichte nach Australien gedrungen sind."(40) Literature as cultural mediation worked for English and Anglo-Celtic writing only. The function of the narrative history of the first German settler in Australia is to demonstrate that bi-culturalism was established by intermarriage.

Becker allows his characters to tell their own and their family's history because it is part of the "adventure" that is Australia, the "adventure" of gaining a multicultural identity in this country. His choice of narrative genre was strongly motivated by readings of travelogues and adventure stories while he was still a child. In that sense there is a degree of autobiography in his portrayal of the novel's protagonist. As Pannwitz comments: "Wie selten kennt man die tieferen Anlässe für seine Handlungen! Ich habe schon als Kind alle Reisebeschreibungen und Abenteuerbücher verschlungen, die ich irgend in die Hand bekam."(Ibid.) In Becker's writing the concept of "adventure" has gained in specific meaning. Exploring the history of other people and their countries may lead to finding one's own identity.

Pannwitz's subsequent visit to Adelaide serves as motivation to present the history of South Australia and its capital. In particular, it allows Becker to record the German migration to that state under Pastor Kavel in 1838 and the beginnings of the Australian gold-rush as a result of the findings of the German geologist and mineralogist Johannes Menge who arrived in Australia in 1836. Chapter Seven explains the special background of South Australia: "Süd-Australien wurde im Gegensatz zu Neu-Süd-Wales und Victoria nach einem festen, vorher entworfenen Plan unter Kultur genommen."(109) The latter phrase reveals remarkable implications, most prominently the commitment to a fully imported culture. Becker not only presents reliable, factual information, he displays a good sense of social history. Thus he refers to the so-called "Schillingsmann" whom he explains as "einen jener berüchtigten Wucherer, unter denen sich leider auch Deutsche befanden".(46–47) There were many such profiteers in the colonies; migrants exploiting their fellow migrants are part of the social pattern of "importing culture". Becker never misses an opportunity to make reference to local newspapers, both English and German. Occasionally their reports form part of the novel's narrative.

As with other German-language writers describing Australia, Becker includes a personal account of the shearing season. The novel offers an authentic, if somewhat impressionistic description of the "Schurzeit".(66) It includes detailed information about working conditions, payment and the kind of character attracted to the work as a shearer.

The need to find German equivalents for uniquely Australian terms presents the author with a major challenge, as "adventurous" as anything the novel tries to relate. Becker offers different solutions to specific challenges. Thus he may choose to explain a particular transliteration: "Bündelmänner — so nennt man die Wanderarbeiter hier"(Ibid.) for the swagman or swaggie. In a variety of instances he simply retains the Australian original, integrating the expression into a German sentence. The range of terms and expressions indicates the extent to which the novel enters Australian life. The author succeeds in his attempt to introduce his reader to the colonial culture of the land and the growing signs of its people's national identity. Becker's novel conveys Australian social history in the making, and it does so with considerable authority. No doubt the retention and explanation of indigenous Australian concepts lend the description an air of authenticity. Another, structurally more important, reason is the integration into the "adventure" of its protagonist Friedrich von Pannwitz of numerous narrative histories, stories, and conversations which grow into what might be termed dialogue sub-plots. Becker tells the "adventurous" history of Australia from the perspective of "eye-witnesses" or someone directly involved, often a member of a particular family who "made history".

The author employs narration as social investigation; his narrators become a team of detectives. Story-telling and the writing of history coincide. Again and again the characters of the novel *request* a story; they want to learn about others and about their own history. "Würden Sie mir die Geschichte einmal erzählen?"(289) may be taken as the formula-type assumption of the novel's narrative structure.

There are numerous types of stories. Becker tells the history of the cities of Sydney, Melbourne and Adelaide. The protagonist is repeatedly reminded — and with him the reader of the novel — that these stories are always told for a didactic purpose. "...die Geschichte...ist sehr lehrreich."(264) It is a basic literary concept which is implied in such a statement, an assumption which informs the structure of Becker's novel. Every person von Pannwitz meets has a story to tell, often his own. "Old-Joe, Sie hatten auch noch eine Geschichte!"(264) He does, of course, and he enters the chain of narrative histories that make up the people of Australia. Social narration is, apart from anything else, itself an historical feature of life in early Australia, around the camp-fire as much as in the polite society of the larger cities. Becker's subject is social history, and he lets it tell its own story. There is a veritable trade or exchange of personal representative histories. They are offered as oral literature, for entertainment, for enlightenment and for identification. Social history is made up of personal stories which belong to everyone. The story also becomes something of a trading commodity. "Weiß niemand eine Geschichte?"(251) In response someone offers "eine Art Gespenstergeschichte vielleicht?"(Ibid.)

Often the story is told simply by reading a newspaper aloud, a reading of social history in print which in turn immediately leads to narrative dialogue and personal "stories". It must be added that where O.E.H. Becker writes without recourse to narrative sub-structure his style may be called journalistic. His concept of "objective reporting" (as opposed to subjective story-telling) is derived from newspapers. Becker's prose is that of a reporter in a new country, his novel a travelogue and adventure story in journalistic interviews. Above all, his writing is crowded with "facts"; *Das australische Abenteuer* fulfils its main ambition to pass on as much information about a distant continent and its people as possible. Not surprisingly, therefore, little attempt is made to create an imaginative literary style. Not only is the narrative form of the novel disarmingly naive and transparently constructed, the language Becker employs is uninventive, colloquial and superficial. The book's concept of style is conditioned by an extensive reading of travelogues and adventure books; as the protagonist explains: "Ich habe schon als Kind alle Reisebeschreibungen und Abenteuerbücher verschlungen, die ich irgend in die Hand bekam."(40) Works such as Kurt Faber's *Im australischen Busch* and other publications by the Rainer Wunderlich Verlag Tübingen give an indication of the kind and quality of writing Becker's novel is influenced by. Apart from a stock holding of "adventure novels" in most German bourgeois libraries, series such as the "Deutsche Jugendbücherei" reinforced and almost institutionalised a preoccupation with journalistic descriptions of experiences in far-away countries. The "Karl May" mentality has remained a central feature of German "Sehnsucht".

One difference between the stock-in-trade travelogues dealing with a more or less exotic Australia and O.E.H. Becker's novel is that the hero of *Das australische Abenteuer* decides to settle in the far-away land. In other words, this book is ultimately — and it could be argued primarily — a narrative of migration. In terms of the novel, the "adventure" leads to the discovery of a new "home". Becker succeeds in depicting the various stages of settlement and integration. After extensive conflicts of loyalty between the old country and the new country it is the love for another human being which determines the final outcome.

The "old new home" receives its (European) identity from — among other influences — the protagonist's "Heimat"; Australia derives its cultural aspirations from the countries of her migrants. It is by such orientation that the "adventure" of growing into an Australian identity can take place. It is important, therefore, not only for the adventurous immigrant and eventual settler but also for the native-born white Australian, to know and to remain mindful of "woher wir alle stammen". Becker's hero suggests that it will take a long time before the new country has reached the cultural maturity of being "independent". The Australian "adventure" is an identity in the making, the privilege and challenge of taking an active part in its shaping, to establish a "new order". There can be no doubt that Becker attempts to construct a narrative paradigma of cultural migration. Becker rightly draws attention to the correlation between colonial conquests and immigration. Australia may not have attracted as many fortune hunters as North or South America, but it had its share. There was no real conflict between the deportation of convicts on the one hand and colonisation for profit on the other: both served the Empire. Becker repeatedly, almost programmatically, advocates Australia to his German readers as "ein wahres Paradies, das nur der Bewohner wartete, die es nutzten!"(217) Parts of his description sound like propaganda pamphlets for intending immigrants.

The significance of Becker's novel lies in its successful attempt to combine social history with narrative fiction. Throughout the work implicit or explicit references are made back to events in European history. The Australian "adventures" are thus related to corresponding struggles for freedom, revolutions and national conflicts. *Das australische Abenteuer* remains a European novel, not least in its belief that the best way of identifying a country and its people is by the narrative means of history. Where a newly settled country is in the process of developing its own history, the history of European mother countries interacts with that emerging self-concept, lending it identity and cultural authority. Such transference makes the settlement of Australia part of European history. Becker's novel is a paradigmatic demonstration of this process. History itself is exposed as a colonial device: the extension of one culture's influence becomes "the adventure" of making history elsewhere.

Chapter Two

Blood and Culture: The Old Language in Search of the New Land

> "Meine Heimat liegt im Unbekannten, in einem Land, von dem ich so gut wie nichts weiß."
>
> Esther Landolt, *Namenlos*

THE FORTIES

In some ways German-Australian literature during the forties continued much along similar lines to the preceding decade. That is to say, nationalism, racism and *blood and soil* ideology remain the dominating themes. There are noticeably fewer publications, an obvious consequence of the war. Among the reduced range of titles adventure books for the young play a prominent part. In addition there are collections of poetry (in German and in English), records of German-language theatre activities in Australia and several novels dealing with European-Australian relations. A striking feature of young adult fiction during the forties is the emergence of a new kind of adventure tale, somewhat less exotic, relying instead on documentary and authenticated accounts.

Chronologically, it is German theatre in the Diaspora which needs to be considered first. Among German-language settlers in Australia attempts are made to recreate the cultural climate of Central European theatre, albeit on the level of semi-professional performances. It is, historically speaking, a remarkable effort, modelled to a considerable extent on the theatre of the Jewish ghetto. What is most astounding is the early date of this enterprise (*The Viennese Theatre Sydney*, 1941) and the fact that it lasted for some forty-five years. Austrian immigrants succeed soon after their arrival in establishing Viennese cabaret and theatre productions on a regular basis. Some sketches and plays were written by members of the company — in German.

The outstanding figure of the period, however, is without doubt the Swiss-Australian *Rosmarie Meyer* or *Esther Landolt*, the name under which she published four novels, two of which — *Ewige Herde* (1942) and *Namenlos* (1947) — deal explicitly with Australia. The prominence of Swiss and Austrian German-language writers during this period is hardly a coincidence. Nor is the prevalence of English-language poetry by first and second generation German-Australians. Their poems are in fact isolated from the mainstream of either Australian or German contemporary writing. They are documents of an archaic imagination, not only in a literary sense. Poets withdraw from both native and host country; indeed, from history. Classical European mythology is invoked in a vain attempt to re-create a sense of "timeless" beauty and reflection. Problems of bilingualism or biculturalism are not addressed. Instead, the Australian bush is aestheticised as a spiritual refuge, celebrated in a language translated from German Romanticism. Dreams are invoked and worshipped as guides to nature's inherent creativity. (*L. L. Politzer*, 1944) Another concept of poetry envisages an emerging Australian "race" similar to the Greeks of classical antiquity. Australia will create a "new man" capable of creating his own, non-European, culture. Yet this poetry, too, aims to transform experience into timeless paradigm. It includes translations from the Greek and the German. Greek culture is to be rejuvenated in verse. Much of this kind of poetry reads like a formal exercise for its own sake. Social and historical specificity are brushed aside to create an untimely ("unzeitgemäße") composition of "beauty".(*Walter Stölting*, 1947) Even an Australian-born poet of German parentage prefers to revive folkloristic myths in bush ballads, odes and fables, applying a neo-classical style to Australian themes. Greek, Egyptian and Aboriginal mythologies intermingle freely. The celebration of local flora and fauna rarely sounds Australian. Nature is to be worshipped in the "elevated style" of European, i.e. German, Classicism. Poetry becomes a statement of sentiment, emotional and rhetorical, with limited scope of imagination.(*Werner Fels*, 1949)[1]

In prose works, too, the forties witness the invocation of "timeless" qualities in Australia. It is interpreted, and applauded, as a land and a people without history. The loss of a native home is sublimated into a migration of metaphysical dimensions. Australia becomes a place of transformation and rebirth; its very existence, distance and vastness allows the war-weary European a new mythical relation to the land. Because of the brevity of white Australian history, the country is spiritualised and aestheticised; the new settler integrates into seasons and droughts, bushfires and floods of a "higher will". The escape from Europe ends in such partaking in a natural mythology.(*Esther Landolt*, 1942/1947) Where history is invoked, it is Australian colonial history, narrated as adventure tales for young readers. No critical view is offered, the author poses as compiler, editor or arranger of "authentic" historical documents. History, like Australia, is beyond immediate reach, an exotic adventure taking place elsewhere. Australian history thus is presented as a journey to adventureland, reinforcing the vision of antipodean "otherness". In post-war Germany history is suppressed, displaced into a realm of juvenile fiction: it is what happens to other people, far away.(*Hans Franke*, 1948) Yet in another book for children Australia is presented for the first time as a country of migrants in which the young are accepted by, and integrated into, a new culture. Such narrative fiction may also be interpreted as the hope of Germans that their children will grow into a different society and ultimately restore some of the lost respectability of the German people.(*Max Albert*, 1948)

The forties thus prove a period of transition. Strong echoes of the immediate past continue to be heard. Other writers, especially Australian authors of German descent, prefer to withdraw from contemporary social politics. While refugees from Nazi Germany try to reconstruct their literary culture in Diaspora, post-war German writers once again turn to the young in fictional anticipations of reconciliation and a new beginning.

VIENNESE THEATRE SYDNEY (1941–1986)

Of all literary genres, drama has the most difficult stance in exile and migration. By its very nature the most social of all art forms, it presupposes an audience of cultural cohesion. Only in ghetto situations, in a migrants' Diaspora, can the theatre assume its inherent function. Unperformed plays are a frustration of cultural communication, an intrinsic contradiction of the very aim and function of the theatre.

The Viennese Theatre, "Kleines Wiener Theater", was founded by

Austrian migrants who had settled in Sydney in 1941. Co-founders were Alfred and Else Baring, Gerhard and Erna Felser. During the forties full-length plays were only rarely performed. As Owen Grant says, "The first programs consisted of little more than a chain of amusing and witty cabaret numbers, loosely strung together."[2]

In the following decades that was to change. Whilst retaining its special Viennese flavour of cabaret-revues, the Theatre progressed to semi-professional productions. The pattern that emerges is a program moving from popular Austrian-Hungarian-Czech plays to a classical and modern repertoire, including productions in English. From the fifties on, every year two or three different productions were staged. The Viennese Theatre moved away from being a mere ghetto institution by involving itself with universities, literary societies and other theatre groups, moving interstate and commercial English-language productions.

Karl Bittman writes in *The Viennese Theatre. A transplant of a special kind*:[4]

> Else Baring, who had been a professional actress in Austria at the beginning of a promising career, not only took many prominent roles in productions but also became the forceful and inspired director of many plays and revues the Viennese Theatre staged over the years. The near professional standards the ensemble achieved was in no small way due to her coaching and unerring advice.

Alfred Baring was a civil engineer by profession, but turned to writing for the theatre; so much so that he had a play accepted by the studio of the Burgtheater in Vienna. It was by the standards of a migrant company a large organisation, with a strong commercial base and effective programme and executive committees. Alfred Baring wrote a short survey of the Viennese Theatre under the heading *Deutschsprachiges Theater in Australien*. The title is misleading, if only because various German Departments at Australian universities were in the habit of staging annual productions of German plays, some reaching very high semi-professional standard. (The University of Melbourne's Department of Germanic Studies, under the headship of Professor Richard Samuel, had a distinguished record of German-language drama productions, especially in the fifties and sixties).[5] However, as a record of the Viennese Theatre of Sydney, Baring's reminiscence remains a valuable document.[6] In July 1986 the "Kleines Wiener Theater" was finally disbanded. Karl Bittman and Owen Grant sum up the nature of the Theatre's achievement as follows:

It not only provided a community theatre for its fellow immigrants and played a significant part in their integration and their continuing interest in the art of the stage, but it also contributed significantly to cultural diversity through keeping a foreign language theatre going for almost half a century.[7]

ESTHER LANDOLT

Of the four novels written by this author, two have an exclusively Swiss setting, one alternates between Switzerland and Australia, and one takes place entirely in Australia. The first novel, *Das Opfer (The Victim)* appeared in 1937, the second, *Delfine (Delphine)* in 1939; both were immediately recognised and celebrated as typical Swiss narratives with Swiss themes, characters and locations. It is important to relate these two early novels to Landolt's later "Australian" works, as they display all the characteristics of her 1942 novel *Ewige Herde (Eternal Herd)* and her novel of migration *Namenlos (Nameless)* published in 1947.

Das Opfer could be described as a tragedy of classical dimension set on a farm in central Switzerland. Its central theme is the fateful juxtaposition of "unfassliche Fremdheit" and "vertraute, liebende Nähe" in human relationships. From the beginning, then, Landolt's main themes are established; her later experience of migration merely reinforces them. It is significant that in this novel the reader is told of the destruction of a native farm which leads to the enforced emigration of the two youngest sons. Even at this early stage emigration is a threat, the consequence of not protecting one's native inheritance.

Another feature of Landolt's first novel retains significance in her later work: the thematic, stylistic and poetic concept of the *image*, the *Bild*. Esther Landolt writes a narrative style overladen with metaphors, similes, analogies, images and symbols. Similar preoccupations exist in Landolt's second Swiss novel, *Delfine*. Here too, the image becomes identified as home — and vice-versa. These first two Swiss novels reveal from what angle and against what cultural and literary background this writer perceived the Australian landscape, the agonies of migration and the promise of a new home.

Ewige Herde

This novel appeared in 1942, at the height of military, political and moral conflict in Europe. The book is characterised by its theological and mythological pretensions. There are extensive quotations from the Bible and frequent reflections upon the interrelationship between Man and Nature. In many ways *Ewige Herde* resembles Patrick White's novel *Tree of Man* (1955); both works share themes and preoccupations, both invoke the Australian landscape as a mythological paradigm. It is in literary style and quality that the books differ. Landolt's Swiss German language is traditional, European, a quotation of, or homage to, Classical and 19th century German literature, the expression of a faith in the soil shared by fascist aesthetics and sociopolitical ideology. This is not to say that Landolt's narrative style is fascist; rather, it displays some of the preoccupations of contemporary writers in neighbouring Nazi Germany and Austria. There is a great deal of *Blut und Boden* philosophy in *Ewige Herde*, albeit transferred (and to some extent transformed) into an antipodean context. The novel's plot is a kind of latter-day *Elective Affinities*; it tells the story of Ann Katrin, the young Swiss who, after the death of her father, travels to Australia to visit her sister Irene who lives with her Australian husband Warren MacLeigh on a property in Victoria. She shares the hardships and triumphs of their rural life, only to fall in love with her sister's husband and to witness Irene's tragic love for Kent O'Dowd, the heir of a neighbouring property. But the real subject of Esther Landolt's book is the Australian landscape, the country and its animals, the herds of cattle and sheep,the native flora and fauna, the natural cycle of growth and destruction.

Ewige Herde invokes a continent as exotic as it is distant. There is a great deal of useful and reliable information about Australia in this book. The novel can serve as a sympathetic introduction to the land and its people. It seems appropriate that Landolt concentrates on Australia's rural population at the time; in the forties the country was still carried on the proverbial sheep's back. There can be no doubt that the author knows what she is writing about. Her personal experience shines through everything she describes. If the book never "reads" Australian, the reason lies in the laboured style of analogies, similes and metaphors. In content and form Esther Landolt has written a European novel transported into a politically safe and distant Australian setting, without, however, abandoning the *topoi* of German highbrow and popular writing. *Ewige Herde* aims to achieve authenticity by (cultural) translation. In terms of its protagonist's experience the novel is undeniably successful. The narrative tone throughout is that of an educated Zürich bourgeois, not without empathy for the Australian way of life. But this act of identification remains a literary construction. It is the transparency of this stylistic composition which lends the book its peculiar honesty and integrity, even where it quotes, thematically and formally, from the trivial novels of German popular literary culture.

In Landolt's novel Nature is Fate and Fate is Nature; it would be futile to challenge such existential force. *Ewige Herde* is, despite its title, a self-confessed anti-social narrative. Relations and communication with other human beings hardly rise above the level of tending cattle; it is, the author argues, almost impossible for people to understand each other. As in Nazi ideology, blood and soil constitute the nature and consciousness, the very identity of Man. It is significant that the protagonist's first unhappy experience of love in her native Zürich is described in these terms. Ann Katrin's eventual fulfilment in a love for the Australian Warren MacLeigh is similarly based on a shared harmony of blood and soil. The Swiss Fred is exposed as a man destroyed by the city and its commerce. Fred's mother and brother have remained on the land; Ann Katrin's visit to their farm near Rapperswil is an act of identification. People of honour and trust live in the country.

The description of Ann Katrin's voyage to Australia is in the same inflated rhetorical style as many passages attempting to invoke the distant and exotic continent. Not only is the sea-god invoked, the narrator celebrates in far-fetched metaphors, frequently bordering on the comical, the marriage of the Sun-Queen with the ocean, and the sky is likened to a festive ballroom in which angels are playing the harp with long white hands.(32) There is a great deal of *kitsch* in the novel, a manifestation of the author's *Bildungsbürgertum* with its ambition for "unusual" or "imaginative" expression. Even without such excesses the style is aesthetically and syntactically conservative.

Ewige Herde is crowded with narrative similes, most of them attempts to convey the exotic nature of life in Australia. All the basic components of daily life are thus "elevated" to a poetic-mythological level. It is above all the Australian landscape which leads to an understanding of new physical and spiritual dimensions. When the author refers to the landscape by itself she describes it as "something spiritual", as the expression of an "eternal longing for the future", as a "reflection of constant change within itself": "Die Landschaft hatte etwas Geistiges, sie war die ewige Sehnsucht nach dem Kommenden, Spiegelbild des ewig Wechselnden in ihr selbst."(143)

In trying to find German equivalents for Australian concepts and terms, Esther Landolt is engaged in a fundamental transcultural exercise. As her own language demonstrates, there are occasions where it seems more appropriate to adopt the foreign term along with the foreign or new object. The history of loan-words continues to be written. One may argue with the author regarding particular choices; what is important is the realisation of the need not merely for translation but for cultural mediation and transformation.

Like many other German-language writers, Landolt introduces the *topos* of inheritance. It raises the general question of ownership of the Australian land, without, however, extending it to a discussion of Aboriginal land rights. This is the basic contradiction of her novel: it aims to present a totally different non-European landscape and culture, but does it in a style of European literary decadence. The conflict between the two sisters personifies the author's own ambivalence in her attitude to the New Land.(74) Her central experience remains an existence beyond all limits of European conception.

Landolt's narrative style is saturated with analogies and similes. It weighs it down and is the source of much irritation. Yet it is also a clear indication of the search for intercultural references, to mediate between the unknown and the familiar. (It could be argued that Australia still has not been fully authenticated by an essentially European literature.) The pity is that in *Ewige Herde* the mannerism of analogies becomes tedious because, paradoxically, they exist for their own sake. Nonetheless, Esther Landolt's novel treats the theme of cultural mediation seriously, albeit in blatant contradiction of its own wisdom. To compare where there is nothing to compare can only lead to falsification and distortion. *Ewige Herde* is a continuation of Landolt's earlier pastoral novels set in her native Switzerland. Thus the work emerges as a spectacular demonstration that its language and imagination cannot authenticate, or do justice to, life in Australia.

Esther Landolt introduces another theme which is of general significance in German-Australian literature: the rebirth of the migrant, the renaissance of an individual's commitment to life, the growth of a new consciousness. Such change of heart or renewed identification is the realm of the German *Bildungsroman*, the novel of education and didactic moralising. Many German-Australian narratives return to this traditional genre, in itself the attempt of a literary and formal renaissance. Their failure to find a contemporary version of the educational novel leads to further inability to authenticate Australia in German-language narration.

Like other novels written during the forties, Landolt's *Ewige Herde* makes occasional reference to the outbreak of war in Europe, implying a safety and peacefulness which is part of the very nature of this land. Shearers and bushies tell stories of war around the camp fire; the soldiers are dying elsewhere.(212–214) Sufferings on this soil are caused by natural disasters, such as droughts or floods, bushfires or frost.(246) It leads to an acceptance of life which is not stoic but derives from an affinity with the land; man's blood and nature's soil intermingle to raise "the eternal herd". *Ewige Herde* narrates the metaphysics of existence, the "inner truth" of nature.(265) The novel attempts to emulate the (alleged) simplicity of nature, but its language (literally) contradicts its own mission. Its author does not want to change anything, her ambition is to find different ways of describing the inevitable.

Thus it is that Esther Landolt's novel assumes some characteristics of the *Heimatroman* in popular German literature, not least in the desire to express itself "poetically". The mystification of life is a major feature of such trivial writing, as is its glorification of the soil and life on the land. Nature is the setting of human passions which, in turn, are man's nature. The motherhood of Nature provides man and beast, it resolves all conflict. Landolt simply transfers this idyllic cliché to an Australian setting, not without occasional glimpses of realism, but on the whole in the attempt to "poeticise" and glorify the *status quo*. It is part of such *Heimatroman* preoccupation and ideology that a property is inherited and defended, for ownership (of land) must be extolled as an "eternal" value. Esther Landolt's *Ewige Herde* mediates the *Heimatroman*, the rural, regional novel of German popular literature, to an Australian setting: the result is a formal alienation *and* the retention of familiar clichés, an apologia of the literary, social and cultural *status quo*. Landolt is a conservative writer in this specific sense.

Namenlos

This is the second novel written by Esther Landolt in Australia but published in her native Zürich. Unlike its predecessor, *Ewige Herde*, only a part of the narration refers to Australia. As a migrant novel, *Namenlos* (1947) offers a broader view of the motives that can lead to the decision to leave one's country of birth. To the author Landolt there can be no greater trauma than to be uprooted, to be alienated from one's native soil. As her earlier two Swiss novels show, all human passions are related to the land which is our home. Emigration thus is the ultimate upheaval and loss of identity.

The return to the protagonist's country of birth cannot resolve the conflict; such a "marriage" between his native Switzerland and his new home Australia is also doomed to failure. Esther Landolt creates a paradigmatic narrative figure whose attempts to correct the errors of his migration and to right the wrongs of his own fate by the adoption of another orphan from his native community merely reinforce a pattern of conflicting identity and the complex consequences of alienation.

Australia again assumes the significance of the impossible, the exotic, far-away and strange place no one knows anything about. It is an almost metaphysical promise of redemption and at the same time a symbol of shame. Landolt succeeds in presenting an image of Australia which combines redemption with dishonour — no doubt a precise description of the contradictory experiences and expectations of many immigrants, not only from Switzerland and not only at this particular time. In the context of her village novels Esther Landolt composes a symbolic pattern of the migrant's social and cultural background. All migration begins with desertion and betrayal.

The novel sensitively invokes a wide range of representative experiences of migration and cultural displacement. The village setting of her protagonists' first home not only accentuates the trauma of alienation, it also corresponds to historical fact: most migrants did originate from such a social background.

Landolt deals with an anxiety which is a central aspect of migration to Australia: the loss of history, the absence of an historical continuity, the lack of a living culture. For most new settlers life in Australia becomes ahistorical, nostalgic rather than a commitment to the contemporary or future aims of a society and culture in which they remain, at least for the first generation, a guest or an outsider.

The strength of *Namenlos* lies in the description of paradigmatic conflicts of migration. The novel's stylistic and formal weaknesses seem less fatal when seen in the context of this achievement. Esther Landolt has written "the" novel of migration — for all its flaws and literary pretensions. It could be argued that many of the work's inconsistencies and incongruities are themselves expressions of migration and cultural alienation. Had Landolt remained in her native Switzerland, she would have continued writing a prose akin to contemporary popular novelists of some quality, such as John Knittel (whose works, significantly, all either deal with Swiss rural themes or have exotic settings [South Sea Islands, Africa, Egypt or Morocco]) or C.F. Ramuz. The marketing of Esther Landolt's work by her publishers Orell Füssli and Humanitas Verlag Zürich confirms that it was in such company that her writing was perceived. The very title of this 1947 novel indicates the loss of identity experienced not only by migrants generally, but by emigrating writers in particular. It could be argued that Landolt tried to overcome this dilemma by transforming her experiences in both hemispheres into the setting of a kind of world village, in a desperate attempt to retain links with her own cultural origin. Her earlier (1942) novel *Ewige Herde* would seem to support such a view.

The male migrant is mythologised as the "eternal wanderer"(445), the woman, according to Esther Landolt, herself a Swiss woman forced to migrate by marriage, is of a steadier nature who remains close to life's origins.

L.L. POLITZER

Autumn Leaves, In Introspective Mood

There are two collections of published poetry by L.L. Politzer: *Autumn Leaves* with no date of publication and *In Introspective Mood* which appeared in 1944. Both volumes were released by Pan Publishers Melbourne. The English language verse is characterised by what can only be termed a pretentious naivety. It could be argued that his publications hardly deserve closer attention, as they are so evidently of negligible quality. Yet Politzer seems a representative voice of the German-born writer attempting to find voice in English by applying archaic aesthetics based on German Classicism to artificially induced "poetic" experiences.

The poems in this volume are a broken (not breaking) voice in isolation. A second language is used without reference to its sociocultural context, rather as an extension of the author's native tongue. The poems read like schoolmasterly reflections of German poetry over a hundred years ago. Politzer's literary isolation would have been no different in his native Germany; his publications in English merely accentuate the "untimely", i.e. outdated nature of his poetics. Much of this poetry is inarticulate cultural rhetoric, the inflated language of academic abstraction and *Bildungsbürgertum*. European mythology is transferred to Australia without apparent conflict. It forms part of a "poetic" gesture employed throughout. The poet's experience itself seems to be, paradoxically, inarticulately verbal, a projected or wished-for language; yet, in the hands of this writer, incapable of verbal expression. Politzer's poetry aims to celebrate language, but has no verbal or imaginative means of doing so.

The poem "Australia" offers a vision of grotesque idealism and literary distortion. Europeans arriving on the shores of Australia see "a paradise so vast/a playground/for man and beast". The native population is described as black outside, but white "within": "It's(sic) natives, black in pigment/but white within/live carefree lifes(sic)...". Like his language Politzer's Australia has little to do with the realities of social, historical or sensual, imaginative life. Despite their ostensibly Australian settings, few poems address themselves to a particular place and make it recognisable. Emotionalism and intellectual reflection are the poetic locale of Politzer's verse. In all of his poems, punctuation, grammar and spelling are, at best, arbitrary, thus adding to the overall irritation of the reader.

Autumn Leaves includes a ten-page section of "Letters", a collection of prose poems or poetic reflections. They were all written, or are ostensibly placed, in the Dandenong Hills. The language of his prose is not very different from his poetry: conservative, archaic, manneristic. Most of Politzer's writings are "a confession of emotions", the place of their outburst is of little importance. As a result, Australia as a physical, identifiable landscape, or as an historical, political society, does not appear in either poetry or prose.

The central word in Politzer's prose poetry is "longing". He sees himself as a "wanderer" in the Byronic Romantic tradition, wearing, as he admits, "that mask of convention". In his final "Letter" the author revealingly considers that "ideal phantoms will compensate for much in life". It is difficult not to see in his own "Autumn Leaves" a collection of phantom ideals and the expression of an inarticulate longing.

In Introspective Mood is another collection of poetry and poetic prose by L.L. Politzer, published in the year 1944. Its title is an accurate indicator of style and themes. In its mixture of ambitious, ill-adapted language the poetry manages to express the poetics of the author. Politzer never addresses himself to his obvious problems of bilingualism and biculturalism. Some of his prose reflections are attempts at cultural criticism. Politzer blames America for having "coarsened" everyday life. He draws connections between "its slang", "the saxaphone" (sic) and "the crooner". The language of contemporary society, in all its aspects, is abhorrent to him. While John Dos Passos in America and Alfred Döblin in Germany developed narrative techniques incorporating the sounds of city low life, L.L. Politzer is anxious to revive the language of the past. Yet he gleefully borrows the American term "gangster" to describe "the political adventurer of today", "the financial freebooter", "all parasites of society".(13)

Other texts address themselves to middle age, war, nature, religion, cars and "feminine emancipation"(21). In Introspective Mood confirms Politzer's habit of desensualising nature, of turning the experience of the Australian bush into an emotional or intellectual abstraction. One cannot help but feel that Politzer's writing would have benefitted greatly from closer contact with everyday social life. Unfortunately, he preferred to leave behind all "city shams" and gain "new strength... from nature's bosom". It may well be that "we get our fill of creation's never ceasing fount"(22), but Politzer's introspective mood does not lead to new insights or understandings.

WALTER STÖLTING

Poetry

Almost all of the many unpublished poems by Walter Stölting are inspired by classical Greek literature and the aesthetics of German Classicism. They read like transliterations or belated variations of their models. Overwhelmingly written in German, Stölting's verse appears defiantly indifferent to contemporary arts and politics. It is spectacularly at odds with the cultural realities of the early decades of the twentieth century. Following the poetics of Goethean Classicism, Stölting aims for "timeless" beauty and validity of thought. He can write in the style of Homer, Hesiod, Pindar or Sappho, handling the dactylic hexameter, the elegiac couplet or the iambic trimeter and the trochaic tetrameter with consummate ease.

Stölting's poetry is most accessible in the author's own transcript for H. von Ploennies.[8] Although copied in 1947, some verse goes back to the twenties, written in Hamburg, in South America or in Scandinavia. Other poems were actually written in Australia, notably during the author's internment from 1939 to 1945. Only a handful are in English, retaining a classicist style. The language is that of the *Iliad*, without any concession to contemporary usage. Stölting raises the spectacle of perfect re-creation in a vacuum of ahistorical aestheticism. Many of his dedicatory or "occasional" poems (*Gelegenheitsgedichte*) are sonnets bearing the imprint of Goethean thought and language. There is a perfection of verbal and metrical craftsmanship which triumphs even over the most painful personal circumstance. The literature of his education has become his "home"; as a writer he remains "rückverbunden", united with, and indebted to, the past. Stölting thus presents the extreme case of a gifted poet coping with emigration, alienation and social conflict by living the discipline and shelter of conservative literary form. Sublimation of cultural estrangement and political challenge through ahistorical aestheticism is a feature not only of German emigrant writers, — it forms part of a general response of middle-class, bourgeois intelligentsia to the threat of social change. Stölting's formalism must be seen as an articulate, reactionary expression of cultural and political withdrawal in a migrant situation. To what extent this exercise was a conscious act must remain speculative. In an undated letter to von Ploennies, Stölting discusses the quality and relevance of his work: "Ob, was ich schrieb, gut ist, wird die Zeit lehren. Gefällt es uns auch noch über Jahr und Tag, ist alles in Ordnung. Das will viel sagen...".[9] Even these sentiments are essentially classicist. They indicate the poet's hope that his work will survive the changes of history.

The poet's preoccupation with European Classicism and German Romanticism dominates his writings in Australia. As early as 1927, Stölting writes his own version of the death of Socrates, "Tod des Sokrates". It is another work of archaic near-perfection, relating not to Melbourne, where the poem was written, but to literary Greece of antiquity. The twelve stanzas read like ancient relics, employing the language of a different age.

Stölting appears to have written primarily for himself and for a few friends to whom he dedicated many of his poems. The voice of his verse is clearly aiming to be that of an I-*persona*, an objective subjectivity, not an autobiographical documentation. The very act of writing is experienced as an objectifying transformation of self; the personal assumes a universal character. His obvious homosexual leaning does not articulate itself in a special voice; it is integrated into the generalised subjectivity of neo-classical eroticism. It is, yet again, a means of controlling emotion and suffering. Poetry remains Stölting's way of coping with life's challenges; in a very real sense, it replaces life. It is this extreme response which makes his position among German-Australian writers unusual. A conservative literary sensibility is used to overcome the challenges of migration, isolation and alienation.

Not counting his translations from the Greek and German, there are only seven poems among Stölting's manuscripts written in English. They, too, show a degree of sophistication, albeit in the same archaic manner as his German verse, unusual for someone writing in a second (or third) language. They were written between the years 1944 and 1952, in Adelaide and in Sydney. Any emotion is formally controlled by the literary masks of antiquity. It is Greek culture which is rejuvenated in the poetry; youth cannot be extolled any other way. Ultimately, Stölting aims to let his verse praise itself; his real love, his real concern is the art of writing. In that sense, he is always a poet glorifying his craft. What matters is the degree of perfection his poems achieve, their subjects are of much lesser concern. The challenge lies in being able to write about any of the "classical" themes and to follow the formally prescribed patterns. This is why Stölting's poems rarely convey the energies of authenticity; the reader senses that they are "set pieces". Their formal perfection adds to the artificiality of the verse.

It seems tragically appropriate that Stölting's final poem in English should articulate a bitter farewell to the gods of antiquity. At long last the writer has realised that Greek mythology and German Classicism are no longer effective, living models. The untimeliness of these gods is admitted in grudge and anger; the poet's resentment allows only for occasional, almost coincidental humour. It is a defiant gesture, not a discovery which might have led to new poetic style or form. As it stands, it must be considered Walter Stölting's self-chosen epitaph.

Hans Franke

Das Ende des Kapitäns Cook

In line with a redefined concept of adventure and the general sense of disillusionment after the war, 1948 saw the publication of a book in a series promising "spannende Abenteuer, Erlebnisse, Entdeckungen und Forschungen, die den Blick für die weite Welt öffnen und Ansporn sind, das Leben zu meistern".[10] *Das Ende des Kapitäns Cook* by Hans Franke forms part of such a didactic intent. Young German readers are to be instructed in the art of mastering life by modelling themselves on the "heroic adventures" of explorers and scientists. The series "Junge Welt" consists of narrative adaptations of biographies or other documentary material. The aim is not to publish fiction, but an inspiring record of model lives. Among the new heroes are Rudolf Diesel, Robert Koch, Marie and Pierre Curie, Karl Zeiss, Sebastian Kneipp and Friedrich Gerstäcker. Gandhi and Livingstone stand side by side as representatives of a "new world". The authors of these semi-documentary narratives (*biographische Nacherzählungen*) are basically compilers, editors and arrangers.

Franke's compilation bears the important subtitle "Alten Quellen nacherzählt" and identifies, on a separate page at the beginning of the book, the sources with precise bibliographical reference. *Das Ende des Kapitäns Cook* thus goes out of its way to assure its young readers that it is a trustworthy record of adventurous facts. It forms part of a radical reassessment of the very concept of "Abenteuer" and replaces the colonial travelogues or the exotic fiction of the earlier part of the century. The excitement of personal involvement remains a vital ingredient in the post-war German *Abenteuerbuch*; it is merely authenticated as a record of verifiable factual events. The very act of narration assumes a documentary character: the author Hans Franke speaks on behalf of the historical Heinrich Zimmermann, he reports on authentic narration. In a postscript Franke again stresses the validity and originality of his sources, whilst also pointing to Zimmermann's lack of literary sophistication. He thereby hopes to justify his own stylistic improvements.

Australia, "New Holland", and the South Sea islands generally are invoked as part of the world which "uns allen unbekannt und seltsam erschien und unsere Träume mit kuriosen Vorstellungen erfüllte".(14) In "Van Diemansland", January 1777, Zimmermann experiences his first contact with Aborigines ("erste Begegnung mit Eingeborenen",18).

The ship's surgeon, William Anderson, informs Zimmermann, "daß sie den Eingeborenen von Neu-Holland völlig ähnlich seien".(10) The German's impression of the Tasmanian coast is that of an exotic island, totally un-European. Yet William Anderson links it to European mythology:

> Mister Anderson meinte, wie die alten Dichter von Faunen und Satyren erzählen, die in Baumstämmen leben, so sehe man hier die Wohnungen der Menschen in hohlen Bäumen: nur ein elendes Geflecht von Stäben schütze den Eingang.(20)

The Antipodean exotic as a natural correlative to European mythology is a forced relationship not only in German-Australian literary contacts. It is perhaps an understandable attempt to "translate" the exotic into a native cultural terminology, without taking away its mystery.

To the extent that Australia plays any part in these journeys to adventureland, it forms part of the Antipodean vision of otherness. As the German sailor says: "Man gaukelte sich immer wieder dieses Paradies vor...".(31) Part of this "paradise" is the promise of "adventure", or the freedom to dream. Hans Frankes *Das Ende des Kapitäns Cook* allows free, albeit reconstructed, expression of that dream, but integrates it into factual, historical information. He sums up Cook's achievements in sober language, tempering his narrator's excitement: "Er fand, daß Neuseeland kein festes Land ist und untersuchte Neuholland."(142) It is in the spirit of post-war German explorative adventure that Cook's "discovery" of Australia should be acknowledged by such understatement.

MAX ALBERT

Abenteuer in Australien und Alaska

1948 saw the publication of a curious book for children, Max Albert's *Abenteuer in Australien und Alaska*. It was published in post-war Berlin, continuing the tradition of German adventure stories for the young. The only thing Australia and Alaska have in common is that both are far-away places and thus, by definition, the right "exotic" locale for adventure, far enough away from Germany's immediate past enemies, thus not likely to cause political embarrassment, even in *Jugendliteratur*.

The remarkable feature of the Australian narrative is that it deals with the adventures of migrant children. The story's plot takes place in Melbourne's port suburb of Williamstown. Significantly, no exact time is ever mentioned, — the events take place in the history of "boys' own" adventure. The narrator ends his account with the declaration that his story really happened, as may be verified from an article in the undated, fictitious paper "Handels- und Seefahrtszeitung", published in Oslo. The history of post-war German popular literature records an upsurge of so-called "Tatsachenberichte" in journals and mass-circulated light fiction. It was part of the experience of disillusionment which made German survivors of the war turn to "real stories", to "facts", to "eye-witness reports" which, more often than not, proved to be merely another brand of fiction.

Albert introduces fictional characters of identifiable social background. The author's Australia is a country of migrants, suggesting a post-war setting. It is the adventure of migrant boys the author relates. Even allowing for the kind and level of this form of popular literature, the turning away from clichés of Australian travelogues and adventure stories (for young and old) is remarkable. The migrant family background is never idealised. The plot offers an interesting twist: it extends the original motivation for migration and "adventure" to a second generation. The changed perspective reveals the relativity of adventure and "the exotic". The responsibility for both is transferred to children. Max Albert's book not only takes place in migrant circles of Australia; in accordance with historical conditions, Australia's migrants and their children live in virtual ghettos. There is little evidence of intercultural contact.

There is a serious and revealing undercurrent in this seemingly harmless and naive children's story. The "adventure" of a migrant boy leads to integration and acceptance outside the migrant ghetto. Max Albert's story ends with the friendship of migrant children and a recognition of their respectability by Australian society. It is this "adventurous fairy-tale" which makes the book noteworthy in the history of German-Australian literary relations during the forties.

Werner Fels

The Lady With the Red-brown Hair and Australian Poems,
The River-side Sage

Werner Fels was born at Daylesford in 1878 and died at Newport in December 1948. He studied art at the National Gallery under Bernard Hall, but did not pursue it as a profession. 1949 saw the publication of a "Memorial Edition" of some of Fels' poetry, *The Lady With the Red-brown Hair and Australian Poems*. It appeared in Melbourne, with an introduction by Cyril E. Goode. In his foreword Goode speaks of a number of manuscripts Fels was preparing for publication at the time of his death. Among them was a verse drama called "The Haunted Swagman", a long narrative poem in blank verse entitled "Fisher's Ghost" and many bush verses and medieval ballads. "It was all grist that came to his poetical mill," writes Goode, "Greek, Egyptian and other mythologies, stories adapted from Aboriginal folk lore or old bush yarns."(3)

The title poem of Fels' memorial selection is a theme taken from the Arthurian Cycle. In form and content derivative or imitative, Fels demonstrates his art of literary reconstruction. He refers to it as "legend", and it is as reteller of legends that he finds his characteristic style. "The First Waratah" bears the subtitle "An Aboriginal Legend". Written in octosyllabic lines with simple a–a b–b rhymes, the epic ballad combines naievety with monotony. Fels aims for a poetic synthesis of Aboriginal and Classical European mythology. In most of his ballads the charm of folk songs is revived by an artfully deliberate simplicity. At the same time there can be no doubt about the origin of Fels' legends: his poetic inspiration were books. The highly stylised revivals of folkloristic myths remain bookish in language and theme. This applies to his attempts at bush ballads ("Harry Power") as much as to his odes and fables. Many of his ballads end on a high moral note, following the model of Friedrich Schiller.

Despite the general seriousness of tone and the intellectuality of learned references, Fels does display occasional glimpses of humour and wit. But, on the whole, Fels prefers to address himself to the classical themes of poetry in a classical "elevated" style. Fels uses European mythology to avoid closer contact with Australian nature. Yet this very attempt to superimpose a European cultural structure onto an emerging Australian art was in itself an Australian characteristic. As Judith Wright says of Australia's nineteenth century poets:

"Traditionless they dared not be; they could not strip themselves of preconceptions and look at their new situation with new eyes, nor perhaps was it desirable that they should."(3–4)[11] Many major Australian poets, from Christopher Brennan to A.D. Hope, James McAuley and Vincent Buckley, have kept the tradition of European Classicism alive. Unlike them, the Australian-born 'German' Werner Fels lacks the imaginative ability to integrate such vision into a sensuous perception of the historical and natural landscape.

By far the most interesting poem on the subject of flowers is his adaptation of Goethe's *Das Veilchen*, "The Lowly Weed. A Fable".[12] Again, the anthropomorphised imagery assumes mythological dimension. It provides an interesting twist in comparison to its model. Whereas Goethe's "Violet" ends on an intensely erotic note, invoking a masochistic *Liebestod*, Fels' weed-flower is transformed into "a herb/To heal and cure the sick". Goethe's poem laments the waste of erotic and imaginative energy, Fels praises "the greater power/Than outward loveliness". Fels replaces the Goethean eroticism with didacticism. Almost all of his poems carry a moral, often a religious tone. Ultimately, they address themselves to what the poet calls the spirit of divine creation. The poetry thereby becomes celebratory and, more often than not, rhetorical.

An earlier war-time publication, *The River-side Sage* (1942), may be called a Melbourne "regional" poem. The poem offers a critique of contemporary civilisation. Over thirty-two stanzas Fels rhymes his reflections, drawn between hope and despair. He singles out the economic world depression, unemployment and "the horrors of war". Unemployment is described as "this century's bane and curse". *The River-side Sage* is certainly a very different kind of verse from most of Fels' later writing: it expresses a social concern and a general political awareness unknown in his other poetry. The city is no more than a convenient back-drop to the poet's philosophical and sociological reflections, — comparable, in that sense, to T. S. Eliot's "Unreal City" of *The Waste Land*.[13] Needless to say, Werner Fels' poem lacks the imaginative quality and depth of vision found in Eliot's or Gottfried Benn's *Zivilisationslyrik*. It is most likely that Fels was familiar with both writers; perhaps some of his outbursts against "modernism" in literature (cf. "The Modern Poet") were a response to their work. Unlike Eliot or Benn, Fels creates a personal voice expressing itself in conservative metre and rhyme ("to vent one's thoughts in measured rhyme", "The Modern Poet"), without, however, achieving any poetic or moral authority. The elevated style has the opposite effect: it unwittingly creates an impression of trivial rhetoric and everyday small talk.

Bearing in mind the social and philosophical preoccupations of poets such as William Baylebridge and Bernard O'Dowd, both contemporaries of Werner Fels, it is perhaps understandable that Fels should have attempted a major poem of similar character. But, like his approximations of Hugh McCrae's and the Norman Lindsay circle's return to Greek and Roman pantheisms, his endeavours failed as a result of one overriding, irredeemable flaw: a limited talent of poetic imagination.

Chapter Three

The New Challenge: Boys' Own Geography and Domestic Reconstruction

> "Das sieht hier aus wie in Deutschland..."
> Heinz Lüneburg, *Australien*

THE FIFTIES

This decade opens with a publication which, on the face of it, is little more than a textbook for schools. Yet *K. H. Pfeffer's* study (1950) "domesticates" the exotic and looks at the antipodean continent as an important political, economic and cultural "neighbour". A new closeness in German-Australian relations is established. Parallels between Australian and German trade unionism are projected. Australia's social history is presented in strictly "objective" academic terms. Australia's culture is her geography, as yet largely undeveloped. White Australians lack a cultural will to define their values; they are seen as subservient to European cultural decadence. Geographical travelogues overlap with writings for the young. They reflect the programmatic attempt of post-war Germany to open up the world to a generation born during the war and to make it accessible again to older readers who survived a Nazi-censored and restricted perception of other countries. A noticeable reluctance to pass judgement on critical aspects of Australian society, its treatment of Aborigines in particular, appears to be prompted by Germany's own recent record in these areas. Only socialist books from East Germany (GDR) use that very fact as the motivation for outspoken criticism of racism and political suppression. In other German-language publications injustices, even genocide, are passively acknowledged. More importantly, great tasks await young pioneers or rebuilders. There are clear analogies to German post-war reconstruction and implicit appeals to young readers to participate in the creation of a German "economic miracle" (*Heinz Lüneburg*, 1951).

Translation, too, serves the political and economic needs of the time. Australian history is invoked as it deals with freedom and guilt, punishment and a new beginning. Australia as a country of migration reflects Germany's immediate past. It is a nation of people whose freedom is based on guilt and punishment. In colonial Australia and post-war Germany occupation forces became liberators. In both countries a political re-education of a vast portion of the population determined future directions. Australia becomes a code for rehabilitation and regeneration. The history of the protagonist has been "forgiven"; he may build a new life. Adenauer's Germany as a period of capitalist restoration and conservatism endorsed the political logic of innocence restored in the name of a new allegiance[1] (*L. and A. Fankhauser*, Charles B. Nordhoff/James Norman Hall, 1953)[2]. Adventures in Australia continue to be linked to didacticism, preparing the young for the challenges of the future. In this context, strikes are portrayed as a crime against the sanctity of labour. In narratives of "young adult fiction" sociopolitical conditions are depoliticised and "elevated" to the realm of emotional morality. Social unrest is an infection to be eradicated. It is easy to see how such values were designed to influence the young German worker in the making. In a dislocation of conflict exotic adventures lose none of their domestic application (*Fritz Raab*, 1957).

To become Australian is the equivalent of leaving a European past of crime and guilt behind. Like "denazification", migration and settlement on the other side of the world amount to an expurgation of a troubled history. Such transition or passage can become the central theme even in narratives for the young. Economic conquest and cultural colonialism are seen as creating a new innocence, even at the expense of a "foreign" indigenous people (*Franz Hutterer*, 1959).

K. H. Pfeffer

Australien

This 1950 publication is part of a series of geographical textbooks for schools and universities ("Kleine Länderkunden", edited by W. Evers). In eight sections it deals with the history of the continent, its position in relation to South East Asia and its status as a British Dominion, the natural landscapes of Australia, the Aborigines, the interrelationships of states and nation, trade and commerce, federal politics and the emergence of an Australian culture. Some of Pfeffer's language tends to be pseudo-philosophical ("Werden und Sein der Landschaft",26), occasionally messianic ("Die Frage des australischen Schicksals",9), but on the whole the author stays clear of the kind of cliché-ridden rhetoric all too frequent in books of this kind. Pfeffer rightly suspects many German writers about Australia of exaggerations and falsifications, and he warns against simplistic slogans with which to summarise a complex land and its people. The very distance has meant that few readers could test the validity of travelogue reports and interpretations. Pfeffer exposes some of the sensationalism and over-indulgence in the exotic. He has a particular reason for a more realistic assessment of Australia. He sees it not as a country on the other side of the world, but as a "Nachbarland"(8), a nation relating to the interests of Central Europe, "in der Mitte des Interesses der Gegenwart".(7) Australians are not fringe dwellers, but residents of Europe, albeit in an outpost of the "Old World". They exist "innerhalb der Europäerwelt".(8) Pfeffer's *Australien* is written within such framework; it "domesticates" the "exotic" and makes this country an important "neighbour" of Germany. "Es kommt darauf an," he argues, "die Eigenart des Nachbarlandes in Achtung zur Kenntnis zu nehmen."(Ibid.)

It is a claim the book largely fulfils, although, inevitably with textbooks of this kind, most of the data presented is long outdated. His key argument is that Australia's fate will be determined by three factors: her isolation, her Asian neighbours and her European cultural ties. Australia's fate is her geography; the geographer K. H. Pfeffer therefore attempts to analyse or to circumscribe this "fate". As a professional text the study is virtually without fault. The author restrains himself from making any unsubstantiated predictions; as an academic, he prefers to list the options with a description of the possible consequences.

Discussing the Aboriginal population, Pfeffer openly admits to a

European's inability to enter Australia's native culture. Yet he does offer an accurate account of white injustice in dealings with Aborigines. He describes it as something almost inevitable, a cultural dilemma with a predictable conclusion. Genocide is reported in a scholarly style of factual information. The author does not discuss cultural conflicts, he merely lists them, along with other data on Australia. Even when describing the Aboriginal painters Albert Namatjira and Edwin Pareroultja as "künstlerische Begabung im europäischen Sinne"(Ibid.), he does not address himself to a more involved conflict of racial culture.

The geographer Pfeffer reminds his readers that, contrary to reports of almost all writers about Australia, cities developed a special lifestyle from the very beginnings of colonisation. There was no migration from the country to the towns in Australia, as was the case in Europe. Life started in the cities, and so it makes no sense to speak of "Landflucht". Pfeffer further insists that the deportation to Australia in the eighteenth and nineteenth century was not a criminal but a social matter. It is the social development of Australia which interests him above all else. He presents a well-informed analysis of the political will forging a concept of national unity and identity. The carriers of this will were blue-collar workers, the petty bourgeoisie, industrialists and farmers — a non-class-oriented social force. This is how Pfeffer explains why Australian trade unions play such an active part in the economic politics of the nation. Social politics never aimed at overthrowing the capitalist system; it concentrated on "equal" rights of the workers in it. Again, the author makes no attempts to comment on the nature or extent of such "equality". In the fifties West German trade unions followed the same path, endorsing small-time capitalism as "equality" within the system. It is easy to see why Pfeffer should look upon Australia as a political "neighbour".

The chapter dealing with Australian culture discusses religion (representation of various denominations), education generally and teachers' training in particular, libraries and learned societies, theatre, music, fine arts and literature. It suffers from the detached registering of facts where a critical discussion would have prompted a more passionate response from the reader. As it is, various names are quoted, artistic "schools" are listed, but the background and genesis of Australian movements and individual artists remain unexplained.

There is one exception to Pfeffer's academic "neutrality". He expresses severe doubt about the wisdom of sponsoring

"Australianisms" by the creation of special chairs at universities, literary prizes and exaggerated publicity. It is possible that he rejects an "Australian bias" on the basis of recent German experiences in the realm of cultural politics. Whatever his reasons, he believes that the "creative imagination" should not be influenced by such attempts to create a cultural identity. But he does no more than express reservations. It is a pity that Pfeffer does not consider the desirability or otherwise of a "European cultural settlement" in Australia. The possibility of an emerging indigenous culture is never envisaged. Pfeffer gives an accurate description of the culture of Australia's middle class. He is most sensitive in his appreciation of the "earthiness" of Australian culture which continues to orientate itself on the bush and country. He sees very clearly how a cultural identity derived from such ideals must clash with the cultural experiences of Australian intellectuals. It leads, he suggests, to serious conflict when there is little chance to confront European cultural decadence with a vigorous native alternative. By clear implication, then, K. H. Pfeffer argues that, as yet, Australia lacks a cultural will, a recognisable collective identity in the realm of arts and letters, science and religion — in the articulation of living values.

Heinz Lüneburg

Australien. Neuseeland
(Jims Abenteuer im Land der trockenen Flüsse)

German-Australian literature in the fifties consists of geographical travelogues and writings for the young. The two overlap in a programmatic attempt of post-war Germany to open up the world to a generation born during the war, as well as to older readers who had been exposed to a censored and restricted view of the world. It is important to realise the true nature of many *Jugendbücher* during this period: while ostensibly aiming for the young, they also consciously, if implicitly, addressed themselves to the older generations, to the survivors of the war.[3] Just as Nazi youth literature carried a message of immediate relevance to the parents, this post-war writing for juvenile readers included many adults among its consumers. To fully understand Lüneburg's publication, it is necessary to remember that from the beginning of this century German popular culture developed a tradition of picture-books propagating national achievements (such as trains, cars, ships, planes, colonies, fashion, science and the arts) based on a collection of dockets (*Bons*) from cigarettes or chocolates, which could be "converted" to special "illustrations" and cards for collectors' volumes, issued by the companies. After the Second World War this tradition was revived. Lüneburg's *Jims Abenteuer im Land der trockenen Flüsse* (1951) is in fact a publication of the "Margarine Union AG Hamburg", a book provided by the "Sanella" company in which to glue the pictures gained by a collection of dockets printed on the wrappings of margarine. The company had its own "Bilderdienst"(72), an exchange service of pictures. This book, then, is a commercial by-product of widest distribution, accessible to any customer or citizen, irrespective of social class or background. The themes of such collections are by definition "popular", or aimed at popular consumption. Their "literature" is an extension of consumerism — and hence made to serve the purpose or philosophy of capitalist investment. The collectors were guaranteed a share of the world; reading became a commercial proposition. The world was up for sale. Education became acquisition; knowledge was accumulated buying power.

In this context Lüneburg's narrative about Australia serves a special social purpose. *Jims Abenteuer* follows the pattern of listing Australian features, mainly of flora and fauna, verbally as well as pictorially. It is easy to see how these Australian plants, animals and human activities are strung together as a kind of running commentary on the illustrations. The "plot" is even more transparently constructed to serve as a lesson in geography or national customs (*Landeskunde*). On the level of such self-imposed restriction Lüneburg's book fulfils its purpose. Like a slide-show it offers glimpses of life in a foreign country, often changing abruptly from scene to scene. On a purely informative basis, *Jims Abenteuer* presents excerpts of representative encounters with Australia.

Interestingly, the author writes about Aborigines in North-West Australia who speak (some) German. He explains that they were visited by the first German naturalist expedition since the war. Lüneburg offers an idealised version of Ludwig Leichhardt's expedition to the Gulf of Carpentaria. According to his fictionalised variation, Leichhardt was the only one who survived the journey.

The author includes a few Aboriginal legends in his introduction to Australia, notably the mythological genesis of the Southern Cross.(21)

Information about Aboriginal culture is sketchy but factual. It includes an account of various tribal dances and ritual ceremonies. Lüneburg's presentation of Aborigines is sympathetic, although he does not record the horrendous history of their suppression by the whites. His account demythologises the widespread stories of cannibalism among Aborigines. He stops short of blaming the white settlers for the horrors their cultivation of the stolen land has caused. There is a brief episode dealing with the transportation of kanakas to the cane fields of Queensland, but the narrator again refrains from making any critical comment. "Aber Australien will weiß bleiben!"(40) the reader is told and left to draw his own conclusion.

There are brief historical references to James Cook, Dirk Hartog and Abel Tasman, thinly integrated into the travelogue. But this pictorial travelogue concentrates on the present, aiming to introduce an Australia to young Germans which is a continent of promise, a country of the future and the home for young, optimistic workers. In an environment of historical and natural violence new generations forge their fate. Injustice, even genocide, is alluded to, passively acknowledged. But "life goes on"; there are great tasks awaiting enterprising young pioneers or rebuilders. Lüneburg's collection of narrative images is a clear analogy of post-war German reconstruction, an appeal to young readers to seek out adventures in their own land, to lend a hand in the creation of a German "economic miracle".

L./A. FRANKHAUSER (TRSL.)
CHARLES B. NORDHOFF — JAMES NORMAN HALL

Kolonie Sydney

The translation of Nordhoff-Hall's novel *Botany Bay* (1941) deserves to be included in a history of German-Australian literature. *Kolonie Sydney* is the German version, freely translated by L. and A. Fankhauser. It appeared in 1953, published by the Heinrich Scheffler Verlag in Frankfurt. Nordhoff-Hall were well-known in Germany; their novels *Meuterei auf der Bounty* and *Schiff ohne Hafen (Mutiny on the Bounty*, 1932; *Men Without Country*, 1942) had been extremely popular, leading the authors to be compared to Joseph Conrad. The publisher's blurb describes *Kolonie Sydney* as an "Unterhaltungsroman" (popular novel) of unusual quality, emphasising its moral concerns and sensuous characterisations. Nordhoff-Hall wrote a work of historical fiction by combining aspects of travel literature with elements of the adventure novel. In 1953 *Botany Bay*, or *Kolonie Sydney*, was produced as a film, one of several novels by the authors meeting "Hollywood's formula for romantic-adventure films".[4] *Kolonie Sydney* could be described as "visual writing"; its narrative style is sensuously formative, uninterrupted by abstract reflection, eminently readable, without great intellectual or imaginative demands on the reader. Even in translation it comes across as a well-written, carefully constructed novel of professional routiniers.

Charles Nordhoff and James Norman Hall met during the First World War in France. Both are American writers who in 1920 moved to Tahiti, where they settled and collaborated in a series of popular novels, "mostly about the South Seas".[5] Iowa-born Hall published verse, short stories, novels, children's books and the autobiography *My Island Home* (1952), as well as a wide range of essays. Nordhoff wrote several South Seas novels independently during the decade 1919-1929. Paul L. Briand's *In Search of Paradise* (1966) describes the nature of Nordhoff's and Hall's collaboration.

In this context the book is considered as an important contribution to German-Australian literary relations. Fankhausers' translation is highly competent, retaining the original's vitality, without forfeiting its ethical assertions. It is symptomatic that this work should be released in Germany during the early fifties, dealing, as it does, with the themes of guilt, freedom, punishment and a new beginning. The book's popularity has helped shape the German image of Australia as a country of migration, while reflecting on Germany's own immediate past. Australia, the reader is told, has produced a new race whose freedom is based on punishment and guilt. It must have been easy for Germans to identify with the sentiments expressed by a successful convict settler: "Mein Mißgeschick...oder war es mein Glück?"(6) The "economic miracles" of Germany and Japan are directly related to the defeat and destruction of industry during the Second World War and to the determination of the population to find comfort and to regain strength in work. The occupation forces in Germany were soon transformed into liberators, the former enemies became friends. Australia's colonial history thus offers a paradigmatic analogy to Germany's post-war situation. It was a parallel not missed by the readers of Nordhoff-Hall's *Kolonie Sydney*. The Allied "colony" Germany followed the Australian pattern rather closely, as the

Nuremberg trials, "denazification" and political re-education affected most of the population.

The co-authors invent a fictional biography for their protagonist which is representative of that of many First or Second Fleet Australians. The novel describes conditions in English prisons (New Gate), the class-oriented judiciary, the passage to New South Wales, life in the penal colony, contacts with Aborigines and the experiences of free settlers. Although all plot and most characters are thus representative of well-documented history, *Kolonie Sydney* is never reduced to mere illustration. The characters are alive, the events carry real impact in the context of a fictional composition. All the factual information about the First Fleet(64) pales into insignificance compared to the novel's central theme of the crimes of the judges. It is justice itself which is "deported". Nordhoff-Hall's protagonist settles in the penal colony, his "punishment" transformed into ultimate happiness and fulfilment. In the context of German literature, such an interpretation of a penal colony was seen to be dramatically different from Franz Kafka's parable of unredeemed punishment.

From a post-war German reader's perspective *Kolonie Sydney* assumed a dimension of renewed hope and defiance. (It goes without saying that Nordhoff-Hall were totally unaware of any such connotations; what matters here, is the specifically German response to what in terms of authorship and plot must be called an American-Australian novel.) "Verbrecherpioniere" (the title of the novel's tenth chapter) may sound too harsh an analogy for post-war German economic reconstruction, until it is realised that the "Verbrecher" are presented as having been misjudged. The one central feature of the narrative protagonist is that he continues to escape punishment (cf. 157 etc.). The narrator thus offers an eye-witness account of historical misjudgement and the restoration of justice in a "penal colony", a kind of concentration camp. Chapter Fifteen deals with the Second Fleet and the famine suffered by the settlement at the time of its arrival — another experience Germans could identify with in the years immediately after the war. The question of justice in war, including the class struggle, takes up most of Chapter Seventeen. It is difficult to imagine that German publishers and editors were unaware of (valid or invalid) "parallels", similarities or analogies. They appear to be the strongest reason for the translation of Nordhoff-Hall's *Botany Bay* — just as American, British and French films were carefully selected for post-war German consumption.

Australia thus becomes a recognisable code of rehabilitation and regeneration. Any attempt to escape from (German) history is not only doomed to failure, it is unnecessary. For the history of the protagonist has been "forgiven"; he may build a new life and prosper with the support of his former enemies. At "home" treachery is rewarded. "Justice" is profitable once again. The concept of property is not examined, it is the ownership of "law and order". Adenauer's Germany may be characterised as a period of restoration and capitalist conservatism. It is possible for the protagonist and his wife to become "free settlers" acquiring wealth and its incumbent "justice". Innocence is restored in the name of a new alliance.

DAVID MARTIN

I look at Australia / Australien und wir heutigen Australier

Although David Martin's main contribution to German-Australian writing is his novel *Where a Man Belongs* (1969), two publications during the fifties deal explicitly and autobiographically with the author's concept of Australia. Born Ludwig Detsinyi into a Hungarian Jewish family, he was educated in Germany and considers German his native language. He moved to Australia in 1949.

In the following year Martin published a personal response to this country, "I look at Australia", which appeared in the March-April 1950 issue of the journal *Unity*. His account reveals an astonishing empathy and understanding for one so recently arrived. If he calls Australia "a strange country", it is because he immediately grasps the contradictions that make up its character and the culture of its people. "A country of poets," Martin writes, "without lovers of poetry."(4) Like the European migrant, Australia's white civilisation is not yet clearly coordinated, its views not yet in focus. "Foreground and background do not merge. No longer and not yet."(Ibid.) An identification with Australia is thus easy; country and settler share the same contradictions. One of them is a simultaneous loss and gain: the loss of European ties and the gain of getting to know a totally different world. Martin detects early losses in Australia's native culture: "The Australian balladists of one generation ago are half forgotten," he notes, "while the recording machine goes out to save the songs of the Aborigines, older than the Iliad."(Ibid.)

He describes Australia as "perhaps the only country in the world where man's struggle with nature has led to a draw".(Ibid.) But he knows that man's eventual "victory" will be inevitable. After only two years in the country David Martin's sensitivity and sociocultural identification with Australians lead him to declare: "Gallipoli has not made the Australian, it has not made a nation; only a casualty list."(Ibid.) It is a claim he repeats in the 1957 German publication "Australien und wir heutigen Australier", where the author's identification with Australia is stated even more programmatically in the title. Martin's pacifist and socialist convictions are spelt out quite explicitly. It is a conviction worthy of respect even if it can be shown to be wrong. David Martin's Australian is a myth in the making and the revival of earlier folklore. But there is already a recognisable image of the true Australian. The author interprets it as the effects of a shared natural environment. "It is an error to speak of Australian 'individualism'", Martin argues; there is, instead, a kind of collective assertion of apathy — another characteristic contradiction. Perhaps the most enthusiastic endorsement of a vision of Australia David Martin derives from "the works of Australia's writers".(Ibid.) With clear reference to German spiritual longing he insists: "This is not a metaphysical yearning, even though it is not tangible to the impatient visitor."(Ibid.) To love Australia "is to love a promise, a prophecy"(Ibid.); it is, and will remain, a love in the making. Martin shares the belief

> that the eventual evolution of Australia, the great upward thrust which is bound to come and which lies now coiled like a spring and out of sight, will coincide with mankind's moment of maturity, with the evolution of Man as a being capable of co-operation.(Ibid.)

Such cultural mythology may be an unexpected faith expressed by the author of *The Young Wife*, a novel of cultural conflict and social discrimination. But like his communism (which Martin later abandoned), his vision of Australia reflects an act of identification to be varied and developed, to be affirmed and criticised.

"Australien und wir heutigen Australier" appeared some seven years later in a publication of the *National Olympic Committee of the GDR* on the occasion of the Melbourne Olympic Games held in 1956. David Martin attempts to draw "ein Bild des Volkes"(52) rather than the image of the country. As in his earlier essay, he stresses that Australians do not yet have a clear concept of themselves; their self-concept is not yet in focus. Martin insists that there is such a being as *the* Australian, but he qualifies this conviction by saying that a truly national character is still in the shaping. He describes Australia and the Australians as "ein Experiment". The ingredients of that experiment are known, "nicht aber ihre endgültige Verbindung".(53) Part of that concept of a social experiment led German-Australian writers like David Martin, Walter Kaufmann and Joachim Specht to an idealistic involvement with communism,the former two with the Communist Party of Australia. Australian-born writers like Frank Hardy and Judah Waten shared this commitment. (Walter Kaufmann's "Literaturbrief aus Australien"[6] offers a stimulating well-informed account of the "Gruppe realistischer Schriftsteller Australiens", including the sociopolitical genesis of Stephen Murray-Smith's *Overland*.) David Martin attempts a general characterisation of the Australian concept of mateship, pointing to its temperamental and ideological influence on the trade union movement. It is rare to find such empathetic understanding of what is indeed a basic quality in being an Australian. Given this enormous cultural importance of mateship, it is easy to see why writers like Martin and Kaufmann assumed their Australian identity (and they remain more recognisably Australian than most other German-Australian authors) along with political commitments: the two were inseparable. As Martin says: "Der typische Australier ist ein Demokrat besonderer Art."(Ibid.) Needless to say, then, that the writings of these German-Australian novelists are characterised by sociopolitical and ideological engagement. Their style could be termed social realism.

Where Martin describes the Australian landscape he offers a rather different perspective from that offered by native authors. Thus he sees the bush as "clean, silent and challenging like the ocean".(Ibid.) Martin contrasts the Australian bush with the Corsican "Maquis", the jungle and the savannah — the latter two frequent descriptions of the outback or the Australian countryside by German travelogue writers. Martin links the history of white Australians to the nature of the land, emphasising, for example, that Australia never had a peasant community comparable to Europe's. Instead, Australian farmers are largely mechanics. Martin's historical characterisation of the Australian people interprets the Eureka Stockade 1854 as "Australiens Schwur zur Eidgenossenschaft", an extravagant claim even in its metaphorical sense, but related back to the author's mythological appraisal of mateship: the Stockade was an event "wo der Kameradschaft ein neuer Sinn verliehen...wurde".(Ibid.) He rightly stresses that from the early gold-digging days "eine starke nichtbritische Beimischung" made up the characteristic mixture of Australia's population, among them many

German gold-diggers ("deutsche Goldbergleute", Ibid.). It is this melting of different cultural backgrounds which Martin admires and defines as the "australische Typ".(57) The Australian Dream defined by Australian writers is strongly endorsed by Martin, linked back to his own commitment to socialism and the sociological genesis of the Australian trade union movement. Martin admits that this Dream could not be realised, but insists that it has not died either. It has remained part of the spirit of the Australian people.

From this assessment of Australian history and cultural consciousness it is clear that for David Martin the "gesamte Grundton des australischen Lebens" is shaped by the "australischen Werktätigen".(Ibid.) Even if such a description of Australia as a workers' country may have become increasingly questionable, Martin's basic assumption still holds true: "Die australische Kultur ist sehr unmittelbar eine Volkskultur."(Ibid.) He himself has pointed to some of the contradictions of this culture, in this essay and his earlier biographical sketch "I look at Australia". "Es ist ein Land," Martin concedes by way of warning, "wo es nicht immer leichtfällt, die Dinge — geschweige denn die Welt — in der richtigen Perspektive zu behalten."(61) The quality and kind of much German-Australian writing is a result of that challenge. Its best works offer an imaginative perspective of counter-reflection.

Fritz Raab

Betty und die 12 000 Schafe

In many ways the most interesting comment on this book is to be found in an advertisement which appears on its final page. It consists of quotations from the *Salzburger Nachrichten*, reviewing not the individual book but the series "Abenteuerliche Welt", published by the Verlag Styria Graz. Raab's *Jugendbuch* is indeed one of many, with no special qualities of its own. All the more important, then, to characterise its representative nature. The authors of this series know the countries they write about from personal experience and claim to narrate factual accounts. It is for this reason that the review calls them "neat" or "tidy" authors — writers who, by implication, remain critically detached from the concept of imaginative fiction.

Die sauber arbeitenden Autoren, die die von ihnen beschriebenen Länder aus eigener Anschauung kennen, erzählen tatsächliche Geschehnisse frei nach.(173)

It is a recurrent claim in German-Australian literature, linked to the very distance and exotic nature of its subject. The stranger the story, the less believable it becomes. Many authors thus aim to turn their narrative travelogues into *Tatsachenberichte*, factual accounts or verifiable documentations. Underlying their notion is the popular dictum that facts may be stranger than fiction. The majority of German authors writing about Australia do see themselves as eye-witnesses who testify from their own observations. As this act of verification, and, indeed, the decision to travel to "the other side of the world", is linked to the central concept of "adventure", the writer becomes an "adventurer" — and, as such, to a greater or lesser extent, the heroic subject of his reader's admiration. The author shares his adventures with the reader, he verifies the truthfulness of the events his book describes.

"Real" adventure is defined as meeting a challenge, clearly a didactic interpretation. "Das echte Abenteuer (ist) die Bewährung an der Aufgabe."(Ibid.) It follows that the adventurous author must, in that sense, also be a teacher, leading his readers to the challenges they cannot meet by themselves. The combination of friend and teacher makes the writer an authority of great trust. In turn, it tends to reduce the reader to a grateful, overawed student. That is why such books of popular literature may address themselves to both young and older readers, but retain their intrinsic, conceptual adolescent dimension. Authenticity and didacticism are seen as the qualities which elevate the series "Abenteuerliche Welt" above the "usual level of the genre". As always, travelogues and adventure stories are linked together, with the implication that they share a genre-oriented dilemma of inferior quality. The review speaks of "Bücher, die alle Vorteile der Reise- und Abenteuerliteratur haben, doch weit über dem normalen Niveau dieses Genres stehen."(Ibid.) It is not spelt out what the "advantages" of travelogues and adventure books consist of, except that they seem to have the power to carry the reader outside the "prosaic and materialistic world" ("nüchternen und materialistischen Welt", Ibid.) of his normal life. Escapist popular literature "usually" does not concern itself with artistic merit. The characteristically German response is that authenticity and didacticism may replace aesthetic qualities. It is fair to say that not only Fritz Raab's novel and not only Styria's series "Abenteuerliche Welt" have followed this pattern. Most narrative works of German-Australian literature adhere to the same formula. They are thus written with clearly defined readers' expectations in what might be termed a context of cultural collusion.

The imaginative strength of Raab's text is, indeed, limited. There are no surprises in *Betty und die 12 000 Schafe* (1957), either in terms of plot or of characterisation. Once again, various aspects of Australian country life are described, Australian terms defined, and Australian "oddities" related. The "adventure" is a learning process for young and old. Lessons in geography and social history reappear throughout the novel, reinforcing its claim to the didacticism of true "adventure". Like many other works of German-Australian literature, Fritz Raab's *Betty und die 12 000 Schafe* sees the transmission of factual information as one of its main functions. As a generalisation, it could be argued that most narratives succeed on this level — to a greater or lesser extent. It is in the realm of literary fiction that many of them fail rather badly. The authors lack the artistic and imaginative skills to create plot and characterisation of social, aesthetic and historical credibility.

Raab's novel shows strong signs of female emancipation, with an implicit didactic message to his young German readers. The fifties in Germany were a period when, due to the deplorable death rate of men during the preceding war, women began to assume positions of social, economic and political responsibility. The catch-phrase was that women had learnt "ihren Mann zu stehen", to replace men in all aspects of life. It is thus no coincidence that Fritz Raab's novel about Australia propagates the independence of a young woman in the professional sphere. Once again, the "exotic" serves to reinforce domestic needs. It is in this specific context that the strike threat of the shearers' union takes on its political significance. German unions have rarely reverted to strike action; to this day, it seems a morally dubious option. The "economic miracle" of Germany which began in the fifties was made possible largely by the cooperation of unions and the active recruitment of women into areas of national productivity. It is a "German" foreman who in genuine bewilderment asks the question: "Henry, glaubst du wirklich, die Gewerkschaftsleitung wird den Streik ausrufen?"(123) Betty, by now in charge of her father's station, is willing to appease the shearers. "Viel wichtiger ist," she reminds herself, "daß der Arbeitsfriede erhalten bleibt."(140) The term "Friede" (peace) itself has connotations few Germans in the fifties could remain insensitive to.

Striking is declared "unfair"(143) because it threatens an activity Germans consider of highest moral dimension: work. "Peace at work" must be preserved at all cost. The issue thus is not the payment of a bonus or an improvement of working conditions, but the very attitude to the sanctity of labour. The threatened shearers' strike is exposed as the manipulation of an antisocial traitor. Concrete sociopolitical conditions are depoliticised and "elevated" to a realm of emotional morality. Society is transformed into an almost spiritual "Gemeinschaft", a cultural community; the class struggle is replaced by a "Gefühl für Kameradschaft", a personal, private "solidarity". Social unrest is seen as an illness, a social infection which must be eradicated. Raab's Australian sheep farmers and shearers are social partners whose conflicts must be resolved "ohne Streit".(157)

This short novel for young adults is an ideological mouth-piece of the fifties, reflecting the work ethic in German-language countries in Europe. Its "adventure" consists of meeting the social and political challenge of the time — "die Bewährung an der Aufgabe".(173) *Betty und die 12 000 Schafe* is much more than a naive story for the young, an adventure tale from a far-away continent. The very title, with its reference to large figures an implied wealth, gives a clue to its underlying social philosophy. The time has come for young women to join the process of national productivity, to take the place of their fathers and to take part in the creation of an "economic miracle". Raab decided to write a *Jugendbuch* and to select Australia as its setting. But in writing a book for the young, he also addressed himself to the adult reader; and in opting for a dislocation of conflict, he merely followed a well-established pattern of German *Abenteuerliteratur* of domestic application. Australia is an antipodean reflection of contemporary social problems in the German-speaking nations of Europe.

FRANZ HUTTERER

Die große Fahrt des Richard Hook

Hutterer's work is one more narrative for young readers, or, as its subtitle defines it, "Eine Jugenderzählung von Treue, Kameradschaft und Wagemut". It fits neatly into Germany's economic and political awakening, the general *Aufbruchstimmung* of national reconstruction, during the fifties. *Die große Fahrt* (1959) stresses the loyalty of a son to his father who is wrongly accused of being a criminal. The author thus combines writing a fictional account of Sydney's early years of settlement with an implicit appeal to German adolescents to remain faithful to the "fatherland". For in this story Australia becomes, quite literally, Richard Hood's "fatherland" — the land to which his father is sent as a convict. Hutterer's young protagonist manages to smuggle himself aboard the brig "Norfolk" to join his father in his enforced resettlement in the colony of New South Wales. The novel follows the fortunes of father and son, free settlers and convicts, during their passage to Australia and eventual settlement in the new land. "Die große Fahrt" is a journey into regained innocence and freedom.

The author integrates his fictional plot into historical fact. Indeed, one of the strengths of this book is its quality of authenticity when dealing with historical data and descriptions. The account of Sydney in the year of 1795, a mere seven years after the settlement's foundation, is valid and precisely observed. The narrative invokes a different landscape from the devastated Germany after the Second World War, but the scene of a primitive beginning was familiar to its readers. Yet, for all the deliberate parallels and allusions, *Die große Fahrt* also records specifically Australian conditions and British-Australian relations. Hutterer's novel recaptures in fictional form parts of Australia's colonial history. Comparisons with post-war Germany are never made explicitly. It is the very choice of subject which invites them, as well as its historically correct preoccupations. Australia is celebrated as "ein Land der Zukunft"(8), the land of the future. Without labouring the analogy, the "great passage" to such a future of freedom and reconstruction carries with it prisoners ("Gefangene",10) of past conflicts. Richard's father is "unschuldig"(12), innocent of the crimes he has been accused of and punished for. The son's plan to clear his father's name or to stay close to him in his unjust defeat is transformed from expiation to a positive vision of a new beginning. The emigration from guilt carries its own triumph. "Treue" (faithfulness) is the key virtue for the young, if they want to help their fathers' cause. "Kameradschaft" is another vital prerequisite for conquering the past and building a better future; the author links the German concept with the emerging Australian values of mateship.

Hutterer's book ends with exonerated father and loyal son deciding to stay in Australia as "die neuen Siedler". Their remaining loyal to a land previously described as a place of "Verbrecher"(7) is in itself proof of moral integrity. To become "Australian" is the equivalent to leaving a European past of crime and guilt behind — especially where they have been exposed as unjust. Migration and settlement on the other side of the world is not quite the same as what came to be known in post-war Germany as "denazification", but in this book they amount to an expurgation or overcoming of a troubled past. The central theme of Franz Hutterer's narrative thus remains "the passage", although almost half of the book deals with the migrants' new life in Australia. Implicit parallels with the post-war German situation do not get in the way of detailed descriptions of historical circumstances.

The narrator's invocation of the Australian countryside follows the familiar pattern: it is largely a stock-taking of flora and fauna. Underneath the novel's juvenile entertainment lies a continuing political dimension which the reader may, or may not, appreciate. The inversion of seasons is interpreted as a broader opposition to European values and life-style. Hutterer's understanding of the Australian bush extends to its social consequences, and, in the broadest sense, to its political implications. That is very unusual in German-Australian literature, especially in adventure stories for the young.

It is perhaps not surprising, then, that Australia's native population too is dealt with in rather more sympathetic terms. The naive assumption of Europeans that the continent may have been uninhabited is ridiculed. Yet the near-genocide of the Aborigines has its roots in commercial exploitation and cultural disorientation, neither of which this book addresses. For all its tolerance and goodwill, Franz Hutterer's narrative reinforces the European fantasy that economic conquest and cultural colonialism can create a new innocence for those whose native people are steeped in guilt.

Chapter Four

Migrants, Adventure and Social Conscience: German Workmanship

"Haben Sie schon einmal darüber nachgedacht,
daß dem Menschen überall die Erde erst durch
Schweiß, Tränen und Blut zur Heimat wird?"
Kurt Lütgen, *Korroborri. Buschreiter in Australien*

THE SIXTIES

During the 1960s German-Australian literature continues to celebrate "new beginnings", treating the fresh start in a new land as an almost spiritual event, with missionary overtones. Part of this vision of migration and settlement is the morality of work. Figures of European colonists and explorers are drawn as mediators between Christian and Aboriginal spirituality, reflecting parallel attempts to reconcile a European concept of work for profit with an Aboriginal understanding of work for need.(*Kurt Lütgen*, 1960) Translations (from the English and the Dutch) illustrate that German authors follow a general pattern of writing about Australia: the "genre" is by now clearly defined and well-established, allowing at most for minor variations. Not only German writers found the range of travelogues, documentations or works of fiction about Australia frustratingly limited. Books appearing in German translation further demonstrate that the style of young adult fiction appears to be a general consequence of writing migrant novels or travelogues as the adventurous record of a learning process, a kind of second adolescence.(*Karel van der Geest*, 1960) Protagonists are usually around twenty years of age, designed to attract the interest of young and older readers alike. Australia itself is defined as an adventure. It includes an acceptance of social and racial diversification, an early statement of "multiculturalism". Australia is a place of social experimentation implying its own moral lesson. The strange character of the continent, its flora and fauna and the relationship between Aborigines and white Australians remain central themes. Some authors advocate a kind of enlightened tribal culture and a willingness on both parts to tolerate and to respect each other's values. The experience of migration is summarised as a transformation of consciousness and the realisation of cultural tolerance.(*Maria Wolkowsky*, 1961) Significantly, some German books subsequently appear in English translation. The perspective is no longer exclusively national.(*Wolkowsky, Kaufmann, Specht*) Novels dealing with explorers and settlers present the outback as a contest of existential dimension. The violence of the land is seen as inseparable from the freedom it offers. A special kind of intelligence and temperament characterises the Australian; German writers begin to appreciate such qualities more and more and show a new respect for Australian culture. On the other hand, German settlers are also drawn in more positive terms than before. The villain of a book can be an Australian whose bushcraft demonstrates a criminal survival which has its own history on this continent. The Australian challenge lies in the discovery of a new innocence and a new justice. It is no coincidence that authors frequently integrate variations of *Robinsonaden* into their fictional narratives: they serve to demonstrate the tension between Aboriginal and white Australian culture, a native and a foreign attitude to the land.(*Hans W. Ulrich*, 1963) The social and the spiritual complement each other in many interpretations of Australia. Travellers and settlers, migrants and native white Australians are presented as either "pilgrims" or "passengers". Attempts are made to link severe criticism of an "incomplete" Australian culture with a spiritual concept of non-identity. The result is a bewildering sociotheology, a judgemental bourgeois "vision" of German *Bildung*. It is expressed in an ambitious style of conceited mannerism, illustrating the inappropriateness of applying models of the post-war German novel to a vastly different subject. Symptomatic tendencies to "overwrite" indicate unresolved cultural conflicts, a continued alienation from Australian society.(*Alice Ekert-Rotholz*, 1964) Other authors choose a native Australian as protagonist, in search of his own country. Such a journey of cultural self-discovery is linked to the fate of an Aborigine. It is noticeable that the interference of whites in Aboriginal culture is perceived as a major social crime. More than before, German-Australian novels enter the discussion of cultural politics. An Australian social and political identity becomes inseparable from Aboriginal culture. (*Alfred Hageni*, 1964)

The socialist tradition of GDR authors reaches its height in the sixties and seventies: *Walter Kaufmann, Joachim Specht, Frederick Rose* and *Helmut Reim* offer their distinctive response to Australian social history and politics. The concept of a lived and living literature leads to a special interest in a genre of eye-witness narrative description: the reportage.(*Walter Kaufmann*) It continues a style perfected by *Egon Erwin Kisch* and suits the writers' preoccupation with social realism. The reliance on personal experience favours a leaning towards the autobiographical, although it is the paradigmatic nature of events which interests the socialist author. Often the model character of an experience is expressed in the precise and intense form of the short story. Specifically German problems are transferred to Australia, without losing their immediate social impact. The overcoming of the past and a political commitment to a new society involve an ideological conversion reflecting the writer's own life. Each book is a renewed ideological identification of its author. Conversion to communism in the Australian context places most of these works in the forties, so that many narratives are more or less fictionalised biographical retrospectives.(*Walter Kaufmann*) The experience of migration is presented as a social adventure. Discrimination against migrants is linked to the suppression of Aborigines: both assume the role of scapegoat in Australian social politics. Australia is not presented as an exotic destination of literary tourism, but as a place of political and ideological conflict. Anti-racist and anti-nuclear solidarity are endorsed as socialist responses to multinational capitalism and US military control over Australia.*(Joachim Specht)* Adventures are no more than the "pre-text" for a raising of consciousness and the propagation of socialist values. Anthropological and historical treatises serve the same function, as do travelogues and edited translations of Australian prose. They all aim to expose the contradictions of Australian capitalist society which are explained as a cultural lack of historical consciousness. A belief is articulated that Australian culture can only emerge in conflict, that its very nature consists of a struggle of liberation.(*Frederick Rose*, 1966) Australia's colonial history continues to be related to contemporary ideological conflicts between socialism and capitalism. Editorial skills serve social documentation. Australia's history is seen as reflecting European conflicts of power from the sixteenth to the nineteenth century. Glossaries and annotations add up to an authoritative interpretation of Australian history from a socialist position.(*Helmut Reim*, 1964) The GDR contribution to German-Australian literature lies primarily in the demythologising of Australia, in replacing the exotic *topoi* and stylistic clichés with concrete sociopolitical analyses. Even where it deals with Aboriginal mythology, it does so in restitution for a culture all but destroyed by white colonialism, capitalism and militarism.(*Ernst Adler*, 1966) The creative imagination of Australia's indigenous population is transmitted to demonstrate the diversity of cultural consciousness: intercultural mediation serves international socialism.

The delicate theme of German-Jewish relations is not expressed directly in a work by a German writer. Although *Kaufmann* and *Specht* know that not all German migrants were automatically anti-fascists, it is in the writings of a Hungarian-born, German-educated Australian Jew that anti-semitism is dealt with candidly and sensitively. *David Martin's Where a Man Belongs* (1969) is that kind of novel about Germany and Australia. It not only rejects the barbarism of German "culture" as a place where man may belong; he also fears for migrants, Jews and other "minorities" in an Australia which often projects its own identity in the aggression against those who have come to search for theirs.

As an oddity it should be noted that during the sixties (1967) the German-American author *Anna West* published a short story entitled "The Compound". It appeared in Clement Semmler's edition of *Coast to Coast 1965-1966* and was subsequently translated into German as "Der Wohnblock" and included in Frank Auerbach's anthology *Eine Frau im Busch und andere Erzählungen* (1970). Anna West migrated to Australia in 1964 and subsequently returned to the United States. It is quite clear that the setting and social criticism of her story relate to North America, and this makes the German editor's comment "Auch eine so unstete Biographie ist für die australische Literatur symptomatisch"(419) nonsensical. The poor literary quality of the work further reflects on Auerbach's judgement to include "Der Wohnblock" ("die einzige bisher veröffentlichte Arbeit der jungen Autorin", Ibid.) in his selection of 'Australian' narrative prose.

Kurt Lütgen

Korroborri. Buschreiter in Australien

As the title implies, Lütgen's novel (1960) centres around "bushriders" and Aborigines in the early nineteenth century.[1] It is, in one sense, a colonial narrative, combined with the theme of historical exploration. The new beginning is not merely a personal change of life, it is consistently interpreted as a service to mankind in general. Lütgen's protagonist is a pathfinder whose explorations prepare the way for European settlement, especially for those who are in need of a fresh start: the socially deprived and the politically persecuted. He shares a vision of European humanism and the revolutionary dream of freedom, but then learns that this concept of freedom is at the expense of Australia's indigenous population. The conflict of his vision is the subject of this book. The new beginning he explores is inseparable from the threatened end of Aboriginal culture. "New beginnings" is an expression of rebirth, regeneration and rehabilitation — for Europeans. Lütgen treats the new start in a new land as a spiritual event, with missionary overtones. The protection of Aborigines has to be accommodated within that quasi-religious and moral concept.

Lütgen's invocation of the Australian landscape relies heavily on similes, perhaps an appropriate style in a work of cultural mediation. Early in his narrative Lütgen debunks the central myth of Australian bushlife. Australia's bush is described in terms of European analogies which are themselves cultural mythologies: "wie ein Stück aus dem Totenland, aus der Unterwelt der Sagen".(32) This land is to be conquered "um Geld zu verdienen".(37) There is profit in the destruction of a foreign culture. This is the key philosophy of European colonisation. Missionary posts and military conquests serve the same economic purpose.

There is an unmistakable ambivalence in the author's attitude to work. More specifically, he is troubled by ownership and labour in a colony. It is a major question in the politics and ethics of migration. Many white settlers came to Australia because they were poor; the very motive for emigrating was to gain property and wealth. Work was the price to be paid for such sought-after reward; it became its moral precondition. The white settler's morality was based on the correlation of labour and wealth. Yet, all too soon there were workers and squatters among them; property was not distributed equally or fairly. Despite such inequality, the whites remained united in their determination to gain wealth at the expense of the Aborigines. Migrants from Europe saw themselves confronted with native migrants in Australia — and ironically used the tribal walkabouts and hunting migrations as justification for taking their land. The Aborigines' work is to hunt when they are hungry, but this possibility of work is taken from them by the work ethic of an imported European culture. The resulting cultural alienation is described in the very appearance of many natives: "Die meisten Schwarzen trugen zerlumpte und verschmutzte europäische Kleidung...".(89)

Criminal exploitation is transformed into narrative plot. Cultural disownment is enacted. Lütgen's hero pleads with his fellow white settlers to understand that if the natives have broken the white man's law, it was out of need. They can no longer do *their* work, to hunt when they are hungry.

Like Leichhardt, the migrant protagonist is haunted by the land: he is obsessed with its exploration, aware of the commercial value of his discoveries. There is, in addition, a distinctly metaphysical quality in this search for the unknown. Australian cattle-drives are reminiscent of the Boers' *Voortrekkers* in South Africa, a movement which became ideologised into the very identity of the white colonialists. German author and German reader remain sensitive to such parallels, especially since South-West Africa features as familiar territory in many German colonial novels and "adventure" books.

White explorations are seen as a tool in the hands of a Christian god; the good and brave man acts on behalf of his creator. Mastering life means following a higher will. The journey of discovery is revealed as a spiritual pilgrimage. Like Patrick White's Voss, Lütgen's protagonist is presented as a European colonist and explorer who tries to mediate between a Christian and an Aboriginal spirituality. The love of the land is a haunting call to discover a new home; Australia becomes a religious obsession. The "ownership" of such a spiritual home remains ambiguous: the European "work" of knowledge fuses with the Aboriginal "work" of need. Pilgrimage and corroboree endeavour to capture the spirit of the land. Remarkably, Kurt Lütgen remains sensitive to the native affinity expressed in the novel's title. White Australians remain "boundary riders", seeking ownership by profitable work.

Karel Van Der Geest

Stampfende Hufe

Although this novel is a translation — by Bruno Loets — from the Dutch, it deserves to be included in a history of German-Australian literature. One reason is its large edition; it was published by the Sigbert Mohn Verlag in 1960 and enjoyed extensive distribution. The other is the model-type treatment of Australian themes. *Stampfende Hufe* (1960) reinforces the impression that there is, for certain European writers, basically only one story about Australia, with prescribed ingredients, *topoi* and cliché characterisations. Writing about this country is like filming a western: the "genre" is clearly defined and well established, it allows at best for certain minor variations. It is worth following this paradigm in van der Geest's narrative, as it shows that not only German writers found the range of Australian travelogues, documentation or works of fiction frustratingly limited.

Like many German migrants, Dutch settlers continue to relate to the home they left behind. The place of birth remains home ("Nach Hause", 16, 277). Like Germans, the Dutch mourn the loss of their colonies, and the term "Kolonist" is used in an entirely positive sense. The author invokes a colonial atmosphere reminiscent of Dutch Indonesia when he describes the population of Alice Springs.(229) There is a variation of the "lost in the bush" theme when a plane crash complicates the plot.(251) The reader is told that by comparison with "Arbeitslosigkeit und Armut" in Holland, life in Australia has its advantages.(256) The hero's homecoming ("Heimkehr", 267) relates to his new country, while his parents leave for a trip home to their beloved Holland ("Nach Hause...Endlich — endlich wieder mal nach Hause!", 277). Two generations of migrants relate to a different concept of home. The son becomes an Australian, his parents remain Dutch settlers in Australia. *Stampfende Hufe* culminates in the joys of integration and the affirmation of a migrant's cultural origins.

It is as a model of the formula-type treatment applied to the concept of a survey of German-Australian adventures that van der Geest's popular novel takes its place in a survey of German-Australian writing. The very fact that it is a translation contributed to its representative character: many German prose works about Australia do in fact read like translations. They encounter most of the difficulties of cultural mediation, above all expressions, values and ideas distinctly native to a country and its people. The frequent appendices with lists of

Australian names, colloquialisms, phrases and sayings are a reflection of the awkwardness of the narrative style and bicultural reporting. Finally, van der Geest's *Stampfende Hufe* may be read by young and adult readers alike, a further characteristic it has in common with most German books on the subject. As German and Dutch culture are closely related, such similarities may not be surprising, but there is evidence that writers of other migrant cultures in Australia display comparable perspectives. A history of German-Australian literature would do well to bear that in mind. In a sense, the migrant is reduced to the level of a second adolescence, just as travelogues are essentially the record of a learning process. Writing about migration and settlement in a foreign country invariably leads to a style of young adult fiction.

Maria Wolkowsky

Australisches Abenteuer

This is a model travelogue-novel about Australia, its protagonist twenty years of age, designed to attract the interest of young and older readers alike. The "adventure" alluded to in the title is Australia itself, its landscape, nature and population. In the tradition of early publications about Australia, Maria Wolkowsky's book contains many photographic illustrations, drawings and sketches. They are an important part of the author's aim to describe an unusual country.[2] *Australisches Abenteuer* was first published in German; it appeared in the K. Thienemanns Verlag Stuttgart in 1961. Victor Gollancz London republished it in 1965 under the title *Australian Adventure*, in the author's own translation. In the English version the names of the protagonists are changed, and the plot is somewhat varied and extended. Whereas the German book ends in an appeal to (German) migrants to retain their cultural traditions and contribute them to an emerging Australian tradition, the English novel closes with an affirmation of Aboriginal culture and a vision of a harmonious, brotherly coexistence of whites and blacks. The final paragraph of *Australisches Abenteuer* reads like an early statement of the philosophy of "multiculturalism". Where the author addresses herself to an Anglo-Saxon readership, she is more concerned with the relationship between Australian settlers and the native population. She is concerned that the first Australians are not made to feel strangers in their own land. The vision of racial and cultural harmony may be naive, especially where it addresses itself to Aborigines living in the cities, but there can be no doubt about the integrity of the appeal. In both German and English, the "adventure" Australia carries with it a didactic concern, the dimension of a social experiment which contains its own moral lesson.

From a literary point of view, *Australisches Abenteuer* consists of a disarmingly transparent narrative formula, with little stylistic pretension. The novel employs most of the well-worn clichés of characterisation and plot. Wolkowsky introduces early the "lost in the bush theme"(cf. 147), complete with the obligatory rescue by an Aborigine. Wolkowsky seems to think that Australia's natives should remain within their stone age culture ("Ihr müßt dort bleiben, wo euer Platz wirklich ist.", 37), but does not consider the destruction of that very culture by the white man. She invokes a romantic vision of tribal life that is no longer possible. Her celebration of "Corroborees"(51) is part of the exotic to be found in Australia, an "adventure" worth observing. The author's sympathy for the Aborigines cannot be doubted, but it is the simplistic goodwill of a traveller collecting first impressions. The Aborigines are a vital part of the "otherness" of Australia, the "strange" nature of the land which makes a visit truly "adventurous".

Wolkowsky's long list of peculiarly Australian features, habits and values includes a full translation of "Waltzing Matilda", complete with sheet music.(61-64) The meaning of Australia's "inoffizielles National-Lied"(63) is explained in great detail. The author further describes the "Rundfunkklinik des Fliegenden Arztes"(58), the "Billy-Tee"(61), the "Platypus, Schnabeltier"(69), the "Kookaburras"(73), the "Tote Herz"(105), "Schafscheren"(114) and "das Tier, das aussieht wie ein lebender Teddybär", the "Koala"(141). It is the standard inventory of German-Australian travelogues. *Australisches Abenteuer* concentrates on two major themes: the strange character of the land and its people, and the relationship between white Australians and Aborigines. It is a clash of cultural consciousness and knowledge, rather than of cultures per se. The author seems to propagate a kind of enlightened tribal culture, aware of the ways of white Australians and willing to tolerate each other's values, occasionally utilising them for its own benefit. Maria Wolkowsky combines an early version of multicultural relations among the whites with a positive and respectful preservation of Aboriginal culture, allowing for supportive contacts between all Australians. Yet in this vision the land itself retains the mystery and exotic quality which inspired her to write the book. At the heart of *Australisches Abenteuer* lies the experience of a changed perspective, a transformation of consciousness, the realisation of cultural tolerance. Strangeness and affinity are Australian correlatives. To settle in this land means to bring to it native cultural values — and to see them integrate into a broader culture, change and grow into a wider vision, adapt and transform into an Australian civilisation. Wolkowsky's protagonists do not return to Germany. They have become Australians without noticing it ("und wir, wir haben es gar nicht einmal gemerkt!",166). The young German migrants are anxious to contribute to an emerging culture, to help shape "nicht unsere, sondern Australiens eigene Tradition".(Ibid.) Maria Wolkowsky's narrative traces the early stages of cultural integration. The exotic is adopted and transformed into native qualities. *Australisches Abenteuer* is a migrants' book propagating the promise of change and the challenge of a new cultural identity. Unlike many other German-Australian writers, Wolkowsky does not dwell on cultural conflicts, but appeals to the migrant to find his place in a society which respects a diversity of values. That she includes the Aborigines in this multicultural vision of a native-migrant Australia is remarkable and sets her apart from the bulk of German-Australian writing.

HANS W. ULRICH

Notruf an alle

This narrative (1963) has all the usual ingredients of a German adventure tale about Australia: the gold-diggers, the bushfire, the "Never-never", the heroes lost in the bush and constant reminders of antipodean inversions, especially in flora and fauna. As it addresses itself to young readers in their teens, the didactic intent is ever present. The author precedes his novel with a map of North-West Australia and makes frequent use of explanatory footnotes or translations. Yet is must be conceded that Ulrich does capture typologies of Australian men living in the outback, and his description of a joint expedition of German and Australian entomologists offers revealing comments on various aspects of cultural and social contrasts.

The landscape of the North-West Australian outback is not only the setting of various adventures, but leads to an interpretation of Australian values and characteristics. The "Never-never-Land" is a place of cruel irony and brutal challenge. To live with and to outwit this country is a matter of survival and has determined Australian intelligence and temperament. The malice of the land has to be controlled by the spite of man. Ulrich's book is an attempt to balance the different kinds of wit and ingenuity that make up life in Australia. In particular, *Notruf an alle* presents the difference between a moral and a criminal resourcefulness in man. The outback thus reveals or identifies human qualities, it measures the particular kind of intelligence which guarantees survival. Freedom and the risk of losing one's life are inseparably linked and make up the special excitement felt by those who choose to live in the Australian bush or desert. Ulrich conveys some of the violence of this land, but also the love it can inspire, a kind of desperate, passionate loyalty.

Writing about a little-known, far-away country still means giving priority to factual information (even if it could be found in similar publications of earlier dates), around which any fictional plot and characterisation must move. This precedence often leads to a certain heavy-handedness and transparency in the construction of the narrative. What is noteworthy is the author's programmatic attempt to draw parallels between Australia and Germany. Writing about another country invites searching for contrasts and resemblances; the foreign place is used to reflect on the seemingly familiar. Travelogues are, in that sense, compositions of self-alienation. Ulrich stresses the Australians' casualness (35), thereby reminding his readers of the very formal character of German social behaviour. What matters most is an Australia which challenges Germans — especially young Germans — to prove their stamina and ability to work. There are, in most travelogues and novels about Australia, strong overtones of the German *Bildungsroman* (pedagogic novel). Travelling to, or living in, Australia leads to the hero's self-fulfilment; he triumphs over the adversity of not being at home. It is no coincidence that Ulrich's protagonist remembers a family of his neighbourhood who had migrated to Australia but returned after two years disillusioned and disappointed. Going to a foreign country, even settling there, is seen by many Germans as an existential challenge on a socio-philosophical or even theological level. It is this attitude which may still determine the special nature of German integration and assimilation in Australian society.

Ulrich's account of Aborigines lacks depth, but is not without sympathy. He does refer to a "kindliche Geisterglaube", a childlike belief in ghosts adhered to by the natives, but he also stresses their lack of interest in any possessions. The author draws attention to the seemingly insurmountable conflict between the work culture of the white man and the free lifestyle of Aboriginal tribes. There is thus a conflict between the novel's work morale, presented as the challenge of surviving in a foreign country, and the natural freedom of a native population. In terms of presenting Australia's Aborigines, the author is restricted in the praise he may bestow upon them, without losing the central didactic purpose of his narrative. The discussion of race is inseparable from the concept of "the Australian challenge". The White Australia Policy of the past encouraged such equation. As Ulrich states: "Jeder Australier betrachtete den Erdteil als 'weißen Mannes Land', denn die Urbevölkerung starb mehr und mehr aus."(59)

Entomological research into the state of termites takes up a vital part of this novel, addressed to young Germans. The analogy should not be stretched, but Ulrich himself refers to "von Menschen geschaffene Staatswesen"(70), thus encouraging a reading of implied reference to Germany. Nor would it allow merely an allusion to one part of post-war Germany. The young German migrant, Jürgen Wenk, promptly comments: "Aber...das ist doch die Idee des kommunistischen Staates, Herr Doktor."(Ibid.)

It is interesting that the villain of Ulrich's narrative is an Australian. It allows the author to present some of the negative qualities of a country he otherwise admires. The Australian personifies the malice, spite and knavery of the outlaw who has conquered this land in his own manner. He is responsible for bushfires, a thief and a murderer. His "bushcraft" demonstrates a criminal art of survival which has its own history in Australia.

Ulrich does not resist the temptation to integrate his own *Robinsonade* into the wider confines of the novel. The chapter "Das Wrack" is an updated version of the theme. Rescued by a native (an unmistakable reminiscence of Hans Bertram's earlier *Flug in die Hölle*), the novel's protagonist is able to expose the false Australian and wrong kind of survival in this land. The hero thus redefines and reembodies the nature of "the Australian challenge". He personifies a new innocence and a new justice. The research expedition now reveals its true meaning: it helped rediscover a brave new, work-oriented man who has come to Australia misunderstood and misjudged, but leaves the country a true model hero for young Germans. "Wir haben Ihnen bitter Unrecht getan," the leader of the scientific expedition assures Jürgen.(147) It is difficult to ignore the designed implication for a rejuvenated, economically vigorous Germany.

HELMUT REIM / JOHN MORGAN / WILLIAM BUCKLEY

Ein australischer Robinson

Helmut Reim is one of a group of GDR writers concerned with the introduction of Australian life and letters to German socialist society. Among his credits are a translation of the writing of Banumbir Wongar (together with Elfi Schneidenbach and Hannelore Winter) and various annotations of publications about Australia. His translation of John Morgan's *The Life and Adventures of William Buckley* (1852) is an expression of his commitment to Australian culture. It is much more than a mere translation; apart from an extensive introduction, it includes an authoritative commentary integrated into the narrative. The title page describes Reim's contribution as "Übersetzung und Bearbeitung", — translation and adaptation. The book thus is a model case of cultural mediation and forms part of the GDR's remarkable interest in Australian themes, especially where they touch upon relations between white colonists and Aborigines.

The importance of *Ein australischer Robinson* (1964)[3] therefore lies less in making a literary and cultural curiosity accessible, praiseworthy as such undertaking may be, but rather in the wealth of information contained in its extensive glossary and the socialist interpretation of Australian history presented in the foreword, introduction and annotations. Reim's knowledge of Australia shines through most of his comments and explanations. He motivates the publication of the book by placing it firmly in the colonial history of the state of Victoria and its capital Melbourne. Buckley was witness to important historical events; he thus assumes the significance of a representative character belonging to the pre-colonisation period. Reim thereby turns the literary topos of the "Robinsonade" upside down: instead of an apolitical withdrawal from society it serves as a means of historical and social orientation. It is significant that the Aboriginal tribe of Wathaurungs, offering life and shelter to the white convict, did not survive the colonisation of Australia. It is the experience of witnessing the arrival of the first white settlers and the establishment of sheep and cattle stations by English squatters, driving Aborigines off their land, which makes Buckley's "adventures" among white and black Australians of paradigmatic importance. Reim thus introduces him as "ein wirklicher, historisch verbürgter Robinson Crusoe" whose fate as adopted member of a primitive tribe reflects upon the aspirations and effects of an emerging European society in Australia.(6) Significantly, Reim informs his readers, Buckley became respected by the Aborigines only towards the end of his stay with them, when an invention of his contributes to the maintenance of the tribe. This is not the same as the later commercial exploitation of the land by white settlers. Rather it is, in line with socialist values, a personal effort to secure a better living for the collective. His social standing among the whites at the end of his "Robinsonade" is very different. After the colonists have exploited his knowledge of the land and the native population, Buckley becomes "dispensable"; like the Aborigines, he now stands in the way of an emerging squattocracy. It is impossible for him to make a meaningful contribution to white society. Reim thus illustrates the exploitative nature of capitalism and the supportive character of (tribal) socialism. Australia's colonial history serves to demonstrate the continued conflict between two ideologies. Buckley is the proletarian anti-hero whose personal history illustrates the fate of someone who is a political "Robinson": his life story has model character for readers in a socialist society.

Along with such political interpretation, Helmut Reim offers a well-informed analysis of *Ein australischer Robinson* as an adventure novel. He compares it with Defoe's classic tale, stressing that William Buckley does not encounter an "imaginären Freitag"(6) who offers himself as his servant. From his socialist perspective it is of great importance that the hero does not himself exploit the services of someone else. He further likens Buckley to Grimmelshausen's Simplicissimus and to Cooper's Pathfinder ("Lederstrumpf"), or rather, his historical model Daniel Boone. Like Simplicissimus, Buckley is a naive, uneducated, enterprising young peasant who survives a long list of adversities by good fortune and ingenuity. Reim draws a parallel between Daniel Boone's leaving of Kentucky and William Buckley's departure from the colony of Victoria for Van Diemen's Land. In both cases the protagonist leaves the scene of his trials and achievements to spend the remaining years of his life in meagre circumstances elsewhere. There is no reward for mediating between natives and white settlers.

Reim wishes to preserve the character of an old travelogue ("den Charakter eines älteren Reisewerkes",8), treating the work as an historical document. His editorial skills are to serve a social documentation; it therefore goes beyond philology, the retention of contemporary names, spellings and expressions. Along with these authentic qualities of an historical travelogue Reim seeks to present ethnographic data of an Australian tribe of Aborigines. The communal life-style of these natives is seen as an integral part of the social model adopted by the protagonist. Buckley's unscientific but valuable observations of the tribal life of the Wathaurungs amounts to the only documentation of an extinct people. "Eingestreut in Buckleys Memoiren kommen sie in ihrer Gesamtheit einer wenn auch lückenhaften Stammesmonographie gleich."(9) Individual biography and tribal monograph complement each other. It is this perspective which is of interest to the socialist author. The "adventures" of William Buckley consist of his failed attempt to live two different lives: that of the landowners, colonists or migrant settlers and that of a native community in which only collective ownership holds any value.

Helmut Reim's Introduction presents a twenty-page survey of Australian history, from the arrival of the First Fleet to the present day. It may be read as an authoritative interpretation from a socialist position and is therefore of major importance in the context of German-Australian literary relations. German GDR authors writing about Australia respond to this assessment of white settlement of the continent. Reim warns against various attempts to come to terms with Australia by applying slogans unsupported by factual knowledge. He laments the unavailability of "populärwissenschaftliche Bücher und Reisebeschreibungen über Australien".(Ibid.) Widespread ignorance of the continent in the GDR is therefore to be expected. Yet Australia's history, the author argues, reflects European conflicts of power from the sixteenth to the nineteenth century. Once again, it is the model character of Australia which motivates the GDR author's interest. It is the long-sighted end of Europe's social and political binocular, presenting an historically paradigmatic development at a distance. Australia illustrating, at a "safe" distance, the power and class struggles of Europe motivates GDR writers' interest in this country. Reim argues that the first period of Australian history is in fact part of British history. The GDR author has little difficulty relating Australia's colonial history to contemporary ideological conflicts between socialism and capitalism. His interest in the figure of William Buckley lies in the paradigmatic nature of his "adventures". Throughout Buckley's narrative Reim offers his own authorial annotations or editorial intrusions, so much so that virtually half of the book is made up of Helmut Reim's writing. It is quite legitimate, therefore, to speak of *Ein australischer Robinson* as very largely his own work. (On another level it may be considered somewhat risky to base a far-reaching interpretation on the alleged dictation of an illiterate man, rewritten and translated: Reim is editor, author, translator, interpreter, critic and cultural historian in one.) Reim's annotations show extensive and reliable historical research and do not shy away from lengthy background information to explain Buckley's motivations and predicaments. Often Reim interrupts the narrative with literary cross references, such as when he calls barking "dogs" or dingoes an essential requisite whenever Australian literature tries to invoke the melancholy loneliness of the bush. He refers to Stephan von Kotze's humorously revealing comment on this *topos* of Australian writing: in 253 bush ballads there were "253 klagende Dingos am Rande des Grabes...und heulten".(55) The author further offers reliable information on the life-style of Aborigines, especially on their spiritual culture. Flora and fauna are explained, frequently with references to German-language publications. Most of the commentary concerns the history of Australian settlement and Aboriginal culture. Occasionally it offers detailed anthropological data (such as fishing methods among the Wathaurungs, "die wahrscheinlich die kulturgeschichtlich älteste Form des Angelns nicht nur in Australien, sondern überhaupt verkörpert",87). Significantly, Reim includes a lengthy bibliography (267-268), underlining the "non-fiction" character of the book, in particular its Marxist-Socialist methodology and its historical, anthropological and scientific assertions. His Postscript ("Nachwort") is an exhaustive survey of anthropological, geological, botanical and zoological features of Australia, relying frequently on Soviet research. It forms a major part of Reim's contribution to German-Australian relations. The accessibility of Soviet Russian publications and findings is not the least of this book's qualities.

To indicate the extent of Helmut Reim's original work associated with the translation of John Morgan's *The Life and Adventures of William Buckley* it may be of interest that of the 237 pages of text, more than half is made up of editorial comment. This proves that the original is little more than a "pre-text", a point of reference, an historical and literary document, used to interpret Australian social history. Reim's analysis along socialist lines updates what could otherwise have been read as an excursion into literary and exotic antiquarianism. The aim of *Ein australischer Robinson* is not to salvage a literary curiosity, nor to glorify the adventures of a social outsider. It rather amounts to a programmatic interpretation of contemporary Australian society and as such is an essential background document for other GDR works on the subject, fictional or non-fictional.

ALFRED HAGENI

Zauber im australischen Busch

In this novel it is not a German traveller or migrant, but a native Australian who explores the country and its people. Hageni draws attention to the fact that many Australians know little of their own land. His protagonist undertakes "Entdeckungsfahrten" on which he experiences things he previously had only heard about, visiting parts of the continent known to him merely as names or images. The vastness of Australia motivates his curiosity. After a period of discovering parts of his native country he is determined to return to the bush and earn a living. Like the great European tour, travelling around Australia has been an obsession for many Australians. Both journeys are part of a cultural self-discovery at a time of increasing national consciousness. Hageni links his protagonist's search for self-knowledge to the fate of a young Aborigine. The consciousness of the white Australian is inextricably correlated to that of his black charge. The interference of whites in Aboriginal culture is seen as a major social crime and forms the central theme of the novel. Harry is responsible for Joey's expulsion from his tribe. The "magic" of the Australian bush alluded to in the title is not the wonder and beauty of nature but the witchcraft of native medicine-men capable of banishing a tribal initiate from his indigenous environment. The topic of the novel is not romantic, but a study of cultural alienation in one's own land.

According to the publisher's blurb, *Zauber im australischen Busch* (1964) deals with "die Gegensätze und Widersprüche" of Australia. The author[4] made a conscious attempt to redefine a country which had already attracted an extraordinary list of slogans, especially in the history of German-Australian literature: "Das Land des Selbstmordes", "Das Land der Zukunft", "Der menschenscheue Kontinent", "Das Land des sozialen Wunders", "Das Land der lebenden Fossilien", "Der Kontinent des Goldes..., des goldenen Vlieses,..., des goldenen Weizens" and "Das Land der Gegensätze". Hageni's concept of Australia is epitomised by the Aboriginal term "woomera". He writes about a continent of contrasts and contradictions, not only in its flora and fauna, but also in its social history and cultural values. His refreshing approach to choose an Australian hero reveals the voice of the narrator as non-Australian, thus establishing a kind of imaginative critical dialogue as part of his very fiction.

There is a special touch, then, in the Australian's residence as tenant of a migrant couple, the Danagys, in one of the western suburbs of Sydney. The native Australian son finds his temporary home with "Neuaustralier"(45) and looks for his home and identity in the company of a young Aborigine. It presents the question of an Australian self-concept in an unusually progressive context, especially for a German writer of the early sixties. There are in this novel strong, if inconsistent, overtones of class-oriented social criticism, ultimately negated by the protagonist's return to his father's capitalist cattle station. Yet the contradictory endorsement of cattle breeding as a kind of "working class" alternative to academic training for capitalist middle class professions reflects not only on a notorious Australian anti-intellectualism, it also keeps alive the myth of individual self-discovery as a worker in the bush. The squattocracy is traditionally recruited by jackeroos discovering their Australian identity before taking up an inherited wealth. Hageni's protagonist follows this path precisely. In his life, too, capitalism and ownership come after the discovery of a cultural self. His Aborigine companion is an important part in this journey of discovery.

Much of the novel is concerned with what might be called the Australian's cultural education. More specifically, he is shown to grow into a predefined national myth. That, too, is "Zauber im australischen Busch". It is a land described as left to itself and following rules of its own making. The significance of this account cannot be overrated, for much of Australia's cultural identity is derived from it. To be left alone and to form oneself by one's own laws has remained an Australian ideal. It explains the anti-historical, insular attitude of "true" Australians, the reliance on myth and "magic in the bush". Although in a different way from the Aborigines', the native flora and fauna in its exotic, almost fossilised character are merely the back-drop to this mythological drama, a kind of sign language serving as means of orientation. Even the bushfire fulfils the function of establishing or verifying a cultural identity: "Ein Buschbrand gehörte zum Leben eines Buschmannes wie der Busch selber."(116) It forms part of the "Zauber im australischen Busch", an experience identifying the Australian, in much the same way as the Aborigine derives his identity from a totem. Black and white means of identification are not very different in the Australian bush.

It is the land which heals both young men, the black and the white Australian. Yet it is a transformation with different consequences. The narrator emphasises that the land's didactic healing power is unobtrusive but lasting. The bush is also the white Australian's "Traumland". When the young hero returns to his "wirkliche Leben", it is to his father's cattle station "Air-Beef" and the commercial exploitation of the land. The native leaves his European clothes near a tree and returns to a different kind of "real life". The Aborigine remains true to the "magic of the bush", whereas the young white Australian "uses" it to assume an identity which allows him to exploit its commercial potential. Yet in his marketing the white Australian retains a (contradictory) affinity with the bush. He derives his Australian identity and part of his national myth from the "Eigenart des Landes". Alfred Hageni thus has given his narrative an unusual dimension of cultural politics which has lost none of its relevance. His *Zauber im australischen Busch* is unusual in not having any German characters. It is much more than merely another "Australian adventure". The novel attempts an imaginative discussion of an Australian culture and, derived from it, an Australian social and political identity. Its importance lies in having put the question, in liberating itself from the repetitive and rhetorical slogans of journalistic or impressionistic travelogues.

ALICE M. EKERT-ROTHOLZ

Die Pilger und die Reisenden. Roman aus Sydney

Die Pilger und die Reisenden (1964) strives for elegance and critical awareness; in fact, it does it so strenuously that it may be said to suffer from heavy-handed pretension and a hyperconstruction projecting a complexity of social and philosophical reflection the novel does not in fact possess. Certain key phrases or quotations, often from classical

European literature, are structurally formalised and presented as experiential formulae, expressed as variations of individual narrative personae. Unfortunately, the author lacks the skill to lend each narrator a distinctively personal voice. As a result, the elaborate composition of a concerto of narrative instrumentation is exposed as authorial monologue. Although there is little divergence in the actual tone of voice, Ekert-Rotholz heads various sections of her chapters with musical titles invoking European culture. The formal structure of the novel appears superimposed to enact certain key themes. It is an unwitting admission of the artificiality of her own narrative. All too obvious repetitions alienate the reader who quickly grows tired of characters being sacrificed to the ambitions of thematic structure.

Unlike most German authors, Ekert-Rotholz does not hesitate to criticise Australian society. In fact, *Die Pilger und die Reisenden* aims to be a critical portrait of social relations in this country. The author's criticism can be sharp, even bitter. The cult of youthful exuberance is exposed as brutal suppression. Ekert-Rotholz repeatedly attacks Australians' hostility towards migrants. The attitude is seen as part of a defensive hierarchy of recent settlers: as the whole country consists of migrants, the most recent arrivals find themselves at the bottom of the social order. The author draws analogies between the country, the cities and the people. She links the ambivalence towards the adopted country, especially the fear of its darker sides, to the cult of mediocrity and approximation ("she'll be right"). Australians, Ekert-Rotholz argues, do not seek precise knowledge. "Wir sind zu schnell mit uns zufrieden," says John(32), motivating the complacency of most of his fellow-countrymen. To have a little knowledge is enough. Anything more is dangerous.

The migrants in this novel resent an absence of history in their new country. Yet their reactions range from passionate over-identification to critical rejection.

Perhaps understandably, there is a general uncertainty in the stylistic level of Ekert-Rotholz's narrative. The desire to apply European sophistication to a novel about Australian society is not without its grotesque instances. The author is on safer grounds when she writes about the alienation of post-war migrants. Frequently Ekert-Rotholz employs a pseudo-religious and "poetic" language while trying to describe a social process. The novel's title sets the tone. Its language fluctuates unhappily between the "visionary" and the "clever" manipulation of trivial best-sellers. The work suffers from a severe stylistic unevenness. The author comments: "In diesem Kontinent waren alle gleich gut oder gleich mittelmäßig"(156), but her own writing strives vehemently to be startlingly different. It would have been stimulating to compose a novel about Australia in exclusively European, i.e. German, style and perspective. But Ekert-Rotholz adopts what she believes to be Australian narrative features and "assimilates" them into her bourgeois "vision", without achieving the kind of tension and conflict which could have expressed the cultural and sociopolitical problems of European migrants settling in this country. Only very occasionally does she try to convey such conflict in other than rhetorical effects. When describing the city named in the subtitle of her work Ekert-Rotholz invokes an "exotic" reading of Aboriginal mythology. It is a characteristically awkward mixture of European and Aboriginal-Australian imagery and style, the kind of pseudo-poetic metaphorical narrative which makes her open the chapter "Eine Stadt wie Sydney" with the botched analogy: "Nach Annes Abreise war Rigby so frei wie der Kookaburra im Busch — nur lachte er nicht so viel."(191) Nor is such comparative imagery an isolated instance. In the final chapter of the Second Book she writes: "Candy wußte genauso viel wie ein neugeborener Koalabär."(245) The "local content" of her narrative style continues to lead her astray.

Alienation from European (literary) culture rarely manifests itself in deliberate stylistic form, apart from occasional chapter headings. The author misses the artistic opportunities of manifesting cultural alienation as a vital quality of her narrative craft. European culture is merely quoted as a point of reference, almost as an alibi. The novel plays on the formal difference between design and execution, first and final version, "Entwurf und Ausführung". It is further evidence of conflict in the act of narration, culminating in the revealing statement "Kein Entwurf — Ausführung"(275). The novel's formal design is not fully recognisable in its final version, the execution of the work appears to have overruled any coherent conceptual structure. Yet the quality of the actual narrative does not seem to address itself to anyone. Racism, arrogance and kitsch come together in a disturbing mixture of literary insensitivity. The author's cultural criticism of Australia remains journalistic.

All ("jeder") Australians, the author argues, derive their self-concept from an emotional and cultural home elsewhere. Ekert-Rotholz continually argues that no proper development of an Australian identity has taken place and that no migrants can commit themselves to an "incomplete" culture. She totally rejects the possibility that it may well be this very incompleteness which could allow newcomers to take part in the definition of an identity in the making and accept this active participation as "Australian". The only possible paraphrasing of an "Australian" quality she tentatively accepts is summed up in her comment: "In Australien war alles anders...".(341) Her criticism of Australian culture is scathing. Referring to a press obsessed with crime and sport, she notes: "Die Presseleute waren zu intelligent, um es nicht selbst zu wissen. Sie schrieben in der Hauptsache für die Abonnenten — ein altes Lied in einer jungen Zivilisation."(362) It takes a special kind of confidence to assert that such journalism is not practised in Europe, especially in Germany. Such attacks form part of the novel's central theme that Australia is a place of non-identity. The search for identity is not recognised as a means of orientation. The European migrant assumes the existence of a predefined white Australian culture and finds himself at a loss when he discovers that a national cultural identity exists only as a search, a quest, a pilgrimage — as something still in the making. The "traveller" is asked to relate to the "pilgrim". Ekert-Rotholz does not explicitly state what she frequently implies, namely that the very obsession with a ready-made cultural identity is a European fallacy, a fixation based on a static concept of culture.

Alice Ekert-Rotholz's novel *Die Pilger und die Reisenden* bears the sub-title "Roman aus Sydney". It is a confused and confusing novel, struggling to express a vision as well as the cultural alienations of a European writer of travelogues. The author herself is part "pilgrim", part "traveller"[5] who, like her hero, the architect Rigby, designs a city in which all formal aspirations give way to a crude directness of casual accommodation. Her Sydney novel tries to construct a poetic bridge expressing thoughts of steel, a cultural mediation of imaginative understanding. It is a spectacular failure, leaving the reader to discover his own city of vision.

Ernst Adler

Die Legende vom Bumerang

Writers from the German Democratic Republic have shown a special interest in the culture of Australia's Aborigines. Their socialist ideology interprets the fate of natives in a global context of capitalist expropriation. The Aborigines thus form part of a world-wide struggle for liberation. Capitalism and racism are seen as correlated. The destruction of Aboriginal culture, the suppression and exploitation of Australian natives as cheap labour form the subject of many publications about Australia, both fiction and non-fiction. The GDR was among the first to feature the translated work of "Banumbir Wongar" (Bahumir Wongar). Eberhard Brüning claims of Wongar:

> Es ist daher weder zufällig noch verwunderlich, daß das eigentliche Zentralthema der Erzählungen Wongars die Zerstörung der natürlichen Umwelt und der Lebensbedingungen der Ureinwohner durch monopolkapitalistische Profitsucht ist.[6]

It is this concern which motivates much of what GDR's own writers have to say about Australia (Joachim Specht, Walter Kaufmann, Frederick Rose). Ernst Adler presents his adaptations of Aboriginal legends and myth in this wider context. Along with a critical appraisal of the labour movement in this country, the Aborigines are the central theme of GDR writing about Australia. The destruction of a culture by capitalist profiteering has ideological implications reaching beyond the specific example. Socialist authors deal with Australia as a model. Adler's collection is an attempt to help restore or record a vital part of Aboriginal culture. Its very existence is an indictment of Australian collusion with multinational capitalism. Politically, it is conceived as an act of solidarity with a people suppressed by anti-socialist forces.

The author's introduction leaves no doubt about the political dimensions of his book. Adler calls the decimation of Australia's native population from around 350 000 in 1780 to about 30 000 pure-bred and approximately 50 000 half-castes some two hundred years later "den ärgsten Schandfleck in Australiens Geschichte".(5) The shame of white Australia lies at the centre of *Die Legende vom Bumerang* (1966). It presents the naive beauty of a culture largely destroyed by colonialism, capitalism and militarism. Maralinga features prominently in Ernst Adler's accusations. Together with mining leases, testing for atomic research has led to the most extreme forms of cultural disorientation, he explains. He does not specifically refer to the first atomic explosion conducted in Australia in September 1956, alluding instead to Woomera's testing ground for British rockets. No mention is made of the nearby joint United States/Australia Defence Space Communications Centre. Walter Kaufmann and Joachim Specht have been more specific in their exposure of nuclear testing and its effects on the native population.

Adler describes the Aborigines as "Menschen, die...Opfer der Gier und Grausamkeit ihrer Unterdrücker geworden sind".(7) He stresses their ability to adapt to coexisting with the white man. Their Stone Age culture does not prevent them from living in the twentieth century, if proper nutrition, medical assistance and education are provided. However, Adler accuses the Australian authorities of not having done enough in this area. "Man braucht die Eingeborenen als billige Arbeitskräfte," he reports, "als Saison- und Gelegenheitsarbeiter".(Ibid.) The exploitation of their labour links them to the international working class; in 1966, Adler points out, they did not enjoy any civic rights and thus did not have the protection of medical insurance or pension. Racial suppression, he argues, invariably leads to cheap recruitment of labour. Any form of racism is thus a major concern of socialism. Adler goes so far as to speak of a "Rassenfanatismus" in Australia, based on "kolonialistische Habgier".(8) He does not shy away from didactic moralising, occasionally adopting the general rhetoric of a politician or a preacher. His appeals are directed as much at GDR readers as at white Australians. The author is motivating the writing of his book, justifying it ideologically as a task of international socialism.

Adler makes an interesting point when he draws attention to the fact that in Aboriginal myths and legends there are no "evil" animals, an essential ingredient of most fairy-tales in other cultures. It is debatable whether it makes sense to speak of "australische Märchen"(Ibid.), given the European, and specifically the German, history of that concept. It could even be argued that Adler turns against his own reasoning on the political nature of his collection when he states that these Aboriginal "Märchen" are for young readers.

Ernst Adler reminds his readers that he has lived in Australia for many decades. Like Banumbir Wongar (Sreten Bozic), he claims to have had close contacts with Aborigines. The stories of his collection are presented as a record of his friendship with the natives. Adler hints at some cultural editing in his translations when he speaks of attempts to make these "fairy-tales" accessible to German readers, especially the young. It is fair to say that Adler's renditions read as authentic. There is, however, a certain self-consciousness in the manner of their presentation. Adler presents a documentation of "fairy-tales", an anthropological documentation of cultural myths. Yet he himself retains throughout the posture of a German "Märchenonkel", someone who entertains the young by telling fairy-tales. In that pose lies his cultural mediation — and alienation. The narrator Adler is almost always a part of the stories he tells (cf. "Heute will ich euch von einem Stammesführer namens Wakulikuli berichten...", 24). He bears witness, authenticates, verifies. In that sense his book is as much a travelogue as anything else, with the difference that Adler offers a subjective documentation of a threatened native culture in a foreign land. In some stories it becomes impossible to distinguish between the Aboriginal voice and the German narrator. Strictly speaking, it is almost always the German author telling the story of an Aboriginal narrator, a kind of "double I" perspective, which characterises Ernst Adler's *Legende vom Bumerang*. His meta-narrative style creates special perspectives, mostly didactic in purpose. The I is an inseparable part of the myth, even though it, too, can prepare the listener for the purpose or theme of its story. The point is that Ernst Adler's collection frequently does not distinguish between the various kinds of individual narration. As the Aborigines express their culture in a tribal identity, their collective I is a characteristic and authentic part of the legends. There is no doubt that the literary voice is distinctly European.

Die Legende vom Bumerang must thus be read as a document of imaginative identification, based on political solidarity with a suppressed culture. The author calls his writings "frei nacherzählt" (title-page), alluding to the ambivalence of their narrative voice. Readers will recognise in this volume an anthropological and literary rescue attempt, evidence of a distinctive culture worth defending and preserving. In its broader context Adler's book is an indictment of white Australia's capitalist and racist exploitation of a largely defenceless people. If profit should indeed be the motive for such genocide, this collection of "Märchen, Mythen und Legenden der australischen Ureinwohner" (subtitle) suggests that there are other benefits to be gained from keeping the expression of Aboriginal humanity alive. Their creative imagination can be transmitted to other people and add to an understanding of the diversity of cultural consciousness. German-Aboriginal communication is merely one example of such intercultural mediation. The political implications need no elaborating.

Frederick Rose

Ureinwohner, Känguruhs, Düsenclipper

Although originally written in English, this work (1966) belongs to the history of German-Australian literature. More specifically, Anneliese Dangel's translation fits into the special tradition of GDR writings about Australia. Frederick Rose is an Englishman from London who migrated to Australia in 1937 and returned to Europe in 1956, settling in Kleinmachnow near Berlin. He accepted a post as Professor of Anthropology at the Humboldt-University in Berlin and returned to Australia in 1962 to renew his anthropological research into Aborigines. Frederick Rose's identification with the German Democratic Republic is both ideological and professional. As a Communist, he considers the GDR "mein Zuhause".(8) But he also calls Australia the "Land meiner Wahl".(Ibid.) And on his occasional return visits to England he notes not merely alienation; he realises: "auch England war meine Heimat".(Ibid.) Like Walter Kaufmann, Rose worked for a year as a wharfie on the Sydney waterfront and like him, he found his social and political home among the solidarity of the waterside workers. Rose distinguishes between Menzies' Australia in which he was persecuted as a Communist (cf. 8) and the country of trade unionists and socialists which welcomes him back on his return visit. "Ja, ich war wieder zu Hause," the author comments, "und als mir Stan Moran meine Gewerkschaftskarte aushändigte, wurde mir klar, daß dies mein Australien war."(11) It is clear, then, that Frederick Rose's book about Australia offers an ideological perspective in accordance with his experience and political conviction.

On his return to the GDR he is asked to write a "Reisebuch" about his renewed impressions of Australia. The Communist anthropologist is aware of the challenge. He feels that his six-year absence has led to a kind of historical detachment, allowing him to see changes in Australia unnoticed by a total newcomer. Frederick Rose admits to a selective view of Australia, to his own special, professionally and ideologically determined perspective of the land "of his choice". Rose is an author who would have been called by German conservatives a "vaterlandslose Geselle", a migrant who continued to "migrate", who left his native England for a better life in Australia and left that country for his ideological home in the German Democratic Republic. His assessment of Australia thus gains a special significance, as it reflects the author's view of an intermediate, transitory state between capitalism and socialism.

In an historical survey Rose argues strongly for the emergence of an indigenous Australian culture. He resents the European arrogance of defining Australia as an intellectual desert. Among the representatives of a distinctly Australian literary culture he lists the authors Katherine Susannah Prichard, Frank Hardy, Dymphna Cusack and others whose works have been translated and appeared in the GDR. A central theme of Rose's book is the belief that Australian culture can only emerge in conflict, that its very nature consists of a struggle of liberation. Rose writes almost prophetically about the struggle of an emerging Australia theatre.(21) He is critical of Australia's secondary and tertiary education system, especially of the lack of university graduates in science and technology. Rose's Australia is a country of bourgeois materialism. He derives the class struggle of the sixties from his reading of Australia's short history. Paradoxically, he maintains, the lack of historical consciousness, the "Mangel an Geschichte"(25), brought about a number of further contradictions and conflicts. A country of barely two hundred years' history cannot achieve cohesion and consensus among its classes. They themselves have not become an historical force. The exploitation of convicts by the squattocracy seems to Rose a transference of European class war to the penal colony. Australia's 1848 "revolution", the Eureka Stockade, is seen as petty bourgeois and democratic, rather than socialist, but still as the force which raised a revolutionary consciousness among the workers. Rose reminds his readers that of the thirty-four casualties among the diggers, four were Germans and twenty Irish. He draws attention to the historical and ideological inconsistency that alongside the development of democratic unionism Australia's labour movement began to formulate its "White Australia Policy". The fact that the Labor Party carried this racist policy as part of its platform until 1965 Frederick Rose cites as an ideological absurdity and a lack of historical consciousness. In his brief historical survey he concentrates on the first *class* conflict of Australian workers with the employers from 1890 to 1894. He acknowledges the correlation between this struggle and the emergence of a new national consciousness in Australian literature at that time. The new social realism is interpreted as a political phenomenon, epitomised by Joseph Furphy's well-known definition: "Stimmung — demokratisch, Akzent — aggressiv australisch". Rose exaggerates the effectiveness of Australia's Communist Party, founded in 1920; the claim that only after that event "real progress" ("echte

Fortschritte",42) was made in the labour movement is wishful thinking. He is on safer ground in his assessment of the Great Depression in Australia, which defines the emergence of the so-called New Guard as an Australian form of fascism ("eine australische Form des Faschismus",45). His report on Egon Erwin Kisch's activities in 1934 forms part of the history of labour in Australia, concentrating on the working class's anti-fascist stance against the Attorney-General R. G. Menzies. "Menzies," Rose writes, "war der Inbegriff der Reaktion und Fortschrittsfeindlichkeit in Australien."(48) His writing about the defeat of the Labor Government in 1949 carries the special excitement of personal experience. The author has by now become an eye-witness and, indeed, a participant in the historical struggle. Menzies' attempts to outlaw the Communist Party of Australia are described as a "Musterbeispiel echt faschistischer Gesetzgebung".(48) As a party member Rose experiences political persecution. The Petrov-Affair is seen as "die nächste Runde im Kampf gegen die Partei".(50) Like Walter Kaufmann, it led Frederick Rose to turn away from the intellectual section to the proletarian base of the party. In November 1954 he joined the Sydney Waterside Workers' Union. Kaufmann wrote a short story about the wharfies' support of Indonesia's struggle for independence. Rose comments: "Typisch für den Einfluß der Hafenarbeiter auf das politische Leben Australiens war ihre Rolle 1945 bei der Unterstützung des indonesischen Unabhängigkeitskampfes."(53) They share the same experience of international solidarity and "die Solidarität der Hafenarbeiter gegenüber Farbigen".(Ibid.) Rose and Kaufmann undergo the same political education in Australia; they are contemporaries, compatriots and comrades in the same struggle. His return in 1962 to these waterside workers is thus more than a gesture, it is the renewal of an ideological commitment. (Disappointingly, Rose does not extend his political analysis beyond the dock workers' strike of January 1956. It is fair to say that the Australian Communist Party never regained the prominence it held during the thirties and forties. Frank Hardy's disenchantment with the party led to the publication of his autobiographical look back in anger, *But the Dead Are Many* [1975].) The early part of *Ureinwohner, Känguruhs, Düsenclipper* makes the most interesting reading, although Rose's later sections retain the energy of individual experience and personal commitment.

The narrative style is largely episodic, occasionally anecdotal. Rose's habit of incorporating biographical sketches of Australian characters adds to the historical authenticity of his book, while at the same time drawing a composite picture of legendary or mythological figures personifying the "exotic" and eccentric aspects of life in the bush. The author captures the spirit of life in the outback, both of the land and of its special people. Not surprisingly, the anthropologist writes with special authority on the Aborigines, discussing their plight both in general culture and in specifically political terms. Aboriginal culture is threatened by contemporary capitalism, more precisely by a "Kolonialismus in seiner spezifisch australischen Form".(106) Detribalisation is a continuing process which had its beginning with the arrival of the white man in this country. Rose consistently refers to the Aborigines as "die Australier".(123) His anthropological observations are written in popular language, retaining an episodic style. He conveys a wealth of scientific information in eminently readable form and links his reports to political comments of great urgency.

There is a certain parallel between Kisch's and Rose's treatment by the Australian authorities. Menzies' role in the Kisch case is somewhat mirrored by Paul Hasluck's attitude in Rose's attempts to gain permission to revisit the Groote Eylandt people with whom he had lived in 1941. (Hasluck was then Minister for Territories.) "1962 in Zentralaustralien" — the book's table of content lists it as "1962 in Zentralasien"(!)(289) — is the final section of *Ureinwohner, Känguruhs, Düsenclipper*. It contains a retold episode of Bill Harney's meeting with Albert Namatjira(186f.), the topos of "Alltag auf einer Viehstation"(190ff.), a family chronicle ("Aus der Chronik der Liddles",200ff.) as a representative part of Australian history and new perspectives on the relationship between Aborigines and white Australians(204ff.). Rose argues that Aborigines came into contact with organised white labour as a result of road construction around Darwin in the early forties. The strike of Aborigines in 1951 has, he claims, its roots in class-conscious white workers spreading the idea of unionism among the native labour force. Rose anticipates the struggle for land rights and the claim of sacred sites such as Ayers Rock. While at Angas Downs, he establishes contact with tourists from interstate and overseas. Among them are many Germans; he records the homesickness of a woman who left the GDR a few years ago(209) and the political discussions with a West German woman ("sofort war eine heiße Diskussion über die deutsche Frage im Gange",210). The spectacle of a heated argument over the divided Germany in front of Ayers Rock carries its very own kind of ironic overtones. Frederick Rose continues to relate Australia's political and social conflicts to a

German perspective; as a socialist, he perceives an international struggle of ideological dimensions cutting across national cultures and problems of individual countries. In a brief chapter on Aboriginal spirituality and missionary influence he illustrates the genesis of a "cargo cult" mentality which the author believes is far more widespread in Australia than hitherto acknowledged. Rose's assessment of missionary work among Aborigines, especially of Hermannsburg, the German Lutheran mission founded in 1877 by Kempe and Schwarz, is surprisingly positive. He appreciates the educational work, above all the teaching of English and Aranda, whilst expressing severe doubts about the wisdom of attempted conversions to Christianity. In his final chapter Rose places Albert Namatjira in the context of Hermannsburg, trading the origins of the Aranda school of painting. In a sense, the declaration of equal rights for half-castes in 1952 marks a natural close to the author's preoccupation with the destruction of Aboriginal culture and the treatment of non-whites in Australia.

In a Postscript 1965 Rose reviews the situation ("Nachwort 1965",268ff.). He links the treatment of Aborigines to his own. Like his fellow-writers of the GDR, he attacks the Australian press for its ideological bias and ignorance. Rose was called a "Petrov spy", and it was alleged that he was held against his will somewhere behind the Iron Curtain. Like Kisch, Rose exposes the absurdity of that claim by holding press conferences and being interviewed on radio and television. And like his famous predecessor, he quickly becomes a *cause célèbre* and an embarrassment for the government. After his political activities in this arena he returns to the Aborigines, especially on Groote Eylandt. He finds evidence of cultural, social and political emancipation. In an optimistic vision he sees a united front between Aborigines and Australian workers. He finds it encouraging that Aborigines have travelled to Africa to learn from the experience of decolonisation. Frederick Rose believes it possible for the Aborigines to realise their demands for equality. He claims that in only thirty years they have moved from a tribal society to an "international movement against colonialism, racism and exploitation". The book ends with a quotation from Kath Walker's poem "Aboriginal Charter of Rights"(277). His Australia is a decolonised society of cultural respect and an international fraternity of workers.

David Martin

Where a Man Belongs

Although David Martin is Hungarian by birth, he was educated in Germany. He left his second country at the age of twenty, escaping from the Nazis in 1935. After spells in Holland, Hungary, Israel and Spain, he settled in London in 1938. Martin worked as a journalist and writer, including a period as *Daily Express* correspondent in India. He moved to Australia in 1949, settling in Melbourne. Of his many book publications, the novel *Where a Man Belongs* (1969) deals most explicitly with the subject of German-Australian relations.

It is the story of two men, the Australian bookkeeper Paul Burtle and the German-born Jew Max Stiegelman, whose uneasy friendship takes them on a journey to Europe — for one a return to childhood, for the other an escape from the solitary defeat of imminent old age. Max is an Australian writer narrating their shared history. Intriguingly, Walter Kaufmann's first novel, *Voices in the Storm*, published in Melbourne in 1953, later appeared in the author's own translation under the German title of *Wohin der Mensch gehört* (1957) — "Where a Man Belongs".[7] The writers knew each other while in Melbourne. It seems likely that both German-Australian novelists chose to write their version of the same subject, relating their German past and Jewish identity to Australia and contemporary post-Nazi Germany. (There is no suggestion of 'plagiarism' in either work.)

Paul and Max meet at work; their offices are small partitions in a room, with little chance of privacy. Max's friends call his office his "Kafka Cubicle".(3) The oppressiveness, forced intimacy and underlying menace of their respective working area are indicative of the disturbing relationship between the two men. Max reflects early on his presence in the tiny downtown office in Melbourne: "...I often asked myself what I was doing here, in this country and this town, of all the ones where the storm might have carried me?"(5) Martin's protagonist, too, is a "voice in the storm". Although he expresses affection for his new home, he is told by Paul "You're a foreigner".(12) Throughout the novel, the point is repeated that Max is "not Australian"(147), — by Germans and Australians alike. Paul introduces his friend Max to an Aborigine with the words: "The New Australian, the one who writes."(74) That is as close as the migrant German Jew comes to being accepted as Australian. Paul, on the other hand, criticises Australian women for "lacking... a certain *je ne sais quoi*... integrity, or call it warmth".(12) His objection to the Australian concept of womanhood extends to literature: "Had I ever read an Australian book in which there appeared one genuine, full-blooded, womanly female?" he asks the narrator.(16) The novel reflects stereotype judgements prevalent at the time of its writing. David Martin records them in the form of dialogues or statements by his fictional characters, without identifying himself with any of them. Bearing in mind the title of his narrative, this reservation seems notable.

Where a Man Belongs assumes a characteristically brutal irony from allusions made to Goethe's novel *Elective Affinities* (18), applied both to the awkward friendship between Paul and Max and to Paul's courtship of the German woman Gudrun whose name and address he obtained from an introduction magazine, "mainly for New Australians".(19) One of the functions of their friendship is Max's attempt to teach Paul German so he can communicate with his bride-to-be. Not surprisingly, Martin's novel is crowded with German words and expressions. They are integrated into the narrative syntax. The difference between English and German thus becomes a continuing point of discussion. "What was friendly enough in English could sound distant in German," Max informs his friend when asked to assist in writing a love letter to Gudrun.(23) In a German hotel room Max finds a Bible in Luther's translation. Reading the psalms, he is made aware of his instinctive bilingualism:

> *Er führt mich auf rechter Straße um seines Namens willen.* He leadeth me in the path of righteousness. But *rechter Straße* is not the path of righteousness, nor is it the road of truth. It is the true road. I was still held by a compulsion to transpose from one of my languages into the other. Unable to shake it off, and wearied by grappling with the verses in their black Gothic armour, I closed the book...(114)

He remembers a letter he wrote to his stepmother while he was still a child. Now as an English-speaking adult, he reflects on the stylistic affront his juvenile letter had aimed for:

> *Dein Dich nicht liebender Stiefsohn.* The diabolic beauty of the syntax inverts and embellishes a family formula: *dein Dich liebender Sohn.* This is how every letter must end. I have avenged myself also on something I can never write without wrathful hilarity. It is better in English; your loving son, your son who loves you, but *dein Dich liebender Sohn* is stilted, ridiculous, outrageous.(137)

Later, on the boat to Aden, the narrator finally recaptures the impulse to write, after having been unable to express himself for so long:

>...it flowed unhindered, not only in English, but, miraculously, in German, for the first time in more than ten years. Before we were well into the Red Sea I had finished a poem of some two hundred lines in which both languages mingled, a strange hybrid, but one which did not displease me, unpublishable though it was.(213)

The attitude to language is a reflection of the degree of acceptance of the Australian writer's German Jewish past and of German culture, past and present. When he is back in Germany, it is the *words* for food and objects, for customs and habits which move him, as do the simple German folksongs.

It is highly appropriate that the narrator should be identified as a writer: not only the curious friendship but also the strange love Paul experiences is seen in specifically literary terms. As Max, the authorial narrator, says: "...I would have been an oaf not to see the artistic possibilities in what I was doing, the latent story beneath."(24) Like Walter Kaufmann, David Martin's *persona* of narrative author freely refers to his own published work and treats the present account as a novel in genesis. *Where a Man Belongs* is also the portrait of an artist as an older man, more precisely, of a bilingual writer fluctuating between his native and his adopted culture. It is this dimension of the novel which gives its plot and characterisation special significance. Instead of consuming his native culture, taking its achievements for granted, the author has to discover and appreciate the modest claims of his new country "in cities unknown to the mellow graces of history".(Ibid.) Many migrants will recognise their own cultural adjustments in this statement. More critically, Max qualifies his response to German-European and to Australian culture:

>...in Australia one did not have to confront reality through a subgrowth of secondary cultures, it was a loss but also a gain. It was a land where the book remained more important than the writer, and the writer at least not less important than the critic. The forest of vicarious experience had not yet become impenetrable.(177)

He may not be acceptable as an "Australian", but the German-Jewish immigrant knows where his home is. *Where a Man Belongs* continues to address itself to the theme of national identity, with uncompromising directness. The Australian Paul identifies himself as a "returned Digger" who admires German "discipline"; German migrants he argues, are "more like us", differentiating them from "Southern Europeans".(26) Max's response to Paul's admiration of German discipline is: "I went to school there, Paul."(Ibid.) Later, when crossing into Germany, he tells a customs officer: "I went to school in your country." To his readers he adds: "(I often said I went to school in Germany, rarely that I grew up there.)"(96) The book cover of *Where a Man Belongs* states that David Martin "was educated in Germany". The author's ambivalent feelings for Germany are in clear evidence in this novel, and elsewhere. Like his protagonist, David Martin changed his name from the Hungarian original of Ludwig Detsinyi. German is his native language, but he started writing in English during his late twenties. Clearly, his use of language reflects a sociopolitical attitude to the culture which murdered millions of fellow-Jews in Germany.

David Martin displays no self-righteousness in his uneasy response to, and memory of, Germany. It is a relationship of love and murderous violence. The Nazi woman Gudrun sings for Max much-loved German folksongs, in particular his "favourite", Eichendorff's "In einem kühlen Grunde", — a song of love betrayed(cf. 160-161). Revisiting Germany after all those years in Australia leads Martin to the realisation that retaliation does not change anything.

Martin's largely autobiographical protagonist is, of course, aware of the challenge he will face upon his return to the country of his youth. "I had steeled myself against this homecoming more than against any other," he remembers, "but now I was glad that I was returning a foreigner: Odysseus alive, but Penelope dead and Argus, the dog, eaten by maggots."(123) European mythology is used to express his alienation, but also his joy at being someone else, no longer a German. David Martin does not shy away from the open wound of German-Jewish relations: if he is unable to forget or to forgive, he goes out of his way to present the opposite argument. He does not propagate a belief of collective guilt, he merely finds it impossible to return to the place of the crime. Too many painful memories interfere. The *"Barmitzvah* boy, who today becomes a man in Israel" cannot forget "the white bosom under black lace of an Austrian cousin": "Suckle me, *Kusinchen,* I hope I shall dream about you tonight. (Your Buchenwald, your Dachau, are far away.)"(133-134) Walking the streets of Berlin, the city of his youth, he is "like a man who, coming out from an anaesthetic, learns to distinguish by familiar symbols where reality begins and nightmares end".(139) Part of the alienation is summed up in his solicitor's remark: "Germany is booming as never before".(126) Confronted with an antiseptic, hygienically cleaned and immaculated Germany, Martin's fictionalised self is hit by "an attack of homesickness".(144)

Part of the ambiguity of post-war Germany is its fraternisation with the military of former opponents. In a haunting chapter Martin describes a meeting between old Nazi soldiers and the Australian Paul Burtle, Gallipoli veteran and member of the R.S.L. Unlike Max, Paul has little trouble in identifying with German *Frontsoldaten*. Reconciliation in the name of militarism and glorification of a murderous past is something David Martin chooses to have no part in. But he is aware of this kind of dubious camaraderie among former enemies. It is a special kind or eros which manifests itself in brutal confrontations.

So where does "a man belong"? What is Max's real home? It is a question put mainly to migrants and Jews, especially to Jewish migrants. In a key passage of the novel the following dialogue between the German Nazi woman and the German-born Australian Jew unfolds:

> "What do you really believe?"
> "That there is nothing, literally nothing, that human beings will not do."(Ibid.)

In the light of this exchange, the novel's title assumes a desperate, almost hopeless meaning. So long as man belongs to man, there can be no guarantee of a home for man. It is this homelessness David Martin alludes to in what the *Oxford Companion to Australian Literature* calls his "most autobiographical and ambitious novel, ...both complex and searching". David Martin treats the controversial theme of a seduction, in the broadest sense, into reconciliation or forgetfulness with sensitivity and vigour. He forces his narrator Max to expose the "cliché about the past and the future".(176) It is the young German girl Maria who presents Max with his greatest challenge. She is the voice of the new generation of Germans who were born during or after the war. David Martin leaves the reader in no doubt about the sincerity of her appeal:

> "I am praying for all the Jews. That they should be happy. That their wounds should be healed. That God should give them the strength to forgive us, and that he should forgive us too."(178)

And, later she continues:

> "I have love, but not enough. I would need all there is in the world to take away your hate. To take it on myself. To take it, of course, for what Germany did to you, and for what poisons your spirit."(179)

Max's response is honest, open and direct: "I see it more simply," he answers. "We Jews have no saints, only prophets. And we don't turn the other cheek. That's a Christian precept."(Ibid.) Martin allows the young German woman a pathos few readers will be able to dismiss. For she thinks she has to remain in Germany, at the scene of the crime, if it can ever be atoned for. Working for a few years in Israel she dismisses as "too easy a solution".(180) There can be no doubt that for many young Germans the question of atonement is of paramount importance. David Martin does not endorse a kind of gentile Yom Kippur, but he does recognise the spiritual, social, cultural and political needs of the children of murderers. It is an extraordinarily generous comprehension which nonetheless does not lead to forgiveness. As Max tells Maria: "You don't need forgiveness, not mine nor any other man's."(179) The crimes cannot be atoned for by the children. *Where a Man Belongs* is a novel of badly timed love.

Part of the theme of national and cultural identity relates to a Jew in Australia. David Martin leaves no doubt about his views on whether the same kind of persecution could happen here. Max's attempts to remind his Australian friend that "there were some Jews at Gallipoli too"(Ibid.) are lost on a closed mind. Paul reflects the uncertainty of an Australian identity, projected in the aggression against those who know, or search to find, "where a man belongs".

David Martin's 1969 novel thus raises questions which still have not been answered, although it may be assumed that Australia is beginning to be identified in other than negative terms. Victorian R.S.L. President Bruce Ruxton's reactions against a policy of multiculturalism serve as an uncomfortable reminder of the continuing topicality of Martin's character of Paul Burtle and his R.S.L. concept of nationhood. The fictional journey into the past proves of unceasing relevance to the present, — in this country as well as Germany. *Where a Man Belongs* exposes the state of national cultures in relation to an individual human being. It is, in that sense, a novel about Australia and about Germany. The barbarism of German "culture" this century proves that is cannot be the place "where a man belongs", but the volatility, naivety and susceptibility of a very recent white Australian culture in matters of social discrimination do not augur well for a safe and confident adoption of national identity by migrants, Jews or other "minorities". It may yet take a while to drive home the vital point that these "minorities" together make up "the nature of these living ties".

Heinz Nonveiller

Jener Teil der Welt

Born in Graz in 1938, Nonveiller emigrated to Australia in 1955 after the death of his father. His short story "Jener Teil der Welt" is the translation of "That Part of the World" which first appeared in *Meanjin* and subsequently in A.A. Phillips' selection *Coast to Coast 1967-1968*. Nonveiller published his first prose works in English around 1957. His narratives deal with what his German translator and editor Frank Auerbach calls "das moderne Einsamkeitsgefühl heimatloser Existenz in Australien".(413)

The story is largely autobiographical. It centres around a protagonist who sees himself as a man without a home: "Das möchte ich besonders betonen: Ich war ein Mann ohne Land, ohne Heimat."(390) As such, he is dangerous, especially when he challenges other people's sense of belonging. Nonveiller describes the alienation produced by meaningless work and argues "daß ein Mann mit einer Heimat sich eigentlich nicht mit so etwas abfinden sollte".(391-392) His "Heimat"-concept thus goes beyond a place of birth, nationality or regional loyalties. It relates to the joy of life and a natural fulfilment of human aspirations. The narrator presents a vision of Australia those who were born here do not possess and, he claims, do not deserve. In a radical inversion he predicts an emigration of the country from its native population:

> "...ich fand heraus, daß sie alle — obwohl sie Männer mit einem Heimatland waren — ihr Recht auf dieses Land verwirkten. Ein Land, in dem man nicht wirklich, nicht richtig lebt, das man nicht verschönert und nicht liebt, ein solches Land ist in der Gefahr, einem verlorenzugehen. Ich überlegte, wie lange es wohl dauerte — eines Morgens würde die ganze Nation (mit wenigen Ausnahmen) erwachen und sich in einem fremden Land finden...".(392)

The protagonist and narrator Janos (401) works together with Jack Johnson as proof-reader for the newspaper *The Daily Truth*. Their attempt to correct the untrue versions of Australia leads to the destruction of their friendship and Jack Johnson's marriage to an Austrian. Katherine, Janos discovers, has a home because she suffers from homesickness. Unable to localise his own homesickness, the narrator encourages his friend's wife to read Austrian books and to regain contact with her native culture. As he strengthens her alienation, she loses interest in her suburban marriage and in particular her sexual passion. In a sensitively poetic interpretation the author lets the husband declare: "Solange sie Heimweh hatte, war sie ganz in Ordnung. Sie war sogar leidenschaftlich. Aber jetzt, nachdem sie kein Heimweh mehr hat...".(399) Female sexuality is described as prompted by a kind of homesickness. Nonveiller links this imaginative observation with an interpretation of Australia as a land for the homeless. Having destroyed his friend's marriage by prompting his wife to return to Austria, Janos informs his friend: "Jack — dies ist nicht Ihr Land. Es ist *mein* Land."(402) He disowns the claims of native Australians who have become "die Opfer ihrer eigenen Nutzlosigkeit"(403). The senseless life-style of suburban pursuits and indifferent work shared by many Australians leads the narrator to proclaim: "es gibt ein Land für die, die keine Heimat haben. Und das ist dieses Land."(Ibid.) Australia thus becomes home for the displaced who suffer from a homesickness which cannot be located geographically: this country is transformed into a state of mind.

Heinz Nonveiller's story reflects the boredom and relative affluence of Australian society in the sixties. He expresses an unusual self-confidence at a time when "New Australians" were made conscious of their place. It is rare indeed that a migrant author can boast: "Aber ich war ein freier Mann, und deshalb konnte ich ihnen ihr Land wegnehmen, ohne einen Finger zu rühren...".(Ibid.) Nonveiller's response to Australia during the fifties and sixties is this urge to "rearrange" what he considers to be the proper perspective on this country. "Ich hatte alle Dinge an den Platz gerückt," Janos says in the story's final sentence, "wo sie hingehören."(Ibid.) The protagonist dispossesses not merely a husband from his wife, but a country he loves from its insensitive (white) population. It is an unusually defiant gesture and impassioned plea on the part of an Austrian-born writer translating his own cultural vision into a violent criticism of Australian society. Written in English, the story loses none of its impact in German and represents a highpoint in German-Australian *Kulturkritik*.

Other important stories by Heinz Nonveiller have not yet been published in German translation, among them "In Regions of Hiding" (first appearance in *Coast to Coast 1961-62*), a Kafkaesque rendition of the experience of migration, and "The Naked Walls" (in: M. Lord's anthology *Modern Australian Short Stories,* London 1971), an autobiographical account of the author's alienation as a migrant in Australia.

Paul Hatvani

Das Ameisenfragment

Although other important narrative sketches and biographical reflections on his exile and subsequent permanent residence in Australia appear in the following decade, Paul Hatvani's *Ameisenfragment* must be considered the most important literary work of his long life in Australia. After decades of silence Hatvani's prose composition first appeared in *Literatur und Kritik* IV/1969.

It opens with the description of a symptomatic fear of loss, "Angst vor den Dingen, die nicht nehr sind".(336) It is an anxiety closely related to the author's own need to come to terms with his new life and to preserve the values, memories and cultural ties with his native Vienna. Significantly, it is language which he sees as a means to overcome such fear, specifically the grammatical construction of German, the creative logic of expression learnt in childhood.

Das Ameisenfragment centres on a range of "games" which are used to define and to escape the world. It is very much the German Expressionist who creates his own literary *Spiel* to reflect on what he left behind: his youth, his involvement in one of Germany's most exciting art movements and his persecution as a Jew. It is an exercise in creative disillusionment induced by conflicting impulses.

Hatvani formulates the double quotation of memory when he asks himself: "Darf man denn nach den verlorenen Zeiten recherchieren, den gestrigen Tag suchen? Diese Ordnung sollte nicht gestört werden, geschieht es, so ergäbe dies tiefes, spätes Leid."(337) This self-critical aspect of his reflections remains present throughout the *Ameisenfragment*. It is implied in his reference to a fraternity of Expressionist art: "Man war in Formen verliebt; Formen sind da, einen Stil zu schaffen und über Stilfragen hat es sich immer gut debattieren lassen."(Ibid.) But despite such reservations it is only through "style" that Hatvani can attempt to do justice to the past, to write again about his need to invent another *Spiel*. If anything has changed since the early days of his participation in the movement, it is a new sense of irony and humour, a heightened consciousness in the employment of "style". Now Hatvani feels there can be nothing dogmatic or predefined in his attempt to "express" "Sinn, Erinnerungen und Bekenntnisse"(338) of his life. His stylised retrospective continues the verbal infatuations of earlier times and introduces a sober reassessment. He speaks of the "Ereignisse, die wir nicht hindern konnten, sich mit uns zu ereignen", but concedes "die Programme sind Programm geblieben". In a characteristic mixture of irony and passion he laments: "Wie riesengroß ist doch die Bibliothek der ungeschriebenen Meisterwerke." Yet he also admits: "Kunst geschah in einem Vakuum."(Ibid.) Leaving such ambivalent history behind, Hatvani speaks of new allegories of time: "die nahende Zukunft" will appear "in fremder Verkleidung".(339) Exile and migration are presented as an intellectual and artistic composition, as part of the author's literary and cultural biography. It is this quality in Hatvani's writing that makes his account of German-Australian resettlement so special; no other author has managed to write about cultural dislocation and the challenges of migration with the same imaginative strength. Hatvani's personal reflections are an inseparable part of Germany's literary history.

In the context of German cultural conditioning Hatvani's move to Australia carried expectations raised mainly by juvenile fiction and colonial literature. "Gebiete aus Indianergeschichten, Abenteuer der Afrikaforscher, Südsee-Romantik tauchten wieder auf."(Ibid.) However, migration to Australia demythologises such clichés: "Aber es gab große Enttäuschungen," Hatvani reports, "— statt um Romantik, Abenteuer und Tomahawks handelte es sich um Papiere...".(Ibid.) He acknowledges the "angelernten Vorstellungen" and in particular a German preoccupation with the "exotic" — "man bildete sich ein, es müsse nun alles 'exotisch' sein".(Ibid.) Alienation could be perceived as something positive and exciting. It meant the escape from a threatening home, not merely during the period of fascism in Germany. Revealingly, Hatvani recognises in the "Fremde" an image *related* to his native culture: "Eigentlich aber hatte auch die Fremde ein freundlich-verwandtes Gesicht."(Ibid.) The otherness is acknowledged as an inseparable part, a constant point of reference, of German culture. Hatvani stresses that artists of his generation were in need of new discoveries. Their search for new beginnings coincided with the desperate quest for survival of others who did not fit into the prescriptions of a Nazi "culture". In many cases the two coincided. Hatvani himself took flight in more ways than one: "So hieß es also, neue Gebiete zu entdecken. "(340) Sadly, Australia proved unable to inspire the literary artist to a discovery of new imaginative concepts. The "ants" he invokes in this fragment are in the first instance analogies to thoughts offering dubious direction ("Gedanken gleich den Ameisen", 339).

In the second part of his narrative Hatvani refers to them again, this time in a less obviously metaphorical sense. He describes a scene where ants enter a small opening: "eine kleine, fast unsichtbare Öffnung, durch die Ameisen aus- und einwanderten".(341-342) The symbolism is verbally explicit and later extended into a search for the rules of migration: "nach welchen Regeln also diese Ameisen ihre unterirdische Welt verließen".(342) The ants are being watched by a "Herr E.", the narrator calls them "kleine unansehnliche Ameisen ohne tiefere Bedeutung... an diesem stillen Orte... des fernen Erdteils".(Ibid.) Hatvani links the migration of such "insignificant" ants to the "fates" ("Schicksale") which have brought Herr E. to Australia: "die ihn hierher, nach Australien, gebracht haben".(Ibid.) The narrative perspective, both on the level of the author's own retrospective reflection and of its fictionalised account, is the presence of a German-Austrian exile in Australia. The two accounts frequently overlap. The correlative function of the two kinds of ants is expressed in straightforward parallels ("...die letzten Jahrzehnte haben uns gelehrt, daß 'Auswandern' im wesentlichen ein Vorgang ist, der nach feststehenden Regeln verläuft", 344) and in the collective pronoun employed by the narrator ("haben *uns* gelehrt"): migration is described (or assumed as) a shared experience. After a consideration of the effects of "Auswandern" the text continues: "Ob es zum Beispiel bei den Ameisen so etwas wie 'Auswandern' gibt?"(Ibid.) Hatvani's central narrative symbol is more than a stylistic device to "belittle" his experience of migration. The author does not simply adopt the analogous image; he creates it in order to problematise it, it is above all a point of reference, artistically and intellectually. As the title implies, it is a fragmentary comparison, an incomplete analysis.

The narrator shares his accommodation in an Australian guesthouse, a clear reference to the status of migrants like himself in their new environment. A separate section opens with the cryptic observation: "Über die Ameisen, mit denen sich Herr E. so gerne beschäftigte, ist zu sagen, daß nun auch andere Gäste der Pension begonnen hatten, sich mit ihnen zu beschäftigen."(346) Hatvani's imaginative treatise on migration is not a self-centred monologue. His narrator quotes various opinions, only to occasionally offer his own view by way of authorial intrusion: "es wäre müßig gewesen, ihn (i.e. Herrn E.) überzeugen zu wollen, daß zwischen biologischen und sozialen Gegebenheiten ein entscheidender Unterschied bestehe".(347) In detaching himself from the narrative's apparently own fictional identifications, the author not only passes judgement on the Nazi-ideology which forced him into exile ("das Absurde eines biologisch regierten Menschenstaats", Ibid.), he also emphasises the deliberate construction of his verbal composition, in a sense *quoting* the literary art he once believed in. This historical self-quotation is not merely the expression of disappointment, it also demonstrates a newly found sense of irony and humour (different from the aesthetic wit of German Expressionism). Literature, "Dichtung" itself is an "Ameisenfragment": "kein Modell einer staatlichen Struktur, kein Ausgangspunkt für symbolische Spekulationen und kein Vorbild für utopische Phantasien".(Ibid.) Properly understood, then, Hatvani's *Ameisenfragment* constitutes a qualified dissociation from the missionary zeal and artistic faith of Expressionism — and from any kind of idealistic writing. It is a complex document of literary, imaginative survival: how to write when a belief in writing has gone. Hatvani's correlation between migration and literature is as forceful as it is tenuous — by design. Part Two of his narrative ends with a disillusioned yet defiant answer to its own question "Wie steht es nun mit diesen Ameisen?" (348); the author's mouth-piece declares: "ich wurde... der Schwierigkeit (gewahr), sich mit nichts als mit der Sprache verständigen zu müssen." (349) Ironically, that is one of the key discoveries of migrant writers, although clearly of relevance in most cultural contexts. Paul Hatvani's *Ameisenfragment* ends with a moral interpretation of the past. In his own "Vergangenheitsbewältigung" he recognises "daß man gemeinsam zu einer Vergangenheit verurteilt wird" and the need "daß man sie abbüßen muß, auch wenn sie weit zurückliegt".(Ibid.) There is no personal past in isolation from a social and cultural context. His version of a "collective guilt" is explained in radically simple terms: "Beim Denken hat es begonnen...".(Ibid.) It is an assessment of German cultural history (not merely of the immediate Nazi past) as challenging as it is essential. And yet: Hatvani's "ants" are in the first instance "Gedanken"(339), strains of thought, "Denkspiel"(336), wilful and imaginative reflections like his own prose narrative. In an ultimate reversal his intellectual and artistic scepticism is bound to acknowledge: "Gestehen wir es uns ein: es handelt sich wieder einmal um ein Spiel...".(350). The collective guilt of an unconquered past meets the individual innocence of the literary artist who believes he possesses the power to creatively articulate the present; both are "Gespenster, die noch nicht tot sind, sondern noch da und nicht dort".(Ibid.) They are "the ants", forever marching into directions difficult to change. Literature itself is made up of such an individual and collective will, a tribe of which Hatvani is himself a member.

"...noch da und nicht dort": in his later essay "Nicht da, nicht dort: Australien"(1973) Paul Hatvani lists the many difficulties in attempting cultural transformation. He remained a German writer exiled in an Australia of too many "ants".[8]

(Hatvani's narrative text "Irrwege", published in *Akzente* 1/18 (1971), transforms most of the *Ameisenfragment's* reflections into imaginative fiction, a surrealist prose of Kafkaesque overtones.)

Chapter Five

Look Back in Wonder: Visitors from Another Republic of Letters

"Ich bin ja nicht hergekommen, um hier zu sein;
ich bin hergekommen, um nicht dort zu sein!"

Paul Hatvani, *Nicht da, nicht dort: Australien*

THE SEVENTIES

Two developments feature prominently during the seventies: a number of major representatives of post-war German literature (including Austrian and Swiss authors) address themselves to the theme of Australian-German relations, and a group of German-, Austrian- and Swiss-born writers living in Australia begin to assert themselves strongly in the context of a self-conscious Australian literature.[1] As well, returned migrants from the GDR continue to publish works with Australian themes and settings. Among other generally accessible publications the reports of an Austrian behaviourist and zoologist offers a special perspective on Australia's wildlife and the economic and political concerns of its population.[2]

German writers stress the change of mental prospect imposed upon them by their (usually brief) visits to Australia. They are reluctant to speak of Germany when drawing comparisons, preferring instead to refer to Europe. Confronted with the vastness of Australia, they adopt a continental stance; they see themselves not as Germans, but as Europeans. Sketches of cities capture the cultural identity of life in Australia, along with biographical fragments, narrative glimpses of representative migrant careers. Such impressions are not without factual mistakes or subjective misconceptions, always pre-conditioned by a European perspective. Old clichés about the Australian landscape are revived, cities are not accepted as cities by European standard. The landscape is interpreted as *ersatz* for culture. European-German writers find it impossible to operate with any concept of culture which is not theirs. Thus their writing about Australia inevitably centres on aspects of European culture, judging the country by its measurable achievements in this area: opera, literature, architecture, film. There is an historical impatience with the Australian continent, culminating in the restless appeal formulating the motivation of most European migrants: when will Australia's future become present reality? (*Horst Bienek*, 1972).

The past excesses of exotic adventures set in Australia are wittily led ad absurdum. German-Australian writing has reached full circle: irony, black humour and German regional wit ingeniously play with the very concept of adventure which had proved for so long the basis for an interest in the Australian continent and its people. The absurdities or laughable improbabilities of Australian adventure novels or travelogues are mocked and, in an act of cultural alienation, transferred to Central European situations.(*H. C. Artmann*, 1969/70) It is a noticeable feature that during the seventies Australia becomes a humorous point of reference, the target of literary wit, often directed at inner German literary establishments. A fictitious journey of Goethe to Australia proves as much a mockery of the worship of literary heroes as a stylistic tour-de-force in which Australia is simply a word invoking certain exotic qualities which in turn are alluded to, and played with, to comical excess. The total verbalisation of Australia has in itself a burlesque effect. Perhaps unintentionally, the humour of a travelling Goethe not ever reaching Australia and spending his time asleep in hotel rooms does amount to a valid statement about German-Australian relations. Serious literary treatments of Australia by major German-language writers have remained rare and are a recent phenomenon. (*Michael Schulte*, 1976)[3] All too often German authors preferred to select a single image (such as the kookaburra) to express a "philosophical" view about the nature of man, instead of offering accurate description or choosing Australia as subject of their narrative work.(*Siegfried Lenz*, 1968) Emphasis on imagery confirms the fact that serious German writers look upon Australia primarily as a source of inspiration of metaphorical expression or stylistic innovation: the exotic is applied to language in the context of German literary culture. It is the less ambitious and less distinguished authors who deal directly with Australia, its history, geography and society. What all German writers share is an Australia which leads them back to their native culture; the foreign nature of their antipodean experience acts like a filter, intensifying their commitment to the familiar. The more accomplished novelists and poets retain elements of the exotic by integrating them into their writing, either as wit or as stylistic alienation. The general pattern of development may be summarised by two lines taken from *Horst Bienek*'s cycle of poems called "In Australien":

> Weit bin ich gegangen, das ist wahr,
> und zurückgekehrt zu den alten Wörtern.
> *(Lern von den Wombats)*

European mythology is revived to express Australian experiences. (*Horst Bienek*, 1975) [It makes an interesting comparison to analyse the essential Australianness of novels and poems written by Australian writers dealing with their responses to Europe, i.e. Kate Grenville, Beverley Farmer, John Tranter, David Malouf, Andrew Taylor etc. Even more revealing and complex are the writings of "migrant" authors revisiting Europe, i.e. Antigone Kefala, Rudi Krausmann, Dimitris Tsaloumas, Cornelis Vleeskens, Manfred Jurgensen etc.] Only one writer applies his wit to disown European culture.(*Peter Bichsel*, 1977) Among Australian writers born in German-language countries a trend towards English language games or linguistic exercises develops, especially in poetry. *Sprachspiel* or a Wittgensteinian philosophical and existential dimension finds its lyrical or staged manifestation: a "play" of, and on, voices, on paper, on stage, on radio.(*Walter Billeter*, 1973; *Rudi Krausmann*, 1975) Other authors apply their linguistic sensitivity and bicultural consciousness to translation and the mediation of literatures.(*Margaret Diesendorf*, 1967-1981) Their own poetry and prose retains cultural and stylistic qualities of their native country, not surprisingly, as much of their work is in fact a translation, either by the author or by someone else, from the original German.(*Walter Adamson*, 1973-1976; *Rudi Krausmann*, 1975-1977) Surprisingly few writers separate clearly their Australian from their German output. (*Manfred Jurgensen*, 1973-1979) The list of publications strongly suggests that German-language-born migrant writers found it easier to write poetry in English. Few have actually published full-length novels, preferring short stories or other forms of prose sketches. Even rarer is their adoption of drama; where they appear as authors of plays, the script is often an extended monologue or *Sprachspiel*. (*Rudi Krausmann*, 1978;

Manfred Jurgensen, 1963/1985)

The GDR writers published short stories (translated from the English) and new versions of earlier novels (again translated).(*Walter Kaufmann*, 1974-1977) As well, various adventure novels appeared, some of which could be termed extended stories. (*Joachim Specht*, 1971-1978) These Australia returnees continue to develop a concept of "Abenteuer" which consists of social challenges and demands an ideological commitment. The exotic dimension is upheld as packaging of explicitly political conflicts. The "Australian adventure" draws the reader into realistic sociopolitical struggles; the antipodean continent is the exotic setting of world-wide domestic politics. A behaviourist's analysis of Australia at the beginning of the decade offers a semi-scientific approach to "the Australian way of life". The aim is to present a paradigm of Australian manners, linking fauna and human population. Underlying such intention is the continuing concept of Australia as a continent of "curiosities". Cultural ethology establishes connections between animal and human behaviour, and also offers perspectives of comparative cultural studies. It could be argued that in the early seventies German-Australian literary relations extended for the first time into the realm of what during the following decade came to be known as "multiculturalism".(*Kurt Kolar*, 1970)

The seventies thus were a fruitful, in some ways even a decisive period, pointing the way towards new directions: a greater involvement of major contemporary German writers, a new consciousness and confidence among "migrant" authors, the continuation of a tradition of social realism and a merging of academic textbook with popular science. These developments are not without contradiction or conflict; cultural clichés are demythologised while new myths are being created, and the concept of culture itself remains controversial. Yet these very tensions make this period in the history of German-Australian literature one of the most exciting decades.

SIEGFRIED LENZ

Das Lachen des Kookaburra

With the reading tour of Siegfried Lenz in 1968 a major figure of contemporary German literature arrived in Australia. His hosts were German Departments at most State Universities, prompting Lenz to write "heute, zurückblickend (habe ich) beinahe das Gefühl..., der überwiegende Teil der Bevölkerung bestehe aus Germanisten."(33) His narrative sketch "Das Lachen des Kookaburra", first published in *Die Zeit*, later in the twenty-fifth anniversary issue of *Merian* (Sonderheft), although casual in tone and lightweight in literary design, demonstrates the transformation of a cliché into imaginatively poetic symbolism, of superficial travelogue impressionism into a creative conception of new discoveries. The much-maligned kookaburra is treated here as a literary motive carrying a formally designed impact, the "message" of artistic composition.

Before Lenz refers to the bird he addresses himself to the question of how a travelling writer should prepare himself for a visit to Australia. "Ein fremdes Land steht auf dem Programm," he opens, "eines, über das man nur vom Hörensagen Bescheid weiß."(31) His instinctive response is to allow for a *prima vista*, for "die Chance... des unvoreingenommenen Eindrucks aus der ersten Begegnung heraus".(Ibid.) But he is not quite honest: in a rhetorical question he asks whether it would make sense "die sympathisch knappe Geschichte des Kontinents (zu) studieren"(Ibid.), suggesting that he has already done so. His narrative account of Australia derives much of its playful and flirtatious character from the author's good-natured deception. On the one hand he stresses the importance of experiencing the unfamiliar, the foreign and the exotic: "soll man sich heimisch fühlen in einem fremden Land, da Fremdheit doch eine spezielle Bedingung des Erlebens ist?"(Ibid.) He does not want to minimise the cultural and social difference, arriving at the strikingly different (and literal) definition "sich original beschreiben zu lassen".(Ibid.) The author's imagination will allow itself to be described by a different country. On the other hand he has to admit to a "circumstantial" knowledge of the kookaburra, introduced from the start as "ein notorischer Freund des Menschen".(Ibid.) Lenz does not mention the source of his (unwanted) intelligence, expressed as it is in poetic irony. His journey to Australia, then, is not quite unprepared; his expectations are not based on a *tabula rasa* — in fact, Lenz's story relies on this very "secret" and his defensive desire to see a kookaburra. The sketch, comparable in many ways to the witty and anecdotal narratives of *So zärtlich war Suleyken*, does fulfil the author's own criterion: "daß man selbst etwas investieren muß — in eine Begegnung, eine Landschaft, ein Erlebnis — damit ein Eindruck oder Abdruck entsteht".(Ibid.) For Lenz allows the host country to shape his experience; in the end, the reader has learnt as much about the author's character as about the Australian kookaburra. The narrator lets himself be defined by a strange environment.

That in itself makes Lenz's travel concept very different. He does not come to Australia with preconceived ideas, with the desire to define and to judge. He opens himself up to a different place and receives the gift of a poetic self-reflection. In the story the kookaburra is introduced as a literary motive, an imaginative point of reference for an experience which extends beyond geographic location. No wonder the narrator has to admit that this kookaburra "drängte sich immer wieder...vor".(32) It is not its "German" prosaic description: "sein Schnabel, was die Härte angeht, (kann) mit einer Heckenschere aus Solingen verglichen werden"(Ibid.) which leads him to believe he may have travelled to Australia "nur wegen des Kookaburras". It is rather, as a literary motive and a poetic inspiration, the "lachende Schlangentöter", the "gutgelaunte Menschenfreund"(Ibid.) which draws him to the strange land. His images relate to a European mythology which carries with it its own spiritual sense of the exotic.

Siegfried Lenz manages to voice his impressions of Australia and to pass on factual information about the continent within the framework of his poetic symbolism. With careful design he speaks of a "schutzlose Kontinent" and its disarming "außerordentliche Gastfreundschaft." (Ibid.) He lists most of the recurrent Australian themes: "Goldrausch", "Einsamkeit des Busches", "eine großartige Verlassenheit", "einen Buschbrand" and the "Koalabär".(Ibid.) Lenz even notes that: "Der schutzlose Kontinent hat sich gegen Asien geöffnet...".(Ibid.) Searching for the kookaburra proves incongruously difficult, the "everpresent" bird is nowhere to be found. The narrator speaks of a "Kookaburra, den ich in Adelaide fast zu sehen bekam"(33), for he suspects that the bird's laughter was staged by his host, as an extension of a generous "Gastfreundschaft". The German writer thus reverses Australian nature: it is man who imitates the kookaburra. Lenz's playful variation broadens the entire perspective of his story, effecting a general humanising of nature. What he suggests is not a European mythologising along traditional anthropomorphic lines, but an interdependence between man and nature which makes a strict separation unconvincing. Thus his remark: "Sie ist in der Tat beispiellos, die australische Gastfreundschaft"(Ibid.) carries its own subtlety, and his comment about the generosity of Australian hosts contains overtones of a more embracing sense of symbiosis: "Es kam mir mitunter so vor, als wollten sie durch mich etwas über sich selbst erfahren...".(Ibid.) When he invokes the Australian landscape, Lenz describes the dead trees as "Graphik eines langsamen Todes".(Ibid.) Man and nature have learnt to read each other.

Thus it is against this carefully, albeit flirtatiously, prepared imaginative setting that the story's conclusion gains its full impact. For it is only in the "kümmerlichsten Zoo, den ich je sah"(34) that Lenz finally witnesses a kookaburra, on a rainy day in Queensland.

The "notorische Freund des Menschen"(31) is held captive; his laughter has to be imitated by those he was meant to guard. Lenz invokes a symbol of alienation and violence: "Ein Vogel war einäugig, der andere ließ den Flügel hängen."(34) This sight allows him to lend a literal meaning to a German saying: "Diese Vögel hatten wirklich nichts zu lachen."(Ibid.) The symbolism of "Das Lachen des Kookaburra" is no less effective because of Lenz's apparent light-hearted narrative style. It is significant that he ends his story with a renewed definition of the kookaburra as "meinen australischen Sehnsuchtsvogel".(Ibid.) Perhaps even more revealing is the author's (factually incorrect) afterthought that the "Lachende Hans" is a name, "den er wahrscheinlich deutschen Einwanderern verdankt".(Ibid.) Lenz's prose sketch thus functions as a parable not merely for human longing in general, but also for German migration to Australia in particular. Few German-Australian writers can equal Lenz's lightness of touch and imaginative symbolism of style. The sheer quality of his poetic imagination raises this short piece of narrative prose above the reiterative, cliché-ridden travelogue accounts of so many other German visitors.

Kurt Kolar

Kontinent voll Kuriositäten/Australien neu entdeckt

The first edition of this work appeared in 1965 in Vienna ("Im Wollzeilen Verlag") bearing the subtitle "Tiere, Menschen und Probleme in Australien". It was republished by BLV in a second edition five years later under the new title *Australien neu entdeckt*. The subtitle now characterises the nature of the book: "Ein Verhaltens-forscher im fünften Kontinent". With the exception of its Introduction, "Eine Brücke nach Australien", the nine chapters of *Australien neu entdeckt* are the same as those of *Kontinent voll Kuriositäten*. Some of their titles may help indicate the style and subject-matter of the work: "Ein Kontinent als Raritätenkabinett", "Papageienland" and "Europäer in Australien". For the purposes of this study the Introduction and the chapter dealing with European migration to Australia are the most interesting. All references are to the updated second edition.

Kolar explains his fundamental approach to (and interest in) Australia when he states in his introductory "Eine Brücke nach Australien" that he views the world with the eyes of an animal lover: "Meine Brille ist die eines Tiermenschen...".(7) His behavioural studies never separate man from animal, human aspirations from the living conditions of animals, and from the beginning he likens the curious nature of Australia to "die große menschliche Kuriosität Australiens: Aus einer Sträflingskolonie wuchs in zweihundert Jahren ein moderner Staat mit hohem Lebensstandard!"(Ibid.) Little wonder, then, that he sums up his knowledge of the country under the heading "Australien... ein Kontinent voll Kuriositäten".(Ibid.) He follows this assessment with a presentation of his own credentials as comparative behaviourist and the history of the "Institut für Vergleichende Verhaltensforschung der Osterreichischen Akademie der Wissenschaften".(Ibid.) Kilar practises what he terms "eine ökologisch ausgerichtete Verhaltensforschung"(10), insisting that man remain the centre of all scientific behaviourism: "Wichtigster Forschungsgegenstand...ist natürlich der Mensch."(11) He introduces the term "Kulturethologie"(12) to explain the nature of his study of Australia. It is the interrelationship between the human population of Australia and its natural environment (both flora and fauna) which Kolar is most interested in. Thus he can speak of the "Papageienland Australien."(13) He accepts (or assumes) the existence of a *homo Australiensis*, an Australian species of humanity heavily influenced by its natural environment. In a sense, Kurt Kolar may be considered one of the first visiting ecologists whose environmental concerns offer a unique perspective on Australian culture.

His chapter "Europäer in Australien" varies from the usual historical survey of European immigration precisely in this vital point: the very presence of a foreign race on the continent, the act of migration itself, is seen as an ecological threat to the environment. Kurt Kolar's Australia book differs from all other publications in this very radical, future-oriented approach, placing the Australian population firmly in a fragile ecological balance. In discussing the arrival of the First Fleet Kolar emphasises: "das neue Land war ein natürlicher Kerker".(135) Later, that prison became itself imprisoned by the presence of European migrants and their descendants. "Die Ankunft des weißen Mannes in Australien, ganz gleich ob Sträfling oder nicht," maintains Kolar, "hat das natürliche Gleichgewicht im Lande empfindlich gestört."(136) His is the classical "green" argument: "Die englische Forelle verdrängte den einheimischen Schwarzfisch aus den Bergwässern, als Ausgleich und Ersatz für den beinahe ausgerotteten Koala erhielt Australien das Kaninchen."(Ibid.) He sees the genocide of the Aborigines as an inevitable extension of the white man's refusal (or inability) to come to terms with the nature of the land.

Australien neu entdeckt reads as a disturbingly contemporary study, its title implying at least two kinds of new discoveries concerning this land. Although Kolar is a zoologist, his observations regarding human habitation are no less valid. Thus he notices the significance "daß in der City, also im Geschäfts- und Büroviertel, keine Leute wohnen."(141) Such a life-style creates its own peculiar culture, or a suburban sub-culture typical of Australia throughout the sixties and seventies. Not surprisingly, Kolar attempts to characterise the kind of person likely to migrate. He arrives at a typology comparable to his behaviouristic studies of animals. Kolar may well be stating the obvious, but our recent history of green politics demonstrates the need to reclaim the self-evident. His chapter on Europeans in Australia reminds German (and Australian) readers of the destructive impact of migration. Nor is it only on this continent that foreigners have threatened the uniqueness of native culture and indigenous nature. It is a general pattern Kolar is anxious to expose; Australia serves as a dramatic example of a global challenge.(147)

Kurt Kolar's *Australien neu entdeckt* offers a unique perspective on Australia and Australians. Its approach is unequalled in the history of German-Australian writing. As such, it holds a special place; its pronouncements and reflections are of immediate relevance to anyone interested in this country. Kolar's rediscovery of the continent is of concern not only to animal lovers. His environmental perspective was clearly ahead of its time; the book has since achieved the status of a "greenies' guide" to a country once thought to be indestructible.

H. C. Artmann

Im Golf von Carpentaria

Artmann's story "Im Golf von Carpentaria" appeared in the 1969/1970 editions of his collection *Die Anfangsbuchstaben der Flagge*, subtitled "Geschichten für Kajüten, Kamine und Kinositze". Readers familiar with Artmann's style have learnt to expect highly imaginative and witty variations of fictional "alienations", and ironic to sarcastic narrative challenges to literary genre and general culture clichés. A precise description of the author's intentions is to be found in his introductory text which serves as a kind of overture to the collection. In its seven sentences Artmann speaks of "ein ausländischer schmuggler", "ein wilderer, neu in dieser region", "ein gestrandeter spion", "ein ausgebrochener sträfling", "einer, der aus dem all zurückkehrt und sich nicht mehr zurechtfindet" and "ein blinder trunkenbold", summing up his variations of alienation and disorientation in the (cliché) formula "seltsames spiel und walten der natur, die nicht aufhört, dem menschen immer und immer wieder neue rätsel vorzusetzen... ".(7) The story "Im Golf von Carpentaria" (which should really be titled "*Am* Golf von Carpentaria") is the second of thirteen prose narratives in the volume. Like the others, its aim is to entertain by mock "adventure", applying the imagery, distortions and logic of comics along with other forms of popular "reading". The accumulation of clichés (in setting, plot, character and morality) amounts to an uncomfortably recognisable imagery of escapism characteristic of contemporary German society. Artmann's wit addresses itself to verbal and attitudinal clichés; phrases like "das leben geht seltsame wege"(25) are not only taken literally but reinforced by the kitschy logic of comic strip phantasies: "aber es kam, wie so häufig im leben, glücklicherweise anders".(24) The author mocks a naive faith in the future along with a specific social ignorance. His story incorporates disillusionment to reaffirm an escapist phantasy, exposing its unwitting humour and cultural violence. In a sarcastic gesture the narrator equates "leben und abenteuer"(26) — the very basis for most of German-Australian literature. The adventure he alludes to is little more than a flight from sociopolitical realities and the responsibilities of a cultural commitment.

It is this unmistakable criticism of contemporary German culture which makes Artmann's story important in the context of German-Australian writing, for, although "Im Golf von Carpentaria" shares the imaginative logic of Michael Schulte's "Goethes Reise nach

Australien", the Australia invoked by the narrative is more recognisably the expression of uninformed escapism or the exchangeable cliché of a predefined "otherness". As a result of that, the very nature of "adventure" — or the German concept of *Abenteuer* — is exposed as commercially and culturally predetermined, as a confrontation with "the other" which carries neither respect nor risk. Rescue or salvation are guaranteed. For all its enjoyable humour, then, Artmann's narrative carries strong overtones of sociocultural criticism — the more stinging the greater the author's range from irony to sarcasm.

His four protagonists are stock-in-trade characters drawn from the personnel of US television movies, cartoons and "adventure novels"; they are "diese vier, die letzten der im sturme gesunkenen *Archipelagus*, einer luxusyacht, die die sensation von San Francisco gebildet hatte".(12) The heroine Millicent Naish is "die platinblonde freundin des texanischen ölscheichs O Shea".(13) Marooned on the beach of Arnhem Land, they search for the "nächsten menschlichen, versteht sich, weißen siedlung".(12) Racism is implied, along with sexism and violence, as an essential ingredient of escapist adventure. Millicent is captured by an exotic tribe, "einer verschollenen prädiluvialen oder sogar noch älteren rasse des fünften kontinents".(15) She is referred to as "die hellhäutige beute".(Ibid.) The "Nkwyi", as the narrator calls the native Australians, are athletically built, of seven foot height and blue skin, with "kolossal langen angehobenen geschlechtsteilen".(16) They also carry long tails. Artmann's Australians are a primitive tribe of animalistic appearance and intelligence, un-European and inhuman.

The Australian landscape is basically jungle. It is a threatening otherness, an exotic nature, invoked to visualise the protagonists' dislocation. The natural setting of an exotic adventure remains part of the genre's cliché. Artmann's narrator refers to it as "diese tückische grüne stille"(18), emphasising its hostility to "civilised" visitors. Australia's fauna complements such image:

> Größere spezimen der tierwelt hatten sich allerdings noch nicht blicken lassen, wogegen es von klettermolchen und baumeidechsen wimmelte, chamäleonartigen wesen, die man kaum von ihrer umgebung unterscheiden konnte, die aber unheimlich lautlos an den jahrhundertealten stämmen auf- und abhuschten.(Ibid.)

The far-away continent is a wilderness inhabited by violent barbarians. The Europeans are engulfed by an evil nature; they move through an "infernalischen wald".(Ibid.) The native tribe is led by a "schamane"(19), indicating a primitive religious society. "Ein emuhaft grosses Ei"(20) forms part of a strange ritual clearly drawing nature into tribal consciousness. As this Australia is uncivilised, it has roads which "hierorts jedermann als straße bezeichnet hätte, *nicht* aber anderswo"(20-21). To the civilised non-Australians the tribal city of Nkw appears "wie ein wilder, absurder traum".(21) The same could be said of Artmann's story. It illustrates phantasies of cultural alienation as an "adventure" of racial and social superiority. Much of Artmann's humour derives from an incongruous vocabulary, "confusing" language and history. The natives who abduct Millicent Naish are called "die vier aboriginen sindbads".(Ibid.) The description of the "Nkwyi"(16) is a mixture of futuristic and archaic vision. As part of an adventurous violence the female victim has to appeal to the reader's base sexual instincts: "eine brust leuchtete entsprungen aus dem verschmutzten stoff des weißen tropenhemdes".(Ibid.) But in the end it is the lack of civilised hygiene, the "mangel an toilettenmöglichkeit"(22) which is at least equally "shocking". Language, the means of human communication, is seen as the ultimate alienation."'Oarrngh!' sagte der teufelsschaman... 'Oarrngh mmmflullwl ahrhkpp nn-nschn!'"(Ibid.) The narrator reproduces the sounds of a complete break-down in communication. "...waren das wirklich worte? Waren diese tierhaften laute noch ausdrucksformen eines menschlichen geistes?"(Ibid.) Australia thus becomes a country where Europeans cannot relate to a native population. As can be seen, much of the grotesque humour is beginning to assume some validity.

H.C. Artmann's comic vision "eines nie erahnten Australiens"(23) does serve a serious function. It seeks to reveal the underlying motives and implications "dieses wahnwitzigen abenteuers"(25), the cultural assumptions of German (European) voyages to Australia (and elsewhere), the very basis of Continental longing for the exotic. Recent Hollywood films have applied a similar logic to their concept of "adventure", reducing other cultures to the level of mere back-drops for the exploits of one of its own kind (*Romancing the Stone* etc.). Naturally, the white European female victim is rescued just in time, she escapes "in die arme der drei aus allen himmeln fallenden pyramidenbesteiger!"(24) Symptomatically, the "pyramidenbesteiger" are immediately reclassified as alpine climbers ("... [sie] hatten bereits ein gutes drittel ihrer alpinen leistung hinter sich gebracht.",Ibid.); foreign culture is transformed and translated into German idiom. Artmann exploits the assumptions of intercultural adaptations, themselves, he feels, a symptom of cultural imperialism or commercialism: one of the displaced and culturally threatened Europeans, Billy, "entpuppt sich... als geradezu überdimensionaler sanikwong-kämpfer"(25), thereby rescuing the entire group and defeating the natives with his own integrated brand of exotic combat. Australia is the fictional code for a strange place, part paradise ("man...aß von früchten, die es hier in jeder menge gab",Ibid.), part primeval unearthly wilderness ("des erdfern anmutenden waldlandes",23). Its exotic character expresses a radically different life from the fully developed "superior" European culture. The humorous contempt with which Artmann treats the logic of his narrative serves as critical tool in his exposure of the "adventures" of popular culture. "Ein australischer kreuzer, der aus diesen und jenen gründen, das leben geht seltsame wege, eine abteilung marinesoldaten an land geschickt hatte, nahm die vier erschöpften gestalten an bord."(25) Salvation is at hand because it constitutes a basic assumption of European culture. Man explores the earth in order to be saved. This cultural commodity is turned into a demand, it waits to be consumed. Artmann demonstrates the sale of cultural clichés, the conventions of trade in phantasies of self-identification.

The story's conclusion or literal dénouement functions as the alienation of an alienation. The reader is taken back to European popular culture; he has just witnessed the screening of a film. The cultural status quo is thus affirmed. In a characteristic twist Artmann devises a dialogue between "die kindergärtnerin Francesca" and "ihren begleiter, den sie vor knapp drei stunden im foyer des *Cinema Gardenia* kennengelernt hatte".(26)

"Was hatten diese blauen wilden mit Millicent Naish eigentlich vor?"...
"Das kann ich ihnen ohne weiteres sagen," versetzte dieser und entblößte seine langen weißen zähne: *"Oarrngh mmmflullwl ahrhkpp nn-nschnl!"*
Es war entsetzlich anzusehen, als er den großen regenschirm achtlos auf den überschwemmten blätterbesäten kiesweg warf...(Ibid.)

The ending is more than sexual comedy. It transfers the bizarre and the uncivilised to the "cradle of civilisation", European culture. And in consequence of this logic it relocates a consumerist Australia to a cinematographic projection in the heart of Europe. Phantasy sells — and determines behavioural patterns, cultural consciousness, "home". Australia as a code for "adventurous" alienation, as a comic-strip setting in the trade of phantasies and as the longing for escape in popular German culture is another extreme example of "not reaching" the real Australia, not being interested in the sociopolitical reality of the Australian continent and its people. As in Schulte, it merely serves as a witty, albeit critical, point of reference, a literary image borrowed from *Abenteuerliteratur*. Needless to say, Artmann does not mock Australia, he merely uses it to expose the cultural conditioning of popular experience.

HORST BIENEK

Writings on Australia

Horst Bienek visited Australia twice: in 1971 and in 1975. On both occasions he was prompted to address himself to the experience on his return to Germany. In 1972 he published an *Erlebnisbericht* essay in the influential journal *Merkur* (26/2) entitled "Versuch den Fünften Erdteil zu beschreiben". Unlike many other German visitors, Bienek opens his account with a programmatic admission: "War ich nicht eingetreten in dieses Land wie in eine Fiktion?"(151) For a writer, such "Fiktion" can amount to an invitation to invent or to imagine, to distort and to pretend. Horst Bienek is one of the few German authors who resists this professional temptation. He prefers instead to articulate his bewilderment, his dislocation and his sense of cultural ambiguity. The result is not only a more honest account of Australia, but also a better quality of writing than the usual travelogues.

Bienek registers: "Man fühlt sich ausgesetzt, irgendwo, eine Art Inselgefühl stellt sich ein. Es kommt hinzu: von hier ist alles fern. Das verändert die Optik und auch das Denken."(Ibid.) The statement is symptomatic in its openness and discovery of the need for different criteria of judgement. The author acknowledges the correlation between geography and culture, more specifically between the physical environment and the intellectual perspective. In a later poem, "Under the Southern Cross", written after his return trip to Australia in the summer of 1975, Bienek repeats the phrase: "von hier ist *alles* fern".(139) In the poem's final line the stress may have shifted, but it is the same insight, the same first impression, the same uneasiness the writer registered on his initial arrival in this country. His poetry and prose together constitute an imaginative response to a continent which clearly left a lasting impression in his mind.

Among Bienek's first impressions is an all-embracing sense of egalitarianism in Australian society. Ironically he comments that Australia seems to have perfected at least one of the three demands of the French Revolution. He quotes from D.H. Lawrence's letter to his sister-in-law in 1922, taking comfort that despite such conformity this writer still found Australia an exciting place to be. Horst Bienek's account of Sydney is anything but monotonous; he meets writers, artists, film-makers. His description acknowledges a life-style full of energy, enthusiasm and creativity. It is a reflection of Bienek's own status as one of West Germany's best writers that he avoids the stylistic trappings of literary tourism. His Sydney is inhabited by people, not made up of tourist attractions. Biographical sketches constitute a major part of Bienek's Australia, offering glimpses of successful and tragically dislocated lives. Among the ones he lists is "Paul Hirsch, der sich als junger Schriftsteller Paul Hatvani nannte, mit Kurt Wolff und Franz Pfemfert befreundet und viele Jahre Mitarbeiter im 'Sturm', im 'Jüngsten Tag' und in der 'Aktion' war".(156) It is difficult not to share a sense of tragedy and failure when confronted with the fate of many who welcome Bienek as a visitor from the past.

But Bienek attempts a broader analysis of Australian society in the seventies. He rightly relates his assessment to migration as the common base of European culture in this country where he distinguishes, at least in relative terms, between "Neu-Einwanderer" and "alteingesessene Australier".(157) Curiously, Bienek describes Australian *Germanistik* as "ein immer begehrteres Studienfach... , was man sich nicht so recht erklären kann".(Ibid.)[4] His "Versuch den fünften Erdteil zu beschreiben" is an authentic survey of one decade of Australian life; the seventies come alive again in many of his recollections. Unlike other German-Australian writers, Horst Bienek's impressionistic style captures the essence of certain aspects of Australian life. His account of late afternoons outside Flinders Street Station is inspired by precise observation transformed into imaginative insight.

Among his most astute comments is his definition of the Australian landscape as a "Fetisch", an "Alibi", and "Ersatz-Religion".(160) Bienek admits: "Zugegeben, ich habe mich davon anstecken lassen, zunächst"(Ibid.), only to protest later: "Landschaft als Fetisch, als Vergötzung — ich wehrte mich dagegen."(161) Unfortunately he does not continue the discussion; it would have been interesting to see whether he does not recognise cultural interrelationships between (say) Dostoevsky and Petersburg, Kafka and Prague, Joyce and Dublin or

Flaubert and Paris. Bienek would probably argue that these are all city cultures, but such metropolitan cultures are themselves a reflection of their natural environment. His critical descriptions of Australian cities as "alles ist Suburbia, überall ist Suburbia, das frißt sich kilometerweise krakenhaft in die Landschaft"(152) could have thrown light on Australia's city culture as an expression of the tyranny of natural landscapes. Instead, Bienek quotes Patrick White's *Tree of Man* to illustrate the Australian landscape as a state of mind. (In passing, he defines Patrick White as "der australische Faulkner".[161]) Bienek's Australia is a writer's discovery.

In a section entitled "Zahlen, Daten, Fakten" Bienek still emphasises the tyranny of distance. His perspective remains not only European, but specifically German. "Von Melbourne nach Brisbane ist so weit wie von München nach Casablanca," he notes.(Ibid.) Such comparisons may be of interest to Germans, but they only serve to demonstrate that different criteria apply in Australia. They are at best misleading. The author's discussion of the Sydney Opera House exhausts itself in financial figures and amused reflections on the difficulties of its construction — neither uniquely Australian features. Even a writer of Bienek's calibre is less convincing when relying on statistics, rather than on the imaginative strength of his own observation.

The final part of "Versuch den fünften Erdteil zu beschreiben" carries the title "Die dritte Entdeckung Australiens". It addresses itself to Australia's cultural and national self-discovery of the past decades. In an astute prediction Bienek claims that Australians are moving from a European history to an Asian future; their very concept of time reflects this process of cultural transformation: "Zeit ist hier schon Verströmen, in sich selbst Ruhen, die Zukunft gewinnen — das hat bereits etwas Asiatisches. Und so werden sich die Menschen bewußt, langsam bewußt, daß sie aus Europa kommen und nach Asien gehen."(Ibid). Bienek does not find a new sense of national consciousness in Australia during the seventies; instead, he notices signs of economic independence and a resulting confidence in dealing with Britain and the United States.

Horst Bienek ends his survey by repeating a question from Patrick White's *Voss: "Australien, ein Land mit Zukunft? Aber wann wird die Zukunft Gegenwart...? Das beunruhigt mich.* (So die Frage eines Neuankömmlings zu Anfang des 19. Jahrhunderts; es ist auch meine Frage, heute.)"(166) His literary question attempts a literary answer.

"Ich habe nicht aufgehört, darüber zu schreiben," he states in his final sentence.(Ibid.) His cycle of poems "In Australien", now [5] included in his collection *Gleiwitzer Kindheit. Gedichte aus zwanzig Jahren*(1976/78), forms part of that continued response.

"Lern von den Wombats" opens with a Brechtian pose, the individual voice announcing a representative fate, the discovery of a general truth:

> Weit bin ich gegangen, das ist wahr,
> und zurückgekehrt zu den alten Wörtern.

Bienek invokes an Australia of primary concerns, primeval nature, a far-away place leading him back to the basics of life and to a few fundamental words in existential language: "Die Erde. Die Sonne. Das Gras. Die Wüste." His poetry needs to interpret and to re-learn verbal sense and natural signs: "die Zeichen...enträtseln". The didactic tone of the poem carries with it an underlying threat. Bienek warns of a betrayal which lies in the very nature of man's (in)ability to read his truth.

> Lerne: schon
> im September verrät dich das Licht
> an einen messerblitzenden Himmel.

While this poem was written, the author worked on the manuscript of his novel *Septemberlicht* (1977). Bienek's own biography explains his fear of human treachery (at the age of twenty-one he was sentenced to twenty-five years in a Siberian labour camp), but this poem extends its imaginative range beyond personal history. It is really a poem redefining reading and writing: "Die Füße unterm Schreibtisch/fangen zu faulen an", "die Todesnachrichten beim Grillfeuer/...lesen". Australia unsettled the poet's European sense of language and challenged the very nature of his art. The poem advocates a return to nature which will lead to a sharpened sense of man's fragility, to a more sensitive perception of human mortality. "Lerne vom Licht," it concludes, "vom Regen/und von den erdhaften Wombats."(135) The Australian landscape appears to Bienek as a new language, a basic yet complex idiom he is anxious to understand.

In the poem "Unterwegs", a title of carefully studied double sense, he expresses his frustration over the ever-presence of words. But these words include "die Zeugenschaft der Bäume./Gum Trees. Eukalyptus. Geisterbäume." There is deliberate ambiguity over the source of the poet's despair. "Wörter. Nichts als Wörter." He needs to escape from his European language of civilisation and abstraction, yet he finds an Australian nature which is both terrifying and mysterious: "Schwarz die verbrannten Stümpfe. Waldrebus." Bienek celebrates an ancient tongue which has been destroyed by man. It is now a riddle we have to learn to solve. "Lies in den Zweigen. Lies die Ringe!" We have lost the ability to read the spirit of a primeval nature. All we can do is decipher our own destruction. The short poem is tightly held together by the frame-like opening and closing lines:

> Wörter. Nichts als Wörter.
> Zähle die Feuer. Zähle die Feuer!(Ibid.)

It is more than likely that Bienek also detaches himself from a more "fiery" language in poetry, sensing the destruction of fundamental correlations and the "unnaturalness" of such imagination.

"Lake Eyre" too ends on a Brechtian didactic note: "Glaub an die Bücher!" But there is no contradiction. In this narrative poem readings "in alten Büchern" are authenticated by an Aborigine's reading of "magische Zeichen". Bienek continues to correlate the language of man and the language of nature. He finds his epiphany in the outback, learning to read the signs. In dissecting death the vision of life will reappear. An Aborigine tells the poet how to tear out the heart of the dead to flood Lake Eyre and "den Mond herunterziehn, tief,/und fruchtbar wird das Land, ringsum." It is the salt of life and death which the native guide relates back to nature and the constellations. Remembering his youthful readings ["(Sammlung Diederich.)"] the poet has to acknowledge his lack of faith ("Glaub an die Bücher!"). In one of his most haunting and imaginatively correlative adaptations Bienek ends the poem with the self-critical appraisal

> Und ich denke daran, mit etwas mehr Mut
> wär ich es vielleicht gewesen,
> der einmal Sonne und Mond vereint hätte,
> dort im gleißenden Salzlicht vom Eyre-See. (136)

His "In Australien" sequence shows what can be done with travel writing when a gifted poet addresses himself to the experience of a different country, when he opens himself up to the spirituality of its nature. Unlike most German-Australian writers, Horst Bienek possesses the imaginative strength to meet such a challenge.

Even "Sydney. Opera House" centres around "Die eine Sprache/und die vielen Zungen". In this poem Bienek reverses the earlier process: this time he begins with the quotation of a European myth ("Ikarus stürzte ins Meer."). But Greek mythology, German music and European culture are transformed by a new civilisation. Its daring leads to its own vision; the poet senses the dawning of a different, antipodean culture. As with all previous poems, light retains its ambivalent symbolism. It remains unclear whether "Licht" betrays ("verrät") or enlightens and revives ("werden die Erinnerungen hell"). It is still twilight,

> Dämmerzeit, in der sich dies Land
> die Augen reibt und erschreckt
> etwas von seiner eigenen Kühnheit
> zu ahnen beginnt. (137)

Bienek's Australian poems are readings in intercultural relations, imaginative "alienations" of culturally predefined language. Yet in "Ausflug nach Woollongong" the poet reads Australian signs with disturbing ease, as they affirm his own limitations in a strange land. Paradoxically, it is this knowledge which links his reading to the old language he has left behind. The fragile nature of our being, the terminal character of human life unites even the most divergent cultures. As always, Bienek's reading and writing are of existential dimensions.

"Under the Southern Cross" summarises the poet's travels in Australia, searching for "Heimat" in a foreign continent. It is at night (away from the "betrayals" of the light of day?) that he explores his presence. "Expeditionen nurmehr nachts,/übern südlichen Himmel." Bienek attempts to locate, to define himself in relation to the stars. "Ah! Sterne und Sätze." He turns the inherited words ("Der Centaurus. Indus. Crux und/Corona Australis... Cepheus. Die Geliebte des/Großen Bären. Andromeda. Cassiopeia, die Vertraute...") into new discoveries, measuring his losses and the pain of searching for the truth. Home is "ganz unten, ein Kindertraum". As with his previous poems, Bienek instructs and directs himself. This time the lesson reads: "Sieh nach unten!" But "unten" in down-under Australia means "Die rote Erde Australiens", holding a painful truth in which the German poet has a part: the distance between man and his home, wherever he might be. The poem concludes with an insistence on a very sensuous tasting of this unpalatable truth, affirming a human geography of dislocation:

> Mahl die Wahrheit zwischen den Zähnen,
> lange, wie Sand; Sand. Spuck ihn aus, Woomera-rot.
> Die Wahrheit: von hier ist *alles* fern.(138-139)[6]

Like almost all German visitors to Australia, Horst Bienek is fascinated by the fate of Ludwig Leichhardt. It is the literary transformation of the historical character which is of main interest to him. He finds himself "Auf den Spuren/von Voss, der Leichhardt geheißen/und aus dem finsteren Deutschland kam." Bienek has been responsible for a modest interest in Patrick White translations in West Germany during the seventies and eighties. The opening stanza of "Voss, auch Leichhardt geheißen" is an homage to the Australian Nobel Prize winner which draws a composite figure of Leichhardt, Voss and White. Its final three lines allude to the self-imposed loneliness and isolation of Patrick White:

> Hinter den weißen Rolläden tickt
> die Schreibmaschine des Aus-Gezeichneten.
> Seine Einsamkeit ist noch größer geworden.

Following the tracks of the German explorer, Bienek relates back to his earlier "Lake Eyre" poem. In a kind of self-quotation appropriate for a coherent sequence such as this, the poet reinvokes the signs of Aboriginal vision embracing nature, the constellations and man in search of his home:

> Was man jetzt hier findet,
> ist verbrannt, verkohlt, ausgeglüht,
> dein Herz, Bruder, malt
> mit den schwarzen Farben von Dubbo
> den Himmel herunter, löscht ihn aus.

Like his words, the words of German or Australian writers, and the words of mortal human beings, the remnants of our explorations will be burnt; our future lies in ashes. "*On the road*" we are following paths of dust; our presence is not more than a torch of sand.(139) Death is ever-present, every day carries with it premeditated or accidental murder: " — aufblitzt am Hals das Rasiermesser." Bienek draws parallels between the German revolution of 1848 which Leichhardt missed and the German explorer's own wilful challenge to Australia's tyranny of distance. He not only compares "Die brennenden Herrenhäuser in Deutschland" with "die flammenden Horizonte der/Großen Simpson-Wüste". The poem draws a further explicit analogy between civilisation's murder weapon "das Rasiermesser" and "die Sichel im Hals..., geschwungen von einem trance-verzückten *Aboriginal*". Bienek thus continues to relate to White's literary myth, reinforcing it by stylising a native bus-driver to a "Nachfahr"(140) of the murderer of Leichhardt. The poem acknowledges in its title the need of mythological language and imaginative vision to express the mystery of human existence. The tracks of Leichhardt or Voss may be rediscovered by the poetic spirit of writers like White or Bienek.

The sequence "In Australien" concludes with "Sydney, im Juni". On one level it is little more than an enumeration of sights and sounds, of suburbs and buildings. Bienek lists all the places he has visited, rehearsing "die neuen, noch ungewohnten Wörter". For it is language he has come to gather, new words and expressions he has gained. He makes no attempt to explain them, to lend them a meaning other than they carry by their very invocation. Words are suburbs of a city language. Once more the poet, equally in love with the verbal composition and its city, records his presence. And finally, in a gesture of protective identification, he acknowledges his own homelessness, appealing to the new words to offer him shelter, to protect him, to make him a resident in their city.

> Ich möchte sie schützend
> wie ein Dach
> über meine Verlorenheit ziehen. (141)

It is a gesture which sums up Horst Bienek's affection for Australia, the imaginative inspirations of his visits to this country and the spiritual dimensions inherent in an antipodean language he retains on his return to Germany.

Significantly, Bienek integrates a few glimpses of this Australian "language" into another poetic sequence entitled "Flucht, vergeblich". As the heading implies, the theme of these thirty-six poems is flight, or rather, the impossibility of escape. It is easy to see why the ex-prisoner Bienek should be obsessed with escape. His two Australian sections throw light on the poet's decision to accept an invitation of the Goethe Institute to travel to Australia and New Zealand. The journey was undertaken as part of a flight from social, cultural and spiritual alienation. Bienek is amazed that imprisonment and war are themes of little urgency in the southern hemisphere. His surprise balances Australia's political naivety with a European's envy over such innocence. But Sydney is no escape for this poet. In the matter-of-fact reporting style of the sequence Bienek invokes a Polish migrant woman reciting the rosary underneath the Sydney Harbour Bridge, waiting for her death. Her dislocation is further evidence of the impossibility to escape; the three lines in Polish add to the sense of alienation. The thirty-fourth poem ends with the devastating line: "Die Versteinerungen hören nicht auf."(99) Sydney here is a very different kind of city; the poems themselves seem petrifactions rather than invocations or celebrations. The sequence "Flucht, vergeblich" is made up of verbal constructions in which Australia is no more than part of a world-wide prison from which there is no escape. It is fair to say that for Horst Bienek Australia has had both a stifling and a liberating effect. His writings about this country, in poetry and in prose, demonstrate the impact it has had on him, both as a writer and as an individual. The strength of his work lies in this very balance of the artistic, the personal and the sociopolitical. Bienek clearly is one of Germany's most formidable writers to have addressed himself to Australia as a country, a people and an emerging culture. He died in December 1990.

PAUL HATVANI

Nicht da, nicht dort: Australien/In Feindesland/
"...gesenkten Hauptes"

Paul Hatvani, born as Paul Hirsch 1892 in Vienna, published in Expressionist journals such as the *Sturm* and *Brenner*. Since his migration (1939) and subsequent residence in Melbourne he became known again mainly for his influential essay "Über den Expressionismus"(1965). He has since published short pieces of prose, excerpts from his work *Die Ameisen* and the autobiographical reflection on his host country *Nicht da, nicht dort: Australien.* A critical edition of the works of Hatvani is currently being prepared by Pavel Petr and Stephen Jeffries.[7]

Nicht da, nicht dort: Australien appeared in the final 1973 issue of the German literary journal *Akzente*, the theme of which was "exile", literary and political, and new scholarly approaches to the study of exiled writers. Hatvani opens his biographical essay with the important observation that an essential part of a culture are its fictions, the loss of which in exile can lead to a special kind of dislocation. He further distinguishes between "Exil" and "Fremde", suggesting that his exile in Australia has changed to a residency in a foreign country. The implications are that exile ends when it is possible to return to one's native country, but Hatvani himself exemplifies that there is also a cultural "exile" or ghetto, an imposed exclusion from the intellectual

Zürich, den 7.Juni 1939

Frau Esther Landolt

M e l b o u r n e

Sehr geehrte Frau!

    Wir beehren uns Ihnen mitzuteilen, dass der Aufsichtsrat der Schweizerischen Schillerstiftung in seiner Jahressitzung vom 3./4.Juni beschlossen hat, Ihnen für Ihren Roman "Delfine" (Zürich, Humanitas, 1939) einen

<u>Buchpreis von 500 Fr.</u>

zuzuerkennen.

    Wir überreichen Ihnen den Wert in Gestalt der beiliegenden Anweisung auf die Schweizerische Volksbank Zürich und bitten Sie um Empfangsanzeige durch Unterzeichnung und Rücksendung der hier ebenfalls beigeschlossenen Quittung.

    Genehmigen Sie, geehrte Frau, den Ausdruck unserer ausgezeichneten Hochachtung!

Schweizerische Schillerstiftung
Namens des Aufsichtsrates
Der Präsident   Der Aktuar

<u>Beilagen:</u> 1 Check
           1 Quittung

<u>Eingeschrieben</u>

Letter of *Schweizerische Schillerstiftung* to Esther Landolt, 1939

337 Dandenong Road. Armadale.
Melbourne.

23. November, 39.

An die schweizerische Schillerstiftung,

Zufällig geriet heute die inliegende Quittung in meine Hande und ich erkenne beschämt, dass ich vergass, Ihnen dieselbe zuzuschicken, wofür ich Sie um Verzeihung bitte.

Die Zuteilung des Buchpreises für meine "Delfine" war mir eine unerwartete und ganz tiefe Freude. Ich schreibe momentan an einem grossangelegten australischen Roman der im Innern dieses Erdteils spielt, wo das Land unvorstellbar weit ist, die Schafherden nach Zehntausenden zahlen und auf den Bäumen Scharen von Papageien wie unzählige grosse bunte Blumen sitzen. Indem ich mit glühender Hingabe an dem neuen Werk arbeite und mich quäle, wenn ich nicht das erreiche was mir vorschwebt, ist mir, dies sei der beste Weg Ihnen zu danken für die Ehre die Sie mir erwiesen haben.

Mit herzlichem Dank und vorzüglicher Hochachtung

Esther Landolt.

Letter of Esther Landolt to *Schweizerische Schillerstiftung,* 1939

Werner Fels, Sydney, 1938

Walter Kaufmann, Berlin, 1985

Joachim Specht, Dessau, 1988

Margaret Diesendorf, Sydney, 1986

Rudi Krausmann, Sydney, 1989

life of the host country.(564)

The reasons for Hatvani's emigration need no explanation, but his escape from the Nazis led him "in ein anderes Koordinatensystem". (Ibid.) He finds himself in a culturally different environment and in danger of losing his identity, not only as a German writer. (Symptomatically, Leslie Bodi calls Hatvani an "Essayist und *Dichter*", while referring to German-Australian writers as "Autoren" and "Schriftsteller" — that, too, an expression of cultural "Koordinaten"...) Hatvani defines exile in contrast to being abroad. Exile means being forced into cultural alienation, while going abroad usually leads to cultural enrichment. Until recent times migration also implied a desperate need and did not allow the exercise of freedom. Paul Hatvani's presence in Australia is the extension of exile; he cannot be classified a migrant writer. This fact alone makes his position in the history of German-Australian writing unique.

Hatvani stresses the challenge of "ein Wechsel des geistigen Klimas".(565) It is not difficult to imagine the *Kulturschock* experienced by the established writer of German Expressionism when confronted with Melbourne in the late thirties. He tries to reassure himself: "es gibt doch auch für dieses Land ein Außen, in dem gedacht, gefühlt, gedichtet wird, gemalt und komponiert!"(Ibid.) Exile in Australia meant a life "gegen das Denken".(Ibid.) Hatvani's knowledge of the country was, like that of most German émigrés, severely limited. He is presented with an Australia of European, culturally his own, making. It is, or was, a country of adventurous gold-diggers, a place of European cultural colonialism, waiting to be explored and exploited. But most of all, Hatvani confirms the overriding character and attraction of Australia: it is far away from Europe. Whether exile, migrant or traveller, most Germans in Australia have come to distance themselves from their native land and culture. It is this negation (even if enforced) which colours their entire outlook on the country and its people. To be "europamüde"(Ibid.) does not mean to be vitally interested in Australia (or any other place). Even Paul Hatvani speaks of "das bevorstehende Abenteuer"(568) of his imminent resettlement. In his case "adventure" refers to the unknown, retaining some of the word's original sense, whereas the majority of other German writers about Australia apply a concept of *Abenteuer* which predefines experience: their various encounters merely confirm knowledge and expectations.

Hatvani's early impressions of Australia quickly lead to more embracing discoveries. His claim that Australia reveals sociocultural structures of its source country is clearly of general validity for all colonised nations. Adopted traditions replacing and predefining history are an enforced national identification further adding to the alienation of migrants from other cultural backgrounds. The "untimeliness" of the Australian identity is exemplified in the prolonged retention of its pioneering image: "Man spielt Pionier auch lange noch nach der 'Eroberung': denn man will sich doch auch ein wenig als Eroberer fühlen."(Ibid.) Hatvani's own need to remain part of German culture is not really very different. Earlier he explains "die Grundlage unserer Existenz" as the opportunity to share in the cultural identity and development of his country: "weil wir mitdenken und mitwirken durften!"(565) But Hatvani's conflicts with Anglo-Australian culture go much deeper and lie elsewhere.

Nicht da, nicht dort: Australien combines a subtle analysis of language with an appraisal of historical repetition and retardation. In a critical assessment of the English language and what he calls the "angelsächsische Sprachdynamik" Hatvani makes a startling discovery:

> daß die Sprache unbedenklich Wörter, nicht aber auch die an sie gebundenen Vorstellungen und Begriffe aus anderen Idiomen übernimmt und so tut, als wäre dies das Natürlichste auf der Welt. Man mußte also auch umdenken lernen und nicht nur die Fremdsprache.(569)

It is perhaps less important whether this observation applies to Australian English only as it is to recognize the fact of intercultural linguistic alienation. Hatvani's assessment can be the very basis of creative tension, as exemplified by much of Australia's contemporary multicultural literature. His refusal to continue or to extend his writing career in English further adds to "ein Leben am Rande", as he describes his life in Melbourne.(571) As he admits, that would have involved "umdenken lernen"(569), using a second language as a means of reassessing the assumptions and realities of a native culture. Unlike social developments in Australia, it would not involve repeating things already known. Strangely, Hatvani claims to belong, together with other exiled intellectuals and artists, to the "geistig unabhängig Orientierten".(Ibid.) Perhaps it is a reference to the title of his biographical reflections, an attempt to negate the negation.

Australia is seen as an extension of European history. It would be interesting to know whether Hatvani abandoned his Eurocentric interpretation of Australian history towards the end of his life. His biographical review ends on a note of qualified detachment. He endorses another exile's definition of their presence in Australia: "Ich bin ja nicht hergekommen, um hier zu sein; ich bin hergekommen, um nicht dort zu sein!"(571) It is this (understandable) "otherness" of Australia which determines Paul Hatvani's critical acceptance of his host country.

Against this background Hatvani's prose narrative "In Feindesland" (1968) assumes additional dimension. The need to become invisible in a home country that has turned into enemy territory can be fulfilled only by traders whose cloaks and codes originate from "nowhere", who sell alibis of absence and exchange masks of non-entity manufactured in a place far away.

Such "innere Emigration" anticipates the need for a more radical escape. The "Nirgendwo" will take physical, geographical shape. The author refers to a geography of thought: "im Feindesland war das Gesetz ein Koordinaten-System mit tödlichen Bestimmungen und Du warst darin eingesponnen."(72) In *Nicht da, nicht dort: Australien* Hatvani speaks of "ein anderes Koordinatensystem"(564) replacing the tyranny of cultural alienation in his home country. What he lists as an essential requirement for the exile, in Australia or elsewhere, is anticipated by the reign of terror in his native culture: "Man begann, mit Begriffen zu spielen, die aus anderen Bereichen gekommen waren; Denken war mit einem Male eine Tätigkeit geworden, deren Gesetze von Außen her bestimmt wurden." It is important to correlate Hatvani's "Fremdland" and "Feindesland", to see the immediate connections between "inner emigration" in Nazi-Germany and eventual exile and residence in Australia. Self-documentation and fiction inform each other. Language's political and cultural reality creates one literature, one vision, one understanding: "Man hatte...Vokabeln erlernen müssen, deren Zweck noch nicht vollends erfaßt wurde."(73) The experience of learning to express himself in a language he does not fully trust or understand is anticipated in the desperate need to camouflage his native tongue. "Man wagte nicht aufzutreten, ging man in dieser ungewohnten Sprache spazieren; aber man hatte bald erlernt, sich so auszudrücken, daß die andern nicht merken konnten, wie wenig wir von ihrer Sprache auch richtig verstehen wollten."(Ibid.) For all the acknowledged difference between the exile's situation in Melbourne and the persecuted's dilemma in his native Vienna, both reflect each other, both dictate related points of reference. Not surprisingly the *Ameisen* fragment "In Feindesland" ends with an expulsion from the native culture's paradise. The consequence is to venture forth into a different "world", to migrate as exile to a foreign place where similar conflicts are re-experienced not by a tyranny of enemies but as a means of preserving the memories of home and of co-existing in the unfolding of a different culture. The new language of Australia has its own history, it cannot be translated into German cultural consciousness.

It is even possible to recognise some of Hatvani's disappointment and disillusionment as cultural and political exile in the "moral" of his narrative sketch "...gesenkten Hauptes"(1968). For the "antipodean" reversal of a "Freudenhaus" into a "Melancholisches Bordell" — with the author's significant comment "wie doch die deutsche Sprache manchmal in die Irre geht!"(76) — leads to an advice to the hostesses strangely reminiscent of the exile's and refugee's need to be humoured, to be comforted, to be "accepted", if not "loved". It is difficult not to read into such a text an analogous logic of the migrant refugee's status in the "Freudenhaus" host country and the culturally dislocated artist's sombre knowledge of the ultimate nothingness of being: the "joy" of survival is dampened by the "melancholy" of mere existence. The range of Paul Hatvani's imaginative adaptations of exile needs no further illustration.

Wolf Heckmann

Haie fressen keine Deutschen

First published in 1974, this report of a solo flight in a power glider from Germany to Australia was reissued as a paperback in 1982, going into a second edition two years later. Heckmann's *Erlebnisbericht*[8] thus proved of great popular appeal. Of its twenty-two chapters, only the last three deal explicitly with Australia. The book is essentially an adventurous tale written specifically for flying aficionados, telling tales of great stunts and anecdotes of pilots' feats. In his Introduction Rudolf Braunburg alludes to the "exclusive" nature of such adventurous explorations. "Das Buch ist voller magischer Namen. Die, freilich, werden nur vom Insider als solche erkannt."(12) His reference to the "initiated" is little more than a marketing exercise, designed to increase sales figures. Yet it appeals to the very concept of adventure and the exotic, promising the reader "etwas...von dem, was heute so oft und mißverständlich über die falschen Lippen kommt: Freiheit".(13)

Heckmann offers his initiated readers or devotees the *ersatz* freedom of an armchair adventure, a flight across the world, a flying visit to the antipodes.

The author makes no pretence to literary ambitions; his style is colloquial, racy and direct, occasionally uncouth and self-flattering. His knowledge of Australia is based on earlier visits, the return flight designed to renew contact. It is clear that Heckmann found Australia an attractive place and its people likeable, congenial. "Wie alles, zu dem man eine erste heftige Zuneigung empfindet," he explains, "wollte ich es näher kennenlernen."(210) He claims a kind of elective affinity for Australia. A European population transported into "eine brutale, nicht zu bändigende Natur"(Ibid.) is viewed as "ein interessantes Experiment".(Ibid.) The author sees in that the uniqueness of what he calls the "sixth continent". He characterizes the Australian language as similar to the "'Cockney'-Jargon der Londoner Unterklasse,...geprägt von bildkräftigen Wortschöpfungen".(211) Heckmann believes he has discovered the result of white Australia's cultural transportation: it is a casualness bordering on indifference. He tells the story of the 1974 cyclone destroying Darwin and the casual determination of its inhabitants to rebuild their city in the same place. Instead of European stubbornness he senses an acceptance of life's trials and a good-natured willingness to start again.

Descriptions of Australian wildlife are colloquial, continuing the conversational style of the book as a whole. He shows little interest in (or knowledge of) particular species; when he uses actual names, he often gets them wrong. Thus he speaks of the "'Barramandy',...einem Raubfisch, der im Meer kapitale Größen erreicht".(Ibid.) But for all that he is seeking "das richtige, urige Australien", flying "Südkurs, mitten durchs Land".(213) Confronted with Aborigines, Heckmann ventures his own anthropological reflection. It would be unfair to call his sentiments racist; perhaps they could best be called European or what he himself terms Nordic.

> Im Prinzip ist das die Wurzel des Übels: Wann immer Menschen verschiedener Entwicklungsstadien zusammentrafen, waren wir aus dem Norden (um des Überlebens willen zu Aktivität und Innovation gezwungen) die Mobilen und Aggressiven. Australien wurde so eindeutig und unwiderruflich ein Land der Weißen (und nicht das schlechteste). Aber wo haben die Schwarzen ihren Platz darin?(214-215)

It reads like an apologia for the supremacy of the white race, at least in relation to the original Australians. Heckmann maintains that whites are better at handling alcohol, but is anxious not to be misinterpreted: "diese Feststellung hat nichts mit rassischer Überheblichkeit zu tun".(215) He does acknowledge the belated attempts on the part of the Australian government to support Aborigines in their search for justice. The author does not go into any detail; his discussion of Australia's racial problems remains general and superficial. Towards the end of Chapter Twenty Heckmann speculates:

> Gewiß, zwei bis drei Generationen weiter wird alles anders aussehen.
> Schon heute kann man in den größeren Städten Farbige in allen Berufen treffen.(216)

"In allen Berufen?" Such a claim is demonstrably untrue, and Heckmann's prediction regarding the future of Australia's Aborigines is largely rhetorical, based as it is on inadequate knowledge of the facts.

But Heckmann's main interest in Australia is as the destination of his flight. Chapter Twenty-One bears the title "Ein Pferd auf der Runway". Much of the country is observed from behind the cockpit of his glider, and not all perceptions are profound: "sie brauen ein gutes Bier da unten in Australien," the flying author notes, "mehr nach unserer Art, richtig mit Kohlensäure und eiskalt serviert...".(219) When he does land in small places like Daly Waters, however, he uses the opportunity to describe Australian characters from a closer angle. He is particularly impressed by the outback truckies and road trains.(221) And Heckmann is one of the few German travel writers who manages to convey the effects of Australian swearing in translation. This is how he reproduces the language of an outback publican:

> Ihr wollt sicher alle beschissene Zimmer die könnt ihr kriegen aber die beschissenen Zimmermädchen sind mir alle weggelaufen und das beschissene Bettzeug ist nicht gewechselt und ich krieg erst übermorgen beschissene neue Mädchen.

Heckmann adopts the vocabulary to good comical effect:

> Wir versicherten einhellig, daß uns das beschissene Bettzeug nichts ausmache.
> Inzwischen hatte er auch den beschissenen Zustand seines Kochs mit sicherem Blick erkannt: "Trinkt noch ein beschissenes Bier auf meine Rechnung, Jungs, und morgen früh mach ich euch selbst ein beschissenes Frühstück."
> Wir tranken sein Bier und machten uns auf ins beschissene Bettzeug, denn alle wollten früh raus.(Ibid.)

In a conciliatory and humorous twist he ends the chapter with a characteristically Australian anecdotal joke about German-Australian relations.

"Ja, Deutschland... Ich war schon zweimal da. Beim erstenmal war es aber schwer, reinzukommen."
"Wieso," fragte ich verblüfft, "als Australier kannst du doch keine Visum-Schwierigkeiten gehabt haben."
"Das war's nicht," antwortete er, "ihr Bastarde hörtet nicht auf zu schießen." ("You bastards kept shooting.")
Wir tranken einen mächtigen darauf, daß wir so etwas beschissenes nicht wieder machen wollten.(224)

Heckmann does capture the tone of Australian wit exceedingly well, as he is at his best throughout his narration whenever he adopts a colloquial style. He relates a number of other anecdotes, among them legendary stories of the Flying Doctor Service. Unlike Hans-Otto Meissner and other German writers he praises the wide variety of cuisine available in this country, agreeing that it used to be very limited indeed. It offers him the opportunity to endorse the development of an Australian multicultural society. "Durch die verstärkte Einwanderung aus Europa," he notes, "ist mit der australischen Küche, ungefähr in den letzten anderthalb Jahrzehnten, ein Wunder geschehen."(220) His repeated visits have made him realise the dramatic changes that have taken place over the last twenty years.

Heckmann's affection for Australia leads him into various attempts to characterise the national temperament. Problematic as such generalisations are, he nonetheless offers a number of valid statements. One of them concerns the anti-authoritarian attitude shared by most Australians: "Das ist ebenfalls ein Charakteristikum australischen Nationalcharakters: Im Zweifelsfalle hält man gegen so etwas wie 'Obrigkeit' lieber zusammen."(226) He links this apparent lack of discipline to the fighting qualities of the Australian soldier, reinforcing a national myth. He sees the German enemy as a challenge of superiority to be defied by a uniquely Australian cameraderie and mateship. Although he never actually uses the word, Heckmann's admiration for the Australian character is based (almost exclusively) on this sense of comradeship. It applies especially to the flying fraternity: to fly in Australia is to be among brothers. This feeling of acceptance, of being looked after by like-minded comrades or mates leads him to say, more than once: "Ich fühlte mich jedenfalls bei den australischen Behörden sicher wie in Abrahams Schoß...".(228) In a way, Australia is to this author "ein Land für Privatflieger".(226) Perhaps some German readers extend such a statement to a metaphorical level; it could add up to a sociological and cultural truism. "Alles ist darauf eingerichtet, auch und gerade bei den 'Kleinen' die Fliegerei so problemlos wie möglich zu machen."(Ibid.) It is indeed this metaphorical interpretation that can lend Heckmann's "adventures" in Australia an additional and perhaps most authentic dimension. The magnificent man in his flying machine does have a particular view of Australia with its own logic.

Wolf Heckmann's *Haie fressen keine Deutschen* is no literary masterpiece. Much of it reads like escapist juvenile "adventure". Australia remains throughout a point of reference, a destination, the challenge of a place far away. It is a flyer's Australia Heckmann introduces, ranging from Darwin to Daly Water, Parkes, Sydney-Bankstown, Canberra, Kalgoorlie and Perth. His descriptions of the land and its people are restricted to contacts made along this route. They are largely impressionistic and anecdotal, yet of undeniable authenticity. Within such confines Wolf Heckmann sings the praises of his flying goal, the destination of his long-distance record, the re-established contact with like-minded adventurers and pioneers.

CARL HEINZ KURZ

Australische Silhouetten

In a brief collection (1975) the author attempts a kind of poetic travelogue or imaginative reporting.[9] The short prose sketches aim to capture representative scenes and moments of a visit to Australia. They are complemented by Kurz's own graphic work which, like the prose, must be described as illustrative rather than evocative. "Bastionen des Lebens" reflects on a year-long drought in the centre of Australia. Unfortunately, neither thought nor language rise above the commonplace. Despite the well-meaning, if naive, conclusion that one has to learn to look at Australia with "non-European", "non-German eyes", Carl Heinz Kurz fails to do just that. His sketch-book is a collection of good intentions, socially as well as artistically. Kurz's Australia is German impressionism alluding to a vision that does not exist. None of his verbal or graphic sketches reveals any degree of urgency or motivation. The reader is left wondering why the book appeared at all.

Like so many German writers Carl Heinz Kurz is obsessed with size, distance and paradox. His interpretations of Australian abundance and need are preconditioned, following the slogans of popular travelogues. His language lacks any imaginative strength, and is characterised by what might be termed anecdotal authority.

Occasionally, Kurz centres his reflections on a journalistic concept: "Wachablösung" seeks to poeticize the "changing of the guards" in a comment on Australia's younger generations. But the author does not even allude to the possible nature of change, to a difference of values and to the significance of such a new beginning. As a result, the text never rises above the banal observation that the young are challenging the old — in any society, at any time. There is nothing particularly "Australian" about Kurz's sketch. "Eine alte Frau nur..." captures the scene of an old Aboriginal woman with her starving grandchildren, trying to protect and to feed them, while waiting for members of her tribe to return from the hunt. (Incongruously, Kurz insists on spelling "Känguruh" "Kängeruh"...,18.) Although this portrait too is highly stylised and not without sentimentality, it does convey the poetic pathos the author is aiming for. (The accompanying drawing totally fails to give expression to the unique Aboriginal features; woman and children look remarkably German.)

"Nacht belauschter Geheimnisse" is a text of great potential. It deals with a situation on an outback farm: the use of the two-way radio for private and for public purpose. A young woman eagerly awaiting the call of her boyfriend has to hand over the radio to a stockman. The total lack of confidentiality is stressed. Kurz transforms this frustration into a poetry bordering on kitsch. There is no call for the daughter, who waits up till late. "Sie wartet. Vergebens. Der Himmel Australiens ist voller belauschter Geheimnisse."(22) The impact of this projection gains added strength from the author's description of the young son using the radio the following morning in routine appointments of the open air school. Kurz succeeds in presenting a topos of Australian travelogues with some imaginative authority because he relates it to an individual situation and confronts his poetic interpretation with everyday reality. The final sketch of the collection is entitled "Zu kurz und zu spät". It addresses itself to the fate of Aborigines. Again, the gesture overrules reliable information, empathy and literary style. To say that Aborigines "vegetierten... im australischen Busch"(23) because they were kept away from the white man's settlements is to reveal a remarkable insensitivity regarding native bushcraft and the Aboriginal life-style. The final rhetorical question retains this superficiality of perception and language: "Zu kurz ist ihr Leben. Zu spät jegliche Hilfe?"(25)

Kurz's collection aims for a poetry of sentiment. The "silhouettes" referred to in its title wittingly or unwittingly allude to the lack of precision and substance in the texts. The sketches are projections of shade rather than light. They offer no new insight or understanding of Australia and her people. The author has made it a habit to collect literary snapshots from his journeys; among his other verbal scrapbooks are: *Amerikanische Impressionen, Asiatische Miniaturen, Afrikanische Reminiszenzen* and *Europäische Variationen*. His *Australische Silhouetten* seem to signal that he has exhausted his continental sketches. Travel notes may indeed be one of the most appropriate and effective forms of intercultural mediation. But it needs a keener eye and a better informed mind than this author's to elevate such glimpses, reports and reflections to the level of art.

MICHAEL SCHULTE

Goethes Reise nach Australien

The title of Schulte's collection of *Erzählungen* is a literary construction, alluding in a playfully witty manner to the unknown, the unlikely and the unbelievable. The author embraces all continents in his narrative prose; earlier stories bear the title "Amerika: Speisebrücke", "Europa: Der Fenstersturz zu Prag", "Afrika: Lexikon der Rauchzeichen" and "Asien: King und Kong die Gelackmeierten". The tone is set for a special brand of literary humour.

Published in 1976, *Goethes Reise nach Australien*'s title story (the final in the collection) mocks and satirises the cultural hero of German bourgeois *Bildung*. The awe-inspiring figure of Goethe is demythologised. The narrator reveals that during his famous Swiss and Italian journeys Goethe was actually asleep. In a style similar to Thomas Bernhard's, Schulte devises a fable of comical scenarios, assuming the voice of a respectful and objective reporter. For his journey to Australia, we are told, Goethe hired a number of scientists whose task it was to report to the *Dichterfürst* all the events and sightings of the day. But their main duty was to dress and undress their master, to accommodate the poet's sleep. Schulte calls into doubt the prime quality of Goethean observation and reflection: the immediacy of experience and the spontaneity of thought. All essentially Goethean qualities in literature and science are replaced by "Goethes ungeheurem Schlafbedürfnis".(109) He dreams the world and its discoveries. In his provincial hotel accommodation he studied "die Tapeten".(114) Schulte's persiflage adopts the tone of a German historian or high school teacher, undermining cultural authoritarianism. Australia is really no more than a code signifying escape from Germany and its bourgeois culture. Schulte designs a "plot" in which Goethe's escape to Australia is motivated by his intense dislike for howling dogs, only to find that "überall ist Vollmond, und überall bellen die Hunde".(117) His highly qualified scientists can merely report that the foreign landscapes are all more or less "wie bei uns in Deutschland,...nur manchmal, damit es nicht allzu auffällig wurde, erwähnten sie eine Palme oder ein paar Ameisenbären."(120) It is really Goethe's planning of a trip to Australia which takes up most of the narrative's humorous attention. Not the destination matters, but the genial resourcefulness to avoid making new discoveries. To Schulte's Goethe everything is already known or can be approximated by virtue of other people's encounters. The world is not worth being explored because the great genius carries it within him. The story thus concentrates on trivial, comical and irrelevant preparations for "Goethes Reise nach Australien".

As part of his preparations Goethe reads "den Band 'Australische Sprichwörter',...erschienen in der Reihe 'Weisheit der Völker'."(127) With an eye on Goethe's own "Maximen und Reflexionen" the narrator records the German poet's agitation over these Australian aphorisms: "Wenn er nachts im Bett lag und nicht einschlafen konnte, klappte er dieses Buch an irgendeiner Stelle auf und las australische Aphorismen. Aber die Aphorismen regten ihn derart auf, daß er sofort wieder zur Weinflasche greifen mußte."(Ibid.) Schulte quotes some of the nonsensical antipodean aphorisms — curiously reminiscent of Rudi Krausmann's "sentence constructs" (*Three Plays*, Sydney 1989) — to illustrate the absurdities of cultural alienation.

> *Ein Känguruh mit dem Pfeil des Jägers im Bauch geht nicht gerne spazieren.*
> Oder
> *Eine große Blume ist nicht inmer ein kleiner Baum.*
> Goethe wurde, wie gesagt, äußerst wütend, wenn er derlei las.(128)

The apparently nonsensical nature of such formulations (such

"Australianisms") is contrasted with the great interest they provoke among academics: "Die Wissenschaftler diskutierten oft und lange über die australischen Sprichwörter."(Ibid.) Once again, Schulte derides the "scientific" (humourless and artistically insensitive) discipline of Goethe research (i.e. Germanistik and related "Wissenschaften").

The discovery of Australia is presented in a similarly satirical style(129), followed by speculations whether Goethe and his fellow-scientists would have been allowed into the country ("Männer, die nicht zupacken", Ibid.), given the sevenfold surplus of men in relation to women during the early years of Australia's Europeanisation. Schulte invokes a despairing Goethe in Singapore, uncertain when and whether to complete his *Faust*. The narrative's flippancy is directly correlated to a literal sense of alienation: Goethean German culture is seen to be totally out of place, thereby assuming comical dimensions. In a hilarious sketch Schulte projects a Goethe not only finishing his *Faust*, but also preparing his will in a Singapore hotel, after he has decided to die in early 1832. Needless to say, even the fictional Goethe does not reach Australia — that is to say, he never achieved leaving himself and his indigenous culture behind. Schulte delights in playing with mock profundities, debunking German literary mythology. Goethe spends the rest of his life sitting in the foyer of a Singapore hotel, watching the sunsets and leaving his armchair only to go to the toilet. The story ends on the same note of satire that sets the tone and logic of the entire narrative:

> "In Australien hätte ich auch keine schöneren Sonnenuntergänge gesehen," sagte er sich, wenn er abends vom Klo kam. Das war sein Trost, bis er im Sessel in der Eingangshalle des einzigen Hotels von Singapur den kleinen Kontinent und die fünf Wissenschaftler langsam vergaß.(139)

Such good-natured derision of German literary culture is a rare and unusual feature in the history of German-Australian literary relations. Schulte's narrative is an extreme example of Australia serving as a mere point of reference, a verbal image, a sign of the incongruous, far-fetched and ridiculous. Australia, then, has become a mere device to satirise German cultural pretensions. Together with H. C. Artmann, Michael Schulte transforms the exotic image of Australia into an intrinsically imaginative concept of the absurd. The social and political reality of Australia is of no interest to these authors; the country is reduced to a verbal device in their satirical exercise of German *Kulturkritik*.

Peter Bichsel

Immer noch liegt die Oper von Sydney südlich der Alpen

In Peter Bichsel one of Switzerland's (and German literature's) wittiest writers came to visit Australia in 1977. The result of his readings at various Universities and associated travels in this country is a delightful short story included in his highly successful collection *Geschichten zur falschen Zeit* (1979). It is a narrative as shrewd as it is entertaining. Its subject is Europe's wrong perception of Australia — in a sense, it summarises much of what is problematic in German-Australian writing. Bichsel is one of the few German-language writers who is prepared to look at Australia from a non-European perspective, indeed, to use his experience of this country to severely criticise Eurocentric cultural arrogance.

As the title of his story implies, Bichsel challenges the European perspective of cultural geography. He is sensitive to a different concept of culture and in particular scorns the European hybris of seeing itself as the centre of the world. To define such a view is comparable, he suggests, to the papal dogma of a flat earth. Bichsel's discovery of Australian culture is a source of strength: "Es scheint mir auch," he reflects, "daß die Idee von der total hoffnungslosen Welt eine europäische Idee ist."(153) He appreciates that in Australia there is little fear of impending doom, no European *angst* of a global holocaust: "Der Untergang Europas wird hier nicht mit Weltuntergang verwechselt."(Ibid.)

The Sydney Opera House thus assumes the symbolic significance of a European monument to culture completely out of place in Australia. It is uncharacteristic of this country's own social values, in its monumentalism paradoxically an expression of inferiority. Bichsel calls the building forced upon Sydney a classic case of cultural colonialism.

Bichsel's story is an impassioned plea for an Australian culture in the making. Its author realises that the collective term "die Australier" is even less meaningful than foreigners referring to "die Schweizer" or "die Franzosen". He knows that the Australian population is a multicultural mixture in the process of defining itself. Unlike other visiting writers, Bichsel is full of praise for most of this country's cities. Vaguely echoing Paul Hatvani's view of a nineteenth-century Australia, Peter Bichsel delights in the "echte, belebbare Städte, Sydney vor allem, aber auch Melbourne. Städte aus dem späten 19.

Jahrhundert...".(Ibid.) He claims to have found in Australia the very kind of city which has been destroyed in Europe. Whatever the validity of his claim, it is clear that Bichsel feels at home in Australia — and he feels guilty that he should be surprised by that. "Es gefällt mir hier," he says early in his "Geschichte zur falschen Zeit", "und ich schäme mich, daß es mich überrascht."(151) Perhaps it took a Swiss writer, used to multiculturalism in his native country, to remain open to cultural diversity and to reject the clichés of national identity. Like Siegfried Lenz, Peter Bichsel carried with him one piece of foreknowledge of Australia: the image of Sydney's Opera House. "...es ärgert mich hinterher," he explains, "daß auch sie zu dem ganz wenigen gehörte, was ich vorher von Australien wußte, und daß genau diese Oper mit daran schuld ist, daß ich mir ein falsches Bild von Australien gemacht hatte."(Ibid.) Lenz did not find what he was looking for, Bichsel found what he was not looking for. Both writers escape the malaise of most German tourists and authors: "nur Dinge (zu) erzählen, die sie vorher schon wußten".(Ibid.) Bichsel's story, then, is about "falsche Vorstellung"(Ibid.), the difficulty of perceiving authentically, of shedding cultural conditioning. As such, it is arguably a prose work of critical significance in the history of German-Australian writing.

Among his challenges to European cultural interpretations Bichsel takes issue with the assumption that Australia has no history of its own. He defines history as a quintessentially European discipline. Bichsel refers to the "fürchterliche Geschichte"(Ibid.) of Australian participation in five wars("Burenkrieg, im Ersten und im Zweiten Weltkrieg, in Korea und in Vietnam"), only to emphasise that these conflicts were global rather than Australian and that global still means European ("die Welt zu sein, das ist der Anspruch von Europa", 154). He thus alludes not only to an Australian history apart from Europe, but also to a concept of history which is no longer European. The very nature of human experience may be in a state of redefinition. If Australia inspired Peter Bichsel and prompted him to write "man kann hier wirklich leben"(Ibid.), it is his trust in a new cultural geography, a new people's consciousness, a new kind of living. Instead of the usual fictional variations of German-Australian dislocation this author presents his readers with a witty and inspiring vision of cultural relocation.

Chapter Six

Tourist Guides and Television Images: Full Circle

"Wildnis, wie sie uns in den
Fernsehfilmen gezeigt worden war... "

Jürgen Seidel, *Ausgewandert*

THE EIGHTIES

With the dramatic increase in travel from Germany to Australia, the eighties reflect a strong growth in what may be termed "literary tourism". Actors, television hosts and journalists feel the urge to write about their "adventures" in Australia. The greater accessibility of the country extended the range of German-Australian publications. Most of the writing can be described as journalistic, with strong biographical overtones. Traditional travelogues and popular introductions to the continent continue to appear, varying in quality and aim. Manneristic presentations emphasise the "cleverness" of personal reports. They often lead to highly dubious assertions, such as the formulation of Australian pride in an alliance with the United States, a national affection for the American Big Brother (!): "Der Stolz auf den großen Bruder oder Die kaum erwiderte Zuneigung für die USA." (*Klaus Viedebantt*, 1981) Travelogues have always recorded experiences and information that date quickly. Together with their often subjective impressions, they prove the least reliable accounts of Australia.

Since this country is being visited by more and more German tourists (including relatives of migrants), travel books seem less concerned than ever with the presentation of factual material, concentrating instead on stylistic effects and aiming for sophisticated wit. Such ambitions are not always successful. Because the journey to

Australia has lost much of its exotic quality, unusual perspectives of describing the land and its people replace the adventure of getting here. Journalistic wit rates highly in the publication of personal experience. Whilst most travelogues and popular geographical textbooks make every effort to present the latest information and a generally contemporary image of Australia, a photographic and textual anthology consciously reinvokes the exotic appeal of myth and legend, the "adventure" of a far-away place. Symptomatically, it quotes from earlier German-Australian literature, occasionally accompanying falsely identified images and illustrations. (*Achim Sperber*, 1988)

Tales and detailed accounts of German migration to Australia are surprisingly rare in the history of German-Australian literature. A collection of stories dealing with the subject of migration appeared in 1982, edited by a working party of proletarian writers ("Werkkreis Literatur der Arbeitswelt".) Reflecting on German migration in the late sixties and early seventies, it suggests that there is no escape from the global conditions of capitalism. Migration as a solution for personal or social problems seems no longer possible. Not surprisingly, these stories end in the return of the German migrant to his native country. (*Jürgen Seidel*, 1982)

It remains a remarkable fact that migration for economic gain or political survival has rarely been the subject of German-Australian writing. Where it was not seen as an adventure, leaving one's home country for another was considered to be shameful, unpatriotic, even treasonable. The actual act of migration has, for the most part, been sublimated or excluded in German writing about Australia. Authors of travelogues may comment briefly on the background of German migration to this country; very few settlers ever choose to write about it. In 1986 a book appears which is all the more remarkable: the biography of an Australian descended from early German migrants who migrates back to Germany and lives there for almost forty years — only to eventually return to her native South Australia. (*Vera Bockmann*)

Other publications include travel notes by film stars with literary ambition. They rarely rise above gossip and repetition of clichés about Australia. Their stylistic level can be both unpleasantly pretentious and disarmingly naive. It is clear that these books are not read for their subject-matter; author and reader collude in a voyeuristic endorsement of the "star's" egocentricity.(*Luise Ullrich*, 1983) So-called information about Australia reaffirms stereotypes and false expectations: "Vom

Strandgut zum Millionär". A love for the country soon translates into a publicity gimmick for aging stars. Given that most autobiographies of "stars" are little more than belated publicity campaigns, the commercial exploitation of a "second home" by a German film and television actor can hardly be called unusual. At least his business interests are discussed quite openly.(*Joachim Fuchsberger*, 1988) Under such circumstances it is not even necessary to be the sole author of the book.(*Eckhart Schmidt*, 1988) In publications of this kind Australia is little more than *le dernier cri* at a literary cocktail party hosted by (and for) so-called "Prominente", figures of Germany's public life. Knowledge of the country is usually gained from German migrants acceptable to the "stars" because of their financial success in Australia. The views thus offered are, to say the least, predetermined or "filtered". New discoveries or responses, originality in style or perspective cannot be expected.

The eighties also feature the first — and so far the only — soft porn version of the "Australian adventure", written, even more surprisingly, under the pseudonym of a woman. Sadly, the book is one of the most impoverished in the history of German-Australian literature: its (German or English) language proves as faulty as its "facts". The "erlebte Reise" is described with much involuntary humour, remarkable crudity and a self-revealing pretentiousness of Austrian middle-class bourgeoisie. An extreme has been reached in the non-treatment or non-topicality of Australia. It is literally no more than a pretext for other concerns. (*Liz Scholz*, 1986) The book itself may not be of any consequence, but it demonstrates, albeit in a radical manner, the reluctance or inability of many German-language writers to address themselves to the social, political, geographic and cultural reality of Australia. For all their qualitative and thematic differences, this kind of writing and the highbrow literature of the seventies (*Bienek, Lenz, Artmann, Schulte*) share the avoidance of Australia as a theme of socio-historical verification. The country is either no more than a conveniently "exotic" backdrop, or it is treated as an intellectual, aesthetic or utopian idea. The result is that after 150 years of German-Australian literature, very little real information or specifically German interpretation of Australia has been forthcoming. The majority of German-language writers were content to repeat received myths and clichés or to choose Australia as a more or less fictional locale for the exotic. As a result, the literary quality of German works dealing with Australia tends to be indifferent to poor, a few notable exceptions notwithstanding.

Even the most successful German travelogues, published in large editions, continue to be plagued by an attitude of cultural arrogance and know-all gestures. This condescending attitude often finds itself in blatant contradiction to factual knowledge of the land and frequently ludicrous opinions. (*Hans-Otto Meissner*, 1983-84) The attitude of most German writers seems to be that of an audience judging a spectacle from a different or mixed culture. There is little evidence of a willingness to adjust, to look for different standards of evaluation. Occasionally, a returned "migrant" writes with greater inside knowledge of the reality of Australian life, without, however, offering a less conceited perspective. The tone, even in a work of "fiction", is usually condescending, stylistically sloppy, pert or insolent. To the end, a novel of migration is defined as *eo ipso* a novel of adventure, Australia is no more than an extension of German social conflicts acted out in a more primitive environment. There is, on the whole, little wonder, little real interest in the country itself. In the last decades the increasing assimilation of German and Australian society, supported by intensive travel and tourism, has led to an Australia as a kind of German "outpost", ready-made, packaged and no longer in need of closer investigation. The result is that whereas in the past the clichéd difference of Australia was sold as adventurous exotica, it now has lost most of its intrinsic excitement, serving as little more than a curious backdrop to essentially German social conflicts. (*Till Reinhard*, 1988) As the accessibility of the Australian continent has become greater, the distance less daunting and travel conditions more attractive, the country has lost much of its exotic appeal. It has become part of the international tourist itinerary or features as an extension of German family life. In contemporary German literature Australia exists either as stylistic alienation or as ironic description of personal experience.

Australian writers of German-language origin are carried by the new "movement" of "multiculturalism". On 28 November 1979 the Australian Institute of Multicultural Affairs was established, which lasted until the end of 1986. In March 1987 the establishment of the Office of Multicultural Affairs within the Prime Minister's portfolio was announced. The founding of the literary journal *Outrider* in 1984 was a direct manifestation of the policy of multiculturalism. (*Manfred Jurgensen*) Poetry and prose in English seek to address problems beyond the immediate experience of migration, although it frequently remains the initial perspective. Occasionally childhood memories of

Germany mingle with later conflicts in personal growth, transforming migration into a metaphor for psychological and emotional dislocation. (*Angelika Fremd*, 1989) Other poets and novelists break out of the narrow confines of multiculturalism and migration, without surrendering their bilingual writing (*Diesendorf, Krausmann, Jurgensen, Adamson*). If it is true that Germans are among the earliest to integrate into Australian society, German "migrant" writers of the past thirty years now show a similar anxiety to take their place in a broader concept of Australian literature. It goes without saying that their work is written in English, seeking a wider readership than the migrant community or the country of their birth. It could be said, then, that the trauma of changing one's country, as well as the excitement and curiosity of travelling to a new continent, have largely lost their literary and social significance. Continental, rather than national, identities have added their weight to this development. It is no longer German-Australian ties that matter, but Australia's relations to a European culture and the recognition of this country's own complex "multicultural" identity.

Klaus Viedebantt

30mal Australien und Neuseeland

One of the better travel guides about Australia in German, Viedebantt's *Australien und Neuseeland*, offers introductions to six broad subjects: Australia's history, Australia in the context of nations ("Australien in der Nationengemeinschaft"), Australia's federal states, Australians and their country, Australia's economy and the Australian Life-style ("Australiens Alltag"). Or, as the title of the book would have it, the author discussed Australia (and to a much lesser extent New Zealand) under the heading of thirty-three journalistically phrased themes. Klaus Viedebantt (who is married to an Australian) wrote his guide while working as a travel journalist for the reputable West German weekly *Die Zeit*. He attempts to formulate clever phrases, "headline" definitions designed to attract the reader's attention. Each of his thirty-three titles is meant to epitomise characteristic features, problems or oddities relating to Australia. Typical examples are: "Jubiläum im Schlaraffenland", "Der Kontinent der Knastbrüder oder Wie Historie zum nationalen Komplex verkümmert", "God save the Pommie's

Queen", "Politik — nein danke", "Intellektuellen-Sumpf und Banker-Langweile", "Auf der Apfelinsel lockt die Sünde", "Grieche sucht Griechin", "Dem Reinen ist alles Rhein", "Darüber reden nur die Wilden" and "Miesmacher im Land der Seligen". The book suffers from this "racy" flippancy and the urge to be witty. Pseudo-literary allusions and manneristic alliterations ("Büffel, Bauxit und viele Besucher") add to the impression that the author is determined to display his verbal virtuosity. Put in more positive terms, Viedebantt's guide aims to entertain as well as to instruct.

There can be no doubting the author's good knowledge of his subject. If there are recurring clichés about Australia, they are on the whole valid truisms, rather than ill-informed distortions.

The Foreword motivates the reader's interest in the subject by referring to the political importance of he Pacific region generally and of Australia in particular. "Australien und seine Nachbarländer fangen jetzt erst an, die Weltgeschichte mitzugestalten."(12) It is from this global perspective that Viedebantt writes about Australia. His information is on the whole reliable, even though already (and inevitably) dated. It is more in the area of cultural and sociopolitical interpretation that the author is occasionally off the mark. Thus he fails to appreciate the intended irony of Donald Horne's coinage "the lucky country": "Seine Bewohner nennen es voller Stolz und ohne Ironie 'the lucky country', und sie haben damit mehr Recht, als sie vielleicht selbst ermessen können."(14) He comes closer in his observation that Australians travelling in Europe feel they are being stylised into exotic beings: "...daß sie in 'ihrer' weißen Welt unbeachtet seien: reich, mit der 'richtigen' Hautfarbe versehen und rechtschaffen, aber dennoch 'Exoten'. Das schmerzt ein wenig."(15) Viedebantt rightly asks the question: why, if Australia has been "ein klassisches Auswandererland"(Ibid.) for so long, is it still so little known in Europe? He offers three main reasons: "die geographische Lage, das kulturelle Umfeld und die politische Situation".(Ibid.) His travel guide therefore addresses itself to these subjects. He writes authoritatively about the British arrogance towards Australian culture and the Continental indifference to Australian art and culture as well as to Australian politics. The author's own journalistic background proves of real benefit: it is rare to see a German writer include the press in his discussion of cultural and political relations between Australia and Germany. The book also includes informative data on trade and other bilateral concerns. Published in 1981, some of its report concerning the Bicentennial has to be corrected: Viedebantt writes there will be no re-enactment of the First Fleet ("Also keine neue First Fleet", 18). A few of the titles he recommends for further reading need updating, among them Manning Clark's now completed *History of Australia*. But such faults are inevitable in a travel-guide and do not detract from the good quality of the book. It is perhaps somewhat problematic when the author tries his hand at more general and complex interpretation, such as at the end of the first section: Australia, he argues, still suffers from a "Minderwertigkeitsgefühl gegenüber Großbritannien" and draws the conclusion: "Aus der Geschichte der ersten Jahrzehnte hat sich ein nationaler Komplex entwickelt."(32) Whether this is still the case towards the end of the twentieth century is debatable, although clearly Viedebantt would be right had he confined his remark to earlier decades.

Under the heading "Dem Reinen ist alles Rhein oder Australien — deine Deutschen" (the latter phrase clearly modelled on a West German series dealing with the culture of individual *Länder*) the author offers an historical sketch of the German presence in Australia. Refreshingly, he distinguishes between authentic German culture and the ghetto mentality of some migrants on the one hand and the Australian tourist image of Germany on the other. Viedebantt rightly sees a connection between the two; both distortions reinforce each other. He describes "was sich Australier als typisch deutsch vorstellen und woran sich deutsche Immigranten als Erinnerung laben".(190) Commercialisation and misrepresentation go hand in hand.

> Es ist der internationale Folklore-Verschnitt aus bayerischer Seppelhosenschau, rheinischen Reblausrummels und vexierhafter Altstadtronmantik à la Heidelberg. Darauf heben natürlich auch die Namen der durchaus trinkbaren, wohlschmeckenden Weine ab, "Kaiser Stuhl" etwa, oder — noch naiver — "Rheingold". Dem Reinen ist alles Rhein.(Ibid.)

Such critical awareness and assessment of allegedly German features in Australia is rare. Viedebantt also discusses various aspects of German integration into Australian society. He notes that the assimilation of Germans into Anglo-Australian culture invariably means the deliberate abandonment of the German language. Ironically, many members of German Clubs combine attempts at Australianisation with a desire to participate in a ghetto *Vereinsleben*, resulting in a bastardisation of both languages.

> Dafür verlieren erstaunlich viele Deutsche schon in der ersten Generation die perfekte Kenntnis ihrer Muttersprache und sprechen ein

teutonisches Kauderwelsch. Dies ist auch die vorherrschende Sprache in den rund 70 deutschen Vereinen, die sich überall im Lande finden.(193)

The author's evaluation of Australia's German Clubs confirms his social and cultural sensitivity. Their role in German-Australian relations, notoriously overstated in the German-language press and by the club circuit itself, is stated bluntly:

> Als Partner für die Programme der auswärtigen Kulturpolitik taugen diese Vereine nicht, wie die Botschaft deutlich ausdrückt: "Mit den Clubs können wir nur rechnen, wenn wir eine Zillertaler Blaskapelle einfliegen lassen."(194)

Representation of German culture in Australia has to take place elsewhere.

Viedebantt rightly stresses the significance of German trade and tourism. "Australien gilt den deutschen Fernreise-Veranstaltern als eines ihrer zukunftsträchtigsten Reiseziele," he notes and remarks that German tourists must be particularly welcome in Australia because they visit regions less favoured by local holiday makers: the outback and the desert.(197) Although some of the statistics regarding bilateral commerce are no longer correct, the general account of trade relations remains valid. "Die Handelsbilanz zwischen beiden Ländern ist traditionell negativ zu Lasten Australiens" the author reports.(195)

The chapter on Germans in Australia is both well informed and sensitive in its sociocultural interpretations. Viedebantt's general assessment of Australian attitudes to Germans is undoubtedly correct: "die Bewunderung für die Deutschen ist verwoben mit einem Gefühl der Beklemmung angesichts der zweifach erlebten teutonischen Kriegstüchtigkeit".(188) He traces the history of successful German migration, frequently demythologising widely-held assumptions (such as the "falsche Assoziation..., die Deutschen hätten in Australien den Weinbau eingeführt",189). The impact of German migration is noted in the frequency of German-named suburbs in Australia's major cities (Heidelberg, Coburg, Altona, Leichhardt). There is also a very brief discussion of distinguished German migrants such as the Frankfurt geologist Hans Menge or the explorer Friedrich Wilhelm Ludwig Leichhardt. But the reader will find more detailed and authoritative discussion of this subject elsewhere. What is sadly lacking is any reference to the teaching of the German language and culture in Australia's education system. The book also fails to mention the shift in German migration from labourers to businessmen and professionals.

But that can be explained by its date of publication. The founding in 1976 of an "Australisch-Deutsche Handelskammer" is recorded (196); it has since grown with various branches in major capitals.

It needs to be remembered that Klaus Viedebantt's travel guide aims to be a practical introduction to Australian geography, society and culture. There can be no doubt that it succeeds in informing and interpreting intelligently and, for the most part, authoritatively. The book is indeed a useful guide, a reliable survey of Australia in the early eighties by a German travel journalist who possesses a good knowledge of the country and an even better sense of critical judgement in interpreting and evaluating a continent which can no longer be dismissed as far away and exotic.

JÜRGEN SEIDEL

Ausgewandert

1982 saw the publication of five interrelated prose works about German migration to Australia edited by the "Werkkreis Literatur der Arbeitswelt". Their author, Jürgen Seidel, emigrated to Australia in 1969, returning to West Germany in 1973. As the cooperative editorship of a study group of work-related literature implies, this is a book dealing with economic migration, reporting on Australia as a work experience. A West German labourer attempts to escape the problems of industrialised capitalist society by emigrating. However, as the book's own summary suggests,

> Er hat die Probleme, die ihn zu Hause quälen, nicht zurücklassen können. Aber er muß sie nun unter härteren und ganz bestimmt abenteuerlicheren Umständen als daheim lösen.(4)

"Abenteuerlich" here means not predefined, confronting the same problems in a new context, learning the rules of a different system. In what the editors describe as "eine Mischung aus ehrlichem Bericht und spannender Reiseerzählung"(Ibid.) Seidel records his gradual realisation that capitalism is international and emigration does not offer escape.

Yet the narrative is never overtly political; it is essentially an "Erlebnisbericht", the travelogue of a casual migrant labourer in Australia. When their migration is discussed among themselves a group of German-language workers define it as an experience which carries its own logic. There is little point in reflecting upon it in advance. Seidel's book expresses more explicitly the assumptions of many German migrant authors. The country Australia is equated with the act of migration to such an extent that they define each other. Both are "unknown", both present challenges, hence both are "adventurous". The fact that Australia lies in the Antipodes reinforces the correlated need to grasp a new order of things, to participate in a changed life-style and to respond to the "laws" of migration. Opposition and negation are to be transformed into affirmation and identification. It is a new kind of life the migrant is anxious to discover. "Ich kenn es auch nicht," the protagonist says. "Wir müssen uns einfach reinstürzen."(15) *Ausgewandert* makes the important statement that migration is no longer final; it can be reversed where the "new kind of life" is found to be wanting. Jürgen Seidel's migrant status is somewhat closer to that of a guest worker in West Germany. There is little commitment to another country.

The author's response to Australia thus is inseparable from his evaluation of the experience of migrating. "Was ich sah, hatte nichts zu tun mit dem, was ich mir vorgestellt oder auf Bildern geschen hatte," he comments, "aber ich war jetzt nicht enttäuscht, nur überrascht."(10) He remains open to the different logic of Australian migration. His account of the country is symptomatically impressionistic and often influenced by television. "Es gab Plätze, die mich an amerikanische Fernsehserien erinnerten."(Ibid.) He will resort to the same television analogy when reaching Rockhampton in Queensland ("alles erinnerte mich an amerikanische Kleinstädte aus Fernsehfilmen", 17) and on other occasions where the pre-defined image rises in his consciousness interfering with an attempt at spontaneous description. Some account of migrant's life in Australia may be misleading — Seidel continuously refers to "das Hotel Bonegilla"(11), although he later does move into a "Hostel"(18) — but the book offers an interesting survey of representative types of migrants.(12-13) The terms may not always be quite authentic (he calls himself a "Krauter",16), yet the author's personal responses to Australian migration are clearly genuine and of paradigmatic importance. Predictably, Christmas is seen as out of place, quite literally: "Weihnachten, das paßte nicht hierher, es war zu heiß, zuviel Sonne und Trockenheit."(19) It is part of this cultural conditioning which excites him on his arrival in Queensland: "Wir waren im Land der Sonne und der Palmen."(23) Such comment invokes the *ersatz* world of German pop songs and operettas.

Arrival in Australia means to Seidel being responsible for oneself. "Genau genommen waren wir erst jetzt in Australien angekommen," he notes. "(Wir) waren auf uns selbst angewiesen."(26) It is this hovering between self-reliance and dependence which informs his narrative evaluation of migrant life in Australia. Seidel's migration experiences in this country are a collection of different views and responses; they include his own varying assessments of life in Australia. The overriding concern is freedom, the choice to live in any country, mixed with the fear of being "settled" — anywhere. It is never quite clear what else it is that the protagonist is looking for. His narration does not propagate any recognisable social values.

Migration to Australia is little more than a working holiday, a flight from working life in Germany. Seidel gradually learns that Australia is not an escapist society, even though he seeks out places like Green Island where he can say "ich lag in einem Paradies!"(67) He informs Linda Wells, a casual acquaintance: "Australien ist für Deutschland so was wie der Mond, schön und unerreichbar."(77) Yet the distant country of a beautiful Never-Never is to the narrator "wie vier Wochen Urlaub, 'ne Weltreise, die hat mich ja kaum was gekostet".(76) It is an economic migration, in every sense. Describing his stay at Stony Creek, Jürgen Seidel reinvokes memories of childhood and images of television to explain his excitement of living in a strange and exotic place.

> Wie oft hatten wir uns als Kinder eine solche Umgebung gewünscht! Wildnis, wie sie uns in den Fernsehfilmen gezeigt worden war, echte Herausforderungen, nicht eingebildete Gefahren, daran konnten auch Ferien im Schwarzwald nichts ändern. Das gewisse Fremde und Exotische war nie zu finden gewesen.(94)

It is part of this logic that the experience of migration itself shares the excitement and challenge of alienation. The migrant himself becomes "exotic", unable to understand his own motives, his chosen self-alienation. Australia thus functions to some extent as the geographical backdrop to an individual, social and emotional conflict; the migrant assumes dimensions of a German *Bildungsroman* protagonist. Goethe's *Wilhelm Meisters Lehr-* and *Wanderjahre* continue to haunt the cultural consciousness of Germans who emigrate to Australia, irrespective of their social background. (The traditional years of apprenticeship, tradesmen serving out their time travelling through the country, along with students' *Wanderschaften* and travelling journeymen, are of course a strong source of German cultural identity.)

Towards the end of *Ausgewandert* (119-120) the author himself establishes an explicit interaction between literary models and his own experience as a migrant. Back in Perth, he buys a copy of John Steinbeck's *The Pearl*. As he reads the novel, literary plot and actual events intermingle, demonstrating the correlation of literature and migration. It is only when this programmatic connection is understood that the eventual loss of the book assumes its full impact ("der Verlust des Buches",121). It links the loss of a model "home" with the loss of individual authenticity, a self-concept that has met the challenge of alienation and migration. As the narrator insists: "Ich bin nicht einfach ausgewandert...".(127)

The transition from literature to personal experience heightens the individual sense of authenticity. Fellow-workers hide the book from Jürgen Seidel, who attempts to establish an authentic connection between his migrant worker's experience and his writing about it. Without this realisation the author's fears of remaining in the dark threaten to become real. His migration is an attempt to throw light on himself, his writing about it the endeavour to articulate a self-discovery. Identity and self are found against the challenge of "otherness"; the "exotic" is ultimately not very different from "emptiness" and "nothingness". The book's title clearly acquires a second meaning at the conclusion of its protagonist's wanderings, his migrations between the self and the other. The author has "aus-gewandert", he has completed his "Wanderjahre", terminated and met the challenge of "migration". Towards the end of his narrative he describes the imaged landscape in terms which not only revert back to film and television, but do so in a way that the threat of personal and social authenticity becomes hauntingly apparent.

Migration motivated by perceived emptiness leads Jürgen Seidel to the realisation of the need to witness, to perceive the existence of nothingness. The landscape of North-Western Australia conveys this powerful message of a migrant author who felt the need to return to pre-defined, witnessed, sociocultural reality:

> Erst jetzt fiel mir auf, wie still es draußen war. Ich erinnerte mich an einen Film, die Erde vor Jahrmillionen oder so, erst ein brodelnder Feuersee, dann erkaltete sie, und es war alles öd und reglos. Was ich am traurigsten fand, war die Vorstellung, daß damals auch niemand war, der diese Leere erleben konnte und feststellen konnte, daß sie war.(128)

Jürgen Seidel found this "Leere" in Australia and in himself. He bears witness to it in a migration narrative of a strikingly different kind, the documentation of discovery and escape, of otherness and self, of the "exotic" in native consciousness.

LUISE ULLRICH

Unterwegs zu mir

Published in 1983, this travel diary by a well-known German-Austrian actress bears the subtitle "Australische Impressionen". Ullrich published other travelogues (such as a report about South America in 1941, *Sehnsucht, wohin führst du mich?*), novels, novellas and an autobiography entitled *Komm auf die Schaukel, Luise*. Luise Ullrich died in January 1985.

The author of *Unterwegs zu mir* is primarily an actress at home in verbal role-playing. She knows how to entertain with flirtatious self-projections and 'authentic' self-revelations. Her readers are expected to be consumerist voyeurs, 'Publikum', an extension of the film and stage actress's audience. Ullrich's aim is to convey 'sincerity', to allow her 'fans' access to her 'private life', to let them 'share' in her personal experiences. Her decision to travel to Australia is based on an invitation from friends (the book only once gives an indication that the visit took place in 1981 [52]), prompted by the recent death of her husband. But she insists: "Es war keine Flucht vor mir selbst oder der Traurigkeit — ich machte meiner Phantasie ein Angebot."(8) The commercial jargon is symptomatic. It sets the tone not only for stereotype questions like "why Australia?" which follow shortly: "Was wollte ich bloß in Australien? Hatte ich denn überhaupt noch die Kraft, mich für irgend etwas auf dieser Welt zu interessieren? Und warum ausgerechnet Australien?"(9) The phrase "ausgerechnet Australien" is one of the many clichés of German writing about Australia; even the long naturalised German-Australian author Walter Adamson published a book (in German) under this title (translated as *Australia Of All Places*).[1] Not the least revealing part of Ullrich's travel account is her description of German migrants and their attitude to their adopted country. Thus she writes about her friends: "Beide sind dem Paß nach Australier. Sie leben schon seit fünfzig Jahren auf diesem Kontinent, geboren aber sind sie in Deutschland."(10) Even after half a century of living in Australia and being Australian citizens their German values and identification with things German have not changed. Ullrich characterises them in representative comments such as "Erich packte gleich zu und verlud mein Gepäck in seinen Mercedes. Es war für ihn eine Selbstverständlichkeit, im Ausland einen deutschen Wagen zu fahren."(Ibid.) The reader is asked to endorse the values of successful business migration and the explicit public relations advantages for the native country. If there is naivety (rather than cynicism) in such a perception, it is a simple-mindedness shared by many citizens of both nations. At least the author leaves us in no doubt about her values; she not only admires wealth, especially as a tool of public relations (as she puts it), but in addition appreciates that her friends' "PR" for Germany comes free of charge.

Unterwegs zu mir is, as the title implies, a self-centred book. Its Australia is experienced almost entirely through contact with German migrants. The author and her friends are interested in the country, but basically only as backdrop to their own German life-style. For all their business success these German migrants have retained a detachment from Australia which allows them to continue to view their new homeland with German eyes. Much of their life in Sydney or elsewhere could be characterised as a comfortable international ghetto. The ease and frequency of travel between Australia and Germany further encourages a kind of 'double life', a parallel existence of constant comparison and evaluation. Ullrich's own celebrity status and life-style fit easily into this pattern. All observations by the author must be seen in this context, especially against the background of a privileged, wealthy migrant community anxious to retain close contacts with its country of birth.

"Edith mixte manchmal englische Worte in ihre Sprache," Ullrich notes, "das gefield mir."(Ibid.) She thereby addresses a characteristic syndrome of bilingual migrants, especially among adult immigrants, a phenomenon analysed (with reference to German-Australians) in some detail by Michael Clyne in his authoritative study *Transference and Triggering*[2]. Luise Ullrich's approval of this mixing of German and English reflects her German-oriented internationalism, a life-style of 'the rich and famous'. Perhaps it is not surprising that her German-Australian friends appear to have little respect for Aborigines, least of all when it comes to language:

"Luischen möchte gerne wissen, was 'Killara' heißt. Heißt das was?"
"Nee," sagte Erich und drehte sich vom Lenkrad ein bißchen nach hinten, "ich kann mir nicht vorstellen, daß das irgendwas heißt — bei

denen."(12)

The answer may have to be taken literally, that there is a lack of imagination (and motivation) to understand Aboriginal culture. After all, it is hardly a business prospect and of little "PR" value.

Apart from the German migrant ghetto perspective, *Unterwegs zu mir* reinvokes many *topoi* of Australia as an exotic continent.

> Wo war ich eigentlich?
> Im Wendekreis des Steinbocks, fünfundzwanzig Grad südlich vom Äquator.
> Auf den Korallenbäumen saßen rotgrau gestreifte Papageien. Sie machten fremdartige, gurgelnde Geräusche und pickten die schwarzen Fruchtkerne aus den Korallenblüten.
> Rote Kamilien wuchsen auf hellgrünem Rasen. Der süße, betörende Geruch erinnerte mich an Bali.
> Wo war ich eigentlich?
> ...Die Gerüche, die Tiere, die Pflanzen wirkten sehr exotisch auf mich.(15)

Such is her description of Sydney's suburbia. In all its alleged exotic character it is socially native territory for the actress; she is a guest of the kind of affluent bourgeois suburbanites to whom she herself belongs. (She could have visited her colleague, the German television and film actor Joachim Fuchsberger living 'next door', had she travelled to Sydney six years later. [Cf. Joachim Fuchsberger: *Guten Morgen, Australien*, 27-30]). The "exotic" can be consumed in comfort, it is part of the international life-style of successful Germans. Australia's indigenous people do not qualify for such exotic interest. The author herself sees the Aborigines condemned to extinction. "Sie scheinen zum Aussterben geboren, ihre Entwicklung führt ins Nichts."(18) She is further made aware of Anglo-Australians' sensitivity regarding their convict past. The German migrant assures her: "Das andere heiße Eisen, Luischen, sind die Convicts,...die Großeltern oder Urgroßeltern der heutigen Australier."(Ibid.) Ullrich expresses surprise over her friend's analogy: "Dir wäre es sicher auch nicht angenehm, wenn ein Australier in eurem Land gleich vom Nationalsozialismus oder von Hitler zu reden anfinge."(19) Her travelogue is full of such revealing statements by German migrants. To the businessman from Saxony, now living in Sydney, Australia in the eighties is still "Ein Traumland für Auswanderer, krisensicher und stabil. Keinerlei Kriegsgefahr. Verstehst du, Luise?"(19) In fairness to the author, she does show some understanding of the double standards she is asked to endorse. Even though she too refers to a "tipptoppe Gesellschaft"(!, Ibid.), she notices that her friends "sprachen über die Ureinwohner, wie Erwachsene über Kinder sprechen, deren Welt sie nicht verstehen."(21) When she meets other migrant friends, not only from Germany, she detects a symptomatic lack of identification with Australia and its history.

> "Sie sagten vorhin, 'die Australier entwickeln ein Gefühl...'. Warum sagen Sie nicht 'wir Australier'? Zählen Sie sich nicht dazu?"(22)

The question addresses a central theme of the book, a dilemma documented in many encounters, dialogues and reflections. From a sociological point of view, it is in this area that the main interest of Luise Ullrich's travelogue lies. Apart from her own thoughts and reactions, it is a revealing record of cultural and political ambivalence among some sections of Australia's (not only German) migrant community. Ullrich does list the right kind of questions, even if in fact she does not dare ask them: "Ich hätte gern gefragt: 'Wann wird eigentlich aus einem Engländer ein Australier?' Aber ich verkniff es mir."(Ibid.)

The following passage illustrates the almost comical incongruity of perspective in various attempts to initiate the German visitor to an 'authentic' Australia:

> "...Du willst das typische Australien kennenlernen, das ursprüngliche. Willst dahin, wo es echt ist. You are hungry for information, okay, you will get it. Wir streunen morgen ein bißchen durch die Stadt. Ich zeige dir den Zoo."(28)

It is at Taronga Zoo that Ullrich meets her first Aborigine, along with a platypus. Her ghetto Australia does not allow for any experience which is not predefined, precontained and prejudged. Much of her descriptions are therefore little more than clichés of tourist images, i.e. "Im Taronga-Park", "Luncheon Theatre", "La Opera" etc. In between this sight-seeing the German consul organises a press conference for the "Weltstar".(47) Eventually Luise Ullrich does travel in the country, without however reaching beyond the well-established pattern of previous visitors. Predictably, she finds comfort in a kookaburra and kangaroos (172, 184), is entertained by "Goldrausch und Glockenvögel"(69).

The book closes on a note of symbolism and philosophy. Ullrich reflects: "Wie weit doch Känguruhs springen können... "(185) and, safe in her Lufthansa jet taking her back to Germany, she realises: "Es gibt keinen Abschied, es gibt nur Veränderung."(187) Unfortunately, there is very little "Veränderung" in Luise Ullrich's perception and observation of an Australia which retains the restrictions of a well-arranged zoo.

Hans-Otto Meissner

Das fünfte Paradies

This travelogue with its meaningless title represents much of what remains inaccurate, uninformed, misleading and insensitive reporting about Australia. Its equally dubious subtitle indicates the circus-like sensationalism the author may have aimed for: "Australien: Menschen, Tiere, Abenteuer". The enumeration does make up the almost compulsory (and compulsive) ingredients of German travel books about this country. Published in 1983 and, in a revised edition (!) in 1984, the book is spectacularly out of date. It reports on the progress of the Snowy-Mountains-Project, informing the reader that "zur Zeit ein gigantishces System von Dammbauten und Kanälen in Arbeit (ist)".(8) It further assures us that Australia is now at last willing to accept migrants from Italy, Greece, Spain, Jugoslavia and Asia: "Jetzt (sic!) werden auch Italiener, Griechen, Spanier, Jugoslawen und Asiaten aufgenommen."(Ibid.) Meissner is an avid reader of the "'Melbourne Times'".(28) He has doubts about Australian food: "Die fade, farblose Küche der Australier zu unterbieten, dürfte unmöglich sein."(30) Australians, he argues, have not yet discovered that eating can be an enjoyment. "Sie ernähren sich nur."(Ibid.) With that comment he dismisses Melbourne's wide range of restaurants and international cuisine. Australians do not like their wines either: "An den Wein ihres eigenen Landes haben sich noch längst nicht alle Australier gewöhnt, obwohl besonders Rotweine auch für unseren Geschmack recht trinkbar sind."(32) The condescension is typical of the tone in which this work is written. Pubs still have the six o'clock closing time, and women are not allowed in public bars. "...nur für kurze Zeit ist der Ausschank geöffnet... Eine weibliche Person darf nicht in die Stehbierhalle hinein."(Ibid.) Australians offer each other "shots" rather than shouts because the custom demands to be "shot": "Unmittelbar darauf muß der Geladene die gleiche Gruppe seinerseits zu einem 'Schuß' bitten."(Ibid.) According to Meissner, there are no fences in Melbourne or any other Australian cities and suburbs. "Man hat keinen Anlaß," he explains, "sich gegen Nachbarn abzuschließen, ein Zaun würde auch einen schlechten Eindruck machen".(36)

It would be easy to dismiss a book such as this, were it not released by Germany's largest publishing concern, Bertelsmann, known for its large commercial editions. *Das fünfte Paradies* is described on the dust-jacket as "Völlig neu bearbeitete und illustrierte Ausgabe". The work is attractively produced, with colour photographs and in large format. There can be little doubt about its sales figures. It is disturbing, therefore, to see a popular production such as this spread misinformation about Australia under the guise of a travelogue. Even factual names are presented incorrectly. Thus Meissner speaks of "die Dandanong-Berge"(39) or of the "Kukkaburro" (46). The following is a typical example of the author's habit of fictionalising facts in order to entertain. Referring to the kookaburra, he writes:

> Alle Menschen, die zum Haus gehören, kennt er genau, und sicher weiß er mehr von ihnen, als so manchem lieb ist. Denn mit seinen klugen, scharfen Augen sieht er alles und hat seinen Spaß daran.(47)

In the Australia circus of Hans-Otto Meissner the art of anthropomorphic stylisation reaches new heights: the exotic is as hilarious as a clown.

Meissner applies his critical knowledge to many subjects, among them Australian *Germanistik*. He reprimands the German Department of the University of Melbourne for offering a degree course in German comparable to a study of *Germanistik* in Europe.

> Was man in Melbourne den bedauernswerten Studenten unserer Sprache als deutsche Literatur vorsetzt, geht nicht nur mit Simplicius Simplicissimus auf den Dreißigjährigen Krieg zurück, sondern reicht bis zu Karl dem Großen. Ohne Übertreibung, denn zu Lynn Aubreys Studienobjekten gehörte auch das Nibelungenlied im Original. Alles gut und schön für junge Leute, die den Ehrgeiz haben, Professoren der Germanistik zu werden, aber für den Unterricht in der gegenwärtigen deutschen Sprache wohl gar zu gründlich.(37)

The author's concept of the study of German proves as informed as his knowledge of Australia. His pronouncements on Australia's capital cities are as categorical, as they reflect the author's personal preference: "Aber sicher ist Adelaide von allen Großstädten im fünften Erdteil die schönste und auch die jüngste."(17) Sydney is described as offering a very limited range of cultural entertainment. Despite the "völlig neu bearbeitete...Ausgabe" of 1984 the author can only report that "die große Oper von Sydney war bei unserem letzten Besuch noch nicht fertig".(59)

Although Meissner retains words like "Wharfies"(11), he insists on using German translations for well-known Australian landmarks. Thus he speaks of the "Ayers-Stein"(122) and he consistently refers to the outback as the "Weitdraußen".(9) His chapter "Die Deutschen in Australien"(182-195) offers an historical survey of German migrants who distinguished themselves in their adopted country, as well as a sketch of German migration in general. Although Meissner's overview of German migration to Australia is basically correct, his interpretation of Australia's immigration policy suffers from the malaise of most discussions in this book: it is outdated.

Meissner uses his chapter on Germans in Australia to attempt general characterisations of the two peoples — not always with success. His assertion of German superiority ranges from the possible to the unlikely, from the profound to the flippant. "Der moderne Deutsche," he maintains, "entwickelt im Durchschnitt mehr Initiative und vielfach auch mehr persönliche Energie als der gebürtige Australier."(190) The validity of such statements must remain dubious once it is realised that many "gebürtige Australier" are in fact the offspring of complex inter-marriages and often include German migrant origins. It is not clear whether the author's final claim in his chapter on Germans is meant to be taken seriously: "Jedenfalls stehen bei den Mädchen Australiens deutsche Männer in hohem Ansehen."(195) Meissner's overall advice to prospective German migrants is to beware of Australia's modest life-style ("Australien ist ein bescheidenes Land, das alle bescheidenen Wünsche seiner Bürger erfüllt." 194-195) and to stay in Germany if they possess "einen hohen Bildungsgrad".(190) For "auf kulturellem Gebiet (ist) nicht viel vorhanden".(194) Such sweeping and often condescending comments characterise the general tone of the book.

In its volatile mixture of fact and fiction *Das fünfte Paradies* may be read as an imaginative travelogue or an autobiographical novel. Many of its descriptions of animals are indeed lovingly prepared, and the personal narrative retains an anecdotal intimacy throughout. Meissner integrates a number of historical sketches into his report on an almost contemporary Australia. Greater care in the treatment of facts and more thoroughness in its research could have made this book a more reliable source of information, but the author's priorities were clearly more concerned with entertaining his readers. If the

"Abenteuer" of the subtitle simply refers to the presence of the narrator in Australia, "animals" and "adventures" outshine Meissner's accounts of "Menschen" in Australia. *Das Fünfte Paradies* is a highly personal response to travel in this country almost two decades ago. Its stylistic perspective is summed up by the dust-jacket's appraisal: "Selbst das entlegene, verwunschene (sic) Tasmanien ist ihm nicht zu weit." Meissner's Australia is a curious mixture of sensationalism and fairy-tale.

HERMANN GLASER

Abheben zu den Antipoden

Glaser's report aims to collect "Kulturpolitische Augenblicke einer Australienreise".(55) It appeared in Vol. 39/ No. 3 (1984) of the *Frankfurter Hefte* and is characterised by the perspective and jargon of West German "Kulturjournalismus". The selective survey of contemporary Australian culture offers factual information, useful comparisons, judgements based on cultural arrogance (as well as a general lack of a useful definition of "culture") and valid social criticism. Glaser's manneristic style causes more than occasional irritation, but whenever the author restricts himself to reporting his account is reliable, noteworthy and frequently empathetic. "Wer die bewegten Diskussionen der sechziger und siebziger Jahre in der Bundesrepublik über Kulturpolitik miterlebt hat, glaubt sich freilich bei den Antipoden in unsere fünfziger Jahre zurückversetzt"(Ibid.): such a statement is symptomatic of the kind of incongruous and insensitive assessment of contemporary Australian culture. Even in the fifties German culture had little in common with the problems and issues of present-day Australian developments. As so often, it is assumed that German (European) "culture" is transferable to Australian conditions and should act as a model for antipodean aspirations. The German cultural discussions of the sixties and the seventies bore little reference to the realities of German social life; in particular, they failed to address themselves to the impact of "guest workers" on a native culture only recently restored from the abominations of fascism. Glaser's cultural condescension towards Australia is a wide-spread European phenomenon, a representative reflection of "Eurocentricity". His essay rarely rises above a stock-taking of different cultural concerns. The author remains little more than a cultural tourist.

A typical example of Hermann Glaser's arrogance is his description of the kangaroo: "Diese sehen aus wie eine Kreuzung aus Hase, Ratte, Eichhörnchen, Reh, sozusagen genetischer Verschnitt, — aber ausgezeichnet geeignet für einen Kontinent, auf dem man immer ins Leere springt."(56) Defining the kangaroo as "genetischer Verschnitt" is symptomatic; it reflects the author's concept of Australian needs: a cultural blend or adulteration of European values, a "kulturelle Verschnitt" modelled on German authenticity. Even allowing for journalistic effect, it demonstrates an almost polemical unwillingness to consider a cultural concept different from that of Europe. The result is a generally condescending and frequently ironic tone which informs even factual statements and statistical data.

Glaser reports on the introduction of Community Arts Officers and makes the interesting observation: "vor allem Frauen wagen sich in dieses Neuland vor."(Ibid.) It is a comment worthy of note for German and for Australian readers. He sees in it a special kind of cultural pioneering: "Kultureller Pioniergeist, wie er faszinierender nicht in Erscheinung treten könnte!"(57) He completely ignores the fact that it also constitutes an important aspect of feminist culture in a land where women may have been in particular need of sociocultural emancipation (but also where one of the world's leading feminist writers, Germaine Greer, emerged while Germany was involved in the "bewegten Diskussionen der sechziger und siebziger Jahre"). Nor does Glaser appear to understand the cultural collaboration between women and migrants in this country. Instead he speaks of "Sehnsucht nach dem Diskurs".(Ibid.) Whose? Later he reports on a Sydney audience's response to David Williamson's *The Perfectionist*: "...theoretische Gesellschaftskritik wirkt hier völlig exotisch."(62) He leaves the theatre at interval in disgust. Could it be that an Australian cultural consciousness articulates itself differently from a German (or European) "discourse"? He does not address himself to what could have made his essay a genuine intercultural dialogue.

Symptomatically, Glaser uses the German migrants' perspective to characterise Australian culture. "Fern der deutschen Heimat"(58) he notes: "aber etwas fehlt".(62) It is not clear whether this absence could be anything more than a longing for the German landscape and German culture, as is asserted. Glaser sums up: "Australien, du hast es nicht besser."(Ibid.) He never considers the possibility that Australian culture may have something to do with being able to live with "absence" —

and that German migrants are hardly representative of Australian culture. Confronted with the landscape of this continent he can only respond with a European literary quotation: "Warten auf Godot...".(61) He "explains" Russel Drysdale in terms of Samuel Beckett.

Despite such misreadings and misunderstandings Hermann Glaser's report contains many pieces of factual and relevant information about contemporary Australian society. He does quote the consensus of Australian artists, intellectuals and politicians: "Die Zeit sei reif für eine kulturpolitische Neuorientierung."(56) He rightly draws attention to "verbetonierte Stadtlandschaften" in which "Stadtstreicher", juvenile unemployed and prostitutes present a disturbing loss of identity.(60) When he visits the Barossa Valley he senses a greater complexity in the designation "deutsch-australisch":

> Überall typisch deutsche Häuser, doziert der uns begleitende Volkskundler. Erkennbar an den Giebeln und der Lage des Kamins. Ich erkenne nichts. Sehe nur typisch australische Häuser. Aber die Wissenschaft muß es ja wissen.(58)

His lack of recognition is more than journalistic mockery. Glaser notices the integration of German-Australian culture, the "deutsche Tal"(Ibid.) is Australian. He registers an "absence" which is in fact assimilation, variation or simply difference. Unlike many other German travelogue writers, he does record the change. His quoting German migrants of that community assumes additional meaning: "Wie es zu Hause aussieht, weiß man nicht mehr so recht."(59) It reflects a similar difficulty of German visitors who try to describe German Australian cultural assimilation.

Towards the end of his article, Glaser (rightly) argues: "was Faschismus ist, davon hat man in Australien nicht so klare Vorstellungen".(62) He pleads for cultural and sociopolitical specificity: Queensland, for all its corruption and conservatism, cannot be equated with German fascism. Even comparisons with Bavaria, although closer, fail to do justice to the cultural character of an Australian state. It is in this sense that Glaser's final sentence, formulated upon his return to his native Nürnberg, carries its fullest impact: "Von den Antipoden bin ich zu meinen Antipoden zurückgekehrt."(64)

Vera Bockmann

Full Circle

1986 saw the publication of one of the most fascinating titles in German-Australian literature over the last half century or so. Vera Bockmann's *Full Circle* reports on what the subtitle describes as "An Australian in Berlin 1930–1946". The author was born in the year 1903 as "Vera Hoffmann at Siegersdorf near Tanunda into one of the Silesian families which arrived in Australia in 1847 and has retained its separate identity into the seventh generation of Hoffmanns". (Introduction by Decie Denholm, 1) Vera and her brother Erwin "broke the Barossa German tradition"(5), Erwin marrying an Adelaide girl and Vera, returning to her German origins, marrying Otto Bockmann in Hamburg. Vera and Otto met at Port Adelaide when Bockmann was chief wireless operator on the *SS Köln* "on the run to Australia".(7) *Full Circle* is so much more than a biography or a family saga. Its socio-historical importance cannot be overestimated, and Vera Bockmann's narrative style is refreshingly uncomplicated, engaging in its integrity. The "fourth generation South Australian"(15) spent more than half her life in Germany, during the dark years of Hitler's rule over the country of her cultural and spiritual roots. Vincent Buckley refers to Ireland as his "source country"(212)[3]. In an interview with Jim Davidson he speaks of Irish Australians in a manner which would seem to be similar to the Barossa German Vera Bockmann's experience:

> The Gael has put its roots down here; but it still has other roots, and in tracing back your personal roots you're going to get back to *that* place and *that* people, from some out-station of the diaspora.(Ibid.)

Bockmann's return to "her" people shares Buckley's discoveries, but she went to Germany because she married a German and she was forced to stay there during very difficult times for the same reason. Apart from its many other aspects, *Full Circle* is very much a woman's book, tracing her biography back to strangely foreign homes, exploring a complex range of "belonging", freedom and imprisonment. If Germany is her "source country", the Barossa Valley remains her native environment.

> There were vineyards and Hoffmanns as far as the eye could see. None of us thought this to be extraordinary, nor the fact that we had the ability to switch from German to English depending on whether we were speaking to our grandparents and their generation or to our

contemporaries. Our parents encouraged us to remember the advantages of starting off with two languages.(15-16)

There is no conflict on either a cultural or (later) a political level. Vera Bockmann's grandfather "had been among those Germans who had walked all the way to Government House in Adelaide to swear allegiance to their sovereign, Queen Victoria. Two generations later the young bloods considered themselves as pure Australians, although some might have a certain Teutonic intonation."(23) The persecution of these Barossa Australians during the First World War constitutes a shameful chapter in German-Australian relations. Bockmann speaks of a "mass hysteria of hate", "the very word *'Tanunda'* could set the hatred aflame".(Ibid.) Her engagement in 1928 to a German *Schiffsfunker* reads like a fateful opportunity to escape or to return to the land of her cultural origin. The author consistently refers to herself as British, even during the Nazi years in Berlin. Bockmann offers a classic comment on biculturalism experienced by many Australian citizens:

> Maturing in a foreign country leaves its mark on you for ever, whether you like it or not. It leaves you constantly groping for a middle way and getting nowhere, very often finding yourself a misfit, no matter where you happen to be.(32)

She is not quite as explicit in her appraisal of the positive benefits such a background may also carry with it. Her own experiences, especially in the immediate post-war years, clearly illustrate the advantages of being Australian or British in an occupied country devastated by war.

Vera Bockmann's account of life in Germany is always authentic, well-informed and socially sensitive. She comments on a range of "German" characteristics, carefully balancing myth and reality. Her common sense judgement is apparent in the following statement: "Scoff if you must at German thoroughness, it usually pays off, and more often than not great wisdom and foresight is revealed."(36) But the author's main strength lies in her ability to capture the spirit of the age, the sociocultural atmosphere of a particular place in time. (It is a pity that almost all the text in German suffers from spelling and punctuation mistakes, providing a curious contrast to the genuine quality of the narrative text.) Bockmann's study of Prussian history ("Living in Potsdam also meant I had a golden opportunity to saturate myself with Prussian history ...",38) further adds to the credibility and authority of her descriptions: history to her means a knowledge of landmarks, houses, palaces, parks and families. This historical information is passed on in the narrative history of her own life:

> It was in the Garrison Church, at the very spot where the bones of Frederick the Great lay, that Hitler was installed by Hindenburg as Reichschancellor, on 21 March 1933, a ceremony of great pomp.(40)

She witnesses world history in the context of her personal biography and the history of her Australian-German family. When her parents visit her in 1930 she meets them in Naples. Again, family and world history come together: "In Italy we heard favourable reports of Mussolini's achievements. Trains were now on time, there was no more begging in the streets, everything was fine."(43) In all her accounts the author's tolerance and goodwill shine through. "How easy it is for people to be patronising to one another," she notes.(44) She extends her own "full circle" to her father's return to Germany:

> To my knowledge my father was the only one of the Hoffmanns to return to the birthplace of our ancestor Samuel Hoffmann, my great-grandfather. We could trace our family through the old family Bible.(Ibid.)

Visiting the village of her family's origin, she can claim "Here indeed was a homecoming".(48) Ironically the inhabitants of the village thought "the emigrants had all been eaten by blacks".(Ibid.) Home and the exotic clash in a symptomatic need to be reconciled.

Bockmann's assessment of Nazi Germany is an honest reconstruction of her experiences at the time. Like most Germans, she found it difficult to believe in Nazi atrocities. She was clearly taken in by the apparent sense of order, cleanliness and social morality. Yet Bockmann's assessment of the political and cultural situation in Germany shows good judgement. She understands that the "Weimar Republic was weak and unloved".(56) Her understanding of, and participation in, Berlin's social life is based on enthusiasm and identification. "What could compare with 'Unter den Linden'... The shops? Absolute luxury! Berlin had *twelve* newspapers, right wing, left wing, centre, liberal with many variations."(Ibid.) She writes about the theatres, especially Max Reinhardt productions during the winter of 1931-32, and about musical performances by Otto Klemperer, Leo Blech, Erich Kleiber, Richard Strauss and Richard Tauber. There can be no doubt that Vera Bockmann knew Berlin's cultural life extremely well.

It reads like a portent that at the beginning of 1933 Vera Bockmann returns to Australia. This time she is not accompanied by her radio operator husband. Despite the death of her mother the author has little to say about her native country. She clearly feels out of place in what was once her home. All Bockmann has to say about Australia's Great Depression is that it is another reason for her to return to Europe, to Nazi Germany where Otto "had a good position with prospects of superannuation".(63) At her return to Berlin she notices a drastic change of behaviour among her acquaintances. Her own husband nearly lands in a concentration camp as "good Aryan stock gone astray".(70) Bockmann describes the food shortages and other aspects of everyday life in Nazi Germany during the thirties. Native and foreign-born Germans escape from the challenges of politics into the aesthetic realm of music.(74) Giving her account of the infamous *Kristallnacht*, one conclusion becomes inescapable: foreigners in Germany did not behave very differently from the rest of the population; they too did not want to know.(83)

With the outbreak of war "Berlin ceased to be a metropolis, it had become a huge conglomeration of villages somehow held together with public transport".(87) Bockmann experiences a kind of solidarity which cut across all social classes. She offers a detailed everyday account of civilian life in a war-torn country. Her political reflections reveal an intimate understanding of the German mind. Although she regrets the failure to remove Hitler from office, she continues with these thoughts:

> And yet. If Hitler's assassination had been successful, might it not have led to martyrdom and a new 'stab in the back' justification for Germany's defeat, just as the 'Dolchstoßlegende' or 'stab in the back' legend had been used after the First World War?(108)

Bockmann's judgement is rarely clouded by cultural mythology or the ideological influence of those around her. If she complains earlier of being a "misfit", "constantly groping for a middle way and getting nowhere"(32), it must be said that one possible advantage of having matured in a foreign country is precisely this kind of level-headed judgement, a healthy and sane balance between total identification and critical detachment.

The author remains a *Zeitgenössin* recording the authentic events and responses of the age. It is this mixture of participant and witness which makes Vera Bockmann's story so unique and so valuable. It offers a rare insight into the mind of a people, without the need to defend it.

Ironically, Bockmann becomes one of Berlin's famous *Trümmerfrauen*, the women who cleaned up the ruins. Once again, she shares the fate of many German contemporaries.(126) Through the intervention of an Australian news correspondent in Berlin, Vera Bockmann is able to get in touch with her family in South Australia. Her absence from her home country has left her ignorant of many new developments: "We had no idea that a road had been built from south to north, right through the centre of Australia up to Darwin. We knew nothing about the movements of Australian troops in New Guinea and the Pacific Islands."(142) Once more, she has become a stranger to her own people. Perhaps it is possible to draw a distinction between a social and a cultural attachment to a country and its people. If so, it is clear that Vera Bockmann's social loyalties have always remained with Australia, albeit a very "British" Commonwealth. Culturally, her traditions seem to be rooted in German customs and values. Descriptions of the immediate post-war period are again characterised by a tone of authenticity derived from the memories of someone who was a participant. (Vera Bockmann in fact never remains an outsider, as she so often fears.) Her impressionistic summary of life in Berlin 1945-46 conveys the energetic, amnesic spirit of reconstruction so typical of the period. As Vera leaves with her son for England, she witnesses signs of regeneration everywhere.

In 1946 Vera Bockmann returns once more to Australia. After the death of her father in the following year she and her son rejoin Otto Bockmann in 1953. The author picks up her description of post-war Berlin where she left off almost a decade earlier. This is how she sums up the *Zeitgeist* of the divided city:

> There was a sense of enthusiasm and vitality in Berlin during the 1950's that had to be witnessed to be believed. It was later regarded as a miracle, but it was no miracle, just plain hard yakka!(185)

The Australianism in her attempt to do justice to a restored Berlin epitomises her own "conflict of love". In the early sixties she returns to Australia with her by now retired husband, joining in "one of the first family reunions"(187) in the country. Her homecoming is a curious mixture of alienation and recognition. She is intensely aware of the injustice and irony of the Barossa Valley's German status in the context of Australian "multicultural" society. "Postwar German migrants have become well established in the art of making noodles, pickled cucumber, yeast cake, locally known as German cake or Streusel kuchen (*sic*)", she notes and adds: "It makes me chuckle to find the foods which were so despised during and after World War I now so eagerly sought after."(195) She is less amused by the decline of the German language in South Australia, based on a deep-rooted distrust in German-Australians. "It is rare to hear the German language in Murray Street," she observes. "Prejudice dies hard."(Ibid.) But Vera Bockmann is clearly reconciled to her fate and at peace with her life. It is symptomatic that her memoirs should end with a British saying: "What a wonderful innings I have had."(Ibid.) Yet for all the apparent harmony and reconciliation there remains an element of tension, no less characteristic of a life spent in two countries, two cultures and two languages.

As her final reflections lend the book its title, they deserve to be quoted in full. They reinforce Vera Bockmann's lifelong dichotomy of remaining a stranger in her own home.

> The Barossa Valley has turned full circle. And so have I. When walking along Murray Street in Tanunda, I feel like Rip van Winkle because the faces of the children seem so familiar. Upon closer investigation they prove to be the grand-children of my former 'mates'. All the streets are as tidy as they have always been. Many houses which I frequented as a child and teenager are quite unchanged, yet I do not seem to know anyone living in them. I feel a strong sense of belonging, and yet to the passersby I am a stranger!(Ibid.)

Six times Vera Bockmann travelled to Berlin and back, staying in Germany for almost forty years — thereby reversing the normal procedure of migration. Her discoveries about cultural identity and social belonging have a validity beyond her individual life, extraordinary and courageous as it was. *Full Circle* defies any narrow categorisation: it is biography, family history, woman's literature (being one's own "author"), migrant writing, memoirs, sociopolitical documentation and so much more. It is, above all, the record of a remarkable human being.

LIZ SCHOLZ

Australische Liebesergüsse

"Eine erlebte Reise" the author calls her travel fiction, an extraordinarily callous and egocentric document of misinformation, written in a mixture of bad German and bad English, packaged as a soft porn novel. It would be tempting to simply ignore this extreme case of vanity publication, were it not for its very unique position in the history of German-Australian writing. A woman author attempting a soft porn version of her travels in Australia certainly marks an unusual stage of development in such a history. What adds further interest to this poorly produced and poorly written narrative is that it constitutes the outermost version of German clichés about Australia and exemplifies in its very style the kind of linguistic loss of identity and false type of bilingual integration many migrants choose to adopt. (One is reminded of the German-US migrant scenes in Walter Bockmeyer's and Rolf Bührmann's unforgettable film *Flammende Herzen*[4].) Liz Scholz, we are told, is the pseudonym of "eine bekannte und attraktive dunkelhaarige Österreicherin, die von Natur aus romantisch und mit großer Prosperität behaftet ist, aber ihre Abenteuer liebt." (Cover, Weishaupt Taschenbuch Verlag, Graz 1986) The language inside the cover moves on the same level, the syntactic logic of "von Natur aus...mit großer Prosperität behaftet". "Scholz's" erratic switching and triggering *is* the central feature of her style. She opens her narrative account with the declaration: "Jedesmal, wenn ein Golfer mich nach dem Emblem fragte, antwortete ich exactly: '*For every handicap I got one from my husband.*'"(5) The author manages to combine allusions to Emmanuelle Arsan's exotic soft porns with cliché responses to antipodean inversions. "No snow in December" causes her to be "etwas traurig so fern der Heimat, ohne Schnee und dem gewohnten Weihnachtsbaum. Doch alles mußte man einmal mitgemacht haben."(10) She cheerfully exchanges her temporary depression for casual sex on Christmas Eve. The following is representative in style, content and morality:

> Sein schwarzer Tanga fiel herab, und ein Pferdeschwanz stand mir gegenüber. "*Ja, deine Augen sind grün wie die eines hinterlistigen Krokodiles, aber der Teil unter deinem Nabel scheint furchtlos zu sein!*"
> "*Heute ist Christmas, in Europa ist es ein Tag der Liebe und Freude. Ich habe dir, deinem Weib oder Nicht-Weib den Jungen gerettet. Come on and love this part.*" Er tat es, und er war sichtlich besser als alle seine Hengste im Stall.(12)

The passage may explain the compulsion to read this book as pure, if unintentional comedy. "Scholz's" crudity proves incapable of erotic language; Australia's "down under" is transformed into clumsy attempts at descriptions of human sexuality. Her assessment of the country and its people is similarly inept; Aborigines are "gefährliche Leute"(15),

Noosa "Head" is full of crocodiles(22), she visits "Dreaming Island"(33), Australians assure her that she and her husband "speak a welcome English"(37), only to confess "I did it never!"(43), she soon moves to "Northern Australia, neben dem Pazifik"(54) where she learns to eat "Kingspraw"(55) and discovers "kleine unbekannte Schnabeltiere"(60), only to be loved by an "alte Nigger"(74) who has a few language problems of his own. They consume their passion encouraged by sexual and verbal compatibility: "Let's love us."(76) Occasionally "Liz Scholz" is moved to cultural reflection: "als Europäer denkt man bewußter," she notices, "und weniger abenteuerlich als der Australier."(80) At other times the author changes the spelling of cities, names and regions. One chapter is entitled "Pourt Douglas"; its first sentence reads: "Am nächsten Morgen fuhren Larson und ich, frisch geduscht und hübsch gedressed auf der Highway nach Pourt Douglas...".(82) "Scholz" mocks the "Schulenglisch" of natives (83), then applies her own brand of language: "do it you ever believe!"(84) It is not quite clear, then, what she means when she admires Australia because it is "ein doch weniger besteuertes Land".(97) Indeed, as the book draws to a close, the narrator's ability to express herself in either German or English reaches crisis point. "Don't worry, let's drive us to Trinity Beach, have lunch there, a look after my house und am Strand werden wir nach Mango fragen."(100) Mango is actually one of her native lovers who "takes a cup of wine"(101) to recover from what threatened to be deadly exercise.

As can be seen, *Australische Liebesergüsse* is heavy going, even as comedy. The author calls her narrative "autobiographisch, erotisch, einfühlsam und detailliert".(Cover) In fact, her book is the most extreme case not merely of misinformation about a country, but of replacing it with the semi-literate phantasies of the author. In the history of German-Australian writing, this publication reduces the Australian continent to an arbitrary backdrop of sexual projections, a ready-made reference to 'the exotic', the far-away place of *Never-Never* where everything is possible. As such, it is an absolute low point in literary quality and social morality (comparable only to some fascist works in the thirties), but it is also one extreme consequence of a continuing reluctance to deal with the socio-political realities of Australia, using this country as little more than a pretext for other matters, appealing to the 'exotic' for its own sake, turning the tyranny of distance into a narrative diction of ignorance.

Achim Sperber

Mythos Australien

Published in the series "Die bibliophilen Taschenbücher", the book's title is to be taken programmatically. Sperber's verbal and visual anthology was released in 1987, bearing the subtitle "Der archaische Kontinent". Despite its bibliophile aspirations the volume is carelessly presented: a photograph of Brisbane is identified as "Adelaide, South Australia".(83); its literary text and "Quellenverzeichnis" list a "Ludwig Reichardt"(12,147) instead of Ludwig Leichhardt etc. Sperber's concept is not without contradiction; it seeks to document ("dokumentiert",1) a myth ("Mythos"). His photographic essay consists of three parts: "Der archaische Kontinent", "Magie der Städte" and "Pioniere der Wildnis". Despite some confusion over the identification of places Achim Sperber's photography captures a wide range of images that are unmistakably Australian. In the context of a history of German-Australian literature it is remarkable that in the late eighties Australia is marketed as a mythological, archaic continent. Such a concept revives the traditional perception of this country as an exotic place, ancient and timeless, far away from the rest of civilisation. In his Introduction Sperber stresses the vastness of the continent, offering his German readers dreams of escape. "Was sind ein paar Tage Autofahrt durchs Outback gegen eine Fahrt durch Deutschland von Nord nach Süd...?"(7) The author summarises the Australian character in one paragraph; it is shallow, harmless, uncomplicated and insensitive.(8) He reprimands Australia for slaughtering its "Wappentier", the kangaroo. Sperber refers to a "Traumwelt"(Ibid.) of the Aborigines, but he means the effects of widespread alcoholism among Australia's natives. Later he lists "Sydney, Melbourne oder Canberra" as the "großen Städte an den Küsten".(Ibid.) He acknowledges the difficulty of relating his many impressions ("Eindrücke von Australien",9) to one all-embracing image of the continent. He records his own "'Schatzinsel-Phantasien' aus der Kindheit" and "Gefühl von Freiheit"(Ibid.) as personal responses to different parts of the country.

The literary texts accompanying Sperber's photographs are taken from twenty-one German, European, American and Australian authors (Frank Auerbach, Hans Bertram, Jens Bjerre, Friedrich Gerstäcker, "Gilmore" [sic], Ulrich Günther, Alfred Hageni, Rudolf Jacobs, Karl Emil Jung, Egon Erwin Kisch, Stefan von Kotze, Werner G. Krug, Hans von Lippa, Kurt Lütgen, Tibor Meray, Hakon Mielche, Alan

Moorehead, Ruth Parker, Ludwig R(L)eich(h)ardt, Gerda Rob and Mark Twain). It is clear from the selection that no unified or coordinated view is attempted; like the anthology itself, the quotations are to serve impressionistic perceptions. Claudia Zimmermann's choice of texts allows for a wide variety of theme and literary quality.

The most valuable information in *Mythos Australien* is to be found in Volker Raddatz's succinct essay "Zur Geschichte Australiens: Probleme und Entwicklungslinien", reprinted from Roger Bendisch's and Uwe Seidel's travel guide *Australien. Ein Reisehandbuch*(Berlin 1986). Over only twenty pages Raddatz manages to offer a precise and authoritative survey of Australian history. His account is divided into three parts revealing the author's sensitivity and understanding of cultural developments: "Die Eingeborenen", "Die Europäer" and "Weiße und Eingeborene". Raddatz explains the existential reality of Aboriginal dreamtime by quoting two legends, "Die Geburt der Sonne" and "Das erste Känguruh".(126-127) When dealing with the European presence in Australia he quotes from four folklore ballads, "Old England, ade! oder Letzter Abschied"(130), "Jim Jones"(131), "Der Geck von der Bond Street"(135-136) and the shearer's song "Nun da die Schurzeit naht..."(137) In each case he allows the voice of the Australian people to speak for itself. His section covering European migration to Australia is subdivided into four parts: "Erste Kontakte", "Die Besiedlung durch Großbritannien", "Von der Strafkolonie zum Bundesstaat" and "Australien als Bundesstaat". All are well-informed, attractively written summaries of periods in Australian history. Raddatz's final assessment of "Weiße und Eingeborene" incorporates today's multicultural society. It concludes on a note of concern characteristic of the author's sensitivity: "Es wäre in der Tat historisch paradox, wenn im Rahmen einer multi-cultural society die Reste der jahrtausendealten Aboriginal-Kultur weniger Gewicht hätten als die Kultur der kürzlich eingewanderten Europäer und Asiaten."(144)

Mythos Australien, then, is a curious mixture of impressionistic, erratic reporting and authoritative, knowledgable information. There are unforgivable printing errors (especially for a bibliophile edition), but there are also empathetic photographs, shrewd observations and memorable quotations. The book as a whole propagates the otherness of Australia, its ancient history and its present cultural conflicts. As such, it is a thought-provoking anthology, tantalising in its uneven quality.

Joachim Fuchsberger

Guten Morgen, Australien

It can be safely assumed that a personal travelogue by a film actor and television host may attract a wider reading public than a similar work by professional writers. Joachim Fuchsberger's *Altstar* status in the Federal Republic of Germany guaranteed maximum publicity for his subjective account of life in Australia. His flirtatious *Guten Morgen, Australien* (1988)[5] bears the subtitle "Meine Begegnung mit dem Fünften Kontinent". Three of the eight chapters are in fact written by Eckhart Schmidt. Fuchsberger's style is conversational, anecdotal, episodic. It combines journalistic information with the chatter of a talk-show host. The discovery of Botany Bay is described in flippant language, anxious to be witty: "Möglicherweise wollte er (James Cook) seinen Botanikern an Bord, Solander und Banks, eine Freude machen...".(22) It comes as no surprise when the reader is told of a meeting (in Germany) between "Luise Gräfin zu Castell-Rüdenhausen — die Schauspielerin Luise Ullrich also"(27) and Joachim Fuchsberger. Both feel the urge to write about their impressions of Australia; they share friends in Sydney and elsewhere. Like Ullrich, Fuchsberger offers constant comparisons between Australia and Germany. Certain kinds of freedom are, he notes, "für einen auf Verbote und Verordnungen getrimmten Bundesrepublikaner kaum vorstellbar!"(25) On a more personal note he links the spraying of air passengers on their arrival in Sydney with his war experiences as POW: "Ich kam mir etwas seltsam bei der Sache vor. Zuletzt wurde ich abgesprüht, als ich Ende 1945 aus Kriegsgefangenschaft entlassen wurde."(42) The Australian Alps are discussed in relation to Germany's, Austria's and Switzerland's better-known Alps.(44) The author retains his tone of amusing informality: "Ob man da Skilaufen kann? Und ob!"(Ibid.) Fuchsberger is less reliable when it comes to passing on factual information about Australia. Canberra, he claims, is a city of "rund zweieinhalb Millionen".(45) His narrative is forever in search of catchy phrases and journalistic bon mots. "Sydney ist eine Stadt der Akzente"(51) is a typical example. Fuchsberger discovers: "Hier könnte ich leben."(55)

Like other travel writers, Fuchsberger lists predictable items of Australiana; he exploits the "geradezu unglaublichen 'Lachvögel'"(60) to the fullest. His discussion of Sydney society moves on the same level; he delights in listing BMWs and Mercedes as the most prestigious European cars.(66) Life in Sydney, as he reports it, depends on "a view"(Ibid.), apparently not only of the harbour. Australian television plays an important part in his travelogue, perhaps legitimately so for a West German TV 'personality'. Fuchsberger is most interested in "Bryan. Ein Topstar in Australien — der Wettermann."(81) He does respond to other everyday features of life in this country. The Australian "Slanguage"(92) fascinates him as much as the complex distortions of Australian history. "Australien als zweite Heimat" marks a more committed attempt to explain the attractions of this country.(105) Almost all accounts of the German migrant community in this country offer an uncritical endorsement of its ghetto mentality and ethnic club life. Fuchsberger is told: "Unter den 'alteingesessenen' Deutschen gibt es einige, die mit Vorsicht zu genießen sind."(142) Such tactful evaluation is as valid as it is rare.

But Fuchsberger also reinforces national myths. To him, too, "Fernweh" is something essentially German: "eine Ureigenschaft von uns Deutschen".(155) Ironically he refers this longing back to one of his own television shows in Germany, illustrating (unwittingly?) the commercial exploitation of popular culture. Understandably, the author discusses the "Veränderung der Medienlandschaft" in Australia and in Germany.(183) He is particularly interested in "Möglichkeiten zu einem Fernseh-Programmaustausch zwischen Deutschland und Australien"(185) and in the multilingual programmes of SBS. ("Euer Derrick ist der Größte.",183) Although German-made television series are successful in Australia, Fuchsberger rightly senses occasional "wiedererwachende Ressentiments".(186) His negotiations with media 'personalities' such as Mike Walsh to introduce to Australia "eine der erfolgreichsten Unterhaltungssendungen der deutschen Fernsehszene"(190) appear to have failed. Perhaps Fuchsberger's perspective on Australia as an extended television game show proved somewhat limited and naive. In his remaining two chapters he highlights symptomatic national television events: the Prime Minister's crying over the drug addiction of his children(324) and the Sydney-Hobart Yacht Race.(327) As always, the TV host Fuchsberger witnesses events both live and on camera. Wealthy German migrants invite him to follow the race on their boat. It is perhaps not surprising that to the author "Meals on wheels" refers to exclusive catering, illustrating that it is possible to order any cuisine in Australia (or, as his chapter calls it, "Essen wie Gott in Australien"); the more common meaning of the term clearly escapes him.(337) It is a symptomatic faux pas; *Guten Morgen, Australien* is little more than a printed television host show, a socialite's and 'star's' views of a country he does not really understand. Fuchsberger's Australia is centred around Double Bay, Woollahra and Sydney's North Shore. He ends his report on Australia with a discussion of 'Waltzing Matilda' and the new national anthem 'Advance Australia Fair'. The search for a national identity is seen in the responses to these two songs. Bearing in mind his own German national anthem's wording, it is intriguing that Fuchsberger should insist on a discussion of the Australian anthem's second stanza with its reference to "True British courage".(342) But he remains sensitive to Australian-British relations and to the growing aspirations of a new culture. Sadly, Fuchsberger does not address himself to the politics of multiculturalism, nor to the prospect that Australia's identity may yet lie in the unity in diversity of its people rather than in an inherited nineteenth-century European concept of nationhood.

TILL REINHARD

Des Himmels Blau in uns

The publisher's blurb printed on the dust-jacket speaks of "ein Auswanderer- und damit (*sic*) Abenteuerroman". Reinhard's[6] novel *Des Himmels Blau in uns* (1988) continues the traditional equation of emigration and adventure. By the late eighties both have changed dramatically in character. There is little of the hardship and irrevocable loss of earlier migration. Reinhard is in fact an "adventurous" visitor to Australia who eventually returns to his native Germany. (He spends roughly two years in this country, i.e. from 1970 to 1972.) His novel follows the general pattern of a German *Bildungsroman* in which "die Fremde" serves as challenge to a young man's growth into maturity ("reift er zum Mann", dust-jacket). The protagonist Bruno Kostbecher leaves his German home to escape family conflict and professional uncertainty. He migrates to Australia where he visits his stepbrother Hannes Hesse. While staying with Hannes Bruno creates his own family conflict: he falls in love with Ellen, the wife of his brother. Sexuality plays a major part in this book, Reinhard's hero is a mixture of Wilhelm Meister and Tom Jones. Once more Bruno has to leave "home"; he travels across various parts of Australia, meets more women and suffers many contests, until his adventures lead him to Tasmania where a young French woman named Monique Leveille instils in him the urge to grow into responsible manhood. The novel consists of three parts; each is named after a decisive character in the life of the protagonist: I "Sonja"(5), II "Hannes"(99) and III "Monique"(239). It is difficult to agree with the book's publicity that its "Sprache ist ausgefeilt" (dustjacket). In actual fact the narrative can only be described as sloppy and colloquial. Its cheek is not without wit, its racy colloquialisms are not lacking in authenticity, but Reinhard's language never adds up to a coherent narrative style. The author appears to be more interested in anecdotal gags than in devising a unified recital of connected events. One of his characteristic mannerisms is the blunt construction "Wir blenden uns ein:".(13) Despite the length of the novel (315 pp.) it is characterised by abruptness and an episodic, anecdotal quality. The overall impression is that of informal talk.

Bruno's migration remains the specific "adventure" of a German middle-class bourgeois, a tongue-in-cheek "Bildungsreise"(54) of the affluent and well-educated. Indeed, his father lectures him on the traditional motives for emigrating:

> "Die großen deutschen Wanderungsbewegungen, in deren Tradition ja die heute noch gehandhabten Immigrationsprogramme einiger Länder stehen, gingen in ihren Ursprüngen immer auf soziale und wirtschaftliche Spannungen in den Heimatländern zurück."(63)

Reinhard's migrant protagonist is nothing if not educated. He in turn informs his father of German Lutheran migration to Australia and the subsequent split of the church in its new environment. Later he entertains his grandmother with stories of Captain Cook, "Nat (*sic!*) Kelly, dem australischen Schinderhannes"(68), Port Arthur and Robert Menzies ("Eine Vaterfigur wie Adenauer,Oma",69). Australia is presented in a mixture of didacticism and satire. Till Reinhard retains this approach throughout the book; his style aims for education and humour. His "migration" was a laughing matter, albeit with serious moral implications. Not infrequently the educational information possesses its own brand of German humour: "...die Regenfälle in Australien konnten infolge von Monsunausläufern exorbitant sein, was er dem Verkäufer erzählte, und der vernahm's mit Staunen."(73) Like so many German travellers to this country, Bruno Kostbecher suffers from a "gewissen australischen Theorieüberdruß"(76) — the author recommends Thomas Mann's *Zauberberg* as antidote.

The entire First Part of *Des Himmels Blau in uns* deals with the socio-cultural background of the protagonist's eventual "migration".

Part Two sees our hero in Brisbane urging a young lady not to marry a graduate from the University of Queensland, for

> sonst endest du wie die Weiber in Jindalee oder Kenmore: reich, zwei Babys auf dem Hals und bis auf die Knochen gelangweilt.(106)

He lectures her on the evils of suburban life while he is in bed with her. Already he begins to realise that his language has deteriorated as a result of contacts with Brisbane's German Club: "die Tonart der alten Herren vom Stammtisch im Deutschen Club der Subtropenstadt (hatte) abgefärbt".(Ibid.) Some of his fellow migrants object to the treatment they receive on arrival in Australia. Employing the jargon of West German economic racism, they protest: "wir sind doch keine Kümmeltürken, sehense mal...".(112) Reinhard exposes the exploitation of migrants by migrants. A German-Australian, "der inzwischen zur Vertrauensperson avancierte Landsmann"(125), recruits cheap labour from recent arrivals. Such revelations lend the novel a social importance beyond any literary quality. The author's description of Brisbane's suburbia shares such critical awareness. Thus he speaks of "diese Filmlandschaft von Jindalee, dieses hitzetrunkene Pseudokalifornien: australisch-schläfrig, jedoch von sanfterer Gewalt."(142) He captures the special kind of boredom associated with a suburban life-style:

> hügelauf, hügelab, an *avenues, roads, drives, squares* und *crescents*, von Jindalee bis Indooroopilly, von Kenmore und Chapel Hill bis runter nach Capalaba, da wütet die Seuche, die Langeweile heißt, und sie befällt vor allem die Frauen... (Ibid.)

Reinhard includes a severe criticism of the Queensland Police Force which he sees as a symptomatic expression of violence grown from individual and social frustration.

Throughout his account the Australian male is shown to be insensitive in his dealings with women. The narrator generalizes from his observations of life in the country. Bestiality and homosexuality are held not to be uncommon.

> Das ganze Jahr über stromerten die Männer im Busch rum, Känguruhs und Karnickels schießen, ließen sich abends vollaufen und machten's ab und an mal mit'm Schaf oder 'ner Abofrau und meistens untereinander.(148)

Australia is perceived to be a rough place, lacking cultural sophistication and social commitment. Christmas brings threatening thoughts of a suburban existence in Brisbane, Australia.

Till Reinhard projects representative qualities in his characters. Occasionally his narrative states explicitly: "In solchen Momenten ist Hannes Australien und Bruno Deutschland. Hier die ungebändigte Pioniergestalt, da der zivilisationsumkränkelte Abiturient."(165) It is clear that the author's flirtatious didacticism aims for a paradigmatic logic of his *Bildungsroman*. His witticisms and cabaret-like gags cannot hide an essentially bourgeois concept of morality and education.

"II Hannes" describes the Great Brisbane Flood of 1974, variations of a suburban life-style and a trip to the country. A visit to the Queensland country town of Texas on the New South Wales border prompts the following satire:

> Und auch die halbhohen Schwingtüren vor den Pubs, die flachen Holzhäuser mit den Regenwassertanks und die breiten Cowboyhüte, die kernige, sonnenverbrannte Männergesichter beschatten, erkennt jeder wieder, der schon mal mit Hollywood eine Landpartie gemacht hat.(187)

The style is typical of Reinhard's ironic quotations of stock characters, plot and situation which soon become indistinguishable from the clichés his narrative is trying to mock. There remains throughout the novel a laboured attempt to be clever and comical, with the result that the entire work suffers from its playfully grotesque artificiality. Reinhard has none of Günter Grass' unified imaginative vision which alone can make consistent distortion a powerful narrative device. His frequent accounts of sexual intercourse constitute a verbal tour de force for its own sake (incongruously modelled on Grass).

Perhaps the most interesting theme of Part II is the author's brave attempt to address himself to Nazi loyalty among some older German migrants. When Bruno's brother Hannes discovers his father's activities as a Nazi, he accepts this inherited guilt as part of his own identity. Isolated by his Australian environment, he finds it impossible to talk about the family curse. Paradoxically, the only option is to accept his imposed sympathy for German fascism: he joins the local German Club. With extraordinary frankness Reinhard writes:

> Sie lebten ja mitten unter ihnen, die Leute mit der Narbe oder der Nummer unter der Achsel. Im Deutschen Club in Brisbane... Gelegentlich...löste der Suff ihre schweren Zungen, und die alte Totengräberherrlichkeit feierte fröhliche Urständ'; dann schmetterten sie, von der warmen Tropenluft zusätzlich erhitzt, "Wenn das Judenblut vom Messer spritzt..." durch die Versammlungsräume...(233)

Whatever the weaknesses of *Des Himmels Blau in uns*, its courage is commendable. The pity is that because of the overall ironic and pert tone of the novel its impact is not as forceful as the author would have wished. Nonetheless, Till Reinhard remains one of the few German writers facing up to the taboo of Nazi migrants in Australia, at least in passing. (Angelika Fremd's narrative *Heartland* invokes the experience of an adolescent growing up against the background of Nazism in her own migrant family rather more fully.)

Part Three describes the protagonist's eventual growth into manhood, not only in a sexual sense. His travels around Australia are called "Irr- und Kreuzfahrten", an educational pilgrimage of the *tumbe* hero in search of his true identity. The plot follows the traditional pattern, albeit in youthful exaggeration and distortion. As so often in this novel, the reader recognises the pattern or cliché. His enjoyment is designed to be found in variations of the stereotype, but the author simply does not provide enough openings to new imaginative perspectives.

It is in Tasmania that the hero eventually reaches his self-discovery. The novel's first part was addressed to his mother *Sonja*, its last section carries the name *Monique*. Finally he writes to his mother from Tasmania, linking the most important women in his life. In the present tense the story of Bruno Kostbecher, i.e. the *tumbe* protagonist "tasting life" (Kostbecher = Desgustation = Kostprobe), relates its climax in his love for Monique Leveille. In characteristic style this culminating event is expressed by the manneristically deflating sentence: "Bruno und Monique sind sich nähergekommen".(290) Yet it is enough for the hero to abandon "das solipsistische Kreisen um sich selbst, das Teil seiner Natur zu werden drohte, mit vielen Wenns und Abers".(309) In "Hobart Town" he realises his need to be responsible for another person. "Arktischer Sommer, denkt Bruno, ich taue auf."(312) With his usual attempt at cleverness the author describes his *Bildungsroman* protagonist's self-realisation in comic bashfulness: "Ich bin ein balzender Pinguin, und ich finde zu mir."(Ibid.) It is difficult to decide whether Monique's dead frog *Jean-Jacques* is a further attempt at satirising literary and cultural myth by varying and thereby reviving it. The only certainty is that the author releases his readers with a description of Bruno and Monique as *"two bloody lovers"*.(315) A very Australian ending to a very German novel.

Angelika Fremd

Heartland

Born in Seelow Mark (Prussia) in 1944, Angelika Fremd 'migrated' to Australia with her parents at the age of fourteen. *Heartland* (1989) is a collection of interrelated prose sketches. In an episodic narrative Fremd recaptures her adolescence as a German migrant in the Victorian Dandenongs. *Heartland* can hardly be called a novel in the traditional sense; rather, it is an interconnected incidental narrative collecting a series of events in the protagonist's life. Occasionally these biographical instalments prove to be almost anecdotal in character. As the title implies, *Heartland* records the anxious integration of its heroine into the Australian way of life. It is the story of a social and biological adolescence in which opposing attitudes to the New Land reflect unresolved political, moral and personal conflicts within the migrant family. The Heinrichs carry with them to Australia German Imperial and fascist ideologies; the drama of post-war German social and moral crisis is acted out in a small Victorian township, exposing deep-seated cultural and ideological prejudices, values literally out of place in an environment of primeval beginnings.

Self-assertion and sociopolitical as well as cultural identification are presented as an act of liberation, enforced against the conditioning and corruptions of the past. Fremd presents the extreme case of migration as an escape into freedom; her protagonist recognises Australia as "heartland", a place which allows her to overcome the tyranny of her native culture and upbringing.

Heartland ultimately deals with the expiation of a family curse, more universally, with the problems of evil and the morality of a social sensibility. The text rarely extends beyond the level of the adolescent protagonist's perspective and thus offers no deeper insight into the complexities it alludes to. But these forty-four episodic sketches, loosely held together by a curiously literary yet adolescent narrative voice, do add up to a haunting tale of displacement, alienation and liberation. They set womanhood and migration into a new and disturbing context.

Angelika Fremd has published a number of poems dealing with the same subjects treated in *Heartland* ("Mutter", "Liebe")[7]. Her prose still lacks complexity and style; indeed, one reviewer characterised the novella *Heartland* as adolescent fiction.[8]

Chapter Seven

International Socialism and Migration: The GDR Connection 1956-1987

> "Loyalität gegenüber Australien schließt nicht Vertrauen in die Sowjetunion aus."
>
> Walter Kaufmann, *Kreuzwege*

WALTER KAUFMANN

Born on 19 January 1924 in Berlin, Walter Kaufmann grew up in Duisburg, escaped as a child from Nazi Germany, first to Holland (1940), then to England, from there to Australia (1942). The child was adopted in 1926 by the Jewish solicitor Kaufmann. His parents were deported to Theresienstadt; after the war Walter Kaufmann learnt that they had been subsequently murdered in Auschwitz. Together with other unwanted antifascists and German emigrants, the eighteen-year-old left England aboard the steamer "Dunera", bound for Sydney. Kaufmann spent his first months in Australia inside an internment camp. Subsequently he worked as a farm labourer and fruit picker, before joining the Australian Army. After the war he found work as street photographer, docker and seaman. He attained Australian citizenship, which he still holds to this day. His colourful working experience shines through all of Kaufmann's writings, in particular his knowledge of the waterfront, his period as a butcher's labourer in an abattoir (cf. "The Beef-House" in *The Curse of Maralinga*) and his time as a tug-boat deck-hand and seaman on the Australian coast.

Encouraged by the Melbourne Realist Writers' Group, which Walter Kaufmann joined after demobilisation, he began writing the novel *Voices in the Storm* in 1949 and completed it two years later. He received special support from Frank Hardy and David Martin. (The German version of the novel did not appear until 1977.) In an interview, held at the author's Berlin residence on 6 January, 1988[1] Kaufmann explained his commitment to communism as a direct result of his experiences as seaman and soldier. During the time of Stalingrad he was particularly moved by the plight of refugees. Strong personal influences emanated from the trade union movement, above all from Ralph Gibson, E.V. Elliott (Sydney), Bill Burt (Melbourne) and Jim Healy (Sydney). If the Australian Communist Party had a period of strength, it was during the time Walter Kaufmann became associated with it. During the forties and fifties its importance could not be underrated. Kaufmann partook in the class struggle, not merely by his writing.

In 1955 the Australian Seamen's Union delegated Walter Kaufmann to the World Youth Festival in Warsaw. There he met many anti-fascist communists who had survived the concentration camps. Kaufmann had an immediate affinity with them, admiring the courage and integrity of victims determined to liberate themselves. From Poland he travelled to the USSR where he spent two months. Still in 1955, Kaufmann returned to the city of his birth; in Berlin he established first contact with the German Democratic Republic. Two years later, he settled in Berlin, where he still lives today. Walter Kaufmann was not a member of the SED, but clearly a strong supporter of his (third) country of choice. Living in the GDR with an Australian passport allowed him freedom of movement and other privileges not shared by ordinary citizens of the socialist German State. Kaufmann left Australia in 1956. After fifteen years as an Australian author writing about Germany he now reversed his literary relationship with the two countries. It is fair to say that Kaufmann enjoyed an exotic image among his readers in the GDR. He himself sees his entire life as one prolonged adventure. Among his strongest literary influences Kaufmann counts Ernest Hemingway, Jack London and William Saroyan — with the latter he claims a special, personal affinity ("artverwandt"). These authors inspired Kaufmann to his own writing. He stresses that he had no formal literary training, no initiation into the art of writing.

Kaufmann has been an avid reader ever since he can remember. Yet he claims that he does not write for readers. To him, a writer is someone who *finds* things, who relies on personal experience, who realises himself in writing. Kaufmann quotes Flaubert's affirmation "Madame Bovary is a part of myself" to explain his literary identification. But he is anxious to demonstrate that his own novel *Kreuzwege* (1961/1962) (translated from the English *Crossroads*) is not obviously autobiographical. He explains how his own childhood experience made it possible for him to live a literary double-life: he can invoke a knowledge of both proletarian and bourgeois backgrounds. In his novel he splits himself in that sense, into a half-brother and a brother, one ending in Auschwitz, the other living in Australia, only to return to a socialist Germany.

It is not surprising that Kaufmann's concept of a lived and living literature should lead him to a special interest in a genre of eye-witness narrative description: the reportage. Among his many travelogues and reporting accounts are: *Begegnung mit Amerika heute* (1965), *Hoffnung unter Glas* (1966), *Gerücht vom Ende der Welt* (1969) and *Unterwegs zu Angela. Amerikanische Impressionen* (1973). Kaufmann sees in his reportages a fund of stories; he is constantly looking for short stories based on fact, on what he calls "actuality". It fulfils, in his own judgement, a double function. He is searching for a "wider view" offered by stories of people in other countries, and thus replenishes his own narrative material. His books on Israel and on Northern Ireland describe people of different background in the context of historical turmoil. "Together, they are burning issues." That was what fascinated Kaufmann about the United States, too: the violence of the Kennedys' and King's assassinations, George Jackson and Angela Davis. He writes about more than these murders and civil rights and Vietnam protests. History and personal story come together in what Walter Kaufmann likes to call "faction".

Kaufmann writes as no other German writes. His concept of literature is steeped in an Anglo-Australian tradition. According to his own claims, he actually translates from English into German when he chooses to, or is asked to write, in his native language. Kaufmann sees his bilingualism as an advantage *and* a handicap. Writing in German is a struggle for him, he insists. And he adds that, although he still feels at home in his second language, he writes better in English than he speaks it. After he left the Australian army, Kaufmann explains, he became "totally Australian". As he had left school at the age of thirteen, he could be said not to have been culturally preconditioned. In many ways, that proved to be a great advantage. Kaufmann likes the English people, but he prefers the Irish. He thinks he could not write about England, but he has written about Ireland. He actually lived in Belfast for three months and feels a special affinity with Irish poetic images, literature and music. His love for Ireland found expression in two books: *Irish Journey* (1979) and *We Laugh Because We Cry* (1977) (*Irische Reise, Wir lachen, weil wir weinen*). Despite the difference in background, there is a certain similarity between the West German writer Heinrich Böll and the Australian/GDR writer Walter Kaufmann: they share their faith in working people, their preference for the short story — and their love of Ireland.

Although Kaufmann denies having written poetry, some verses of his did get published in *Angry Penguins*. It is clear, however, that he wishes to disown them. His short stories were published in *Meanjin*, *Overland* and in three issues of *Coast to Coast*. His first short story, published in Australia, not only won a prize[2] but to this day expresses his political, literary and moral credo: *The Simple Things* deals with friendship, integrity, honesty and betrayal. Again, Kaufmann is anxious to clarify that it is not an autobiographical story. What matters to him is that both boys reject the inroads of fascism.

Among the socialist writers Kaufmann met in Warsaw, Berlin and the USSR were Willy Bredel, Anna Seghers, Ludwig Renn and Eduard Claudius. Their example made him decide to stay in the German Democratic Republic. During our conversation in Berlin he was emphatic that he writes "because I can't do anything else". When asked how he can reconcile that with the wide variety of his labours, he replies that he "was gathering experience". He insists that he never simply experienced life as a seaman or a butcher's labourer in an abattoir: "I perceived life and work with the eye of a writer". Nonetheless, work remains the major source of his 'factional fiction'. Kaufmann remembers that he took on the job of a photographer because he had to work on Saturdays only, which meant that he had the rest of the week free for his writing.

While he was in Australia, Walter Kaufmann concedes that he had no particular interest in Aborigines. Maralinga and the story covering the event were mainly concerned with the nuclear issue. In those days Kaufmann's central preoccupation was the plight of the Jews. His hitherto last novel, *Tod in Fremantle* (1987), "happened" to him, as he puts it. It is the result of his return visit to Australia in 1984. Solidarity emerged as a natural, inevitable moral response. It is strange that this novel, dealing with 'suicides' of Aborigines in custody — a subject of overwhelming urgency in Australia during 1988 — has not yet found a publisher in this country. There can be no doubt that the fate of Aborigines has become a major concern for Walter Kaufmann.

It is with satisfaction and pride that Kaufmann points to the fact that since his first novel in 1956/57 (*Wohin der Mensch gehört*) he has been able to live on his writing. His books have appeared in large editions. Walter Kaufmann remained a full-time writer. The "exotic" image of his works in the GDR is perhaps understandable when one remembers that the predominant theme of that country's literature was for a long time what came to be known as "Republikflucht" — escaping to the West. By contrast, Kaufmann offered adventure, solidarity and the Antipodes, equally acceptable to the Party State and to its people. It was an 'escapist' literature of a different kind, yet ideologically and politically of recognisable, immediate relevance to life in the GDR. Kaufmann is a popular, professional writer: he has published novels, short stories, narratives, reportages, television and film scripts and several books for children. Often travelogues and children's literature overlap, of necessity in *Stefan*. *Mosaik einer Kindheit* (1966), but also later in *Das verschwundene Hotel*, *Patrick* und *Entführung in Manhattan* (1975).

What Walter Kaufmann's total output demonstrates is an all-round professionalism as a writer. It is perhaps significant that Kaufmann's contribution to the GDR-anthology *Writers About Writers* (edited by Baldauf) is entitled "Das unbestechliche Gedächtnis" ("Incorruptible Memory").[3] His fiction and 'faction' derive their impetus from the moral reliance and guidance of memory. Kaufmann's literary memories articulate the social conscience of a victim and a survivor, of a migrant and a homecomer, of an Australian and a German.[4]

Voices in the Storm

In 1953 the Australasian Book Society in Melbourne published Walter Kaufmann's first novel, *Voices in the Storm*. It is the story of a group of underground fighters against Hitler. At its centre stands the experience of a Jewish boy who sees his family disintegrating before the onslaught of Nazi violence.

It is significant that "a living link" is said to exist between fascist Germany and Menzies' Australia in the fifties. (Menzies won the 1949 elections; he remained Prime Minister for the next 16 years. In 1951 Menzies signed the ANZUS Pact, a defence agreement between Australia, New Zealand and the United States. The Menzies government sent Australian troops to fight the communists in Malaya,

Korea and Vietnam.) The socialist publishers see Kaufmann's book as a powerful tool in the conflicts of national politics.

It is clear that Walter Kaufmann's first novel formed part of the political landscape in Australia at the time. It lays claim to a moral legitimacy and integrity of the anti-fascist Communist alliance. As such, the publication of *Voices in the Storm* was as much a political as a literary event.

Kaufmann succeeds in his attempt at a narrative integration of historical events and personal happenings. Through the perspective of his naive child protagonist the rise of Nazi dictatorship is drawn in a simple, paradigmatic manner. *Voices in the Storm* gives the impression of a barely fictionalised social report, its narrative style creates authenticity by interrelating individual but representative fates derived from the conflicts of the period. Kaufmann's faithful recreation of the atmosphere includes quotations of German advertising from the thirties ("Persil remains Persil", 43). The author's keen eye for detail lends the novel its characteristic realism. Yet most narrative scenes and figures may be said to be paradigmatic in nature. Kaufmann's chapters are carefully chosen settings, each describing different aspects and stages of a nation sliding into fascism. The place of action is always an expression of a sociopolitical condition.

Kaufmann raises the kind of questions that have been asked over and over, such as: why did the Jews not leave in time? His novel gives a convincing answer in its realistic reconstruction of the fear of an entire epoch. Among the many remarkable qualities of Kaufmann's narrative in *Voices in the Storm* is the author's ability to sketch a wide span of model behaviour. In that sense, most of his characters are representative types, and the novel does indeed add up to a gathering of voices, of paradigmatic attitudes, in the storm of rising fascism. Kaufmann's novel is a collection of representative portraits, young and old, who together make up the dominant opinions and behaviour of Germans under Nazi rule.

There is also a dimension of the work which has much in common with popular adventure stories. The resistance fighters against fascism are natural candidates as heroes of narrative fiction. Kaufmann is aware of this potential — and of its dangers. It is fair to say that he balances his didactic protagonists between historical realism and ideological idealism. There is an inevitable typology of simplistically drawn characters, but the author's eye for details usually rescues them from becoming clichés. Similarly, many dialogues read like set speeches, only to be saved by a turn of phrase or the sudden intrusion of precisely observed manners or motivations. For all the integrity and narrative powers of Walter Kaufmann, it apparently remains extraordinarily difficult to portray Nazi characters without turning them into caricatures. (This may well be the reason why satirical accounts of fascism have proved so much more successful and "convincing" — one thinks of Günter Grass' novel *The Tin Drum*.)

Writing about a German Jewish boy in the thirties means descriptions of victimisation and persecution. Kaufmann excels at reporting such incidents. One senses the full weight of the author's own experience behind such accounts. It is the impression of authenticity which lends this novel weight, credibility and moral authority. Like his protagonist, the narrator appears as historical witness.

Walter Kaufmann's novel appeared in 1953. Part of its purpose was to agitate, to be *parteilich* in the sense of Georg Lukács and socialist realism. It is only fair to bear that in mind when reading the book over 35 years later.

The apparent defeat of Jews, communists and other anti-fascist resistance fighters in Nazi Germany, faithfully recorded in this novel, assumes the nature of an appeal: the reader of *Voices in the Storm* is drawn into the contemporary conflict of the novel's historical theme. If the forces of evil had not 'won', even on the level of fictional narration, there would have been no need for protest, for commitment on the part of Walter Kaufmann's international readers.

The Curse of Maralinga

This is the first collection of Kaufmann's short stories, initially published in German in 1958 (republished in 1977), released in English by the "Seven Seas Book" series in Berlin in 1959. It consists of eighteen narrative sketches, mostly with an Australian setting. Other stories are recollections of a troubled childhood in fascist Germany. Kaufmann himself draws attention to his "first story written at the height of the Second World War", *The Simple Things*:

> It is really no story at all. It is an avowal of trust in the *other Germany*, a peaceful, democratic one. It was written in the seclusion of an Australian country town, written at white heat some days after I received word that my parents had been deported by the Nazis. Through it, I tried to reach out across the world to those who defied fascism in the face of death.[5]

It is, indeed, representative of many characteristics of Walter Kaufmann's style and motivation of writing. Primarily, the art of narration is seen as an act of identification. Kaufmann's stories not only bear witness, their perspectives are a clear expression of moral and social commitment. As narrative historian he sees his task in keeping the past alive. In reinvoking historical conflicts he is able to articulate their sociopolitical dimensions and take sides with the progressive forces of a socialist humanism. As in so many other works, Kaufmann in this short story records instances of loyalty between Communists and Jews. A central theme in his writing is the acceptance of a changed social identity. Himself of a middle-class bourgeois Jewish background, the author again and again describes the process of an ideological conversion based on experience, often rooted in childhood incidents and observations. If his stories seem at times all too didactic, the reason is to be found in this commitment. Kaufmann has demonstrated outstanding qualities as a writer of fact and fiction; there can be no question, then, that such demonstrative moral affirmations are the deliberate statements of a socially committed author. It is perhaps not surprising that some of Kaufmann's short stories are reminiscent of the early Böll: both writers share a trust in proletarian values and a concern to formulate and keep alive the lessons of the past. (Of course, many of their stories were written at the same time, albeit Kaufmann's at least partly in Australia.)

The strength of *The Curse of Maralinga* lies in its succinct characterisations, the empathetic creation of personal conflict and the precision of its social realism. Work is one of Kaufmann's principal themes: its part in man's self-realisation as well as man's exploitation as worker. Part of this preoccupation with work is the recurrent expression of confidence and trust in the unions. Identification and commitment, the hallmarks of Kaufmann's prose, are demonstrated rather than realised.

The Curse of Maralinga combines criticism of US-capitalism with Anglo-Australian racism in a powerful account of the exploitation and genocide of the Aborigines. The main protagonists are little more than narrative mouth-pieces expressing stock-in-trade views and values of the ideological enemy. Kaufmann uses the opportunity to describe Australian anti-Americanism at the time. The suffering of Aborigines as a result of nuclear testing is a subject treated only by the German-

Australian socialist writers Walter Kaufmann and Joachim Specht.⁶ *The Curse of Maralinga* conveys in barely controlled passion the anger and mourning over a dispossessed people. As its title implies, it is a curse cast over white Australia as well.

Much of Kaufmann's prose reminds one of Gertrud Leutenegger's assessment of socialism as "a red psalm"³. For Kaufmann, the experience of migration loses much of its potential hazards because he is at home in international socialism.

Walter Kaufmann's prose is carried by a tone of masculinity. His protagonists live in a man's world. Not surprisingly, conflicts of love for a woman and mateship loyalty are usually resolved by a courageous commitment and return to the comrades. The woman shares in, or may be part of, the adventure Kaufmann's men are seeking, but she is not a home to them. Women seem to lack the strength of a socialist brotherhood, they do not, in these stories, inspire loyalty, courage or faith. There is no harmonious relationship between men and women in *The Curse of Maralinga*. Women act as victims, models, provocateurs, as motivators and challengers, as *catalysts* of male decision-making and behaviour, not as genuine partners in work or love.

The shortest story of this collection, *The Sweets*, re-presents the themes of identity and role with a magic twist of fairy-tale logic. It is a simple, beautifully written parable of seduction in the context of childhood playfulness and trust. (One is reminded, by way of contrast, of Ingeborg Bachmann's violent childhood memory recounted in her novel *Malina*⁸ where instead of sweets the girl is offered a slap in the face.) Kaufmann ends his brief narrative with a reconciliatory response to the parent's attempt to denigrate the beauty of the boy's experience:

"I shouldn't wonder that she thought you a beggar boy, a stray, neglected waif."
"Nonsense," said the boy with great assurance, "I was the Prince!"(111)

The story's dedication further emphasises the symbolic intent of this childhood scene.

Kaufmann continues to be preoccupied with *the politics of role and identity*. He respects the ability and courage to change. One of his stories is dedicated to the Hungarian-German-Australian writer David Martin. David Martin went to Spain, where one of his first poems was nailed to a tree on the Madrid-Valencia road and read by passing soldiers and ambulances.⁹ Instead of Zionism, Kaufmann's protagonist joins the forces of anti-fascism and socialism, even though he is a Jew.

It is the woman who is fanatical in her role as fighter for the state of Israel.

Kaufmann's eighteen stories in this collection bring together an impressive range of character portraits and recurrent themes of social and political conflict. From his own experience Kaufmann describes the work of dockers, seamen, farm labourers and street photographers. It is *at work* that his protagonists experience the world and humanity. The author's obvious love for Australia does not blind his perception of political corruption and, in particular, of the cold-blooded genocide of the Aboriginal people. His stories portray human beings either in the state of slavery or in the process of liberation. Kaufmann's literary and political mediation between Australia and Germany is based on a vision of socialist equality, a humanism of brothers and workers.

Wohin der Mensch gehört

The first German-language version of *Voices in the Storm* appeared in 1957 under the title *Wohin der Mensch gehört*.[10] The novel is dedicated to the memory of Kaufmann's adoptive parents, "J.K. und S.M.K.", emphasising the autobiographical dimensions of the work. The book consists of two parts ("Teile"), the first covering, in condensed form, most of the characters and plot of *Voices in the Storm*, the second dealing, as a completely new theme, with the protagonist's internment and subsequent fortunes in Australia. In effect, then, Kaufmann has written a new novel within a novel, or added a lengthy and revealing narrative account of his experiences in his country of adoption. The two parts are of roughly equal length (the "Zweite Teil" is in fact 21 pages longer) and replace the five parts of the English-language original.

Among the few changes in Part One is the different name of the novel's boy protagonist: David Ruben becomes Stefan Hermann (a closer approximation of Kaufmann?). *Wohin der Mensch gehört* seems to follow a clearer ideological pattern. The ideological war is not only declared in the German novel, it is fought out in its pages. Another shift of emphasis occurs in the importance Stefan Hermann attaches to books and writing. In particular, Stefan's readings of travelogues shelter him from the brutality of his immediate surroundings. Kaufmann's description of the exotic in literature as a means of escaping political reality touches upon a major theme — and ambiguity

— in German literature. The young boy's rejection of school knowledge is directly linked to his discovery of a world of literature. One dimension of *Wohin der Mensch gehört* is, indeed, a kind of "Portrait of the Artist as a Young Man": art and politics are correlated; the human spirit expresses itself in both. It is in that context — and in the context of the current dogma of "sozialistische Realismus"[11] — that one of the novel's characters carves the bust of Ernst Thälmann.

The first half of *Wohin der Mensch gehört* adheres to the ideological prescriptions of socialist realism, propagated at the time. Part Two of the novel gives a narrative account of the protagonist's arrival in Australia in late 1940 as a refugee. Kaufmann allows his protagonist to ask himself questions of lasting significance in the context of German emigration to Australia.

> Was, dachte Stefan in der Stille des Zeltes, macht mich zum Antifaschisten? Meine Vergangenheit? Daß ich freiwillig ins Heer eingetreten bin? War ein Emigrant selbstverständlich Antifaschist?(219)

Like his fellow-GRD-writer Joachim Specht, Kaufmann knows that no such assumptions can be made.[12]

It is mateship, more specifically workers' solidarity, which leads to an understanding of contemporary Australian society and Stefan's place in it. His contact with seamen and other workers continues to remind him: "Auch dies gehört zum Krieg...Der Klassenkampf...".(253) Kaufmann draws migrant characters who see themselves as part of an international union of workers. The novel suffers from a somewhat simplistic typology of narrative figures; there is a lack of complexity in Kaufmann's characterisation. This, in turn, affects the composition of language and plot. The narrative class struggle does not allow for subtlety. Kaufmann sketches scenes from the Australian Communist underground (the CPA was banned at the time) not lacking in romantic idealisation. Literature and sociopolitical reality have merged, one bears witness to the other. Kaufmann also records his literary beginnings in Australia in a kind of fictional self-documentation.

Walter Kaufmann's first novel *Voices in the Storm* (1953) may be said to exist in at least four versions: apart from the Australian original, it appeared in three German variations — in 1957 under the title *Wohin der Mensch gehört*, in 1965 as *Unter australischer Sonne* and in 1977 as *Stimmen im Sturm*. *Unter australischer Sonne* is in fact Part Two of *Wohin der Mensch gehört*, with few minor changes.

It is perhaps not surprising that incestuous cross-references should occur where the same book is extended to so many different publications. Little wonder, too, that Kosch's *Deutsches Literatur-Lexikon* has difficulties listing Kaufmann's publications in their proper sequence.[13] What can be said is that Walter Kaufmann not only translated, transliterated, rewrote and republished this first novel several times (partly for commercial, partly for political reasons); *Voices in the Storm* clearly was, and remains, the most important work of his career, both on a personal level and in terms of its literary quality.

Voices in the Storm was rewritten and translated by the author and republished in 1977 by the Verlag der Nation Berlin under the title *Stimmen im Sturm*. It also appeared in the GDR series *Roman-Zeitung* as Heft 377 (8/1981). The German version of Kaufmann's first novel follows the same structural pattern: it, too, consists of five parts, but the narrative is reduced by five chapters. It is unusual that an author does his own translations; in the case of the bilingual Walter Kaufmann such an undertaking almost inevitably led to an actual rewriting of the work. *Stimmen im Sturm* is certainly not a literal translation, rather a kind of literary transformation. It offers little comfort and makes no attempt to idealise the sufferings of Jews and other victims of fascism. There is, not surprisingly, a marked tuning-down of ideological rhetoric. Instead of an expression of faith and confidence in Stalin, *Stimmen im Sturm* adds a passage which reads like a homage to Walter Kaufmann's own background: the story of adoption of a workers' child named Gert or Gerhart(Chapter Twenty-Four). The German novel thus relies on (fairly transparent) parallels and complementary narrative figures. In some respect it appears more radical in its criticism of a collective German guilt.(141/244)

Ruf der Inseln, Am Kai der Hoffnung

The GDR literary historian Joachim Schreck claims there is no other prose writer in the Socialist Republic who has concentrated as much on the genre of the short story as Walter Kaufmann.[14] He rightly draws attention to the Anglo-American tradition, but fails to add that in Australia, too, the short story has enjoyed continued popularity and has a tradition of its own. Among the stories Kaufmann himself lists as separate or major publications are: *Ruf der Inseln* (1960), *Feuer am Suvastrand* (1961) and *Die Erschaffung des Richard Hamilton* (1964). They are also the titles of prose collections. *Am Kai der Hoffnung*

(1974) bears the subtitle "Stories" and is in fact a selection of Kaufmann's better-known pieces.[15]

Considering that the first German novel (Schnabel's *Insel Felsenburg*) had an island setting, far away from the social and political realities of the reader's everyday life, Kaufmann's demythologising of exotic Pacific islands is a prose work written against the tradition of German novels.[16]

Die Erschaffung des Richard Hamilton is characteristic of Walter Kaufmann's narrative role-playing. It is a short story about a writer of short stories who invents a pseudonym for his authorial *persona*. Some of the statements made in *Die Erschaffung des Richard Hamilton* correspond very closely to views Walter Kaufmann expressed in an interview.[12] The following, for example, seems a case in point:

> Damit meinte sie, daß ich das Schreiben von Geschichten als meine eigentliche Aufgabe betrachten und anderen Arbeiten lediglich nachgehen sollte, um Stoff und Erfahrungen zu sammeln.(77)

The general tone of the story is flirtatious and humorous. There is a passing reference to "Luke Devanny, den bekannten Kurzgeschichtenautor, den ich sehr bewundere"(85), — possibly a hidden homage to Gavin Casey, the Australian short story writer Kaufmann admired.[18] There are unmistakably autobiographical ingredients, such as the protagonist's experiences as a street photographer in Melbourne. Despite the playfulness and humour, the author manages to integrate into his narrative self-reflection an account of Australia's treatment of communists in the fifties.

Some of Kaufmann's stories are impressionistic portraits of characters, drawn from the perspective of workmates or friends, social witnesses responding to someone's changed circumstance. Kaufmann's figures are always identified by the reactions they inspire in other people. Social witnessing creates identity. A different attitude or a change of heart is expressed by the adoption of a new name. Kaufmann's aesthetics and politics of masculinity imply that there is a certain restlessness inherent in all men and that women are determined to destroy it, that it is their nature not to share in it. Kaufmann describes women as imprisoning men. They appear to have no place in the world of exotic adventure or the erotic realm of freedom.

The title of the volume thus gains a very specific significance. For the seamen land means hope of adventure or the return to safety. For the many victims whose fate Kaufmann invokes in this collection the title carries a more symbolic meaning, often at odds with the reality of their situation. *Am Kai der Hoffnung* is a selection of seamen's stories glorifying the camaraderie of men sailing to exotic parts of the world, sharing adventures, triumphs and failures. Of the seventeen short stories only a handful do not explicitly deal with the lives of wharfies, seamen, their friends and their women. Kaufmann's narrative style is an effective mixture of precise observation and paradigmatic intention. Instead of psychological motivation, his characters are shown to act in response to social challenges. Their "inner" life is shaped by external events. Walter Kaufmann draws his figures as political beings in the broadest sense. With great economy the author describes them in a representative state of crisis: as workers, as women, as members of a suppressed race, challenged to make a far-reaching decision. The "quay of hope" is an expression of the ability to choose; only those who have no choice and no control over their own fate are real victims.

In the tradition of the Anglo-American short story Kaufmann's openings are almost always *in medias res*. He makes extensive use of dialogues, thus adding to the dramatic impact of the narrative. Characters are sketched rather than portrayed in detail. Most of the stories have a surprising or unsettling conclusion, often with strong moral overtones. They all illustrate a model kind of behaviour, good or bad, and they all aim to demonstrate man as a social being. Kaufmann's narrative gesture often includes direct addresses to the reader, albeit expressed in authorial role-playing. The narrator is identified as another figure in the story; the tale involves the *persona* of the story-teller. Kaufmann is at pains to show that the author, too, is part of the social events he is reporting. There can be no "objectivity".

It should be said that Walter Kaufmann's short stories translate well, even where he has not rewritten them himself. His language is basically simple and straightforward, with mainly short sentences, uncomplicated syntax and few mannerisms. The popularity of his prose is hardly surprising; it is eminently readable, without being superficial or trite.

The 1974 edition of *Am Kai der Hoffnung* (paperback version 1981) contains fifteen additional stories. They are all translated from the English, this time not by the author himself. Where Kaufmann's stories become overtly ideological the narrative rhetoric cannot disguise a genuine sense of commitment. What some readers may dismiss as political five finger exercises of minor literary value is to Kaufmann an affirmative act of identification. This is not the place to discuss the aesthetics of ideology. It must suffice to note the inferior quality of language in such prose, the predictability and transparency of plot and characterisation and the awkwardness in attempts to symbolise and to idealise. Similar problems exist where other ideologies are being propagated: it is by no means a dilemma confined to socialist writing. These less successful stories do not question Walter Kaufmann's major talent as a prose writer, they merely put his literary achievement in a self-chosen context and perspective. For it is above all as a short story writer that Walter Kaufmann's outstanding contribution to German-Australian literature will be measured.

Kreuzwege

As one of Kaufmann's most successful works, *Kreuzwege* deals with a programmatic theme of socialist literature: the overcoming of the past and a political commitment to a new society. *Kreuzwege*'s subject is ideological conversion, it tells the story of Ron Prentice's liberation by joining the Australian Seamen's Union. The author's biography indicates a similar career. His protagonist's change from a farm labourer to a seaman reflects Kaufmann's own experiences in Australia. The cross-roads alluded to in the title relate to Ron Prentice's private and professional life; in both realms he is confronted with the challenge to commit himself to social and moral values. The conversion to communism is the overriding theme of all of Kaufmann's prose. In that sense, his writing may be seen as a continual form of self-justification, a reflection on his ideological development. Writing and publishing in a socialist society involves the constant need to demonstrate the authenticity and reliability of a narrated commitment. The author has to identify himself ideologically with every new book. *Kreuzwege* never shakes off its ideological superstructure. Its twelve chapters are in fact a progression towards personal political commitment. The "moral" of the book *is* that the personal is the political.

Kreuzwege may not be the most convincing story outside its ideological determination, but it does add up to a series of semi-documentary social sketches of Australia in the fifties. Not surprisingly, its protagonist reads Theodore Dreiser in his berth aboard the *Epoch*.

Like Joachim Specht, Kaufmann refers in particular to the Aboriginal artist Namatjira whose work gains symbolic significance in the struggle for freedom of the native people of Australia.(103-104) By continuing with his analogy between documentary films and social reportages, Kaufmann succeeds in turning style and form into narrative plot. He indulges in a form of fictional self-reflection. There are two kinds of documentation taking place at the same time, both transformed into fiction. Such narrative perspective turns plot and characterisation into documentary political reflection. Kaufmann thus emphasises the model character of his fiction.

The mixture of autobiographical and ideological fictionalisation lends *Kreuzwege* its special quality. Kaufmann's own trip to Moscow in 1955 is given model character by a writer whose narrative compositions are in fact attempts to discover ideological patterns in personal experience. It is Kaufmann's way of authentification. Perhaps his adoption by members of a persecuted section of society sensitised him to the need of re-adoption and ultimate approval. Walter Kaufmann may be said to have practised the art of adoption at least twice: in Australia and in the GDR. His conversion to communism is an act of ideological adoption which he describes in various forms in his prose. There is, in all of Kaufmann's writing, a demonstrative quality, anxious to be recognised and endorsed. Applied to *Kreuzwege*, the author sees his task as looking beyond the exterior to explain the nature of communist solidarity. But the novel fails to do this: it is precisely as statements and as "external" observations that its style aims to effect ideological conversion. The schematic style continues throughout the book. It leads to clichés and naive simplifications. Kaufmann is a competent craftsman of the narrative trade, but in this novel he lapses into some of the worst features of popular writing. *Kreuzwege* is not so much a novel of indoctrination as a narrative report on the general pattern of indoctrination. Political conversion is presented along the lines of the classical *Bildungsroman*. The genre of the *Bildungsroman* is itself a fictional pattern; the narrative structure reinforces the representative quality of its protagonist's growth.

Truth is presented as the ultimate conflict of *Kreuzwege*; the novel acknowledges and describes at least two different kinds of truths — in a preconceived ideological framework. *All* narration is biased; it is in the nature of prose fiction that its perspective must remain authorial (even where it attempts to be "objective"). Kaufmann's narrator records, as it were, his own ideological commitment, without serious attempts to create characters or plot capable of questioning it. His protagonist loses his love because a woman betrays the cause and cannot be trusted. Katherine's womanhood is the reason for her betrayal. Once again, Kaufmann's patriarchal sexism simplifies what should have been a very complex problem. Another woman is a traitor to the cause of socialist seamen.

Flucht

This novel, first published in Leipzig 1984, republished in the *Roman-Zeitung* (Berlin, Heft 4/1987 [445]), is the story of a writer confronted with the choice of adopting or betraying a country, a society, an ideology. It is the recurring theme of most of Walter Kaufmann's prose. In one form or another, the author is the protagonist of his own work. Kaufmann presents surprisingly varied versions of the same semi-autobiographical narrative composition. *Flucht* deals with a major dilemma of the GDR society, *Republikflucht*, the escape of its citizens to the West, by linking it with the author's own return from years of emigration in Australia and his erratic love for a black American singer, Elena Crawford. The illegal escape of his friend Hartmut Berg to West Germany challenges the author-narrator's own concept of home and identity. His desertion of his wife and daughters for the love of Elena adds another intimate dimension to the concepts of social betrayal. As always with Kaufmann, the private sphere reflects political, ideological conduct. Implied in Kaufmann's treatment of the theme is the question whether a writer (or any other artist) can afford to lose his sociopolitical and cultural identity for the sake of an exotic concept of his craft.

By 1984, Walter Kaufmann's attitude to Australia — or his own Australianness — has been reduced to a matter of convenience. In fact, he specifically refers to Australia as "die Fremde".(216) With such loyalty to the GDR State, the author naturally rejects Hartmut Berg's escape and terminates the friendship. At the same time, he finds the subject of *Republikflucht* a rewarding, indeed a fascinating, topic for a literary report. He is interested in "die Beweggründe zur Republikflucht — ein Thema, das mich in letzter Zeit...beschäftigt (hat)."(173) Thus *Flucht* relates its own narrative genesis. Kaufmann's autobiographical references are easily recognisable: the trip to the United States, invoked in Chapter Two, alludes to his reportages *Begegnung mit Amerika heute* (1965) and *Gerücht vom Ende der Welt* (1969), both republished in one volume under the title *Manhattan-Sinfonie* (1987). Not surprisingly, in these reportages Kaufmann refers to himself as "unser Autor"(6), following the example of Egon Erwin Kisch. In his fictional prose, too, he consistently sees the author as a narrative figure of his own work, playing his part, like any other character. His self-consciousness has been fictionalised and functionalised.

Flucht could be described as a kind of handbook or introduction or narrative commentary on the style and books of Walter Kaufmann. On one level, it is a novel of barely fictionalised self-propagation, linked with an ideological self-justification. The socialist author is anxious that his writing should find readers at home, his home, an adopted home. His travelling is done to lead him back to "ein Zuhause".(181) Elena falsely associates him with "the wandering Jew"(Ibid.); Kaufmann rejects the Jewish image for the sake of a socialist home. That home is a GDR reader who may not travel himself — at least not yet. Kaufmann's travels of flight come dangerously close to an ideological apologia for the exotic. *Flucht* is, in the most literal sense, a work-in-progress. It is, as such, also an attempt to explain or to define a style which grows out of the experience of travel. Kaufmann's "talk stories" may have their origin in far-away Australia, but they can be put to ideological use in the GDR. They are "talk stories, die nicht zuletzt auch deutlich machten, was einen wie mich in dem Land hielt, dem Hartmut den Rücken gekehrt hatte."(102) Kaufmann seems to hint at the ability of documentary fiction to expose conflicting ideological identifications, both in terms of aesthetic form and of social politics. That is how Kaufmann sees his own writing: as reproduced information, fiction authenticated by facts. And part of that information is the background of each of his narratives: it is not vanity which makes him refer to so many of his prose works in a novel, rather the urge to relate them back to their original context, an event, an adventure, a journey, a flight.

Significantly, he acknowledges that it is his writing ("meine Arbeit") which has made him acceptable in the GDR: it has inspired trust in him as a man, as a socialist without GDR passport, as a traveller escaping the lures of ownership and exploitation. His travels are an exotic freedom for most of his readers, but as they only lead back to where they are, they partake in this joint flight of fancy. The reader's escape while reading is matched by the author's flight home while writing about the illusion of personal freedom. *Flucht* thus amounts to a structural and ideological concept describing the interrelationship between Walter Kaufmann and his readers, as much as between Walter Kaufmann and his works of narrative fiction.

Tod in Fremantle

This novel bears the subtitle "Chronik einer Nachforschung"; an apt description for a narrative trying to reconstruct the murder of a young Aboriginal. Kaufmann has written a social and political detective story. *Tod in Fremantle*, published in Leipzig in 1987, is a timely novel dealing with "suicides" of Aborigines in police custody, an issue which led to a Royal Commission and continued to haunt Australian society in the eighties. It is Kaufmann's strongest work yet. Surprisingly, the book has already been translated; perhaps less surprisingly, it has not found a publisher in Australia.[18]

In characteristic Kaufmann fashion the reader is drawn into the genesis of the work, and the narrative is recognisably autobiographical. But the author's role-playing follows the general principles of Egon Erwin Kisch. The personal is used to report (and to authenticate the report of) social conflict, to document what appears as narrative fiction. The subtitle stresses the "chronicle" aspect of the narrative — and it further indicates that this work of fiction is in fact an "investigation". *Tod in Fremantle* is a relatively short book; its eight chapters extend to only 125 pages.

Like many other migrant authors, Walter Kaufmann did not succeed in his ambition to find an Australian reading public. Unlike other "bi-" or "intercultural" writers, he did gain a large readership back in the country of his birth. Yet the subject of most of his literary works deals with the Australian experience. Like his retention of the Australian passport, a vital part of his imagination remains linked to his "second" country. *Tod in Fremantle* is as much a critical self-reflection on his identity as a writer about Australia, possibly even as an Australian writer, as on the fate of the Aborigine Ricki. Not that Kaufmann ever treats the murder of his protagonist with anything other than outrage, respect and profound concern. The closest analogy is his writing about the treatment of Jews in Hitler Germany: it is a central theme in his (early) work, linked to the author's personal background. Kaufmann's own "history of writing" is inseparable from his social, political and artistic commitment to the "writing of history", a history he himself witnessed and experienced.

His determination to investigate the fate of Ricki is seen as a special kind of "Abenteuer "(33). To offer a narrative documentation of "Völkermord"(35) becomes the ultimate moral and literary challenge for Walter Kaufmann.

Kaufmann's *Tod in Fremantle* is another work asking the all-pervading, urgent question of identity. The alienation of the Aboriginal protagonist is an extreme case of cultural and ideological confusion. There is something grotesque about Ricki asking when it will snow in his native land. He suffers "weil ihm alles so fremd war".(75) The absurdity of an Aboriginal boy speaking the German dialect of Saxon in Coolbellup highlights his loss of identity. Kaufmann handles the conflict between a physical, "biological" or cultural home and a society in which there is no racial suppression with great insight and only occasional rhetoric. But he cannot resist the temptation of referring to the ideological conflicts between the two Germanys.

Kaufmann's narrative investigation aims to separate "Vorstellung und Wirklichkeit" — a critical aspect in the writing of social history. (81) The aim of *Tod in Fremantle* is to report and to expose. Like Egon Erwin Kisch, Walter Kaufmann's reporting is authentically personal and ideologically committed. His chronicle attempts to bear witness, it lays claim to the statement "So war es!"(95) The authorial narrator collects voices as evidence, arranging them in a particular composition. There is a curious ambivalence in his interpretation of the crime committed on Ricki: on the one hand, it is linked to the genocidal treatment of Aborigines by white Australians; on the other hand, Rick's inability to find, or to regain, an Aboriginal identity is linked to his abduction from the GDR. The novel illustrates the dilemma of the Australian Aborigines: in a white man's country they live torn between apartheid and integration.

Kaufmann is anxious to convey the concept of a *social* murder, the destruction of a human being by political and cultural violence. His report concerns a crime committed by a whole society. It is difficult to argue with this approach, even if the ideological interpretation of its investigation will be challenged. *Tod in Fremantle* remains a powerful, deeply disturbing document of narrative "faction". Walter Kaufmann has written a social reportage in the tradition of Egon Erwin Kisch, as well as a detective and adventure story. Once again, he has shown an excellent knowledge of contemporary Australian society and established a very special brand of German-Australian relations. There is an urgency and authenticity in this book which distinguishes it from the bulk of contemporary writing about Australia.

Joachim Specht

Joachim Specht was born 1931 in Weinböhla (Kreis Meissen). He received his secondary education in Radebeul and Dresden. After the destruction of Dresden during the Second World War Specht's family moved to Dessau. There Joachim Specht was trained as a fitter and subsequently applied for permission to enter university. When this was rejected, he moved to Hamburg. In 1951 he became unemployed; the following year he signed a two-year contract with the South Australian Railways and left aboard the MS "Nelly" for Australia. From April 1952 Joachim Specht worked at Mile End (Adelaide), Orrorro, Peterborough and Cockburn. He joined the Australian Workers Union. At the end of 1955 he returned to Hamburg, initially to find a wife. While in West Germany his family in Dessau was looking for someone who could manage their locksmith's trade. Joachim Specht moved back to East Germany, accepted GDR citizenship, married and took over his family's business.

Specht's first writings go back to his participation in a "Zirkel der schreibenden Arbeiter" at Dessau in 1960, run by the author Werner Steinberg. He established contact with the publishing company "Verlag der Nation" in Berlin which released his first collection of short stories *Peterborough Story* (1963). Together with its paperback version *Australisches Abenteuer* the collection has sold over 150,000 copies. When in 1972 his family business was transformed into a state-owned company ("Volkseigener Betrieb") — after a previous merging into the PGH ("Produktionsgenossenschaft des Handwerks") — Joachim Specht became a full-time writer. By 1965 he had become a member of the "Arbeitsgemeinschaft junger Autoren im Bezirksverband Halle" (an association of young writers around Halle) and in 1968 he was awarded full membership of the GDR Writers' Association ("Schriftstellerverband der DDR"). Joachim Specht has published eleven novels, three volumes of short prose and numerous short stories. He co-authored the GDR television series *Hannes Scharf* (with his mentor Werner Steinberg) and *Der Sheriff*. In 1983 Specht was awarded the Wilhelm-Müller-Prize of the city of Dessau. His best-known works are: *Peterborough Story* (1963), *Australisches Abenteuer* (1966), *Die Gejagten* (1967), *Stippvisite* (1968), *Jemenitisches Abenteuer* (1969), *Der Fünfer* (1971), *Blütenhölle in Banusta* (1971), *Wasser für die roten Wölfe* (1972), *Buschbrand* (1974), *Perpetuum mobile* (1975), *Leuchtfeuer Eastern Reef* (1976), *Paraipagody* (1978),

Der Einzelgänger (1978), *Wunder dauern etwas länger* (1981), *Korallen-Joe* (1981), *Das Camp am Burdekinfluß* (1982), *Der Steinbock ist ein Talismann* (1983), *Daniels Weg in die Steinzeit* (1985), *In den Korallenriffen* (1987), *Heißes Erbe* (1988) and *Segelflug unterm Kreuz des Südens* (1990). Many have an Australian setting and deal with Australian social problems.

Peterborough Story

Joachim Specht's first book is a collection of short stories based on his migrant experiences during the years 1952 to 1955 when the author worked for the South Australian Railways around Peterborough.[20] The central theme of his narrative account is the exploitation of migrants. "Man wollte ihn ausnutzen, ihn und andere Auswanderer," maintains an introductory report on the migrants' passage to Australia.(8) The following stories keep an uneasy balance between fascination with the country and an ever-growing awareness of exploitation on its behalf. Migration means above all exploitation of labour. Specht's characters gradually learn to defend themselves; they become more and more involved in the organising of workers and the protection of the underprivileged. When Specht leaves Australia to return home, he becomes a citizen of the GDR. His experiences as a migrant worker in Australia, his involvement with the Australian Workers Union and his gradual understanding of the meaning of socialism prove a turning-point in his life. All his books deal in one form or another with this self-discovery, which Specht sees as a model for others.

If *Peterborough Story* is 'migrant literature', one of its most interesting features is the author's situation of looking at his own people and country 'from the outside'. Migration itself is, of course, a paradigmatic experience of alienation. But not only Brecht realised the great learning potential of alienation. Cultural and political self-estrangement is a crisis which leads to a newly defined self-concept. That is Specht's main concern, not only in this book: again and again he traces such a process of autodidacticism, the learning experience which led to his own ideological conversion.

The title story addresses itself to the discovery of fascist migrants among the contracted labourers brought into the country after the war. Specht not only exposes the naivety of Australian immigration procedures, he fears that the very migrants who should have never been allowed into the country will one day become its leading citizens. His stories continually refer to the dubious background of many migrants and the political and moral bankruptcy of post-war Germany in particular. Specht's German heroes have to face up to their native country's inhuman past. They are either on the run from this past or they are confronted with it by the presence of older Germans among the migrant population of Australia. Immigration and Australia thus become a challenge, a social and political watershed. In this context political events in Australia (such as the Petrov-affair) are invoked; they assume a different significance in their changed perspective of migrant biculturalism. The derogatory term 'New Australian' becomes indicative of a new way of looking at Australian problems. Significantly, Specht's 'New Australian' needs to be able to relate "seine Geschichte"(89), "eine gute Story... eine stichhaltige!"(90) His 'story' has to be both fiction and alibi; like the author's prose, it must combine composition and documentation. In such an understanding lies the basis of all of Joachim Specht's writing about Australia. His 'story' concept owes a great deal to the American short story, which exerted a particularly strong influence on post-war German literature.

For Specht, the "Story" is the social identity and history of an individual. It implies communication with others. Human relationships consist of reading and writing, listening and narrating life compositions. Specht propagates a social literacy. Unlike Max Frisch, he does not expose the irony of personal fiction, but, like Frisch, he recognises authenticity in "Geschichten". The difference is that for Specht there can only be one "Story" which is ultimately true. It has to be "stichhaltig".(Ibid.) It must form part of a socialist history which cannot be questioned. The personal "Story" of Specht's many protagonists is inseparable from the "Streikstory"(107) or "Streikgeschichte"(108) of the working class struggle. It is an ideological form concept which allocates to literature the function of sociopolitical illustration.

As in all of his writings about Australia, *Peterborough Story* contains many accurate descriptions of life-style, scenes and events in the new country. Characteristically, the cliché account of a bushfire is treated with a social and moral difference: it is the 'story' of an insurance crime. Specht's "Geschichte"(118) serves to demonstrate the collusion between police and white-collar criminals; it links commercial ruthlessness and the capitalist system to the murder of a mute Aborigine and the suicide of a young white who has witnessed the crime.

Specht transforms traditional Australian themes into parables of social conscience.

It is a very German Australia which thus emerges from Joachim Specht's narrative prose. There is no escape from the "böse Vergangenheit"(205) of his native country. For even while they are working for the South Australian Railways German migrants raise contemporary political issues relating to the existence of two Germanys.

The fourteen stories of this collection were first published in 1963; they have since reached their seventh edition (1986). The experience of Australia emerges as an eye-opener to the migrant writer Joachim Specht. His migration gains the significance of a political education. The popularity of his narrative prose in the GDR confirms the ideological model character of this type of story-telling. The exotic or far-away merely serves to confirm what is already known. The author of *Peterborough Story* is a "model" GDR writer.

Die Gejagten

This novel reached its eighth edition in 1985; it was first published in 1966. *Die Gejagten* (*The Hunted*) is one of Specht's most successful book publications. It is also one of his earlier works and contains ingredients, formal and thematic characteristics which the author adheres to in most of his narrative fiction. *Die Gejagten* tells the "Story" of its protagonists' political enlightenment, their gradual social awakening and the need for a world-wide socialist solidarity which is anti-racist and anti-nuclear in its self-concept as an international peace movement. Australia is presented as a country with certain social practices, not as an exotic destination of literary tourism. Specht's first narrative work, *Peterborough Story*, describes the migration to this country as a sociopolitical experience and Australia has remained a place of social conflict to this author. Its political problems are of paradigmatic significance. The setting of fiction serves as 'pre-text' for the raising of consciousness in a world-wide context.

As in other works, especially in *Daniels Weg in die Steinzeit*, a conceptual pattern emerges which is reinforced by the narrative plot and characterisation. In his treatment of racist exploitation of the Australian Aborigine Specht illustrates the ambivalent part played by the (mostly Lutheran) missions. He sees in them a preliminary stage of social commitment. His heroes grow out of a religious calling and discover, often unwittingly, their broader political 'mission' in life. Being a missionary or being at the mercy of a missionary leads Specht's protagonists to a cathartic conflict, to a first transformation of their social consciousness. The narrator does not condemn the missions. The novel traces the heroes' development from individual isolation to social solidarity.

Joachim Specht manages to turn a fictional textbook communist career and, in terms of GDR-prescribed literary aesthetics, of socialist realism into an eminently readable, entertaining yarn. Despite pre-determined political patterns and far-fetched designs of social consciousness the novel retains a strong air of authenticity. The author's first-hand knowledge of Australia and its sociopolitical problems always shines through and saves the book from being mere propaganda. It is this transmission of facts and information about Australia which gives Specht's books their special significance. In the light of continued widespread ignorance about this country in Europe such precisely observed, if fictionalised reports serve a cultural purpose which should not be underestimated.

Joachim Specht's fictional travelogues go beyond literary introductions to far-away countries, they attempt to be documentations of concerns to which native readers can relate.

The author raises a number of vital issues in this novel which have remained unresolved (not only in Australia) to this day. His commitment to international socialism does not blind him to the racism of many workers. Specht also describes the fate of many so-called New Australians (175f.), especially the isolation and deprivation of immigrant workers in the outback mining towns. (He is sadly wrong, however, in his optimistic assertion "Deutsch ist hier im Lande eine Universalsprache geworden."201) *Die Gejagten* is a travel book concerned with civil rights, a novel about life in Australia as it is experienced by the socially underprivileged. It offers a narrative account of issues and concerns which affect readers in all parts of the world.

Blütenhölle in Banusta

This "Abenteuerroman" appeared in 1973 and deals with colonial exploitation of Papua-New Guinea in the period prior to independence.

Although the novel begins and ends in Australia, it is concerned with Australian attitudes to its northern protectorate. (Surprisingly, Specht does not mention the German presence in New Guinea at all.) Once again, then, the author's narrative fiction is designed to describe the sociopolitical values of Australians. *Blütenhölle in Banusta* presents an Australian administration in collusion with American 'development companies' determined to exploit a defenceless indigenous population.

The book successfully invokes the colonial atmosphere in Port Moresby and elsewhere. The independence movement is represented by a white Australian doctor who supports it — it is not allowed to speak for itself. He is one of three protagonists who discover the need for political action if mankind is to be truly liberated. Joachim Specht has written yet another political parable set in the antipodean tropics.

There is a 'migration' from Australia to New Guinea comparable to the migration from Europe to Australia, the subject of many of Specht's other novels. Both can be experienced as a journey of political enlightenment; "home" is a commitment to recognise, expose and adjust "sozialpolitische Ungerechtigkeiten".(60) The tropical setting again proves no more than a device to lure the youthful reader towards the 'excitement' of ideological discoveries, to the 'exploration' of a new human environment — only to realise that the same forces rule the living conditions of man all over the world. In this novel Specht deals with a theme which remains central to all his writings about Australia, the "Landraub"(75) black natives suffer at the hands of a white colonial population. More specifically, the author of *Blütenhölle* reveals such injustice in New Guinea "weil er die Kluft zwischen ihrem (i.e. the natives') Pfahlbaudasein und den Prachtpalästen der Gesellschaften als ungerecht empfindet".(Ibid.) It allows him to demonstrate the classic beliefs of Marxist ideology.

Papua-New Guinea gained full independence in late 1975; at the time Specht's novel appeared internal self-government had already come into effect. The author's concerns must be seen in this context. *Blütenhölle in Banusta* offers a narrative account of "eine gefährliche Raubbauwirtschaft".(104) Multinational mining companies threaten intertribal peace and the democratic aspirations of a new nation. Australia's collusion with this economic exploitation is criticised. As always, Specht aims to show the *pattern* of exploitation, in whatever context. His narratives address themselves to their reader: "Urteilen Sie selbst!"(176) All of Specht's writings are informed with didactic, ideological zeal, they aim to stimulate or 'excite' the reader into political commitment and action. He warns that Papuans are no longer overawed by the power of white colonialists. Specht's interest in the Papuan worker is more than rhetoric. The author knows the natives' working conditions and pay. Australian society is used as point of reference. The novel enacts a political mission: "Die Papuas müssen endlich ihre Freiheit haben."(210) *Blütenhölle* presents narrative fiction as a model for gaining political self-consciousness. The relationship between Australia and Papua-New Guinea corresponds to that of the reader's reaction to this book: both are challenged by an intrinsic appeal to a sense of responsibility.

Buschbrand

When Specht wrote this novel of adventure ("Abenteuerroman") he had already found his narrative pattern: Australia was the setting for capitalist crimes against ordinary workers, migrants and Aborigines, aided and abetted by equally criminal nuclear or biological warfare testing on behalf of the United States. The writer's communist propaganda is obvious despite more or less sophisticated attempts to 'integrate' its rhetoric into the plot, characterisation and style of his prose works. *Buschbrand* presents a great many political and cultural clichés of Australia, yet despite stock situations and stereotyped figures the novel does succeed in creating authentic settings of social conflict.

The reason lies in Specht's ability to observe and to describe minor details, to be precise in his reporting on cultural mannerisms. He is like his part-Aborigine tracker Martin Usendo: sensitive to minute forms of 'evidence', persistent in his search and as an outsider all the more perceptive. In addition, Specht seizes every opportunity to pass on historical facts and events of Australian life, thus letting his novels act as cultural mediators. All his works provide a great deal of factual information about the fifth continent. Specht's presentation of contemporary Australian society may suffer from frequent oversimplification, but the general tone and direction retain credibility. Occasionally the author employs well-worn local phrases in translation, thus further adding to the impression of genuine documentation.

Empathetic authenticity is contrasted with cliché responses to the hackneyed question "How do you like this country?" The European author satirises a grotesque ritual of polite deception and delusion by not appraising the "lovely" landscape but referring instead to the more questionable aspects of 'the Australian way of life'. The beautiful or exotic is balanced by familiar social and political grievances. *Buschbrand* includes frequent reference to the treatment of migrants by native Australians, linking their discrimination to the suppression of Aborigines: both assume the role of scapegoat in Australian social politics. 'New Australians' and 'Original Australians' alike are the source of unresolved conflict; neither have been fully integrated into contemporary society.

The United States are presented as the real source of social unrest in Australia. The economic dependency on American export trade restricts local freedom at all levels. Specht's narrator makes this comment in the context of wide-spread contamination of Australian agricultural and pastoral land as a result of American tests in bacteriological warfare in the country.

The author's own aims are obvious: to provoke Australian political consciousness into independence and resistance and to illustrate the evils of American economic and military intervention worldwide. As Specht's readers are GDR citizens (so far his books have not been translated into English), it is the latter purpose which is of greater and more immediate relevance. The economic crime committed by the Australian sheep-farmer which cannot be disguised by the bushfire is a reflection and the direct consequence of US crimes committed against the Australian economy. *Buschbrand* strongly implies that any fire the Americans are likely to light to cover their offences would destroy more than the Australian bush. Joachim Specht presents the destruction of the McWire family as the fictional pattern of a greater threat to the survival of an independent Australia committed to a just and humane society.

Leuchtfeuer Eastern Reef

This narrative was first published in 1976; it reappeared in a new paperback edition (Verlag Das Neue Berlin) together with *Wasser für die Roten Wölfe* in 1980 under the subtitle of "Zwei Abenteuerromane". Only *Leuchtfeuer Eastern Reef* has an Australian setting. It is a short novel made up of a collection of six stories within a story (*Rahmenerzählung*), each an act of identification, the biography of interrelated individuals rescued by the lonely lighthouse attendant Jim

Parker. Form and content are following principles of 19th century German Romanticism. Credibility is stretched to breaking point, coincidence becomes part of the exotic. It is one of Specht's least political works. *Leuchtfeuer* may be regarded an adventure story with little depth, escapist entertainment typical of popular literature. Yet in the context of his overall development as a writer Joachim Specht demonstrates in this novel more clearly than anywhere else his concept of the "story". In a sense his favourite literary genre is the real and only subject of this book. For the lighthouse of the title symbolises the guidance, enlightenment and direction of the 'story'. Jim Parker is an author who collects the narrative lives of other people only to relate them to himself, to make them part of his 'story'. The little island 'Eastern Reef' may indicate the author's exotic isolation, but in fact life's stories come to him on this reef and expect to be told and retold by him. Jim Parker's story includes the stories of others who have come to be rescued by his art of communication.

As in his other narrative works, Specht's concept of the "story" or "Geschichte" is partly based on journalism (reportage), partly the formal essence of verification or authenticity. His writings about Australia are, of course, largely autobiographical, almost always based on first-hand experience. He can vouch for their 'truthfulness'. Specht's definitions attempt to define a narrative form of social realism in which the reader's own 'story' is the basis for an evaluation of its literary counterpart. Literary form is recognised as the expression of a social relationship. Those who are 'rescued' from loss of direction exchange their stories in an act of recognition. These tales are recorded as accounts of real events even if they appear in fictional form. For fiction is the exotic setting of truth. In the end the "story" or "Bericht"(338) has to be recognised as true and verified as real. *Leuchtfeuer* takes the logic of such aesthetics to extremes. The exotic 'adventure' triumphs over its didactic purpose. Specht's book makes for superficially adventurous reading, occasionally bordering on unwittingly satirising its genre. For all its attempts at a socialist progressive narrative the novel remains conservative in fictional form and plot. It fulfils the reader's expectations of light fiction: adventure is escapism which through coincidence assures him "that all's arranged in one clear view"(Yeats). Despite Specht's many clues designed to assist in the detection of the real purpose of his collection of stories *Leuchtfeuer*'s language lacks imaginative authority to enforce this guidance. Style and content remain linked to the pattern of popular literature (*Trivialliteratur*). In Günter

Grass' terms, the novel offers no resistance (*Widerstand*) against pre-established models of 'easy reading'. The exotic is itself a favourite device of literary entertainment. German literature, not only about Australia, has a history of invoking the far-away and exotic as *topoi* of escapism or self-fulfilled longing. In popular writing unknown settings abroad serve as powerful erotic stimuli; it is important to realise, however, that so-called high literature continues to make use of foreign environments to serve its didactic purpose(Hesse).

Daniels Weg in die Steinzeit

Like most of Specht's other works of narrative fiction, this novel combines a great deal of factual information about Australia with a somewhat youthful sense of 'adventure' and an ideological commitment to aspects of socialist politics. The book was first published in 1985 and is written in the context of a Christian Protestant peace movement that assumed significant influence in the German Democratic Republic around that time.

The book cannot be accused of subtlety, either in its literary or its political qualities. As part of the assumptions of the German genre of the *Abenteuerroman* the narrative has to identify good and evil,right and wrong, without which any didactic intention would be impossible. Like most adventure novels, *Daniels Weg in die Steinzeit* stretches credibility on more than one occasion. What makes the book uniquely German is its apparent intention to be recognised as a *Bildungsroman*, a novel of didacticism demonstrating 'the getting of wisdom' in a predetermined way. The paradigmatic nature of Daniel's experience is even emphasised typographically: the book's title has the first two words printed in capitals.(3) Although the author is clearly aiming for young readers, the sociopolitical moral addresses itself to all who are willing to join in the adventure of recognising suppression, discrimination and exploitation wherever it occurs. Daniels "Story" is the counter version or anti-book of his father's "Lebensbericht".(196) The hero of the *Bildungsroman* responds:

> Nein, Dad, so ging das heute nicht mehr. Die Welt befand sich im Aufbruch, die junge Generation ließ sich nicht mehr besänftigen, weder durch Sprüche noch durch ein Referendum, sie wollte Freiheit und Gleichheit, und das sofort.(199)

The moral seems clear. Yet Specht hints at a somewhat more complex dilemma, the immediate relevance of which needs no labouring for a citizen of the German Democratic Republic. The political implications of this novel must be recognised not only in the immediate 'fictional' Australian context.

Stylistically the novel is written in colloquial language, with little pretension to poetic subtlety or literary complexity. Specht's aim is summed up by a statement of his protagonist: "Was hier geschrieben steht, entspricht den Tatsachen."(215) Daniel refers to a newspaper article and in fact Specht's novel shares many qualities of the journalistic *Tatsachenbericht* — it could be described as a narrative reportage. There is indeed a certain similarity between Egon Kisch and Joachim Specht: both attempt to write a social report in which fictionalisation and narrative role-playing serve the function of political enlightenment. It must again be stressed that Specht's novel contains a great deal of factual information about Australia. It is significant that at the end of the book a newspaper report is endorsed for its honesty and correctness. Specht obviously sees himself as a truthful reporter. His fiction retains qualities of historical authenticity. *Daniels Weg* captures the atmosphere of the Whitlam government's enthusiasm and idealism. Explicit reference is made to Gordon Bryant and other historical figures, lending the book further 'documentary' quality. The author Specht sees himself as a kind of witness, an empathetic outsider, a sympathetic foreigner, a comrade-in-arms of the socialist-communist *Internationale*.

Albert Namatjira's representative fate is also identified as a "Story"(189), a story which leads Daniel to the realisation that he cannot change society by being a missionary on an outback Lutheran Station in Hermannsburg. It is Albert's "story" as much as his own which leads Specht's hero to move to Canberra, the nation's capital, to fight, together with his lover Jeanette, for the rights of the underprivileged and exploited. An Aboriginal guide informs him "daß es heute Gewerkschaften gebe, die auch die Forderungen der Aborigines unterstützten".(178) Daniel's 'path' is the classical path of enlightenment; his "Weg in die Steinzeit" turns out to be his progress to a future in Canberra, to a personal commitment in social politics. Albert Namatjira's paintings are contrasted with the photographs Daniel is ordered to take as evidence of a dying culture. The "Story" of Namatjira is the story of "eine Art Wende im Bewußtsein der Ureinwohner".(186) The "Story" thus is ultimately concerned with the image of man, the self-concept of black and white Australians and the nature of their relationship.

Daniels "Erkundungsreise im Auftrag der Mission"(136) conveys to the reader central social conflicts in contemporary Australia. Specht does not present a tourist's image of the fifth continent. His book is well informed about tribal customs and the problems between white and black Australians. If his characterisation is at times too simplistic, it is largely an expression of socialist "Parteilichkeit" (Lukács). Specht's treatment of racial politics in Australia retains an immediate relevance in the context of his own country. "Friedensfreunde, und das wußte Daniel nun genau, wurden von der Polizei als Staatsfeinde betrachtet."(127) Linking the peace movement in Central Europe with racial problems in Australia makes this narrative a political document.

Chapter Eight

Joining the "Mainstream": First-Generation Australian Writers 1967-1989

> "Sweet are the uses of adversity".
> *As You Like It* (II.i.)

MARGARET DIESENDORF

Margaret Diesendorf's published work shows that her writing frequently suffers from the malaise of bilingual interculturalism: there are clear signs of cultural and literary conflicts in her poetry. Yet her verse often gains its own special quality from the author's non-integrated European background and the urge to draw complex or witty allusions to classical mythology. In an interview[1] she quotes the recently deceased Austrian writer Thomas Bernhard to explain the tyranny of cultural origin: "One's definition by one's country of origin is a lifelong yoke". Diesendorf retains many characteristic qualities of her native Viennese culture, above all, its humour and its musicality. She explicitly affirms "two cultures" in her life and in her work. The European qualities in her writing include a pronounced, occasionally playful, intellectuality, a leaning towards classicist aesthetics and a preference for philosophical themes. She draws attention to certain parallels between Austria and Australia, defining the former as "an outpost against Eastern Europe", the latter as "an outpost of European civilisation in an Asian environment". Both countries began as colonies, both share "the anthropological amalgamation of many racial elements". Diesendorf therefore feels that "Austrians settle in rather well in Australia. And these parallels," she maintains, "create...strong similarities in the two literatures — vast areas to be critically explored." Her own interests in Australian literature include the *Bulletin* school, Patrick White, Randolph Stow, Christopher Koch, Thomas Shapcott, and, more recently, Kate Grenville. Margaret Diesendorf is "passionately interested in the contemporary poetry of this country". Her involvement with Australian literature, almost from the beginning, did much to reduce the sense of creative isolation, although it could not be said that her own work has ever been perceived as fully integrated into the "mainstream".

Judging her early poetry as "too sentimental", Diesendorf experienced her involvement with fine arts and art history as an imaginative stimulus demanding greater formal and intellectual control, leading to a new kind of inspiration she calls "potenzierte Imagination". Her art poems do not seek to describe, but aim to pass on to the reader the nature of their original inspiration. Diesendorf's verse is strongly musical, characterised by a pronounced syllabic musicality. Each poem attempts to articulate, or celebrate, a key thought, presented in what the poet calls a form of verbal 'dance'. Diesendorf actually speaks of a communication with "the divine". Her poetry is designed to enlarge the divinity within us, to reveal the divine idea of living. Diesendorf is not a descriptive poet; there are no nature themes in her verse. Rather, she presents the idea of a landscape, deriving an imaginative vitality from nature. During her childhood the Hungarian puszta left a lasting impression on her, in particular the vastness of the flat country, the rolling planes and the distant horizon of the steppe. Not surprisingly, Diesendorf found it easy to respond to the Australian outback and its "transition to the sky". She claims an affinity with the culture of the Aborigines, sharing their attitude to nature. Margaret Diesendorf lost contact with nature while living in the suburbs of Vienna. By studying the Romantics she assumed a theoretical love of nature. Only in Australia has she developed a positive response to the natural landscape, but even now it remains largely the idea and spirit of nature which fascinate her. In much the same way she now carries the idea of Europe within her. Among the many painters Diesendorf admires, Lloyd Rees, Olsen Ouburn and Pablo Picasso stand out, Reed for his landscapes, Ouburn for the Jewish memory of the holocaust and Picasso for his dancing movements, especially in the lines of his vases. The poets exerting the strongest influence on her work are in German

Goethe (whom she calls her "guide"), Schiller, the Romantics, C. F. Meyer and Rilke (whom she has translated). In Australian literature A. D. Hope, Gwen Harwood and Grace Perry emerged as her models. She admires Hope for his poetic discipline; Perry translated her (as she translated Perry) and was a long-time collaborator and friend. Among philosophers Diesendorf lists Kant, Jaspers, Heberling and Scheler as formative influences. To her philosophy is "another approach to the same thing" that poetry is dealing with — the basic (German existentialist) assumption of Heidegger. She values Paul Heberling's "Sozietät des Menschen" and Scheler's "Wesen der Person" most highly. Her own poetry addresses itself to philosophical themes; indeed, it is in this intellectual and spiritual quality that Diesendorf's poetic style is to be found. As a poet, she wants to "understand our being" and traces a development "from the bottom of the well to light". She self-consciously follows Schiller's didactic aim to achieve the highest degree of individualisation. "Light" and "individualisation" merge in her poetry as the enlightened individual, inspired form. The poem is, to her, an imaginative realisation of that aim.

To date, Diesendorf has shown little interest in prose. She believes that part of a novel is a kind of gossip, narrative chatter. She affirms he own commitment to ideas rather than to "communication chatter". Surprisingly for a Viennese, she has not written for the theatre (although she did produce plays in Sydney). To her, poems are "addresses to others".

Light

Born in Vienna in 1912, Margaret Diesendorf emigrated to Australia in 1938. She holds a doctorate from the University of Vienna, was a language teacher in Sydney and has lived in this city since as a freelance writer and translator, radio and television broadcaster, lecturer and reader. Over the past fifty years she has been Associate Editor of *Poetry Australia* (1967-1981) and of *Creative Moment* (USA). She has published numerous poems, articles and short stories, originals in English and translations from the French and German. Surprisingly, only two book collections have emerged from Diesendorf's extensive literary activities: *Light* (1981) and *Holding the Golden Apple* (1991). Her overall influence thus far exceeds the publication of these two volumes of poetry.

Light bears the Ezra Pound quotation "Take thought:/I have weathered the storm,/I have beaten out my exile." Indeed, it is difficult not to think of Margaret Diesendorf's Viennese background as anything but a "multicultural" asset. Whatever personal experiences the poet may have had during her early years in Australia, her work does not identify her as an artist in exile. Unlike many other German-language migrant writers, Diesendorf feels at ease in English and only rarely gives an indication that it is her second language (or third, she is fluent in French). The collection has two parts: "On Canvas", made up of twenty-six poems, and "Nineveh", comprising thirty-six poems.

"On Canvas" is a celebration of fine arts and music. It is hardly a coincidence that Margaret Diesendorf has translated Rosemary Dobson's volume *Child With Cockatoo* (*L'Enfant au Cacatoés*, translated with Louis Dautheuil), many of her own poems are congenial responses to paintings. It is striking how frequently Diesendorf models her verse on the writings of other poets or on other works of art. *Light* opens with a poem entitled "The Rose", based on Rilke's "Das Rosen-Innere". A comparison with the German original indicates the extent to which Diesendorf's lines are a creative translation, a *Nachdichtung*.

What is significant about such re-creation is the discipline and craft of language composition. Diesendorf is an outstanding sculptress of language and an empathetic renderer of original tone as well as of intellectual intent. All of her poems are the product of verbal chiselling, to the extent that even some of her original work occasionally gives the impression of being translated. "Translation" means much more in the case of Margaret Diesendorf than the term usually implies. Nor is it simply a matter of stressing the poetic quality of her translations. Many of Diesendorf's poems are transformations from one art form to another (*Nachdichtung*). In a process of regenerative creative inspiration art is the centre of a circle of adaptations, variations and modifications. It is a development of organic redefinition, a rebirth of the one reality, a regeneration of the one energy.

The title poem of Margaret Diesendorf's first collection addresses itself to the mystery of such a life-giving force. "Light" is a verbal painting enacting, or radiating, its meaning. As creator of images and vision, light is recognised as a vital part of creative power.

Margaret Diesendorf's poetry is a collection of momentary enchantments, written against the "betrayals" of a reality in which they have no part. "Form" is of paramount concern in this poet's writings, but not as a falsification or distortion of human experience and the realities of human suffering. Poetic transformation does not mean fraudulent misrepresentation of the factual or the passionate; on the contrary: poems like "Musée du Louvre" lead the reader back to the "reality" of the human spirit — a painted Christ whose mouth not only breathes life upon the perceiver, but also calls out for help.

When the poem does "respond" to painting, it adopts its theme and represents it in language's own composition. Monet's *Camille sur son lit de mort* is merely the pretext for the poet's own reflections on death. Yet she responds to a creative, artistic mediation of death, not to the event itself. Even in death, it is a reality already shaped into sensuous and aesthetic, intellectual form. What Diesendorf can achieve by appearing merely to "describe" a picture, is demonstrated most impressively in "Femme au chat". On one level, it is a precise and sensitive verbal reproduction of Pierre Bonnard's painting. Yet at the same time Diesendorf has written a most sensitive, powerfully disturbing poem about domestic violence. The poet knows of the violence that plays its part in artistic transformation, the energy of inspiration which can also be the power of sublimation. She addresses herself to the artist's "alter ego's brutality/oh animal in man conquered by the brush", to ask whether it is "painting" or "woman" that makes the artist do what art wants ("Pablo Picasso"). Diesendorf's poem marvels at the correlation between destruction and creation, at the ultimate unity of these seemingly contradictory impulses. It is this artistic reconciliation of forces shaping the destiny of man which the poet pays homage to — in the full knowledge that such harmonious control only ever occurs in art, "on the canvas". The title of the collection's first part thus assumes a less descriptive, rather more critical meaning. Beauty and life "on canvas" have not been achieved in social and political "reality".

The female artist is no less in possession of potentially violent power. But, as "The Portrait" shows, Diesendorf sees herself — apart from any biography — as having been left, deserted by "the male" and thus "wounded". Violence has already been done to the woman artist prior to, or as a part of, her creative output. "The Portrait" goes beyond the poet's own image, reflected in another art form, to articulate the situation of the female artist in general.

The woman as victim of love is a recurring theme in Diesendorf's poetry, without any allusions to the politics of feminism. In "Modigliani Nude" it is the male artist's infatuation with his own creation which leads to an ambiguous form of autoeroticism; yet the congenial poet can restore a balanced, harmonious response in her invocation of the nude, long after the death of painter and model. For in her lines "the red roses" of the nude "burn in her canvas lap".

When Diesendorf writes about specific places, she paints a picture of them: the poem becomes a verbal canvas. Her imaginative transformation is radical, turning "the real world" upside down. Instead of metaphorical analogy the poetic logic of her vision leads to its own consequence.

The miraculous creative spirit comes as an act of liberation, as a "release from bondage/to be read on the white canvas eternally". ("Walking up to the Cemetery...") The language does not distinguish between painting and writing. It is a female power which brings about changes of appearance, metamorphoses of erotic violence. All inspiration is related; the poet herself continues to be inspired by other artists' inspiration, as much as by nature and religion. Diesendorf's poetry demonstrates the spiritual affinity between painter and poet, celebrating an eros of creativity.

Yet Diesendorf's eroticism is essentially aesthetic. Her painting poems begin with description, progress to invocation, and end in speculative thought or empathetic interpretation — a transference to the poem's own dimensions. This poet is in possession of a language of sensuous intellectuality — or, rather, as she would have it, possessed by it. All of Diesendorf's poems have a sense of urgency and commitment to their subject which carries with it its own excitement. This, and the invariable element of surprise, mostly towards the end of the poem, convince the reader of the inspirational nature of the verse. Characteristically, Diesendorf's wit does not allow for a clear separation of awe and humour.

Her images of magic and splendour are dangerously close to those of terror and fear. Diesendorf's poetry moves between the two, mediates, interprets, harmonises. It seeks to convey an inspirational vision, a seduction to knowledge. Transformation is always miraculous, and this poet is a verbal prophet, a witness, an enchantress, an enticer, a conspirator of sense.

Part Two, "Nineveh", opens with a terse variation of the collection's title concept:

> *Wisdom*
> Like a lighthouse it can
> signal only to the seeing.

It is a Goethean maxim that recognition can occur only among equals. Goethe, of course, went so far as to claim that the eye itself must be light, a view he never changed, despite Newton's discovery.

"Litany for Ezra Pound" is clearly a major poem in the volume; Diesendorf calls it "my principal poem in this book"[2]. The poet feels a close affinity with Pound's tragic life, in particular with his exile.

Characteristically, she dismisses Pound's fascism in a dialectic of poetic and philosophical truth. A key statement of Diesendorf's poem reaffirms the special role of woman in the search for truth, above all the truth of experience: "being woman/and aware of the torment that comes/from the relentless pursuit of the ideal...". The female poet seems to be predisposed to special tolerance and compassion for those who suffered failure. Her homage extends not merely to Ezra Pound (as the dedication to Howard Sergeant shows), it is addressed to "language and craft", to "memory and passion", to the "superior...vision". Diesendorf has her own part in all of them, and the light entering the cave is the same as that which shines through her own poem.

Frequently Diesendorf is content to capture the mood of a particular moment. The poem articulates the quality of feeling, using the poet's own experience as catalyst, as part of a correlative construction. Considering the author's biographical background, there is remarkably little reference to politics and persecution in the poems dealing with the most turbulent and barbaric times in her native culture's history. In "Ancestors" there is, however, an expression of profound uneasiness and a disturbing sense of personal involvement. Diesendorf shows the sufferings, the consequences of fascism, racism and other forms of suppression. She does not, in her poems, confront the social and political causes of such misery. Her poetry is full of compassion and empathy, it does not address itself to the politics of social conflict. It may speak of "the suavity of the snake"("Litany for Ezra Pound"), but does not venture outside traditional mythology to specific political concerns. A comparison with the work of Hans Magnus Enzensberger, for example, illustrates the extent to which Margaret Diesendorf avoids any literary articulation of political concerns.

Places — landscapes, cities, houses, farms, interiors and exteriors — hold a special fascination for this poet. A great many of her poems are devoted to them. They are a record of humanisation, the attempt to imbue a dwelling or a terrain with the qualities of imaginative individuality. There is a lightness of touch in this poetry which belies its careful composition. Diesendorf writes with studied casualness, the ideal tone for this kind of *Gelegenheitsdichtung*. In a sense, the poem is a verbal composition allowing language, albeit at different levels, to quote itself. Diesendorf's social criticism expresses itself in the distortions of a poetic vision. In her interview with Rudi Krausmann, Margaret Diesendorf singles out "the humour and the musicality" as the most decisive influences of her native Austrian culture. There is, indeed, evidence of much humour and wit in her writing.

Like the inspiration of a specific locale, human relationships, the meeting of people, offer the poet the imaginative scope of identification. Frequently, they take the form of an homage. At other times, a poem can simply attempt to describe the fleeting nature of some human contact. Diesendorf is fond of using animal metaphors to suggest the alienation of personal relationships ("Meeting"). She regenerates a poetic mythology by transposing it into a contemporary context, without forcing the present into an archaic stylisation. Diesendorf acknowledges her affinity to other classicist writers in Australia, among them A.D. Hope, James McAuley and Gwen Harwood.[3] Her poetry is full of "desirous thought"; it comes alive only through "suffering/and sacrifice". There can be no doubt that the poet has submitted herself to both. "Venus Incommunicado" gives more than a hint of the kind of artistic and intellectual passion necessary for her poetry to emerge and to claim validity. Most poems of *Light* seek to elevate human experience to a spiritual level, to discover (potentially) divine qualities in all parts of life, even in terror and in dejection. It is, in that sense, an affirmative, celebratory collection with strong religious overtones. Diesendorf does not "widthdraw" into literature, she turns (back) to it to validate experience, to test its imaginative credentials. There are different kinds of deaths in strange countries: Diesendorf invokes the spirit of nature and of civilisation. Curiously, the poet refers to Australia, and her own place in it, only very rarely. Perhaps that in itself is a comment. When she does describe a scene from her domestic life, conflict and suffering are again expressed in an act of identification with animals, literature and brutal alienation. "I am now capable of a hardness, a decisiveness, a cruelty almost," Diesendorf claims,[4] "that I would not have been capable of had I remained in Austria. Some poems are really hard... . The reason may be that as a displaced person one has to harden oneself to survive."

The bitterness of a self-discovery in imprisonment is gently mocked; there is no sentimentality, rather a sense of irony. Unlike most migrant writers Margaret Diesendorf never allows herself the luxury of self-pity or nostalgia. Her poems are "really hard" because she has shunned the concept of a ghetto literature and the pitfalls of self-righteous lamentations. For all the borrowings from European mythology, for all the adaptations of classical themes and forms, the poetry of Margaret Diesendorf has remained that of a very gifted loner, an artist addressing herself to fellow-artists, wherever they are.

Holding the Golden Apple

Margaret Diesendorf's second collection of verse, made up of three sections of love poems ("Pervigilium Veneris", "Cupido Cruciator" and "De Reditu Suo"), is a truly representative volume of the poet's imaginative range. Written mainly in 1988, they make no secret of their classical orientation (the book is dedicated to the late Robert Graves). "The White Goddess" is in fact omnipresent, as are many references to other artistic mythologies, music, painting and Christian symbolism. On one level, it could be argued that throughout the collection art is quoting art; Diesendorf's poetry is often an exercise in artistic self-reflection. The impulse of these poems is clear enough: a desire to project, create and transform identity (of nature, thought, art and love), thus communicating with a need which is perceived and experienced as existence itself. Love here is a largely Platonic relationship of erotic thought and poetic reflection. Behind it lies an historical and spiritual loneliness threatening the very being of the poet. The many references to other art and artists attempt to force a relationship of meaning which is the essence of survival in love. The poet "dresses herself" in congenial works to cover a fearful nakedness. Her addresses are in that sense spiritual exercises, desperate compositions to create and to defend a meaningful life. Diesendorf *lives* her poems of invoked love and splendour, she attempts to "seduce" the divinity of beauty to judge her a living partner in the senses' creation.

These poems, then, appeal for a kind of recognition, an identification that is Margaret Diesendorf's definition of love. Her urge to find correlatives and analogies unfortunately lead her to an over-use of similes; there are literally hundreds in the collection. As this habit is recognised by the reader, its stylistic impact diminishes, although the reasons for such frequency may be appreciated. *Holding the Golden Apple* possesses all of the weaknesses and strengths of Diesendorf's poetry. If Rilke's concept of poetic criticism is accepted ("Love alone can grasp it"[5]), it still matters what concept, indeed what *art* of love the reader is to endorse. The voice of these poems is unmistakably Central European, classically educated, philosophically oriented and philologically trained. The poems' thoughts are mostly interrelated references, imaginative cross quotations or playfully complex allusions to European philosophy, art and letters. For all their apparent spontaneity this makes them not immediately accessible to every reader. Added to this, there is a preoccupation with the poet's self which in the setting of modern German literature is totally acceptable, but continues to meet with reservation, even suspicion in the Australian context. Temperamental differences aside, there remains a cultural restriction to personal outpourings in Anglo-Australian writing (which, however, is beginning to lose its dogmatic hold, not least, one suspects, under the influence of so-called multicultural poets and novelists). Diesendorf is sensitive to the mythology of the poetic I; even her autobiographical references are imaginatively integrated into classical art, quotations of kindred spirits. The frequent allusions to her "dancer's feet"(20) are a sign language praising nature's artistic transformations.

Her best poems are characteristically complex and precise, often short and witty, they are imaginative definitions of the need to relate. By contrast, the language of her longer prose poems seems one-dimensional and flat. Thus the poet can instruct herself "to settle down to/work forgetting my chronic ills"(22).In all her verse allegories and angelic spirits abound; there is a ready-made metaphysical universe in which the poet feels at home, from which she can quote with ease and occasional wit. *Holding the Golden Apple* is a title which implies not only quotation but also faith. Diesendorf's language hovers uneasily between traditional imagination, orthodox diction and specifically modern colloquial Australian. She has no difficulty speaking of "the kingdom of the word"(34) and "the poet's throne"(Ibid.) — and mean it, yet in the same poem employ a phrase such as "incredibly real".(Ibid.) Contemplating the validity of quoting Greek myths in an Australian setting Diesendorf attempts to mingle Aboriginal with European mythology.(40) The Australian forest is presented in medieval and Wagnerian terms: "the trees have their male/counterparts, smoother & taller/(stiffened like/Tristan's manhood at the sight/of Iseult's moist lips);...".(95) It is doubtful whether such cultural quotations succeed in conveying the authentic nature of an Australian landscape; it rather appears to be a form of nostalgic alienation, an incongruous imagery unable to express the truth of contemporary experience. Appropriately, the poet concludes one of her verses with the resigned knowledge "I must lie with your idea".(26) The entire volume of love poetry is such a consummation in mind and spirit, more precisely, with the Platonic eros of an inherited knowledge.

Diesendorf's verse is a poetry of likeness, a recollection of early teaching and lived education. It is important to acknowledge the subjective authenticity of Diesendorf's language and experience. There can be no question about the truth and depth of her feelings. What is both fascinating and disturbing is the situation of a gifted migrant poet whose lengthy stay in this country could not undo the "outdated" and "studied" diction or thought of an exiled European imagination. Diesendorf's poetic style would be as decadent (*epigonal*) in contemporary German-language literature as it is in Australian writing. The poet failed to share in the development of her native tongue's post-modernistic concept of poetry. She is suffering the fate of being stranded in a static Diaspora of history and *Bildung*. Symptomatically, there is a correlation between Diesendorf's reliance on European mythology and her extensive over-use of genetive metaphors: both reflect basic attempts to establish relationships and to construct poetic meanings where "native" writers prefer to expose the absence of both. Many of Diesendorf's love poems simply do not read as if they were written in the late eighties of this century. Instead of the aimed-for "timelessness" of classical imagery they frequently run the risk of sounding trivial or like expressions of contemporary consumerist pop-culture: "the sun of your love" corresponds to "the nude of your dreams".(28)

There is a vast amount of learning in Diesendorf's poetic references, even where they occasionally produce unintentional humour. Like an imaginative, emotional formula one poem summarises "it is as if...".(31) In a way, that is what all poetry has been about — rightly so, for as long as the analogies are recognisably relevant and contemporary, i.e. imaginative creations of the author addressing her live readers. Yet Diesendorf's love poetry reads as follows:

> You were the snow-white bull,
> my Zeus in disguise;
> like the seagod's offspring...
> (I...let you) recall
> that I am not Europa...
> (32)

The "as if" formula of such mythological allegories or personifications amounts to little more than learned quotation in the name of beauty and education. It is not so much elitist as archaic, imagery taken from the poetic museum of classical history. Where Diesendorf attempts to be more contemporary (or less antiquated), her lyrics can sound like throw-away pop-songs ("in the sea of love"; cf. Don Gibb's 'classical' country and western title "Sea of Heartbreak"). Where Margaret Diesendorf employs semi-religious mythology she deserts her own poetic strength, replacing creative precision and the power of observation and analysis with rhetorical profundity and emotional ambiguity. Instead of "absolute" poetry (with all its assumptions and implications) Diesendorf could be writing contemporary verse — sceptical, inquisitive, verifiable, modest, fragmentary, preliminary, 'relative' poetry. The fact is that she is quite capable of doing that. There is not enough imaginative realisation to redeem the fundamental doubt about this collection by a clearly gifted poet. Too often "Love will enter the glass dome/of the museum artefact."(41)

Her previous volume *Light* continues to dictate the thought and stylistic form of her later poetry. However, even if this "light" is spiritually and intellectually linked to enlightenment and the Holy Spirit, the association remains largely verbal. There is no sociopolitical, cultural specificity, not enough realisation of the predefined and rearranged verbal resource. In one poem the lyrical I senses her artistic isolation: "I'm left/alone/in the centre/of the magic/circle...".(46) In terms of cultural history the inherited magic has lost its "centre" a long time ago. The poet succumbs to the construction of visionary quotations, dream-like *déjà vus* of literary history.

The woman's voice is dramatically different from the liberated tones of her younger sisters. Artistic and religious orthodoxy are endorsed, albeit with occasional, often flirtatious variations. The patriarchal myth of womanhood is essentially confirmed.

Occasionally Diesendorf's verse integrates German into its art of quotation. Individual lines appear in parallel translation:

> Blood ripples over stone
> *Blut rieselt über Stein*
> & it is night
> *& es wird Nacht*
> ......
> we were chosen
> *wir sind erkoren*

>   to be a part of life frozen
>   to be a work of art
>   (53)

It is not always clear why German intrudes into these poems, nor are the quotations made explicit. (It is difficult not to recognise in the final lines Manfred Jurgensen's poem "(montreux)" (from *a winter's journey*,1979) which ends

>   was i chosen
>   to be a part
>   of life frozen
>   to works of art
>   (52).)

The final section of *Holding The Golden Apple* actually contains the 'same' poem in German and in English(102/103), "Sieh' uns da" and "See us there". In a real sense, much of Margaret Diesendorf's poetry must be seen as a highly creative form of translation, not merely of her own poems or those of other writers, but of literary cultures. Her quotations and integrations of the work of other artists are not plagiarism, they form an essential part of Diesendorf's multicultural consciousness and imagination. Hers is an integrational creativity, a constant interrelating of German, French, English, Greek, Roman and Australian literary myths. In her isolation as an Austrian-Australian migrant poet she seeks to unify and keep alive her consciousness, her European education, her very identity. That she chooses the form of love poetry adds a tragic dimension to her work, for it is a love not always reciprocated. As she says in one of her translated poems, "to hold/& uphold the heavens/it takes two"(103). That also applies to two cultures, to her loving need to harmonise Australian and German literary culture. Therein lies the highest aim of this poet's voice: "to hold" and to "uphold", to participate and to preserve, to innovate and to maintain. Diesendorf's creative gifts would have benefitted greatly from frequent return visits to Central Europe; they would have allowed her to be more responsive to more recent trends in German writing.

Margaret Diesendorf's poetry has raised translation and quotation to the level of art. She is a multicultural artist *par excellence*. The archaic return to the history of her native culture is largely responsible for the stagnation of an imagination unable to wholly adapt a new literary tradition, especially one so young and contradictory as Australia's. Her fate, therefore, is tragically paradigmatic of many artists in exile or Diaspora ("Then I sing — my loneliness."56) What shines through all of Diesendorf's writing, however, is a strong creative talent stifled by cultural alienation, yet assertive enough to articulate (albeit often in archaic or antiquated terms) a Central European classical humanist literary tradition, its myths and values, its art, philosophy and religion.

MANFRED JURGENSEN: WRITING IN ENGLISH*

When Manfred Jurgensen came to Australia in 1961 to study Arts at the University of Melbourne he spoke fluent English, but had written little in this language apart from exercises at his Grammar School in Flensburg, and during his year as an Exchange Student at Roosevelt High School in Iowa. As a boy in North Germany he wrote poems in the mode of German Romanticism. In Melbourne he began to write modern lyrics in English which found a place immediately in the student magazines. Many of his poems were distinguished from the general run by a concern with language and exile and, after his conversion to Catholicism, by a sensuous spirituality.

Concern with language as an instrument in human affairs was expressed in an editorial note Jurgensen wrote for *Melbourne University Magazine* in his final Honours Year in which he majored in German, English and Political Science. The comment is a general concern shared by all language users, and of a different kind from the problems he faced with others writing in a non-indigenous language. By 1930 the political corruption of language had begun to preoccupy thinking people, adding another dimension to the perennial complaint against the purity and efficacy of language made by writers who had lost the robust Renaissance faith in the resources of human speech to communicate truths. In the 1960s the sociological and semiotic investigations which were feeding into Structuralist and Post-Structuralist interpretations of the problem of written texts had not, in general, begun to affect creative writers in Australia.

Writing from the intellectual and ideological furore of Melbourne University in the sixties, Jurgensen used the vocabulary of the time to ask readers to contribute "at least half the effort" in ensuring that

---

* This section was written by Elizabeth Perkins.

tolerance and acceptance of the relativity of truth would restore intellectual vitality to university debate: "Words are built around personalities rather than ideas of vitality, become reflections of lost and blurred concepts, and in this lies their abuse." This concept of the role of transmitter (writer) and receptor (reader) might now be expressed through the prevailing end-of-century discourse in which the idea of *vitality* becomes the idea of *vigorously deconstructing* utterance or text in the process of reading. In emphasising the role of the reader, Jurgensen's comment is a reminder that the author-centred, author-controlled nature of literature has always been largely a myth, although a powerful one.

This issue of the place of the author has central importance when reading the work of a writer like Manfred Jurgensen. His poetry and prose fiction reiterate the belief that everything in the writing comes from outside the writer, whose role is to be the medium for whatever communication is made. In Jurgensen's writing this means that not only inspiration, whatever that may be, but words, sentences, and the whole form of the utterance originate outside the writer. This idea may be referred back to the Greek belief in inspiration. On the other hand, it may be interpreted in terms of Machereyan theory, or through any of the theories between the sixth century BC and the twentieth century AD that see any utterance or text as a complex product of the contemporary moment, a product in which any overt intention of the author may be challenged, changed or subverted in the process of writing. Jurgensen's work, which is often ostensibly author-centred, is also often radically deconstructed by the other voices admitted into the writing through the wide sociological concern of his texts.

Certainly in different generations, theory places a different emphasis on the components of the literary creative act. The difference that exists between early Greek attribution of inspiration to divine afflatus, Renaissance attribution to the human-centred yet transcendent nature of human language, and Machereyan attribution to complex, pre-existing literary and social forces, is chiefly an ideological difference. If "transcendent" means "possessing almost inexplicable power", what Jurgensen calls "almost demonic" power, Jurgensen's work acknowledges the possibility of each of these ideological positions. He interprets the process of his own creativity or literary production by attributing the work to something other than the independent genius of the author. As he himself has commented: "I am conscious that the voice that articulates itself in my poetry is not entirely my own voice.

But it is a voice that addresses itself to somebody, and I suspect that in the first instance it is speaking to me and I see myself as my first reader." This may be interpreted as a mystic statement, or as an explanation of the way in which one writer experiences the interaction of contemporary discourse in the process of his writing. When Jurgensen's work is examined closely, it is seen as a compellingly egocentric network of discourses which the idiosyncrasy of the writer's consciousness dyes with its distinctive coloration. It may be literally so that the social moment — not necessarily an historical contemporary one — writes itself through this poet, and that the first text is as surprising to him as it is to the external reader.

Another aspect of this creative process is explained in Jurgensen's comment on the title of his third volume of German poems, *Innere Sicherheit* (1979). The inner or internal security evoked in the title refers both to the individual and to the state, and Jurgensen added: "The innermost personal state of a citizen is also the most political; unlike most Germans, I've never accepted the separation between the public and the private, the subjective and the political." The process is not as simple as merely being a writer who acts as a medium for the public moment; and the evidence is not merely seen in the use of metaphor and simile drawn from the political arena. Jurgensen's work is the site of conflict between a voracious ego demanding attention to and expression of personal identity and sense gratification, and an almost self-annihilating and disciplined superego consumed by awareness of public responsibility. While this conflict may be concealed in the work of most poets, it is only barely concealed in Jurgensen's. Its exposed condition is perhaps due to the way in which his writing reiterates the belief that his identity and his work can best be expressed as a "quotation"; that is, as the re-statement of intellectual and emotional acts preceding his own existence and that of his work. It could be said that the ego is the more exigent because of the belief that it lives only through the articulation of innumerable collective discourses.

Manfred Jurgensen's earliest poetry in English was, overtly at least, concerned with issues other than the nature of literary production, although the acts of writing and reading often provided imagery for the poems. In general, too, his awareness of migrant status in Australia was subsumed in the poetry by the concept of the migrant status of human life in the universe, and of the transitory, migratory nature and power of love. The idea of exile in many senses appears in this early work.

In 1964 his play *Rückkehr ins Exil* (Return into Exile) was performed at the Union Theatre in Melbourne, and in 1967 he dedicated a sequence of lyrics, "Exile and Other Places", to his friend and lecturer, the poet Vincent Buckley. As Jurgensen had taken up a Swiss Government Scholarship at Zürich in 1966, after extensive travel, it is difficult to attribute the sense of exile and alienation in any poem to a specific country. Moreover Jurgensen's doctoral studies under Emil Staiger at Zürich led to a thesis on Goethe's Aesthetic, and months of research into German Romanticism where the image of journeying and homelessness often assumes metaphysical significance for poets who never leave their birthplace. Whether or not the poet himself felt exiled and alienated, there was every reason why the discourses of exile and alienation in eighteenth, nineteenth or twentieth-century form might speak through the poetry.

In style and competence the seven varied lyrics in "Exile and Other Places" are typical of much Australian poetry published in journals like *Twentieth Century: An Australian Quarterly Review* in which they appeared in the Autumn issue for 1967. Thematically, flight, suspension of responsibility and direction are balanced against fixity, inevitability and self-determining responsibility. Specific images suggested by the poet's journey from Australia to Zürich in 1966 are reinforced by those images related to Classical and Catholic myths and images of sensual eroticism which, together with the vocabulary of political ideologies and the language in which language itself is discussed, have so far remained the staples of Jurgensen's writing. A painful period of hospitalisation in Melbourne in 1963 contributed other staple images of violence, constraint and helplessness consonant with images generated in Europe during and after the war.

signs & voices

In 1968 Jurgensen took up a lectureship at the University of Queensland and began his contribution to the development of poetry in Brisbane which he has maintained for over twenty years. Many of his poems appeared in *Makar*, the University's literary journal, and in other Queensland anthologies, and in 1973 his first collection of poems in English appeared under the title *signs & voices*. Evoking semiotic and spoken communication, the title summarises the role of the poems in signifying both the poet and his inner life and also the external world of which he is almost hyper-sensitively conscious. One problem that underlies the articulation of voices, and that prompts the poet to turn to non-verbal signs, was the problem that continued to preoccupy many poets at this time in most parts of the world. The difficulty of writing poetry in the damaged languages of the twentieth century was intensely felt in post-war Germany by poets like Grass, Enzensberger, Krolow, Brecht and Celan, whom Jurgensen has named as influencing his own work to some degree. Moreover Jurgensen was especially attentive to the language of signs since the medical condition of a gifted member of his own family made it necessary for him to communicate in sign language. Yet Jurgensen's personal concern with the problematics of language was shared by many Australian poets who had come to know post-war European poets directly or through the Modern European Poets series of translations, so that the poetry of Paul Celan, and the poetics of writing after Auschwitz, in which Celan's name is central, also affected Australian poets in their search for a language which might not sabotage what they said or betray them into saying what they did not mean. The problem is compounded for a poet writing in a second language, and for a poet whose personal experience often becomes the metaphor for his exploration of the outer world. A minor, wry example of attempting to rectify language is the changes in the poem "Academics", published twice in 1968, which begins, "In their appointed chair of public service", and which became "In our appointed chair" when printed in *signs & voices* in 1973.

A more intense concern for the verity of the poet's language is seen in the poem "dedication" published in *Square Poets,* a Queensland anthology edited by Maureen Freer in 1971. "Dedication" was not included in *signs & voices* but is central to the communications in that collection. The poem transcends its private origins and expresses a fear of betraying its readers and a fear that language can never yield the meanings it promises. The person addressed and the "demon of forgiveness" are both the speaker's self and the external Other, the reader, with whom the voice fears it cannot honestly communicate. In the mirror of the poem, both the "I" and the "eye" of the speaker, and the eye of the reader, may meet in some way and resurrect lost integrities.

Barely half a dozen poems in *signs & voices* do not foreground what might be called the "fictional I", a literary concept to which Jurgensen has given theoretical attention in his study *Das fiktionale Ich* (1979)[6], a commentary on the diaries of Goethe, Kierkegaard, Kafka,

Mann, Frisch and Handke. The most fruitful reading of Jurgensen's poetry is possible if notions of the "confessional poetry" of Robert Lowell's *Life Studies* (1951) are set aside. It is more tempting to invoke the German concept of the "verlorenes Ich" or the "lost I" which is epitomised in Gottfried Benn's poem of that title written in 1943 as a desperate attempt to drown (or sustain?) the poet's voice within the chaos of history. In the Foreword to *Das fiktionale Ich* Jurgensen writes of the diary as a form of literature which embodies the search after the lost I: "the I that lies between Fiction and Being". In context, Jurgensen's phrase is: *Das Ich zwischen Fiktion und Sein*. The English translation suggested here introduces the ambiguous verb "lies" which sums up the dilemma of self-expression in language. Yet Jurgensen's poems do not constitute a diary, and whether or not the poet is searching for a hidden I, for a personal identity, it is perhaps an unnecessary distraction in the present context of writing and reading to initiate a reading of the poems from this point of view. It may then be more fruitful to set aside even the tempting concept of the fictional I and see the "I" — or "i" as it is often written — of Jurgensen's poetry as simply a dramatic device which suggests immediacy of experience and which balances the concept of quotation which denies immediacy. The use of the first person address also suggests that however evasive or fictional the poem is, it nevertheless desires to mime the possibility of direct communication with the reader.

The vocabulary, images and network of discourses that make up the poems in *signs & voices* are those found in the early poems. The poems are adept at selecting and combining precisely those images and fragments of a discourse that one would associate with the situation of each poem, but the emphasis, juxtaposition and intensity are unique to Jurgensen's writing. Separation of parent and child, of lovers, of the individual and society, of intellect and feeling, are recurrent themes, together with illness and possibilities of other morbidity in marriage, academia or in the observations of the tourist. Yet through the interplay of recurrent images the act of inscription and interpretation emerges as the dominant theme. This includes all varieties of recording, translating, coding, de-ciphering, reflecting and imaging, so that the collection, read as a whole, replaces notions of reality of experience with the probability that all reality is a process of constructing experience. As one poem says, life is praised "as a quotation," an act which is not confined to the lecture room. The poems in *signs & voices* insist that they cannot be mistaken for experience itself, except insofar as the reading constitutes an experience. But they also seem to go further and deny the immediacy of any experience. This insistence that life is a perpetual quotation or reflection of experiences inscribed in an earlier time and place may be a means of sheltering from the impact of the immediate, or it may be a lament for the loss of immediacy. Jurgensen's belief that his poetry records a voice that articulates itself to him, and that he is his first reader, complicates the issue of immediacy. The vocabulary of inscribing and re-inscribing, mirroring and reflecting, could derive in the first place from this process of composition.

The poem "identity" begins: "i am writing against myself/ an amateur photo". Hospitalisation and reversion to an infant state of helplessness give rise to the lines: "our characters rehearse/ their manuscript of second childhood." Love making is seen as a literary act, a written contract, but it is important to realise that this need not prevent the joyful celebration of the act of loving:

> afterwards
> we breathe the knowledge of our act.
>
> confirmed
> the signatures of our bodies
> certify
> freedom from contracted struggle.
>
> after the dictated gestures
> we serve the sentence of our deed.
> rising
> our silent witness reads
> the glowing signs of truth.

Another gentle lyric, commemorating the end of a love affair, creates more than literal meaning with the lines:

> you do not write
> the borrowed rain transmits my monologue.

Here "writing" carries the weight of a whole relationship, and the disappearance of the relationship is imaged in the monologue which will be obliterated as well as transmitted by the speaker's tears or by the invalidating "borrowed" rain of his physical environment. The impact of *signs & voices* is disturbing when it is read as a record of an ego struggling to assert its identity through innumerable discourses and in a borrowed language — borrowed not only from another country but also from earlier generations of a native country. Yet there is some consolation here too, as though the sense of living through quotation does finally become a shelter and a home, and an awareness of discourses does at least permit the traveller to find an appropriate voice in any environment. Such a traveller is never entirely deprived of some form of articulation whether he is caught in the doldrums of domesticity:

> The gaspipe yawns from its
> natural sea and vomits
> into the kitchen stove.
> soon our thanksgiving dinner
> will be roasted...

or the South China Sea:

> here life is artfully created
> as a chinese opera
> where signs and voices represent
> the refuge of identity.
>
> boarding the ferry back to kowloon
> i see in every sail that boasts
> upon this harbour of confusion
> the taming of a magic dragon,...

To a sensibility where identity is a refuge, not an exposure, the identifying signs and voices can only be borrowed quotations. What the poems cannot answer is whether this is the general condition of articulate humanity or the personal dilemma of a relatively few, but they do assert that to some sensibilities this is the nature of social existence, and they are thus remarkably consonant with some theories about the nature of literary production.

a kind of dying, Break-Out

In 1977 Jurgensen published his second collection of English poems *a kind of dying*, and the first version of a novella, *Break-Out*, which he was to revise in 1987. The epigraph to the poems is two lines by Anne Sexton which supply the title: "This singing/is a kind of dying." There is an intensification of the sharpest elements in the first collection, and the play of wit is tormented and remorseless rather than relaxing. The best of the poetry is a tour de force executed, it seems, against overwhelming odds. Rhyme, rhythm and word-play mime lack of control, but the poems finally are seen to be disconcertingly well controlled. The first section, "ward twelve", evokes some six or seven weeks of hospital confinement:

> this new guy's got a way with words
> and almost murder he's a hopeless case
> of all the overcrowded wards
> why did they have to send him to this place
>
> don quixote riding on ward twelve
> a writer of all wrongs
> he keeps imagining himself
> a righter of false songs...
>
> when we ask him not to dream aloud
> he says he'll soon be gone
> then he reads a crazy poem out
> without rhyme or reason

Sometimes a lyrical poignancy surfaces, as in the poem where the trees or patients address the "painstaking gardeners and punctual warders"; staff inside and outside the walls, patients and plants, are brought together in one beautiful metaphor:

> do not rake all our passionate leaves
> to the same smouldering heap of indifference... .

The later poems in *a kind of dying* use the language of violent erotic engagement as a major discourse interwoven with a more compassionate discourse of love counterpointed by the language of the mundane and commercial world. Although images of transcription and reading persist, the poems no longer foreground this act as they do in *signs & voices*, but assume that to live as quotation *is* the mode of existence. Yet it is a mode that leaves the projected subject vulnerable to hurt and violence.

a winter's journey

A winter's journey in 1979 marks a new phase in Jurgensen's writing in English. Where earlier and indeed some subsequent work is preoccupied with the notion of the self as a construct of quotations, *a winter's journey* is a more self-disinterested although not depersonalised collection of lyrics, which exemplifies Julia Kristeva's idea of intertextuality or transposition.

The poems are in essence a mosaic of quotations in which related earlier texts, literary, graphic and musical, are absorbed and transformed. In *a winter's journey* any notion of subjectivity may fruitfully be replaced by the idea of intertextuality which emphasises the strength of the creative act involved in producing the poetry. The process of transposing discourses or other material into a new text demands an exacting kind of originality, since traces of the transposed material must be seen clearly within the new work to demonstrate a genuine transformation. It is not surprising that the word *Spuren*, meaning traces, trails, or scents is found often in Jurgensen's writing in German. *A winter's journey* approaches a formal parody of Schubert's *Winterreise* and the lyrics of Wilhelm Müller to which Schubert composed the song-cycle. This intertextuality balances the personal diary form of the poems indicated in the subtitle and the dates preceding each poem that suggest the sequence refers to specific days between December 1976 and June 1977. *Winterreise* begins with a comparatively complex setting of Müller's four eight-lined stanzas in the song *Gute Nacht* (Goodnight) and ends with the exquisitely attenuated words and music of *Der Leiermann* (the Organ Grinder). Jurgensen's *a winter's journey* reverses this form with an aubade comprised of twenty-one-syllable lines, and ends with resonant, meditative twenty decasyllabic lines addressed to the "you" to whom the aubade was written. The cycle, which has been discussed more fully in a chapter in *The German Presence in Queensland* (1988) edited by Manfred Jurgensen and Alan Corkhill, is a complex mimetic work showing that intertextuality can become a fine socio-aesthetic act.[7]

In dramatic contrast to Schubert's traveller who journeys towards death, Jurgensen's traveller sees himself as embodied language journeying from the monosyllabic cry of infancy to the sophistication of the adult who reflects "i wrote the pages of my diary/ in search of myself." Yet, when the speaker asks "was it i or he/ who memorised the anger of our pain?" the cycle closes with the same sense of tentative, diffused identity found in the poems of childhood. In tracing self and not-self or Other through the two hemispheres and winter seasons, Jurgensen's traveller experiences the social and political world as sharply as the world of his own emotional and intellectual being. The cycle includes poems like the following, dated June 1977 and subtitled "restoration", a reference to work done on the buildings of the University of Queensland:

> today i saw a worker holding
> an iron bar so delicately
> balanced in his hands. the scaffolding
> which climbed across our grand views lately
> was taken down. almost all windows
> were broken while it was erected
> around our towered extravagance.
> another age clawed undetected
> into the dated stone. decay grows
> steadily until its own advance
> can progress no further. death restores
> life-masks of similar countenance.
> paid by the hour, workers are earning
> more than their keep. the tower's entrance
> and its glass have hardened to the cores
> of this establishment of learning.
> the sandstone cleaned, its motto's carving
> proclaims, while half the world is starving:
> 'truth is great and mighty above all
> things.' whose truth? whose writing on the wall?

Without encasing the traveller in his own shell of identity, *a winter's journey* leads in an intellectual progression towards the Other, nevertheless there emerges from the poems a poetic voice as resonant and passionate as any heard in the works of German and English Romanticism. The traces of Shelley's "Ozymandias" echoing in the poem "restoration" demonstrates not only the delicate intertextuality of this song-cycle, but the historical fact that romanticism itself is a densely textured engagement of the putative self with the outer material world of politics and power.

south africa transit

South africa transit published in Johannesburg was the second collection of Jurgensen's poems to appear in 1979, the result of a term as Visiting Professor at Witwatersrand. This collection emphasises the ineluctable weaving of political and social discourses into the texture of personal and private speech. For the visitor to South Africa, Otherness and alienation are made visible with shocking clarity, but this, paradoxically, forces them to see that their attempts to separate private lives from the public discourse of apartheid requires blindness that should be impossible but often is achieved. This is summed up in a trenchant epigram addressed "to a black student":

> your skin is borne
> out by your being
> the sight you scorn
> still blinds your seeing
>
> pity the white
> with his big white lies
> he has no sight
> for he has no eyes.

Stylistically, the poems in *south africa transit* are diverse, although the vocabulary is typical of Jurgensen's earlier work, with a new emphasis on the image of eyes and seeing. In the sardonic "tourist's report", for example, the speaker says comfortably: "i went on a white man's safari/i only shot with my imported eyes." For a different kind of tourist, apartheid Africa is a region of geography and of the spirit where age comes quickly with the understanding that one is separated for ever from what one might have been:

> i would have liked to tell someone
> why suddenly on a winter's night
> in africa i have grown old
> why all the things that i have done
> seem foolish now and nothing right
> but i'm alone and it is cold.

The central piece of this collection is "variations on a love poem", a structured poem of four ten-lined stanzas each shaped by lines of increasing but not mechanically rigid syllabic count. The speaker sees that his personal isolation is cognate, in every sense of the word, with the apartheid of Johannesburg:

> a part of
> apartheid
> i trace my origins
> back to the coloured leaves
> that fell on rain-wet pavements
> in the foggy streets of autumn
> when time was beautiful decay
> child's play in ever-present parks
> boot-kicking the skeleton's abundance
> with anger and letters and leaflets to burn

The coloured leaves kicked about by children link the speaker's birthplace in northern Germany to the street brutality around him in Johannesburg. Although only the skeletons of leaves are literally present, they evoke human skeletons which may then be associated with the anger and leaflets of political demonstrations. For the Australian reader, the city of Johannesburg reminds of the Queensland premier, Johannes Bjelke-Petersen, whose repressive regime in Jurgensen's home State was characterised by illiberal proscriptions against street demonstrations.

The second stanza openly asserts the speaker's isolation and the hope that his fear of other races will not make him indifferent to what happens in the streets. The rapid line movement links him to the protester who "squatters" in front of his hotel burning, literally, and also with anger, the same letters and leaflets the speaker knew in another country. At the most private level, the angry letters are also those that pass between the estranged lovers in their different continents.

In the third stanza the political situation is identified with the speaker's separation from the desired Other whose face resembles his in that he shares with her a no more sinister burning than that of the sun. In the last stanza, however, the poet succumbs to what he experiences as the dark magic of divided Africa, a continent whose sunlight, darkness, geographical separateness, and racial and political division, image those things which undermine human love. The last two lines of the poem have the same ambiguous message to lovers as is found in the ending of Donne's poem, "The Canonisation":

> a part of
> apartheid
> i fall for the same line
> apart from apartheid
> we discover native ground
> deep in the south of africa
> and spell out this dark continent
> casting its magic on our love
> so lovers may read the teeth of our skin
> with one face and one faith and sunrays to burn

If Africa is a pattern of human love, the burning face, faith and sunrays of the final line disturb more than they comfort. Moreover, the inverted phrase, "the teeth of our skin", suggests not only the dangers of racism but also a strong reservation about the depth of sensuous love. In this last stanza reconciliation and love struggle with the discourse of apartheid and European concepts of negritude and Otherness adumbrated in words like "line", "deep", "spell", "dark" and "magic", so that the poem's final statement is complex, disturbing and honest.

the skin trade

The skin trade published in 1983 is one of those bold experiments that can only be carried out successfully by a poet like Jurgensen who is experienced in the controlled, ironic expression of strong passion. As the brief title suggests in itself there is nothing new here in discourse or vocabulary, but the intensity, compression and concentration on the last seven days of a long relationship are remarkable. The book was designed by Phoenix Publications which Jurgensen founded in 1981, and the fine layout, cover design and quality of type and paper are integral to the statement of the poems. The cover reproduces Bernini's *St Theresa in Ecstasy*, a marble sculpture of a religious sensuality that often disconcerts critics, something that may also be true of Jurgensen's poetry. Although the poems in *the skin trade* express the pain and rage of the deserted lover, they are even more remarkable for their profound absorption with the sensuous experience of the female Other. It is more than the male gaze, stricken and enraged as it is, that is felt here: it is rather the male desire to become the wrinkled, scarred, aged, and above all, experienced body of the female:

> your skin is a map
> on which history
> replays its war games.
> each touch is a trap,
> the shed mystery
> when love still bore names.

In his anger, the male splendidly performs the old rituals of the patriarchy, alternately addressing the woman as:

> fallen angel, angelica,
> doomed to the glory of being
> female.

and as one who follows "the oldest profession":

> i don't cry
> over whores;
> all befores
> i have paid
> with my pride.

In the context of the poems, the disclaimer is to be recognised as a palpable untruth. Moreover the speaker has been defeated in the struggle for the female by the phallically named new lover, Rod, who is attacked and belittled as a mode of ego-salving revenge. There is pathos too in the deserted lover's pain and in the loss of the woman's daughter whom he regards as his own:

> in love, despair, in pleasure and
> in pain i shall forever trace
> with blind, appealing, outstretched hand
> the beauty of my daughter's face.

Although the poems are arranged in sequences tracing the lover's response and relationship to the departed beloved, the mood fluctuates from poem to poem. Almost mid-way through the cycle is placed the poem "learning, knowing, acting," which ends in a moment of quiet acceptance. The final poem in the collection "angelica or: writing in english" returns to this moment in which the possibilities of the relationship, whether realised or unrealised, are celebrated.

> your body is a grave
> for the ever-silent truth.
> teach my life to be brave,
> to retain the mystery
> of the word that cannot be.

The skin trade is set in the context of the city and suburbs of Brisbane, one of the longer poems being an extract called "the valley" from the cycle "shine on, brisbane". Here the patriarchal discourse gives way to a wiser, less arrogant speech. Abandoning the "mystery" of the patriarchal "word" which is asserted in the final line of the book, the speaker in "the valley" finds himself at one with the male immigrants of the "cosmopolitan" coffee-shop. Addressing Luigi as "poet of unaltered love,/teacher of signs" the speaker ends with the hope of a future that seems to be withheld in the poems that concern the passion existing between the male and the female protagonists:

> your casual grace
> alone gives meaning to this place.
> i am your guest, kim, boris, john:
> our living days have just begun.

The love and friendship that exist between the male characters is "unaltered" both in the time-sense of unchanged and in the sex — or gender — sense of lack of alterity. *The skin trade* is a brilliant text written in a patriarchal discourse which demonstrates that the tragedy at the heart of the male-female relationship is inevitable while the patriarchal discourse holds the privileged position in all such relationships.

The Unit

Jurgensen returned to this problem of patriarchal discourse in an one-act monodrama called *The Unit*, published in *Outrider* in 1984 and first performed in 1988 by the actor John Lavery directed by Pam Lythgo at the Townsville Theatre Company. Michael, the deserted lover in *The Unit,* realises in the course of an evening that he cannot survive as a single unit, but with the lost Anouk, however troubled the relationship was, he experienced a kind of unity. The harmony within the disharmony of their love which his narrative chronicles, is ironically challenged by sound effects of hammering, exaggerated telephone bells, monotonous heartbeats, and a cacophony of sirens that gradually invade the unit until Michael hurls himself from the balcony of the high-rise apartment. In dramatic contrast, the play opens with a pleasantly-cadenced, whimsical scene as Michael waters the house-plants and addresses a patriarchal God:

> Well, God, if you don't exist, it's time again to invent you. You probably owe your existence more to my loneliness than I owe mine to your reality.

Like the lost love in *the skin trade*, Anouk has grown old with a female experience that fascinates Michael as he carefully spells it out:

> God, when I think of her body! Everytime she got undressed, I thought of "Hiroshima, mon amour". After two marriages, five children, an abortion, one hysterectomy and fifty-four lovers, she was held together almost entirely by varicose veins and stretch marks.

He is astonished that he was attracted to a woman whose appearance so failed to measure up to masculinist expectations, and his interest in other women also surprises him. He reluctantly admits that perhaps he did "love" Anouk, although her psychiatrist warned him that "Anouk is the sort of woman one simply does not love. Because it's suicidal." Michael trusts the psychiatrist's advice since the man "sees enough middle-aged housewives who've taken an overdose." Secure in this patronising view of women, Michael interprets Anouk's behaviour as hallucinatory, hypochondria and play-acting to a captive audience. He admits that he himself was "too involved in [his] own performance" to pay full attention to hers, and this may account for her departure. That Anouk's reasons for leaving may have had little to do with him does not seem to occur to Michael, who cannot understand even at the end of the play why she suddenly stopped "playing" her part in their drama. He sneers at what he sees as her new role played with the "sissy" new lover who does the cooking for her.

Like the Angelica of *the skin trade,* Anouk has a daughter to whom Michael is deeply attached, but Anouk, he says, lost interest in her children once past babyhood. That mothers, contrary to the demands to patriarchal conditioning, can relinquish children when they have grown beyond initial dependency, shocks the masculine sensibility, as if this maternal insouciance threatens the support that the male feels is due to him from the female. Michael, facing the problem of preparing his own meal, suddenly screams like a bad-tempered child, "I WANT MY DINNER!"

Out of his need for the kind of relationship he had with Anouk, Michael creates the metaphysical proposition that "A man wasn't born to live in units," echoing the God of *Genesis* who bestows on Adam the "gift" of Eve, saying "It is not good that the man should be alone."

In a powerfully orchestrated and flexible monologue, Michael represents Anouk's role in their shared drama, until

> ...suddenly she didn't want to play anymore. She no longer wanted to be a part of me. Said she wanted to be herself, whatever that might mean. So she took her whorishness with her. And I'm left with my killer instinct, my murderous need to be loved.

The audience, of course, cannot see the whole of this relationship since all that is known is conveyed through Michael's mind which gradually disintegrates during the play. Again, Jurgensen's script emphasises, with intellectual wit and emotional intensity, the limitations of the patriarchal discourse. The dramatic possibilities of *The Unit* equate with the compelling modern lyricism of *the skin trade* and reinforce his exploration of almost identical situations.

Movement in the monodrama is provided by Michael's domestic pottering and his pursuit of the gecko, Igi, who becomes his companion, and culminates in Michael's frenzied plunge from the balcony. Surrealist effects develop as Michael apparently watches on television the arrival of the fire-engine which, realistically, might be expected to come if Michael were threatening to leap from the balcony. In this climactic ending Michael's search for a conventional family group — mother, father, child, warmth — is caught up in a wild denunciation of his own quite different destructive passion. The isolation of private lives in units controlled by an impersonal Body Corporate is also contrasted with the possibilities of the family-centred group.

Although *The Unit* exposes the personal tragedy of a man imprisoned by his dependence on a destructive relationship which he can only enunciate through patriarchal discourse, it also involves some dramatisation of Jurgensen's staple concerns with political violence, and with the self that is known only through quotation. Intertextuality contributes to the script, although it is less concentrated than in *a winter's journey*. Michael recalls a strange event in Florence which began as lunch with Anouk in a pavement café and disintegrated, in his mind at least, into a weird carnival scene in which a troupe of artistes gave a mocking performance of the diners:

> At first I thought it was funny; they really were good actors. Then I became convinced that they were actually mocking us. I just wished they would have gone away. They were beginning to spoil my appetite. Suddenly I noticed that their "food" consisted of little cakes in the shape of cars, houses, churches and even people. It was horrible how they devoured men and women, even children. It was obscene; somebody should have stopped them. But no one complained; on the contrary, some guests threw money to the performers and the waiters smiled benevolently.

The recollection evokes a scene in Mann's *Death in Venice* and other narrative incidents in which bourgeois travellers are mocked by Italian carnival figures. An uglier political echo is heard as Michael pretends to instruct the gecko:

> Repeat after me: a good gecko is a dead gecko. That's right, children. Now try this one: once a gecko, always a gecko. Altogether now: Once a gecko, always a gecko. Good, you're improving.
> A good woman is a dead woman. A good life is a dead life. A life dead is a dead life. A good dead is a dead good.

The brief scene demonstrates how political slogans of hate and enmity finally destroy those who internalise them.

In *The Unit* the political level is, on the whole, subsumed in the personal, although the connection between private violence as characterised in the relationship between the man and woman, and public violence is inherent in the script. The concept of self-quotation is, however, at the heart of the play. Like the speakers who recur in other texts by Jurgensen, Michael looking into a mirror, sees himself as a quotation:

I don't look well. But then, what do you expect? (thinks) I wonder whether one can imitate oneself. I mean, turn oneself into an actor. After a while you couldn't just imitate any longer; you'd have stopped copying and it would be real. Enacting yourself would become a way of realising yourself.

At the height of his anguish he speaks his most climactic emotion through a quotation: "Each man kills the thing he loves," he quotes from Wilde's "Ballad of Reading Gaol." As he staggers towards the balcony he calls to Anouk:

Anouk, where *are* you? We invented love, you and I, don't you remember? Once you understood, you knew your lines, you let yourself be killed.

Although Michael's suffering is presented as genuine, one of his last impassioned cries is also a quotation, the title of an early Fassbinder film: "Love is colder than death." The play asserts that although Michael believes he and Anouk "invented love", their invention, or his part in it, was confined to the discovery of lines and phrases already embedded in the patriarchal discourse of passion. Eventually, Anouk "didn't want to play anymore." The audience might indeed imagine that Michael has also invented the figure of Anouk. Although her silence in the play challenges the patriarchal discourse through which Michael speaks, it cannot subvert it.

The high melodrama of the ending is adequately prepared, and what might have become an over-heightened text is relieved by Michael's frequent undercutting of his own solemnity, as in the anticlimax of this speech:

Love was always a kind of death, a kind of dying. I couldn't imagine it any other way. Anouk could. I couldn't. That's how it always was: big drama all round, screams, appeals, fire, threats. Our love was pretty noisy. No wonder people talked about us.

The Unit is a powerful stage piece, providing a vehicle for a bravura performance by the actor and compelling theatre for the audience.

waiting for cancer

The collection of poems called *waiting for cancer* (1985) explores language as a means of both apprehending and constructing reality and meaning. The poems together debate the possibility that language or "the word" has mystic power over matter, but challenges this with the possibility that contemporary language has been corrupted and deprived of its power to point to absolute truths. Neither the metaphysical and political implications of the debate account for the metaphysical and political implications of a feminist questioning of language which at its extreme equates with the concept of speech in the post-lapsarian world. Nevertheless, within its own parameters, *waiting for cancer* is a striking achievement, accessible to the general reader but also involved in a fairly intricate intellectual pursuit.

The ten parts of the collection are thematically self-contained, although each contributes to the overall debate about language, and their titles indicate preoccupations typical of earlier work: "object-lesson", "liebestod", "outrider", "traffic", "the splendour of the fall", "outback", "dedications", "splinters", "xenia" (epigrams), and "l'affaire d'amour".

"Object-lesson" introduces a concern touched upon in Jurgensen's poetry in German but new to his Australian work. The *Dinggedicht* or poem about the objectivity of objects — as compared with our subjective apprehension of them — exists partly to prove how difficult or even impossible it is to reproduce in art the "reality" of any thing untouched by the artist's mind and medium. Eventually such "thing-in-itself" poetry supports the theory that no reality exists outside the observer's experience. Jurgensen's "object-lesson" sequence does not attempt to assert the absolute independence of objects, and in fact uses objects like the chair, the table, the TV and the wardrobe as sites for sociological and political commentary or to revisit family history. Yet, once this is done, the individuality of the object is asserted. One of the finest examples is the opening poem, "the chair" which begins by replacing the "chairness" of the chair with a definition possible only in the discourse of semiotic and verbal literacy:

> aborted exclamation mark,
> it stands like an unnoticed sign
> typed on an unlined carpet —

But after noting that the chair "casts the alphabet/ by which three generations lived," and tracing its history in family "greed" and the need to preserve, the poem still uses the language of language, the poem to assert the independence of the chair:

> its form is coded to outlast
> all knowledge that has gone before

and truths that come to pass.

The poem "communion" recognises that the thing can only express itself:

> in every thing there is,
> native and foreign tongues
> await their self-release;

but it concludes that this "self-release" is brought about by "the miracle of speech" in which "flesh becomes the word." Unless the poet believes this, of course, poetry is impossible. But a reconciliation between the arrogance of naming in language and the enabling act of language is suggested in the title poem "object-lesson" dedicated to the writer Lolo Houbein whose short story collection *Everything is Real* was published in 1984:

> i trace the aim of your design
> with new-found patience and respect
> for all the meanings that define
> themselves, . . .

Unlike the "design" of the woman writer, the speaker says his attempt to describe and name was "reckless," and the poem shows his attempt to grasp that "the thing itself . . . is created/as one innumerable part/to which all parts are related/as wholly as a work of art." The possibility that the universe may be comprehended as a work of art that does *not* beg for the artist's shaping hand is, nevertheless, not one that the writer can maintain if he or she is to remain a writer. So the poem concludes with an echo of Browning's Andrea del Sarto who also believed that a man's reach must exceed his grasp, despite the patience and respect with which the grasp is attempted. Here the speaker discovers

> the beauty of a measured rule,
> the splendour of its craftsmanship,
> the use of a discovered tool,
> the missing word within my grip — .

Perhaps the silent break at the end of the poem is one of the most serious statements in the collection.

An interesting poem titled "dualism" engages with Kant's division of perception into "sense" and "reason" or, as the poem puts it, "truth". In Kant's metaphysics, "the world became the ghost/of thought" and lost its "truth". Kant's apriorism meant that he ruled out possibilities of becoming, and "he thus missed/the being that man is", so that only artists can restore the unity of sense perception and the creative mind:

"for what [Kant] divides/ their truth condenses./ they are the world's brides."

The last image suggests either a transcendence of gender roles or a usurpation of the feminine; more interesting is the possibility that in using the medium of language the female artist may be seeking a quite different truth from that pursued by the male writer.

The other parts of the collection grapple with less metaphysical issues, but all consistently see the world in terms of language, and language itself is the most frequent subject. "Dictionary" carries the epigraph from Theodor Adorno: "After Auschwitz, poetry can no longer be written," and all the poems assert their belief in language against this possibility. Where "dictionary" interprets the language of the prison camp as "emasculated", some might wonder if it were not the very masculinity of language that brought Auschwitz into being, but on the whole the poems struggle to express with compassion their pain, irony and longing. Language rather than "the word" appears at its purest when it is heard as a pre-Oedipal, pre-logocentric cry or call, as it occurs in the lyric "midnight" from "outback", which concludes:

> it was as if the word
> had come to set me free,
> a native spirit heard
> the call and let me be.

waiting for cancer, as it title implies, positions itself between a belief in a future benign use of language and a fear that language is cankered beyond redemption. Four lines in English titled "inquisitors' dialogue" catches up an earlier German poem called "Leda" from "Zürcher Gedichte" in the *Stationen* collection (1968):

> 'who's the young witch
> burning at the stake?'
> 'it is language
> suffering its make.'

In the German poem the ambulance arrives too late to save the witch; in *waiting for cancer* the collection as a whole suggests that if language is given proper attention it may yet be snatched from the burning.

Selected Poems 1972-1986

In 1987 the Greek-born Australian poet, Dimitris Tsaloumas, edited a volume of Jurgensen's *Selected Poems 1972-1986*. In his Introduction Tsaloumas indicated the stubborn pursuit of artistic refinement he saw in Jurgensen's poetry, and an intellectual passion balanced by an intelligence founded on a rich emotional apprehension of life. The selection points up a concern with language as one of the dominant themes of the poetry, both as a metaphysical phenomenon and as a specific problem for a bi-lingual poet. The selection also emphasises the incidence of nature in Jurgensen's poetry, although it is not the nature known to Romanticism but nature absorbed in the medium of language and inscription. Among the earliest work are found descriptions like these:

> the solitary gum
> recites a monologue
> of melting bark
>
> on the rocky silence
> lizards score
> their fiery punctuation

and in the latest and previously uncollected poems:

> the evening tide delivers letters
> sent from another continent . . .
>
> rustles in the pandanus trees pass on their code . . .
>
> the stars proclaim our calendar walking the waves
> with dolphin saints . . .

Tsaloumas intended the collection to act for the reader as an ordering device on the impetuous flow of work written over some fourteen years, so that the direction of the poetry might become clearer. Rather perhaps the selection indicates the variety and subtle adaptations and echoes recurring in the work written over these years, and the range of subjects and experience filtered through an intensely self-conscious mind. If Jurgensen's global field as a specifically political and sociological poet is less evident, it is because Tsaloumas believes that

> Jurgensen derives most of his inspiration from three main areas of experience: illness and death, love and sexual passion, and an unhappy past in curious conflict with an unsatisfactory present which, as I have already pointed out, involves the conflict of two cultures and the problem of identity.

Tsaloumas adds that there are many aspects of the human condition that interest Jurgensen, but finds in the poems centred on the themes he singled out "a greater sense of urgency and vividness of realisation." *Selected Poems 1972-1986* represents some of the best of Jurgensen's poetry in English.

The Partiality of Harbours

Two collections appeared in 1989, *The Partiality of Harbours* and *My Operas Can't Swim,* in both of which contemporary events and recollections are trapped and coded in the network of language that, for this poet, is not merely thrown over experience but is the very nature of experience. In the first poem of *The Partiality of Harbours*, titled "beirut, mon amour", the dramatic and tragic cityscape is the site of a love poem, and the opening lines state a recurrent thesis in Jurgensen's poetry:

> three a.m. the factual world is begging for release.
> our pulse recites the sentences of streets. at last we are
> no more named creatures of description. the breath of dawn
> is measured by dust, while darkness stays, shelled in the
> otherness of words...

The speaker, a poet acutely aware of the battle-torn city and its besieged people and wrapped in an intimate love affair, identifies himself and his craft with the violence:

> can poets kill with words? we watch the snipers keep their time,
> a yelping triumph's aimless repetition...
>
> what is the cause of poets? to be a traitor to the cause?
> the cause of words? or be a terrorist exploding sonnets for the
> glory of the deaf and dumb?...

Although the final stanza sees the poet a victim of this violence, there is the chance that he and his "word" finally will possess all that the city holds and suffers:

> the poet's executed, his head
> caught in the rubble; time to praise the soldier's courage.
> beyond the mountains, in the desert's split horizon, the word's
> disciples wait for the untimely miracle.

Whether the awaited "word" is Islamic or Christian or the word of any other ideology, it is also the poet's medium. The ending is ambivalent:

readers may reject or assent to the word of the poet.

The Partiality of Harbours is characterised by an idiomatic but almost classical dignity of phrase which is lyrically and dramatically impressive. The poems proceed phrase by phrase, concluding with a shapely sense of cadence not unknown in earlier work, but commonly subordinated to more energetic and impassioned statement. The title refers to the German harbour of Jurgensen's birthplace and the Danish harbour on the opposite coast. Because the images in Jurgensen's poetry are drawn from many countries and discourses, and, as was noted in his very earliest work, his concern with loss, alienation, exile and wandering is both real and metaphysical, there are few pieces that insist on being read with absolute specificity. One that might be thought to do so is "parents", describing a young boy's early memories of an ice-bound harbour in war-torn Europe, where "mum's singing in the heated kitchen" and "father is dressed in ice" and known only through "letters from the front". In the last line, however, as the mother enters the boy's bedroom which he has left open to "the snow's reckless invasion", her singing dies, and the poem ends "our love will be war." This prognosis loses its specificity immediately, since all love in Jurgensen's poetry is a site for war, including of course "love of country", which is analysed in the poem of that name. It is here that passion itself is described as a "poem of precise exclusion/ recognised by different needs." Yet Jurgensen's poems themselves, while often precise, are never exclusive. On the other hand, they are directive: there is little place for the Rorschach slot reading practice where poems are mere shapes to be interpreted by individual sensibilities. Although the fullest reading is gained after fairly wide acquaintance with his work, each poem is precise enough to stand independently. This precision and non-specificity are illustrated in "to a poet", which links this specific poet's birthplace near the border of Germany and Denmark with his present home, on the coastal margin of a nation celebrating the bicentenary of its sea invasion of a country whose native inhabitants have been both marginalised and banished to the interior:

> some are banished to the interior,
> free to mock the limits of reflection
> of those who live by margins judged in daily balance,
>
> the minutiae of radical precision,
> native residents of border towns
> who grew into a knowledge of the partiality of harbours,

> while in the certainty that redraws the horizon
> heartland's outposts vainly memorise the sea
> blown with a dry wind sailing on untimely land.
>
> our vision's skeleton will not be buried
> in unmeasured space; its crossings lines
> to mark the sovereign code, sails and keel declare the craft.

The resonant vocabulary evokes many things, yet the poem directs its readers without confining them to specific meanings. This is so even in poems commemorating known figures, from the stern but gravely understanding "demjaniuk in jerusalem" to poems to fellow artists and friends like Ingeborg Bachmann, Vincent Buckley, Brett Whiteley and Margaret Diesendorf. Even the quite specific details of "visiting the poet m.d." allow its closing lines to resonate with the echo of many lives:

> between the shut piano and the weeping willow
> i watch her train the heavy-handed hours
> into moving arches of infinity.

Poems whose precision does not impose specificity but which preclude Rorschach reading are among the most stimulating of contemporary Australian writing, and Jurgensen is one of the most prolific of our poets. His editor's hope that the *Selected Poems 1972-1986* might "tidy up the stream" of his work, although helpful at the time, has been frustrated in the long term by the quantity and diversity of these later collections. The surface tension of the passion, wit and intelligence ensures that the poems flow, but as collections *The Partiality of Harbours* and *My Operas Can't Swim* tend to break the banks of a reader's attention and inundate that market-place whose currency is not money but an eager and receptive curiosity.

My Operas Can't Swim

Yet this is the poetry of its time and place: prolific in supply, global in reference, local and regional in detail, inclusive in its intimacy but exclusive of personal interpretation. Rejecting consumerism — "consumption's poetry recited in abundance" — it supplies itself in consumerist quantity. It is also cognate with contemporary life in showing that few experiences are not invaded by voices whose ubiquitousness renders their alien intrusion familiar. An example is "the apparition", an evocative description of a drive through the old German farming district of Marburg, west of Brisbane, where the speaker sees floating in the afternoon light the apparition of a migrant child whose century-old tombstone stands in the cemetery. In another age, such a meditative piece, enriched by the intertextuality of familiar Chagall paintings, would be profoundly adequate. The observer's sensibility, and the living past and present landscapes, however, are invaded by the car and its radio:

> engine running, i watch your head escape
> past the wound-down windows, the
> every-hour-on-the-hour news,
> the old-time hits and windscreen tests of now,... .

"The apparition" is an example of the contemporary nature of the poetry in *My Operas Can't Swim*, much of which contains a similar abundance of intellectual, emotional, sensory and imaginative stimuli. The title refers to a flooding of the Brisbane River which inundated suburban homes and set afloat recordings of operas owned by the poet Val Vallis, an event commemorated in the poem "moving". As the city expands with concrete and inflated real estate values, the poem asks "where can we live but in the property of song?" Like Eliot's shards shoring the ruins of his culture in *The Waste Land*, Jurgensen's words and quotations are both monuments to and bulwarks against the invasion of a civilisation without which they would not exist. The creative effort of erecting these collections is impressive and its impact almost overshadows the shape and quality of individual poems, but the appearance of both volumes in one year facilitates public recognition of the contribution his work makes to Australian literary culture.

A Difficult Love, Break-Out

The two novella in English that Jurgensen published in 1987 under the title *A Difficult Love* are closely related to his poetry and the stage play *The Unit*. *Break-Out* is a revision of a 1977 novella which satirises the tentative liberal *frisson* felt by the bourgeoisie during the Whitlam era. Its allegorical form was clarified and heightened in the later version and its satiric edge sharpened. The four central characters are an academic environmental town-planner named Dan Winter, a real estate man, Ray, a career woman, Marion, and a housewife, Helen, who is

Ray's wife. The allegorical figures are Boredom, Heat, Success, Love, Decision, Fear and Dr Teeloeffel (Dr Teaspoon) on whose couch the patients measure out their lives. These figures interact with the characters to represent the non-material qualities of their Brisbane environment.

Dan, ironically depicted as the hero of the suburban saga, epitomises the betrayal of the Whitlam fellow-travellers. From his academic tower he has the vantage point of over-view and philosophical framework for the shaping of Australian urban life, but he wastes his substance in purveying cheap sexual excitement to the desperate housewife Helen, and in pursuing Marion with an ersatz liberal relationship which she rejects for the solid domesticity offered by Barry. The satiric and farcical Happy Century Real Estate development is immediately recognisable, but the satiric portrait of Dan's academic betrayal, although even more scathing, is less obvious, because something of the failed hero, the anti-hero, still clings to him in the narrative:

> We still have not learnt to live with nature, including our own, Dan thought. The only love we are capable of is a life-assurance, a promise to build wall-to-wall protection against the risk of natural disasters. Well, he thought, they may have called it Paradise, but we're living in a disaster area right now. I want to make love to this woman, I want to be part of this natural disaster. My need for her is real, it is not only possessive. Our love will not lead us anywhere, if not to ourselves.

The political satire was recognised by reviewers, and although Jurgensen sees *Break-Out* as a minor work, it is at least one of the few Australian political satires to parody heavy-breathing sexual encounters within an allegorical and romance framework.

A Difficult Love, together with Rosa Capiello's *O Lucky Country*, is one of the most powerfully written books about contemporary migrant experience in Australia. Like the Italian novel, its intense reaction to the Australian social environment takes it beyond realistic representation to an impressionism which is occasionally almost surrealistic. The emotional desperation of the unnamed central figure, a German lecturer at the University of Queensland, and his scathing attacks on the materialism and immaturity of middle-class and suburban Brisbane, were sympathetically recognised by many migrants and long-settled Australians. The lecturer's narrative voice is relieved by other voices contributing to the portrait of the almost voiceless doomed Amalia, a passionate, dangerous self-destructive Other whom the narrator identifies with that part of Australia and of himself with which he cannot come to terms. The central figures continue the exploration of the kind of violent male and female relationship that Jurgensen's work in English began in *the skin trade* and *The Unit*. In *A Difficult Love* it is the woman who kills herself, the wife who flees the country, and the man who survives with his new-found love, the gentle, committed and independent Ushi.

A Difficult Love is rare in Australian writing in its attempt to identify its historical, factual representation of the Queensland Government's repressive measures during the 1985 Electricity Workers' Strike with the relationship between the narrator and three women. The romance framework sends the narrator desperately seeking his Ushi in the hedonistic yet strife-torn city while he re-lives his other destructive love for Amalia. The tendency of the narrative of passion and love to frustrate the liberal thrust of the novel has been discussed in an article in *Australian Writing 1988* edited by Manfred Jurgensen and Robert Adamson, and from the feminist perspective the novel is restricted by a patriarchal ideology and discourse from which its narrator cannot free himself.

Although the tone and angle of attack do not change, there is some relief in the parts of the novel that deal with the narrator's experience in the Australian outback, and the monologue about the filming of Central Australia given by the German film-maker:

> Yes, I'm like everyone else: a European exploiting the land and taking its profits to the city. Did I not mine the Australian landscape with my camera? Who knows whether my team hasn't left scars similar to those of the multinational mining companies? Whether you drill for copper, bauxite or uranium, all mineral resources are used to create or to destroy. In the deep caves of this continent lie the seeds of transformation. We make the country speak, and this is what it says to us. My camera drilled for an expression as much in need of development and just as capable of creation or destruction. Where do the two languages meet: the land's own, making use of its people, and the people's, making use of their land?

This recognition of the problem of the arrogant or colonising property of language in any of its forms, and of its enabling property, is one of the most interesting reflections in a novel which carries a good deal of impassioned meditation.

To read *A Difficult Love* not as realism, but as intellectual impressionism, places in a better perspective the tension and heavy anguish of the narrator's attempts to analyse passion, social and private fascism, and commitment to some form of truth. The chief narrative voice is that heard in certain poems by Jurgensen, but where the brevity of the lyric is a perfect medium for this voice, the romance novella is not. The novel is, nevertheless, an important literary text to emerge from the political and social ethos of Queensland in the eighties. Its validity does not depend upon some impossible objectivity that might be ascribed to a sophisticated migrant whose natural perspective is international, but on the writer's sensitivity to the forces at work within himself and in his society. This, in fact, is the key to opening up a great deal of Jurgensen's work.

Manfred Jurgensen: Writing In German[*]

General Introduction

Manfred Jurgensen is an author and a man now equally at home in Australia and Europe. He has lived and worked on both continents. His German is as fluent as his English, and he writes both fiction and non-fiction in each of these languages. The experience gained from his travels back and forth on the physical, emotional, intellectual and perhaps even spiritual level has produced an ever-fragile but ever-onward synthesis, of great relevance to any consideration of "multicultural" or "migrant" writing (however one likes to define the term — an issue Jurgensen deals with constantly in his role as editor of the literary journal *Outrider*). Jurgensen is both the stable migrant who has settled permanently in Australia and the curious visitor who never ceases travelling — a seeming paradox reflected in all his writing. He is on the one hand the migrant who by way of a slow process of assimilation learns to gain a truer and wider appreciation of Australia than might otherwise have been possible; he is also the native-born German who gains objective distance from his 'homeland', and thus sees a different reflection than the native German who remained, or the Australian who has never visited Germany. The inner struggles of identity as well as the outwardly-expressed insights and perceptions that often result are reflected back for the reader's consideration (or thrown back by the narrative I at the author with a

---

[*] This section was written by Marga Lange

remarkable sense of irony) in virtually all of Jurgensen's numerous works.

A consistent complexity in thinking, style, subject matter, theme, setting, and characterisation dominates most of Jurgensen's academic non-fictional writing, as well as his poetry, drama and novels. Style and content in virtually all of Jurgensen's numerous works are multi-layered, multi-faceted; abounding in symbolism and subtle cross-references. His writing is thus capable of being emotionally fascinating and intellectually challenging to most readers.

Jurgensen's language is employed in service to an existential and Existentialist search for self. His writing, mirroring life, is a process of discovery about aspects of himself — the nature of his relationship with himself, his art, others, and the places he finds himself in. His perception of himself, of Australia, of Germany, of his peers, of his relationship with other people — from the most intimate levels of love between two people to the wider socio-political-economic concerns common to Western culture — are explored to varying degree in all his fictional works. There is no subject matter that is taboo to this author: his themes generally include the overall quest to define identity, objective analysis versus subjective recognition, intellectual consideration versus sensual knowing, sexual passion and social propriety, the political conservative versus the rebel, dreaming and reality, sanity and madness, language and silence, exploring and role-playing, restriction and breaking-out, the creative versus the consumerist self, self-expression and social restriction, apathy and commitment, sin and absolution, faith and despair, living and dying, wounding and healing, death and renewal, love and hate, loyalty and betrayal, presence and absence, loneliness and separation, marriage and divorce, abortion and having children, life in the suburbs contrasting with visits to exotic places, travelling and arriving, in both a literal and a metaphorical sense.

The difficulties that the narrative I experiences in reconciling such apparent contradictions create the underlying "plot" of a poem or a story in Jurgensen's writing. The protagonist willingly suffers his existential dilemma in order to achieve a more positive and meaningful relationship with himself, his partners, his society, and his places of residence. The despairs and successes of his characters are at times very personal, yet reflecting the experiences of his own generation, or even that of modern man in general. Jurgensen in most his fiction is making a passionate statement about "what is". This usually lends a sense of immediacy and emotionally moving quality to his writing, in particular his lyrical yet sharp-witted poetry. Jurgensen also frequently extrapolates, makes side-comments, or inserts long passages without dialogue, especially in the novels *Versuchsperson* and *Wehrersatz* and in the travel diary *Deutsche Reise*.

The "narrative I" of Jurgensen's fiction generally wants to arrive and belong, but paradoxically is condemned to travel constantly in order to discover who it is that wants to arrive where and why. One is constantly reminded of the "authentic" quest for self of the contemporary Existentialist author, philosopher, or psychologist. The conservative "bourgeois" mentality frequently conflicts with the rebel "outsider" mentality; being a migrant itinerant with being at home, the politics of earning a living with the desire for truthful being. The consumerist mentality is frequently contrasted with creative self-sufficiency. The desire to know oneself is often manifest through conflict with another.

The setting for Jurgensen's fiction is generally Europe or Australia; stopovers only are made elsewhere. The modern (Western) political system as experienced by the fictional characters generally forms an important part of the background of his writing, either implicitly (as in most of the poetry volumes) or explicitly (as in the novels *Wehrersatz*, *Break-Out*, and *Versuchsperson*, and the travelogue diary *Deutsche Reise)*. The Australian and German mentality, and the stereotyped as well as individualistic behaviours these countries have produced, remain a major concern of the author's, featuring prominently in Jurgensen's early play *Rückkehr ins Exil* (1964), as well as in the more recent German novel *Versuchsperson* (1986).

His German writing, like his English work, extends from academic literary criticism and critical anthologies to such diverse literary expressions as drama (*Rückkehr ins Exil*, 1963), the novel (*Wehrersatz*, 1978; *Versuchsperson*, 1986), the diary (*Deutsche Reise*, 1990), the film (*Das Gift der Heimat*, 1989), and, above all, poetry (*Stationen*, 1968; *aufenthalte*, 1969; *innere sicherheit*, 1979; *Erste Gegenwart*, 1988).

Rückkehr ins Exil

(*Return to Exile*, Department of Germanic Studies, University of Melbourne, 1964; pp.39. A play in 3 Acts, first performed on 15 July 1964 at the Union Theatre, University of Melbourne, directed by H.

Koopmann).

In spite of being Jurgensen's first, and in many ways immature, work, key themes and stylistic tendencies are already clearly present. The theme of travelling is intertwined. There are frequent references linking the quest for identity, travel, and migrants in exile here, as in Jurgensen's later works. Jurgensen's use of symbols, puns and layers of meaning is already apparent. Identity is a game, but a serious one, for Jurgensen. The themes of death (physical or metaphorical), transformation and renewal are already established in this early work. It is easy to get lost on this path, but the narrator generally maintains his sense of irony and self-awareness, so typical of Jurgensen's later novels. Lack of definition of self (in the Frischean sense, a theme most fully developed in Jurgensen's later novel *Versuchsperson*) is, if anything, a virtue.

Another typical feature of Jurgensen's writing, here as elsewhere, is that the plot is of less importance than the psychological interplay of characters. The expression of the author's ideas generally takes precedence over characterisation. The question of what is reality, what is fantasy, and the conflict of perception between the "outsider" and "society" — a key theme in Jurgensen's work — is of central importance.

A sense of critical self-irony and barbed wit, sharpened and refined in Jurgensen's later work, is already apparent in this first play. Definition of the *self* in relation to *the other* remains, as always, the overriding concern. "The other" is not only another person, but can also refer to various aspects of the same self which the author feels free to explore. This very characteristic play with identity is rather neatly summarised by the lines Byron reads out loud at the end of Act I:

> Oftmals hab ich nachts im Bette
> schon gegrübelt hin und her,
> was es denn geschadet hätte,
> wenn mein Ich ein Andrer wär.

Rückkehr ins Exil invokes a critical analysis of the "exile" of language, the "home" of the poet and playwright.

Stationen. Gedichte

This small volume(1968), like its sequence *aufenthalte*(1969), gives the overall impression of being cosmopolitan in outlook, diverse in setting, and self-reflective in nature. A variety of themes, both personal and social, are immediately evident; that Jurgensen intends the personal and concrete to reflect the greater social whole becomes clear at first reading. Jurgensen has a great capacity to appreciate his given location and experience to its fullest degree; his imaginative participation becomes indistinguishable from his creative output. All his "stopovers" in life contribute consciously to his sense of identity; the self Jurgensen is constantly constructing, modifying, and reflecting back to himself, his "Mitwelt", and his reader.

Places Jurgensen visits are not merely geographic locations, but have added significance as "stopovers" on the emotional, intellectual or spiritual level. Occasionally, they are places of alienation, disappointment, or those of no consequence in one's travels.

aufenthalte. gedichte

The first and last poems of *aufenthalte* sum up the notion of travel in the wider sense, i.e. in relation to personal and cultural identity. Thus "adresse"(7) asserts that all fixed addresses form a kind of imprisonment: the right kind of "furniture" is bought, and security is exchanged for an awareness of life and death. The final poem in *aufenthalte* carries the name of the whole volume, and its basic theme: that of the pilgrim traveller searching for his lost paradise, for a spiritual — as much as physical and emotional — home.

The hope is expressed that poetry can make some sort of contribution to the journey through life; thus the poems are described as "tracks in the sands of time".(39) The socio-political element is particularly evident.

Many of the poems in *aufenthalte* are invocations of or reflections on sexuality. Jurgensen's willingness to be sexually explicit in his writing is an ability he develops further still in the later novels *A Difficult Love* (1987) and *Versuchsperson* (1986). Like the major erotic authors analysed by Jurgensen in his authoritative work of literary criticism, *Beschwörung und Erlösung. Zur literarischen Pornografie/A Like Madness. Essays on Literary Pornography* (1985), Jurgensen never presents erotic descriptions for their own sake. His sexual references are integrated into a wider concept of Eros and identity.

Stylistically, Jurgensen's frequent use of symbolism is striking in originality. Meaning is intensified by complex and overlapping images. All of the poems in *Stationen* use some kind of rhyme; by contrast, *aufenthalte* is less traditional, using free verse as well as rhymed verse. Another difference is that *aufenthalte*, unlike *Stationen*, uses no capital letters whatsoever. Both volumes still retain traditional punctuation and an accomplished sense of rhythm. The influence of a study of the classics in literature and language, as well as contemporary lyricism, is evident in Jurgensen's style and subject matter. Not unlike the modern film-maker, Jurgensen at other times uses visual statements which rely less on verbal commentary than on a phenomenological portrayal of the direct experience of the object.

innere sicherheit

Innere sicherheit(1979) appeared a decade after *aufenthalte*. Many of Jurgensen's old themes re-emerge. The lyrical I, like modern man, is now vulnerable: "nach jahren/nackten steins/werfe ich/blätter und/falle auf/pflaster die/mich treten".(7) The double meaning of the word "pflaster" here (concrete footpath, bandaid), and the complexity of meaning created from just one pun is a characteristic feature of Jurgensen's writing.

Being a "migrant" is a state of mind, the "migrant's" homelessness parallels the ego's homelessness: "alle drei jahre ziehe ich um" (21); "verdinglichte abwesenheit /heimatboden... aale züngeln/ in fremdes salz".(42) There is some hope of "arrival" for the metaphysical traveller nevertheless: "durch den leisen dauerregen/ein gerücht von ankunft".(42) The poem "türken in flensburg" reflects the narrator's complex view of migrant worker and native German: "sie sind hier zu hause/im ausverkauften/niemandsland".(32) The lyrical I comments rather sarcastically on "geregelte verhältnisse"(27); he does not wish to be pre-defined to that extent, however painful the consequences: "gebrochen sehe ich/den ungeheilten schmerz/und gebe mich nicht/zu erkennen".(34) His true home lies within: "heimatliche landschaft/die ich in mir trage".(29)

The lyrical I feels "inwardly secure" enough to prefer any kind of passionate self-expression to a cautious conventional response. Human vulnerability, loss and pain are symbolised by nature and the frequently occurring images of bleeding and death: "gesichert verblutet deine existenz"(15).

Where there is survival, or even death, Jurgensen sees the possibility of transformation and renewal. This applies to man's spirit as much as to physical nature; the different levels of meaning support and enrich each other.

Compared to Jurgensen's earlier poems, the style in *innere sicherheit* has become simplified, pared down to essentials. Symptomatically, the titles of some poems are simply numbers. (It is more than likely, therefore, that the entire collection should be read as a unified sequence.) Symbolism, irony, puns, double meanings still abound, while all punctuation, classic harmonies and rhymes have disappeared. So has much of the earlier youthful idealism and illusion. The title of the volume carries distinctly sinister overtones: the term "innere sicherheit" denotes not only personal safety, but also the state's security and implies reference to police, intelligence officers and political censorship.

Erste Gegenwart

The themes of *Erste Gegenwart* (1989) are still recognisably those of the earlier German poetry volumes, published a decade apart. As in *innere sicherheit* (1979), and in contrast to *Stationen* (1968) and *aufenthalte* (1969), the style and statements are pared down to essentials. The use of symbolical language is still predominant, but embellishments of emotion, thought, and language are virtually absent. The new simplicity and restraint, combined with an honesty of feeling, produce a sense of understatement that can be surprisingly moving and suggestive in meaning. At other times something is stated so simply or briefly that the poetry is to be found in, or released from, the objects themselves. The poem traces the protagonist's failure to communicate in a way that produces the beauty of flowers. He is forced instead to "love the weeds" that grow in his relationship with "the other", and accept these as possible expressions of love. We now see the poet coming to terms with the art of the possible. The possibility of resolution is also the promise of a greater invisible whole. The lyrical I wants to "see" the greater reality: "frost schützt/bis ich sehe".(ii) "Home" becomes a word implying original and final metaphysical unity. It carries overtones of childhood, a lost Eden, Goethe's and the Buddhist's timeless self-sufficient satisfaction in the moment (*Augenblick*), the opposite of "travel", and the author's quest for identity in his journey through language. These are inseparable themes in *Erste Gegenwart*, and written into virtually every poem.

Paradox and ambiguity, like separation and reunion, remain an essential aspect of Jurgensen's definition of home, self, and the relationship with another. The poet has to keep travelling: "immer wieder/den äquator überqueren".(i) Implied is a secular, physical and cultural transcendence, a crossing of the borders of conditioned knowledge. In that sense his journeys are "excessive". He knows his arrivals may well be ends: "in ankunft enden", and that the light that beckons him on is also the source of his betrayals: "die sonne mein judenstern".(Ibid.) But to end in new beginnings is also an expression of hope and faith. The journey thus is a difficult one, so the sun feels cold (the seeming paradox is resolved by the inherent logic of the extended symbol): "in kalten strahlen/sucht die wintersonne/ein heimatliches wort".(iii) It is the travel of a language of knowledge.

Wehrersatz. Roman

The setting of Manfred Jurgensen's first novel(1978) is that of his first homeland: the landscape and townships of Germany and Denmark, notably the city of his birth, Flensburg, and the surrounding waters. Much of the action takes place aboard the local ship "Libelle". The chief character, a young man called Gerhard Schlicht, ferries back and forth on the "Libelle" to remain deliberately homeless. He does so to oppose his own military conscription, which he has been called upon to undertake. Gerhard, like the author, rejects the Germany of the time.

The importance of travel to identity is once again obvious. Characters changing the direction of their journey ("umsteigen") is also more than a physical gesture; Jurgensen's narrative figures (in *Versuchsperson* as much as in *Wehrersatz*) generally do so at psychologically critical turning points. References to travel are always a hidden clue to a character's true intention. It is the kind of symbolism Jurgensen delights in, and which abounds throughout this novel. Keeping on the move can be viewed as tantamount to self-exploration, or as escape from traditional duty.

Gerhard is also the narrator, and to some extent his story coincides with the personal history of the author. In an interview Jurgensen comments that a person remaining in international waters like his protagonist Gerhard would have been legally able to avoid seizure, although Gerhard's ferrying back and forth across the Danish/German fjord was a fictional creation of the author's.

The quotations selected in lieu of a preface justify moral objections to German conscription, a major theme of *Wehrersatz*. Jurgensen comments on the contradiction of Franz-Josef Strauß's public political statement — "Whosoever takes a gun into his hand again, deserves to have his hand fall off" — in relation to the fact that Strauß became Minister of Defence for West Germany soon after. Jurgensen states "it is this kind of hypocrisy that I found in West Germany I wanted to write about". The last line of the novel is implicitly political, offering the hope of a united and pacifist Europe: "Ich ging den Kai entlang, Richtung Europastraße Drei."(128) (The Epilogue of the later *Deutsche Reise* (1990) also comments retrospectively on individual behaviour, including Jurgensen's, in the context of the German political system of the time.)

In *Wehrersatz*, this political theme forms the basis of the main plot. However, the sub-plots — the relationship between Gerhard and various others — assume greater importance as both the novel and the protagonist develop further. As Gerhard discovers more about others, and experiences the consequences of how he relates to them, they function as a mirror for his own self. The existential quest for identity as the underlying theme is again revealed.

Gerhard consciously chooses to exercise his own power as an individual by challenging the power of the State (a theme even more fully developed in the later novel *Versuchsperson*, where a number of key characters are active terrorists): "Ich war mir meiner eigenmächtigen Sonderstellung als steuerhinterziehender Fahnenflüchtiger durchaus bewußt."(9) His comment illustrates Jurgensen's sense of humour, a wit informed by social politics and self-deprecation.

As Gerhard flees an anonymous intimacy with the State, his belief in, and need for, a more personal intimacy reveals itself. Significantly, his attempts to find social roots take place on land, symbolising more fixed notions of identity than when he is travelling on trains, planes or boats. He is relatively free while out at sea, out of reach of government, home and family. The hero does not dare to submit his identity to either orders (conscription by the government of the day) or offers (the manipulative wealth of Christine's family and social class).

He remains independent too in his lack of commitment to Elise, even though his relationship with her has become increasingly intimate.

Jurgensen is able to convey different degrees of intimacy and alienation. The phrase "erkennen" (recognise) is used in the sense that the Existentialist Martin Buber uses the concept "encounter", or "authentic dialogue" of one Self with the Other. Where Jurgensen employs the expression "Selbstzitate" (self-quotation) — here as throughout his poetry — alienation from self or others is usually indicated. Excessive identification with one's own point of view produces self-quotation and repetition in love. This kind of "Wiederholung" is a central theme occurring throughout Jurgensen's work. After several failed partnerships, drugs, and a suicide attempt by the protagonist of Jurgensen's later novel *Versuchsperson* these errors of communication are comprehended, and the "Versuchsperson" transforms himself, willing now to learn from women. Freedom, experimentation, transformation, the other, and the self are inextricably linked. Gerhard's plea of "conscientious objector" is finally upheld by the State: society has accepted his voluntary alternative — conscription to the service of love, his "Wehrersatz".

Versuchsperson. Roman

Versuchsperson (1986) is the first part of a trilogy which examines the nature of identity in relation to male and female sexual behaviour and role playing over the last fifty years or so. In the wake of feminism, it seemed appropriate to the author to re-define masculinity and manhood in the context of present-day Western society. (Jurgensen has published a number of books and papers on feminism.)

Part Two, *Mannesalter*, deals with middle age, and on a level beyond the individual, with the historical role of the male. *Mannesalter* shows what it means to be a male person in present society, and attempts to redefine the male protagonist so he can assume a new place in history.

Part Three, *Kinder*, is a utopian vision of the author's, by his own admission. This final book of the trilogy presents a new generation of people who have no need to define themselves in terms of sexual role play, who possess a natural and instinctive harmony. Because of the loss of tension in themselves, they have no need of violence, and are therefore able to relinquish all violence in their relationships. Jurgensen says he intended the novel to show that this way of relating can be liberating, but can also produce a certain loss of vitality. He now invokes a definition of peace where orderliness is accepted as part of life. By contrast, the earlier novels *Wehrersatz* and *Versuchsperson* portray the protagonist as opposing the dominant social order — the "Versuchsperson" is still a rebel in terms of identity, and the terrorist G. a political rebel against the government.

Yet Jurgensen remains himself somewhat the rebel. His self-expression as author includes a prerequisite need for a certain "creative tension", produced by the polarity of opposites. So the conclusion of *Kinder* remains "highly ambiguous". The style of loving by the new generation, however peaceful, is questioned for lacking that "creative tension" inherently present in the conflicts of love, however painful, as portrayed in the earlier novels.

As implied by the title, *Versuchsperson* is the attempt to discover a viable identity, rather than operate in bourgeois fashion with pre-defined types of relationships. The theme of identity is already struck with a tone of satiric irony on the first page. The conflict between individual self-expression and the attempt of authority and government to limit this is at once apparent (both are previously developed themes of Jurgensen's). The final chapter in the novel shows two homeless characters beaten to death by passing drug addicts. Jurgensen's statement is, intentionally, a frightful one. The novel shows that "not only individuals are capable of terrorism but also the State". The violence of man against man is not simply confined to something as predictable as "outsider" (homeless "drop-out") versus bureaucratic official (police), but is here extended from one type of social "drop-out" to another. It includes explicitly and implicitly domestic violence (suffering in love, which characterises the major relationships in the novel), scientific violence (the harmful nature of the laboratory experiments that Eberhard is subjected to), and political violence. The terrorist activities of G. and his German Baader-Meinhof group, planning to bomb a political meeting, are no less violent than the secret service who pursue them viciously, on behalf of a (violently) self-righteous society that would be happy to see them hang. The callous interrogations and sinister obsession with power displayed by Dr Grambauer and his group exhibit the same inherently violent nature, irrespective of means and ends. The main narrator too, commits violence against himself, in the form of a suicide attempt — although this follows the exploration into his "Menschenlabor" where he courageously attempts to study his own past relationships and personality. The protagonist at least becomes aware of the violence done to others by particular ways of relating.

The novel is written on three interacting levels, akin to sub-plots, which each develop their own internal narrative and consistency. Firstly the failure of the narrator to define himself in a meaningful way and to avoid identifying himself with one particular ego or partner produces conflicts so severe as to result in attempted suicide. Secondly, it is the story of the "Evangelienmann", or E.-van-Gelien of the German Baader-Meinhof terrorist group, and of how the State does violence to the individual by subjecting some of its opponents to highly debatable experiments, all in the name of State Security (cf. Jurgensen's poetry volume bearing the title *innere sicherheit*). Thirdly, *Versuchsperson* deals with the problem of a writer creating a persona, and doing violence to the identity of his real-fictional characters in that he is defining them for the reader. Jurgensen states that the process of creating a protagonist is a contradictory one, inherently violent as it is erotic.

In the context of modern literature, on reading *Versuchsperson* one is reminded of Max Frisch's novel *Mein Name sei Gantenbein* (English title: *A Wilderness of Mirrors*) — and Frisch has been an important figure in Jurgensen's critical writing as well as in his personal life. Both novels are constructed around a sharp-witted bantering protagonist who tries out different aspects of identity and relationships within the context of a limited socio-political framework. The authors are indulging in an existentialist kind of "perverse" playfulness, deliberately taken to frightening extremes at times. There are also connotations of Kafka, not only in the repeated use of the phrase "Urteil", but in the sense of very fragile victims being subjected to the terrors of the powers-that-be.

The theme of personal love, as well as man's love (or otherwise) for his fellow-man, is even more fully developed in *Versuchsperson* than in *Wehrersatz*. There is less literary symbolism in *Versuchsperson*. The author draws the devastating consequences of a male consciousness unable to alter its power-oriented concept of masculinity. Manfred Jurgensen says: "I wanted to write a non-sexist book". He adds that it is not easy for a man to write in this way about women, any more than it has been easy for contemporary feminist or non-feminist female writers to avoid doing occasional violence to the male character in their books. As in *Wehrersatz*, love is seen as the only meaningful survival of an individual identity. Jurgensen's novel *Versuchsperson* deals with the social politics of that love.

Deutsche Reise

Deutsche Reise (1989) is an ad hoc gathering of Jurgensen's impressions of places and events, based on a trip through Germany and Switzerland (after long periods of residence in Australia) during the months of June to July 1986, and again November 1987 to January 1988. A supplement entitled "Hier — oder Auf der anderen Seite" is written from the alternative perspective of Jurgensen having come from a life in Europe to begin another in Australia. The section begins with a flashback to his early 1961 days in Melbourne, followed by intermittent flashbacks through to the present period (1988) in Australia. The actual book was written between June 1986 and April 1988.

The Epilogue summarises his response to being born into a generation often referred to by some Anglo-Saxon historians as "Hitler's children", in a place he obviously loves, but cannot help observe critically. The distance and comparison afforded by a life in Australia has permitted the author to develop a constructive objectivity towards his old homeland. At the same time, his early education, personal ties, and constant visits to Germany have yielded an affection and insight which greatly enrich the resulting diary-travelogue. This combination provides a highly stimulating reportage, subjectively honest and offering valuable socio-political feedback. *Deutsche Reise*, apart from its publication in Switzerland as a book, has also appeared in serialised form in the German weekly *Die Woche*, Sydney.

Stylistically, *Deutsche Reise* rapidly moves from one time, person, and place to another. Given the intended spontaneity of the diary form of writing (Jurgensen also published a book on the aesthetics of the diary, *Das fiktionale Ich. Untersuchungen zum Tagebuch* [1979]), the reader should not expect outer consistency or completion, but rather a collage of images and thoughts, drawing attention at times to some essential characteristic of a particular city or event. The influence of Max Frisch's style is again evident, in this case his two *Tagebücher*. As the title implies, the book is meant as a variation of Goethe's *Italian Journey*, and like its model it attempts to characterise a people and its culture.

Deutsche Reise is probably Jurgensen's most explicitly social and political book to date. His satire is no longer concealed by symbolism (as in *Wehrersatz*), political plots (*Versuchsperson*), or alternating romantic sub-plots (*A Difficult Love* and *Versuchsperson*). Jurgensen knows that the journey he started three decades ago from Germany to Australia and back again will never be finished. He asks his reader to recognise that there is no end without a new beginning, that there can only be a "migration" in this specific sense. Above all, his frequent use of subjective narration and his preoccupation with identity emphasises Jurgensen's fundamental belief that "the personal is the political". Yet it would be a gross misunderstanding to read his paradigmatic works as fictionalised autobiography.

Diverse as ever, Manfred Jurgensen has also written the script for a film called *Das Gift der Heimat* (*Native Poison*) (1989). The title itself is a pun: it suggests that the influence of a culture is two-edged: positive in the "gifts" offered and consumed, negative in the residual "poisons" that all imperfect systems must invariably produce.

WALTER ADAMSON

Walter Adamson was born in 1911 in Königsberg, educated at a German high school and was for ten years employed in commerce. He left Germany for Italy in January 1938 and arrived in Australia in July 1939. As a migrant Adamson took on various unskilled jobs in factories. In 1944 he joined the Australian army as sergeant/interpreter for Italian. During that time he studied accountancy part-time with the Army Educational Service. After his discharge in 1947, Adamson joined an import/export company in Melbourne, but left soon after, in 1949, for South America. There Walter Adamson taught English as a second language in the British school of La Paz, Bolivia. He returned to Australia in 1953 and worked for some sixteen years as sales representative for import companies. Since 1969 Adamson has been writing full-time.

Walter Adamson is a bi-lingual writer of poetry and prose. To date, he has published three books in Germany and four in Australia: *Die Anstalt* (1974), *Ausgerechnet Australien* (1974) which grew out of the original *Das australische Einmaleins* (1973), and *The Institution* (1976, republished in 1986), *Australia Of All Places* (1984), *Adamson's Three-*

Legged World (1985), and *The Man with the Suitcase* (1989). Various short stories and occasional poems have appeared in German and Australian journals.

Of his bi-lingualism (which is not "total", two of his three books in English are translations by Sonja Delander) Adamson says he is a "violinist playing a piano". After over forty years in Australia he still finds it difficult to write spontaneously in English, even though his occasional poems and his short stories are written in that language. His German suffers from lengthy isolation; Adamson calls his German poetry "dated" — it is modelled on Rilke and other poets admired during the period of his early manhood in Germany. Adamson claims that the writings of Ernst Wiechert, Thomas Mann and Hermann Hesse influenced his development as a prose writer. Generally, he endeavours to use a non-colloquial language; by force of circumstance as well as by choice Walter Adamson prefers to use a language away from its context. He argues that his English is "more cosmopolitan than Australian".[9]

His first piece of writing was a novella crowded with landscape images: *Nidden*, a German-language reinvocation of the regional countryside of the author's youth. *Nidden* refers, of course, to the East Prussian landscape, especially to the region of the bay between what used to be East Prussia and Lithuania. Adamson wrote this lyrical narrative recollection in Melbourne during the years 1941 and 1942. It is the story of a painter who falls in love with the daughter of a famous writer — Thomas Mann had built a house at Nidden — and escapes with her from the Nazis. The author describes his first narrative as "a romantic landscape story". Like most of his German-language publications, it appeared in the *Ostpreußenblatt*, a paper for Germans banished from East Prussia (*Heimatvertriebene*). As this newspaper addresses itself to a minority of refugees whose first generation is about to die, it is fair to say that Walter Adamson's work in German has not, to date, received wide circulation or recognition.

Almost all of Adamson's poetry in German also appeared in the *Ostpreußenblatt*. It addresses itself to regional themes, such as the "Kurische Nehrung", part of the East Prussian landscape of the author's youth. Like the paper, the poems are conservative and provincial. Adamson continues to publish short stories in the *Ostpreußenblatt*.

After a reading tour in German in 1973, introducing himself to his refugee readers, Walter Adamson's *Die Anstalt* appeared in a small German edition (Bläschke Verlag). In a feature article of the Melbourne

Age the author stated that he wrote English poetry, "but could not bring himself to translate his German novel *Die Anstalt* into English".[10] Through this article he met his future translator, Sonja Delander. *Die Anstalt* became *The Institution* and was first published in 1976 by Outback Press. Delander continued to translate Adamson's short stories which began to appear in a number of Australian journals. *Ausgerechnet Australien* was published in Sonja Delander's translation as *Australia Of All Places* and became one of Hodja's educational reading titles in 1984 — Hodja (Richmond) specialised in publishing and distributing multicultural reading packages, mainly for schools. In the following year Adamson collaborated with the Melbourne designer and illustrator Stephen Pascoe, producing a slim collection of verse entitled *Adamson's Three-Legged World*. It was published by the small Abalone Press (Cheltenham, Melbourne) in 1985. During the following years Adamson published a number of short stories in little magazines such as *Access* and *Luna*. His break-through came with the republication of *The Institution* by Penguin Books in 1986 which meant that the novel had now received wide distribution in Australia, England and the United States. In December 1986 Walter Adamson was the Feature Artist of the journal *Outrider*; along with an interview of the author by his translator, the feature included four short stories and two poems as well as a critical essay on *The Institution*.[11] A collection of short stories, *The Man with the Suitcase*, was published in 1989 by Houghton Mifflin.

Adamson is the author of one play which to date remains unpublished and unperformed. It deals with a migrant who suffers a stroke and loses command of the English language. He is married to an Australian-born wife with whom he can no longer communicate. A German nurse is employed to look after the patient in a wheel-chair. Patient and nurse fall in love. Although Adamson would not offer more information about this play (indeed, even its title remains, as yet, uncertain), its plot, summarised on the basis of the author's own description, gives a clear indication of one central theme in the works of this writer: the fear of losing a language and its resulting further isolation of the migrant artist. Although Adamson has never published a play, it is worth pointing out that he did gain experience as an actor (both in English and in German) at the American Theatre and the Austrian Theatre in La Paz, Bolivia.

Adamson's literary style may be characterised as witty, entertaining and frequently anecdotal. Among his home truths, the truism of "laugh and the world will laugh with you" ranks high. Adamson believes part of the function of literature is to entertain, his main fear is to bore the reader. It is fair to say that *The Institution* is by far his greatest achievement. There is a considerable variance in the quality of Adamson's writing, both in German and in English.

Das australische Einmaleins

This first narrative account of Walter Adamson's response to Australia is characterised by linguistic weakness, stylistic awkwardness, repeated spelling mistakes and a general uneasiness in the use of the German language. The book, printed by the University Printery of Giessen, appears to be a self-publication. It is badly in need of editing, and it is not surprising that Adamson should have tried to "rescue" its publication by adding to it and re-releasing it a year later as *Ausgerechnet Australien*.

Das australische Einmaleins (*Australian Multiplication-Table*) uses a colloquial language in a socio-political vacuum — a characteristic feature of much migrant writing. Adamson writes an anecdotal, even chatty, style. This book is clearly a narrative, largely autobiographical, sketch by an author who is no longer at home in his native language. As such, *Das australische Einmaleins* is of considerable documentary value. It is as a personal document that the text has been conceived. The booklet is hardly a novel, or novella; it reads like an accumulation of episodes and anecdotes, concluding abruptly, albeit with a migrant's "happy end": marrying a native and inheriting a farm. *Das australische Einmaleins* is the printed version of a table conversation, the uneven record of a likeable raconteur.

Australia Of All Places consists of two parts, the first corresponding to the German text *Das australische Einmaleins*. Sonja Delander's translation amounts to a revision of the original manuscript: text is added, large parts are cut. The edited English version reads much tighter and appears linguistically more relaxed. Part Two of *Australia Of All Places* records the migrant's return visit to Europe, as a kind of counterbalance or counter-version to the earlier description of settlement in Australia. It is a somewhat self-conscious, witty collection of cliché situations, episodes which have been told, and written about, by many migrants of different ethnic background.[13] Adamson has introduced a strongly didactic element into his narrative. The narrative voice transforms the autobiographical author of Part One into a fictional character, while turning itself into another imaginative figure. At the same time the narrator of Part Two assumes the identity of a social and moral consciousness.

Australia Of All Places is exactly what its publisher claims it is: a record of "the experiences of a migrant settler".[14] It lacks the dimensions of fictional art, of an imaginative narrative experience. Its final paragraphs report or summarise a poetic vision the book itself is unable to provide. This evasion of a creative and imaginatively intelligent articulation of the experience of migration haunts the history of German-Australian literature. Its language states where it should realise, it reports where it should authenticate, it offers documentation where it should formulate a vision.

Adamson claims to be interested only in the "country of the mind".[15] In his novel *The Institution* he has no difficulty changing the setting from Germany to Australia as part of the work's translation into English. He simply adds a few gum trees to the (sparse) landscape to indicate a different backdrop. Plot, characterisation and theme of his writing exist almost entirely in an intellectual context. Adamson stresses that *The Institution* does not "flow from the migrant experience." (He adds that *Adamson's Three-Legged World* "...could have (been) written on the moon."[Ibid.]) We have reached a crucial aspect of migrant writing: some authors elevate or remove their themes from either country to a different dimension altogether. The experience is not imaginatively realised, but reflected upon — mostly, in what appears to be a defensive gesture, with a self-mocking humour or an ironic self-stylisation. If such a reflection grows to intellectual, moral and sociopolitical complexity, the literary work will carry considerable weight and assume its very own identity and quality. Adamson's *Australia Of All Places*, for all its entertaining virtues and stylistic ambition, never moves beyond a "good yarn". It merely reaffirms stereotype behaviour and expectations. There is too little intercultural mediation, too little intellectual (or sensual) novelty in this narrative which promises to deal with "Australia, of all places".

The Institution

Walter Adamson's *The Institution* was first written and published in German (1974); its English translation appeared in 1976 with Outback

Press and was re-released in 1986 by Penguin Books Australia. Like all parabolic novels, *The Institution* can, and should, be read at various levels. Adamson's work possesses the logic of wit, rather than of systematic thought. If his narrative is at times strongly reminiscent of Kafka, Huxley and D.M. Thomas, it is carried by a quality Germans are presumed to be lacking, not only in their literature: a humane humour of philosophical dimensions. Whatever else *The Institution* may be, it is a book as entertaining as it is disturbing. Eminently readable, it is carried by a tone of demonstrative (as opposed to didactic), yet amused concern. The voice of the narrative *persona* lures its reader into an ambiguous identification (cf. "We must be clear about that." — 37, "as we know" — 32 or "We say..." — 31), for it is not at all certain who actually tells the story, or, indeed, whether the story should be told in this particular manner. In a subtle way the reader becomes responsible for the narrative perspective, for its style and hence the nature of its statement. The 'joke' is, literally, on him; the novel's imaginative form is at the reader's expense. Adamson's wit emerges as a stylistic, structural device.

If "we" are in some way responsible for, or part of, 'the Institution', we need to know who "we" are. Throughout the novel figures introduce themselves, only to add in an almost formula-like manner: "In reality we are called something quite different".(17) We are, it would appear, both 'inmates' and 'outsiders', both 'mad' and 'sane', both 'innocent' and 'guilty' — without even knowing which is preferable. Is the world outside a safer place than 'the Institution' or vice-versa? Or could it be that, in the end, the world *is* 'the Institution'? All that can be said is that we share a questionable identity. No wonder, therefore, that mirrors are the most prized possession for the inmates of 'the Institution'. Are "we" narrators, or are "we" being told?

It is appropriate that the name of Adamson's protagonist is "Schiller". Not only does it invoke the German Classical poet and dramatist, the German verb *schillern* also conveys the idea of iridescence and change. One interesting interpretation of the novel's parabolic plot and characterisation may be derived from Schiller's own comments on language and migration, on art and identity. Considering Walter Adamson's biography — the author first came to Australia in 1939, went to South America in 1949 and returned to Australia in 1959 — the experience of a migrant writer does not seem a coincidental ingredient of the narrative's complexity. (It may also be said of the author, as of many migrants: "In reality my name is quite different." -17) In Chapter Two Schiller's response to the language of his new land is described:

> Since his emigration, he had been much concerned with his mother tongue; why heart unhappily rhymed with smart. There were many examples of this type, greatly testing the poetry of the language. And now he could add another rhyming problem to the others: why nude with rude? Or even the other way round.(8)

The "mother tongue" could not have been English, assuming that the novel's setting is Australia (the reference to "eucalyptus forest"[18] would appear to justify this assumption), yet in Adamson's native German a different rhyme pattern applies. What matters, however, is the acquisition of a new language and the need to think differently. Schiller's response to the 'foreign tongue' may be said to be that of a writer, more particularly that of a migrant writer.

> Schiller felt himself pierced by the penetrating eyes of the head physician. Right down to the bone. Rhymes with stone. A further discovery. (9)

The Institution offers an account of such discoveries. The artistic nature of Schiller's personality is of great significance, he is even called "a genius".(24) His art is music, but a music performed in silence, comparable to a literature produced in a foreign language. The music is not heard, the writing is not understood. There is no need to labour the point: Adamson's protagonist experiences the fate of an 'ethnic author' in need of translation, in search of an audience. In Sonja Delander's translation Walter Adamson has gained admission into 'the Institution' of Australian literature.

It is part of the migrant writer's frustration to feel like Schiller "The sooner I learn to live without a pencil, the better." (36-37) With the help of twins Schiller's composition is being heard. The migrant artist is "quite satisfied" with the Gemini "who seemed to enter well into the spirit of the composition".(42) It is not difficult to recognise the interpretative art of the sensitive translator. Indeed, the twin image seems particularly appropriate as an expression of faithful recreation. The German *Die Anstalt* (1974) and its English counterpart *The Institution* (1976), the author's German novella *Ausgerechnet Australien* (1974) and Sonja Delander's translation *Australia Of All Places* (1976) are literary "Gemini" in the works of this migrant writer. Walter Adamson reads and lectures to book clubs and other interested groups;

he has been writing full-time since 1969. Against such a background Schiller's performance "before the assembled community"(42) assumes a specific significance. Indeed, if there is any validity in the interpretation of Adamson's Schiller as parabolic protagonist of the migrant writer, one would expect fairly concrete references to Australia or at least a paradigmatic context which could be recognised as being applicable to Australia. It needs to be borne in mind, however, that it lies in the very nature of parables to remain open to as wide a range of application as possible. The 'Institution' represents above all an institutionalised life-style; its motto, often repeated and proudly propagated by medical staff and patients alike is "here everybody can do what he can do".(73) For European migrants that promise has been the epitome of Australia. As such, the hopes and aspirations of newcomers to this land coincided with native self-projection and social mythology. To migrant writers, too, Australia, or Australian literature, proved 'an Institution'. In it, "amateur interest had...a certain professional quality".(45) The critic Toneless appears as the personification of institutionalised art. Schiller's unexpected composition presents great challenges to 'the Institution'. Chapter Seven offers a fictionalised account of the response to 'ethnic literature' in Australia:

> "What happened last night in the common room has caused a shock epidemic."
> "Granted. After years of silence somebody has finally taken the initiative, and provided a little chamber music."(53)

Artists who are not 'natives' perform "without instruments".(54) There is threat of a "shock epidemic"(53), "the patients are becoming impatient"(55). One cannot help recognising in the awkwardness of 'the Institution's' reaction aspects of hysteria among representatives and 'defenders' of a so-called mainstream Australian literature. Yet the migrant artist asserts: "It was an experiment". His fellow-artists reply: "And you succeeded... Shall we hear more from you? I do hope so!"(48) Readers of Adamson's *The Institution* may well agree.

But it would be unwise to insist on such a reading of the narrative, all the more since its central symbol is such a two-sided reflection. In a sense, the final chapter of the novel offers its own imaginative interpretation. However, as such, it does not attempt to go beyond the paradigmatic. It could even be said that trivial thoughts or popular expressions are put into the mouth of an unnamed "man" who bears an uncanny resemblance to Schiller or who, at any rate, seems to know the personnel of 'the Institution' ("Some say the world is a madhouse", 190). Chapter Twenty-four is a curious combination of fictionalised autobiography of the protagonist and philosophical reflection. The "Gemini" are 'explained' by the fact that "he had two sisters. They were twins who so resembled one another that they could fool anybody".(192) But not everything can be explained.

> Perhaps I don't exist, he thought. There was a time once when I did not exist. That was not so far back. Sixty years, perhaps, but what are sixty years compared to the long time when I was not I? If I did not exist for so long, how did it happen that I am today?(191)

These are the thoughts of an old man waiting "for something"(190). The 'Institution' retains its significance as a reflection of existential uncertainty. It is hardly a coincidence that the old man is (also) a writer. The reader remembers Schiller's loss of a precious pencil at 'the Institution', a loss which paradoxically led to a new form of art. Now writing, composing and painting are explicitly seen as part of the same need to express the uncertain identity of man.

> On the desk top lies a whole pile of closely written sheets of paper. It was fascinating to write without knowing what he really wants to write. Writing was good. Perhaps even better than playing the piano or painting. In any case it made no less sense, even if perhaps not more.(193)

The (possible) senselessness of all art (and existence itself) leads author and reader back to 'the Institution'. Whoever "they" (194) are who come to take Adamson's protagonist away from the safety of his suburban home, they reside in the mind of the artist, in the creative consciousness of man. As such, they may be demonic beings, haunting spirits, but they are forces by which we live. They make us lose and find ourselves again. "And so it is a good thing that Prof. Longbeard's institution exists."(190)

Clearly, the narrative figures of *The Institution* are not meant to be individual characters but representative types. Adamson aims to present a pattern of human behaviour. As a result, social criticism, irony or recognisable references to recent events are an integral part of this novel. At times it could be said that certain instances of typology verge on caricature, occasionally individual comments develop into social generalisations of demonstrative validity. A figure, later introduced as "Adviser... In reality he was of course called something quite different" [like Henry Kissinger?](80), is described in the following terms: "... the man's brand of insanity was of a type which had always been considered eminently useful in politics"(71). The criticism lies in the characterisation and needs no further comment. The various names of Adamson's figures are self-revealing: Professor Longbeard is an obvious variation of the legendary literary figure Dr Bluebeard, Dr Esau is "so called because of his strong growth of hair"(6), the dwarf's name of Chimpanzee is a self-explanatory reference to monkey-like behaviour, the music critic is called Toneless for equally apparent reasons and the Gemini twins propagate their double-nature in their very name. Others are referred to by formula-like phrases or expressions, such as "Nurse Helen of (or: with) the flying cap"(60-62), described in the manner of a *leitmotiv* as "the young thing". The "full-breasted Matron" is always presented in military terms. Even minor figures, patients of the lunatic asylum briefly sketched for one appearance only, carry allegorical names ("Guinevere Whore", 56). One reason for these names lies in their immediate, if somewhat laboured humour, another, perhaps less obvious, motivation is the stylistic effect of such moral typology: it lends the novel the tone of a Miracle Play or a traditional Morality Tale. Its moral pretension appears all the more at odds with the author's real intentions of allegorical role-playing. For it is ironic that the novel's central theme deals with the uncertainty of who we are while its various characters seem to proclaim their identity in their very names. The absurdity of language's inability to do justice to the complex and contradictory nature of individual existence is demonstrated most clearly in an exchange between the dwarf and a student he meets in the 'outside' world.

"By the way, what am I to call you?"
"U. And to avoid misunderstanding: it's spelt with just the letter 'U'."
"Well, as you like. My name is Chimpanzee. In reality I am called something quite different."
"Chimpanzee? What are you really called?"
"You can also call me 'you'."(93)

Apart from the comic effect the author is aiming for an understanding of the 'institutionalised' arbitrariness or manipulation we accept as the basis of social relationships and of our experience of life in general, Adamson's humour expresses a very serious philosophical, existential concern.

There are unmistakable overtones of Schopenhauer's philosophy when Schiller tells the young nurse: "... life is only illusion."(74) And Thomas Mann's sanatorium of the Magic Mountain seems to have influenced the narrator's conviction:

> Life itself, existence, are they not illnesses themselves? The coming to life of an inorganic substance, matter goaded into life, the rebellion of basic elements let us be clear about that there is much in all that which is unhealthy. Relatively one is healthy or ill, certainly.(77)

Whoever speaks on "our" behalf in *The Institution* believes that man "is incurable even in health".(Ibid.) Adamson's novel retains this existential dimension throughout, often in statements which combine philosophical consciousness with humorous social criticism — a mixture curiously appropriate for an Australian writer. Thus the reader is told about life in the 'real' world: "Everyone practised the playing on non-existent instruments."(78) The book's final chapter reads like an authorial intrusion into the formalised and fictionalised voice of the narrator. It contains a statement which reads like the key to Adamson's own thoughts as well as to the embracing perspective of his novel: "It was in the irrational that life's reason made itself most felt."(193) This understanding is the basis of much of Adamson's humour which is also applied to the book itself. For it, too, emerges as an 'Institution', an organised, dictated and projected way of destroying and creating consciousness. The reader becomes an inmate of *The Institution* for as long as he is reading it. As Nurse Helen says of her patient: "He had a sense of humour."(5) Even though this humour can lapse into occasional overkills (cf."a very large dwarfess, the largest he had seen in his life" 29; or Dr. Esau's remark "No rest for the wicked, day and night. It's like a lunatic asylum." 24), its overwhelming function is that of enlightenment. The absurdity of existence is not merely philosophical speculation or intellectual and artistic amusement; it has expressed itself historically in crimes against humanity and is in danger of repeating itself. It is with reference to Germany's political and moral past that the narrator explains:

> When something is senseless, it can't become more so. No, it has to happen. You know, when I was young it did not have to happen. But nobody did what was necessary, although there were plenty to warn us. "Doom merchants" they were called.(75)

History is invoked with a deceptive playfulness of Reason. It is the pattern of events, the exposure of a paradigm of irrational forces which matters. Adamson does not go into concrete detail. The same applies to the prediction of another holocaust: the threatened extermination of a thousand million people within ten years (69) is presented for what it is — the insanity of criminal politicians. Yet its fictionalisation as a joke seems dangerously reckless. There comes a point where satire coincides with, or comes close to, reality. It could be argued that it is at this stage that it becomes most effective, but it is also here that it ceases to be satire. On the other hand, the cynicism of mass murder is expressed by the narrator's tongue-in-cheek casualness and black humour. Reason may reveal irrational human behaviour; the dilemma is that its demonstration does not appear to have the power to prevent it. Adamson's playing with concepts of sanity and insanity may be in the name of Reason, yet this Reason avoids any moral considerations: it, too, is 'institutionalised' logic.

Clearly, this is an important book which deserves the widest reading public. It is unmistakably European in its very conception and style. The humour is the voice of historical experience, its artistic form a rejection of all notions of aesthetic or moral realism. Adamson's *Institution is* a Beckettian 'End Game', the clownish acrobatics of a desperate knowledge. As such, it offers Australian literature a new dimension, an Absurdist direction informed by Kafka and Wittgenstein. The unique tone of the novel stems from its intellectuality and the author's ability to sustain a remarkable tour de force.

An awkward elegance? It does seem appropriate for the subject and concept of this unusual novel. It is on the level of deliberate errors and misunderstandings that Adamson's humour operates. When two Heads of State plan a world war the following logic of language applies:

"You want us to be the aggressor? That's not fair!"
"Please, don't be offensive, dear colleague."(133)

Logic is seen as a sinister game of synonyms, disguising the violence of Reason. Insanity emerges as the only escape from this kind of 'sense'. Adamson derives his black humour from, and applies it to, language. It is not just the innate ambiguity of speech his novel exploits. The author of *The Institution* is mindful of the fact that language is man-made and demonstrates its ever-increasing manipulation to the point of absurdity. "Freedom is the only thing a prisoner has," argues one of the novel's characters. "If we take away his freedom, the prison walls will drive him mad."(110) Statements such as this share their cynical logic with cold-blooded politicians whose press secretaries announce a bilateral attempt at mass destruction as "a new trade agreement...concluded to mutual satisfaction".(134) The social and political use of language, Adamson argues, is insane and, occasionally, criminal. At the same time he demonstrates his misgivings that it is in language's very nature to lend itself to exploitation and abuse. Perhaps this is the ultimate 'insanity' of *The Institution:* it is a language composition by a writer who does not trust his medium. To Adamson, language is the 'Institution' which brings about the manipulation of truth and the distortion of reality. In saying this, he knows only too well that 'truth' and 'reality' are also words, concepts of speech. A novel, then, indeed all literature, is a deliberate manipulation of language, the art of altering our perception of truth and reality. On this level, *The Institution* is a human comedy of errors as well as a humorous self-deprecation of the artist and his work. Yet it is a sign of the strength of Adamson's novel that despite such brutal, if comic, exposure it continues to convey a sense of truth and reality beyond all words. Like the German philosopher Immanuel Kant ("He and I both come from the same city",122), Königsberg-born Walter Adamson sees himself as an apostle of enlightenment who believes in the truth and the reality of the idea. The senses, language and the world conspire to confuse the meaning of life, thereby making it more enjoyable, liveable. This is the genesis of Adamson's humour: Man does not wish to live the idea of his being, he longs to express himself in a language which offers a sensuous experience of the world. The narrator of *The Institution* knows what he is saying when he addresses his readers in an act of collective identification as "we outsiders".(135) And the writer is like the director of 'the Institution', of whom it is said that he "had, from being the puppeteer, become a puppet."(137) Clearly, it is more than a casual remark when the reader is told: "we use the word paradoxically, because an important grain of truth is often dormant in a play with words".(141) Adamson's *Institution* is a play with words bearing witness to the paradox of human knowledge. Chimpanzee's proud exclamation "I am a paradox!"(173) is not only the comic highlight of a discovered identity, it is also the key to an understanding of the parabolic nature of the novel. The semi-detached manipulation of the narrative voice is an authorial intrusion of a special kind. It reads like a programmatic self-reflection of the writer Walter Adamson when Chapter Twenty-three addresses itself to the reader: "We only speak in this fashion, because this is the way they spoke outside. Are we making fun of them?"(174) Well, if "we" are, we are making fun of ourselves.

That this work deals, above all, with the nature of language, enacting its inherent ambiguities, is demonstrated one more time towards the end of the novel. The 'outside' world has suffered the fate of nuclear destruction. Confronted with this situation, the narrator declares: "Only the regular call of a wood owl was a reminder that once in the dim, distant past the word had been created."(181) Adamson's book is a "tale"(186) of the creation and uncreation of language, a parable of the migrant status of all writers — moving from philosophy to language or vice-versa. As Nurse Helen asks: "Why did you emigrate, Mr Schiller? Away from your hometown and your philosopher?" The answer may be taken quite literally: "That's a long story, my child."(124-5) — Walter Adamson's "long story" of *The Institution*.

Adamson's Three-Legged World

This collection consists of thirty poems: nonsense verses, aphoristic lines, surreal definitions and ironic nursery rhymes. Unlike his other poetry, especially in German, these intellectually and linguistically playful compositions are engagingly fresh, often bright with witty confidence and thriving on spontaneous associations. They are as far away from Adamson's early landscape poetry as possible; significantly, not a single poem is addressed to nature, the countryside or any one particular place. An unbalanced world is exposed, along with our distorted assumptions and perceptions. The reader is drawn into the critical humour of the poem. Using German and English words to rhyme for comical effect is only part of the general delight in, and simultaneous alienation from, language which makes up the character of the poem. It is easy to see that a migrant poet using a second language, acquired late in life, can be almost predestined to employing this kind of verbal wit. No word is taken for granted; words are allowed to turn their double meaning against aesthetic expectations and assumptions of reason or propriety. It would be appropriate to call Adamson's poetry a verbal cabaret.

Part of the charm of *Adamson's Three-Legged World* derives from taking things out of their usual context, indeed, isolating an object, activating it on its own or to anthropomorphise parts into independent agents. Another source of humour can be the deliberate mishandling of the poetic craft, i.e. changing a word to make up for a wrong syllable-count. Literal understandings open up new, incongruous, fantastic perspectives.

The strength of Adamson's humorous verse at its best lies in an outrageous manipulation of language, not merely changing meaning but forcing a particular reading. Most poems introduce what might be termed a "partnership" between two (or more) words, concepts or phrases and stage various exchanges, mock dialogues and distorted reflections.

There are unmistakable echoes of Joachim Ringelnatz (pseudonym of Hans Bötticher, 1833-1934) in this poetry: a similar kind of frivolous irony with moral overtones, a like brand of grotesque language and a dimension of satire may be recognised. Behind the spectacular cleverness of many of these poems lies a complexity the unsuspecting reader is invited to explore.

The Man with the Suitcase

Walter Adamson's short stories follow the same line as his longer narrative prose: they are mainly anecdotal, often recollected episodes from the past, sometimes surrealist or written from a distorted perspective. Occasionally they have the magic of fairy-tales about them ("The Old Man's Secret Talent"). Adamson's habit of seeing the individual in a universal context finds new expression in his stories. There is an almost relentless exploitation of linguistic ambiguity and tension which replaces traditional ingredients of short stories, such as characterisation and plot. Frequently it is language entertaining itself.

Adamson's first volume of selected stories appeared in 1989, containing some twenty-one narrative sketches. Like most prose by Adamson, the collection has strong autobiographical dimensions. The author's self-consciousness is such that he feels the need to explain his 'non-German sounding' name in a kind of foreword entitled 'To Whom It May Concern'.

The Man with the Suitcase contains some of Adamson's strongest work. His range of narrative style is impressive; it extends from the lyrical-reflective manner of "View From The Top" to the satirical mode of "A Trifling Error", from the grotesque tone of "Stalemate" to the surreal wit of "The Old Man's Secret Talent", from the gentle, somewhat uneasy dealing with a Jewish identity of "Shalom" or "The Revolver" to the philosophical and socio-critical treatments of the theme of time and migration, as in "The Promise", "Tobias Yesterday", "Matilda Stops Waltzing" or "Shadows In An Empty City". As always with this author, language is a central theme, as are history and death. Walter Adamson treats these topics with gentle humour and occasional poetic vision. If there is an overall sense of loss and not belonging, *The Man With The Suitcase* accepts this fate gracefully, finding that it is in the nature of things. However, such gentle knowledge and philosophical amusement does not mean that Adamson has no eye for the absurdities and criminalities of contemporary society. What Adamson's prose lacks in subtlety and complexity it regains in sheer pathos and a gesture of compassionate humane concern. Some stories are little more than intellectual-poetic impressionistic glimpses, narrative reflections, fragments of elegiac thought. Occasionally the reader may wish a somewhat more dramatic tension and direction to these stories. Having said that, it needs to be stressed that Walter Adamson's imagination, at its best, has a Swiftian slant. "A Trifling Error" revives Swift's Lilliputians as "the Giant family" who "had emigrated from their homeland...to the great Land of Dwarves".(31) It is a humorous parable of some migrants' bi-culturalism, written in the tone of a fairy-tale, with a light touch of humour and heavy didacticism. Other stories are a faithful narrative dealing with the gradual acceptance of "foreign" foods and customs during the sixties. Much of Adamson's prose is important as an illustration of recent social history.

Among his many themes exchanged or mistaken identities play a prominent role (presented most effectively in the story "Only Poodles"). Conflicts of identity are the stock-in-trade of most migrant writers, but Adamson manages to extract from it more humour, wit, tolerance and compassion than most. His almost impish wit and mischievous imagination do much to balance an otherwise heavy-handed didactic concern. Yet too often Adamson limits the impact of his stories by deflating mistrust in his own and his reader's imagination. Stylistically, he shows a tendency to succumb to colloquialisms in serious attempts to be profound. Adamson employs the narrative posture of a collective consciousness, drawing the reader into his own accounts and thereby reinforcing fixed images and concepts.

Almost all of his writings are attempts to recapitulate or to recapture moments of the past. The profound sense of loss is usually balanced by (an occasionally facile) humour. All too rarely Adamson deals with his inheritance of German culture and offers a critical assessment of Germany's recent history. He describes his own fate and the assessment of his new home, an Australia which he still can only define negatively as non-European:

The southern hemisphere, the empty bottom of the world, that dismal outpost of human habitation, swallowed us and cut us off from the wicked splendour, the goddess that bears the greatest name in human history still: EUROPA.(Ibid.)

In a way Adamson's writing could be paraphrased as a dialogue with a dead lover, friend, or fellow-countryman. It proves, among other things, that his humour is grim, a means of surviving, the ultimate acceptance that he remains unable to find a new identity. Death comes early to this author, long before the act of dying.

In one sense at least Walter Adamson is an 'existentialist' writer, a narrative voice forever exploring the nature or the (im)possibilities of existence. Not that Adamson has philosophical pretensions, despite his self-conscious identification with Kant in whose city of Königsberg he was born. What poses as philosophy in Adamson's writings is really a good-natured, humorous, humane brand of tolerance. "Perhaps" is a key-word in his language; he favours playful or comforting assumptions such as "what if?". The author knows that he (we) know(s) nothing, or very little, and that it is this absence of certainty which we share, which identifies and unites us, to a point. The reader senses that literature is the comfort of the author, a kind of verbal imaginative metaphysics or, at the very least, an entertaining, mildly amusing speculation.

Adamson's philosophical abstractions or quotations tend to render most of his prose works unspecific, irrespective of their setting. They seem to exist in a vacuum filled with the language of loss and disorientation. The reader senses the 'filter' of Adamson's nature descriptions, the intellectual and cultural 'archaeology' at work in his reflections, dialogues and invocations.

Poetry and Prose in "Das Ostpreußenblatt"

It may seem appropriate that for the German-Australian migrant writer fleeing from his native East Prussia one continuing literary life-line should be *Das Ostpreußenblatt*, a refugee paper catering for readers who have settled in West Germany but retain the ambition (to differing degree) to return to their homeland, now a part of the Soviet Union. It is by its very nature a conservative paper whose contributions, political or otherwise, are ideologically informed by its brief to keep alive the memory of a former home.

With the death of many refugees this longing to return to East Prussia has been gradually replaced by an affectionate identification with a regional culture and its history — not unlike many Australian migrants' cultural loyalty to the country of their parents (or the Anglo-Saxons' 'homeland','mother country'). Most of Adamson's poems in German are Romantic reinvocations of a lost home, or of a unified sensibility. They fit the conservative paper's context in which they appear. Adamson's main imagery is nature. A conservative, traditional, almost archaic language is employed to express alienation with the present time and place. When Adamson writes about his native Königsberg it is a city "von Zeit und Raum verlassen", a poetic "Bild, so schön und unzerstört". ("Königsberg",1976) One of his poems is entitled "Bilder"(1976); programmatically Adamson's verse seeks to revive a style of poetic realism. Poets such as Theodor Storm or Conrad Ferdinand Meyer are frequently alluded to. Not surprisingly, Adamson likes writing in strict rhyme and metre, following the pattern of German Romantic poets. He also endorses the "Unsterbliche Götter" of German Classicism("Das Licht",undated). His *Heimatlyrik* relies most heavily on the combined stylistic and thematic influence of Romanticism and Classicism.(cf."Kurische Nehrung"1975, with its strong overtones of Eichendorff). The desire to make time stand still informs most of Adamson's verse; his remembrance of things past leads to a kind of creative quotation, the attempt to statically re-write the native poetry of the past. Resignation and affirmation are balanced in a moment of composition.

Adamson's *Alterslyrik* (it seems the poet never had a different style or perspective) is preoccupied with time and the apparent absence of absolute values, either morally or spiritually. Adamson's amoral didacticism is a central feature of his verse; the poem itself is the resolution of conflict. Signs and tracks are all humankind is capable of producing and leaving behind; the poet can do no more. It is an act of complete identification with time, accepting death and the need to comfort not only the dying, but also the forces of death. Adamson's poem is traditionally a song of praise, letting language and its metric time affirm its own kind of perfection and comfort. A politically, historically identifiable concept of time lies outside the poet's interest. Instead, he follows the traditional pattern of praising the seasons. All parts of nature relating back to his childhood landscape inspire Adamson to similar acts of human identification. But the ultimate and primary purpose of these exercises remains "Das schöne Wort". (12.5.84) East Prussia is invoked as a landscape of death in four seasons. Distance is a grave: it is not that death is (still) far away, but rather that vast distances such as "Übersee" are deadly. Walter Adamson laments the loss of home, using the language of Wiechert, Hesse and the Romantics. The poet's own awareness of the archaic or "dated" nature of much of his German verse adds to it a dimension of tragic dislocation. Why does he continue to write in this vein? The answer is the same as for most bilingual, bicultural German-Australian authors: it is difficult not to fall into the pattern of stylistic retardation (to a greater or lesser extent) while living outside one's native literary culture. Adamson cheerfully addresses himself to themes of "timeless values", reflecting his continued endorsement of Classical and Romantic German styles (and values). His traditional use of rhyme further indicates that for him the world is still at one, the universe still in harmony. It is as if a dissociation of sensibility had never occurred; the words are all still there, the same old words, and they can still be trusted. Adamson's "infinity" is not the relativity of twentieth century science and technology, it is the eternity of faith, a wishful thinking of knowledge, a harmonised, aesthetisised and mythologised vision of things that no longer exist. Walter Adamson's German poetry remains apolitical throughout, it shuns social issues, indeed, the complexities of contemporary existence. It does so with the craftsmanship of an accomplished student of an art which grew out of a different life, a different time, a different culture and society.

During the 1970s Walter Adamson published twenty-one short stories in the *Ostpreußenblatt*. In addition he published a revealing autobiographical account of his native grammar school in Königsberg ("Die einzige Doppelanstalt") and a programmatic essay on language as home ("Unsere Muttersprache als Heimat").

In his essay on German as mother-tongue Adamson argues the identity of language as man's ultimate home. His native Königsberg, although close to Russia, Poland and Luthuania, did not, as he recalls, allow for multilingual and hence multicultural contacts. He is particularly interested in the situation of Germans who had to leave their country and learn a foreign language in order to survive. Adamson raises a question of fundamental importance to most migrants: "Ist man untreu, wenn man sich von dem abkehrt, das es nicht mehr gibt, nicht wiederkehrt?"(24.12.77;11) In contrast to his poetry he accepts the loss of his first home, the past as past, the finality of historical events. But he is comforted by the knowledge that each individual life is a totality, and as such continues to include things that no longer prevail. He recognises the deadliness of trying to hold on to what is gone forever. His essay affirms the individual property of language, a personal identification, the authenticity of a "first" or "mother-tongue" ("in der ersten, der Muttersprache", Ibid.) which will remain an inseparable part of us to the end. Revealingly, he claims that despite his daily use of English, despite his Australian-born wife and despite his bilingual writing, German for him expresses "das· Ureigene, das Unveräußerliche,...eine von Zeit und Raum abgesonderte, unantastbare Heimat...".(Ibid.) It is Adamson's belief in a mother-tongue beyond the limits of time and space, a German which has stopped developing, growing and changing in response to complex historical, sociopolitical circumstances, which leads him to write in an elegiac, archaic, curiously outdated (not at all "timeless") style.

The task of mediating between languages remains a central preoccupation of this 'multicultural' author. How can "truth" be ascertained in words that at best remain approximations? Almost all of his own writing has been subjected to translation, with remarkable effects. An appointment as court interpreter leads him to realise the enormity of his responsibility. He discovers that "die Wahrheit im Wort und das Wort tief in der Sprache, nur in der eigenen Sprache verwurzelt ist".(Ibid.) His story "Der Dolmetscher" covers a key experience of his bilingual writing and his own activities as a translator.

Imprisonment and freedom correlate in the migrant artist's adoption of a new country; the escape from suppression is tempered by a sense of loss. Cultural predefinition can have a crippling effect on the attempt to develop as a writer in a different language. Adamson lends each narrative in German and in English a distinctively unique flavour, a character closely determined by language and its sociopolitical culture. It would be a valuable exercise to carry out a detailed analysis of Adamson's (and other bilingual authors') prose transliterations. Adamson's dialogues are all 'Ich's coming alive in language, bearing witness to the contradictory authenticity of a bilingual, bicultural writer in Australia. He makes specific reference to a continuing German longing for the exotic which can be in conflict with moral responsibilities, turning transformation into escape. Another recurring motive is the relationship between age and art. The author has no answer regarding art's relationship to time. He merely asks which is ultimately more real and important — and he accepts his own passing. Adamson's attitude to age, death and art is characterised by gentle questioning and graceful acceptance. He finds meaning in artistic consciousness, even playfulness, rather than historical knowledge. Like Hesse, one of his models, his prose seeks to teach, to comfort and to inspire.

Of Walter Adamson's German short stories published during the eighties almost half have been translated into English and have appeared in various anthologies, journals and collections in Australia. They include "Der Dorftrottel"(21.3.81; "The Art Critic"),"Das Versprechen"(2.5.81; "The Promise"), "Das Geheimnis des alten Mannes"(7.8.82; "The Old Man's Secret Talent"), "Es sind ja nur Pudel"(11.1.86; "Only Poodles") and "Tobias Gestern" (3.5.86; "Tobias Yesterday"). His *Ostpreußenblatt* publications include travelogues and personal reminiscences. Adamson's response to Germany is tellingly ambiguous. It appears to him like a well-oiled machine, a country difficult to fault. Yet there is an underlying disquiet in comments such as "Soviel Perfektion ist beinahe beängstigend."(Ibid.) In this society of perfection, affluence and stability he notices "Gesichter" which seem to be "zu ernst". And he wonders: "Streß? Womöglich Angst? Wovor?"(Ibid.) Committing more than a stylistic faux pas he characterises Germany thus: "Es geht über alles, über alles, was wir bisher in Europa gesehen."(Ibid.)

In a literary essay dealing with Germany's past, ("Im Namen der Vergangenheit",13.3.82) written by an exiled author of part-Jewish background, Adamson avoids and evades a direct and more complex reflection of Nazi Germany. He is aware of the enormity of such an omission — and of its artificiality. It is, indeed, a literary 'trick', a device of narrative structure, relating his personal past in Königsberg and his non-involvement with Germany's Nazi legacy to a work of art. Political consciousness is transformed into personal reminiscence. The migrant writer Walter Adamson is not prepared to confront German Nazism more directly. He describes himself as someone who survived the end of *his* world at the end of *the* world, "einer, der am Ende der Welt das Ende seiner Welt überlebte."(Ibid.) He now worries about the ultimate holocaust, the end of the world, the destruction of the planet. The writer of the past directs himself to a collective future of mankind "im Namen der Vergangenheit". Walter Adamson's short stories in German convey the author's central idea that all art is a form of memory, the attempt to recapture a time and a language lost to another time and language.

Fairy-tales remain an important formal vehicle of this author's thoughts about time, home, identity and reality. Walter Adamson knows how to use the inherent wit and irony of the fairy-tale in an almost Swiftian manner. In many of his short stories there is a sense of imprisonment, his protagonists are often perceived as captives of time and place.

If Walter Adamson has an embracing philosophy, it is this act of keeping alive, or giving birth to, something worthy of seeing the "light" of time, history and eternity. As he says in "Gedanken aus Übersee"(1973), we have all become existentialists, living for the moment. Adamson's antidote to an indulgent memory is a commitment to live in the here and now and a belief in what he terms natural resurrection.

It is in this context that the author admits: "Heimat, was ist das für ein fremdartiges Wort!"(1986). He is determined to partake in a personal resurrection, as natural as the seasons. The Tolstoy allusion is more pronounced toward the end of his story "Wie einer es erfuhr..." where even a reverse order of seasons cannot negate his vision of spiritual rebirth: "Ostern. Gibt es auch für mich hier diese Auferstehung aus der Trauer um Verlorenes...". It is a wish expressed with the fervour of a prayer. Walter Adamson's German prose may indeed be seen in such terms, as a rising above losses and a commitment to regrowth, regeneration and rebirth.

WALTER BILLETER

Born in Sierre (Switzerland) in 1943, Walter Billeter emigrated to Australia in 1966. He is best known for his literary translations of German writers, especially Paul Celan and Konrad Bayer. Billeter lives in Melbourne, where in 1974 he co-founded with John Jenkins the literary magazine *etymspheres* and later edited the *Papercastle Mimeographs* series. In 1977 he co-edited with Kris Hemensley and Robert Kenny the anthology *3 blind mice*. Billeter published *Sediments of Seclusion* (poetry, 1973), *Dreamrobe Embroideries & Asparagus for Dinner* (with John Jenkins, 1974), *Australian Novemberies* (prose, 1978) and *Radiotalk: 10 Pieces for magnetic tape* (1980).

Etymspheres was dedicated to new writing, including both

theoretical and practical aspects. The mimeographed magazine bore the subtitle "The Journal from the Paper Castle". Its first issue included Paul Celan's *Meridian*, three essays on prose forms by Arno Schmidt, work by Bernhard Noel, Paul Buck, Kris Hemensley, Bruce Beaver, David Miller and others. The following issue featured a survey of English publications by Kris Hemensley, prose by Walter Billeter, and essays and reviews by Finola Moorhead, John Jenkins, David Miller and others. Still in 1974, an anthology "hovering around the roots and branches of surrealism" appeared as *etymspheres* 2/1; it bore the title *Dreamrobe Embroideries & Asparagus for Dinner*. The collection brought together contemporary and avant-garde work by European and Australian writers, but it also included translations of Ludwig Tieck. Among the authors represented were Hans Arp, Okopenko, Beltrametti, Middleton, Tranter, Jenkins, Maiden, Hemensley and Krausmann. *etymspheres* was conceived as appearing in two concurrently running series, one a journal, the other an anthology.

Not surprisingly, Walter Billeter describes himself as neither a European nor an Australian writer. He attaches himself to what he calls a "personal canon" and a small group of (international) writers. Billeter is passionately against monocultures of any kind, and advocates compulsory language learning. (His wife is a Greek-Australian actively involved in a bilingual programme in Melbourne.) It is from personal experience that the Billeters claim that bilingualism is achievable by children in fourth grade, with a subsequent maintenance of proficiency in two languages. Walter Billeter's Swiss background means that multilingualism could be taken for granted. He is particularly sound-sensitive and is especially interested in sound compositions. Contemporary music serves as immediate inspiration to his own work. Billeter attempts to transform musical composition into the structure of his writing.

His editorial work with various journals and anthologies must be understood as experimental work in a kind of literary laboratory. In Billeter's translations the personality of the author is vital. Paul Celan touched Billeter most deeply. It is easy to see why Celan's individuality and work should be so attractive to Billeter. A clear separation between poetic theory and practice is impossible or nonsensical in the writings of Paul Celan. In particular, Celan called for what Walter Benjamin termed "translatability", an integration and congenial transformation or transliteration of one artistic language into another. Walter Billeter's work consists largely of such "translations".

It is therefore a programmatic attempt at cultural mediation. If there is some contradiction in Billeter's position as a German/Australian literary mediator, it is that he rejects commercial publishing, thereby limiting the effectiveness of his activities.

Billeter's *Paul Celan Prose Writings & Selected Poems* offers bio-bibliographical notes as well as a list of English translations of Celan's work (up to 1977). It includes Celan's Büchner Prize speech "The Meridian" and his "Edga Jené and the Dream of the Dream" (translated by Jerry Glenn). An understanding of Celan's poetics is an essential prerequisite for an intelligent reading of Walter Billeter's poetry and his concept of literary translation. Celan's statement "Art, you remember, is a puppet-like, iambic-pentametrical and...childless being" ("The Meridian",27) does much to explain the aims of Billeter's literary art. His collection *Sediments of Seclusion* (1973) seeks to eliminate metaphorical writing; in its very literal quality the language progresses on its own terms. Language is perceived as a construction, a self-reliant composition creating its own absolute "reality" or "being". Arno Schmidt's works are acknowledged as a considerable contribution to a new language; they form part of what makes Billeter's own style. In Walter Billeter's poetry and prose the migrant writer's obsession with language leads to an absolute realm of words, a verbal culture of total *Versprachlichung*. Mediation is not between two "mainstreams" of literature, but a transformation of avant-garde language into its intrinsic self-existence, in relation only to itself, even in translation. Language to Billeter is the unrestricted oneness which is also its otherness. It does not express or convey anything other than itself.

In his recording "Words & Sounds of the Australian Landscape" (ABC, January 1988) Billeter aims to end surface meanings; the sound composition was written against "meaning". Contrary to expectations, emotions actually increase with a loss of predefined meanings. The "words" and "sounds" are not illustrations of a landscape; they are themselves a verbal countryside of constitutive character. It is clear that Billeter uses layers of recordings, often employing techniques of "blotting out", resulting in a phonemic construction of haunting (and occasionally musical) quality. Not surprisingly, Billeter lists Helmut Heissenbüttel, Günter Grass and Thomas Brasch among his German influences, along with Ludwig Hohl, Robert Walser and Peter Bichsel (his Swiss-German references) and the Romantics Ludwig Tieck and Arthur Schopenhauer. Jean Paul, too, serves as early model. Needless to say, the entire Vienna Group (*Wiener Schule*) of linguistic philosophers and artists remains a constant point of reference. In Australian literature, the strong influence of Kris Hemensley is unmistakable, as are the writings and personalities of Laurie Duncan and John Tranter. Billeter's "Words & Sounds" could have been called, in the words of another Australian poet (Barry O'Donohue), an "Addiction to False Landscapes". Sociologically, this language of verbal totality can be explained not as a multilingual migrant writer's identification with a different society or a new culture, but as an identity escaping into compositions of speech. Billeter is not at home in one language or another, his being resides in the very nature of tongues. The author "migrates" into continents of words where he settles as experimental verbal architect. It is in the structure of language that Billeter's poetry and literary art resides. Much of his work is made up of sound compositions, with contemporary music a strong influence on his own verbal constructions. Few Australian poets have been so explicitly sound-sensitive as Walter Billeter.

1984 saw the first performance of Billeter's *European Carousel*, a composition made up of "nine postcards from Europe", dedicated to Kris Hemensley. The work consists of an interaction between two projections, of the cards and of their text. The text itself exists in two related forms: on tape and in type. The readings are strongly influenced by the German prose of Arno Schmidt and Rolf Dieter Brinkmann. Billeter's text consists of his own reactions to Switzerland, in particular of his responses to postcards.

His early *Sediments of Seclusion* ends with an elegy reaffirming Billeter's anti-metaphorical style. *Australian Novemberies* (1978) is a prose piece basically derived from the *Age* newspaper during November 1975, the *Encyclopaedia Britannica* article on Australia, passages from history books concerning events that have taken place in November, etc. The text treats this material in a number of ways, ranging from collage, fictions, variations to cut-ups and fold-ins. *Australian Novemberies* is a special brand of political writing: it is not the content which problematises certain issues. Billeter employs devices of traditional narrative, adding to it interrelated material. By phonic or other means of verbal sound the author "alienates" reading expectations; the text begins to question itself. There are two "characters" or voices: Finnegan (taken from Joyce's novel *Finnegan's Wake*) and Pamphlet. The prose fiction leads to newspaper material and vice versa, creating "versions" of the model. Billeter then typed the text on A3 pages and cut them into twelve squares, thereby composing rows from one to twelve, leaving out certain rows etc. Through "fold-ins" a new text is produced. Billeter's manipulation of documentary and fictional texts leads to what the author calls a "dialectic text", alluding to a synthesis of verbal authenticity. This wilful style can be interpreted as a formal protest against what Walter Billeter perceives as weaknesses in contemporary German political writing. His highly eclectic translations from German literature relate primarily to more or less "eccentric", manneristic authors who do not represent the "mainstream" of contemporary writing. (It is highly revealing that Walter Billeter should attempt to create a narrative *roadie* film, moving language to unfamiliar places, never allowing meaning to settle.)

Like Rudi Krausmann, whose *Everyman. A Sentence Situation* Billeter's "paper castle mimeographs" first published, the author's obsession with language is a curious contradiction: it mistrusts its medium so profoundly that this very volatility makes for its own kind of creativity. Translated into the position of a migrant writer in Australia, this leaves Walter Billeter in a state of permanent, albeit "creative", alienation. The author does not settle. There is more than humour in the title of Billeter's, Hemensley's and Kenny's anthology *3 blind mice*. The authors themselves remain experimental animals, inseparable from the matter under analysis, language beings testing themselves along with their tool. In hindsight, there can be little doubt that this collaboration was responsible for one of the most innovative, exciting and impressive literary anthologies ever published in this country. Sadly, Walter Billeter's contribution limited itself to translations of Celan, Bisinger and Becker. They are important and authoritative translations, but there is no explicit "statement" or direct articulation of Billeter's own concepts and aims. All the reader learns is that Billeter has his "feet in Australia/head in the world" and "wouldn't have it otherwise" (8) — a tantalising approximation of the writer's more complex position.

What then is Walter Billeter's contribution to Australian literature? In the first instance he is undoubtedly a great mediator between German-language and Australian avant-garde literature. His introductions to the writings of Konrad Bayer (*The Head of Vitus Bering* and *the philosopher's stone*, Westgarth 1979, pp.53-63), Paul Celan (*etymspheres*, Melbourne 1974ff), Gerald Bisinger and Jürgen Becker (*3 blind mice*, pp.130-164), Arno Schmidt, Hans Arp and Ludwig Tieck (*etymspheres,* op.cit.) are major contributions to the area of German-Australian literary relations. In addition, Billeter has published "Notes on some German Writings since 1950" (*Ear in a Wheatfield* 17 [Autumn 1976],pp.80-94 and *The Merri Creek or Nero*, Melbourne 1977, no pagination ["Personal Experience and Social Perspectives"]), discussing works by Konrad Bayer, Peter Bichsel, Horst Bienek, Johannes Bobrowski, Paul Celan, Erich Fried, Eugen Gomringer, Andreas Okopenko, Heinz Piontek, Arno Schmidt, Wolf Wondratschek, Rolf Dieter Brinkmann, Jürgen Becker, Hans Magnus Enzensberger and a variety of German literary anthologies and books of criticism. Despite such apparent involvement with contemporary German letters, Billeter claims: "...apart from translation which covers a substantial part of my activities, I've got very little to do with German literature (that is, apart from reading and studying it). My stance is somewhat opener than that...".[17] By his own definition, then, Walter Billeter is a language or sound composer of Swiss-German background whose translations and mediation serve to throw light on his verbal constructions. Billeter's writing is characterised by a poetic thought that will not allow a narrow differentiation between theory and practice, poetology and art. It is a literature reflecting upon and relating to itself. Like Celan's work, Walter Billeter's writing is meditative rather than theoretical. His main achievements in the context of an Australian literature lie in sound compositions, of which "CONTEMPA FIELDS"(1973), "hurmus"(1977-84), "HUMBUG"(1981), "This stillness" (1987), "It is so quiet here" (1987) and "Xenophony" [Part Two of "Radiotalk"] (1977-84) are perhaps the strongest. These sound pieces may have been influenced to some extent by H.G. Helms' *Fa:m Ahwesgwow*, but Billeter acknowledges it "more as a knowledge that it was feasible to do such things".(Letter to M.J., op.cit.) In *Australian Novemberies* he offers the following equation:

> Australia is a verbal situation in political distress. It is also a political situation in verbal distress. Even a verbal situation in verbal distress. But it is not a political situation in political distress.

He explains that he came to know Australia through books, but he truly discovered it

> through the people & their media — it was their language which enabled me to write this text & demonstrate some of its possibilities. If only they listened! They might hear.

There can be no doubt that Billeter's work is directed towards Australia; it sees itself as part of an Australian literature. The quotation acknowledges his isolation ("If only they listened!"), but it is an isolation relative to the position of the avant-garde writer, irrespective of the culture he is working in. Billeter's sound score *Contempafields* was performed several times during the seventies, although it did not get published. He also read poetry from *Sediments* to improvised music. Writing about himself in 1977, Walter Billeter states: "his close attachment to contemporary music is well known to intimate friends, though apart from musical schema in *Sediments* has yet to surface overtly in his writings."(*The Merri Creek Or Nero*, op. cit.) It is in the area of sound compositions and language constructions that Billeter's main contribution lies.

Rudi Krausmann

Like Margaret Diesendorf, Rudi Krausmann is of Austrian birth. His emigration to Australia was somewhat reluctant. Born in Mauerkirchen in 1933, Krausmann first came to Australia in the late fifties (1958) and returned to Europe on three different occasions: in 1960 to Salzburg (where in 1962 he briefly worked as a journalist at the *Salzburger Nachrichten* [Lokalredaktion]), in 1964 to both Salzburg and Vienna and in 1972 to Berlin. Krausmann's mother was from Berlin, his father from Mauerkirchen. A knowledge of this personal background of the writer's family may help appreciate the characteristic style and preoccupations of his work. It is important to realise that the general information published in his collections that "Rudi Krausmann came to Australia in 1966"[18] is incorrect. In the light of the writer's various stops and starts it seems significant that he actually began his publication in Australia with a little-known novel *Die Erfolglosen*, published in serialised form in the German-language ethnic paper *Die Neue Welt* in Melbourne. It may be a startling revelation to many of Krausmann's readers that this author has in fact kept a thirty-year diary written in German, inspired, as he suggests, by Ernst Jünger. He seems to have started with his entries around 1960; they cover the local art scene, meetings, reflections and personal responses to his life in Australia or while travelling. Even more surprising is the revelation by the author that almost all of his English poems were first written in German — often a very long time ago. It appears that Krausmann makes selections from poems collected in manuscript book form. Certain poems seem to him more appropriate for translation into

English than others; no doubt his choice is not determined by linguistic deliberations alone. Krausmann has an acute sense of the artistic 'scene' at a particular time and in a specific place. He appears to harbour few illusions about the nature of his literary 'exile' in Sydney, and occasionally it may seem that he has resigned himself to an 'irrelevancy'. Needless to say, there is a great deal of Austrian self-irony and self-negation in such projection, which as a cultural conditioning is much more than a mere pose. At other times Krausmann can be seen at the forefront of artistic activity, acting almost as his own impresario. The Salzburg/Berlin axis continues to assert itself.

As editor of the (now defunct) magazine *Aspect*, a journal devoted to art and literature, Rudi Krausmann has made a substantial contribution to the artistic and literary life on a national scale. Indeed, one of the features of this magazine was to draw European writers or artists into a dialogue with their Australian counterparts. This laudable editorial policy did not always succeed, yet there can be no denying that *Aspect* did create a broader awareness of world literature in a literary community which continued to be parochial and cliquy. *Aspect* began its quarterly publication in 1975 and appeared on a regular basis for almost a decade. Fine arts has always exercised a very strong influence upon this writer, as witnessed by his many poems (and interviews) dealing with painters and their work. Curiously, music never had a similar hold over Krausmann, despite his Salzburg connection. As he says in his *Description Of A Voyage*,

Musical phrases were served for the tourists at the religious walls.[19]

Occasionally one senses a certain lack of musical quality in some of Krausmann's verse, but this may well be the result of his continuing translation(s). He explains some of his literary abstractions as the expression, or the consequence of a cultural exile. Like a painter, Krausmann needs to write in (seeming) 'abstractions'; much of his poetry and language compositions are "gegenstandslos", i.e. 'without object' or 'devoid of application'. It is the expression of a language which itself is in exile; it cannot address itself to a native sensibility.

The titles of his main collections of poetry may indicate the sense of isolation and uneasiness which continues to dominate the work of Rudi Krausmann: *From another shore* (prose poems by Krausmann, drawings by Brett Whiteley, published in 1975, and among the strongest of his works), *Paradox* (poems by Rudi Krausmann, illustrations by Lorraine Krausmann, his former wife who is a graduate of Fine Arts, published in 1981) and *Flowers of Emptiness* (published in 1982 with a cover by David Aspden and including Concrete Poems "taken from a series of silkscreens entitled *Night Poems* exhibited at Hogarth Galleries, Sydney, in 1974"[20]). These are not the titles of a native voice.

Realities(1984) is a longish poem written entirely in German and translated as and when the occasion arose.[21] Again, the title may convey almost programmatic implications. All that is left of the original German in the poem's final version is a (badly misspelled) quotation from Friedrich Nietzsche, a quotation which goes a long way to describe Rudi Krausmann's themes and fears:

> Das Eis, das heute noch trägt, ist schon
> sehr dünn geworden. Der Tauwind weht, wir
> selbst, wir Heimatlosen sind etwas, das
> Eis und andere allzu dünne Realitäten aufbricht.

This poet sees himself as part of a group of "Heimatlose"; homeless not only in the sense of having lost, or left behind, a so-called 'homeland', but of being exiled by the 'realities' of life itself. Krausmann's poems are unmistakably Germanic; their philosophy or 'abstractions' often lead to expressions as startling as they are awkward: "behind airtight doors/reality narrowed". 'Reality' to this poet in exile has become a "pantomime" which may linger on the tongue, but cannot be spoken or made authentic. It is the exiled bi-cultural poet who proclaims, paradoxically, that "the new silence/has few listeners". Krausmann's poetry operates on the level of an all-embracing *Kulturkritik*: that is its strength and its weakness. German-language poetry very often is a translation of thought into language (or vice versa). As a result, especially in a further translation of such poetic translation, images and phrases can occur which, to others, may lack the very quality of poetry: "instead of the family photo/progress is framed". Yet the same style of writing is responsible for lines such as "in the New Year/the sea has withdrawn/and fish have designed sayings/on the sand".

It is part of this exiled language that it has little trouble employing terms such as 'truth' (not only in *Realities* but also in the very opening of *From another shore*), 'the soul', 'beauty', 'hope' and 'dreams'. Krausmann uses them philosophically, as terms of an essentially intellectual aesthetics, the heritage of a German concept of literature. Added to this, however, the poet makes extensive use of surrealist images — it is no coincidence that he likes his work to be accompanied (rather than 'illustrated') by drawings, to be contextualised in a broader composition of 'fine arts'. "Hope sweeps over the streets/against sober eyes": there is also, occasionally, the influence of Gottfried Benn's *Zivilisationslyrik* (Benn is the poet whom Krausmann acknowledges as one of his models and on whom he has written a revealing poem, *In Memoriam Gottfried Benn* [in *Flowers of Emptiness*]). Krausmann's 'Realities', poetic or otherwise, do suffer from the syndrome of 'genetive-metaphors', not often enough to affect the overall authenticity and compositional integrity of his work, but mostly as an irritant which may well be an inseparable part of this kind of writing.

Perhaps one way of describing Krausmann's poetry is that it employs, or seeks to employ, 'vertical' words, language and images "passing through...the zenith", which hold "position directly above (a) given place or point".[22] There can be no doubt that Krausmann's 'vertical' words authentically verify a cultural crisis the poet has transported into the Antipodes. The profoundly un-Australian quality of Krausmann's poetry is a language which has long since learnt to distrust itself. Australia is 'unequipped' for the language of abstraction, the desperate articulations of 'exile' as presented by Rudi Krausmann. His *Realities* do not come to terms with the reality of Australia. He transports and translates European post-fascist aesthetic and political preoccupations of Austrian/German literary culture into an environment where its language appoints its own 'exile'. It is revealing how often Krausmann employs the term — another genetive-metaphor — "of emptiness" in his imported writing. His (hitherto latest) collection *Flowers of Emptiness* (1982) expresses it most categorically; but his poem *Realities* also speaks of "the leaves of emptiness" — which "fall" (of course) "and love/is illusion in cross-section". This is the 'poetic' language of the European *salon* or *café-house*, the 'intellectual' discourse of the literary avant-garde — half a century or so ago. There is far too much of "a deep-frozen noon" in Krausmann's 'European' *Zivilisationsekel*. As he admits, he does have "abstraction on (his) fingertips". This exiled poet still "speaks", still "meets", but he appears to be unwilling or unable to confront the landscape and the ruin other than in a language which itself — translated or not — has been landscaped and ruined.

From another shore (1975) is a collection of what could best be described as prose poems. The literary form itself was, and has remained, less than popular with Australian writers. Krausmann's volume is made up of three parts: I Day, Night, To A Muse and Conquests; II Description Of A Voyage, Season Below Zero, Ways of Exile and The Fish and III From Another Shore. The book, wrongly announced as "prose"[24], is modelled on work of the French (West Indies) poet Saint-John Perse; it opens with a quotation from *Vents* (published some 30 years prior to Krausmann's collection). It is part of Krausmann's contradictory or paradoxical situation that he can quote from a French work which affirms poetry's power and its destiny to draw upon all forms of knowledge: psychoanalysis, history, phenomenology, autobiography. "It is perhaps the one art of synthesis able to show at moments of intense illumination the once-complete form of our shattered world."[25] For Krausmann writes against this very concept of faith.

The book is characterised by a radical determination and an intellectual energy which articulate themselves as a veritable onslaught against the reader. Jacques Hardre explains: "By considering words as images having an autonomous life of their own and by bringing together word-images of widely removed species, the surrealist poet creates new images of a remarkable ignascent quality. This, rather than the use of metaphors, or other figures of rhetoric, is the basis of surrealist imagery."[26] His definition may help in a proper assessment of much of Rudi Krausmann's prose poetry in this collection. Added to such surrealist imagery, a Germanic philosophical abstraction (with a rhetoric of its own) characterises the writer's language. "Courageous ideas decayed in the air."(42) It is a poetry of non-realisation, imaginative rhetoric, the gesture of words. Occasionally the exotic quality of the language is indistinguishable from the awkwardness of translation: "Once the voyages were festivities in front of the foreheads."(Ibid.)

It makes interesting reading to compare Les A. Murray's "Exile Prolonged by Real Reasons"[27] with Rudi Krausmann's "Ways of Exile". Krausmann is undoubtedly right in declaring "Poems are not made to fill the gaps of civilisation."(Ibid.) But these are insights Europe, and in particular German culture, arrived at after the Holocaust and the Second World War.

From another shore refers back to Krausmann's return to Australia in 1965 and was written (translated or completed) on Scotland Island. The poet describes this journey as "a voyage into nothingness which demanded adventure from the impossible walls".(55) It seems that his alienation had reached a point of ultimate crisis. Unable (or unwilling) to live in either Europe or Australia, he found himself on an island made of words which did not communicate. The suffering over such isolation is unmistakable. Physically and intellectually, but above all artistically, there can be no return. Thoughts cannot be unthought, even where their urgency may not (yet) be felt.

Krausmann has not stopped writing; he has instead continued to isolate himself or allowed himself to become isolated by his language. Rudi Krausmann remains on his island between the shores, refusing to accept either one as 'home'. *From another shore* constitutes the philosophical, aesthetic and socio-political protocol of a writer who lost his language and in translation found that it was not worth having. Words 'translate' and 'abuse' each other. A vast verbal construction collapses as it mocks its own scaffolding.

In 1977 the short-lived Makar Press Brisbane published Rudi Krausmann's *The Water Lily and other poems*. The title-poem of this collection reappears in the later volume entitled *Flowers of Emptiness*. It is indeed a key to Krausmann's self-concept as a poet, an excellent poem worthy of being republished and anthologised. It is written in a style of negative affirmation characteristic of most of Krausmann's poetry which should not be mistaken for rhetoric. The dialectic may occasionally wear thin; often it carries a powerful impact. Austrians generally have a penchant for finding nothing more exciting than boredom — it promises limitless possibilities. So it is that "a 'poetry that does not matter'" is in fact "the absolute luxury". Only 'boring' poetry can be luxuriously exciting. The poet can choose "between/sand & sand/water & water/or/dust & art".

Krausmann is at his strongest in short 'definitive' poems which combine precise observation with intellectual, political or social elegance and wit. His animal poems — originally part of a sequence entitled *Structures* — leave no doubt about the excellence of his epigrammatic imagination. The majority of these animal-poems reappear in the collection *Paradox* (1981) under the heading of "Man and Beast". (In *The Water Lily and other poems* the sequence opens with the laconic lines which explain the nature and the purpose of the following poetic reflections "the beast/observes/man/and sees/another beast/which thinks desperately".) Equally witty and sharp are many of Krausmann's 'geographical' poems taken from a series of poems bearing the title *Maps*. (*Maps* is also the title of a collection of poems completed in 1987. It, too, contains many reprints from earlier volumes.)

Imaginative paradox remains a central quality in Rudi Krausmann's poetry. There is an acute sensitivity to contradiction and absurdity as to the inherent humour of apparently non-sensical propositions. The volume *Paradox* possesses the quality of imaginative paradoxical redefinitions. Its logic embraces a somewhat constructed irony. The rejected is affirmed and the affirmed rejected.

Krausmann's poetry sees itself as a record of alienated dreams. Yet his "homeland" was "lost" long before the poet's decision to emigrate. The attempt to solve the "homeland's" loss of cultural unity cannot be achieved as the poetry of another, "new country". Krausmann's European alienation cannot be healed, reconciled or expressed in a poetic style which Australian readers can only treat as intellectually, aesthetically and politically 'exotic'. Krausmann has entered a literary culture which for all its European 'influences' has largely remained outside the Continental history of art, philosophy and social politics. That is not the least of Rudi Krausmann's tragic paradoxes. Wittgenstein, Benn and Adorno did not impinge on Australian writers.

Whilst it may be said that the following volume *Flowers of Emptiness* (1982) continues his formal and thematic preoccupation, it also changes direction. The title-poem, curiously reminiscent of T.S. Eliot, articulates the statement of an old man, a tired observer and critic of 'culture'. The poem contemplates a civilisation in disintegration where "the best have no future". The artist himself considers "not peace, but the void". In Eliot's poetry the 'culinary' aesthetic qualities help arrest, or even contradict, the indifference. But Krausmann's *The Void* is no *Love Song of J. Alfred Prufrock*; it lacks urgency and paradoxical realisation, in both imaginative and philosophical terms. The poem's doubt and cultural satiety, its boredom and disgust are literally of no consequence.

Rudi Krausmann has formed close contacts with a number of Australian painters, gallery owners and art critics. His journal *Aspect* was an attempt to bring the visual and the literary arts together. It published numerous interviews, frequently with overseas, mainly European, painters and writers. His own prose-poem collection *From another shore* which appeared around 1975 features drawings by Whiteley, of which it is said: "They were not specifically designed for this book but have provided visual encouragement to the prose."[29] It could be argued that Krausmann's creative language occasionally bears a resemblance to (some of) Whiteley's visual compositions. What is new in Krausmann's *Flowers of Emptiness*, at least in the directness of its expression, is the social concern and compassion for the underprivileged. The poet demonstrates the correlation between such identification and his (self-)doubt about the relevance or present function of art.

It is striking how little Krausmann's poetry has been influenced by Australian writers. His *Found Poem* is in form and content a direct imitation of Horst Bienek's *Vorgefundene Gedichte*.[30] Bienek visited Australia twice and for a short while acted as Munich correspondent of *Aspect*.[31] In following the patterns and ideas of contemporary German writers Krausmann introduced new poetic forms to this country.

Even the statement "poetry today" is "a flower/of emptiness" is based on a derivative metaphor, a variation of the flower-motive from Goethe to Novalis, from Baudelaire to Benn, from Loerke to Celan ("Die Niemandsrose", 1964). Repeated outbursts like "nothing more to say"("Materialism", "News") emphasise the despair of the exiled poet, 'exiled' not merely because he migrated to Australia. Krausmann took his sense of cultural 'nothingness', his "flowers of emptiness" with him when he left his native Austria. He had learnt to become an 'exile' even at home.

Krausmann's commitment to multicultural art adds a further dimension to his own sense of alienation. For all its simplistic assertions and rhetorical quality, his declaration in *Aspect* 29/30 (1984) does carry some weight as a program of cultural politics:

> As long as art is a reflection, illumination or provocation of life as we experience it daily and not a promotion of trends or academic or esoteric theory it is inevitable that artists from backgrounds such as these (migrants) will play a more important role in our multicultural society in future.

Ironically, Krausmann's work, more than any other migrant's, promotes "trends or academic or esoteric theory". The statement's criticism is far too general, offering no names; it alleges, accuses, applauds in the manner of rhetoric. Yet there can be no doubt about the author's personal commitment to an "artistic expression" which "should not be separated from living", — even if such faith can only be expressed in his art's own "flowers of emptiness".

Rudi Krausmann's *Everyman* first appeared in 1978 in the Melbourne series *Paper Castle Mimeographs*, designed and produced by the Swiss writer and translator Walter Billeter. In 1989 the complete trilogy *Everyman*, a comedy of education, The *Perfection*, a comedy of progress, and *The Word*, a comedy of words, appeared under the title

Three Plays. Krausmann himself considers the trilogy among his most important work as a writer in Australia. His word-plays have been produced several times, as "sound environment" in the manner of Ernst Jandl or Helmut Heissenbüttel, both on tape and live on stage. Some have been broadcast by the ABC's Radio Helicon and the New South Wales Drama Theatre. Krausmann's main interest lies in the staging and enacting of language, in the presentation of a very Austrian *Sprachspiel*-consciousness. *Everyman* is defined as a "sentence situation". Like the other two comedies, it grew out of Krausmann's association with Billeter, Hemensley and Kenny.

The title of the work not only alludes to the popular morality play of the 15th century (of Dutch origin), but also to Hugo von Hofmannsthal's "updated" morality play *Jedermann. Das Spiel vom Sterben des reichen Mannes erneuert*, the Austrian dramatist's work published in 1911. Both in the Anglo-Saxon and in the Austrian-German tradition, it is instantly recognisable — and as such capable of alienation and variation, a different adaptation to changed circumstances. Hofmannsthal's play is frequently performed as one of the highlights of the Salzburg Festival; its staging has assumed the status of a cultural ritual, raising celebratory expectations in the audience. Krausmann, mindful of his cultural background, is writing against this Salzburg consensus. His "sentence situation" is a play on and with words, producing linguistically logical nonsense by following the reasoning of grammar. They can be enjoyed as good fun, for a while. The truth is, however, that relatively soon weariness and fatigue set in, as the cleverness of formal constructions begins to try the patience of reader or listener.

Wittgenstein's *Tractatus logico-philosophicus* ends with the famous line: "Worüber man nicht sprechen kann, darüber muß man schweigen." ("What one cannot express in language one must not talk about.") In what might be termed poetic polemic, Krausmann only speaks of those things which cannot be expressed in language, or rather, if they are expressed in language amount to non-sensical sound construction. While Wittgenstein urges us to throw away the scaffolding of his "sentences"(§6.54), Krausmann's verbal plays celebrate their artificial syntactical connection. The sociopolitical implications are not spelt out, but form an important part of Krausmann's texts. The final "song" of *Everyman* is a forceful mixture of Brechtian polemics and verbal nonsense à la Jandl. Its compositional ingredients (or verbal motives) are a strangely confusing yet powerful mixture of linguistic terror in the name of social, political and moral enlightenment. The staging of linguistic "comedies" must remain problematic; experience in Europe and Australia has shown that recordings seem to be the more appropriate form of publication for this kind of literature.[32]

Like Walter Adamson, Rudi Krausmann writes in German and only later translates his works into English. He is currently seeking a publisher for his German-language diaries of three decades. Whether this experience of self-translation is at least partly responsible for his scepticism about words in general and the effectiveness of literature in particular must remain conjecture. What is beyond doubt is that Rudi Krausmann has found his artistic identity in this expression of variance, lamenting and celebrating the unreliability and the essential viability of language, the contradictory nature of human expression.

Conclusion

Cultural alienation is relative. Most Italians, Poles or Germans who emigrated to the United States in this century were able to retain a double identity without too many conflicts: they were Italian *and* American, Polish *and* American, German *and* American. As a result of early decolonisation, the Civil War and a much closer proximity to Europe, the United States had assumed a cultural identity which was recognised and could enter the consciousness of most other nations. By contrast, Australia remained a cultural non-entity in Europe until at least the middle of this century. Emigrants to the United States knew what it meant to be "American"; in this country a consensus on what it means to be "Australian" has not yet been reached. German-Australian writers thus addressed themselves to an "otherness" unable or unwilling to define itself. Frequently they found it easy to distort or to falsify the nature of this land and of its people. The deliberate misrepresentation of Australia as a monocultural society of English character contributed to many migrants' sense of alienation and displacement. Its far distance and lack of self-identification lent itself to fictional stylisations of the "exotic".

Despite a number of Germans writing about Australia during the eighteenth and nineteenth century (C. F. Behrens, Johann Reinhold and Georg Forster, Adalbert von Chamisso, Friedrich Gerstäcker, the Swiss-German Theodor Müller, Hermann Püttmann, Amalie Dietrich, Stefan von Kotze and Rudolf de Haas), it is during the period of German colonialism and subsequent Nazi expansionist aspirations that a body of literature develops in which German perceptions or cultural transformations are articulated. Regarding the earlier literary output, Professor Augustin Lodewyckx's assessment "die Ernte ist, wir müssen es gestehen, eine magere"(182) proved correct. Yet as general background to the development of a German-Australian literature over the most part of this century these earlier authors retain their historical significance.[33]

Much of what has been discussed and analysed in the present

survey is of sociological interest only. As with the works of eighteenth and nineteenth century writers, the literary quality varies considerably. But a history of literature is inevitably (and properly) part of a broader history of culture. Any account of German-Australian writing is in effect a history of intercultural relations. Similar surveys have been conducted in recent times for most other migrant or "ethnic" literatures in this country. Together they are an important contribution to a more embracing, more meaningful and more authentic definition of a truly Australian literature. This study sees itself as part of that process.

What has emerged is a changing image of Australia reflecting Germany's own sociopolitical and cultural aspirations. "German" in this literary and cultural context invariably relates to all German-speaking countries. It was necessary, therefore, to bear in mind the specific nature of East or West German, Austrian or Swiss conditions prevailing at particular times. Nor was it possible to assume that the nature of migration remains the same. With a change in motivation the experience itself assumes a different character. Attitudinal judgements predominate in the writings of migrants and visitors alike. Australia, the host country, remains a target of perception. Frequently, it is little more than an *Aufhänger*, a pretext, a point of reference to voice frustrations, entertain speculations or propagate a faith. A vital part of such projection is of course the readership these publications are aimed at. As has been shown, they too change from decade to decade: from colonial and fascist propaganda to appeals for "adventurous" participation in the rebuilding of a nation, from travelogue tourism to role-playing "stars'" self-propagation, from cultural retrospectives to visions of a multicultural literature. The majority of works were written for German readers, presenting the exotic to the domestic market. By its very nature the socialist writers of German-Australian literature address themselves to an international proletarian readership. Not surprisingly, many of their publications appear in both German and English. The group of "multicultural" authors write predominantly in English, as they consider themselves to be part of an Australian literature. They want to be read by Australian readers, only occasionally publishing in German with a specifically German theme prompting them to revert to their native tongue. In all cases the selected readership influences the nature, the scope and quality of the writing.

The key concept in all of this writing is *die Fremde*, an "otherness" perceived and experienced as strange, challenging or reassuring. In German terms too Australia features as a "Never-Never"; its remoteness is both its attraction and its insignificance. It is a place of banishment and rescue, exile and escape, damnation and salvation. Visitors catch a glimpse of this contradiction, German settlers learn to live with it. German-Australian writing about this continent has one fundamental theme: how to deal with a "foreign" culture. Its responses range from the denial of an Australian culture to an enthusiastic vision of a new antipodean culture. Writers either seek to conquer it or propagate a creative integration. Almost all German authors view Australia as an extension of European culture, and this makes migration to this country the very basis for any interpretation. Yet, strangely, few address themselves in more than a cursory manner to this central issue. What is noticeable is the ever-increasing sense of European rather than German cultural consciousness addressing itself to an emerging and acknowledged multicultural society in Australia. Australians, of course (following the example of British insularity), tended to refer to German, Italian or Polish migrants as "Continentals", assuming a collective cultural identity of all European newcomers to this country. With the recent "unification" of Europe that cultural classification has gained at least in formal validity. If writers continue to experience "the other" in Australia, it is either the expression of a cultural construct reflecting the *need* for alienation as part of the process of identification, or the recognition of something non-European in this country's history of civilisation. Either way, the German contribution to assessing Australian culture will be witness to an independent identity in the arts as well as in other manifestations of social consciousness. It is legitimate, therefore, to read German writing about this country as part of Australian history, without denying its place in German literary records. Its present and future significance in this country's cultural history must be considered greater than in a German-European context. A large part of a people's identity derives from its perception by others. German-Australian writing thus contributes to the continuing development of Australia's cultural image.

With the prospect of an emerging global monoculture sponsored by multinational capitalism a literature's strains of origin are a precious commodity. The description of Australia by German and other literary cultures does express particular aspects of this country's development at various stages in its history. Even distortions or misinterpretations reflect the "other" quality which is authentically Australian. If Australia has contributed to German literature a variety of cultural themes, German writings have documented many of the unique cultural features of this continent. The present survey forms part of such a history of cultural mediation. Travel means movement, progression towards a destination frequently unknown. The "foreign" quality of other countries, their society and culture as well as their natural landscape, are a strong motivation for travelling. The overwhelming majority of German books about Australia are travelogues of one kind or another. Their account of the "other", the antipodean stranger, serves to confirm the domestic image of self. The curiosity of the armchair traveller relates to an established cultural identity — as does all reading. The "foreign" country thus perceived can in turn read a great deal from another culture's response to its identity. It is symptomatic not merely what is considered to be "exotic", but, more importantly, how a (literary) culture relates to it. German-Australian literature is a paradigmatic history of ideological, artistic and spiritual responses to the definitive powers of the "other". To trace the transformations of domestic interpretations, frequently expressed in terms of cultural arrogance, to a creative, imaginative adoption of what was considered to be different makes fascinating reading.

Notes

INTRODUCTION

1 Lodewyckx's final comment on German-Australian literature up to 1930 — "...die Ernte ist, wir müssen es gestehen, eine magere."(182) — is both a quantitative and a qualitative judgement which supports the assumption and scope of the present study.
2 Such designations and descriptions continue into the second half of the century, cf. Klaus Immelmann, *Im unbekannten Australien*, Darmstadt 1960, Peter Grubbe (Klaus Volkmann), *Der vergessene Kontinent Australien* or Achim Sperber, *Mythos Australien. Der archaische Kontinent*, Dortmund 1987.
3 Cf. J.H. Voigt, *New Beginnings/Neuanfänge. Deutsche in New South Wales und Queensland*, Stuttgart 1983.
4 Hans Mayer, Grundpositionen: Außenwelt und Innenwelt. In: H.M., *Von Lessing bis Thomas Mann. Wandlungen der bürgerlichen Literatur in Deutschland*, Pfullingen 1959.
5 Michael Hamburger, *Reason and Energy*, London 1957.
6 Cf. Manfred Jurgensen, The Politics of Imagination. David Goodman/D.J. O'Hearn/Chris Wallace-Crabbe (eds.), *Multicultural Australia: The Challenges of Change*, Melbourne 1991, pp.21–30.
7 Cf. Wim Wenders' cinematographic images of the United States and Werner Herzog's visual interpretation of Australia (*Wo die grünen Ameisen traümen*, 1984) as well as Achim Sperber's anthology, op.cit.
8 Cf. John Moses, German/Australian 'Cultural Policy' and the Count von Luckner Visit to Queensland in 1938. Manfred Jurgensen/Alan Corkhill (eds.), *The German Presence in Queensland*, Brisbane 1988, p.98 and August von der Flatt (J. F. W. Schulz), *Jugenderinnerungen und Allgemeine Beobachtungen*, Tanunda 1938, p.11.
9 Cf. Jacques Delaruelle/Alexandra Karakostas-Seda/Anna Ward (eds.), *Writing in Multicultural Australia*, Sydney 1985.
10 William H. Wilde/Joy Hooton/Barry Andrews (eds.), *The Oxford Companion to Australian Literature*, Melbourne 1985.
11 *Aspect* edited by Rudi Krausmann, *Outrider* by Manfred Jurgensen, *Poetry Australia* co-edited by Margaret Diesendorf, *etymspheres* by Walter Billeter.
12 Cf. Jeffrey Garrett's reports on Kinder- and Jugendliteratur in Australia (*IJB Bulletins* 1984ff.). The migrant concept of "new beginnings" shares much with the social and cultural assumptions of juvenile fiction.
13 Geoffrey Dutton, An Unjustly Neglected Writer, Eric Otto Schlunke, Literary Quarterly 12, *The Weekend Australian*, April 2–3, 1988. Dutton

also prints *Extracts from Eric's Diary, 1957*, Juliet Schlunke's account of her father, *Re-encounter with Rosenthal, Two Letters* of Eric and Olga Schlunke and the author's short story *A House In The Country*.

14 Frank Auerbach (ed.), *Eine Frau im Busch und andere australische Erzählungen*, Tübingen/Basel 1970, pp.141-149.
15 There are numerous studies into this area, notably by Noel Macainsh and, more recently, by Irmtraud Petersson. Irmtraud Petersson, *German Images in Australian Literature from the 1940's to the 1980's*, Bern 1988.
16 Among its early book publications are Gerhard Stilz/Heinrich Lamping (eds.), *Australienstudien in Deutschland. Grundlagen und Perspektiven;* Alan Corkhill, *Australia and the German Literary Imagination (1754-1918);* John Moses, *Prussian-German Militarism 1814-18 in Australian Perspective*; Noel Macainish, *The Pathos of Distance. German-Australian Literary Affiliations;* Volker Wolf (ed.), *Australien. Deutsche- zumeist literarische-Impressionen aus 150 Jahren;* Gerhard Stilz (ed.), *Mensch und Natur in Australien* and Kerry Montero, *Das Bild der Südsee in Adelbert von Chamissos "Reise um die Welt"*.
17 John Tranter. Der falsche Atlas. Translated by Hans Magnus Enzensberger. *Akzente* 5 (1984), pp.466-474.

THE THIRTIES

AWAY FROM EUROPE: ADVENTURE, DISCOVERY AND GERMANS IN AUSTRALIA

1 Cf. Arnold von Skerst, Das Deutschtum in Australien. *Wir Deutsche in der Welt* (ed. Verband Deutscher Vereine im Ausland), n.p., 1938 and John Moses, German/Australian 'Cultural Policy'...op.cit. The following is a typical example of fascist German-Australian "poetry":

Zum Ersten Mai

Der Tag der Arbeit wird festlich begangen!
In Hitler'schem Geist soll jeder gelangen
zu'r Ueberzeugung, dass Arbeit stets adelt!
Im Dritten Reich wird das Nichstun getadelt!

Ein Volksgenosse muss arbeiten wollen!
Muss arbeiten können auch ohne zu grollen!
Muss Arbeit und seine Verrichter verstehen!
Der Faule wird nie seiner Strafe entgehn!

Ob Arbeit der Faust, ob Arbeit der Stirne!
Vernunft muss leiten alle Gehirne!
Nur Einig, können sie Werte zeugen!
Gewinnsucht muss vor Gemeinnutz sich beugen!

Der wiederwärtige Klassendünkel,
Der Standeshochmut in jemem Winkel,

Sie sind zerbrochen und werden vernichtet!
In Arbeit das Volk ist nun gleichgerichtet!

"Der Arbeits-Dienst" gibt jedem die Probe,
Auf das er sich dann für's Leben gelobe:
Kamerad zu sein! Dem Volke zu dienen!
Die Arbeit zu achten! Vergangenes zu sühen!

Heinrich Helmuth Tobler, Sydney (*Die Brücke*, Vol.2 No. 10 27.4.1935, pp.22. Original spelling.)

2 Cf. Egmont Zechlin, Um den "Platz an der Sonne": Das Kaiserreich 1871-1918, Hans-Adolf Jacobsen/Hans Dollinger (eds.), *Deutsche Geschichte von 1871 bis heute*, München 1982, pp. 15-27.
3 "Aber sie arbeiten für andere, und das kann der deutsche Kolonisator nicht vertragen." Alfred Herzog, *Mädels, Ochsen und Halunken*, Berlin 1937, p.12.
4 It is a feature of German culture to reconcile escape and longing, home and 'the other', world and metaphysical absence.
5 Cf. W. Vahldiek, *Um Gold*, Reutlingen 1931; J. Velter, *Australien kreuz und quer*, Köln 1931; A.E. Johann (Alfred Wollschläger), *Känguruhs, Kopra und Korallen*, Berlin 1936; Colin Ross, *Der unvollendete Kontinent*, Leipzig 1930 and others.
6 Heinz Geck, *Umweg über Australien*, Berlin 1937, p. 11 ("das Blut hungrig auf Abenteuer").
7 J.C. Martin, *Grünhorn in Australien*, Reutlingen 1931, p. 7.
8 Heinz Geck, *Umweg über Australien*, op.cit., p. 187, 190 etc.
9 Ibid. (p.144ff.) and J. M. Velter, *Die Farm der guten Hoffnung*, Bern 1935.
10 A. E. Johann (Alfred Wollschläger), *Känguruhs, Kopra und Korallen*, op. cit., p.69 ("diese deutschen Kraftzentren").
11 Ibid. ("Das Heldenepos eines deutschen Forschers wartet immer noch der Enthüllung...", p.112)
12 Published by Verlag J. P. Bachem, Köln.
13 Published by Ensslin & Laiblins Verlagsbuchhandlung, Reutlingen; it includes titles such as *Wild-Süd/Abenteuer fahrender Gesellen*, *Sturmvogel Abenteuer in Wild-Süd* and *Kampf um Wild-Süd*. There can be little doubt about the deliberate variation of the North-American "Wild-West" genre.
14 Published by Ensslin & Laiblins Verlagsbuchhandlung, Reutlingen. Vol. 230 includes the following information: "Im ganzen 268. Hefte dieser obenerwähnten Sammlungen wurden von 53 Jugendschriften-Prüfungsstellen aus den bis 1. Oktober 1929 erschienenen 270 Heften ausdrücklich empfohlen." It reflects the qualitative and quantitative judgement of contemporary popular juvenile fiction.
15 Published by Ensslin & Laiblins Verlagsbuchhandlung, Reutlingen, edited by Josef Viera. The series is described as "Reise-, Siedler- und Jagdabenteuer der exotischen Wunderwelt aus der Feder berufener, die kolonialen Länder aus eigener Anschauung kennender Verfasser". (J. C. Martin, *Grünhorn in Australien. Auswanderer-Erlebnisse*, Vol. 91, p.33.)

16 Published by Hermann Hillger Verlag, Berlin and Leipzig; edited by the German "Dürerbund".
17 Listed in, among other titles, W. Vahldiek, *Um Gold*, Vol. 92, pp. 33-34.
18 "Er sehnt sich nach den Menschen seiner Rasse." Alfred Herzog, *Mädels, Ochsen und Halunken*, op.cit., p.90.
19 Egon Erwin Kisch, *Der rasende Reporter*, Berlin 1930, p.10.
20 Cf. Hermann Sturm (ed.), *Das Fremde. Ästhetische Erfahrung beim Graben, Reisen, Messen, Sterben*, Aachen 1985. Also Alois Wierlacher (ed.), *Das Fremde und das Eigene*, München 1985.
21 The cliché of a "dream" escape to a South Sea island or similar setting (what Günter Grass called Germany's "Fernstenliebe") is equally "at home" in literature, music (especially operettas, cf. *Blume von Hawaii*; and popular songs, cf. "Am weißen Strand von Surabaya" etc.) and the visual arts (including cinematography). It is the epitome of German "longing", i.e. the moody dream of escape, a sense of non-belonging, cf. Heine's "Ich weiß nicht, was soll es bedeuten...".
22 Joseph M. Velter, *Australien kreuz und quer*, Köln 1931, Einsiedeln/Zürich/Köln 1958, dust-jacket of 1958 edition.
23 Listed in Joseph M. Velter, *Die Farm der guten Hoffnung*, Berlin/Leipzi/Wien 1935, p.251.
24 Op.cit., p.250.
25 Ibid.
26 Ibid.
27 Quotation from *Volkswacht*, Trier; Ibid.
28 Jürgen Tampke's and Colin Doxford's history of the Germans in Australia, *Australia, Willkommen*, Sydney 1990, lacks scholarly depth and substance.
29 *Flight To Hell*, a TV-series produced by the Australian Broadcasting Corporation.
30 C.M.H. Clark, *A History of Australia*, Vol. VI, Melbourne 1987.
31 *Kürschners Deutscher Literatur-Kalender 1988*, 60. Jahrgang, Berlin/ New York 1988, pp. 1341-1342.
32 Cf. Christian Siegel, Egon Erwin Kisch — "Meister der revolutionären Berichterstattung", Egon Erwin Kisch, *Landung in Australien*, Darmstadt/Neuwied 1975, p.300.
33 Cf. August von der Flatt (J.F.W. Schulz), *Jugenderinnerungen und Allgemeine Beobachtungen*, op. cit.
34 Cf. John Moses, German/Australian 'Cultural Policy' and the Count von Luckner Visit to Queensland in 1938. Manfred Jurgensen/Alan Corkhill (eds.), *The German Presence in Queensland*, op. cit.
35 Christian Siegel, Egon Erwin Kisch — "Meister der revolutionären Berichterstattung", Egon Erwin Kisch, *Landung in Australien*, op. cit., p.298.
36 Cf. Craig Munro, *Wild Man of Letters: The Story of P. R. Stephensen*, Melbourne 1984.
37 He was invited to a meeting of the Fellowship of Australian Writers.
38 Cf. Theodor Balk's essay "Die zweite Entdeckung Australiens", *Die neue Weltbühne*, 1, xxxiii (1937), p.89.
39 *Kreiskalender Beeskow-Storkow*, Beeskow, 1938, pp. 48-55.

40 A number of German writers idealise the racial features of the Aborigines in the manner of Leni Riefenstahl's African portraits (Colin Ross, Hans Bertram a.o.).
41 John Moses, German/Australian 'Cultural Policy' and the Count von Luckner Visit to Queensland in 1938. Manfred Jurgensen/Alan Corkhill (eds.), *The German Presence in Queensland*, op.cit.

THE FORTIES

BLOOD AND CULTURE: THE OLD LANGUAGE IN SEARCH OF THE NEW LAND

1 Werner Fels is included in this analysis because his writing represents much of what remains recognisably German *Epigonaldichtung*, i.e. his cultural conditioning leaves his poetry outside an Anglo-Australian literature.
2 *Viennese Theatre (Kleines Wiener Theater)*, Twenty-five Years Viennese Theatre, Sydney 1966, p.4.
3 *Viennese Theatre, Diary of Performances staged 1941-1981*, Sydney 1981.
4 Karl Bittman (ed.), *Strauss to Matilda. Viennese in Australia 1938-1988*, Sydney 1988, p. 204.
5 It included semi-professional productions of the classics, Frisch and Dürrenmatt and the premiere of Manfred Jurgensen's *Rückkehr ins Exil*. Among its directors were Burt Cooper and Hector Maclean. (Burt Cooper later produced the English-language world premiere of *Andorra* for the Newman College Dramatic Club, staged on 14-18 April 1964 at the Union Theatre, University of Melbourne.)
6 Alfred Baring, *Deutschsprachiges Theater in Australien*, unpubl. typescript, Sydney 1974 (with Karl Bittman), 17pp.
7 Karl Bittman/Owen Grant, The Viennese Theatre. A transplant of a special kind. Karl Bittman (ed.), *Strauss to Matilda. Viennese in Australia 1938–1988*, op.cit., p.208.
8 Ms. Abschrift H. von Ploennies, Mitchell Library, Sydney. Folder 6 contains the poetry of Walter Stölting, Folder 7 a ms. autobiography of Stölting (254. pp.).
9 Ibid.
10 Published by Verlag Kemper, Waibstadt bei Heidelberg; cf. Hans Franke, *Das Ende des Kapitän Cook*, Waibstadt b. Heidelberg 1948, p.151. Interestingly, one of its titles is Ch. W. Schmidt, *Friedrich Gerstäcker — Zwischen Wildnis und Kultur*, a programmatic concept for the series and much of German adventure in Australia.
11 Judith Wright (ed.), *A Book of Australian Verse*, Melbourne 1962, pp.3-4.
12 Cf. Manfred Jurgensen, Towards a People's Literature. Manfred Jurgensen/Robert Adamson (eds.), *Australian Writing Now*, Ringwood/Brisbane 1988, p.xv.
13 T.S. Eliot, 'The Burial of the Dead': "Unreal City,/Under the brown fog of a winter dawn...", 11.60-61; *The Waste Land* (1922), T.S. Eliot, *Collected Poems 1909-1935*, London 1959, p.63.

The Fifties

The New Challenge: Boys' Own Geography and Domestic Reconstruction

1   Cf. Elisabeth Endres, *Die Literatur der Adenauerzeit*, München 1980.
2   It is no coincidence that 1953 sees the publication of Kurt Lütgen's Cook biography for young readers entitled *Der große Kapitän* (Braunschweig 1953), together with a reprint of Joseph M. Velter's *Australien kreuz und quer* (Köln 1953; Einsiedeln /Zürich/Köln 1958). The most programmatic and symptomatic publication is A.E. Johann's *Große Weltreise* (Gütersloh 1955) which "conquers" the world under the heading of "Entdecker und Eroberer"; Australia is summarised as "Raum für Millionen Menschen".(5) Johann's book experienced a dozen editions during the fifties, a clear indication of German craving for "world", not only among the young.
3   Cf. Gerhard Haas (ed.), *Kinder- und Jugend-Literatur*, Stuttgart 1984.
4   William H. Wilde/Joy Hooton/Barry Andrews (eds.), *The Oxford Companion to Australian Literature*, op. cit., p.523.
5   Op. cit., p.313.
6   Walter Kaufmann, Literaturbrief aus Australien, *Neue deutsche Literatur*, 1/1956, pp.149-152.

The Sixties

Migrants, Adventure and Social Conscience: German Workmanship

1   Kurt (Bodo Heinrich) Lütgen began writing in 1945, specialising in juvenile fiction combining distant places and exotic adventure. Among his publications are: *Der große Kapitän* (1950), *Kein Winter für Wölfe* (1955), *Lockendes Abenteuer Afrika* (1962) and *Das Rätsel Nordwestpassage* (1966). His books have been republished several times, reaching many editions; *Kein Winter für Wölfe*, for example, 17 editions by 1974, and translated into 16 languages. Lütgen's narrative fiction proves the outstanding success of, and continued demand for, juvenile adventure. The author was awarded the German Juvenile Book Prize as well as the Gerstäckerpreis (1956 and 1967). A typical title of the seventies is *Allein gegen die Wildnis: Abenteuer im australischen Busch* (1972).
2   The author's other books indicate her preoccupation with "adventure" and "magic", the usual fare of juvenile fiction. (*Perilous Journey*, *The Enchanted Pancakes*, 1964)
3   In 1843 Amalie Schoppe published her *Robinson in Australien* (Heidelberg), a clear indication of Australia's identification with a literary topos.
4   Hageni's many publications in the area of juvenile fiction includes the title *Zauber der Ferne* (1973), re-establishing the nexus between distance and magic, a fundamental assumption of German literature's concept of the exotic.

5   Alice M. Ekert-Rotholz was the daughter of a British father and a German mother. She lived in Bangkok from 1939 to 1952; in 1959 she settled in England. All of her books deal with travellers, spiritual and worldly pilgrims caught in human passions. Some of her titles reveal this general preoccupation: *Siam hinter der Bambuswand. Ein ostasiatisches Reisebuch* (1953) — it is symptomatic that her publications open with a travelogue, *Reis aus Silberschalen. Roman einer deutschen Familie im heutigen Ostasien* (1954), *Wo Tränen verboten sind. Roman der Wandlungen* (1956), *Strafende Sonne, lockender Mond* (1959), *Mohn in den Bergen* (1961), *Elfenbein aus Peking* (1966), *Der Juwelenbaum. Karibisches Panorama* (1968) etc. Most of her books achieved editions of 100,000.
6   Introduction, B. Wongar, *Der Pfad nach Bralgu*, Leipzig 1981, p.13.
7   Cf. p. 446.
8   Cf. "Eine kritische Ausgabe der Werke von Hirsch-Hatvani wird vorbereitet von Pavel Petr und Stephen Jeffries, Monash University." Leslie Bodi, Zur Frage der deutschsprachigen Literatur in Australien, E.T. Rosenthal (ed.), *Deutschsprachige Literatur des Auslandes*, Bern/Frankfurt am Main/New York/Paris 1989, p.80. Such critical edition would make the writings of an outstanding representative of German-Australian literature (or German-language literature in Australia) more accessible to the general reader. It is to be hoped that some of Hatvani's prose will also be translated into English.

THE SEVENTIES

LOOK BACK IN WONDER: VISITORS FROM ANOTHER REPUBLIC OF LETTERS

1   Rosenthal's assertion "daß der in der Fremde in seiner eigenen Sprache sich schriftlich Ausdrückende sich bewußt abseits stellt von der ihn umgebenden Situation, um sich an Leser zu wenden, deren Probleme etwa den seinigen entsprechen" ignores writers like Walter Adamson, Rudi Krausmann or Margaret Diesendorf (in the Australian context) who choose to publish in both German and English and who do not address themselves to an ethnically restricted readership. The same applies to many Italo-Australian writers (Rosa R. Cappiello et al.). Translation, especially 'creative translation' by the author, is an important part in 'bicultural, bilingual literature. Erwin Theodor Rosenthal (ed.), *Deutschsprachige Literatur des Auslandes*, Bern/Frankfurt am Main/New York/Paris 1989, p.9.
2   More than any other country, Australia's literary image in German writing correlates the 'exotic' of animal and human behaviour. Both constitute extremes of 'strangeness'.
3   Michael Schulte's other publications share the same wit of a literary burlesque, i.e. *Die Dame, die Schweinsohren nur im Liegen aß* (1970), *Drei Nonnen gekentert* (1972) etc.

4   In fact, Australian *Germanistik* had been on the decline during the eighties. During Horst Bienek's visit to Australia the discipline had reached unprecedented heights which it could not sustain.
5   First published in *Akzente* 19 (1976), pp. 42-48.
6   It is tempting to respond with an old Jewish 'joke': "Weit von wo?"
7   Stephen Jeffries, Paul Hirsch-Hatvani. A German-Speaking Expressionist Writer in Victoria. Leslie Bodi/Stephen Jeffries (eds.), *The German Connection*, Melbourne 1985, pp. 92-94.
8   The journalist Wolf Heckmann previously published *Rommels Krieg in Afrika* (1976/77) which he described as "ein Lese- und Erfahrungsbuch", an "historischer Bericht, objektiv" and a "Reportage"(Book-jacket, Lübbe Verlag). It illustrates the author's broad concept of "Erlebnisbericht".
9   Carl Heinz Kurz travelled extensively, publishing novels, short stories, bibliographies, juvenile fiction, travelogues and translations. The publisher describes Kurz's *Australische Silhouetten* as follows: "Diese Arbeit enthält eine Reihe von Erlebnissen aus verschiedenen Landschaften Australiens...er notierte, was er sah und erlebte...Sie werden in schlichter und maßvoller Sprache dargeboten und zeigen so recht auf, daß wir alle mitverantwortlich werden für das, was an Menschen geschieht." (München 1975, jacket cover) The text was written at a time when West Germany revived the discussion of a collective guilt ("mitverantwortlich werden") of the German people.

THE EIGHTIES

TOURIST GUIDES AND TELEVISION IMAGES: FULL CIRCLE

1   Cf. also Ilse Friedrich, *Ausgerechnet Australien*, Reutlingen 1963.
2   Michael G. Clyne, *Transference and Triggering*, The Hague 1967.
3   Vincent Buckley, Imagination's Home, *Quadrant*, March 1979. Cf. also Jim Davidson, *Sideways from the Page*, Vincent Buckley Interview, Melbourne 1983, pp.209-229.
4   Walter Bockmayer/Rolf Bührmann, *Flammende Herzen*, Mainz 1978.
5   Fuchsberger's book takes its title from the Australian television program *Good Morning, Australia*.
6   Till Reinhard is the nom de plume of Till R. Lohmeyer.
7   Sneja Gunew/Jan Mahyuddin (eds.), *Beyond the Echo. Multicultural Women's Writing*, St. Lucia 1988, pp.118-119 and pp.159-160.
8   Philip Thomson, "Outsiders Awash in the Soapy Scenario", *The Weekend Australian* 2/3 September 1989.

INTERNATIONAL SOCIALISM AND MIGRATION:

THE GDR CONNECTION 1956-1987

1. Kaufmann invited Manfred Jurgensen to meet him in preparation of this history. The interview (6.1.88) was informal and remains unpublished.
2. Kaufmann was awarded the Eureka Youth League Prize (together with Frank Hardy). Among his other literary prizes are the Mary Gilmore Award (1959), the Fontane-Preis (1961, 1965) and the Heinrich-Mann-Preis der Akademie der Künste der DDR (1967).
3. Published by Aufbau-Verlag, Berlin.
4. Cf. Fred Dobberstein, *Deutsche Exilliteratur in Australien*, unpubl. M.A. thesis, University of Melbourne 1983 (chapter on Walter Kaufmann, pp.111ff).
5. Walter Kaufmann, *The Curse of Maralinga and Other Stories*, Berlin 1959, back-cover text by author.
6. Cf. especially Joachim Specht, *Die Gejagten*, Berlin 1967.
7. Gertrud Leutenegger, *Ninive*, Frankfurt am Main 1978, p.109 etc.
8. Ingeborg Bachmann, *Malina*, Christine Koschel/Inge von Weidenbaum/Clemens Münster (eds.), *Ingeborg Bachmann. Werke. Band III*, München 1978, p.25.
9. Cf. David Martin, *Poems of David Martin 1938-1958*, Sydney 1959, p.6.
10. Walter Kaufmann, *Wohin der Mensch gehört*, Berlin 1957.
11. Cf. Hans Jürgen Geerdts (ed.), *Deutsche Literaturgeschichte in einem Band,* Berlin 1971, Die Periode von 1949 bis 1961, pp.666-720. Walter Kaufmann is not listed in this history.
12. It is mainly the socialist writers who touch on the sensitive subject of German fascist migrants.
13. Carl Ludwig Lang (ed.), *Deutsches Literatur-Lexikon. Biographisch-Bibliographisches Handbuch. Begründet von Wilhelm Kosch, 8. Band*, Bern/München 1981, p.971.
14. Walter Kaufmann, *Am Kai der Hoffnung*, Berlin 1981, Nachwort von Joachim Schreck, p.215. The paperback edition contains a selection of the hardback edition published 1974 by Verlag der Nation, Berlin.
15. Many of these stories are contained in Walter Kaufmann, *Unter dem wechselnden Mond*, Rostock 1969.
16. Cf. Hans Mayer, Grundpositionen: Außenwelt und Innenwelt, Die alte und die neue epische Form: Johann Gottfried Schnabels Romane. *Von Lessing bis Thomas Mann*, Pfullingen 1959, pp.9-78.
17. Interview with Manfred Jurgensen, op.cit.
18. Gavin Casey (1907-1964), author of *It's Harder for Girls* (1942), republished as *Short Shift Saturday and Other Stories* (1973), *Birds of a Feather* (1943), *Downhill Is Easier* (1945), *The Wits Are Out* (1947), *City of Men* (1950), *Snowball* (1958), *Amid the Plenty* (1962) and *The Man Whose Name was Mud* (1963).
19. *Death in Fremantle* has since been published in full in *Outrider* Vol.VI/Nr.1, pp.145-180 and Vol.VI/Nr.2, pp.77-108.
20. Extracts of *Peterborough Story* were translated into English by Malcolm McInnes and appeared in *Outrider* Vol.I/Nr.1, pp.51-57.

Joining The "Mainstream":

First-Generation Australian Writers 1967-1989

1 Conducted with the author in Eastwood (Sydney), January 1987.
2 Rudi Krausmann, Margaret Diesendorf, *M.A.T.I.A. Literature*, Sydney 1988, p.2.
3 Ibid.
4 Ibid., p. 1.
5 Quoted by Jacques Delaruelle in his Preface to *Holding the Golden Apple*.(unpublished)
6 The formal aspects of the title concept are stressed even further in the 1980 study *Narrative Forms of the Fictional I* (*Erzählformen des fiktionalen Ich*), Bern/München.
7 Elizabeth Perkins, "Three Suns I Saw": Geography, Art and Desire in Manfred Jurgensen's *a winter's journey*. Manfred Jurgensen/Alan Corkhill(eds.), *The German Presence in Queensland*, op.cit., pp.326-342.
8 The treatment of *Native Poison/Das Gift der Heimat* appeared in Manfred Jurgensen, *Deutsche Reise*, Bern/Frankfurt am Main, New York/Paris 1990, pp.67-89.
9 Sonja Delander, Interview with Walter Adamson, *Outrider*, Vol. 3/Nr. 2 (1986) pp.3-8. Cf. also Walter Adamson, Some Problems of Multicultural Writing in Australia, Jacques Delaruelle/Alexandra Karakostas-Seda/Anna Ward (eds.), *Writing in Multicultural Australia*, Sydney 1985, pp.93-95.
10 *The Age*, feature article on Walter Adamson by Stuart Sayers ('Writers and Readers'), January 1975.
11 *Outrider*, op.cit., pp.1-33.
12 Interview M.J. with Walter Adamson, Melbourne, 15 September 1988 (Melbourne).
13 Given Adamson's literary temperament, a collection of short stories would have been more appropriate. Despite *The Institution*, Walter Adamson is no novelist.
14 Walter Adamson, *Australia of all Places*, Richmond 1984 (back cover).
15 Sonja Delander, Interview with Walter Adamson, op.cit., p.7.
16 Sonja Delander translated this story under the title of "The Last Dream". (W.A., *The Man With The Suitcase*, op.cit. pp.82-84.)
17 Letter Walter Billeter to M.J., 30.4.87.
18 Rudi Krausmann, *The Water Lily and other poems*, Brisbane 1977; *Everyman*, Carlton 1978 etc.
19 Rudi Krausmann, *From another shore*, Sydney 1975, p.41.
20 Rudi Krausmann, *Flowers of Emptiness*, Sydney 1982, p.5.
21 Rudi Krausmann, *Realities*, Sydney 1984, pp.39-49.
22 Grahame Johnston, *The Australian Pocket Oxford Dictionary*, Melbourne 1976, p.916.
23 Gottfried Benn, Blaue Stunde, *Gesammelte Werke*, Bd. 1, München 1975, p.259.
24 Rudi Krausmann, *From another shore*, op.cit. (back cover)
25 French Poetry, Alex Preminger (ed.), *Princeton Encyclopedia of Poetry and*

Poetics, London 1975, p.300.
26 Jacques Hardre, Surrealism, Alex Preminger (ed.), *Princeton Encyclopedia of Poetry and Poetics*, op. cit., p.821.
27 Exile Prolonged by Real Reasons, Les A. Murray, *The People's Otherworld*, Sydney 1983, p.58.
28 Cf. Manfred Jurgensen's German poetry collections *Stationen*, Bern 1968 and *aufenthalte*, Bern 1969 and the travel diary *Deutsche Reise*, Bern/Frankfurt am Main/New York/Paris 1990.
29 Rudi Krausmann, *From another shore*, op.cit., p.4.
30 Horst Bienek, *Vorgefundene Gedichte. Poemes trouves*, München 1969.
31 Bienek is listed as contributing editor of *Aspect* during the late seventies.
32 Cf. Ernst Jandl's *Das Röcheln der Mona Lisa. Ein akustisches Geschehen für eine Stimme und Apparaturen* or Helmut Heissenbüttel's *Max unmittelbar vorm Einschlafen*, both produced by Deutsche Grammophon, 2574 003.
33 Cf. Alan Corkhill, *Australia and the German Literary Imagination (1754-1918)*, (German-Australian Studies, Vol. 2.) Bern/Frankfurt am Main/New York/Paris 1990.

Bibliography

PRIMARY LITERATURE

Adamson, Walter, *Das australische Einmaleins*, Giessen 1973.
   Ausgerechnet Australien, Darmstadt 1974.
   Die Anstalt, Darmstadt 1974.
   The Institution, Melbourne 1976; Ringwood 1986.
   Adamson's Three Legged World, Cheltenham 1985.
   The Man with the Suitcase, Ferntree Gully 1989.
Adler, Ernst, *Die Legende vom Bumerang*, Berlin 1966.
Albert, Max, *Abenteuer in Australien und Alaska*, Berlin 1948.
Artmann, H. C., *Die Anfangsbuchstaben der Flagge*, Salzburg 1969; München 1970.
Baring, Alfred, *Viennese Theatre*, Sydney 1966.
Becker, O. E. H., *Das australische Abenteuer*, Leipzig 1939; 1942².
Bertram, Hans, *Flug in die Hölle*, Berlin 1933; München 1977.
Bichsel, Peter, *Geschichten zur falschen Zeit*, Darmstadt/Neuwied 1979; 1983⁴.
Bienek, Horst, "Versuch den fünften Erdteil zu beschreiben", *Merkur* 26/2, 1972, pp. 151-166.
   Gleiwitzer Kindheit. Gedichte aus zwanzig Jahren, München 1976; 1978².
Billeter, Walter, (ed., with John Jenkins) *etymspheres, The Journal of the Paper Castle*, Balaclava 1974 (Vol.1, Nr.1).
   (ed., with John Jenkins) *Dreamrobe Embroideries & Asparagus for Dinner*, Melbourne 1975.
   "Notes on Some German Writings since 1950", *Ear in a Wheatfield* 17 (Autumn 1976), pp. 80-94.
   (ed.) *etymspheres* (Vol.1, Nr.3), "the private as social meeting place", Melbourne 1976 (Spring).
   "Personal Experience and Social Perspectives. Notes on Some Recent German Writings", Part 2, *The Merry Creek or Nero*, Melbourne 1977 (no pagination).
   (ed. and transl. with Jerry Glenn) *Paul Celan. Prose Writings & Selected Poems*, Melbourne 1977.
   (ed., with Kris Hemensley and Robert Kenny) *3 blind mice* Melbourne 1977.
   Australian Novemberies, Melbourne 1978.
   (ed. and transl.) *Konrad Bayer, the philosophers' stone*, Melbourne 1979.
   (ed. and transl.) *The Head of Vitus Bering, a portrait in prose by konrad bayer*, Melbourne 1979.
   (ed. and transl.) Gerald Bisinger, *Sieben Neue Gedichte/Seven New Poems*, Gosport (U.K.) 1980.

Bockmann, Vera, *Full Circle. An Australian in Berlin 1930-1946*, Netley 1986.
Diesendorf, Margaret, *Towards the Sun*, Sumter 1975.
　Light, Sydney 1981.
　Holding the Golden Apple, Brisbane 1991.
Ekert-Rotholz, Alice, *Die Pilger und die Reisenden*, Hamburg 1964; 1972; 1985.
Ey, Karl, *Kolonisten in Ketten*, Bremen 1935.
Faber, Kurt, *Im australischen Busch*, Berlin/Leipzig 1931.
　Als Landstreicher durch Australien, Leipzig 1933.
　Unter Landstreichern und Schafscherern, Reutlingen 1933.
Fels, Werner, *The River-side Sage*, Melbourne 1942.
　The Lady With the Red-brown Hair and Australian Poems, Melbourne 1949.
Franke, Hans, *Das Ende des Kapitäns Cook*, Heidelberg/Waibstadt 1948.
Fremd, Angelika, *Heartland*, St. Lucia 1989.
Fuchsberger, Joachim, *Guten Morgen, Australien*, Hamburg 1988.
Geck, Heinz, *Umweg über Australien*, Berlin 1937.
Glaser, Hermann, "Abheben zu den Antipoden", *Frankfurter Hefte* 39/3, 1984, pp. 55-64.
Hageni, Alfred, *Zauber im australischen Busch*, Düsseldorf 1964; München 1974.
Hatvani, Paul, "Zwei Prosastücke: 'In Feindesland', '...gesenkten Hauptes'", *Akzente* 15/1, 1968, pp. 71-75.
　"Das Ameisenfragment", *Literatur und Kritik* 1969/4, pp. 336-350.
　"Irrwege (1)", *Akzente* 18/1, 1971, pp. 71-75.
　"Nicht da, nicht dort: Australien", *Akzente* 20/6, 1973, pp. 564-571.
Hauser, Heinrich, *Last Port of Call*, London 1938.
　Australien. Der menschenscheue Kontinent, Berlin 1939; 1941.
　Australien. Der fünfte Kontinent, Berlin 1956.
Heckmann, Wolf, *Haie fressen keine Deutschen*, München 1982.
Herzog, Alfred, *Mädels, Ochsen und Halunken*, Berlin 1937.
Heyd, Kurt, *Christophs Abenteuer in Australien*, Berlin 1935.
Hutterer, Franz, *Die große Fahrt des Richard Hook*, Köln 1959.
Johann A. E., (Alfred Wollschläger), *Känguruhs, Kopra und Korallen*, Berlin 1936.
　Große Weltreise mit A. E. Johann, Gütersloh 1958.
Jurgensen, Manfred, *Rückkehr ins Exil*, Melbourne 1964.
　Stationen, Bern 1968.
　aufenthalte, Bern 1969.
　"dedication", "from: 'a house to live in'", "from: 'the death of chiron'", "first autumn", Maureen Freer (ed.), *Square Poets Brisbane 71*, Brisbane 1971, pp. 26-28.
　signs & voices, St. Lucia 1973.
　a kind of dying, Melbourne 1977.
　Wehrersatz, Flensburg 1978.
　a winter's journey, Sydney 1979.
　Das fiktionale Ich, Bern 1979.
　south africa transit, Johannesburg 1979.

innere sicherheit, Darmstadt 1979.
the skin trade, Brisbane 1983.
The Unit, *Outrider* Vol.l/Nr.2, 1984, pp. 99-111.
waiting for cancer, Brisbane 1985.
Versuchsperson, Bern/Kreuzlingen 1986.
A Difficult Love. Break-Out, Brisbane 1987.
Selected Poems 1972-1986 (ed. by Dimitris Tsaloumas), Brisbane 1987.
(ed., with Robert Adamson) *Australian Writing Now*, Ringwood/Brisbane 1988. (Also published as *Australian Writing 1988.*)
(ed., with Alan Corkhill) *The German Presence in Queensland*, Brisbane 1988.
The Partiality of Harbours, Sydney 1989.
My Operas Can't Swim, Milton 1989.
Erste Gegenwart, Berlin 1989.
Deutsche Reise. Das Gift der Heimat, Bern/Frankfurt am Main/New York/Paris 1990.

Kaufmann, Walter, *Voices in the Storm*, Melbourne 1953.
"Literaturbrief aus Australien", *Neue Deutsche Literatur* 1956/1, Berlin 1956, pp. 149-152.
Wohin der Mensch gehört, Berlin 1957.
The Curse of Maralinga, Berlin 1959.
Ruf der Inseln, Berlin 1960.
Kreuzwege, Berlin 1961.
Am Kai der Hoffnung, Berlin 1974; 1981.
Stimmen im Sturm, Berlin 1977.
Flucht, Leipzig 1984; Berlin 1987.

Kempcke, Hermann, "125. Geburtstag — 90 Jahre verschollen", *Kreiskalender Beeskow-Storkow*, Beeskow 1938, pp. 48-55.

Kisch, Egon Erwin, *Landung in Australien*, Amsterdam 1937; Berlin 1948[2]; Darmstadt/Neuwied 1975.
Australian Landfall, London 1937.
Abenteuer in fünf Kontinenten: Reportagen, Wien 1948.
Paradies Amerika/Landung in Australien, Berlin 1978.

Kolar, Kurt, *Kontinent voll Kuriositäten: Tiere, Menschen und Probleme in Australien*, Wien 1965. *Australien neu entdeckt. Ein Verhaltensforscher im fünften Kontinent*, München/Basel/Wien 1970.

Krausmann, Rudi, *From another shore*, Sydney 1975.
The Water Lily and other poems, St. Lucia 1977.
paradox, Sydney 1981 .
Flowers of Emptiness, Sydney 1982.
Three Plays, Sydney 1989.

Kurz, Carl Heinz, *Australische Silhouetten*, München 1975.

Landolt, Esther, (Rosmarie Meyer) *Das Opfer*, Zürich/Leipzig 1937.
Delfine, Zürich 1939.
Ewige Herde, Zürich 1942.
Namenlos, Zürich 1947.

Lenz, Siegfried, "Das Lachen des Kukkaburra", *Die Zeit* 49 (6.12.1968), Hamburg 1968, pp. 63-64.

Lodewyckx, Augustin, *Die Deutschen in Australien*, Stuttgart 1932.
Lüneburg, Heinz, *Jims Abenteuer im Land der trockenen Flüsse*, Hamburg 1952.
Lütgen, Kurt, *Der große Kapitän: Leben und Entdeckungsfahrten des englischen Seemanns James Cook*, Braunschweig 1953.
   Korroborri. Buschreiter in Australien, Braunschweig 1960.
   Pioniers in Australie, Utrecht 1963.
   Südland-Saga, Würzburg 1977/1980.
Marken, Wolfgang, (Fritz Mardicke), *Das große Australiengeheimnis*, Hamburg 1936.
Martin, David, "I look at Australia", *Unity* 3/4 (March/April 1950), pp. 4-11: "Australien und wir heutigen Australier", *Nationales Olympisches Komitee DDR. Olympic Games 1956*, Berlin 1957, pp.52-62.
   Where a Man Belongs, Melbourne 1969.
Martin, J. C., *Himmelsstürmer*, Reutlingen 1930.
   Grünhorn in Australien, Reutlingen 1931.
Mattheus, Peter, *Minnewitt und Knisterbusch*, Leipzig 1930; Berlin/Augsburg 1950.
Meissner, Hans-Otto, *Das fünfte Paradies. Australien: Menschen, Tiere, Abenteuer*, Stuttgart 1965; 1971; München 1983; 1984[2]; 1985[3].
Mühlen-Schulte, H. J., *Drei Millionärsanwärter starten in Australien*, Leipzig 1932.
Nonveiller, Heinz, "Jener Teil der Welt", Frank Auerbach (ed.), *Eine Frau im Busch und andere Erzählungen*, Tübingen/Basel 1970, pp. 389-403.
Nordhoff C.B./Hall J. N., *Kolonie Sydney*, Frankfurt am Main 1950.
Pfeffer, K. H., *Die bürgerliche Gesellschaft in Australien*, Berlin 1936.
   Australien und Neuseeland, Berlin 1943.
   Australien, Stuttgart 1950.
Politzer, Ludwig Louis, *Centenary Journal 1934-35*, Melbourne 1934.
   In Introspective Mood, Melbourne 1944.
   Autumn Leaves, Melbourne 194?.
   My Creed: a poem, Ferntree Gully 1949.
   Collection of Verses, Ferntree Gully 1951.
Raab, Fritz, *Betty und die 12 000 Schafe*, Graz/Wien/Köln 1957.
Reim, Helmut, (ed. and transl.), *John Morgan: Ein australischer Robinson. Leben und Abenteuer des William Buckley*, Leipzig 1964.
Reinhard, Till, (Till R. Lohmeyer), *Des Himmels Blau in uns*, Frankfurt am Main/Berlin 1988.
Rose, Frederick, *Ureinwohner, Känguruhs, Düsenclipper*, Leipzig 1966.
Ross, Colin, *Der unvollendete Kontinent*, Leipzig 1930.
   Das Buch der fernen Welt, Berlin 1931.
   Haha Whenua - das Land, das ich gesucht, Leipzig 1933.
Scholz, Liz, *Australische Liebesergüsse*, Graz 1986.
Schulte, Michael, *Goethes Reise nach Australien*, München/Zürich 1976.
Seidel, Jürgen, *Ausgewandert*, Frankfurt am Main 1982.
Specht, Joachim, *Peterborough Story*, Berlin 1963.
   Australisches Abenteuer, Berlin 1966.
   Die Gejagten, Berlin 1967.

Stippvisite, Berlin 1968.
Blütenhölle in Banusta, Berlin 1971.
Buschbrand, Berlin 1974.
Leuchtfeuer Eastern Reef, Berlin 1976.
Der Einzelgänger, Berlin 1978.
Korallen-Joe, Berlin 1981.
Das Camp am Burdekinfluß, Berlin 1982.
Daniels Weg in die Steinzeit, Berlin 1985.
Tippet, Berlin 1985.
In den Mangrovensümpfen, Berlin 1988.
Sperber, Achim, *Mythos Australien. Der archaische Kontinent*, Dortmund 1987.
Stölting, Walter, *Australien. Das Land von morgen*, Berlin 1930.
Troll, Alexander, (ed.), *Australien. In Busch und Sand*, Berlin 1930.
Ullrich, Luise, *Unterwegs zu mir. Australische Impressionen*, München 1985.
Ulrich, Hans W., *Notruf an alle*, Stuttgart 1963.
In Australien verschollen, Stuttgart 1964.
Vahldiek, Willi, *Um Gold*, Reutlingen 1931.
van der Geest, Karel, *Stampfende Hufe*, Gütersloh 1960.
Velter, Joseph M., *Australien kreuz und quer*, Köln 1931; 1953; Einsiedeln/Zürich/Köln 1958. *Jürgen in Australien*, Köln 1935; 1949.
Die Farm der guten Hoffnung, Bern/Leipzig/Wien 1935; Mainz 1950³.
Viedebannt, Klaus, *30mal Australien und Neuseeland*, München/Zürich 1981; 1983.
Viennese Theatre Sydney (The), *20 Jahre 1941-1961, Jubiläumsprogramm*, Sydney 1961.
Twenty-five Years Viennese Theatre Sydney, Sydney 1966.
Diary of Performances Staged 1941-1981, Sydney 1981.
von der Flatt, August, (J.F.W. Schulz), *August von der Flatt. Anne Gemeende-Versammlung uff der Flatt*, Tanunda 1938.
Meine irschte Reese noach Bethesda und meine zweete noach Hermannsburg, Tanunda 1938.
von Tiefenhausen, Berend, *Deutsche in Australien*, Leipzig 1938.
Wolkowsky, Maria, (Maria Prerauer), *Australisches Abenteuer*, Stuttgart 1961; 1965².
Australian Adventure, London 1965.

GENERAL FICTION, TRAVELOGUES, VERSE

Auerbach, Frank, (ed.), *Eine Frau im Busch*, Tübingen/Basel 1970.
Bahr, Rüdiger, *Der schwarze Bumerang*, München/Zürich 1982.
Baume, F. E., *Burnt Sugar*, n.p. 1934.
Bergius, C. C., *Heißer Sand*, Gütersloh/Stuttgart/Wien/Berlin/Darmstadt 1978; München 1982; Stuttgart/Hamburg/München 1983.
Bischoff, Charitas, *Amalie Dietrich — Ein Leben*, Berlin 1980.
Breucker, Oscar Herbert, *Der Tanzplatz des Satans*, Leipzig 1936.
Brinks, Josef, *Im australischen Busch*, Leipzig 1977.

Brunner, Hans, *Außer der Sonne bewegt sich hier nichts*, Aarau/Frankfurt am Main 1978.
Carsten-Henrich, (Richard Carl/Paul Hengst), *Unter dem Kreuz des Südens*, Berlin 1937.
Faust, Bernhard, *Yilgarn und Meeri. Ein australisches Liebespaar*, Berlin 1957.
Fester, Richard, *Die Steinzeit liegt vor deiner Tür*, München 1981.
Fülles, Mechtild/Schenk, Renate, *Abenteuer Australien*, Bochum 1984.
Geck, Heinz, *Das heiße Herz Australiens*, München 195?.
Geisler, Walter, *Australien, Neuseeland und Ozeanien*, Berlin 1932.
Gilde, Werner, *Für 1000 Dollar um die Welt. Das Leben des J. C. Voss — von ihm selbst erzählt*, Halle/Leipzig 1983.
Gillsäter, Sven, *Beglücktes Auge*, Zürich 1961.
Gluth, Oscar, *Das höllische Paradies*, Bamberg 1955.
Grzimek, Bernhard, *Mit Grzimek durch Australien*, München 1966 (pb 1975).
Gronefeld, Gerhard, "Für Touristen springt kein Känguruh", *Westermanns Monatshefte*, März 1970, pp.19-27.
Grubbe, Peter, (Klaus Volkmann), *Der vergessene Kontinent Australien*, Hamburg 1967.
Harpprecht, Klaus, *Georg Forster oder Die Liebe zur Welt*, Reinbek 1987.
Helling, Victor, *Als erster quer durch Australien. Das Schicksal des deutschen Forschers L. Leichhardt*, Berlin 1931.
Herzog, Werner, *Wo die grünen Ameisen träumen*, München/Wien 1984.
Hufschmied, Julius, *Kleiner Bruder, wo bist du? Roman aus dem Deutschtum Australiens*, Berlin 1937.
Bruder, wo bist du? Abenteuer-Roman, Berlin 1942.
Immelmann, Klaus, *Im unbekannten Australien, dem Lande der Papageien und Prachtfinken*, Pfungstadt/Darmstadt 1960.
Jacobs, Rudolf, *Die Legende vom Känguruh. Begegnungen und Schicksale im Australien von heute*, Gütersloh 1959; 1962.
Jentsch, August, *Ein Mann und ein Traktor auf Weltreise. 2. Buch: Rund um Australien*, Wien 1969.
Johann, A. E., (Alfred Wollschläger), *Abenteuer der Ferne*, München 1978.
Jurgensen Manfred/Robert Adamson (eds.), *Australian Writing Now*, Ringwood/Brisbane 1988.
Kant, Hermann, *Ein bißchen Südsee*, Berlin 1962.
Katz, Richard, *Ein Bummel um die Welt*, Zürich n.d.
Keim, Friedrich, *Über Gold- und Perlgründen Australiens*, Regensburg 1925.
Australischen Häschern entronnen, Berlin 1941.
Keiner, Bernd, *Quer durch den roten Kontinent: unterwegs in Australien*, München 1986.
Keller, G. A., *A poar Reesebilder*, Tanunda 1937.
Kortwich, Werner, *Schangait (sic) nach Sydney*, Stuttgart 1953.
Krug, Werner Gerhard, *Viel Känguruhs und wenig Menschen. Australien, die neue Welt von morgen?*, Hamburg/Berlin 1956.
Leichhardt, Ludwig, *Ins Innere Australiens*, Leipzig 1951.
Schicksal im australischen Busch, Leipzig 1959.
Löffler, Anneliese, (ed.), *Märchen aus Australien*, Düsseldorf/Köln 1981.
Löhr, Adolf, *Erhard in der Südsee*, Reutlingen 1939.

Lütgen, Kurt, *Kapitäne, Schiffe, Abenteuer*, Zürich 1971.
Wagnis und Weite, Würzburg 1971.
Marken, Wolfgang, (Fritz Mardicke), *Das große Australiengeheimnis*, Hamburg 1938.
Nörgaard, Poul, *Lones große Reise*, Gütersloh 1958.
Opper, Rudi, *Gesichter Australiens*, Darmstadt 1982.
Peter, Brigitte, *Setzt die Segel für die weite Reise*, Wien 1972.
Prerauer, Curt a. Maria, (eds.), *Zeitgenössische australische Lyrik*, München 1961.
Ramann, Werner, (ed.), *Reisen in Australien*, Breslau 1932.
Reim, F., *Über Gold- und Perlgründen Australiens*, Dillingen 1925.
Reiners, Wolfgang, *Uru-Uru. Ein australischer Goldwäscher-Roman*, Bremen 1935.
Rober, Karl, (pseud.), *Das Schicksal führt sie nach Australien. Ein abenteuerlicher Roman*, Leipzig 1936.
Rönninger, Hermann, *Buschbanditen. Abenteuererzählung aus Australien*, Reutlingen 1930.
Schreiber, Hermann, *James Cook. Auf der Suche nach dem fünften Erdteil*, Wien 1981.
Seger, Imogen, *Wenn die Geister wiederkehren*, München 1982.
Sielmann, Heinz, *Ins Reich der Drachen und Zaubervögel*, Gütersloh/Wien 1970.
Trebonius, R., *Ins gefahrvolle Australien*, Berlin/Düsseldorf 1954.
Ulrici, Rolf, *Landung in der Wüste*, München 1972.
van Huc-Bethisy, Edelgard, *Endstation Australien*, Stuttgart 1961.
von Cramer, H., *Die Konzessionen des Himmels*, Hamburg 1961.
Wermers, Paul. G., *Ins Land der Känguruhs*, Münsterberg 1960.
Woerner, Charlotte, *Spuren im australischen Busch*, Marburg a.d.L., 1986.
Wolanowski, Lucjan, *Abschied vom Bumerang*, Leipzig 1970; 1973.
Wongar, Banumbir, *Spuren der Traumzeit*, München 1981.

JUVENILE FICTION

Aick, Gerhard, (Gerhard Aichinger), *Wasser für Australien*, Wien/Heidelberg 1957.
Berger, Peter, *Ali reist doch nach Australien*, Wuppertal 1966.
Brinek, Günther, (ed.), *Australien und Ozeanien*, München 1973.
Francé-Harrar, Annie, *Das geheimnisvolle Australien*, Berlin/Leipzig 1935.
Friedrich, Ilse, *Ausgerechnet Australien*, Reutlingen 1963.
Höfling, Helmut, *Todesritt durch Australien*, Bamberg 1954.
Kelbe, Wilhelm, *Der Galgenhügel. Erzählung aus dem australischen Busch*, Reutlingen 1932.
Lütgen, Kurt, *Weit hinter dem Wüstenmond: Geschichten und Gestalten der Erforschung Australiens*, Würzburg 1977.
Wie Sand vor dem Wind, Würzburg 1979.
Meinwerk, Christian, *Alarm in Alice Springs. Ein Abenteuer im australischen Busch*, Würzburg 1961.

Riedel, Curt, *Auf Jagd im australischen Busch*, Berlin 1941.
Rönninger, Hermann, *Buschbanditen. Abenteuer-Erzählung aus Australien*, Reutlingen 1930.
Thür, Hans, *Der Busch brennt*, München/Wien 1954.
von Muralt, Inka, *Als die Sterne dunkel wurden: dramatische Ereignisse beim Goldrausch in Australien*, Würzburg 1980.
Sie nannten ihn Tracy: Menschen im Zyklon, Freiburg/ Basel/Wien 1982.
Woerner, Charlotte, *Spuren im australischen Busch*, Konstanz 1957.

SECONDARY LITERATURE

Auerbach, Frank, "Commonwealth Literature — Präsenz und Rezeption im deutschen Sprachraum. Zum Beispiel: Australien und Neuseeland. *Großbritannien und Deutschland*, 1974, pp. 420-451.
Australian Dictionary of Biography, Melbourne 1972ff.
Argyle, Barry, "The German Element in Australian Fiction", *Wascana Review*, pp.5-22.
Björksten, Ingmar, *Patrick White, die Stimme Australiens*, Düsseldorf 1973.
Bodi, Leslie, "Antipodean Inversion and Australian Reality. On the Image of Australia in German Literature", Walter Veit (ed.), *Captain James Cook. Image and Impact*, Melbourne 1979,pp.76-94.
"Deutschsprachige Literatur und australische Identität", Albrecht Schöne (ed.), *Kontroversen, alte und neue*, Tübingen 1985, pp.106-112.
& Stephen Jeffries (eds.), *The German Connection*, Melbourne 1985.
Brunhoff, Kurt, "Australien — ein Kontinent und seine Literatur", *Der Literat* (Frankfurt am Main), 1971/12, pp.236-239.
Burnley, Ian/Encel, Sol/McCall, Grant (eds.), *Immigration and Ethnicity in the 1980s*, Melbourne 1985.
Brunt, Richard J./Enninger, Werner, (eds.), *Interdisciplinary Perspectives at Cross-Cultural Communication*, Aachen 1985.
Clark, Manning, *A History of Australia*, Vol.1-6, Melbourne 1962-1987.
Clyne, Michael G., *Deutsch als Muttersprache in Australien*, Wiesbaden 1981.
Multilingual Australia: Resources — Needs — Policies, Melbourne 1982.
"Multilingual Melbourne l9th Century Style", *Journal of Australian Studies*, 17 (1985), pp.69-81.
Crawford,R.M./Clark, Manning/Blainey, Geoffrey,*Making History*, Melbourne 1985.
Deklaration der Marxisten-Leninisten Australiens (11. November 1963), Peking 1964.
Dobberstein, Fred, *Deutsche Exilliteratur in Australien*, M.A. Thesis, Melbourne 1983.
Fishman, Joshua, *Language and Nationalism: Two Integrative Essays*, Rowle 1972.
et al (eds.), *The Rise and Fall of the Ethnic Revival: Perspectives on*

Language and Ethnicity, Berlin/New York/Amsterdam 1985.
Fläming, Walter, Der Heimat Bild. Aus australischen Auswandererbriefen, *Tageblatt für den Kreis Jerichow* (8.-24.12.1934), Burg b. Magdeburg 1934, pp. 287-300.
Foster, Lois/Stockley, David, *Australian Multiculturalism: A Documentary History and Critique*, Clevedon/Philadelphia 1988.
Garrett, Jeffrey/Kafka, Susan, (eds.), Kinder-und Jugendliteratur in Auswahl: Australien, *IJB Bulletin 1984*, München 1984.
IJB Bulletin 1985, München 1985.
IJB Bulletin 1986, München 1986.
Australien, *IJB Report*, München 1987, pp.7-11.
Geissler, Otto, *Die Länder und Völker der Erde*, Leipzig 1942.
Gelder, Ken/Salzman, Paul, *The New Diversity. Australian Fiction 1970-88*, Melbourne 1989.
Glazer, N./Moynihan, P. (eds.), *Ethnicity. Theory and Experience*, Cambridge Mass. 1975.
Goodman, David/O'Hearn, D.J./Wallace-Crabbe, Chris, (eds.), *Multicultural Australia: The Challenges of Change*, Melbourne 1991.
Graubard Stephen R., (ed.), *Australia: The Daedalus Symposium*, Sydney 1985.
Günther, Harri, Reiseprosa in der Gegenwartsliteratur der DDR, *Deutsch als Fremdsprache* 19 (Sonderheft), 1982, pp.39-54.
Günther, Ulrich, *Australien heute*, Wien 1975.
Gunew, Sneja, (ed.), *Displacements: Migrant Storytellers*, Geelong 1982;1987.
"Australia 1984: A Moment in the Archaeology of Multiculturalism.", Francis Barker et al. (eds.), *Europe and its others*, Essex Sociology of Literature Conference, University of Essex, Colchester 1985, pp.178-193.
Gunter Sigi/Klein, E., Warum schreibt ihr überhaupt? Deutsch-australisches Schriftsteller-Treffen, *Der Literat* (Frankfurt am Main), 24/4 (1982), pp.93-94.
Haas, Gerhard, (ed.), *Kinder- und Jugend-Literatur*, Stuttgart 1984.
Härtl, H., *Entwicklung und Traditionen der sozialistischen Reiseliteratur*, Berlin 1977.
Harmstorf, I./Cigler, M. (eds.), *The Germans in Australia*, Melbourne 1985.
Houbein, Lolo, (ed.), *Ethnic Writings in English from Australia. A Bibliography*, ALS Working Papers, Adelaide 1984.
Hutterer, Franz, *Das überseeische Deutschland: die deutschen Kolonien in Wort und Bild*, Stuttgart 1903.
Josephi, Beate, *'Suburbia' in der modernen australischen Dichtung*, Hannover 1978, Phil. Diss.(1978).
Jupp, James, *Ethnic Politics in Australia*, Sydney/London/Boston 1984.
(ed.), *The Australian People. An Encyclopedia of the Nation, Its People and Their Origins*, Sydney 1988.
Jurgensen, Manfred, (ed.), *Ethnic Australia*, Brisbane 1981.
Literature and Ethnicity, James Jupp (ed.), *The Australian People*, Sydney 1988, pp.906-909.
Geschichte und Verdrängung: Zur deutsch-australischen Literatur, Dieter Borchmeyer (ed.),
Poetik und Geschichte, Viktor Žmegač zum 60. Geburtstag, Tübingen 1989,

pp. 187-204.
Deutsche Literatur in Australien — die historische Perpektive, Gerhard Schulz/Tim Mehigan/Marion Adams (eds.), *Literatur und Geschichte 1788-1988* (Australisch-Neuseeländische Studien zur deutschen Sprache und Literatur, Band 14), Bern/Frankfurt am Main/New York/Paris 1990, pp. 333-347.
The Politics of Imagination. David Goodman/D.J. O'Hearn/Chris Wallace-Crabbe (eds.), *Multicultural Australia. The Challanges of Change*, Melbourne 1991, pp.21–30.
Kamenetsky, Christa, *Children's Literature in Hitler's Germany. The Cultural Policy of National Socialism*, Athens(Ohio)/London 1984.
Klein, Karl Kurt, *Literaturgeschichte des Deutschtums im Ausland, neu herausgegeben mit einer Bibliographie (1945-1978) von Alexander Ritter*, Hildesheim/New York 1979.
Kooznetzoff, C., *Bibliographical Essay on Germanic Studies in Australia since 1958*, Sydney 1969.
Laila, Yousef Abu, *Integration und Entfremdung*, Göttingen 1981.
Leichhardt, Ludwig, *Die erste Durchquerung Australiens*, Stuttgart 1983.
Lenhardt, Christian, *In Australien verschollen: das Rätsel Ludwig Leichhardt*, Burgholzhausen v.d.H. 1973.
Lohr, Otto, *Deutschland und Übersee. Zur Geschichte deutscher Kulturbeiträge im Ausland*, Stuttgart 1962.
Lommel, Andreas/Mommel, Katharina, *Die Kunst des fünften Erdteils*, München 1959.
Lumb, Peter/Hazell, Anne (eds.), *Diversity and Diversion. An Annotated Bibliography of Australian Ethnic Minority Literature*, Melbourne 1983.
Macainsh, Noel, *Nietzsche in Australia*, München 1975.
Australian Literature and Europe. *The Journal of Commonwealth Literature*, London 13, 1978 (1), pp.50-58.
The Pathos of Distance. German-Australian Literary Affiliations (German-Australian Studies, Vol. 4), Bern/Frankfurt am Main/New York/Paris 1991.
Mannzen, Walter, *Die Eingeborenen Australiens*, Berlin 1949.
Meray, Tibor, *Australien*, Lausanne 1962.
Palmer, N., Some Relations between German and Australian Literatures, *Australian Goethe Society Proceedings* 151, Melbourne 1952.
Passarge, Siegfried, *Australien und die Südsee*, Frankfurt am Main 1934.
Priessnitz, Horst, Die Literatur Australiens. *Literaturen in englischer Sprache*, Bonn 1977, pp.177-198.
Australien. *Commonwealth-Literatur*, Düsseldorf/Bern/München 1981, pp. 29-63.
Reif, W., *Zivilisationsflucht und literarische Wunschträume*, Stuttgart 1975.
Ritter, Alexander, (ed.), *Deutschsprachige Literatur im Ausland*, Göttingen 1985.
Scheible, Hartmut, *Wahrheit und Subjekt*, Bern/München 1984.
Scheller, Bernhard, "Black Theatre" in Australien und die Problematik der Aborigines, *Weimarer Beiträge* 33 (1987), 1, pp. 76-97.
Schmidt, Heiner (ed.), *Jugendbuch im Unterricht, 1950-1965*, Duisburg 1966 pp. 212-215.

& Willie Röwenkamp (eds.), *Jugendbuch im Unterricht, 1970-1972*, Duisburg 1973, pp. 92-93.

Schöps, Joachim (ed.), *Auswandern. Ein deutscher Traum*, Reinbek 1982.

Schulz, Gerhard, Urmythos in Australien. Zum Werk des Nobelpreisträgers Patrick White. *Neue Rundschau*, Berlin, 85, 1974, 1, pp. 163-167.

Schulz, Joachim, *Australien*, Nürnberg 1963.

Senff, Hans-Dieter, *Setting the record straight: the history of the Serbs, the Slav settlers from Germany, and their historic contribution to the early settlement of New South Wales, South Australia, Queensland and Victoria*, Newcastle 1986.

Sherington, Geoffrey, *Australia's Immigrants*, Sydney 1980.

Sivrikozoglu, Cicek, *...nix unsere Vaterland*, Frankfurt am Main 1985.

Smith, Bernhard, *European Vision and the South Pacific*, Oxford 1969.

Sturm, Hermann, *Das Fremde. Ästhetische Erfahrung beim Graben, Reisen, Messen, Sterben*, Aachen 1985.

Tampke, Jürgen, *Wunderbar Country. Germans look at Australia 1850-1914*, Sydney 1982.

& Colin Doxford, *Australia, Willkommen*, Sydney 1990.

Thum, Bernd/Lawn-Thum, Elisabeth, 'Kulturprogramme' und 'Kulturthemen' im Umgang mit Fremdkulturen: Die Südsee in der deutschen Literatur. *Jahrbuch Deutsch als Fremdsprache*, Bd. 9, (ed. A. Wierlacher et al), Heidelberg 1982, pp. 1-38.

(ed.), *Gegenwart als kulturelles Erbe*, München 1985.

Turner, Graeme, *National Fictions*, Sydney 1986.

Valentin, Hartmut, *Länderkundliche Forschungen auf der Kap-York-Halbinsel, Nordaustralien*, n.p. 1959.

Veit, Walter et al. (eds.), *Antipodische Aufklärungen/Antipodean Enlightenments, Festschrift für Leslie Bodi*, Frankfurt am Main/Bern/ New York 1987.

Vermeulen, Hans/Boissevain, Jeremy (eds.), *Ethnic Challenge. The Politics of Ethnicity in Europe*, Göttingen 1984.

von Skerst, Arnold, Das Deutschtum in Australien. *Wir Deutsche in der Welt* (ed. Verband Deutscher Vereine im Ausland), n.p. 1938.

von Stutterheim, Kurt, *Australien*, Berlin 1949.

Ward, Russel, *The Australian Legend*, Melbourne 1987.

White, Richard, *Inventing Australia*, Sydney 1981.

Wierlacher, Alois, *Das Fremde und das Eigene. Prolegomena zu einer interkulturellen Germanistik*, München 1985.

Wilde, William H./Hooton, Joy/Andrews, Barry (eds.), *The Oxford Companion to Australian Literature*, Melbourne 1985.

Wolf, Volker, *Die Rezeption australischer Literatur im deutschen Sprachraum von 1845-1979*, Tübingen 1982.

Zur Rezeption Patrick Whites in deutschen Zeitungen bis 1979. J. H. Voigt (ed.), *New Beginnings/Neuanfänge. Deutsche in New South Wales und Queensland*, Stuttgart 1983, pp. 246-255.

(ed.) *Australien: Deutsche-zumeist literarische-Impressionen aus 150 Jahren*, (German-Australian Studies, Vol. 5), Bern/Frankfurt am Main/New York/Paris 1991.

Index

Aborigines, 8, 13, 24, 27, 28, 31, 32, 45, 48, 49, 53, 66, 67, 74, 75, 85, 87, 88, 94, 96, 99, 100, 118, 126, 129, 134, 135, 137, 138, 140, 149, 150, 151, 152, 154, 155, 158, 159, 160, 161, 162, 163, 164, 166, 167, 168, 170–174, 178, 179, 180, 201, 204, 210, 212, 219, 220, 223, 242, 244, 257, 259, 260, 272, 276, 278, 283, 287, 288, 291, 292, 295, 296, 299, 302, 310
Access, 358
Adamson, Robert, 342
Adamson, Walter, 195, 233, 241, 356–377, 392
Adelaide, 18, 21, 27, 83, 103, 108, 125, 198, 246, 251, 252, 259, 289
Adenauer, Konrad, 133, 141, 264
Adler, Ernst, 153, *171–174*
Adorno, Theodor W., 335, 389
Afrika, 33
Age (The), 358, 380
Ägypten, 33
Akzente, 192, 214
Albert, Max, 110, *127–128*
Alexander II of Serbia, 58
Alice Springs, 85, 156
Altona, 236
Angry Penguins, 272
Aristotle, 102
Arnhemland, 31, 203
Arp, Hans, 378, 381

Arsan, Emmanuelle, 257
Artmann, H. C., 5, 194, *202–206*, 226, 231
Aspden, David, 385
Aspect, 8, 384, 389, 390
Auerbach, Frank, 9, 153, 186, 259
Auschwitz, 269, 271, 318, 335
Australian Communist Party, 71, 176, 177, 270, 279, 281
Australian Labor Party, 64, 70, 71, 82, 176, 177
Australian Workers Union, 289, 290
Ayers Rock, 178

Baader-Meinhof-Group, 353, 354
Bachmann, Ingeborg, 277, 339
Baldauf, 273
Ballarat, 33
Banks, Joseph, 261
Baring, Alfred, 114
Baring, Elise, 114
Barossa Valley, 82, 251, 252, 255, 256
Baudelaire, Charles, 390
Bayer, Konrad, 377, 381, 382
Baylebridge, William, 131
Beaver, Bruce, 378
Becker, Jürgen, 381, 382
Becker, O. E. H., 11, *103–110*
Beckett, Samuel, 250, 367
Beeskow, 89, 91
Behrens, C. F., 39, 393

Belfast, 271
Beltrametti, 378
Bendisch, Roger, 260
Benn, Gottfried, 130, 319, 386, 389, 390
Berlin, 16, 31, 41, 44, 45, 52, 55, 61, 62, 75, 95, 98, 100, 127, 175, 183, 236, 251, 252, 253, 254, 255, 256, 270, 272, 275, 280, 285, 289, 296, 383, 384
Bernhard, Thomas, 224, 301
Bernini, Lorenzo, 327
Bertram, Hans, *44–46*, 54, 161, 259
Bethanien, 19
Bethedsa, 84
Bichsel, Peter, 5, 195, *227–228*, 379, 382
Bienek, Horst, 5, 194, 195, *206–214*, 231, 382, 390
Billeter, Walter, 195, *377–383*, 391
Bisinger, Gerald, 381
Bismarck, 11
Bittman, Karl, 114
Bjelke-Petersen, Johannes, 326
Bjerre, Jens, 259
Blainey, Geoffrey, 40
Blaxland, John, 105
Blech, Leo, 253
Blumberg, 18
Bobrowski, Johannes, 382
Bockmann, Vera, 230, *251–256*
Bockmeyer, Walter, 257
Bodi, Leslie, 9, 215
Böll, Heinrich, 272, 276
Bonnard, Pierre, 305
Boone, Daniel, 163
Brasch, Thomas, 379
Braunburg, Rudolf, 218
Brecht, Bertolt, 209, 210, 290, 318, 390
Bredel, Willy, 272

Bremen 35, 46
Brennan, Christopher, 130
Brenner, Der, 214
Breslau, 83
Briand, Paul L., 139
Brinkmann, Rolf Dieter, 380, 382
Brisbane, 32, 208, 259, 265, 266, 317, 340, 341
Browning, Robert, 334
Brüning, Eberhard, 172
Bryant, Gordon, 299
Buber, Martin, 352
Buchenwald, 183
Büchner, Georg, 379
Buck, Paul, 378
Buckley, Vincent, 130, 251, 317, 339
Buckley, William, 99, *162–166*
Bührmann, Rolf, 257
Bulletin, (Sydney), 48, 50, 97, 302
Burt, Bill, 270
Byron, Lord, 122, 346

Canada, 41
Canberra, 97, 222, 259, 261, 299
Cape Hope, 28
Capiello, Rosa, 341
Carlton, 34, 35
Casablanca, 208
Casey, Gavin, 281
Celan, Paul, 318, 377, 378, 379, 381, 382, 390
Ceylon, 33
Chagall, Marc, 340
Chamisso, Adalbert von, 39, 393
China, 31
Clark, Manning, 40, 45, 46, 235
Classicism, (German), 109, 113, 118, 120, 121, 122, 125, 361, 373, 374
Claudius, Eduard, 272
Clyne, Michael, 242

INDEX

Coast to Coast, 272
Coburg, 236
Conrad, Joseph, 86, 138
Cook, (Captain) James, 18, 26, 47, 126, 127, 138, 261, 264
Cooper, James Fenimore, 43, 96, 163
Corkhill, Alan, 323
Creative Moment, 303
Curie, Marie and Pierre, 126
Cusack, Dymphna, 176

Dachau, 183
da Gama, Vasco, 59
Daiber, Albert, 99
Darling Downs, 27
Dangel, Anneliese, 175
Dante, 59
Danzig, 31
Dark, Eleanor, 100
Darmstadt, 16
Darwin, 27, 31, 178, 219, 222, 255
Dautheuil, Louis, 304
Davidson, Jim, 251
Davis, Angela, 271
Defoe, Daniel, 163
de Haas, Rudolf, 393
Delander, Sonja, 357, 358, 359, 362
Denholm, Decie, 251
Dessau, 289
Deutsch-Australische Studien, 10
Deutschtum, 6, 11, 14, 19, 37, 38, 43, 50, 75, 98, 99, 125
Diesel, Rudolf, 126
Diesendorf, Margaret, 195, 233, *301–314,* 339, 383
Dietrich, Amalie, 393
Döblin, Alfred, 123
Dobson, Rosemary, 304
Donne, John, 326

Dos Passos, John, 123
Dostoevsky, Michaelovich Feodor, 207
Dreiser, Theodore, 283
Dresden, 99, 289
Drysdale, Russell, 250
Dublin, 49, 207
Duisburg, 269
Duncan, Laurie, 380
Dunera, 269
Durack family, 96
Dutton, Geoffrey, 9

Ear in a Wheatfield, 382
Eichendorff, Joseph von, 106, 183, 373
Ekert-Rotholz, Alice, 151, *168–171*
Eliot, T. S., 130, 340, 389
Elliott, E. V., 270
Engels, Friedrich, 63, 66
Enzensberger, Hans Magnus, 10, 307, 318, 382
etymspheres, 8, 377
Eureka Stockade, 65, 143, 176
Evers, W., 134
Ey, Karl, *46–50*

Faber, Kurt, *41–43,* 109
Falkenberg, 91
Fankhauser, L. and A., 133, *138–141*
Farmer, Beverley 195
Faulkner, William, 208
Fels, Werner, 112, *129–131*
Felser, Erna, 114
Felser, Gerhard, 114
Feuchtwanger, Lion, 63
Flatt, August von der (Johann Friedrich W. Schulz), 39, *79–86*

Flaubert, Gustave, 208, 270
Flensburg, 314, 350
Florence, 331
Forster, Georg and Johann
  Reinhold, 18, 39, 66, 393
Franke, Hans, 113, *126–127*
Frankfurt am Main, 18, 138
Frankfurter Hefte, 248
Fränz, Georg, 91
Freer, Maureen, 318
Fremantle, 58, 60, 67, 97, 272, 287
Fremd, Angelika, 233, 267, *268*
Fried, Erich, 382
Friedensberg, 19
Frisch, Max, 291, 319, 346, 354, 355
Fuchsberger, Joachim, 5, 231, 243, *261–263*
Furphy, Joseph, 176

Gallipoli, 142, 184, 185
Gandhi, Mahatma, 126
GDR (German Democratic Republic), 7, 8, 132, 142, 153, 162, 164, 166, 171, 172, 173, 175, 176, 178, 179, 193, 196, 270, 272, 279, 280, 284, 285, 288, 289, 290, 292, 293, 296, 298, 299
Geck, Heinz, *72–75*
Gellert, Leon, 39
German Clubs, 7, 19, 235, 236, 265, 266
Gerstäcker, Friedrich, 39, 99, 100, 126, 259, 393
Gibb, Don, 312
Gibson, Ralph, 270
Giessen, 359
"Gilmore", 259
Glaser, Hermann, *248–250*
Glenn, Jerry, 379

Goebbels, Joseph Paul, 75
Goethe, Johann Wolfgang von, 42, 91, 123, 130, 181, 194, 202, 224, 225, 226, 239, 303, 307, 317, 318, 319, 350, 355, 390
Gomringer, Eugen, 382
Goode, Cyril E., 129
Grant, Owen, 114
Grass, Günter, 266, 275, 297, 298, 318, 379
Graves, Robert, 309
Graz, 144, 186, 257
Grenville, Kate, 195, 302
Grimmelshausen, Hans Jakob
  Christoffel von, 163
Groote, Eylandt, 178, 179
Gunn, Aeneas, 97
Günther, Ulrich, 259

Hageni, Alfred, 152, *166–168*, 259
Hahn, Captain, 19
Hahndorf, 19
Hall, Bernard, 129
Hall, James Norman, 133, *138–141*
Halle, 289
Hamburg, 31, 97, 124, 137, 289
Hamburger, Michael, 3
Handke, Peter, 319
Hardre, Jacques, 387
Hardy, Frank, 143, 176, 177, 270
Harney, Bill, 178
Hartog, Dirk, 138
Harwood, Gwen, 303, 308
Hasluck, Paul, 178
Hatvani, Paul (Paul Hirsch), *188–192*, 193, 207, *214–218*, 227
Hauser, Heinrich, *86–89, 92–98*
Healy, Jim, 270
Heberling, Paul, 303
Heckmann, Wolf, *218–222*

Heidegger, Martin, 303
Heidelberg, 235, 236
Heissenbüttel, Helmut, 379, 391
Helms, H. G., 382
Hemensley, Kris, 377, 378, 380, 381, 391
Hemingway, Ernest, 270
Hermannsburg, 84, 85, 179, 299
Herzog, Alfred, *75–79*
Hesiod, 124
Hesse, Hermann, 298, 357, 374, 376
Heyd, Kurt, *51–52*
Hindenburg von, und Paul von Beneckendorff, 253
Hitler, Adolf, 7, 16, 28, 46, 59, 61, 64, 72, 81, 82, 92, 103, 243, 253, 254, 273, 355
Hobart, 99, 267
Hofmannsthal, Hugo von, 391
Hohl, Ludwig, 379
Hölderlin, Friedrich, 60
Homer, 124
HongKong, 25
Hope, A. D., 130, 303, 308
Horne, Donald, 234
Houbein, Lolo, 334
Hutterer, Franz, 133, *147–149*
Huxley, Aldous, 361

Iowa, 314

Jackson, George, 271
Jacobs, Rudolf, 259
Jandl, Ernst, 391
Jaspers, Karl, 303
Jeffries, Stephen, 214
Jenkins, John, 377, 378
Johann, A. E. (Alfred Wollschläger), *52–55*, 102
Johannesburg, 324, 325, 326

Joyce, James, 207, 380
Jung, Karl Emil, 259
Jünger, Ernst, 383
Jurgensen, Manfred, 195, 196, 232, 233, 313, *314–356*

Kafka, Franz, 140, 187, 192, 207, 318, 354, 361, 367
Kant, Immanuel, 303, 334, 335, 368, 372
Kaufmann, Walter, 7, 8, 62, 64, 69, 143, 151, 152, 172, 175, 177, 180, 182, 196, *269–288*
Kavel, Ludwig Christian, 103, 106
Kefala, Antigone, 195
Kelly, Ned, 264
Kempcke, Hermann, *89–92*
Kempe, 179
Kennedy, John F., 271
Kennedy, Robert, 271
Kenny, 377, 381, 391
Kierkegaard, Sören, 318
King, Martin Luther, 271
Kisch, Egon Erwin, 7, 8, 16, 50, 53, *58–72*, 88, 93, 152, 177, 178, 179, 259, 286, 287, 298, 299
Kissinger, Henry, 364
Klausmann, Adolf, 44
Kleiber, Erich, 253
Klemperer, Otto, 253
Kneip, Jakob, 29
Kneipp, Sebastian, 126
Knittel, John, 121
Koch, Christopher, 302
Koch, Robert, 126
Kolar, Kurt, 196, *199–201*
Köln, 83, 251
Königsberg, 356, 368, 372, 373, 374
Koopmann, Hubert, 345, 346
Kosch, Wilhelm, 280

Kötz, Alfred, 99,
Kotze, Stefan von, 39, 100, 165, 259, 393
Krausmann, Lorraine, 385
Krausmann, Rudi, 195, 225, 233, 308, 378, 381, *383–392*
Kristeva, Julia, 322
Krolow, Karl, 318
Krug, Werner G., 259
Kupang, 44
Kurz, Carl Heinz, *222–224*

Landolt, Esther (Rosmarie Meyer), 103, 111, 112, 113, *115–121*
Lange, Marga, 343
Langmeil, 18
La Paz, 356, 358
Lavery, John, 329
Lawrence, D. H., 207
Lawson, Henry, 100, 105
Leichhardt, Christian, 89
Leichhardt, Ludwig, 14, 27, 54, 89, 90, 91, 92, 96, 99, 137, 155, 212, 213, 236, 259, 260
Leipzig, 21, 96, 285, 287
Lenin, Vladimir Iljitch, 70, 71
Lenz, Siegfried, 5, 194, *196–199*, 228, 231
Leutenegger, Gertrud, 277
Lindsay, Norman, 131
Lippa, Hans von, 259
Literatur und Kritik, 188
Livingstone, David, 126
Lobetal, 18
Lodewyckx, Augustin, 2, 9, *38–40*, 393
Loerke, Oskar, 390
Loets, Bruno, 156
London, 97, 104, 157, 175, 180
London, Jack, 270
Lord, M., 187
Lowell, Robert, 319

Luckner, Felix Graf von, 61
Lukács, Georg, 62, 275, 300
Luna, 358
Lüneburg, Heinz, 132, 133, *136–138*
Lütgen, Kurt, 150, *154–155*, 259
Luther, Martin, 181
Lythgo, Pam, 329

Macarthur, John, 69
McAuley, James, 130, 308
McCrae, Hugh, 131
McKay, 96
Macquarie, Lachlan, 49, 70
Maiden, Jennifer, 378
Makar, 317, 388
Malouf, David, 195
Mann, Thomas, 264, 319, 331, 357, 365
Maralinga, 172, 269, 272, 275, 276, 277
Marburg, Queensland, 340
Marken, Wolfgang, *55–57*
Martin, David (Ludwig Detsinyi), 39, *141–144*, 153, *180–185*, 270, 277
Martin, Johann Carl, *33–35*
Marx, Karl, 68, 70, 71
Masefield, John, 63
Mattheus, Peter, *20-21*
May, Karl, 13, 31, 37, 43, 66, 109
Mayer, Hans, 3
Meanjin, 186, 272
Meissner, Hans-Otto, 221, 232, *245–248*
Melbourne, 34, 38, 51, 58, 60, 63, 68, 72, 73, 97, 108, 114, 121, 124, 128, 129, 130, 142, 162, 180, 208, 215, 216, 217, 227, 245, 246, 259, 270, 273, 281, 314, 317, 345, 346, 355, 357, 358, 381, 383

INDEX

Melbourne Realist Writers Group, 269
Melbourne University Magazine, 314
Menge, Hans, 236
Menge, Johannes, 18, 107
Menge, Joseph, 18
Menzies, Robert Gordon, 60, 62, 175, 177, 178, 264, 273
Meray, Tibor, 259
Merian, 197
Merkur, 206
Merri Creek or Nero, The, 382
Meyer, C. F., 303, 373
Middleton, 378
Mielche, Hakon, 259
Miller, David, 378
Modigliani, Amedeo, 305
Monet, Claude, 305
Moorehead, Alan, 259, 260
Moorhead, Finola 378
Moresby, Port (Papua-New Guinea), 294, 295
Morgan, John, 99, *162–166*
Morrin, Elsie, 69
Moscow, 284
Moses, John, 102
Mücke, Dr, 19
Mühlen-Schulte, Hans-Joachim, *36–37*
Müller, Sir Ferdinand Jacob Heinrich, Baron von, 35
Müller, Theodor, 39, 393
Müller, Wilhelm, 289, 323
München, 208, 390
Murray, Les A., 387
Murray-Smith, Stephen, 143
Mussolini, Benito, 253

Namatjira, Albert, 135, 178, 179, 283, 299
Naples, 253

Napoleon, 69
Nazi, 7, 16, 19, 24, 50, 53, 55, 56, 58, 59, 61, 62, 64, 67, 72, 73, 74, 75, 77, 78, 79, 82, 93, 94, 95, 101, 102, 103, 113, 116, 117, 133, 136, 149, 180, 183, 190, 191, 215, 217, 243, 252, 253, 254, 266, 267, 273–275, 357, 376
Neue Welt, Die, 383
Neukirch, 19
Newcastle, 68
New South Wales, 18, 49, 80, 99, 101, 104, 107, 148, 266
Newton, Isaac, 307
Nicholson, William, 90
Nietzsche, Friedrich, 385
Noel, Bernhard, 378
Nonveiller, Heinz, *186–187*
Nordhoff, Charles B., 133, *138–141*
Novalis (Friedrich von Hardenberg), 390

O'Donohue, Barry, 380
O'Dowd, Bernard, 131
Okopenko, Andreas, 378, 382
O'Reilly, Dowell, 100
Oslo, 128
Ostpreußenblatt, Das, 357, 372, 374, 376
Ouburn, Olsen, 302
Outrider 8, 232, 329, 343, 358
Overland, 143, 272

Palmerston, 27
Papercastle Mimeographs, 377, 390
Papua-New Guinea, 26, 293, 294, 295
Pareroultja, Edwin, 135

Paris, 72, 208
Parker, Ruth, 260
Parkes, Sir Henry, 19
Parramatta, 49
Pascoe, Stephen, 358
Paul, Jean, 379
Perkins, Elizabeth, 314
Perry, Grace, 303
Perse, Saint-John, 387
Perth, 59, 97, 222, 240
Peterborough, 289, 290, 291, 292
Petersburg, 207
Petr, Pavl, 214
Petrov Affair, 179, 291
Pfeffer, K. H., 132, *134–136*
Pfemfert, Franz, 207
Phillip, Captain Arthur, 18, 47, 48
Phillips, A. A., 186
Phoenix Publications (Brisbane), 327
Picasso, Pablo, 302, 305
Pindar, 124
Piontek, Heinz, 382
Pitt William, (Prime Minister), 47
Ploennis, H. von, 124
Poetry Australia, 8, 303
Politzer, L. L., 40, 112, *121–123*
Port Essington, 27, 91
Portsmouth, 47
Potsdam, 252
Pound, Ezra, 304, 307
Prague, 207
Prichard, Katherine Susannah, 63, 176
Pückler, Fürst, 90
Püttmann, Hermann, 40, 393

Queensland, 43, 55, 80, 100, 101, 138, 199, 238, 265, 266, 317, 323, 341, 342, 343
Queen Victoria, 49

Raab, Fritz, 133, *144–147*
Raddatz, Volker, 260
Radebeul, 289
Ramuz, C. F., 121
Rees, Lloyd, 302
Reim, Helmut, 152, 153, *162–166*
Reinhard, Till, 232, *263–267*
Reinhardt, Max, 253
Rheintal, 19
Renn, Ludwig, 272
Riefenstahl, Leni, 46
Rilke, Rainer Maria, 303, 304, 309, 357
Ringelnatz, Joachim (Hans Bötticher), 370
Rio de Janeiro, 25
Rob, Gerda, 260
Romanticism, (German), 124, 297, 314, 317, 324, 336, 373, 374
Rose, Frederick, 152, 172, *175–179*
Rosenblum, L. A., 39
Rösenmann, Pastor, 53
Ross, Colin, *21–26*, 74, 94
Rostock, 97
Rudd, Steele (Arthur Hoey Davis), 83
Ruse, William, 104
Ruxton, Bruce, 185

Salzburg, 144, 383, 384
Salzburger Nachrichten, 144, 383
Samuel, Richard, 9, 114
San Francisco, 101
Sappho, 124
Saroyan, William, 270
Scheler, Max, 303
Schiller, Friedrich, 66, 129, 303, 361
Schleswig-Holstein, 31
Schlunke, Eric Otto, 9
Schmidt, Arno, 378, 379, 380, 381, 382

Schmidt, Eckhart, 231, 261
Schmidt, Hans, 68
Schnabel, Johann Gottfried, 281
Schneidenbach, Elfi, 162
Scholz, Liz, 231, *256–258*
Schomburgk, Richard, 19
Schönberg, 19
Schopenhauer, Arthur, 365, 379
Schreck, Joachim, 280
Schubert, Franz, 323
Schulte, Michael, 194, 202, *224–226*, 231
Schulz, Gerhard, 9
Schwarz, 179
Scott, Walter, 96
SED, 270
Seelow, Mark, 268
Seghers, Anna, 272
Seidel, Jürgen, 229, 230, *237–241*
Seidel, Uwe, 260
Semmler, Clement, 153
Sergeant, Howard, 307
Sexton, Anne, 321
Shapcott, Thomas, 302
Shelley, Percy Bysshe, 324
Sierre, 377
Silesia, 18, 33, 106, 251
Socialist Realism, 275, 279, 293
Socrates, 124
Solander, 261
South Australia, 18, 19, 22, 79, 81, 101, 103, 106, 107, 251, 255, 256
South-West Africa, 12, 14, 28, 31, 155
Specht, Joachim, 7, 35, 62, 65, 72, 143, 151, 152, 172, 196, 277, 279, 283, *289–300*
Sperber, Achim, 230, *259–260*
Spielvogel, Nathan F., 39
Square Poets, 318
Staiger, Emil, 317
Stalin, Joseph, 280

Stalingrad, 270
Steele Rudd's Magazine, 83
Steinbeck, John, 240
Steinberg, Werner, 289
Stephens, Anthony, 9
Stephensen, P. R., 63
Stölting, Walter, *17–19*, 112, *123–125*
Storm, Theodor, 373
Stow, Randolph, 302
Strählow, Charlotte Sophie, 89
Strauß, Franz-Josef, 351
Strauss, Richard, 253
Sturm, Der, 214
Stuttgart, 2, 38, 157
Sutcliffe, Thomas, 69
Swift, Jonathan, 371, 377
Sydney, 25, 47, 49, 50, 58, 65, 68, 69, 70, 77, 89, 98, 103, 104, 105, 108, 111, 125, 139, 140, 148, 167, 170, 171, 175, 208, 210, 213, 214, 222, 227, 228, 242, 243, 246, 259, 261, 263, 269, 270, 303, 355, 384, 385
Sydney Bulletin, 48, 50, 64
Sydney Herald, The, 104
Sydney Morning Herald, The, 64
Sydney Waterside Workers Union, 177, 283

Tanunda, 19, 76, 83, 84, 251, 252
Tasman, Abel, 138
Tauber, Richard, 253
Taylor, Andrew, 195
Thälmann, Ernst, 279
Theresienstadt, 269
Thomas, D. M., 361
Tieck, Ludwig, 379, 381
Tiefenhausen, Berend von, *101–102*
Timor, 44
Townsville, 329

Tranter, John, 10, 195, 378, 380
Troll, Alexander, *98–101*
Tsaloumas, Dimitris, 195, 336, 337
Tübingen, 41, 109
Twain, Mark, 98, 260
Twentieth Century, 317

Ullrich, Luise, 5, 230, *241–245,* 261
Ulrich, Hans W., 151, *159–162*
Unity, 141

Vahldiek, Willi, *31–32,* 33
Vallis, Val, 340
van der Geest, Karel, 150, *156–157*
Velter, Joseph M., 12, *26–30*
Victoria, 80, 101, 107, 116, 162
Viedebantt, Klaus, 229, *233–237*
Vienna (Wien), 31, 188, 199, 214, 217, 301, 302, 303, 304, 383
Viennese, Theatre (Sydney) (The), 111, *113–115*
Vleeskens, Cornelis, 195

Wagner, Richard, 310
Wakefield, E. G., 68
Walker, Kath, 179
Walser, Robert, 379
Walsh, Mike, 262
Warnemünde, 97
Warsaw, 270, 272
Waten, Judah, 143
Webster, E. M., 92

Wehrenalp, E. Barth von, 101
Weimar Republic, 12, 73
Weinböhla, 289
Wentworth, William Charles, 105
West, Anna, 153
Western Australia, 31, 81, 101
White, Patrick, 116, 155, 208, 212, 302
Whiteley, Brett, 339, 384, 389
Whitlam, E. G., 299, 340, 341
Wiechert, Ernst, 357, 374
Wiener Schule, 380
Wilde, Oscar, 332
Wilhelm II., Kaiser, 11
Williamson, David, 249
Wilpert, Gero von, 9
Winter, Hannelore, 162
Wittgenstein, Ludwig, 195, 367, 389, 391
Woche, Die, 355
Wolff, Kurt, 207
Wolkowsky, Maria, 151, *157–159*
Wondratschek, Wolf, 382
Wongar, Banumbir (Sreten Bozic), 162, 172, 173
Wright, Judith, 129

Yeats, William Butler, 297

Zeiss, Karl 126
Zeit, Die 197, 233
Zimmermann, Claudia, 260
Zimmermann, Heinrich, 126, 127
Zürich, 117, 120, **121,** 317, 335